Anne Baker trained as a nurse at Birkenhead General Hospital, but after her marriage went to live first in Libya and then in Nigeria. She eventually returned to her native Birkenhead where she worked as a Health Visitor for over ten years. She now lives with her husband on a ninety-acre sheep farm in North Wales. Her first novel, *Like Father, Like Daughter*, is also available from Headline.

Also by Anne Baker

Like Father, Like Daughter
Legacy of Sins
Nobody's Child
Merseyside Girls
Moonlight on the Mersey
A Mersey Duet
Mersey Maids
A Liverpool Lullaby

Paradise Parade

Anne Baker

HEADLINE

First published in 1992
by HEADLINE BOOK PUBLISHING PLC

First published in paperback in 1993
by HEADLINE BOOK PUBLISHING PLC

10 9 8 7 6 5

ISBN 0 7472 3960 6

Typeset by
Letterpart Limited, Reigate, Surrey

Printed and bound in Great Britain by
Clays Ltd, St Ives plc

HEADLINE BOOK PUBLISHING PLC
A division of Hodder Headline PLC
338 Euston Road
London NW1 3BH

Paradise Parade

Book One 1931–1932
CHAPTER ONE

When Giles Wythenshaw came to the typing pool the clicking of keys almost ceased. Alone Emily Barr kept her fingers moving, as she watched the other typists smiling up at him, hoping to catch his eye as he talked to their supervisor. When he left, she listened to their comments about what he wore and what he'd said. They vied with each other to do any work he brought.

She knew that as sole heir to J.A. Wythenshaw & Son, makers of artificial jewellery, they thought him Birkenhead's most eligible bachelor. From the day he'd started learning the business, the office girls had had one ambition. They all fancied their chances of marrying him and living in luxury ever after.

Many of them had boyfriends already, but they all saw Giles as being on a different plane. He was larger than life, someone to dream about as an alternative to Rudolph Valentino or Douglas Fairbanks. Almost out of reach, but not quite. Flesh and blood, but thoughts of marrying him were close on fantasy all the same.

The other nine girls in the typing pool were green with envy when they heard the news. 'Emily Barr, you've got the luck of the devil!'

Emily had been given what everybody wanted, the job of secretary to the canteen manager. Giles Wythenshaw had just moved there too, and she would also be working directly for him.

On the morning she was to start in the canteen, Emily was so full of nervous excitement she hardly noticed the rain sheeting down as she cycled to work.

'I hate coming to work on foul mornings like this, don't you?' Sylveen Smith, her friend, complained in the cloakroom. She had come fully trained to Wythenshaw's and been appointed as Mr Bunting's secretary.

'Not this morning! Not any morning really, anything's better than staying home.' Emily twisted round so she could run the roller towel round the back of her neck. Rain had trickled down the collar of her best blue blouse. Pools of water were running from mackintoshes and umbrellas on to the tiled floor.

'You're soaked.' Sylveen edged away from her. 'And today of all days. Why come on your bike in weather like this? You haven't far to walk, and an umbrella . . .'

'Quicker to get back. Have to for the shop.' Emily took out her comb and moved nearer the mirror, but there was nothing she could do to make her hair look better. It was short, the colour of dark chocolate and hanging in damp clumps that made it look straighter than usual. Her fringe was sticking out in all directions. Her usual treatment was to damp it down. She tried a little more water to make it lie flat.

'I don't know how you put up with it. Your dad's a slave driver.' As Sylveen applied lipstick, their eyes met in the mirror. 'Still, you're lucky in other ways, today's the day, isn't it?'

It was no secret that Sylveen fancied Giles Wythenshaw. With her looks, the typing pool thought she had the best chance of getting him, and half the office discussed how it might be done. 'A good job you don't worry about what you look like.'

Emily's brown eyes glittered back at her from the

mirror. 'But I do,' she said with feeling. 'I'd like to look more like you.' She looked enviously at Sylveen's blonde waves, and couldn't help comparing her own rosy cheeks and elf-like features with Sylveen's fair skin and fragile beauty. 'But it isn't possible.'

'You could choose your clothes more carefully.' That made Emily smooth down her grey flannel skirt.

'It's the wrong shape, does nothing for you. Needs to be longer.' A scented cloud billowed up as Sylveen patted powder on her pretty nose.

'I could let the hem down,' Emily said doubtfully; she'd been pleased with it when she'd bought it last winter.

'Needs more than that. You're too thin. It's not fashionable any more to have a figure like a boy. Eat more of those chips, fill yourself out. You need to look more womanly.'

Emily grimaced. She hated chips. She loathed the smell of them, couldn't bear even talking about them. She wished for the thousandth time she didn't live in a chip shop.

Beside her, Sylveen was teasing seductive blonde tendrils down her cheeks. She was taller and heavier by a stone. Every ounce enhanced her figure. 'You ought to take yourself in hand.'

Emily was certain she'd done all she could. She'd turned herself into a Janus, leading a double life. This was her preferred persona, office girl in plain cardigan and skirt. Sylveen hadn't noticed how much worse she looked in the shop. 'How?'

'Well, how old are you?'

'Seventeen.'

'You look fourteen. Make yourself look older.'

Emily frowned in the mirror. Surely she looked at least sixteen?

'That's your problem. You look like jail bait.'

'What's that?'

'You know. It's illegal for men to be intimate with girls under sixteen.'

Emily felt the flush run up her cheeks. 'I wouldn't want to be,' she said too aggressively.

'Of course not,' Sylveen soothed, in her breathy voice. 'But you want to look interesting with Giles Wythenshaw about. He's lovely, isn't he? Emily, you are lucky!'

Emily agreed, she had also counted herself lucky to get on Wythenshaw's office-training course when she left school at fourteen.

'I'd better go, he might be there.' They went down the corridor. Sylveen headed for Mr Bunting's office, swaying on her high heels.

Emily went on; the canteen offices were in the factory and not grand. She felt all of a flutter but only Mr Osborne, the manager, was there to greet her. She had to make a conscious effort to keep her eyes away from the red patches his spectacles made where they clipped on to his large nose.

She found the desk she was to use wedged in a small anteroom. Two other rooms opened from it; the larger was used by Samuel Osborne, the other he told her was being used by Giles Wythenshaw.

He showed her the files, pointed out the stationery cupboard, and dictated a few letters. Emily couldn't concentrate: her fingers were hitting the wrong keys, she was buoyed up with anticipation.

It was mid morning when she looked up to find Giles studying her from the doorway. His large tawny eyes held her gaze for a full five seconds, making her tingle with surprised gratification.

'I'm Giles Wythenshaw,' he said, as if he expected her not to know. She felt his hand grasping hers in a friendly squeeze. 'I understand you're to be my secretary.' He perched on the corner of her desk smiling down at her, smoking a cigarette in a jet holder with gold bands. 'I hope we'll get on well together.'

His eyes were wide spaced and slightly protruding;

everybody noticed them. Hot eyes, they called them in the typing pool. Emily felt they were like magnets pulling her gaze up to meet his. With an effort she managed to break eye contact. Sensuality crackled out of him.

He was blessed in other ways; being fond of sailing, sun and wind had bronzed his skin and bleached gold streaks into his handsome head of loose waves. His suits were expensive, his shirts whiter than snow, his fingernails appeared manicured.

She had decided she was not going to compete with the pack where Giles was concerned, but within days she was lost. In slack moments he would amuse her with stories about sailing his boat, and his hot eyes would laugh into hers. There was a warmth about him, it was impossible not to like him. She found herself building whole worlds of meaning into his smiles, revelling in his company. She even began to hope he would feel the same titillating pleasure he gave her. But as the months passed, she realised he was not singling her out with special affection. His handsome tawny eyes worked their magic on every girl he met.

Only last week, Mavis Finnegan had been cheeky enough to ask whether he'd kissed her yet. That was how the typing pool rated progress. Emily wished she could say he had, but she knew she was no nearer that now, than she had been her first day in the canteen office.

She knew she'd been given the job because her tutor said her shorthand was better than average. She also knew now that Giles Wythenshaw never dictated anything. He came into the office to browse through the mail and pencil notes in the margins. 'Potatoes delivered not quality laid down in contract.' Or: 'Ask for samples and price list.' Then she had to formulate his letters.

She made up her mind to be the perfect secretary. She'd make herself indispensable, impress with her efficiency. Giles Wythenshaw might then take more notice of her.

Sometimes he gave her work which could not be described as secretarial. She always did it to the best of her ability, and Giles would smile and say: 'Don't know what I'd do without you, Emily.'

Officially, Giles was one of three management trainees being given experience round the factory. Alex Fraser was another. The difference was that one day Giles would run it. He was currently learning how subsidised dinners were provided for employees, and monitoring the true cost.

Emily found it was her job to keep copies of the bills that came in daily. Giles was supposed to add up what was being spent on food, wages, heating, cleaning and administration, to arrive at a price per meal. It was Emily's job to type his figures into a neat schedule at the end of each month.

When the figures were due for the second time, she had to remind him. His tongue clicked with impatience but he sat down and did the job. The month after, she had to remind him once more.

He frowned. 'I haven't time now. Tomorrow.'

Emily knew by now, he spent most of his day out on the golf course, or in his boat. She started to collate the figures herself, using the new comptometer he'd had installed in his office, feeling her way, trying to follow the method he had been shown by Mr Osborne. She hoped to keep him out of trouble.

'You will check what I've done, Mr Wythenshaw?'

'Of course, Emily. You're a wonderful help.'

The following month, he said: 'You're better at it than I am. How about doing it again?' Somehow, she found herself doing the job thereafter.

Emily was feeding five sheets of paper and four carbons into her Remington to type next week's menu, when the phone rang. The call seemed harmless enough at first.

'Can I speak to Mr Giles Wythenshaw?'

'I'm afraid he isn't in at the moment,' she said. Routine question and routine answer. He rarely came this early.

'Donkin, Internal Audit here. Ask him to ring me as soon as he comes. I need to speak to him this morning.' Emily felt a vague sense of unease.

'Is it the September figures?' She'd sent them up yesterday to Donkin's office, two days late.

'Well yes, though the problem seems to go back further.' That brought her first flutter of alarm. 'I'd like him to explain his method.' Emily froze in consternation.

'Hello, are you still there?'

'I'll give him your message,' she said weakly, knowing the error must be hers, and Giles Wythenshaw wouldn't be able to explain anything.

The next moment she was scrabbling through the filing cabinet for the copies. She must have overlooked something. She studied them till the figures danced before her eyes, but she couldn't see where she'd gone wrong. To think she'd prided herself on being efficient!

She had to let Giles know, though he wouldn't be pleased. Where would he be on a wet morning? Probably still in bed. She asked the operator to put her through to Churton House. She was right, he sounded half asleep.

'What sort of a mistake?' he demanded peevishly. Since she didn't know, it was hard to explain.

'All right,' he said. 'I'll ring Donkin and find out, and then I'll come in and you can explain what you've done.' Emily shivered, his manner had changed. It seemed he wasn't so friendly when things went wrong.

A great ball of dread was growing inside her. How could she have been so careless? She felt all thumbs, and made so many typing errors on the menu, she had to tear it out and start again. Mr Osborne gave her a couple of letters to type, but they were soon finished. Being slack gave her time to worry. She kept looking out of the window, to see if his black Riley Monaco sports saloon was parked outside.

The morning dragged into afternoon. She gave up

expecting him as dusk came. The factory closed at five-thirty, and the machines stopped five minutes before the hooter blew. All day long there was a permanent background hum, made up of the slide and rattle of mechanical rollers, and the rhythmic thump of machinery die stamping brooches from sheet metal. In the sudden silence she heard a girlish shriek and a wolf whistle followed by ribald laughter. This was Giles Wythenshaw's usual reception from the factory girls. Her office door banged back.

'You've dropped me in it, Emily.' His handsome face could have been chiselled from stone.

'What did I do wrong?' she choked.

'I don't know. You should be more careful.' Emily believed she was careful. 'How did you get a cost of 3.1 pence per meal? It's not enough.'

She heard the factory hooter wailing, and panic surged through her. Then came the sound of feet stampeding down the corridor. 'I don't know.'

'You must know. You should check what you do.'

She'd checked everything twice. She'd no idea what had gone wrong.

He was taking a sheaf of papers from his briefcase. 'We'll have to go through the figures and find out.'

Emily stared at the office clock, agonised. Already she was five minutes late leaving. 'I can't now,' she gasped.

'Why not?'

'It's time to go home. I'm sorry, I have to. Won't tomorrow do?' His tongue clicked with impatience.

'First thing, then. Donkin will be here at eleven to get it sorted. Must find out where you've gone wrong before he comes.'

For once Emily was relieved to get away. She grabbed her gaberdine from the cloakroom and rushed to the bike shed. She was shaken by the change in him. Knowing she had no one to blame but herself made it worse.

She was late leaving because he'd come in at the last

minute, and that would put Dad in a bad mood. She stood on the pedals of her mother's old-fashioned bike to force them round. Usually she managed to get away quickly, ahead of the tide of workers. Today she couldn't pedal through, they hampered her progress. It was Friday, the evening air vibrated with shouts and laughter as the crowd surged out through great iron gates, taking her with it.

From the darkening street all Emily could see of Wythenshaw & Son, Manufacturers of Artificial Jewellery, was a gaunt windowless building, the original nineteenth-century factory dominating the skyline downriver towards Birkenhead. An eight-foot wall of smoke-blackened brick, topped with splintered glass, hid the newer buildings in the yard.

The new office had been built in 1904, when Wythenshaw's had added gilt brooches and bracelets to their necklaces of coloured glass.

Emily pedalled slowly along Paradise Street in the middle of the crush. A terrace of two-up and two-down cottages fronted the pavement on one side. On the other, an eight-foot wire fence cut off access to the River Mersey. Dusk veiled the industrial squalor of the foreshore. She could see lights twinkling on the Liverpool side, and feel the keen wind blowing off the river. They passed a small factory that roasted peanuts before the road curved into Paradise Parade.

All along the Parade, a row of shops, the lights were full on. As factory hooters sounded, every counter hand stood poised like a sprinter waiting for the starting pistol. Whether at dinner time or five-thirty, there was a mad rush. At other hours, trade could be spasmodic, they had their good days and their bad, but they benefited from two hours of hard trading, day in and day out, and were grateful for the prosperity it brought.

Emily could see customers pouring into the greengrocer's, jockeying to be served quickly and be on their way. The newsagent was doing a roaring trade with Woodbines and *Liverpool Echoes*. Ethel's Ladies' Fashions had a crowd of girls round its window.

Charlie Barr's Chippy stood out like a beacon. Emily knew he always timed his chips to be crisping when the hooter sounded. Black figures were running to his door. She could see steam clouding the windows, the door opening and the crush inside clammering to be served. The scent of frying rolled along the Parade to meet her.

She turned into the entry behind the shops, slithering on the wet setts. The gate into the back yard scraped the step as she pushed it open. Two empty fish boxes stood against the wall. Hurriedly she pushed her bike into the shed.

At the back door, the atmosphere pungent with years of frying closed round her. Stale odours had seeped into the curtains and the wallpaper, the lino, the hearth rug, and the furniture itself. It had penetrated every room behind and above Charlie's chip shop. It would seep into all her clothes, and her hair if she gave it half a chance.

Warmth and fresher scents came from the shop now, and the buzz of voices.

'Emily, you're late. Hurry up. Get yourself here,' Charlie called in strident tones as she ran past.

'Coming, Dad.' She took the stairs two at a time, unbuttoning her coat as she went. The air funnelled up the stairs bringing warmth from the shop. The odours hung in a heavy pall on the tiny landing, sometimes thick enough to make her gag. Hers was the only bedroom on the attic floor. Hastily she pushed her key in the lock and shot inside, slamming the door behind her.

Inside it was twenty degrees colder than the landing. She kept the window open always. In October, Birkenhead air was damp and smoke laden, but anything was better than the smell of chips. At school the children had said quite often: 'You smell of chips.' She couldn't have them say it at the office.

She had made a draught excluder to fit along the bottom of her door from a laddered stocking stuffed with clean rags. She'd driven damp paper between the skirting board and the floor with a knife. She'd taken to locking the door since the day Gran had taken clean sheets in and left it open.

She undressed quickly. One deft movement put a coat hanger through her blouse. Her grey skirt was hung behind the curtain that served instead of a wardrobe. Off came her stockings.

In her slip, she shot back on to the landing, locking the door behind her. She pulled on the red dress that hung on a nail in readiness, buttoned a print overall over it. Tied a scarf, turban style, over her hair, tucking in every last wisp. This was why her fringe wouldn't lie straight, she parted it too often to push it under her scarf. Hair was notoriously quick to pick up scents.

She pushed her bare feet into broken sandals, thinking what a Jekyll and Hyde existence she led. From neat office worker to drudge in one minute thirty-two seconds. She skidded down to find the shop crammed with jostling customers rapping their pennies against the counter.

'You've taken your time,' her father said, making a token pass with the vinegar bottle over the chips he was wrapping. 'Where've you been till now?'

He was a short man with the beginnings of a beer gut. His hair was a thick straight swatch of iron grey, his face pallid, ill tempered and greasy. He looked as though fish and chips were his staple diet, which they were.

Emily heard somebody call: 'A pennyworth of chips and a twopenny fish.' She started to serve. It was five minutes before she hissed: 'Where's Gran?'

'Not well. In bed.'

That shocked her. Gran must be ill to be in bed during rush hour. She had never failed to be here before.

Charlie Barr slid a scant scoop of chips on to the paper

and hesitated. He mustn't get a reputation for being stingy, so he added a few more before wrapping them in newspaper. The penny clattered into the till, and he was able to take a breather at last. It had been a terrible day, he was dead tired. He hadn't stopped since he'd opened at five o'clock.

Almost immediately, a waiting customer had shouted a warning to him, and he'd turned to see his mother sliding to the floor in a dead faint. She'd banged her head on the corner of the fryer as she fell.

His nerves felt torn to shreds, with half the customers shouting to be served and half demanding he attend to his mother. He'd been unable to move. What did one do for fainting women? He'd never known his mother faint before in all her eighty-two years, and there had been no warning.

Except that she'd complained of feeling unwell before he opened the shop, and said she wanted to lie down. But she'd not needed much persuasion to leave it till after seven, because he really did need her.

He'd felt panic stricken. Who wouldn't, seeing her black straw hat knocked off and streaks of blood daubing her sparse white hair? Luckily, Myra George, who helped in Ted's shop, was in getting some chips for her tea before the evening rush began.

'Fetch Olympia,' he'd croaked, Olympia always knew what to do. But Myra had helped Ma upstairs and put her to bed by herself.

'Working your old ma till she drops,' one man had guffawed to the whole shop. He'd had to ignore it because he was being run off his feet.

Even so, he'd overcooked a whole batch of chips during the mêlée. They had hardened and dried till they were almost inedible, but he couldn't waste them, and he had to get the queue served.

'What about a cup of tea for your ma?' He hadn't noticed Myra come down, but the queue had.

'How is she?' they chorused.

'She's all right.' It was Ma's job to look after the customers who sat down to eat at the tables. She buttered bread for a penny a round, and made cups of tea if they wanted it. The pot happened to be full, so Myra had taken a cup upstairs.

Myra was a cheeky bit though. 'How about being generous with the chips tonight?' she'd said when he came to serve her. And if that wasn't bad enough, she'd opened the package in front of them all and added: 'I don't call that generous.' He'd had to give her a few more, it didn't do to argue with customers.

On top of all that Emily had been late, and when she'd turned up she'd stood around expecting him to tell her all about Ma. It had been as much as he could do to stop her dropping everything to see how she was.

She could be as obstinate as a mule, could Emily. She'd dug her feet in, and at the first opportunity shot upstairs. She was a right little madam, it wouldn't hurt her to pull her weight more. She'd have to while Ma was sick. He had put it to her nicely. Tried to keep her sweet, though she'd chosen today of all days to be late.

'I'll need a hand in the shop, Emily, while Ma's in her bed.'

'I'm sorry I was late. Something happened in the office, I was kept talking about what should be done.'

'All right, but I want you to take a couple of days off. You'll not lose out. Wythenshaw's will pay you just the same.' Charlie was watching her face. For one wonderful moment the little madam seemed to consider it. He really thought she might.

'I can't, Dad.' She'd turned her pert little nose up at him. 'I can't stay off work.'

'Tell them you're sick. Or I'll phone and tell them.' Her brown eyes had met his, full of contempt.

'Just for a couple of days till Ma's better.' He shouldn't

have to plead like this. 'I can't manage on my own.'

She'd spun round on him like a tiger. 'Gran's too old to work. You're killing her. Why don't you get help?'

'I'm asking you to help.'

'No, Dad.'

'Oh come on, Emily, it wouldn't hurt you.'

'In the long run you'll have to pay someone else. You've put it off long enough.'

Charlie pursed his lips. She was always on at him to hire help, he'd heard it too often. She thought money grew on trees. No sense. 'The business can't afford it.'

'Come off it, Dad,' she'd said.

There was something alien about Emily. She could look at him with the eyes of a stranger. Like now. He'd never felt close to her. He'd married her mother and saddled himself with her.

She'd been three years old when he'd first seen her. An elf-like child who spoke with unusual fluency for her age. He'd thought she'd be easy to love. He'd wanted to, because of Alice. Bright she might have been, but she'd showed too clearly what she felt. Her lustrous brown eyes were like windows to her mind. He knew she'd always hated him.

The way she clung to Alice when he was near had turned him off. She'd always been so demanding of her mother's attention. So wary of him.

He'd had so few years with Alice, and always the little madam had been between them, ever present. She'd come into their bedroom in the middle of the night, careful to get into their bed on Alice's side, and not above showing resentment that he was there already. Nobody could take to a child like that. He'd wanted to love her, it just wouldn't come.

'My mummy,' she used to cry. 'She's mine.' He'd had to prise her fingers open to release them from Alice's nightdress more than once.

'Be patient with her,' Alice had pleaded. 'She's shared my bed till now. She's jealous but she's only three, she'll get used to you. Give her time.'

'You fuss her too much, Alice.'

'No. Let's show her all the affection we can. She'll come round.'

'I already do,' he'd protested, but Emily never had come round.

She was nothing like her mother. Alice had been gentler, more easily persuaded to do things his way, and he hadn't pushed her too far about Emily's father. He knew she'd been hurt, it showed.

Alice had bowled him over. He'd been willing to take on anything if he could have her. Willing even to support another man's child. And he'd done that even when Alice was gone. Fed and clothed her all through her childhood. No thanks from her, wouldn't lift a finger to help him now.

Not that he'd come out of it badly. Wythenshaw's had helped because of the manner of Alice's death. She'd gone off to work in the morning and been dead by eleven o'clock. She'd been working in their canteen kitchen when it had gone on fire. He'd been shaken to the core. Only right he should be compensated. Only right they should pay him ten shillings a week to support her dependent child, and take her into their offices when she was old enough.

Emily had tossed and turned late into the night. When the time came to get up she felt heavy with sleep. The house was cold and silent as she ran downstairs.

Because Gran usually did it, she cleared the ashes from the grate in the living-room and laid a fresh fire. Bed was the only reasonable place for an invalid in this house, since Dad didn't like the fire being lit early in the morning. She heated the pan of porridge she'd made last night and took two bowls upstairs, so they could have it together.

Gran was a still, small mound under the bedclothes, her thin white hair spread across the pillow. Her skin was grey and wrinkled like the skin of a tortoise. With her teeth in a tumbler on the chest by her bed, her cheeks sagged inwards, leaving her mouth open. She looked incredibly old.

Suddenly Emily froze, waiting for her to breathe. The mound was too still. Horror was stealing through her. But no, the cheeks moved slowly like bellows. Gran was breathing all right.

She relaxed a little, it seemed a shame to wake her, but Gran would never get better if she didn't eat. She hated to see her sick and helpless.

Gran had hugged her that awful day her mother had died, and promised then she would look after her. She'd been seventy-two, but she'd kept her promise. Emily saw Gran's rheumy eyes open slowly.

'I was afraid I wouldn't live to see you grow up,' she murmured. 'But you'll be all right now.'

Emily shivered, afraid Gran was ready to die now she'd discharged that duty. She couldn't imagine life without her.

When it was time to leave for work, she was reluctant to go. Last night, she'd been tempted, when Dad suggested she stay off, but she knew it wouldn't solve anything. Eventually she'd have to go back. She pushed her bike into the back entry.

'Morning, Emily.' Another bike was coming out from the yard behind Fraser's Grocers of Distinction, two doors up the Parade. She'd known Alexander Fraser as an ally all her life. He was nearly two years older, and had been her childhood companion and mentor. At one time, she'd thought the strong curve of his jaw wonderful, his thick dark chestnut hair handsome. Over the last year or so, she'd not felt so close. They were drifting apart and she didn't know how to stop it. She still saw a lot of him because they lived so close, and he worked at

Wythenshaw's too. Pedalling hard, Emily started telling him what was on her mind.

'God, Emily, they aren't paying you to take that sort of responsibility. It's not your job.'

She sighed. 'There's not much typing to do. Not enough to keep me busy.'

'Don't worry, they can't expect the earth for three pounds a week.' Alex's grin was rather lopsided.

'It's good money,' she said indignantly.

'Not good enough to blame you for mistakes of that sort. You're supposed to be a shorthand typist. Who showed you how to work out those costs?'

'Nobody showed me.'

'I bet they pay Giles Wythenshaw a handsome salary, and he's doing nothing.'

'It's different for him,' Emily flared.

'Very different. For him everything comes easily, it's handed to him on a plate. He's like Peter Pan, he can't grow up. Twenty-three and still wants to play. Can't concentrate on anything but his own pleasure.'

'You sound envious,' Emily said coldly.

'I am. I'd give a lot to be in his shoes, being groomed to run the whole works.' Alex laughed. 'Serve him right for leaving it all to you.'

Once Alex would have understood. Emily pedalled harder, wanting to get away. The trouble with childhood sweethearts was that you grew out of them. Damn Alex. She reached her office.

'Good morning, Mr Osborne.' She could see him at his desk through the adjoining door. Apart from the background clatter of machinery, there was no sound. She tapped on the door of Giles Wythenshaw's room, then pushed it ajar. The two letters she'd typed for him yesterday still waited for his signature. He hadn't even bothered to sign them last night.

Giles had said he'd come in early. Yesterday he'd been

reluctant to let her go before they'd gone through the figures. She couldn't understand why he wasn't here now. She felt on edge, torn between wanting to get it over, yet fearful of the trouble it might bring.

Why should she worry? It didn't seem to be bothering him. There was still plenty of time for everything she could tell him. Nevertheless a lump of foreboding was growing in her throat.

The morning dragged. Mr Osborne dictated two or three letters, but she soon finished them. He went down to the kitchens, and she started to tidy the files; it left her mind free to worry. She could no longer sit still at her desk.

Quarter to eleven. Where was he? She went to the window, expecting every moment to see his car edge into its space outside. At five to eleven she heard steps and voices coming along the passage. She knew already Giles Wythenshaw would not be with them.

'Good morning.' The door of her anteroom swept open. 'Donkin and Coates from Internal Audit. Mr Wythenshaw asked us to be here at eleven.' Soberly clad and serious, they filled all the space. She indicated two upright chairs.

Donkin was in his mid thirties with thin sandy hair and a moustache to match. An up-and-coming executive, he exuded confidence.

'Mr Wythenshaw won't be long.' She looked pointedly at the clock, it was three minutes before time. Would he still be at home, sitting over his breakfast? He had talked of a heavy social life that kept him out late. She dialled the number, conscious of two pairs of eyes both behind gold-rimmed spectacles, watching every movement she made.

'Young Mr Wythenshaw?' Emily knew it was the housekeeper who answered though she didn't say so. She'd rung often enough for that. 'He left for the office some time ago. Early, around nine.'

'Thank you,' Emily said hastily, slapping the phone down before she could say anything else.

The golf club, then. She opened her diary to read the number and closed it before dialling. The men were sitting too close, almost overpowering her. She hoped they had not heard the housekeeper. The phone was in the bar, she could hear the tell-tale clink of glasses as she waited.

A voice said: 'Hello, Wythenshaw here.'

'Oh! Mr Donkin and Mr Coates have arrived. Your eleven o'clock appointment.'

There was a moment's silence. She knew he'd forgotten all about it. 'Let them wait in my office, Emily. Make them some tea, I'll be there in five minutes. Keep them happy.'

'Yes, Mr Wythenshaw.' Donkin was watching her, his fingers steepling, signalling power. Norman Coates's straight hair stuck out like wire. She saw him wink almost imperceptibly. He was Alex's friend, the third of Wythenshaw's management trainees. No doubt, it was he who had spotted the error. That would not please Giles either.

She smiled. 'He's been delayed in a meeting, but he's on his way now and won't be more than five minutes. Sends his apologies.'

She knew he couldn't possibly cover the distance in five minutes, but she felt better now she had made contact. She had time to make the tea and take it in. They had time to drink it too. It was a relief to have her office to herself again.

She heard his car tyres scream to a halt in the yard. He was at her door in moments, signalling to her to come to the storeroom opposite. It was bigger than her office, with shelves piled high with dried goods, flour, sugar, salt and rice in big sacks.

'Emily.' He was breathless. 'You never did get round to telling me what you did wrong.'

'I don't know. They haven't explained it to me. I can hardly ask.'

'You must know.'

'No, you'll have to talk to them. They'll tell you.'

He groaned. 'I'll leave the door open, so you can listen. If I can't handle it I'll have to make some excuse to come out and confer. All right?'

She nodded, 'I'm sorry,' but he was gone.

His voice carried clearly, greeting them, pouring himself a cup of tea from the pot she'd taken in. It would be cold by now. He didn't sound his usual confident self. Emily closed her eyes and wished it was over. She heard the rustle of papers being spread across his desk.

They were asking him exactly how he'd arrived at a figure of 3.1 pence per canteen dinner. He was blustering, showing too obviously he hadn't the slightest idea. Emily curled up inside. She heard him suggest it might be a typing error. Even he must know it was a lot more than that! He was doing his best to lay the fault on her. Then he suggested it could be an error in arithmetic.

'Obviously,' Mr Donkin said, and for a time they were side-tracked into discussing the reliability of the new comptometer Giles had ordered, and the feasibility of having a girl to operate it for him.

Emily covered her face in anguish. Hadn't she asked him to check her figures? She might have known he wouldn't bother.

She looked at the clock. They'd been at it for an hour, and were no nearer a solution now. Mr Donkin asked Giles to explain his method. Emily heard the papers rustle again.

'Excuse me a moment.' He came out closing the door behind him.

Emily could see by his turkey-red face that they had him rattled. He grabbed her by the wrist and headed for the storeroom. There were no windows and, when he closed the door, his face was a pale triangle in the darkness.

'I added all the bills together, and divided by the number of meals served,' she hissed, feeling anxiety ricochet round the store, increasing the jitters she already had.

'What about wages?'

'I added them in. Heating, lighting, depreciation on equipment, everything.' The store was hot and smelled of apples.

'You couldn't have. You've done something wrong. You should have gone into it with me.'

'You weren't here.' Emily felt stiff with tension.

'Come on, don't hold out on me now.'

'I'm not holding out. I'm trying to help. The problem goes back to the first month when you did them. Mr Osborne showed you how.'

'You're not saying it's my fault?'

'I don't know. I think the final figure should have been carried on from one month to the next, but there's more wrong than that. Keep them talking, and you'll find out.'

'For God's sake, Emily!'

She heard him stumble over something in the darkness, as she followed him back to her desk. She found she was holding her breath; both the auditors had their backs to her, it wasn't easy to hear what they were saying. The interview dragged on.

'You'll have to excuse me again, I'm afraid,' she heard Giles say. 'Must be something I've eaten.'

His face was twisting with anger as he swept to her desk. 'Come on,' he snarled under his breath. She followed him again to the store. The door slammed shut, blackness engulfed them.

'You're making me look a bloody fool.' She could hear the fury in his voice. 'You've really dropped me in it. Come on, open up, Emily.'

'Definitely the final figure should have been cumulative,' she was saying. His face came close to hers in the darkness. She could see the angry glow in his eyes. He came closer still, she could feel his breath against her forehead, it seemed threatening. In a wave of panic she threw out her hand to ward him off. She felt her nails scrape against flesh.

His sharp intake of breath told her she'd hurt him. Jerking back in horror she bumped her head against a shelf.

'You little cat,' he spat, snatching the door open. As he turned, the light from the corridor shone on three angry scratches running from the corner of his eye to his chin. One deeper than the others ran with blood.

'What did you do that for?' he gasped, staring at his fingers, smeared with blood from touching his face. His shocked eyes met hers before he twisted away, cannoning into Mavis Finnegan who was on her way back to the typing pool after taking dictation from one of the salesmen.

'What's the matter?' Her eyes glittered with speculation behind their thick spectacles, as she looked from Giles to Emily.

'Nothing!' he spat and went striding off towards the men's cloakroom. Emily was shaking. She could still feel his flesh under her fingernails.

'Did you scratch his face, Emily?' Mavis had short mousey hair, which she wore pushed back anyhow behind her ears.

With an agonised groan Emily ran towards the cloakroom, fighting for self control. She hadn't meant to do him any harm. It had been an accident. She couldn't face Mavis Finnegan or going back to her office, and anyway it was almost time to go home. Already the cloakroom was filling with girls; she pushed her way through them to grab at her coat. She was frightened she'd marked the boss's son for life.

CHAPTER TWO

Emily pedalled furiously, feeling overwhelmed. She'd grown used to normal office life, working hard, building her career, edging towards what she thought of as a better life. The cold damp air did nothing to cool her hot cheeks.

Everything had blown up in her face, and the more she thought about it, the worse it seemed. She'd set out to attract Giles's attention with her competence; instead she'd impressed with her mistakes. She'd scratched his face and, by Monday, Mavis Finnegan would have set the whole office agog with the news.

'You little cat,' he'd snarled.

She couldn't believe the change in him. In her day-dreams he'd never act like this. She began to worry that he'd complain about her. If he did, she would certainly be sent back to the typing pool in disgrace.

The familiar pungent smell of home closed round her. She raced to change into her old clothes, and run down to Gran's room. She sought comfort, sinking down on Gran's bed, and telling her what had happened, letting all her fears flood out.

'Emily! You could get the sack.' Horror gave Gran the strength to pull herself up the bed, revealing a large expanse of pink winceyette nightdress topped with a black wool shawl.

Gran was rarely seen without her shawls. She had two;

a shoulder shawl with a bobble fringe, which she wore in the house as well as in bed, and a larger thicker one to cover it, if she went to the pub or out along the Parade. For serving in the shop she dispensed with both; the heat from the fryer made shawls unnecessary.

Emily had already worried about getting the sack, but had comforted herself with the thought that Wythenshaw's always treated employees kindly. To hear Gran put it in words made the strength ebb from her knees.

In these days of depression, jobs were not easy to get. Her career might end almost before it began. She'd need a good reference from Wythenshaw's, if she were to stand a chance anywhere else.

'What a pity, especially when you'd made a good start,' Gran lamented, her eyes rheumy. 'And working for the boss's son – I had such hopes for you.' Emily hadn't expected Gran to see things as the typing pool did.

'I wanted you to have a better life. I hoped you'd make a good marriage. People like us have to, if we're to have anything.'

Gran had soft slack cheeks, and eyes that didn't miss much, though she couldn't read without her glasses. They were on the chest beside her bed now, tortoiseshell frames, held together with sticking plaster. Really she needed them to see the coins she was being handed in the shop, but she had learned instead the feel of small change.

Emily saw her future stretching ahead in the chip shop; even if she had no job to go to, Dad would see she was fully occupied. Gran was writing off any alternative, and Emily had the sinking feeling she'd lost everything she held most dear.

She had had this feeling before. She had been seven years old on the day she'd heard the fire engines hurtle past her school. Walking home with Alex at dinner time, she saw the usual crowd milling along the Parade. She noticed people turning to look at her with pity in their eyes.

'The blinds are down.' She'd jerked Alex to a halt, fear pulsing through her. She'd never known the shop closed at dinner time. She rushed in the back way, to find her father slumped in a chair in the living-room staring at the empty grate in despair. Gran had pulled her on her knee; Emily remembered being hugged against unyielding corsets.

'Your mother's been killed,' Charlie said baldly. It had taken a moment for the awful truth to sink in, because her mother was never home at dinner time. Gran's face, ravaged by tears, underlined her grief. The feeling of being abandoned came quickly. Desolation followed, and eyes that kept flooding tears however hard she tried to control them. She had not eaten the food Gran put on her plate.

Alex had returned; he had been seeing her back and forth to school since the day she started. Gran would have kept her on her knee.

'Send her back to school,' Charlie snapped. 'Better for her. I can't stand her snivelling underfoot all afternoon.'

Emily remembered the aching devastation. The painful humiliation of being unwanted. Of knowing Charlie believed her loss less than his, and that her grief was a small matter.

'Your gran loves you,' Alex had consoled. 'She'll take care of you.'

'Yes, but she isn't really my gran. He's not my father either. I've nobody of my own now.' That was over ten years ago, but the warmth of Alex's response was with her still.

'You've got me. I'm your friend.' She'd heard the break in his voice, felt the weight of his arm on her shoulders as clumsily he'd pulled her close. 'Come on, kid. I'll see you're all right.'

'Better go and help Charlie.' Gran's gnarled hand patted hers now. 'You know what Saturday dinner time's like.'

Emily went down reluctantly, expecting to find her father in a bad mood. He was scooping a mound of crisp chips on to the warming tray, while the waiting customers sniffed appreciatively.

The fryer he'd bought secondhand last year almost filled one wall of the shop. It reminded Emily of a cinema organ, its pale green enamel decorated with strips of polished chrome. He moved a batch of half-cooked chips to the crisper, and the fat spluttered furiously as more raw ones were flung in.

Emily started to serve, and there was no time to think of anything else. She knew she could do this job and not be found wanting; its familiarity was a comfort. For once she found the frenzied atmosphere soothing. Charlie served like an automaton alongside her.

'Next,' he barked.

'I'll wait for Emily.'

That caught her attention. Sylveen had come in on her way home. Emily knew it riled Charlie to have customers ask for her. He said they did it because she gave over-generous portions. Emily hastened to serve her, so she would go and Charlie forget what he saw as an insult.

'Three pennyworth of chips, and three fish.' Emily picked out three good fish and, after making sure Charlie's attention was elsewhere, scooped generous measures of chips into the bags.

'How about coming down Grange Road this afternoon, Emily? I want a new frock, and we could look for a new skirt for you.'

'I can't,' she said quietly. 'Got to work.'

'She can come out, can't she, Mr Barr? Just for a couple of hours. You close in the afternoon, don't you?'

'She doesn't need any new skirts,' he said. 'Got more than enough clothes already.'

A young workman in dungarees grinned from Sylveen

to Emily. 'I'll come with you. You can choose some new trousers for me.'

'I don't think so,' Sylveen said distantly. 'I'm not sure you're my type.'

'You're mine,' he said, and she laughed, counting her money into Emily's hand.

'Thanks for the offer, Handsome, but I never go out with strange men. See you, Emily.'

'Who is she?' the workman demanded when it was his turn to be served.

'Just a girl I know.'

'Wish I did.' His grin was friendly.

'Chatty to the fellows, isn't she?' another customer added.

'Chatty to the girls as well,' Emily retorted. 'Sylveen's a friendly person.'

'Too friendly by half,' Charlie grunted.

'Not to me,' the workman sighed.

'How do you know her, Emily?' her father demanded suspiciously.

'She works in the office at Wythenshaw's.' Emily expertly wrapped the parcel in newspaper.

'She doesn't live round here?'

'No, she lives in Prenton.'

'Whew, posh,' the workman said. Emily thought so too; Sylveen's home was a new semi-detached.

'She's not posh,' Gladys Wade, Billy's grandmother, said stridently from the back of the shop. 'She's no better than she should be, that one. I know her, our Edith lives near her.'

Emily knew Gladys as a gossiping old harridan who used to serve in the newsagent's next door, but now she helped only with household tasks. She had come in wearing her carpet slippers and crossover floral overall.

'Had a baby she did. Had it adopted, now she's going round as bold as brass.'

Emily couldn't stop her sudden intake of breath. 'Did she?' She hadn't known that.

'You're better off without the likes of her, young man.'

'Oh, I don't know,' he said, handing over his money in exchange for the parcel of chips.

Emily shivered. She had envied Sylveen her looks, and her middle-class background. Her easy-going manner gave no hint of the trouble she'd had. She wondered who the father had been.

'Stay away from her,' Charlie ordered. 'Do you hear? We don't want you led into trouble like that.'

Emily seethed with anger at Gladys Wade, for taking Sylveen's reputation away in front of a shopful of customers. When she came to serve her, she was deliberately meaner than Charlie would ever be with the chips.

'Two bottles of dandelion and burdock please.' On one side of the fryer was a shelf holding half-penny bottles of pop, brilliantly coloured. On the other, a table supported two gas rings. A pan simmered mushy peas on one, a kettle sang on the other.

Emily saw Alex Fraser looking round the shop door. He waved to her but retreated. She knew he could see she was busy and would come back. She wanted to tell him about scratching Giles Wythenshaw. Alex would know what she might expect to happen next.

'Can we have two slices of bread and two teas?' a voice shouted from behind the waiting queue.

'See to the tables, Emily,' her father hissed. Three small tables were fitted into an alcove at the back of the shop, where customers could eat their chips on the premises. Emily poured tea into two thick cups. Snatched bread and butter from the mound prepared during the morning and kept under a damp tea towel. Pushed her way through the waiting queue to the tables.

The alcove wall was decorated with three incongruous pictures. Already the steamy atmosphere was condensing against the glass, toning down the emerald palms and aquamarine sea, the red bathing suits of natives cavorting with beer barrels on a foreign shore.

She had been serving behind the counter for another half hour, when she looked up to find Alex had returned. With an apologetic look in his dark eyes, he handed over a paper bag.

'What's this?' She took it automatically.

'Blackcurrant tarts. Your favourite. For tonight.'

'Why bring them now?'

'Billy Wade has asked me to go out with him.'

Emily bit back the protest. They always spent Saturday evening together, always had as long as she could remember.

Alex's father was Charlie's friend. Even as a child he'd been brought round to play with her on Saturday nights, when his mother went to the pictures. It had become the social occasion of the week: Ted Fraser brought beer round at closing time, and Charlie provided the fish and chips to go with it.

'Billy Wade? What does an evening with him consist of?' She knew she was showing her hurt. She sounded like a fish wife.

'Just a drink at Donovan's. Just for once.' The shop door opened with a rush of cold air. Emily turned to attend to the customer without another word.

'See you around, Emily,' he said shamefacedly. Emily eyed the paper bag he'd given her with displeasure. Alex had been bringing cakes on Saturday nights since he was ten years old.

'After all,' he'd said. 'Dad brings beer.' They'd laughed together, sharing the secret of how on Saturdays Alex put a couple of custard tarts or doughnuts in a paper bag, and hid it below the counter so they wouldn't be sold. It meant they had to eat their feast sitting on the stairs, so Ted wouldn't see the cakes, but they preferred being on their own. Over the years, Alex's mother had found out, but had given permission to take them. Now Alex was working, she knew he paid for anything he took from his mother's shop.

Emily couldn't shake off the feeling she'd been let down for the second time today, and being let down by Alex was far far worse.

It was after two when the shop closed. Charlie took the last of the chips and slumped down at one of the tables. Emily was tired and hungry, but she had to make something for Gran. She went to the scullery and simmered two pieces of fish in milk, but Gran could only manage a few mouthfuls. Emily ate her share too and hurried down again, wanting to get her afternoon work finished.

There was another pan of dried peas to set boiling, and another batch to soak. She wiped down the counter and the fryer, swept out the shop.

One job she quite liked doing was getting the weekend shopping; it made a break to get out along the Parade. Charlie rang up the till and gave her a pound note, and she found a bag.

It gave Emily a feeling of freedom to stand outside Wade's the newsagent next door and read the placards in their window. Not good news: the number of unemployed was growing. The scent of newsprint came wafting out with a customer. As she passed Fraser's Grocers of Distinction, she peeped in to see if Alex was behind the counter. He wasn't.

Sunday was the one day they always had meat. She went into McFie's, the butcher at the end of the row, to buy some stewing steak. Old Mrs McFie served her, wearing an apron spattered with blood. She was stout and ten years younger than Gran, but had been her crony for many years.

'Your gran looked real poorly this morning,' she said. 'I told her I'd send round some lozenges, had them for my bad throat in the spring, and these were left over. Wait a minute while I get them, had to turn out my cupboards but I found them.'

Emily waited in the empty shop, forcing her gaze away from the speciality of the shop, delicious-looking boiled ham. When old Mrs McFie came bustling back, she pressed an opened packet of throat sweets in her hand. 'Tell her they taste terrible, but they'll do her good. Hope she'll be back on her feet soon.' For Emily, shopping along the Parade was a social occasion too.

Outside Tarrant's the greengrocer's, boxes of produce were stacked on the pavement. From them she chose carrots, onions and a couple of lemons to make lemonade for Gran. Cathy Tarrant came to serve her. When she'd gone to school with Cathy, she'd had thick pigtails, but now she had a head of bushy brown curls.

'Guess what?' Cathy's eyes danced with excitement. 'I've got a job. Start on Monday.'

'What as?'

'Dentist's receptionist. Lloyds in Well Lane.'

'Lovely,' Emily breathed.

'Be much better than working for me dad,' Cathy said behind her hand.

Emily laughed; Cathy was a few months older than her and she knew she'd been trying to get a job for a long time. 'All the best for Monday.'

She went along to Fraser's. It was the most stylish shop along the Parade. On one side of the door a brightly coloured metal sign read 'Camp Coffee is Best'. On the other, was a sailor boy advertising Reckitts Bag blue. Alex's mother, Olympia, a junoesque matron of thirty-five, was behind the polished mahogany counter.

'Half a pound of cheddar, please.' Emily drifted to the glass-topped mahogany boxes in which biscuits were displayed. Digestive, eightpence halfpenny for half a pound. Gran's favourite were Crawford's meadow creams but they were tenpence halfpenny.

'How's your gran?' Olympia drew a wire through the cheese, cutting a slice.

'She's got tonsillitis.'

'Gave Myra quite a turn seeing her drop in a dead faint like that. I've told your dad he shouldn't make her work so hard.'

'A packet of Rinso Washing Powder and half a dozen eggs, please.' Emily thought the grocer's shop an Aladdin's cave of delights with mahogany shelves piled high with Skipper sardines, Fry's chocolate, and Libby's cooked corned beef. She sank down on the bentwood chair provided for customers.

'Alex has gone to the match at Prenton Park.' Olympia collected the goods with quick economical movements, and added up the bill. 'I suppose he told you?'

'With Billy Wade?' She hadn't meant to sound so bitter.

'No, he's taken his dad.' Olympia reached behind her for a tin of peaches.

'Give this to your gran for her tea, Emily. They'll slide past her sore throat.' Olympia tucked a loose tendril of hair behind her ear; it was deep chestnut red, very like Alex's, but drawn back in a severe bun.

'Thank you, that's very kind.'

'I'll come in and see her tomorrow. Tell your dad I'll find a girl for him, he's only to say the word.'

When she got back home, Emily found her father already down in the cellar which was their preparation room. With a box of coley at his feet, he was cutting the fish into portions. It was the one job he always did himself. He said other people cut them too big.

'See to the potatoes, Emily,' he ordered. It was the job she liked least. Although Charlie had bought a machine to peel potatoes from a café that had gone bankrupt, it sprayed her with cold water as she fed them in, and then the eyes had to be removed by hand. As she dragged another sack of potatoes down from the yard, she hoped Charlie would make up more batter and not leave it to her. She went on feeding in potatoes till her back ached.

'That'll do. What's the matter with you? I've told you twice you've done enough. It's Sunday tomorrow.'

Emily switched the machine off. Her mind had been on Alex. She'd been miles away paddling in the Mersey. They'd had long expeditions on summer Sundays as children. Walking for miles along the narrow band of fine sand on the Rock Ferry foreshore. Looking for crabs in small pools beneath the broken bricks, rusting bicycle wheels and other flotsam and jetsam that lay on the firm sand below the tide mark.

She was relieved to see her father measuring flour and bicarb into the enamel washing-up bowl to make batter. She was now free to make a cup of tea and put her feet up until the shop reopened at five. Charlie had already put a match to the fire. It was beginning to burn up.

Emily sipped her tea, letting memories of Alex come and go. She had gone with him out to the clean firm sand at the low-water line. To get there, they had to cross a broad band of thick oozing mud that sucked and pulled at their bare feet. She had been frightened; dragging one foot out made the other sink deeper.

Billy Wade called it going 'out lowie'. He told her it was sinking sand, and once three girls had been sucked under and lost for ever. He'd dared her to cross.

Alex had said it was possible, so she went with him, leaving two sets of footprints in the mud, marking the way they must return.

There was the compensation of clambering up the keels of fishing boats and yachts marooned on their sides in the mud. It was exciting to go on board, though they had to keep a sharp eye out. Once an irate owner had stolen up on them, uttering dire threats if they had interfered with his moorings. When he found they had not, he knocked their heads together anyway, for trailing mud on deck.

Always there were the ferry boats hustling importantly on their three-point journey, from Liverpool Pier Head to Rock Ferry pier, and then on to Woodside. Steamers chugged upriver to Runcorn. Gulls wheeled overhead and both Liverpool and Birkenhead drowsed in hazy sunshine.

Today, Birkenhead was known rather derogatorily as a satellite town, because Liverpool had been a bustling port, when Birkenhead was still a bank covered with birch trees. But when iron ships with engines were built in the last century, the ferry service made it easier for the rich merchants of Liverpool to cross the river than reach the outskirts of their own town. Then Rock Ferry had prospered and become a residential resort for the wealthy. It boasted of Royal visitors.

There had been many fine hotels, a splendid sandstone Esplanade, and it had been possible to take donkey rides along the sand to New Ferry. Sometimes she and Alex walked the length of it and rested on the fine sand in the gap. Sometimes they took sandwiches and went on past New Ferry Esplanade, and under the shore fields to the old brickworks. Now the big houses in Rock Ferry were growing shabby, and many were rented by the room. Summer visitors went elsewhere.

In less pleasant weather, if Alex could get them twopence each, they went indoor swimming in Bryne Avenue baths, though she had to do it in her knickers because she had no bathing costume. Alex had taught her to swim there because it was easier than in the swirling Mersey tide.

When Gran found out she had forbidden it, saying she ought to be ashamed, and only a very brazen girl would show her bare body. She had found her an old blouse to wear as well as her knickers.

Emily's thoughts went back to the summer of 1924 when she'd had her tenth birthday. Even the year before,

Gran had said it was quite improper for her to swim in blouse and knickers, and had looked out a cotton dress that she'd worn to Sunday school at the age of six. It had had sleeves and a sash in a pretty print of birds and flowers, as well as matching bloomers. Gran thought if she pulled the bloomers down to hide her thighs, it would look like a real bathing dress.

It had been tight across her chest the year before, and had been rolled up in a drawer over the winter. In the changing room at the baths, it had been a real struggle to get the dress fastened up the front. It was constrictingly tight, and she could hardly move her arms.

She had tried to keep up with Alex jumping in the deep end and racing to the shallow. Emily had felt the seams give at her first jump, and her vigorous breast stroke finished off the bodice. The material had rotted and now tore easily, and at the end of the afternoon, there was precious little to cover her body, which was showing the first changes of adolescence.

Alex had thought it funny until he'd realised how ashamed she was. Then he'd run to fetch her towel to hide her nakedness as she went back to the changing rooms. Back on Paradise Parade, she'd pulled him to a halt to gaze at a red bathing costume in Ethel's window. It was priced six shillings and elevenpence.

'Ask your gran to get it for you,' he suggested. 'For your birthday.' But Gran had already bought her a pretty dress with poppies on, as well as a cardigan.

'You need them more, love,' she'd said. Emily loved the dress and knew she was right, but still she hankered after a bathing costume.

'If I come up on a horse,' Gran had promised, 'you shall have it the very next time I win.'

Emily knew Gran liked a flutter on the horses, but she seemed to lose more often than she won. 'Unless . . . Why don't you ask your dad?'

Emily did, but not with much hope. 'You need shoes,' Charlie complained. 'Bathing costumes are unaffordable luxuries for the likes of us.'

'He's mean!' Alex had said fiercely. 'He could afford it. I'll get it for you, Emily.'

'How?'

'I'll do it somehow,' he vowed. 'Let me think.' By the next day he had a plan. 'Promise you won't breathe a word,' he'd whispered, and explained how Charlie would pay for the bathing suit without knowing.

'He buys dried peas by the sack from my mother, but we also sell them loose in the shop. When you put his peas to soak, fill a paper bag too. I'll sneak them back to our shop, weigh them, and add them to the sack we have open. Mum will sell them without realising she's selling the same stock twice. Then I'll take the money from the till without her being any the wiser. We can work the same trick with the tea and sugar he gets for the shop.' Emily had tingled with fear and admiration of his daring.

'He also buys potatoes by the sack from Tarrant's.' Emily's mouth had sagged open. 'I've arranged with Ken Tarrant that we'll return a couple of bowlfuls daily.' Her hand covered her mouth. Ken was the fifteen-year-old son of the owner.

'Ken will weigh them, and add them to the potatoes being sold loose in the shop. It's foolproof.'

'Ken Tarrant would do that for me?'

'He's keen to get one up on Charlie.'

Emily had been shocked at the time, though she had already practised some of the deceptions they suggested. From every shop along the Parade, children were expected to spend their Sunday afternoons at Sunday school. They all dressed in their best, accepted a halfpenny for the collection, but went to the shore or to play ball in Mersey Park. The money usually went on sweets, or latterly a twopenny packet of Woodbines to be shared round the boys. Emily's big preoccupation was to return home looking clean.

In order to reassure her, Alex had whispered details of another scheme the boys along the Parade used to raise money.

Mr Wade, the newsagent next door, already knew a day's consignment of newspapers could be spirited away a moment after the delivery van tossed them on his doorstep. He'd complained too often to his wholesaler that they hadn't delivered, when they had. Now he made sure the shop was open when the delivery van came.

'Billy Wade sold them on his own account outside Rock Ferry Station. Ken Tarrant even did it outside the ticket office at the entrance to the ferry.' But that had proved too close to home, and he'd been recognised. They'd all been terrified of trouble, but it hadn't come. 'Billy said it was a good source of income while it lasted.'

A few days later, Alex had given her a shilling to put down on the bathing costume. Emily had crept guiltily into the shop. Ethel had measured her, and ordered one on the large size to give her room to grow into it. By the time it came a week later, Alex had given her enough money to pay for it.

He'd taken her to the baths the next weekend, and she'd had the smartest bathing costume there. The bodice fitted modestly high at the neck and had ample overskirts. Guilt had spoiled the gift for her. She'd told Gran that Alex and his friends had clubbed together to buy it for her birthday, but she lived in dread of her knowing the truth. She had worn that bathing suit till last year, when she'd treated herself to the brand-new backless style for the thirties, in blue wool.

From her tenth birthday, Emily had had to spend most of her Saturdays working in the shop. She enjoyed Alex coming round when it closed, and always secreted the best pieces of fish for them both.

Often in the week, if Alex wanted chips, he'd come in and openly tap his penny on the counter. Careful to time his visit so Emily was free to serve him, the penny only appeared to change hands. Billy Wade had wanted her to do the same for him, but she'd refused. She'd never liked Billy much, and even though he had offered the same service for sweets in his dad's shop, she had not been persuaded.

When Alex was fourteen, he left school and went to Wythenshaw's as an office boy. He found they had a scheme to help bright youngsters, and had been sponsored on a night-school course and further training. Now he felt he had prospects. When she started at Wythenshaw's too, Emily had felt very close to Alex. He encouraged her to apply for the secretarial course Wythenshaw's ran for girls.

'We are not going to slave in a shop all the hours God sends,' Alex said. 'We'll have careers, and work from nine to five-thirty with weekends free.'

Sometimes, after they had eaten their fish and chips on a Saturday, Alex took her home, knowing Ted was with Charlie and his mother was at the pictures. The Frasers' living-room was furnished with a comfortable sofa.

She'd been fifteen when Alex first told her he loved her. Still fifteen when they first made love. It happened again, and while Emily leaned back, feeling flushed with love and contentment, Alex was suddenly on his feet, tense and straight faced.

'We can't keep doing this,' he said, agonised. 'You could have a baby.'

'I love you,' she whispered.

'We can't get married now, Emily! What would we live on? It could put you in a terrible position. No, we mustn't do this again, I couldn't bear to see you hurt.'

'It doesn't seem wrong.'

'Look, we'll get married as soon as I'm twenty-one. We

could afford to rent a little place for ourselves. I'll be on good money by then.'

'I'm earning, Alex,' she said.

'You wouldn't be able to work, love, if you had a baby, and there'd be another mouth to feed. No, we've got to be patient. It could happen. Could have already happened.'

Emily shivered.

'Don't we see it happening all the time? Myra, who works in our shop?'

'She managed. Your mother was very good to her.'

'I don't want it to happen to us. I want us to save up, do things properly. Not be rushed or panicked. I want us to have a good life. So there'll be no more of this. We've both got to work hard if we're to get anywhere. I want the best for you, Emily. We mustn't spoil everything. We've . . . I've got to be sensible.'

'You wouldn't think I'd killed a man with my bare hands, would you, Emily?' Ted Fraser unfurled his palms in front of her face. They were gaunt and bony like the rest of him.

'I would,' she retorted, turning to slither coal from the hod on to the living-room fire. 'You've told me often enough.'

'But you don't care.' Ted went to the shabby sideboard to get two beer glasses, with the ease of one who visits frequently. 'You don't listen.'

'I do, Uncle Ted, but it was a long time ago.' She straightened up and her brown eyes flashed back at her from the mirror over the mantelpiece. How dowdy she looked with her hair pushed beneath a turban like this. If Alex had come, she'd have combed it out by now. She washed it on Sundays anyway.

'I can't get the feel of his throat out of my mind. The way he squirmed and fought.' Ted's pale protruding eyes stared at his palms. 'I dug my fingers into his windpipe till my hands ached.'

'It was in the war. You had to do it.'

'The Captain shouted: "Watch out Fraser, get him." And I did.'

'It was a terrible time for you.' Emily knew he was looking for the sympathy she provided. She knew the war had been Ted's heyday, and he was proud of surviving on the Front from 1914 to 1918. Apart, that was, from a bullet wound that kept him in Blighty for eighteen months.

'I just went for him.' Ted coughed as he fetched a bottle opener, his chest sucking and wheezing as he struggled for breath. He'd come home a broken man living on his memories.

'It was your duty. And you did it. You were fighting for your country.' She stood warming her back at the fire. The room was lit by a single bulb covered with a parchment shade in the centre of the ceiling.

Poor Uncle Ted, his pale mournful eyes glittered at her from under brows growing wild. He had deep furrows running from nose to mouth that increased his look of misery. He was bald, with a shiny greyish scalp stretched so tight, his cranial sutures showed through. Only a thin fringe of greyish hair circled the back of his head.

Once Alex had lived in dread of going bald like his father. Emily had been with him when he'd said as much to his mother.

'It won't happen,' Olympia had laughed. 'You've got hair like mine and I've got a good head of hair, haven't I?'

'He might take after Uncle Ted that way,' Emily had said.

'No, there's nothing of Ted in him. You can't see any resemblance, can you?'

Emily had to admit she could not. She had caught Ted washing at his kitchen sink one day, bare from the waist up, great bony triangles of shoulder blades sticking out at the back. She could count every rib, the outline of his breast bone was clearly visible through a thin covering of pallid skin. He was tall but never stood straight; his shoulders drooped over a concave chest jutting his head forward.

'Here we are.' Her father came in with two big platefuls of fish, chips and peas, and slid them on the table.

'What are you having, Emily?' Ted asked, flicking the tops off two of the beer bottles.

'I've had all I want – with Gran.'

'How is she?'

'Worse,' she sighed. 'I think you ought to get the doctor, Dad. Her throat's terrible, she can hardly speak.'

'At this time of night?' His fork stabbed into his fish. 'And it's Saturday, he'll charge the earth.'

'She's very poorly.' She had sat at her grandmother's bedside offering her sips of tea. It had been agonising to watch her swallow.

'I'll call him on Monday, if she isn't better.'

'You wouldn't care if she died.' She rounded on him angrily. He chewed silently, so she slammed out to the scullery to make a cup of tea.

Ted's voice droned on about the war. Mulling it over with Charlie was the highlight of his week. Emily and Alex had heard it all so often, they both switched off when Ted started. She was only listening now to take her mind off Alex's absence.

'It's the gas that did for me.'

Ted had told her many times about being gassed. Of how the Germans waited till the wind was in the right direction and then let them have it.

'We didn't know it was deadly poison. We all thought gas would just knock us out for a few minutes.' She heard Charlie crunch the batter on his fish.

'We thought it was thick smoke at first, curling up from the enemy trenches, and drifting towards us. Till we heard the Captain shouting it was gas fumes, and they sounded the strombos horn.'

'What's that?' Emily asked, putting her head round the door.

'A sort of klaxon, the gas warning.'

'Made me feel groggy, I could smell it.' Ted replenished the beer in their glasses. 'Left men coughing and retching and vomiting and dying in agony.'

'We ran. We all ran, anywhere to get away from that burning curling smoke.'

'It made us all sick, but I got better. Many didn't. Went all through the war, Emily. I didn't think it would do this to me afterwards.'

Emily had put Alex's blackcurrant tarts on a plate which she took to the table. Gran hadn't been able to eat one, and they would stick in her throat. Emily felt Alex had rejected her.

'Didn't hurt Captain Wythenshaw though,' Charlie said. 'Must have had nine lives. Didn't deserve that sort of luck.'

'You mean our Mr Wythenshaw?' Emily asked.

'How many Wythenshaws are there? I mean Jeremy Wythenshaw.'

Emily couldn't believe it. 'I didn't know Mr Wythenshaw was your Captain in the war.'

'Well, he was. We were all in the Cheshires. Fourteenth Infantry Brigade, Fifth Division, B Company. Poor bloody infantry we were.'

'He's a lot older than you, Uncle Ted,' she said.

'And a lot healthier. Must have the constitution of an ox.' There was envy in his voice. 'Sixty if he's a day, and still going strong.

'And I got pensioned off when I was thirty-four. The War Office gives me twelve and six a week, fat lot of good it does me. I'm a wreck, but that's all I get.'

'Different for the Wythenshaws of this world. They get luxury all the way. It's the good living that keeps them fit, Ted.'

'Aye, the riding round in big cars, the cigars and the brandy. He should have caught gout by now, at the very least.'

'It's because he doesn't have to work like us.'

'He does work, Dad,' Emily said, frowning. 'He works hard. Runs a business, the same as you.'

'But he sits in an office and gets others to work for him.'

'I'm glad he does, me and lots of others. Wythenshaw's is the best place to work in Birkenhead.' Emily lost patience with them. 'Why do you hold a grudge against him?'

Charlie sniffed. 'He can afford to be generous to the likes of you. Pay a bit over the odds.'

'He's never been generous to me,' Ted complained. 'And he owes me. Didn't I kill a man for him? He'd have been a goner if I hadn't.'

Emily stood toasting her back at the fire. Ted was making it sound like a boy's adventure story. Perhaps it was all in his mind, a sort of daydream, like she had about Giles Wythenshaw. Perhaps he never had killed a man with his hands. Anyway, why hadn't he used his gun? Soldiers had guns.

CHAPTER THREE

It was a fine blustery morning in late October, with grey clouds scudding across the sky. Jeremy Wythenshaw was striding briskly on his way from James Street Station up to the shop. He enjoyed walking and there was a bounce in his step. He carried a walking stick, but it was an affectation. He gave it a twirl.

It amused him to see Higgins, his driver and general factotum, carrying his briefcase as though it were a great burden. He was having difficulty keeping up, though he himself carried a case of valuables he wouldn't trust to anyone else, and he could give Higgins twenty years.

Jeremy filled his lungs with the scents of tar and rope and seaweed, the smells of a port. Grey gulls wheeled and called overhead, and the bustling crowd gave the feel of being at the hub of the universe. Liverpool had a wonderful vitality that seemed to match his own. He enjoyed his Saturday visits to the shop in Lord Street, and usually went once in the week too.

His first sight of J.A. Calthorpe's always gave him a lift. As the Calthorpe family had been trading on the premises since 1729 and had built up an enviable reputation for fair dealing in merchandise of good taste, high quality and impeccable workmanship, he had continued to trade under their name. The shop had three largish windows, two of them on Lord Street, and a marble step leading to double doors.

Jeremy paused at the first window to look at the two or three pieces of antique jewellery displayed against a background of black velvet. He recognised them, a pearl and diamond festoon necklace with matching ring, earrings and brooch, made in Paris in 1820.

He moved to the second window where a still life in oils, possibly of the Dutch school, was shown on a small easel. He saw his dark overcoat reflected in the glass, and mused that he had bought the shop for all the wrong reasons, yet it had benefits he'd not foreseen.

He knew the difference between right and wrong as clearly as anyone else, but so many things depended on the circumstances and the people concerned. Often what seemed wrong turned out to be right, and what he hoped to be right was not always so.

He had not expected to enjoy the shop so much, to find so much pleasure in continental *objets d'art*. Handling fine china from Limoges and Dresden gave him immense satisfaction. The more he learned about the trade, the greater the pleasure he found in it.

He rounded the corner to glance in the window displaying their bread-and-butter lines. Wedding and engagement rings, watches by Jaeger le Coultre and Rolex. Modern, but all his stock was of superlative quality.

He went inside, enjoying the air of opulence as his feet sank into luxurious carpet. There were five customers in the shop, three separate transactions were being conducted. His staff were in attendance, everything was as it should be.

The wealthy expected polite and knowledgeable service; he liked to know his business provided it. Even after the crash of '29, and in the present depression, there were still plenty of people in Liverpool who had money to spend on jewellery and fine art. He was providing them with a hedge in these uncertain times.

'Sir,' Higgins handed him his briefcase, his fingers stained brown with nicotine. 'Shall I fetch Mr Calthorpe now, sir?' Jeremy felt in his pocket for some money.

'Yes, do that. Get him in a taxi, then pick me up for lunch.'

Poor old Arthur, he was too doddery now to come out alone. It gave him confidence to have Higgins in attendance. Still, he was in his ninetieth year, a good age. Jeremy wondered if he would survive as long. Such thoughts weighed on him more now that he had passed sixty. Probably he would not; Arthur had always lived more abstemiously. Jeremy knew he'd lived it up all his life, indulging himself in every conceivable luxury and was lucky now to be so superbly robust.

He nodded to Mr King, his manager, a man not much younger than himself who had worked here for decades, and smiled at Miss Roberts. Not that he found her thin elegance attractive, but he had always smiled at the ladies.

He took off his Homburg in Mr King's office, and smoothed down the silver hair that still grew rampant thick. He was given to formal dark suits with waistcoats, across which he wore his grandfather's half hunter on a thick gold chain.

Mr King always cleared and vacated his desk when Jeremy was expected. Jeremy opened up the safe set into the wall, and took out the books that King kept there. He opened the case he had carried and locked some jewel cases and a small statuette inside. Then he settled down to see what had been sold since he'd been here on Tuesday.

It was an hour before Higgins was back to say the taxi was waiting at the door with Mr Calthorpe. Jeremy went down and got in beside him.

'Morning, Arthur.' His father-in-law was dwarfed by his thick overcoat. He looked grey, his eyes sunken and dull. Jeremy usually took him to lunch, it was the only time the old man got out. Even at ninety it must be dull to look at one's own four walls all the time. Arthur livened up a little as they ordered steak and kidney pie in the Exchange Hotel. Jeremy called for the wine list.

'A glass of claret will do you good, Arthur.'

The old man smiled. 'Give me indigestion more like.' But all the same, he drank two glasses with every sign of enjoyment. 'You're a lucky man, Jeremy, able to enjoy the good things of life the way you do.'

Jeremy took him back to the shop afterwards for the business of the day. He was sorry Arthur could not get to the office, but that was up two flights of stairs he could no longer manage. The shop itself was on two floors, and the stairs to the first floor were wide and easy. It was the last flight, up to the office and storerooms, that was so steep and narrow. A rope had been fixed to the wall as a handrail, but it gave no great sense of security.

Nowadays Arthur was satisfied to get to the shop at all. Seated behind the counter at the back he came to life. As Jeremy got his latest treasures from the safe to show him, he felt the old man's interest quicken.

'You got this from Paris?'

'Yes, early eighteenth-century soft-paste porcelain.'

'Not much of it left now. Very fragile. Early Sèvres?' Arthur's fingers were like claws against the delicate statuette, but however unreliable his hold might seem, he never let anything slip. It had been right to buy the shop if only to give Arthur pleasure in his old age.

Though he'd had a lifetime passion for the stock, Arthur had not been a good businessman. The shop had flourished in the ownership of his family for two centuries. Arthur would have counted himself a failure had he had to sell it on the open market.

These days, his mind was clear at some moments and gone at others, but face him with some *objet d'art* or piece of fine jewellery, and he seemed to lose thirty years.

Jeremy never ceased to marvel that he always knew exactly what he was looking at and could suggest a price appropriate to the present day. He had lived for the trade all his life and knew it backwards.

'What do you think of this?' Jeremy put a pocket watch in front of the old man, who opened it with infinite care, and took the outer case off.

'Two solid covers hinged together, embossed with rococo ornament. Gold of course.' Arthur took off his glasses, and put his jeweller's magnifying glass to his eye. 'Made in London, in . . . 1724. Looks French, doesn't it? Possibly made for a Frenchman.'

Then he gently prised the inner case open. 'The movement is Swiss, the inner case is engraved and pierced to allow the sound of the bell to escape. Wonderful quality.'

'How much can I charge, do you think?'

The old man chuckled. 'I'm sure you've already made up your mind. Worth five hundred of anybody's money. Splendid condition.'

'I've something rather special to show you today.' Jeremy slid a large case in burr walnut on the counter and opened it.

'A toilet set,' the old man said. 'Splendid.'

'Twenty pieces.' Jeremy started to take them out. 'A silver-framed mirror, comb cases, brushes for hair and clothes, candlesticks, pomade pots, salvers, ewers, caskets. It's all here.'

Arthur picked out a pomade pot and looked at the hallmark. 'Made in Paris, have you got your directory of continental hallmarks? I'm not as familiar with them as I am with the English.'

'It is Paris, 1791, the maker's mark is LJP which I believe is Louis Jeinopurte. Have you heard of him?'

'Yes, fine craftsman.' Arthur's fingernails looked faintly blue against the silver.

'But what's really wonderful about this, is that we have

the original bill made out to a Monsieur Henri Aurele Lasac. It shows the cost of the silver, the engraving cost, and the cost of making everything.'

Arthur replaced his glasses slowly to study the account.

'Five hundred and twenty ounces in all, and it gives the exact purpose of each piece. Marvellous! Three thousand five hundred and twenty francs, twenty centimes. I wonder who Monsieur Henri Aurele Lasac was?'

'A rich man.'

'Enormous luck the bill has survived, adds to the interest and value. Authenticates it.'

'Enormous luck,' Jeremy agreed. Even greater luck that he had not been able to find out anything else about Henri Aurele Lasac. The risk would have been greater if he'd been well known. He shivered, perhaps he was making a mistake? He hadn't been able to bring himself to destroy the original bill, it was an historical document, but it made identification possible. He'd feel safer now if he'd burned it.

Arthur was studying each piece in turn. 'Superb workmanship. Wonderful condition.'

'Always been kept in the case. What can I ask for this, Arthur? I need your opinion. I've never seen anything quite as good before.'

'Have to think about it.' He began to list the pieces. 'Considerably more than the three to four hundred pounds it cost originally.'

Jeremy watched his staff going about their duties and let Arthur add up in peace. He had already fixed on a price for the toilet set, what he wanted was confirmation that he had priced it correctly. At last Arthur came up with a figure.

Jeremy smiled. Once he had needed Arthur's experience. He hadn't known the good from the excellent. It had taken a long time but he was learning to trust his own judgement. If anything happened to Arthur . . . he smiled at his euphemism. Arthur was ninety, there was only one thing likely to happen to him, and Jeremy knew he could now manage alone.

'Just look at the gadrooning on the rim of this salver.' Arthur ran his fingers over it. 'There's not a lot I still hanker for, but I envy the person who buys this.'

Jeremy stood motionless. That was the answer. The toilet set with its bill would be safely away from public scrutiny in Arthur's possession. 'Would it give you pleasure?'

'Immense pleasure.' Arthur couldn't bear to put the salver back in the box.

'Buy it, then,' Jeremy said. 'I'll give you thirty per cent off.'

'I don't know, I'm too old to accumulate more. Got a houseful of lovely things.' Arthur's slack lips pursed doubtfully.

'Nonsense, as you get older there's a lot you can't do, and more you no longer enjoy. You should jump at anything that still gives you pleasure. Owe it to yourself.'

'I'm tempted.' Arthur was trying again to match the pieces to the bill.

'Take it, then.'

His ancient face wrinkled into a smile. 'I think I will.' He felt in his top pocket for his cheque book. 'Be yours again soon, anyway.' Jeremy knew Arthur had willed his antiques to him.

'Not too soon, I hope,' he said truthfully, musing that it was very wrong to destroy anything of historical interest. Almost a sin, but he would have to when it came back in his possession. It wasn't safe, foolish to take the risk.

'I was never able to find stock like this. First class.' Arthur's claw-like fingers stroked his new possession.

'Lefarge & Drogue, in Paris. You dealt with them?'

'I remember them well. Old Marcel Lefarge.'

'He's retired now. I deal with his son, Emile.' Jeremy

twirled a tumbler from the set between his fingers, holding it to the light to see the glass sparkle. Arthur had fired his interest in antique crystal, taught him all he knew about glass. He owed Arthur more than the old man realised.

'I'll have it packed up.' Jeremy closed the burr walnut case; he was relieved Arthur was having it. It was only right he should get pleasure out of all this too.

'Emile? He was a strip of a lad, just come into the business. Of course you often go to Paris, you've built up a good relationship. He lets you have his best things.'

'Perhaps,' Jeremy allowed, but he wasn't going to say too much about Lefarge & Drogue, the truth was too awful to think about. His mind skidded over it, just as it always did. He'd trained himself not to dwell on it. It played havoc with his sense of security. Too late to do anything but benefit from it now.

'I shall go again next week. I feel as much at home there as in Liverpool. Wonderful restaurants and, since the war, remarkably cheap.'

'If I were younger, I'd like to come with you.' Arthur pondered a moment. 'You've got that house there, but no, it's too late now for me.' Jeremy took a deep breath, reflecting that his luck still held.

'You always knew how to get the best out of everything,' the old man chortled.

Feeling a pleasant glow of anticipation, Jeremy crossed the hall to his library. He always enjoyed coming home to Churton after a busy day, to relax for half an hour before dinner with one of his single-malt whiskies, Glenfiddich or perhaps Glenlivet tonight.

A big fire flickered and leapt in the grate, the curtains had been drawn against the winter dusk. It was the room he liked best. Comfortable, with all his old books lining two walls. One table lamp provided a subdued and welcoming pool of light by his drinks cabinet.

He went towards it rubbing his hands, pulling up with a start when he saw the top had been left off his bottle of Laphroaig. And of all things, a bottle of ginger ale had been brought from the kitchen and was open beside it.

'Hello, Father.' Jeremy turned to find his son Giles sprawling in the green velvet armchair he liked to use himself. 'Can I have a word with you?'

'Of course.' He sounded abrupt. Irritation welled up in his throat as he replaced the top on the Laphroaig, and reached for the Glenlivet. He could guess what was coming. He poured himself a drink and went to sit on the other side of the fireplace. He crossed his legs, tried to relax. Just looking at Giles made it impossible.

'I find I'm a bit short.' Giles smiled disarmingly through the smoke idling up from his cigarette in its long jet holder. He could be very charming when he tried. 'Could you possibly increase my allowance? Please.'

Jeremy felt himself bristle with dislike. He disliked the calculating look in his son's tawny eyes, the self-indulgent line to his lip. He hated the pale wavy hair that reminded him of Elspeth, and he hated himself for feeling this way about his son.

How many times had he tried to analyse why he should feel like this? A likeness to Elspeth should endear Giles to him. He'd loved Elspeth, almost to the end.

He'd welcomed Giles into the world. He'd wanted a son to follow him in the business but was afraid of being too hopeful. After all, he'd already been married to Elspeth for six years. What a fuss he'd made of her and the child.

Giles had been a pretty baby whose toes he'd loved to tickle. Later, he'd enjoyed teaching him to play cricket and to swim. Everything had been set fair at the start. He'd wanted Giles to go to a good boarding school. It made boys stand on their own feet, and Giles had always been inclined to hang on to his mother's skirts.

Elspeth had doted on Giles to such an extent that he

began to feel she loved the child more than she did her husband. She had insisted he stay with her, and because she hadn't been well, Jeremy had agreed.

Jeremy sighed. He'd hoped Giles would do well at his day school, and choose some profession, but he hadn't applied himself to anything but games. When Elspeth died of tuberculosis at thirty-seven, Giles had been inconsolable. Perhaps he hadn't tried hard enough with him then.

Giles had grown up with expectations. Who could he blame for that but himself? The boy was lazy, it riled him to see Giles putting out his hand, expecting to be given all manner of luxuries, when he wasn't prepared to do a jot of work in return.

Jeremy had had to work hard all his life. How could Giles expect to do otherwise? A business didn't run itself. Jeremy despised men who couldn't stand on their own feet, and if Giles didn't learn to run the factory, he never would.

Giles had inherited all his faults too. He was self-indulgent, enjoyed good living, was knowledgeable about food, wine and where to find the best tailor. It wouldn't take him long to appreciate the Laphroaig on its own. He loved parties and women, and Jeremy wouldn't have minded about any of that if only he worked.

But no, Giles preferred to sponge, to spend money he hadn't earned. Jeremy tried to swallow his irritation. It was wrong for a father to feel like this.

'I already give you a thousand a year, and that's generous, considering I cover all your living expenses too.'

'I know, Father. You're very generous, but . . .'

'No.'

'What?'

'I'm not going to increase your allowance.'

'Father, be kind to me. You wouldn't miss another couple of hundred. You can't give it away fast enough to charity. You're over-generous to your employees, so why not your only son? It doesn't make sense.'

'It makes sense to me.' He had to hold his irritation in check when he saw Giles returning to the Laphroaig for a refill. 'You've got to learn to earn it, Giles. Settle down and make something of your life.'

'I'm trying. Honestly, Father, I'm trying.'

Jeremy let the Glenlivet roll over his tongue. Nothing had changed. Last year he had talked to Giles, man to man. Spelled it out. He had been twenty-two then, had had time to sow his wild oats, but was still young enough to learn.

Jeremy had made up his mind not to lose his temper with Giles. He would be kind but firm. Giles would change given time, he'd settle eventually. He must have inherited enough sense to ensure that.

Jeremy had set out a training programme for him. Explained how he wanted him to work in each department, manage the factory a bit at a time from the bottom up. Eventually he would take over.

Giles had spent three months on the factory floor, where they die-stamped brooches and bangles from sheet metal. When he'd first enquired about his progress, Billings his overseer had said he was no trouble. It transpired later that he was not often there, and showed no interest. It had been a disappointment, but he'd moved him on to beads.

They'd been working on a big order for pearls from Woolworths. Covering plain glass beads with pearlised paint. Murphy had asked Giles to order more paint and he'd forgotten.

'You've not had any bad reports from the canteen these last few months, have you?'

'Nothing as bad as the foul-up you caused with the pearls. That cost good money.' Two lines were idle for half a day while they tried to get the paint in a hurry.

Murphy had lost his temper and asked him to move Giles elsewhere.

'You see, I am improving.'

Jeremy sighed. 'Perhaps . . .'

'Just a couple of hundred, go on. To encourage me.'

'I don't think it will help.'

'Honestly, Father, it will. Everybody needs to be rewarded.'

'I want you to work. Running the factory will be your reward. Independence, and the knowledge you can stand on your own feet.'

'I think I could do it now. Really, Father, I do.'

'You've still a lot to learn. It's taken generations of Wythenshaws to build the business up; we don't want it to go down the drain. It has to be a gradual process.' Very gradual if Giles was to cope.

'Why do you do it, Father?' Giles's innocent gaze locked into his.

'Do what?' he asked irritably.

'Work the way you do.'

Jeremy swirled the amber liquid in his glass. He was caught on a treadmill. He had started on what seemed to be the right course, now he had to finish the job. Tidy everything safely.

'You've already got more than enough to live on, you've said so. Why carry on working to give it all away? It doesn't make sense.'

Jeremy watched the firelight flicker against the ornate plasterwork on the ceiling. 'I take a pride in running the factory, providing work for the community. And I'm making my name as a philanthropist.'

'What is the point of that?' He heard the hollow ring in Giles's laugh. 'A name for giving money away?'

'There are still things I want from life, Giles.'

'You'll get nothing from giving it away.'

'I get the satisfaction of helping people.'

There was no mistaking his son's disbelief. 'You get no satisfaction from helping me.'

'Believe it or not, if you could be helped, it would give me more satisfaction than anything else. We just don't agree on what would help you.'

'But giving money away?' Giles's prominent eyes held his.

'It might help with a knighthood. I'd like that. Sir Jeremy Wythenshaw. Does it make sense now?' He sighed, he'd said all this to Giles before, but he didn't seem to take it in. 'What's the matter with your face?' There were three scratches from eye to jaw, one was livid.

He saw Giles's fingers feeling up his cheek. It was swollen. 'Nothing to worry about.'

'I'm not worried. How did you do it?'

'Lovers' tiff,' Giles mumbled.

'Really? Who's the lucky girl?'

'She works in the office.'

'That's a change.' Jeremy took another sip of his Glenlivet and wondered about the girl. He hadn't heard anything bad about Giles from the canteen. She might be a good influence, settle him down. A girl who worked for her living, instead of having a wealthy father and nothing better to do but hang round the golf club.

'About the extra two hundred you were thinking of allowing me,' Giles began, getting up again to help himself to more whisky.

'I wasn't thinking of any such thing,' Jeremy snapped, his irritation blowing up in his face. 'How many times do I have to tell you?'

Fury erupted from Giles in response. 'You shower kindness, understanding and love on everybody but me.' He was boiling over. 'You throw money at every charity there is, because it's good for your public image. Yet you're a Scrooge at home. You must hate me, to treat me like this.'

'No,' Jeremy protested, but the door had already slammed behind his son. He groaned and moved to the chair Giles had vacated. He had failed to keep his temper yet again. Where had he gone wrong? He wished he and Giles were not permanently at loggerheads, the fighting made him feel terrible.

Giles took the stairs two at a time to his room. He should have known talking to his father would be like banging his head against a wall. It always was.

He hardly knew why he'd come up to his room. His eyes burned wildly from his wardrobe mirror. Not his, nothing was his, not even the clothes he stood up in. His father owned everything. Decided everything. Ran everything. Was all-powerful.

He pulled his brush twice across his pale waves and rushed downstairs again. He couldn't stay here. He would go to the club, have a drink with reasonable people, though they all thought his father was wonderful. They talked of his humanity and his kindness, his marvellous business brain.

They envied Giles because he was his son, but Father wouldn't give him the crumbs from his table. He kept him like a cat keeps a mouse. Watching him struggle to do the impossible, knowing there was no way he could escape.

Emily had worked herself into a panic by Monday morning. She fully expected the worst. All Sunday she had imagined Giles's handsome face twisting with fury. She had seen, in her mind's eye, Mr Donkin remove his glasses and polish them, his expression one of sorrow rather than anger, as he told her she was incompetent. Then Miss Simpson the office manager would give her her cards. She felt sick with dread.

When she reached her office she was surprised to find everything looking so normal. She changed into the shoes she kept in the bottom drawer of her desk. Never wearing them outside kept them looking new.

The door to Mr Osborne's office was slightly ajar. 'Morning, Emily,' he called from his desk. 'Can you come in?'

With sinking heart she pushed his door; it creaked wider. She looked at the pinch marks his glasses made on the side of his nose, and waited for him to say she'd have to leave after causing such a furore.

He looked up and smiled. 'Have you brought your pad? I've got letters to dictate.'

'Sorry!' Emily fled to her own desk. It took her a minute to find her notebook and pencil. She couldn't even see straight.

It felt strangely unreal to be taking dictation as usual. When the time came to type, she found she was all thumbs and couldn't concentrate. Mr Osborne had left the door to the corridor ajar when he'd gone to the kitchen. Every passing footfall brought her heart to her mouth. The thump thump of distant machinery and the occasional clatter from the kitchen wound up her nerves like a clock spring.

Suddenly Giles was standing before her. He closed the corridor door and peeped in Mr Osborne's empty room. Emily felt cold.

'Sorry, Emily. I was horrible to you on Saturday, went over the top. Panic stations, I was expecting big trouble.' He came to perch on her desk. His tawny eyes burned into hers, prevented her looking anywhere else.

Emily's mouth felt dry. 'You didn't get into trouble?'

His fingers went up his cheek, it didn't look so bad this morning. 'You made your mark.'

'I'm sorry.' They said it together and she laughed.

'Am I forgiven?' He was smart in blazer and grey slacks.

'What about Mr Donkin?' she asked.

'He's sorted the figures out. He's satisfied now they're right.'

'But won't he . . .?'

'He'll do nothing. It's all smoothed over.'

Suddenly Emily relaxed. 'That's it, then?'

'Yes, if you'll forgive me.' His hot eyes held hers. 'I shouldn't have turned on you. I was afraid everything was going to blow wide open. Panic gets to me.'

Emily smiled. She understood what panic did to the nerves, hadn't she had a bad day yesterday?

'Of course you're forgiven.' Nobody could hold a grudge against Giles. He smiled down, pale wavy hair curving across his forehead. Something in him turned aggression off. Emily understood why he was so popular.

'Well, if that's settled I'll just pop into the kitchen.'

'There's mail on your desk,' she called, but he'd already gone. She returned to her typing, but a few moments later Sylveen's blonde head came round the door making her jump.

'Hello, Emily, can I sell you a poppy?' She slid her tray on to the desk. 'You can have a little one for a penny, or one of these for threepence. This size is sixpence, and isn't this one lovely? You must put in at least a shilling.'

Emily reached for her handbag. The tray was like a window box.

'Do you want a penny one? Most of the girls have had them.'

'Yes please.' Her fingers found the coin and put it in the tin.

'What's the matter?' Sylveen's breathy voice asked.

She shook her head. 'Nothing.'

'Where is . . .?' Her blue eyes flicked towards Giles's office and then towards Mr Osborne's.

'In the kitchen at this time of the morning.'

'See you, then.' Sylveen left her door half open. Her high heels tapped away down the corridor. Emily's fingers were back on her typewriter before she realised Sylveen was talking to somebody else.

'Good morning, sir. Would you like to buy a poppy? I hope, sir, you don't object to me selling them in office hours?'

Emily froze. She must be talking to Jeremy Wythenshaw, but he had never come to the canteen office before. She had never spoken directly to him, though she had seen him about the main office. She felt fluttery with panic again. Had Giles got it wrong?

Or could he be on his way to the kitchens? She wanted to look, to see if he'd passed the kitchen door, but she made herself stay where she was, knowing she'd feel worse if he caught her peeping.

Jeremy Wythenshaw had spent Sunday trying to stem his disappointment with Giles. It was very wrong for a father to feel like this about his son. He ought to be thinking of new ways to help him, but he was beginning to doubt that Giles could be helped.

Curiosity niggled about the girl. He had assumed all the girls in their employment were ready to lay down their lives for Giles. It didn't please him that Giles was universally popular, when he thought of nobody but himself.

Yet this girl had scratched his face, he chuckled to himself. Giles must have made a pass at her and been repulsed. He was on his way now to take a look at her.

As he turned the corner, he saw the door to the canteen office open, and a girl, carrying a tray of poppies and a collecting tin, come out. A lovely girl, not too slim, with a skirt that was tight across her flat stomach, but flowed elegantly to mid calf. Her neat shirt blouse was unfastened at the throat, showing just enough cleavage to tantalise.

'I won't sell them round the factory while the lines are running,' she said in her attractive breathy voice. 'I know better than that, but I hope you don't mind me selling them here.'

'No,' he said. She was standing very close to him. Her

perfume was seductive. 'I fought in the war. It's a cause I support.'

'I want to sell lots of poppies. I want Wythenshaw's to raise more money for our old soldiers than any other company.'

He had to smile as he fished out a ten-shilling note to push in her tin. This was just the girl to interest Giles; he applauded his taste. A stunning girl, with a fragile child-like face, quite at variance with her body.

As she leaned forward over her tray, he caught a glimpse of snow-white lace, edging a pale curve of breast. She chose a huge silk poppy for him, and, edging closer till he could feel her body pressing against his, pinned it in his button hole. Her breath was warm against his cheek.

'I think it's a little ostentatious,' he said, when he could trust himself to speak. Picking a more modest bloom, she went through the process of removing one and pinning in the other, her small pearly teeth clasped against a pink tongue.

'I hope you don't mind me saying this, sir.' Big eyes of piercing blue looked into his, giving him a powerful sensual pull. 'But I hear you will soon have a vacancy in your office?'

'Yes.' He felt a niggle of confusion. 'Miss Lovat is leaving to get married.'

'I was wondering, sir, if you would consider me for the job.' That did surprise him. Perhaps Giles had not captivated her affections after all. Her smile was open, her body arched invitingly on high heels.

'I'm a good shorthand typist. Mr Bunting has been very pleased with my work, but I feel I'd like a change. I'd like to work for you.' Suddenly he found it difficult to breathe.

'I think that is an excellent idea,' he heard himself say.

'Thank you, sir. My name is Sylveen Smith. I'll ask Miss Lovat to explain the job to me.'

'Yes, please do that. Have you worked for us long?'

'More than a year.'

Jeremy wondered why he'd never noticed her before. 'Perhaps I'd better have a word with Miss Simpson, see how soon she can find somebody else for Mr Bunting.'

'That would be lovely. You won't find me wanting . . .' He saw blatant invitation in her eyes.

'I'll look out for you,' he choked, and discovered Sylveen could best be appreciated from the back. Short blonde waves ending in a small curl at the back of her neck. Her fashionable black gored skirt floated over high heels, yet showed rounded buttocks moving sensuously against the tight material.

He tried to pull himself together. What sort of a fool was he? But she left him feeling elated, more alive than he had for a long time. He was taking deep breaths as he tried to remember what had brought him to this part of the factory.

He realised now he had not seen Giles's friend yet. He was glad the blonde beauty was not her. With more bounce than usual in his step, he pushed at the door of the canteen office.

The girl leapt to her feet as he went in; he seemed to fill the tiny room. He looked at her doubtfully, stung with surprise. Her elfin face and slight frame were not what he'd expected. He would have thought the other girl more to Giles's taste. This one looked frightened.

'Are you Emily Barr?'

'Yes.' It was only a whisper. She took a step backwards and added, 'sir.'

Intelligent eyes of brown velvet slanted upwards giving her a puckish look. Pixie eyes. Rich brown hair that bounced as she moved, cut in a thick straight fringe. Not dead straight, it curved slightly to her face.

He let his gaze travel down her too-slender figure. She wore a pink blouse with a Peter Pan collar buttoned to the throat. Her tiny buds of breasts hardly showed, not enough for Giles to get his hand round. Jeremy stroked his thick silver hair.

'You've been working for my son, how long?'

'Four months now.' The velvet eyes were showing panic. She backed into the filing cabinet. He wanted to reassure her.

'I'm moving Giles to the design department, just for a few weeks. He's praised your work and asked if you could move with him. Tells me you're a help.' Her mouth opened slightly in surprise. 'Are you agreeable to the move?'

'Yes.' Her voice was thick with eagerness. 'The design department? Yes please, sir.' She was smiling, looking more elfin than ever.

'Yes, well, thank you for working so hard for the firm.'

She was beaming at him. 'Thank you, sir.'

'Tomorrow morning, then, design department.'

He heard her laugh with relief as he turned away.

CHAPTER FOUR

The next morning, as Emily climbed the stairs to the top floor of the old factory building, her mind was on Alex. She'd never before made a move without first talking it over with him. They hadn't planned this together, and that made her nervous about it. She felt she was out on a limb, alone for the first time. She wanted Alex behind her, to point out the pitfalls. She felt lost without him.

Gathering her courage, she knocked on the door of the design office, and found herself in a large room. A middle-aged woman with an Eton crop was pouring boiling water into an enamel teapot.

'I'm Emily Barr,' she told her.

'Hello, we're expecting you. I'm Mary O'Neil, and this is Mary Murdoch.'

Emily turned to see a younger woman taking off the little hat she'd been wearing over one eye.

'Have a seat,' they said, indicating several chairs pulled up to a long table.

Emily hovered, taking in the view of Liverpool's skyline through an enormous window. The Mersey lapped like oil in the grey morning mist. She noticed a small desk in a corner, but there was no typewriter to be seen.

'Is there much typing to do here?' Mary O'Neil looked at her rather strangely as she put a cup of tea in her hand.

'Not a lot, the odd letter from time to time. We get

them done in the typing pool.' Ill at ease, Emily wondered how she'd fill her day.

'Our output is in ideas and drawings.' She waved a hand towards the table. Emily noticed then the folders, the pencils and the drawing paper.

'We sketch our ideas, try them out on each other, often we collaborate,' Miss O'Neil told her. 'If we come up with anything good, we draw it to scale as a template.' She pulled open one of the many tiny drawers in a large chest. 'These are templates. Mr Wythenshaw comes up every week, and decides if any should go into production. Then a steel die has to be made to stamp our designs out of the sheet metal.'

The door opened again and Giles came in; Emily was relieved to see him. In the new situation, she foresaw trouble if he didn't keep more regular hours than he had.

'So you've come to learn about design?' Miss Murdoch smiled, her teeth were over-large, giving her a rather horsey look. 'Your father told us to expect you both.'

Emily was surprised to find the designers treating her as they did Giles. She felt her position had greatly changed. Wythenshaw's had paid her to learn shorthand and typing, and now she had developed those skills, they were paying her to learn about design. She had been proud of working in Wythenshaw's office, but to design the stock they made, well, that was a glamour job she'd be thrilled to learn.

'Is this how you learned?' she asked Miss O'Neil.

'Yes,' she smiled, but when Emily heard she'd trained for three years at Birkenhead School of Art before starting, she had to assume that when Giles was moved on, she would go too, and revert to typing. She must look on this as a pleasant educational interlude.

For the first week, Giles came in each morning when she did, sat up to the long table with her and the two designers. It didn't take her long to notice he showed considerably less interest than she did. Then he started absenting himself without reason.

The two Marys took endless trouble to ensure she understood everything whether Giles came or not. They even seemed to expect her to achieve more.

It wasn't, Mary O'Neil told her, simply a matter of drawing designs for pretty jewellery, other things had to be taken into account. The cost of making a piece was paramount. They were also restricted by the machinery already installed and the tools available. She was taken with Giles on to the factory floor to have this made clear.

'We use base metals here, usually electro gilded or silvered.'

Emily watched a machine stamping out both sides of a locket, including hinge and fastening, in one operation. 'All that remains to be done is to pin the two halves together, and insert the inner fittings.'

'We do lots of curb chain. Bracelets and necklets.' Emily watched half hypnotised as a machine bent and twisted gilt wire.

'This can be adapted to fashion by adjusting the size of the wire and the size of the pendant. We do all sorts of pendants: coins, owls, lizards, hearts, wishbones.

'Fashion is something we have to consider carefully. Brooches in the form of bows are this year's winners.'

Wythenshaw's already had several designs in production. Miss O'Neil set out a row across the table, some in silvery metal, some gilt, many set with coloured stones and pearls.

Giles was late arriving on the Saturday morning Miss O'Neil said to Emily: 'We need a variation of the bow, something a little different. See if you can come up with an idea we can use.'

Last weekend she had noticed a box of chocolates in Wade's window next door. It was decorated with a bow of red ribbon, tied in an unusual almost circular bow. She attempted to reproduce the shape with her pencil, and decided it should be edged with tiny diamond-like stones.

'A pretty curly bow,' Miss Murdoch told her when she showed it to her. 'If you follow the lines through, accentuate the shape,' her pencil expertly began another sketch, 'it will have more life about it. More individuality.'

'You can use this?'

'Not as it is. Too expensive to set so many stones. Get out the pattern plates. See what the machines are capable of providing by way of decorative stamping instead.'

Giles came in as she was laying the plates along the table. 'Why not stamp holes right through the metal?' he suggested, turning the sketch of the bow round in his hand. 'Big holes.'

Mary Murdoch redrew the design, making both the brooch and the holes bigger.

'What about polished gilt?' Emily suggested.

'Light and airy and full of movement, I like it.' Mary Murdoch laid the sketch down with satisfaction. 'I'll measure it up, draw it to scale, have a template made. Work out what it would cost in labour and materials. We'll see how it turns out.'

'There we are, we've cracked it, Emily.' Giles laughed and, bending, gave Emily a congratulatory peck on her cheek. 'This will show Father we haven't wasted our time.' Emily's cheek burned. Miss Murdoch laughed too, but with a hint of embarrassment.

Emily was exultant when the hooter sounded the start of the weekend. She went to the cloakroom to put on her coat, and found Mavis Finnegan next to her, pulling a grey felt hat over her short mousey hair.

'Never thought you'd make it, Emily. Scratching his face must have done the trick, a novel approach after all the wolf whistles.' Emily buttoned up her gaberdine, she'd heard plenty of this over the last weeks.

'It hasn't done any trick,' she denied, but she felt like a

cat who's had two saucers of cream. He had kissed her, and as far as Mavis was concerned, a kiss was a kiss.

It made her feel closer to him, though she'd felt no passion behind it, not even affection. It had been given spontaneously in the flush of their first success. Impossible to explain such nuances to Mavis. 'Never thought you'd get him, not with Sylveen Smith simpering round him.'

'I haven't got him, as you call it.' His kiss hadn't conferred any such understanding. 'Don't you listen to what I say?'

'I suppose you have to deny it, till it's official. He is heir to all this, but you can't deny you've given Alex Fraser the push.'

'What do you mean?' Emily froze.

'Well, I saw him at the Palace last night. Charlie Chaplin was on. He was with another girl.'

Emily was taken aback. Shocked even. 'Who?'

'I don't know. Anyway, what does it matter? You've got Giles Wythenshaw.'

Emily shivered. It did matter. Alex was quite different. She pedalled home furiously. Wanting to put the thought out of her mind. Alex had another girl! She couldn't think of it. She was almost glad of rush hour in the shop, it was impossible to think of anything while she worked through that.

But Alex's defection weighed on her mind all afternoon and evening. Though he came round with his father as the shop was closing, he stood the other side of the counter, aloof and serious, watching as she dished up the fish and chips saved for their supper.

'Thanks,' was all he said as she handed him his share. In recent years, they had got into the habit of eating by the living-room fire with the others. Tonight was the first Saturday for weeks that Gran had felt well enough to come down for supper, but Alex elected to sit on the stairs like they used to as children. One stair higher than her, so they could both sit on the strip of carpet, which was warmer than the varnished wood.

He munched on his chips in brooding silence. Emily nibbled without appetite. She would have cooked something different for herself if Alex had not come. She smouldered with discontent, and thought he might as well have gone out with Billy Wade, or his new girlfriend again. She wanted to kick out at him.

'What's the matter, Alex?'

'You almost marked him for life,' he said, disgruntled. 'What was he trying to do to you?'

'Who?' she asked, deliberately obtuse.

'Giles Wythenshaw of course. Was he trying to kiss you or something?'

'No.' She turned to look up at him, his dark red hair, so like his mother's, swept back from his face, his chin jutting forward obstinately.

'He's giving out it was a lovers' tiff and all is back on course now.'

'I've been moved to the design department with him.'

'I know that,' he said impatiently. 'It bears it out.'

'Bears what out?'

'You're his girlfriend. It's all round the office. The girls can talk of nothing else.'

'Gossip,' Emily said. 'Just gossip.'

'There's got to be something in it.'

'No.' Emily felt a tinge of guilt about the kiss, and told herself again it didn't mean she was his girlfriend.

'I don't believe you. I thought we had an understanding, Emily, it was to be you and me.' Now the void between her and Alex gaped wider, all space. 'You agreed.'

'A long time ago.' She wanted her words to hurt. He had hurt her.

'You mean it's off? Is that what you want?'

'It seems to be what you want,' she spat. 'Mavis

Finnegan says she saw you in the Palace with another girl on Wednesday.' Suddenly Alex was staring over her head in silence.

'Yes,' he agreed at last. 'And did she tell you Billy Wade was there too? It was a foursome.'

Emily moved the chip round her mouth, finding it hard to swallow. A foursome could have included her, as if that made it any better!

'It was hurtful, hearing it from Mavis Finnegan. You might have said. Anyway, who was she?'

'It doesn't matter. She's not important.'

Emily nearly exploded. Not important? She'd been burning up with curiosity all afternoon. Perhaps with jealousy more than curiosity.

'If she's not important, why keep it a secret?'

She watched Alex shrug his broad shoulders. 'She's nothing to either of us, Emily. You don't know her.'

'We don't seem to be getting on well any more,' she burst out. 'Perhaps we're growing out of each other.'

'If that's how you feel,' Alex stood up angrily, 'I'll leave you to Giles Wythenshaw. It seems you prefer his company to mine.'

He strode out through the shop, slamming his empty plate on the counter.

Emily was left sitting on the stairs alone. It took her ten minutes to pull herself together, rebolt the shop door after him, and think of joining the others by the living-room fire. She heard a burst of laughter as she opened the door. It grated; she felt she'd never laugh again.

'I know I've seen better days,' Gran was lamenting.

'So's that hat.' Charlie's laugh had a cruel edge.

Gran was rarely seen without her black straw hat whether in shop, house or outside. She wore it flat on the top of her head. A bunch of red and yellow cherries survived in good condition though their cloth leaves had curled and faded.

'Bought this in 1917 I did, when Charlie married your mother, Emily. Bought it in a hurry because they got married in a hurry.'

'When I came home on leave from the Front,' he nodded, giving Emily a sour look.

Emily tried to pull herself together and join in. She knew it had been the fashion when Gran's generation was growing up, for a woman to keep her head covered. Gran had only just missed wearing a cap.

'Paid a lot for it I did. It's been a good one,' Gran laughed. Sometimes during cold winter spells she replaced it with a black felt cloche she'd bought for the wedding of Moira McFie in 1922.

'You're not going to buy yourself a new one?' Ted asked.

'What's the matter with this? It'll see my time out. No, I've spent me winnings on a nice bit of topside for tomorrow's dinner.'

Last night, Gran had had her first outing in weeks. On Friday nights Emily had always washed up after supper, so Gran could go across to the Bird of Paradise with Mrs McFie and sometimes Gladys Wade too. Emily knew she put a couple of bob on the horses and had two port and lemons.

'Don't ever let me catch you over there,' Gran said to her regularly. 'Drink is no good to you.'

'Why not?'

'After a couple, Emily, it's harder to say no.'

'Say no to more?'

'Say no to anything, especially men. You mark my words, drink spells trouble. Even one.'

'But doesn't it have that effect on you?'

'Yes, if I have to wait for Bert to come in to take my bet, I sometimes put three bob on, when one would have done.' Gran was keen on the horses, getting her information from the sports page of the *Daily Mail*.

'How much did you win?' Ted wanted to know.

'That would be telling.' She winked towards Charlie. Emily knew that if she won a few bob, it went on a roast joint for Sunday. Anything more she paid into a Christmas club. Gran made no secret of paying into two clubs, one with McFie the butcher and the other with Fraser's Grocers of Distinction. 'Might have enough for a turkey this year.'

'What if there isn't?' Emily asked.

'Then a big piece of pork.' Gran wiped at her thin pinched nose, the tip tinged with blue.

'I prefer pork, it's as nice as anything,' Charlie said. 'Better value, less bone.'

'Turkey's more of a treat,' Gran insisted. 'Just the job at Christmas.'

Emily brooded all evening, listening with only half an ear to Gran's chatter, battling with a sense of loss.

She went to bed feeling heavy with hurt, unable to believe she and Alex had said such horrible things to each other. Why had she said she'd grown out of him? It had made him suggest they go their separate ways, and that had slashed her like a razor.

Alex was everything to her. Her friend, her lover, her security. Impossible to believe they'd quarrelled. In all the years of childhood, they never had.

They'd made plans for the future, wanting to change everything about the way they lived now. But everything they planned, they planned to do together.

They were going to train for careers, get good jobs, claw their way up, say goodbye to poverty. They planned to get married when Alex was twenty-one, and buy their own house. They were partners and had meant to stay that way.

Emily knew Alex had given her strength, supported her through bad times. She couldn't imagine life without him. Didn't want to.

The quarrel had opened up a new chasm between them. His angry words had blistered, but she'd felt they'd been drifting apart for some time.

It made her ache to think about it. She'd spent an agonised night, tossing for hours on her flock mattress, hearing the ships' hooters sound their dismal warning in a river fog. In the early hours of the morning she'd fallen into a heavy sleep so that she'd been late getting out of bed. She'd felt lifeless all day, and had to drag herself through her Sunday chores. She decided she would have to try to smooth things over with Alex. She wanted to hold on to him at any cost.

On the way to Wythenshaw's on Monday morning, she wheeled out her bike into the entry, and waited outside his back gate till he came wheeling his bike out too.

'Sorry, Alex,' she told him. 'I said things I didn't mean on Saturday.'

His face seemed unusually grim; he pushed off leading the way over the entry setts.

'I don't like what's happening to us, Alex.'

'I'm sorry too.' He turned with a half-smile then, and she realised she'd hurt him as much as he'd hurt her. She had to pedal hard to keep up with him.

'Why don't we go out one night?' This was the olive branch. Once they'd gone everywhere together.

'There's night school. I've got three nights a week of it.' His reluctance made her feel cold, she thought he'd jump at the chance to bridge the gap.

She made herself to say: 'What about next Saturday then?' Emily knew from one glance at his stricken face he'd already arranged something else.

'Billy Wade wants me to meet him for a drink in the Bird.' She felt a wave of displeasure. She'd never liked Billy Wade, and Gran said he kept bad company.

They had to dismount. A bus was disgorging office workers into the street outside Wythenshaw's. She felt ready to give up under the pall of discouragement. Instead she pushed herself forward alongside him.

'Can't I come with you?'

'You're not eighteen, Emily.'

'There's lots of girls in the Bird who aren't eighteen.'

'No, I'd have your gran on my back. You know she's dead against you going in there.'

Emily could feel her face crumpling with disappointment; she couldn't believe he'd reject her like this. She headed for the bike stalls as fast as she could go.

'Hang on a minute,' Alex called after her, his cheeks scarlet. 'All right, I'll come round to your place with Dad at closing time. I'll tell Billy it's off. We could go to the pictures.'

Emily could feel his discomposure coming across in waves. Somehow they couldn't stop rubbing each other the wrong way. What had happened to them?

Her voice was twisted. 'Thank you,' she managed. 'I'd like that.'

Emily had an uneasy week. They met in the canteen on three of the days, but they could say little with so many other people close. Alex ate quickly and seemed prickly. They might have been strangers.

She pinned all her hopes on Saturday. She knew what she had to do, she had to talk this through with Alex, tell him she loved and needed him. Try to understand how he felt.

A visit to the pictures was not what she would have chosen for this. For them both to sit in his living-room alone and thrash it out would be better, but Alex wouldn't take her there now unless he knew his family was at home too. He seemed to be holding her at arm's length.

On Saturday evening, she wore her office clothes to serve in the shop for once, covering them up with a clean overall. She wanted no hitches.

Alex came with Ted as he said he would at closing time. She looked up from serving a customer to find his dark eyes watching her warily. He seemed more aloof and serious than he had the week before.

She sat next to him at the living-room table, silently eating, shutting Ted's war reminiscences out of her mind.

'Shall we go, Emily?' Alex asked when they'd finished. 'There's only twenty minutes before the last house starts at the Palace.' The Palace in Rock Ferry was their local picture house and within walking distance.

'There's a double bill tonight. Two feature-length cowboy films, Billy Wade says they're good.'

Emily had been going to suggest they go to the Regal in Birkenhead. It made it more of an occasion to go into town, and the typing-pool girls had told her the Clark Gable picture showing there was wonderful.

Cowboy films didn't interest her, but it was a minor disappointment; if Alex wanted to see them she was prepared to go too. What she wanted was a chance to talk to him, to sort out their difficulties.

Emily shot up to her room, shed her overall and put on her gaberdine instead. Ran a comb through her dark hair. Alex was waiting impatiently, standing in the lobby with his coat on.

He pulled her arm through his, hurrying her along when she thought there was little need because the advertisements would run for fifteen minutes before the second house started.

'I can't understand why all you girls are so besotted with Giles Wythenshaw.' Alex sounded prickly. 'He's a spoilt brat. A lazy good-for-nothing. He wouldn't last five minutes if he wasn't the boss's son.'

'You're just like your dad, always going on about the Wythenshaws.' She felt prickly herself.

'I don't like hearing your name linked to his. Everybody

is talking about you. You're spending too much time with him.'

'I'm paid to spend time with him, it's my job. What do you want me to do, give it up?' She was finding it a struggle to keep up with Alex's long stride.

'Of course not, don't be silly.' That made Emily bristle. She didn't want Alex thinking she was silly.

It took an effort to say calmly: 'Alex, we need to talk about ourselves, not about Giles Wythenshaw.' But they'd reached the picture house, and there was no queue to buy tickets.

The cheapest seats cost sixpence. Emily pushed the coin in Alex's hand as they went up the steps.

'These days, girls expect me to pay when I take them out,' he said, trying to give it her back.

'Nothing's changed with us. If one of us is broke, the other pays for both. Didn't we agree? We pay for ourselves if we can.' Emily wished she hadn't said it with such thrust. He'd meant it as a kindness, she should have accepted it as such. They were at each other's throats in a way they'd never been before.

She'd trusted Alex, given him everything she could. Now she was full of hurt because it wasn't enough. What they'd shared was dying.

They were barely seated before the lights went out, and the first cowboy film started. In the darkness she pushed her hand in his, he squeezed it gently, and turned to smile at her. This was more like Alex of old.

Emily found she couldn't lose herself in the confection of cowboys and Indians, when her own problems were so real. But Alex had her hand in a vice-like grip. He was leaning forward in his seat, tense with the thrills of thundering hoofs and showers of arrows.

As soon as the lights came up in the interval, and she opened her mouth to say something, Alex leapt to his feet.

'Would you like an ice-cream?'

The ice-cream vendors were positioning themselves in the aisles. Bright toe-tapping music was crashing out, designed, Emily thought, to lift the spirits after watching so many Indians bite the dust. It was going to take more than music to cheer her.

She let her eyes follow Alex. His dark red hair, glossy under the subdued lights, made him easy to pick out. A line of waiting customers was forming quickly, but he was near its head.

She watched him being served, and turn to come back. A girl waiting in the queue put out her hand to detain him as he passed. She wore a smart hat with a feather, and seemed to have a lot to say. Her hands gesticulated, her fingernails were painted talons. It stabbed at Emily, to see him laugh with the girl, and to realise he was in no hurry to return.

Emily couldn't drag her eyes away, but eventually as the girl's turn to be served came, he left her and came back to his seat.

'Choc ice,' he said, putting one into her hand. 'Your favourite.' It was already melting.

'Who was that?' Her voice sounded sharp in her own ears. It took him a long time to answer.

'Rita Shaw, she works in the canteen.'

Emily bit into her choc ice. 'I didn't recognise her without her overalls and turban.'

She knew she'd let him see her jealousy when he said: 'I had to stop for a moment to chat. I didn't want to seem rude.'

'Of course,' she said. 'You can talk to whoever you want.'

'Emily,' he chided. 'Because I talk to a girl it doesn't mean I want to spend the rest of my life with her.'

She wasn't sorry when the lights dimmed again and the second cowboy film started. But she enjoyed it no better than the first.

She was tired by the time the show was over, but had decided to suggest they walk a little way along the Esplanade. It would be quiet down there, and she'd have peace and all his attention to say what she wanted.

After looking at so much arid Arizona desert, it came as a shock to find the night was wet and dark when they got out. Alex took her arm and hurried her along. Traffic, with headlights cutting through relentless rain, swished along New Chester Road spraying water in all directions.

It was no night for a stroll along the Esplanade. In fact they'd only gone a hundred yards or so before the heavens opened, and there was a real downpour. Alex quickened his step, making her break into a run towards a shop doorway to shelter.

Two girls were already sheltering there. Obligingly they moved back to make room. Emily felt their eyes rake her.

'Hey, Alex,' roared one, a peroxide blonde balancing on six-inch heels. 'You said you'd see us at the Bird for a drink. We waited for you. You promised.'

Emily recoiled. Shocked to find Alex interested in a girl like this.

'No, I didn't promise, I said I might,' he protested. 'I told Billy I wasn't coming. Decided to go straight to the pictures.'

'You'll come next week, won't you?'

'Perhaps,' he said. 'Come on, Emily, it's slackening off.' He took her arm and bustled her out into the rain again. It was still coming down in torrents.

'You didn't say anything about meeting girls in the Bird,' she said, trying to keep up with him.

'They're Billy's friends,' Alex said through clenched teeth.

'Yours too, by the sound of it,' she couldn't help

adding. Seconds later, she knew it was the last thing she should have said. Alex was striding out so hard, she was almost jogging to keep up with him. She noticed Gran's bedroom light was on as they came up the Parade.

In the back entry, Alex's step slowed. She stifled her anger, pausing deliberately at his back gate.

'You're drenched,' he said, his tone cold. In the half dark, she could see drops of water running down his face.

'We still haven't had our talk,' she said.

'Do you want to come in for a cup of tea?'

Emily flinched. 'Do you want . . .' sounded as though he did not.

'Yes,' she said. 'Thank you.' Alex pushed the back gate open. Light was streaming across the yard from both the living-room and kitchen windows.

'Dad's home,' he said, leading the way indoors. Ted was getting his breath back in an armchair by the fire.

'Good gracious, Emily, you're soaked. You're both soaked.'

Alex put the kettle on the gas, and shook both their coats at the back door before running up to the airing cupboard with them.

'Get those wet shoes off,' Ted told her. 'You'll catch your death of cold.'

He was reaching for the poker. Emily took it from him, poked the fire up into a blaze, put another lump or two of coal on. She felt at ease with the Frasers.

'There's a pair of Olympia's slippers there, you'd better put them on,' Ted said with genuine concern.

Emily made tea for them, while Alex took away her cardigan because it was damp across the shoulders, and brought down one of his pullovers to keep her warm.

'Do you want a cup of tea, Dad?' he asked.

'No, I think I'll go to bed. Your mother won't be long. Went to see Clark Gable. Is that where you've been?'

'No,' Emily snapped.

'I expect she's round at Ethel's by now. Usually pops in there for a cup of tea on a Saturday night.'

Warmed by the fire now blazing up and the scalding tea, Emily took pleasure in snuggling Alex's pullover round her more tightly. She felt ungrateful because she wanted Ted to go.

As soon as she heard his bedroom door shut over her head, she went over to the sofa and sat down beside Alex. She put out her arms, snuggled closer and kissed him. It was the best way she knew of showing him how she felt.

For one wonderful moment his arms tightened round her, his lips pressed down on hers, opening her mouth. She was tingling with the joy of success.

His touch burned, and she felt the first pulse of desire. Then roughly he was pulling her closer, till she could scarcely breathe. He was pressing savage kisses on her face.

'You're hurting . . .' she gasped, and suddenly he was jerking away from her, as though her kisses stung.

It stunned her. 'What's the matter?'

'Don't start that again, Emily,' he choked. She tossed away into the corner of the sofa, shocked and hurt, wanting to cry.

'What are you trying to do?' Alex's dark eyes blazed back at her. 'Make me wire-tight with tension? You know I can't stand it. Try to understand. You're pushing me to a knife edge of frustration. Screaming frustration. Stay away from me, can't you?'

Outside, the back gate slammed shut. They heard Olympia's footsteps crossing the yard. Fighting for self-control, Emily was ramming her feet back into her wet shoes. Without tying them or speaking to Olympia she ran past her and out into the rain.

Once in her own home, she tore Alex's pullover over

her head, tossed it into a chair in the living-room, and raced for the stairs.

She wanted to scream. She'd made things a hundred times worse.

CHAPTER FIVE

Jeremy Wythenshaw got up from his breakfast of bacon and eggs feeling replete. He went upstairs at the double, eager to get down to the first business of the day. He thought of his bedroom as a private place. Only Higgins, his man, was allowed in, and he always made the huge bed while Jeremy ate his breakfast.

Elspeth had brought the bed with her, a marriage gift from one of her relatives. Dating from Victorian times, it had gothic mahogany trellises at head and foot. In the years since her death, he'd banished her frilly curtains, and the feminine dressing-table.

Now it was a man's room, plain and orderly, with two enormous wardrobes, a tallboy and a big desk under one of the windows looking over the front entrance. He had comfortable sofas and chairs near the gas fire, several small tables and a standard lamp. If his circumstances had been different he'd be content to live in this room.

A small mahogany bookcase seemed to stand against one wall. Jeremy touched a catch that allowed it to be swung back on hinges just clear of the floor. It hid the safe behind.

Humming a march by Sousa, he opened it with the key he kept on his watch chain and took out two account books. One he kept to give his accountant at the end of the financial year; in the other, the figures were different. He kept it for his personal information and never showed to anyone. He had to battle with his conscience about the two sets of accounts. It was very wrong of him to do it, but under the awful circumstances, he had no alternative.

He tried to work on these accounts first thing in the morning, when his mind was clear and the details fresh. He couldn't afford to make mistakes. Today, with the shop's takings over the last few days to enter, he didn't feel single-minded. Sylveen's face kept coming between him and the figures.

He'd never seen a face where each feature was so in accord with the whole. The small straight nose, delicate eyebrows over wide blue eyes. In repose it had child-like innocence, totally at variance with the ripe promise of her body, and the blatant invitation in her manner.

Meeting her in the corridor yesterday had unsettled him. It was months since his liaison with Olivia had ended. Three at least, and he had told himself he was too old at sixty to have another such dalliance, but Sylveen's aura of simmering sensuality was tempting him.

He finished making up his records, and locked the books up again, knowing all the time he'd do what he always had. It wasn't in his nature to resist temptation, his way was to reach out for anything that offered excitement. He would have to be at death's door to turn his back on the invitation in Sylveen's eyes.

Still whistling Sousa he went downstairs. In the hall, the deferential Higgins helped him into his greatcoat. He was slow and had a lined face for a man of forty. He coughed.

'Are you all right?'

'Yes, sir.' Higgins never seemed very well, and always smelled of cigarette smoke. As he led the way down the front steps to the Rolls, and ceremoniously opened the passenger door, Jeremy hoped he wasn't going to be ill. He was his most useful member of staff. With a peak cap to wear with his black lounge suit, he was transformed from valet to chauffeur. If Jeremy had guests to a meal, he put on a dinner jacket and served as butler.

'To the factory,' Jeremy said, settling on to the sumptuous leather. He enjoyed the time he spent running the business. It gave him great satisfaction to do what his father and his grandfather had done before him. To know they had put up these buildings, and set up the factory lines gave him a sense of continuity. Because of Calthorpe's, he was earning a greater profit than his forebears ever had. It ought to make it all the sweeter, but instead it seemed wrong. Today, he mustn't let himself dwell on his problems and get depressed.

The factory was providing an honest living. He wanted to hand it on to Giles in the way it had been handed to him. Five years ago he had expected the business to make a man of Giles. It was becoming increasingly clear that it would not. He was more Calthorpe than Wythenshaw.

Everybody greeted him as he walked up to his office, and that gave him pleasure too. Yet Giles thought of the place as a prison.

'Good morning, Miss Lewis.' She had straight grey hair and the suggestion of a moustache, but he had selected her as his personal secretary for her efficiency and experience. In ten years her work had never given any cause for complaint, and he hoped she would not retire before he did, for she was almost as old.

'Morning, Miss Smith.' He allowed his glance to linger a moment longer on her. It pleased him to feel a further rush of temptation, proving his libido had not yet settled into old age.

This morning, he had to force his attention on to work. He read through his mail, called in Miss Lewis and watched her pencil scrawling incomprehensible lines and curves to record his words. Then she drew his attention to a matter he'd overlooked, and he dictated a memo to settle that. At last he had finished. She stood up.

'Ask Miss Smith to come in. I want to start a report.' He

could see by the sour look on her face she didn't approve of Sylveen.

'She could do a rough draft and you could type it afterwards if she isn't capable,' he said. That mollified her.

Sylveen seemed to bring a breath of fresh air into his room. Sitting in the chair Miss Lewis had used, she seemed nearer, though the desk still stretched between them. Jeremy knew what he planned to do would be considered wrong. What she offered was explicit. It made him feel alive, almost on fire; doing wrong things added zest to life. Get on with it, he told himself. Ask her, there's no other way.

'Would you have dinner with me one evening?' he said in the middle of a paragraph. Her bright blue eyes shot up from her note pad. He searched them for shock or alarm. Nothing like that, they were shining with pleasure.

'I'd love to. When?'

'Tomorrow?'

She nodded. 'Yes, lovely. Thank you.'

'Where shall I meet you?' He knew she wouldn't suggest he call at her home. Already there was something clandestine about the meeting.

'Rock Ferry Station,' she suggested after a pause. He couldn't suppress his smile. It seemed so youthful and innocent an answer, but he was long past the age of hanging around railway stations for his partners. Anyway, she might be late.

'Wouldn't we both find it more convenient to go straight from here? When the hooter goes, you get your coat from the cloakroom, and come back to my office. We'll have a cup of tea, and let the workers have their mad scramble to leave. Then no one will be any the wiser.'

When she had gone Jeremy leaned back in his chair in a state of exultation. It had been incredibly easy. He was looking forward to the outing. There was something between them already. He had felt it burst into life as she'd pinned the poppy in his button hole. He felt twenty years younger.

By the next morning he was changing his mind. He felt an old reprobate; she was so ridiculously young for him, he was having second thoughts. Walking together, she would look like his daughter, possibly even his granddaughter.

He needed to know more about Sylveen, so he went along to the personnel office. Thumbing through the filing cabinet to find her folder, he noticed a red-haired woman watching him from a nearby desk. Her name was on the tip of his tongue. Pender? To throw her off the scent, he selected five more folders at random and what he hoped was hers too, before striding off to his own room.

He discovered Sylveen was twenty-four. That pleased him, he had feared she was younger. He noted her address in Prenton. That she had had three other jobs, then a gap of six months unemployment before coming to Wythenshaw's. She had trained at Skerry's Commercial College in Liverpool. Her references were good, she was over-qualified to assist his secretary. He smiled to himself; much more tactful to find out this way instead of having to ask clumsy questions.

She came to his room, excited and eager and brimming with life. He had intended to leave before six o'clock when the night watchman locked the gates, but he was afraid the time might drag, it was so very early to go anywhere for dinner.

Sylveen had been making his tea morning and afternoon for the last few days. She made more now, producing chocolate biscuits with it. She ate most of them herself, rocking backwards and forwards in his visitor's chair. He talked on, she seemed genuinely interested in the baubles they were making. It seemed important that she understand the trade.

It was nearly seven and they hadn't moved when Sylveen said: 'You'd have made a good teacher.'

'Have I missed my vocation?'

'No, certainly not. Most teachers couldn't do what you have, but you know so much, and you make it interesting.'

'Perhaps you're the ideal pupil.' Jeremy watched her tidy away all traces of their tea. She was hungry for knowledge of any sort. Hungry for life. He had enjoyed providing it.

Sylveen unlocked the factory gates with his key, and he drove his car out of the yard. There was no sign of a night watchman. He headed towards Chester; he had reserved a table at the Grapes.

'Your car looks different.' Her hands stroked the soft leather seat.

'It is different. Usually Higgins drives me in the Rolls, but if I drive myself, I prefer the Alvis.' It attracted less attention, wasn't immediately recognised as his.

She was impressed, he told her all he knew about the silver eagle Atlantic saloon. She thought dinner and the Grapes Hotel wonderful. He loved her enthusiasm for things he took for granted. It was her youth, he realised, and her search for experience.

He told her about his forthcoming trip to Paris, even toyed with the idea of taking her. He would love to unfold all of Paris before her. She would be thrilled, but no, he couldn't. He'd never taken anyone there with him. It would be too risky.

He debated with himself whether he should take her back to Churton. He had told his staff he would need nothing more, so they would not be about, and Giles could be relied upon to avoid him.

Sylveen would enjoy his collection of baubles, the more successful lines Wythenshaw's had made over the last century. He kept boxes of them in his library. They'd have a night cap, then he'd take her home to Prenton. There would be no pressure on her this first night, unless she showed quite clearly she wanted something more.

Jeremy was surprised to find a note from his housekeeper propped up on the hall table. It was addressed to Giles. He had failed to turn up for dinner when expected. Par for the course. He ushered Sylveen into the library, poked the fire up into a blaze. She was enchanted with the baubles.

'They're beautiful,' her breathy voice enthused. 'Just look at this bracelet, and there's a matching ring. What's the label for?'

He took it from her. 'We made them from 1891 to 1893. Sold two hundred thousand gross. The set cost a shilling.' The metal had stayed bright in the box, the red glass sparkled like garnets.

'They're really pretty.' Sylveen slid the ring on her finger, clasped the bracelet round her wrist, and stretched her arm to show them off.

'You wouldn't want to wear those,' he said, making up his mind to get her something from the shop. Not a ring, girls read more into receiving rings than was intended. A bracelet, nothing wildly expensive, but gold at least.

'I can understand why it sold well. The design is beautiful.'

'Sometimes we resurrect an old design, but not this, we couldn't sell it for a shilling today. Too much work involved, and a bit ornate for present taste.'

That was the delightful thing about Sylveen, she asked all manner of ingenuous questions, and was not afraid he'd think her lacking if she showed ignorance. And she showed her emotions, they passed in a kaleidoscope across her fragile features.

He couldn't remember when he'd enjoyed himself so much. She was a delight to look at, her youthful eagerness was refreshing, her thirst for knowledge a compliment, and she had an underlying sensuality that sparked the atmosphere with electricity.

Emily was sitting at the long table next to Miss Murdoch.

Suddenly she pushed herself upright in the seat; she had been brooding again about Alex. His dark eyes had burned into her back as she'd walked away from him at the bike sheds this morning, yet they'd hardly exchanged a word. Alex was jangling her nerves.

Emily sighed, trying to concentrate on Miss Murdoch's pencil, which was expertly sketching what looked like a brooch with a chain mounted on each side to fasten round the neck.

'Pykes, the jewellers in Grange Road, have several.' Her horsey face was enthusiastic. 'Beautiful things set with pearls. It's the latest fashion. We make the chain, Emily, and we must have brooches being produced at the moment that could be adapted. It wouldn't take much.'

'A fashion Wythenshaw's can exploit?'

'Yes, we could make them cheaply, and possibly sell the original brooch as well as the adapted necklace, as a *demi parure*.'

'What's that?'

'A set, or rather a half set.'

Emily was helping Miss Murdoch sift through their patterns to choose what could best be modified in this way, when Giles came in, his hands in the pockets of his slacks.

'Have you heard?' he asked. 'Your brooch is in production. Do you want to see it coming off the machines?'

'Both of you go,' Mary Murdoch said.

Emily jumped to her feet, thrilled to follow him down to the factory floor. She hardly noticed now the envious glances other girls sent in her direction. Above the crash of machinery and rattling rollers she heard a wolf whistle. Giles, she noticed, grinned in the direction from which it had come.

'Quite an honour for you.' He took her arm and led her towards a machine into which sheet metal was being fed on rollers. It was stamping out rows of bows, and bending the ends back to form a catch on one side and a hinge on the other. The noise was deafening. He bent to shout in her ear: 'Done in two operations.'

Another machine stamped pins out of wire; Emily knew Wythenshaw's had standardised the size of the pins, making them large or small. This limited the size of brooches but reduced costs. Rollers carried the brooches to girls who fed them by hand into smaller machines that attached them together. More girls were pinning brooches on to display cards, a dozen at a time. Others packed the cards into cartons. Emily watched, bemused by the dexterity of their fingers.

Giles picked a brooch out of the tray and put his lips to her ear. 'Keep it as a memento,' he shouted. Emily turned it over in her hand feeling a little disappointed.

'I'd hardly know it. Not at all as I imagined,' she mouthed. Giles threw back his head and laughed.

Without warning, the line jolted to a halt. In the sudden silence the girls whooped with delight, leaping to their feet and rushing for the door.

'The two Marys have adapted it a bit. Simplified the shape, but they were working on your idea. It's quite pretty.' Emily pinned it on to her cardigan.

'Lunch time,' he said. 'Might as well go straight in now.' He was heading towards the staff dining-room where waitress service was provided and the tables set with white cloths.

Emily hesitated; although office staff were entitled to use the dining-room, she had started eating in the canteen when she first came to Wythenshaw's because the same meal cost half the price there.

Canteen staff were entitled to free meals. She could have eaten in either place while she worked there, but had continued to go to the canteen because everybody she knew did so.

She hesitated now because she knew she would have to pay a shilling for her dinner; she explained the situation.

'I've never tried the canteen,' Giles said. 'I suppose I should.' Emily was embarrassed to have him fall in step beside her. What would the typing pool make of this?

She had to show Giles where to collect his own cutlery and plate. As they stood in line to have them filled at the counter, Emily was very conscious of him standing behind her. Every acquaintance she'd ever made seemed to come up to chat, and she had to introduce them to Giles.

'Hello, Jenny,' he said. 'Where is it you work?' and, 'Hello, Joan, I've seen you about the office. Yes, the typing pool.'

They were taking their plates of sausage and mash to one of the long linoleum-covered tables, when she saw Sylveen waving from the queue. 'Keep a place for me, Emily,' she called. They found space at one of the tables.

'I'll keep this for your friend.' Giles tipped up the chair next to him. 'Not much elbow room here.' The canteen was vast and echoed with the chink of cutlery, the scrape of chairs and the buzz of voices.

'The feeding of the five thousand,' he said. 'Enough to give everybody indigestion. Do I have to go back in that line to get my pudding?' he asked. Emily pointed out a different queue, and Giles collected helpings of apple pie for them all.

'Isn't he nice?' Sylveen said, her blue eyes following his progress up the queue. 'You are lucky, Emily, working for him.' Emily felt bombarded with knowing looks from the girls.

Only then did she notice Alex eyeing her balefully from further up the table. His pursed lips and air of grim determination compared ill with Giles's light-hearted chatter.

Alex always used to keep her a place beside him, but today there were storemen ranged on both sides. That slammed home the message. Alex no longer sought her company. She nodded a cool acknowledgment, and tried to stem the tide of sadness that ran through her.

'You know, I think I prefer the dining-room,' Giles said on the way back to the office. 'There's basic civilisation there. I'll take you both tomorrow.'

Emily decided he was making an effort to be more friendly to her.

Giles Wythenshaw changed tack and felt *Seaspray* surge forward as the stiffish breeze filled her sails. He felt in control out here on the Mersey.

'It's a bit chilly,' Phyllis complained, from where she huddled on the steps leading down to the cabin. A babyish blonde he'd met for the first time last week, she was already getting on his nerves with her Daddy this and Mummy that.

He'd endured a terrible morning at the factory studying cheap trinkets. Each piece put into his hand to demonstrate some vital rule he must remember and use. His mind had been paralysed by the earnest faces surrounding him, the patient voices explaining what they expected from him. Even to think of it made him uneasy. There was no way he could provide what they wanted. Design jewellery for God's sake! He neither knew about nor cared for the rubbish. If only Father would give him something interesting to do.

Little Emily was interested, they were women's trinkets after all. He was beginning to fear the two Marys might notice her performance was better than his. What she meant to be was quietly supportive as always, but she was showing him up. Impossible to explain to her where she was going wrong.

He'd thought her bow stupid, but the two Marys had loved it, bending over backwards to say how good it was. Trying to make out he had some hand in it. He lived in hourly dread that Emily was going to come up with other ideas. His eyes settled on Phyllis's throat. It was bedecked with some bauble. Her green eyes caught his gaze.

'Do you like my necklace?' Her fingers pulled at a gold chain that widened out in the centre and was set with pearls. 'A birthday present from Mummy.'

'Nice,' he said; at least it was gold.

'I brought it to show you. It came from your father's shop.'

'Really?' Giles looked at it again, seeking ideas. No, setting all those pearls would be expensive. 'Too good to bring out here in the boat, then.' So was her pink suit, both unsuitable. Easy to see she'd never been sailing before.

'Daddy says your father is a gentleman, he does a lot for the poor.'

'Depends who the poor are.' Giles couldn't keep the bitter note out of his voice.

'Daddy says he sells good stock at a fair price. He admires him.'

'Everybody does.' His voice was wry. That was the problem, he couldn't hope to emulate Father. 'I'm not much like him.'

'Of course you are. The same build, and just the same nose. Mummy was impressed when I said you were taking me out. Said I couldn't go far wrong with you.'

'Little does she know,' Giles said, with enough inflection to sound suggestive, but it hid something else. He knew he'd never achieve what his father had. It rankled. Made him dissatisfied.

This was what he was good at, tacking upriver in a blustery breeze. He'd expected some help from Phyllis, but it didn't matter. He could handle *Seaspray*'s eighteen feet, he'd been doing it for years now. The small yacht had been a twenty-first birthday gift from his father.

They had come up beyond Eastham and the entrance to the Manchester ship canal. This part of the river was less busy. He threw out his sea anchor. He would lie-to here against the leeward shore for a while. Have some fun with Phyllis.

Down in the cabin he wound up his gramophone and put on a Henry Hall record. No room to dance, but he had the bunks. He steered Phyllis towards the galley, pointed out the kettle and the tea. Girls always liked tea, it would warm her up, put her in a softer mood.

But it was not a satisfactory afternoon either, Giles decided later. Phyllis's green eyes had promised heaven, but she'd dug her heels in when he got her near the bunk. Despite the privacy, and the gentle rocking, and the flickering reflections on the cabin ceiling, she had refused. He was allowed to do no more than run his hand up her silk blouse.

She'd complained of the cold. His hand was cold, and she couldn't bear to have her clothing loosened. She needed more on. He'd had to find her a jacket to put over the pink suit. Even then she'd gone on complaining. She'd known it was November, despite the sun at midday. By four o'clock when he started the return journey, the day was overcast and grey. He'd had to scull the dinghy across the receding tide in the dark, and she'd said she was frightened as well as cold.

She'd come round a little with her feet on dry land, and he'd taken her on to the Royal Rock for dinner. He didn't know why, he'd decided he was wasting his time by then. Afterwards, he took her home, then feeling the need of more company, went back to the Royal Rock for another drink. It had been another dead loss of a day.

Giles knew himself to be a creature of habit. Years ago, Father had met him at the top of the stairs, irate at being woken in what he called the middle of the night. Since then he'd made it a rule to switch off his headlights and engine, and let his car roll the last fifty yards to the front door of Churton.

The dark night closed round him. The car crunched

softly on the gravel. It was only midnight and early for him, but he was tired and had no wish for another exchange with his father.

An outside light in the porch was kept burning all night. It lit up the steps and the front door. Giles was steering his Riley into the shadows to the right of it. The shadows seemed unusually heavy.

At the last minute, his foot rammed down on the brake, jerking his car to a stop, bouncing him forward. The rush of adrenalin made his heart pound. He'd only just avoided running into his father's Alvis.

Giles let his breath burst through his teeth. His father was a creature of habit too. His car was usually garaged at night, but then he was usually driven by Higgins. Giles got out slowly. Father only drove himself when he didn't want others to know where he went.

He was climbing the front steps when he saw the chinks of light showing through the library curtains. And crossing the hall when he heard a woman's laugh, a hearty laugh from a woman enjoying herself.

The randy old devil, he thought and almost laughed with her. On impulse he changed direction. This was too good an opportunity to miss. He could get one up on Father, embarrass him. Give his woman the once-over. Let them know he knew she'd be staying the night. Father liked to be secretive about such things.

There was so much about his father that got up his nose, but he had to hand it to him, he carried his years well. He had the energy and enthusiasm of a man half his age, and he put it all into clashing with his son. They couldn't come face to face without it happening.

Giles crossed the hall, putting his feet down noisily so as to be heard. He assumed an innocent expression before flinging open the library door.

'Hello, Father. I was wondering if the light had been left on by mistake.'

His father was rising hastily from the sofa; Giles's gaze went beyond him to his companion. He almost whistled through his teeth again. Softly rounded breasts rose invitingly in the neckline of a lean and flowing blue dress. Her bright blonde hair waved loosely round her head in the latest style, and great dewy eyes met his seductively. She smiled, Giles felt his knees turn to water. It was an inviting smile.

'Miss Sylveen Smith.'

In a daze, he put out his hand, she gave him a friendly squeeze. He had expected a much older woman, with lots of breeding. Someone more like his mother, though he remembered her only vaguely now. He found it hard to believe his father was still capable of attracting such a girl.

'My son Giles.'

Father was jumpy, his white hair glistening in the lamplight. Snow on the roof, Giles thought, but he still has fire burning within.

'Yes I know.' Her smile was intimate. 'I've seen you at work.'

'Really? The office? I've not seen you.'

'You don't go often enough,' his father said coldly.

'Do you know Emily Barr?' she asked.

'Yes, quite well.' Giles knew immediately he had been premature in asking for Emily's services. 'You're a secretary? Who do you work for?'

'Your father.' She turned to smile at him.

He remembered the ogre Miss Lewis who relayed his father's orders, and another quiet girl.

'I've not seen you there.' He'd never forget this one.

'Since last Monday. I spent a year working for Mr Bunting before that.'

Giles felt a powerful surge within him, compounded of envy and wonder. So his father had seen her and fancied her too. He should have spent more time at work, she was worth ten Phyllises.

'You might have told Mrs Eglin you wouldn't be in to dinner tonight.' His father turned in sudden attack. 'Do you realise she cooked a meal just for you? And kept it hot for hours in case you were delayed.'

'Oh dear,' he said. Sylveen's blue eyes met his sympathetically.

'You really should have more thought for other people.'

Giles clenched his teeth at the familiar carping tone, the familiar complaint, but he could see his father shaking, and knew he'd tipped him off balance. He'd shattered the mood Father had been building up.

The girl was watching through lustrous lashes, lying back against the sofa, her hands behind her head. She was providing a sizzling undercurrent that was wasted on an old man.

Giles felt his spirits soar. He wanted to laugh. He'd been searching for years for some way to avenge the insults he had to endure. His father held power over half of Birkenhead, but his grip was tightest on him. He had made him feel less of a man more times than he cared to count.

Now he knew how he could do it. There was one thing he was better at than his father. In any case, all his instincts urged him to go for this girl. He liked her sultry beauty. The fact that Father did too, made her twice as exciting. He would take what his father wanted. That would give him great satisfaction.

'I'm sorry.' He needed to placate him now, give himself time to think this out. 'I'll make my peace with her tomorrow. Meantime, I'm off to bed, I'm tired. Good night, Miss Smith. Good night, Father.'

CHAPTER SIX

Jeremy sighed, aware the library door had clicked shut with unusual restraint. He had been forced to introduce Sylveen to Giles, and it had not pleased him. He was not ready to let the world know of his liaison, the first links were only just being forged.

As a girlfriend, she would not enhance his public image, or help his preferment; what Sylveen offered was only too obvious. With her as his wife, many men would envy him. He'd known it was risky to bring her home, but it had added fillip at the time. As the evening progressed he had been conscious of the emotional atmosphere heightening between them, and wasn't that half the pleasure?

Now Giles had shattered it. Damn Giles. It would take a blind man to miss the way he'd looked at her. He found Sylveen's blue eyes watching him.

'Barging in on us like that,' she smiled. 'Quite ruined our relaxed mood.' Her gaze could draw him out, make him feel hot. 'Shall I get you another drink?'

She swayed over to the drinks cabinet, brought him some more brandy. Sat down again beside him on the sofa. So close against him, he could feel her warmth, smell her fragrance.

Her voice, soft and breathy, said: 'You have some lovely things here. What is that?'

Jeremy relaxed. 'The sofa table? Regency mahogany.'

'I meant the glass.'

'Beakers.' He was specially fond of antique glass. He roused himself, reached out to put it in her hand. 'From Bohemia, late seventeenth century.'

'Such beautiful engraving.' Sylveen held it up against the glow from the fire.

'Mat engraving. Medallions of the Apostles.' He reached for another piece. 'This is a covered goblet, with hollow baluster stem. Made in Nuremberg, again late seventeenth century.'

'Where do you find things like this?'

'Paris,' he told her. There were a few things he loved too much to part with. He'd meant to sell them, but couldn't bring himself to do it. He talked on about his beakers from Vienna, his goblets from Poland, Germany and Bohemia.

Sylveen seemed to know exactly what to do to soothe his irritation. She was helping re-create the atmosphere to get them where they'd been before Giles had interrupted. He kissed her, gathered her up in his arms and kissed her again. She had soft warm skin, the firm resilient skin of youth.

Sylveen showed her energy and enthusiasm for love as for everything else. She was as ready for it as he was. A peach ripe for the picking. He took her up to his bedroom. He should have had the sense to do this as soon as he got home. Nobody would disturb them here. Giles had chosen a room as far away as possible, because he did not want him to know what time he came and went. It worked both ways.

Sylveen was not a virgin, he didn't expect her to be. Making love to her brought a warm rush of affection; he knew he could grow very fond of her. He did not much enjoy driving her home at three in the morning.

'This is the house,' Sylveen murmured. 'Keep going for thirty yards or so, in case the engine wakes my mother.'

Jeremy couldn't bear to think of her mother. 'Can we do it again?'

'Love to.'

'When? Probably be glad of an early night tonight. How about Friday?'

'Yes. I've had a lovely time, thank you.'

Jeremy got up the next morning at his usual time, feeling he'd been given a new lease of life.

The cloth covered only a quarter of the dining-table at breakfast. Two places were always set facing each other, but Jeremy had usually finished before Giles came down. He was helping himself to porridge from the warming dishes on the sideboard, feeling a sharper-than-usual appetite, when Giles came in.

'Morning, Father.' There was a knowing look in his eyes that Jeremy had hoped to avoid. He could sense Giles wanted to ask where Sylveen was. 'I like your taste. Quite fancied the girl you brought here last night. How old is she?'

Jeremy flinched. He'd been a fool to introduce her to Giles.

'Did she go home?'

'Of course she went home,' Jeremy said irritably as he poured coffee. He must not let Giles's needling upset him. 'Where else would she go?'

Giles would have liked to ask whether he'd managed to get Sylveen to bed, but didn't quite dare. He couldn't face an explosion of fury from Father this early in the day.

Last night, he had gone up to his room, but not to sleep. His mind had been reeling from the impact Sylveen had delivered. He was slavering with anticipation. His first idea, to take Sylveen from his father, needed refinement. He thought out his plan carefully. Step one was to make Father uneasy. Tell him outright he admired Sylveen, that she was too young for him. Go on telling him that on every possible occasion.

Then, when Father went to Paris, he would saunter into his office and invite Sylveen here to Churton. Making sure the old ogre of a secretary heard every word, and he would say to Mrs Eglin, the housekeeper: 'I will be bringing a guest to dinner tonight.' He would order something special to be cooked. Make sure all the staff saw him showering kisses on her, especially Higgins. If possible take her up to his bed for the night, and down again for breakfast the next morning.

It would only be a matter of time then before Father found out the hard way. To start rumours round the office, and to let everybody else in the house know first, would increase his embarrassment. Let him feel hot under the collar both at work and at home. He'd pay him back for refusing a small increase in his allowance.

He had five days to wait until Father made his trip to Paris. He watched for Sylveen at work, but decided he would not seek her out until his father had gone. Going to Father's office was tantamount to putting his head into the lion's mouth. Better to lie low for the time being.

Alex Fraser pulled on the new Aran pullover his mother had knitted for him and surveyed the effect in his wardrobe mirror. It looked good and its warmth hugged him.

Everybody told him he was like his mother, that he had her colouring, but somehow the red hair looked better on her. She described it as deep auburn or chestnut, but a man could only call it red. Not that his was carroty, and neither did he have the pale freckled skin that usually went with it. Emily had told him it was a wonderful colour, but it now seemed she preferred Giles Wythenshaw's pale-gold streaks. Alex brushed hard, trying to make it lie flat.

He had his mother's gentle brown eyes, rather too gentle for a man, and neither of them had the fiery temper that traditionally went with their colouring. He hoped in his case, his mother's placid ways were spiked with determination.

He glared into the glass, trying to look like a man who was strong, who has made up his mind what he wants from life and thinks he's on course to get it. At nineteen, he'd too much to achieve to be placid. He had to work his way up, and needed to keep on his toes. He was ambitious about making a success of the job, but the whole point had been to give Emily a better life. She had given up on him, no doubt she was expecting to get the better life more quickly with Giles Wythenshaw.

Was his jaw resolute? He ran his fingers along it as he studied its line in the mirror. He wasn't sure what a resolute jaw looked like, but it felt prickly. He should have shaved again before changing.

He went back to the bathroom. His mother had had a new bathroom suite put in; they had the smartest bathroom in the Parade. Hurriedly he ran his razor over his dry chin; it tugged painfully at the tiny hairs. He tried his father's, and it did a better job. He rubbed in a little of his mother's cold cream to soothe his skin, then wiped most of it off again because it made his chin shine in the bathroom mirror. There was a raw look about him he did not like.

There were other things, too, he didn't like. He'd been saddled with a nature that was too easily aroused, too easily enamoured of the opposite sex. He'd been hooked, smitten and kept in chains by Emily Barr. Nobody else had seen her at fifteen as likely to inspire passion, yet he had had difficulty keeping his hands off her. Even now at seventeen, Billy Wade, Ken Tarrant and several more at work had assured him Emily was no great attraction. Too skinny, too quiet, and rather plain.

They didn't notice how in the sun her chocolate hair could sparkle with dark red lights, how her face lit up when she laughed. He'd hankered after Emily for years, till she'd turned her back, and left him feeling new pin pricks of love–hate. But Emily certainly had something; she'd attracted Giles Wythenshaw and he had the pick of them all.

He'd thought he must have a stronger libido than others, be more lustful, till he'd heard Billy Wade boast of his prowess. Alex could hardly believe the number he claimed: 'Don't be daft, there's plenty of girls who will.'

'But will they with me?'

'Of course. Will with anybody.'

Billy was going out with a girl called Edna who worked at the place that roasted peanuts. Last week, Billy had asked her to bring along a girlfriend for Alex, and they'd all gone to the pictures first. The girlfriend had turned out to be a decade older than him, a peroxide blonde. He couldn't get on with her.

'An old hag,' Billy had agreed, he'd quarrelled with Edna too. 'But plenty more fish in the sea.'

Tonight, Alex was meeting him again in the Bird, and Billy had said he'd organised two good bits of crumpet this time. Alex went out whistling, telling himself he had no reason to feel guilty. A night out would do him good.

It was a fine starlit evening, and the Bird of Paradise was less than a hundred yards from the Parade. A working-man's public house, it was built like everything else in the neighbourhood, of Victorian smoke-blackened brick.

Light shone out into the road from windows with opaque glass in the bottom half. The sign creaking in the breeze from the river showed a bird, a cross between a parrot and a peacock, its plumage faded and smoke-blackened with time.

Alex pushed open the door, there was a burst of laughter above the chatter. Blinking through the blue haze in the bar he could not see Billy's short squat figure, though there were storemen from Wythenshaw's. He bought himself a half of bitter and went to look in the snug.

There was no mistaking Gran's battered black straw hat with its red and yellow cherries, or the big black shawl loosening round her thin body to show another smaller shawl beneath. Her eyes were sharp enough, they fastened on him straight away. 'What you doing here then?' she demanded.

'I don't need permission,' he said, and then regretted his sharpness. Gran was always friendly and generous with chips when she served him. She was fond of Emily too. 'Glad to see you out and about again.'

'A little nip does me good.'

'Let me get you another,' he said.

'Don't mind if I do. Bert's late tonight.' Old Betty McFie was with her so he had to get her another too.

'You shouldn't be wasting your money on us,' Gran told him when the port and lemons were safely in front of them. 'Our Emily's at home.' He didn't quite know what to say to that. 'Mind you, I don't want you bringing her in here.'

'No, Gran,' he smiled, relieved to see Billy Wade making his way across the snug, wearing an open-necked white shirt with its collar turned down over his blazer collar. His lapels were stained with beer drips, his straight brown hair was badly in need of a cut.

'Have you got us one in?' Billy asked.

'You'll not be going round for Emily tonight, then?' Gran asked at the same moment. Alex answered neither, just took Billy's arm and marched him back to the tap room. They got in a couple of pints each. Billy spent a lot of time shouting to someone yards away about Tranmere Rovers' game tomorrow.

He tried to find comfort in the beer as he thought about Emily. He'd tried to explain things to her. He'd told her he loved her and wanted to take care of her for the rest of her life. She couldn't understand that he dared not do something that carried such a risk for her. It could blow up in their faces. He'd seen it happen plenty of times.

A couple of years ago he'd thought, just once to get it out of my system, but it had made his need greater. It was agony keeping her at arm's length. Emily didn't understand that, she was too young.

But she was old enough to put in the knife. She was showing him very clearly that she wasn't prepared to wait any longer. That she'd found someone she liked better. Giles Wythenshaw was turning her head, as he turned the heads of most of the girls working at Wythenshaw's.

'What about the girls then?' he reminded Billy when he brought more beer over.

'Here they come now.' Billy directed his gaze to the door. Alex felt his heart sink with disappointment. He found he was landed with the less attractive of the two. A big girl with plummy lipstick smelling of Californian Poppy. She said her name was Joan. He bought two gin and oranges to start the ball rolling.

It took a long time before Billy deemed the moment ripe. Alex felt bloated with beer, it was beginning to turn acid in his stomach. They started to walk. The night was cold. The breeze off the river cut sharp as a knife through his coat and new pullover.

'Along the Esplanade,' Billy had said. 'Never anybody much along there on a cold night.' The wind was getting up, the tide was out, but he could hear the waves hurling themselves across the mud towards them.

He tried a kiss. That helped, she was a real live girl, though she didn't make his heart race as Emily did. Billy and the other girl were lost in the dark. He was alone with Joan. She told him all about her job as a waitress at the Royal Rock. They sauntered the mile to the gap, without him making much progress. He led the way down on to the sand. Found a place against a wall, away from the path and not in the teeth of the wind.

Although he was freezing, he took off his coat and spread it on the dry sand. He decided it was time to get going in earnest, it was getting late, and he'd never get up for work tomorrow.

He gathered her up in his arms, she held him tight when he kissed her. He was beginning to enjoy himself after all. He felt up her jumper, he knew she shivered at his cold hand but did not protest. He went a little further, tried up her skirt. Suddenly she jerked into sitting position and slapped his hand.

'Here,' she said. 'That's enough. Who said you could go up there?'

He couldn't blame her, but it was a long walk back, and he was very cold, even though he had got his coat on again. Billy Wade's powers of persuasion must be greater than his. The evening was a great disappointment.

Alex was not ready to get out of bed the next morning; it took him longer than usual to get dressed. As he pulled out his chair at the living-room table, the mantelpiece clock chimed once for seven-thirty.

'You're cutting it fine,' his father grumbled. 'I don't know why you can't get up when you're first called.'

'Sorry, Dad, I was late going to bed.' His father was breathing heavily, looking greyer than ever. More irritable than usual, Alex felt an edge of worry about him.

'Whose fault is that? You stayed out half the night.'

Alex frowned; that was one reason, the other was he'd been unable to sleep when he got to bed because Emily had been on his mind. Suddenly he couldn't put a foot right where she was concerned. They were at loggerheads about nothing every time they met.

His mother came bustling in from the back kitchen with two plates. One, with a narrow rasher of bacon and a spoonful of scrambled egg, went down in front of his father. The other, which she slid in front of him, was overflowing with eggs, bacon, sausage and fried bread.

'I can manage well enough, Ted,' she said gently.

Alex looked round the room; nobody would dispute that, the fire was already burning up, the room tidy. His mother believed in keeping a comfortable home.

'Nonsense him going out to work, Olympia, and you paying Myra George.' Alex knew his father was prickly about him working for Wythenshaw's. He'd been over this ground often.

'I earn nearly three times as much as Myra now, Dad,' he said quietly, 'and I'm hoping for more soon.'

'This is a good business, Alex. One day it could be yours. Surely you want to be your own master? Working for Wythenshaw's, you never know the moment you'll be laid off.'

'When can you remember them laying anyone off?'

'Look at Lairds, two hundred laid off last week. Look at the dockers,' Ted spluttered. 'It's the depression.'

'Dad! The depression is making half the shops in Birkenhead bankrupt. Paradise Parade lives on the back of Wythenshaw's workers. If they're earning, so are you. Wythenshaw's never have laid off, but if they do, your shop will feel the pinch.'

'Yes, well, your mother would be glad of more help. The lifting's heavy for a woman.'

'Dad, just look at her. Does Mother need help with the lifting?'

Olympia smiled, there was a Madonna-like tranquillity on her large face. Large hands were forking bacon into a wide mouth. Everything about Olympia was oversized.

Alex could look down on her now but that had only come about recently. She was five foot nine in her size-eight lisle-stockinged feet. She wasn't fat, but she had an ample curving bosom with a breadth across her shoulders Alex would have described as powerful in a man. He had seen her heave sacks of sugar and flour from the cellar store up to the shop. Only now was he developing the ease she had. Each sack weighed fifty-six pounds.

'Leave him be, Ted,' she said softly. Despite her size there was a gentleness about Olympia. A softness in her velvet brown eyes. She was a handsome woman. 'Alex is doing well, picked out for special training. You did agree he should go to Wythenshaw's.'

Ted snorted, clattering his cutlery down on his plate. 'I wouldn't trust a Wythenshaw as far as I could throw him.'

'Why not, Dad? What have they done to you?'

'I know Jeremy Wythenshaw well. Always wanting men for fatigues he was. Used to come round the barracks picking us out, never left me off. Think nothing of marching us five miles, working us all the hours of darkness shoring up the sides of trenches, making the tops firm with sandbags, then marching us back five miles for breakfast. And this while we were supposed to be having a few days' rest.'

'That was the war, Dad. Life was hard in the trenches.'

'You don't have to tell me.' Ted's gaunt blue chin bristled. 'I'm not the man I was. The trenches did for me.'

'Yes, Dad,' Alex murmured. His mother's calm brown eyes were signalling him to give over, Alex understood the problem only too well. Lifting was not women's work. It added to Dad's agony to see her toss heavy sacks about, when he could barely budge them. It underlined his infirmity.

He wondered what they had in common. His mother ran the shop and the home, and organised both of them. Family decisions were usually hers, and his father was growing more dependent on her. Yet she seemed happy, her smile ready, always making time for those she loved. She seemed content. It was Dad he pitied. Of course, he hadn't always been like this.

A bell rang urgently. Alex leapt to his feet and ran to open the shop door, as he expected the baker's van was at the kerb, its back doors open. The van lad was already coming towards him with a great wooden tray of loaves on his shoulder.

'Two dozen large cobs, two dozen large tins, six bloomers, six Hovis.' Alex counted in the daily order, arranging a selection on the counter, putting the rest on shelves beneath. The small wholemeal loaves were still steaming hot and filling the shop with their fragrance. The jam tarts looked crisp and delicious.

It was at moments like this Alex almost wished he had elected to work here. His mother was one reason he had not. This was her life, she did it well and enjoyed it. Whatever Dad thought, she could cope with the shop single-handed. She was only thirty-five to his forty-seven, it would be years before she'd want to leave it. Where would Mum be without her gossiping customers? They put the neighbourhood at her fingertips. Besides, she was ambitious for him, urging him along the path he'd chosen.

'Three dozen plain buns, three dozen currant and three dozen iced.' The van lad collected yesterday's trays, and Alex was scribbling his signature on the delivery note when the first customers of the day came in.

The factories started at eight. Some workers wanted buns and biscuits for their tea break. Alex usually stood in for an hour, while his mother saw to the household chores. Business was sporadic, and Myra George couldn't come in before taking her five-year-old son to school.

In the slack moments, he couldn't keep his mind away from Emily. It was being said openly in the office that against all the odds, Emily Barr had taken Giles Wythenshaw's fancy. He'd heard the rumour several times before but hadn't really believed it. He thought he knew better. Hadn't Emily denied it? Hadn't she confided in him about being afraid of losing her job?

But that was weeks ago, and yesterday, he had to believe the evidence of his own eyes. Giles Wythenshaw holding on to her arm, guiding her round the factory. Picking out one of the brooches and giving it to her. Emily's look of pride as she pinned it on her cardigan.

Then Giles had come with her to the canteen for dinner, and it had taken her fifteen minutes even to notice he was sitting further up the same table. He still couldn't believe she would take Giles seriously, she must see what sort of a man he was.

To Giles the five days before his father left for Paris seemed long. He always looked forward to his absences, because he could do what he wanted without fear of inciting sudden wrath. The house seemed quieter, the staff more relaxed, everything slowed down.

Ever since he'd been a schoolboy, he'd used his father's key box as proof of his whereabouts. Father didn't mean to keep his movements secret, but he didn't always communicate every detail.

In his library, a still life of a nineteenth-century military helmet and sword dominated one wall. Behind it, where most people would have installed a safe, his father had had an office key box let into the wall.

The massive house keys of Churton, the keys to the factory, the shop in Liverpool and the house in Paris, all had their places in the box. All were carefully labelled as Set One or duplicates, all visible but locked behind glass. His father liked to think he was an organised person.

When he went to the shop, he took a set of keys with him, and returned them to the case when he came home. The same for the Paris house; so early on, Giles learned to match up his father's whereabouts to the missing keys.

This time he was so looking forward to his father's absence, that he asked him twice when he intended to leave. It didn't stop him checking on the key case, when he was late coming home one night; he didn't want to find Father had gone a day earlier and he'd wasted time.

On the morning of his father's departure, Giles got up early to eat breakfast with him, and saw him off to the station in his Rolls. Then he drove into work, and went straight to Father's office.

His secretaries' room had panelled walls, smarter desks and filing cabinets, and newer typewriters than the rest of the office, though his father's carpet did not stretch out here.

Sylveen was trying to open a large business envelope with one of the letter openers they were making to give away as Christmas favours. Her smile for him was dazzling. She continued to tear at the envelope without much effect. He took it from her and opened it with one good tug.

'Can't manage, silly me,' she said in her breathy voice. It made Giles feel competent, but he saw what he had planned was not to be. He had gone to great lengths to time this approach in order to have everything as he wanted it, and now that ogre Miss Lewis was not here. He'd come to invite Sylveen out, but he meant the invitation to be as public as possible.

'Father got away all right this morning,' he said awkwardly, deciding to postpone it.

'I don't know what I'm going to do over the next few days without him.'

'What?' He was surprised. 'How long has he been taking you out?'

She laughed. 'Work, I won't have much to do. Though he has left me a report to type and some other odds and ends.'

'Oh!' He felt he'd been wrong footed.

'Better not say too much about your father and me. He wouldn't want it to get round.' Sylveen gave him a conspiratorial smile.

'No, of course not.' How was he to ask, after that? He was making a mess of it. 'Where is the ogre?' He nodded towards her desk.

'Miss Lewis has taken a few days off to go the wedding. Aileen Lovat, you remember Aileen?'

'Yes.'

'She's getting married, and it's a good time for her to take leave when your father is away.'

Giles decided he'd better do what he'd come for. No point in wasting days waiting for Miss Lewis to return.

'I was wondering how you'd feel about coming out with me.' The letter opener went down on the mail, her eyes searched into his. She hadn't expected this.

'I hardly know what to say . . .'

'You're a family friend now.'

She laughed again. 'I'm not sure your father would approve.'

'I'm damned sure he wouldn't.'

'Where were you thinking of taking me?'

His stomach turned over. She was agreeable after all.

'The same place. Home.' Her blue eyes widened as the silence lengthened.

'No,' she said at last. 'I don't think so.'

To Giles, it was a sharp setback. 'Why not? He takes you there.'

'I'm likely to end up as pig in the middle.' Sylveen shook her blonde waves. 'Likely to be in both your bad books if there's trouble. And I don't think your father would like it. Absolutely not.'

'What about what I'd like?' Giles saw his plan coming to naught. He felt as though his father had bested him yet again. Her lustrous eyes were studying him.

'Come to the Argyle with me on Friday, then,' he wheedled, wanting her company for its own sake. 'It'll be a bit of fun. We'll have supper afterwards.' He could see she was tempted. 'Somewhere Father isn't likely to take you. He hasn't got sole rights, has he?'

'No,' she smiled. 'All right, I'll come, but don't tell your dad.' Giles felt a gust of pleasure. She had not exactly thrown herself into his arms, but she was coming.

He booked the best seats at the music hall, and a table at the Royal Rock. Father never went there. He couldn't for the life of him understand what a beautiful girl like Sylveen could see in Father.

She gave him her address, and he went to her house and rang the doorbell. Sylveen let him in immediately; she was wearing the same blue frock she'd worn when he'd walked in on her in the library. It did wonderful things for her bosom. Her perfume was seductive.

She took him into a tiny but smart sitting-room and introduced him to her mother who was working on a piece of tapestry. She was Sylveen gone to seed, a plump and empty husk, with a lined face. He made small talk, feeling ill at ease. Sylveen was back in a few minutes wearing a coat and they were off.

Giles knew he was doing all he could to beguile her. Everything was organised for the evening; he'd even armed himself with a large box of chocolates.

The orchestra was warming up as they took their seats in the Argyle. It was a whining of discordant fiddles, but they soon set about a rousing overture. A hush of anticipation fell on the audience, and the velvet curtains swung open.

Sylveen leaned forward enchanted, as the bouncy opening choruses gave way to a troop of acrobats. Sand dancers followed a pearly king. A Marie Lloyd copy sang a lively tune. Giles studied Sylveen's pretty nose in the darkness, finding her more interesting than the artists on stage. It wasn't just that she was more beautiful than the girls up there nor that Father had staked prior claim.

She tugged at his senses so that he was unable to concentrate on the show. To see her laugh at a joke, or enjoy a tune was more important than enjoying it himself. The way she turned to share a laugh warmed him. The kaleidoscope of interest and amusement on her face, seen in the reflected light from the stage, was paramount.

The music hall lifted them both. As he drove to the Royal Rock afterwards, they tried to sing 'Roaming in the Gloaming' together, as Harry Lauder had. They collapsed laughing because they didn't know the words, though they were generating twice the verve and bounce he had.

Giles knew the Royal Rock well, he asked for and got a quiet table. He felt high on excitement before he even had a drink. He couldn't take his eyes from Sylveen.

'Why did you go out with my father?'

'He asked me.'

'A good-looking girl like you must get plenty of invitations. You don't have to go out with old men.'

'I like him, he's nice, Giles. A real gentleman.'

'He's too old for you.'

'No, he knows how to look after a girl, make her feel pampered.'

Giles couldn't resist: 'I bet he's older than your father.'

'He is,' she laughed, 'but he doesn't seem it. He can enjoy life. My father is all duty and earnest endeavour.'

Giles felt the old familiar churning inside. Father had everything and did everything. He'd meant only to use Sylveen to get at him. Suddenly he knew she was a prize he didn't want to slip through his fingers. He wanted Sylveen for herself.

He ordered a bottle of champagne. He meant to sweep her off her feet. What Father could do, he could do better. The salmon was excellent, the service couldn't be faulted, but the meal was coming to an end. He was nervous now about getting her to take the next step he'd planned.

'I feel lapped in luxury.' Sylveen leaned back on her chair. 'You have a wonderful life.'

'No,' he said. 'It's all work.'

She laughed. 'You don't have to run for the half-eight bus every morning, then work till half-five. And it's all thrift and economy when I get out of work. Do you know what my father keeps preaching?' Giles shook his head.

'That old chestnut about Mr Micawber. Income nineteen and six a week, expenditure nineteen shillings, result happiness. I'm sick of hearing about it. He thinks I'm extravagant. Would you believe it? Extravagant.'

'What does he do for a living?'

'He's a teacher, wouldn't you know? This really is living.' Her eyes went round the dining-room. 'I'm overdue for a bit of fun.'

'Is that what my father gives you?'

'He gets me out of my rut.' He couldn't miss the defensive note in her voice.

'Is that all?'

'I told you, I like him.'

'Go on.' He knew he was pressing too hard. She wouldn't like a man screwed up about his own father.

'I really do. He's interesting to talk to, a big softy.'

'A sugar daddy?' He couldn't stop himself, he felt tense as a drum.

'He's that too, but he's been everywhere and done everything.'

'I bet he has.'

'Are you jealous or something?'

'Yes.' She had a gutsy laugh, he remembered how it had intrigued him the night he was creeping upstairs. It had made him go into the library and meet her. He shared the last of the champagne between their glasses. Tipped the empty bottle upside down in the bucket of ice. Sylveen and champagne were having a heady effect. He knew he'd be devastated if she refused. He screwed up his courage.

'Come home with me,' he pleaded.

'Giles, I can't. What if one of your maids should see me there with you? I couldn't go again with him, could I?'

'And you'd want to?' There was perspiration on his forehead.

'I might, I know he'll ask me. I don't want to queer my pitch.'

'I've told the staff to take the night off. They'll all be in bed now.'

'What about tomorrow morning? You aren't likely to get up at three to drive me home.'

'Is that what Father does? Haha. Haha.'

'Well, you're not the type to do it.'

'No, I wouldn't find it fun. What would you say if I told you I'd booked a room in a hotel?'

'Which hotel?'

'The Victoria in Gayton. Miles away. Nobody there knows me or my father.'

It took her so long to answer, he thought she was going to refuse. 'I might feel a bit awkward, arriving at this time of night without luggage.' She drained off her glass.

'I've got an overnight case for you. Wash things and a bath robe, that sort of thing.'

'You haven't!'

'Yes, in the boot, and I told them we'd be late, because we're driving up from London. Asked for sandwiches and a bottle of champagne in the room.' She wouldn't look at him now. She was doodling a pattern on the tablecloth with the end of a coffee spoon. He could feel his heart racing.

She looked up and her luscious blue eyes laughed into his. 'I'm not sure about the sandwiches, I've eaten enough.'

'Will you come? I'm more fun than my father, I promise you.'

Again she laughed, opening her mouth so he could see her pearly teeth. 'We'll have to see about that,' she said and tears of mirth glistened in her eyes.

Giles got up from the table and kissed her nose, feeling overwhelmed by her lustiness. 'And I know as much about pampering women as my father. You must admit that.'

'You might even have the edge, you're both wonderfully attentive.'

'Do you want to phone your mother? Make some excuse about not going home?'

'Can't, we aren't on the phone. I told her I was making up a foursome, and I'd stay with Sophie Black if it got late. Sophie lives near Wythenshaw's but works at the Co-op clothing factory, so we cover for each other.'

He put her coat round her shoulders. 'I'll bring the car to the front steps for you.'

She hung on to his arm. 'Rather walk to the car park with you,' she said. He unlocked the car door for her.

'And my Riley is as good as his Alvis?'

'Any car is fine by me.'

'I'm a better driver, faster and safer. He doesn't get enough practice, riding round in the back of his Rolls.'

'I'm not much of a judge when it comes to driving,' Sylveen giggled. 'Because I can't.'

'Shall I teach you?'

'Oh, I'd love that.'

'Well, you'll have to admit first that you like me better,' Giles said.

'Of course I do, you're nearer my own age. All the girls at the office like you better.' She leaned across and kissed his cheek. He drove with her head against his shoulder and a feeling of exultation in his gut.

CHAPTER SEVEN

Giles woke up to find himself alone in the bed, though he could see the dent Sylveen's head had made in her pillow. He turned over, feeling drugged with sleep.

'I've been for a bath,' Sylveen was saying. 'Come on, we've got to get to work.'

'It's Saturday,' he groaned.

'Yes, only half a day, but I have to go.'

'Father's away. Come back in here.' He lifted the bedclothes, wanting to make love to her again.

'No, I don't want to lose my job. Miss Simpson will notice if I'm not there. I feel her eagle eye on me all the time. Anyway, somebody has to sort the post and take messages.'

'All right.' Giles reached for his robe and went down the corridor to the bathroom. Over breakfast he was surprised to find Sylveen fresh and eager after a very late night indeed.

'Headaches for breakfast?' she smiled. He did have a bit of a headache; they'd finished the second bottle of champagne before settling to sleep, but they'd had a wild time.

'Sylveen, why don't I reserve this room for a few more nights? Father won't be back for a week. We can go to work from here.'

'If I can get you up in time.'

'I am up. Tell me now, so I can ask the receptionist if the room is free. It's a good idea, isn't it? You can go home and get a few things.'

'A marvellous idea,' she agreed.

Giles grinned. 'You know, you give me a lift. We'll have a wonderful weekend.'

Last night had changed everything. For years he'd been searching for one particular girl. He thought he'd found her several times, but always he'd been disappointed. He saw now, very clearly, that Sylveen was the girl he'd be happy to spend the rest of his life with. He felt bowled over.

He couldn't tell her his first intention had been to get at his father through her. Now he felt caught in his own noose. He wanted to be with her, not sitting at home, bristling with jealousy at the thought of his father taking his place. It was an exquisitely painful irony, and he didn't know what to do about it.

'I love you,' he whispered. He'd already told her several times in the night, but Sylveen grasped his hand under the tablecloth, almost too overcome to speak. She spent the morning in a daze, unable to type properly.

At lunch time, Sylveen walked quickly from the bus stop in Woodchurch Road, along tree-lined roads of new semi-detached houses, with small neat squares of garden in front. All morning her mind had run riot with plans. What she was going to tell her mother. What she would pack. She was brimming with anticipation. She put her key in the lock and let herself in. The kitchen door was open, she could see her mother lifting a casserole from the oven.

'Is that you, dear? Dinner's ready.' Her mother was wearing a loose print overall over a blue wool dress. An executive-type overall with sleeves buttoned to her wrist. She liked something she could remove quickly if an unexpected visitor came to the door.

'Hello, Sylveen,' her father called from behind *The*

Times, as she passed the living-room door.

'Mum, Sophie wants me to stay with her for a few nights.'

'For the weekend?' Her mother's mouth pursed with disapproval.

'Yes, and perhaps till Tuesday. We'll see how we get on. Her mum and dad are going to Blackpool for a few days.'

'Now? In the middle of November?'

'To see her auntie who isn't well. We'll be going to work every day.'

'I'm not sure that's a good idea. You'd be better coming home, dear. Let's see what your father says.'

'Mother, I'm a big girl now.'

'Not too big to make mistakes,' she said sharply. To Sylveen her meaning was only too obvious.

'You don't let me forget, do you?' she shouted as she ran to the stairs. 'I'm going to pack.'

'It's better you don't forget. We can do without any more trouble like that.'

Sylveen slammed her bedroom door. For years she'd been fighting her feelings for Denis Lake. Mum knew exactly the anguish she was stirring when she threw him in her face. Now she was reminding Dad too.

Once she'd believed she'd never feel for anyone what she'd felt for Denis. He'd only had to look at her to make her heart pound. His touch had been electric. She hadn't known passion existed till she met him.

The end had come, painfully traumatic, when she found she was pregnant. Denis had decided his career was more important than she was, and as a fourth-year medical student he couldn't afford a wife. It had all been carefully covered up for the neighbours. She been sent away to a home for fallen women before it became too noticeable. Pretences were made, but the neighbours knew. Sylveen had seen it in their faces.

She was over Denis now, but it had taken a long time. It had put her off men. She had stayed at home with her mother for a year, and found little pleasure in it. She knew some of the girls at Wythenshaw's envied her her smart home, but she found it comfortless.

'What's the point of having a sitting-room if you don't light the fire there?' Sylveen had asked.

'It stays tidy. I've got a nice room to take visitors in.'

'But we never use it. We sit here in the back. You call it the dining-room but it's a living-room with room for only two easy chairs.' She had to sit at the dining-table or on a footstool if both her parents were home. The expensive tea sets weren't used either, nor the new three-piece suite. All were kept for show when the rare visitor came.

'Daddy sees to the mortgage and the rates, dear,' her mother said in self-satisfied tones. 'But I have to save for luxuries.' She meant, save from her housekeeping allowance. 'We have a lovely home.' Sylveen knew she had been saving for a bedroom carpet for years. Her mother thought only the decadent owned a car or a telephone.

Sylveen felt she'd lived through two rotten years. The second, totally boring, had helped to blot out the hurt of the first, but it was leading nowhere and she was no longer young.

She began to feel better as she settled into her job at Wythenshaw's. She enjoyed the company of the girls she worked with, but it wasn't enough. She began to feel life was passing her by, and if she didn't do something, her mother would inculcate her habits of thrift and economy into her, and she'd finish up an old spinster like Miss Lewis.

She accepted an invitation to go to the pictures with Jack Williams, a clerk in the office, because she felt hungry for male company, but he was a dull companion. He thought it a waste of money to eat in a restaurant, when his mother provided meals at home. His prospects at work were nil.

Sylveen's discontent deepened to desperation. She decided she must change her life, and began thinking hard about what she wanted. She had found out the hard way it was better to receive love than to give it. In future, she decided, she would choose a man with her head not her heart.

What she wanted was a partner who would take her out to dinners and dances. She wanted to live it up, and be pampered in luxury. She was sick of scrimping and thrift, and getting value for the little money she had. It was no fun being excluded from doing things because of the cost.

She had thought Jeremy Wythenshaw very attractive, she'd gone to great lengths to get on friendly terms with him, and she'd managed it. He was opening up an entirely new life to her, teaching her all she needed to know to feel at ease in expensive restaurants and luxury houses. She was loving it.

She'd been sorry when he went off to Paris, feeling left in limbo, until the moment Giles walked into her office. She had the same feelings as the other girls at Wythenshaw's; Giles had riveted her attention from the moment he'd started learning the business. She knew she'd have gone for him in the first place if she'd thought she stood half a chance, but every girl in the office was showing interest, and what her mother called 'her trouble', and the two years in the wilderness had robbed her of confidence. She had believed, like most of the girls in the office, that Giles was unattainable. It wasn't enough to worship from afar, as they did. She'd wanted a real relationship, and head and heart said Jeremy was the one to go for.

She recognised Giles's intention immediately. Unbelievable after such long discussions with other secretaries about how to attract Giles, but the seductive tawny eyes were playing with hers. The signs were all there, easy to recognise. He meant to entice her.

She took a close look at him from across her desk, then

couldn't tear her eyes away. She had always found pleasure in perfection, whether it was a painting or a flower. Here in the male form was perfection, glossy hair of light brown sculptured to his head in loose waves. His slightly prominent tawny eyes sparkled with intensity as he leaned towards her.

It had come as an exciting surprise to find him willing to go to such lengths to have her company. She felt her morale take a marvellous boost. It had shocked her that Giles had no thought for the difficulties their friendship might bring. Inviting her to Churton in his father's absence! He was like a child, so eager to get at the cherries, he had no thought for the consequences.

Sylveen saw the dangers only too clearly. She knew she'd be wise to refuse to have anything to do with him. Her friendship with Jeremy was going too well to jeopardise. But Giles could set her on fire, make the soles of her feet prickle with excitement. She was greedy for more. Giles was her own age, he too was ready to provide a surfeit of luxury. He had everything to recommend him. He was more exciting than Denis Lake had ever been, more exciting than Jeremy. His hot eyes could tear her apart.

Last night had been wonderful. With Giles, she would have the best of both worlds, she would have love and money. That thought kept springing into her mind. She could hardly believe it.

'Sylveen, your dinner's on the table,' her mother called. The living-room door shut with a bang. She went down slowly. Sat at the living-room table with a plate of casseroled steak, boiled potatoes and cabbage in front of her.

'Your mother would like you to stay home, Sylveen. We don't know your friends.' Her father's glasses were being steamed up by his helping of casserole.

'Much safer,' her mother said.

'I don't want to be kept safe for the next fifty years, Mother. I want a bit of fun. There's no harm in that.'

'Your dad would be glad of a hand in the garden this weekend.'

'I'm going to Sophie's,' Sylveen said, knowing her case was packed, and Giles would be waiting at the end of the road for her at two-thirty. The thought of staying in a hotel like the Victoria with Giles, was sybaritic luxury compared with this thrifty meal eaten from a checked cotton cloth. She wasn't going to relinquish a treat like that.

The night his father was expected back, Giles returned home, feeling deprived of Sylveen's company in his leisure hours. He'd had a miserable day in the office, seeing Sylveen's beautiful face laughing up at him from every rotten ledger. The one girl he really wanted, and he couldn't claim her openly. She belonged to Father, like all the other good things of this world. To use Sylveen to hurt him was no longer possible.

Fate had stopped him letting the world know from the beginning, before he felt this involvement. Now he worried that Father would cut him off without a penny, and they wouldn't be able to do any of the things they enjoyed. Now it was in his own interests that Father didn't know.

Sylveen, on the other hand, had been pathologically anxious to keep their affair a secret to start with, and had now changed her mind. She didn't seem to appreciate their predicament.

'I'd like to tell your father,' she said. 'I feel so guilty, letting him believe . . . I hope he won't be upset.'

'Sylveen, he'll be livid, and it's never easy explaining anything to him.'

'I shall just say that we're head over heels in love. We are, aren't we?'

'Of course.' He squeezed her hand.

'He'll understand.'

Giles shuddered, it was the last thing Father would

understand. 'No, you mustn't. Not ever.'

He was in the drawing-room having a glass of beer before dinner, when his father came to sit with him.

'Hello, Giles. Everything all right at the office?' He had brought his pre-dinner whisky with him. Giles knew his father preferred to drink alone in the library, and tonight had come specially to talk to him.

'Yes, Father, nothing much happening.' If there was, he and Sylveen had better things to talk about. Giles knew Higgins called in the office to collect a package of mail and messages from his secretary. It would have been in the Rolls when it met Father at the station. He already knew all there was to know.

'What have you been doing with yourself while I've been away?' His father looked tired, and was lying back in the chair, the light glistening on his thick silvery hair.

'Not a lot.' Certainly not a lot he could talk about. Suddenly his father was upright, his blue eyes boring into his.

'You must have done a lot somewhere, Mrs Eglin says you've not been home all the time I've been away.'

Giles felt himself turn cold. It was almost as though Father knew! 'I've taken Emily Barr out a few times,' he said hastily.

'Oh, where did you go?'

'The Argyll. Dinner at the Royal Rock, that sort of thing.' He could see his hand shaking as he felt for his beer. Did Father already know he'd been with Sylveen?

'I'm glad you've got yourself a steady girlfriend,' he said. Giles felt himself relax, perhaps he was worrying unnecessarily.

Emily felt she was getting to know Giles better. He was spending most of every day in the office now, though chatting to her rather than applying himself to work. She knew the two Marys thought him charming.

The day after having lunch with him in the canteen, he'd whispered, 'The dining-room for lunch today. It's on me. Don't let's get involved with the Marys, we have enough of them up here.' When the hooter blew, he'd leapt to his feet. 'Come on.'

When they reached the floor where Sylveen worked, he said, 'Why don't you put your head round the door and tell your friend – what was her name?'

'Sylveen.'

'Yes, that's her. Say we're on our way to the dining-room. You'll keep her a place, and today it's on me.'

'Nice of you to remember,' Emily said, knowing Sylveen would want to come. She enjoyed the lunch, Sylveen was on top form, sparkling with wit and good humour. It surprised her when Giles made no effort to repeat it.

The weeks were passing, and Emily continued to fret over Alex. They rarely cycled to or from work together now, she was beginning to think he was avoiding her. As for herself, she was beginning to think she was obsessional about him. At work, some sixth sense always told her when he was near. Her eyes were drawn to him as though by a magnet. She wished she could get him out of her mind.

Christmas came and went. She and Giles were alone in the design office when he said: 'By the way, my father wants me to ask you to lunch one Sunday. When can you come?'

Emily was dumbfounded. It was the last thing she was expecting. 'At your home?'

'Yes, at Churton.'

She couldn't think, her pencil continued to sketch. She felt she was walking on glass. Yes, she wanted to see where he lived, no question of that. She was thrilled. She'd been working on a design for a bar brooch, she threw down her pencil when she realised it was covered with extraneous lines. 'Do you want me to come?'

'Yes, why not?' She could think of a dozen reasons why not, but it wasn't easy to put them into words. The implications for a start. Giles was singling her out from the crowd. It must mean he liked her. It surely meant he wanted to deepen their relationship?

'Shall we say next Sunday, then?' His tawny eyes were searching into hers. Emily felt she was floundering. A guest at Churton House, the Wythenshaw mansion! She couldn't imagine what it would be like.

'Who else will be there?' She wondered if he intended asking other people from the office. Perhaps the two Marys?

'Probably only my grandfather. My mother's father.'

'Would it be better if I came when he did not?'

'He comes every Sunday unless my father is away. No need to worry about him.'

'I don't know, Giles. There's a thousand things I need to do about the house. Sunday is the only free day I have.' She had to clean her room and do her washing for a start. 'My gran's better, but she can't do much.'

'Come on,' he urged in his friendly fashion. 'I'll collect you in my car and bring you back.' She hadn't told him yet she lived in a fish and chip shop, but she'd have to. 'Shall we say a week on Sunday?'

Emily quailed, wondering what she could possibly wear.

'How can I get to know you better if you won't come?' Giles had a beseeching look in his eyes. Her heart bounced and quickened. 'I really would like you to.' Out of all the girls at Wythenshaw's he'd picked her. Impossible not to feel flattered.

'A week on Sunday, then. Thank you,' she agreed reluctantly.

Sylveen felt swept off her feet. In love again, and this time with the right man. 'I love you,' Giles had said. She would be supremely happy, had her conscience not niggled about Jeremy. She'd had a wonderful five nights at the Victoria.

Coming face to face with Jeremy again was like coming down to earth. He asked her if she'd missed him. It was difficult to pretend she had. Her feelings for him had altered: now he was second best, and she knew she must not let it show. Her time with Giles had robbed her of the joy she'd felt in Jeremy's company.

'Dinner tonight?'

It was Jeremy who decided which nights she would spend with him.

'He's an old man, Sylveen,' Giles smiled. 'Can't manage more than twice a week.'

'A little more than that,' she laughed, but the trouble was she felt sorry for Jeremy. They were both cheating him.

With Giles what she felt was all physical. She felt on top of the world, felt she had energy enough to jump over it. She laughed to herself, thinking it just as well, because she was alternately spending a night with Giles and a night with Jeremy, and none of them were early. Her life was suddenly full and brimming over. They both wanted to make love to her and somehow she was always more than eager.

At the same time she couldn't eat, couldn't sleep and couldn't concentrate. She felt torn between the two. Gentlemanly, old-fashioned Jeremy who was teaching her the ways of the rich and worldly. She still enjoyed his company, but it made her uneasy, because she wasn't treating him fairly.

And Giles said he loved her! To catch sight of him unexpectedly coming towards her in the corridor at Wythenshaw's was enough to start her heart thumping. He said he loved her, and she believed him.

One Wednesday at work, she'd gone to the cloakroom to comb her hair and freshen her make-up, and found Emily there fluttering with excitement.

'Giles has invited me to lunch at Churton.' Her eyes had

been wide with pleasure and astonishment.

Sylveen saw her own face in the mirror stiff with shock and envy, and couldn't speak. She and Giles had talked about Emily of course.

'Our insurance policy,' he'd laughed. 'I like my name linked with Emily's. Safer for you and me. Give the office something to gossip about and make Father think he's hearing the gospel truth.'

'Poor Emily,' she'd said. 'Don't you be leading her on.'

'Course not. Emily thinks of me as a step up in her career. Her ambition is to be the perfect secretary.'

'She's my friend, so be sure you let her down gently.'

'I won't even pick her up,' he'd laughed. 'I call her my staunch little helpmate.'

Sylveen felt stunned, knocked off course, even jealous. She could see no reason why he should invite Emily to Churton.

It kicked all the harder because she would have loved to be asked to meet the Wythenshaw family at lunch. She understood it was not an invitation Jeremy extended to his mistress. He might take her home, he often did, but only when he was sure they would be alone. How had she managed to get cast in the role of mistress, when Emily the innocent waif was cast as a friend? She wouldn't have believed it possible.

'Lucky old Emily,' she managed to say. 'Asked you to lunch at Churton?'

'But I've nothing to wear,' she wailed.

'You must have something.'

'No, I wear my best things to work. If I wear this skirt, he'll recognise it. I don't even have a blouse he hasn't seen.'

Sylveen frowned into the cloakroom mirror, wanting to tell Emily it wouldn't matter what she wore. 'Do you really want to go?' she asked. It was hard to tell whether Emily was really worried about clothes or just making excuses. The brown velvet eyes swung to hers. She could see suppressed excitement in her elfin smile.

'I hardly know myself. I shall be as nervous as a kitten sitting down to dinner with his father.'

'Dinner?'

'Lunch, I mean, Sunday lunch.'

It was on the tip of her tongue to say: 'Emily, don't go, you'll get hurt.'

The gentle brown eyes were showing trust. 'Giles is very nice, isn't he?'

She couldn't hurt Emily's feelings. Poor kid, she didn't have much of a life. It would be a real eye opener for her to see Churton. Instead she said: 'If you're really bothered about clothes, I've got some things you could have.'

'They wouldn't fit me.' But Sylveen saw hope on Emily's pixie face.

'I've got a kilt, black, white and red. I almost offered it to you before, when we talked about skirts, but I was afraid you'd be offended. It wraps round so it fits anyone. It would suit you, and I've got a blouse that's too tight for me.'

Emily stared at her gratefully. 'That's awfully good of you.'

'I've had them ages. Grown out of them. I'll bring them to work tomorrow for you to see.'

'Would you, Sylveen? That would be marvellous. You've never worn them to the office?'

'No, but I'm not sure they're all that wonderful. They are my cast offs.'

'He won't have seen me wear them to the office, anyway.' Emily looked cheered.

Sylveen shuddered, she felt raw with hurt that Giles could do this to her, and at the same time she was bristling with envy and disappointment. How had little Emily managed to succeed where she had failed?

Gran was feeling better and helping in the shop again.

Emily told her about her invitation to Churton as soon as they'd finished the evening stint. Charlie was still cashing up. Gran poked the living-room fire into a blaze and pulled her chair closer.

'You've got to go,' she said. 'Emily, this is your chance. If you don't take it, you'll regret it for the rest of your life. My goodness, a Wythenshaw! What's he like?'

'Everybody thinks he's wonderful.'

'There you are then, and one day he'll own the factory?'

'Yes, I suppose so, he's an only child.'

'Good looking?'

'Yes, very.'

'And he loves you!'

Emily smiled slowly. 'I'm not sure.'

'Of course he does! Why else would he ask you?'

'I don't know. He's very popular. Generous too, and believes in enjoying himself.'

'That's it, then, he's chosen you. You don't know how lucky you are!'

'Gran, I like him, but I'm not head over heels . . .' Gran's lined face came so close to hers, the black straw brim touched her forehead.

'I married for love, Emily. I was nineteen, and thought I'd be happy ever after. A greengrocer he was, and thought to be a catch because he worked for his father, and one day the business would be his.'

'Weren't you happy, Gran?'

'I was at the start, we didn't expect the earth then. You think working in a chip shop is hard, but you don't know the greengrocery trade.'

'Tarrant's do all right.'

'You should try it. In the middle of winter, the shop door stays open with half the stock outside on the pavement. Potatoes always covered with mud, and vegetables icy to the hands. At least a chip shop is warm.'

'You closed earlier at night.'

'Not always. We were open till nine on a Saturday in them days. We shared the house with his father, and the men took it in turn to go to market at five in the morning.'

'Hard,' Emily said, but she didn't really believe it. It could be exciting if it was done in partnership with someone she could trust like Alex. Hadn't they discussed the pros and cons of every small business before deciding on careers with Wythenshaw's? 'Perhaps when we're older,' he'd said, 'if the careers don't work out, and if we can accumulate a bit of capital.'

'It was hard having three children by the time I was twenty-one, and no other woman in the house. While they were babies I kept them wrapped up in a pram behind the shop, but as they grew older they wanted to crawl in the dirt. The storeroom floor was covered in soil and mud and cabbage leaves, and if I didn't keep my eye on them, they'd be off down the road. No wonder there's only Charlie left. I cleaned and cooked and brought up my children and still had to help in the shop. I hated the place, I can tell you.'

'Yes, Gran, but if you loved . . .'

'Love doesn't last. Work and poverty kill it off. If this young man Wythenshaw wants to marry you, Emily, you'd better jump at the chance. At least you'll never want.'

Emily sighed. Gran was right when she said love didn't last. Once Alex had said he loved her, that hadn't lasted. She was a fool to hanker after him still. Better by far if she thought more of Giles now.

The next morning when Emily got to work, Sylveen handed her a brown paper carrier bag. She peeped inside: 'They seem almost new, thanks very much. I've got five minutes, I'll try them on now.'

The blouse was white and frilly but rather large. The

kilt suited her, though she felt it was flapping just above her ankles.

'It's mid-calf,' Sylveen protested. 'The fashionable length this year. I can't wear it because it's too short on me. Your office shoes have little heels. It will look better with them.'

Emily had to agree, it looked better than she'd hoped, though she didn't feel entirely at ease. She'd never owned anything remotely like the kilt, and it was certainly on the long side.

'Will you keep them for me? In your office? Don't want Giles peeping inside the bag, do I?'

Once at home, Gran offered to take the blouse in a bit on the side seams; that helped. 'Can't shorten the kilt,' she said. 'The pleats wouldn't hang right if I tried. You look very nice, Emily. Take a cardigan, that blouse won't be warm enough.'

Emily had a black cardigan that toned with the kilt, but the frilly blouse looked better without it. Dread was building up as the days passed. She'd have to wear her gaberdine on top if it rained and the kilt showed three inches below it.

She spent all the morning of the visit getting ready. She washed her hair, anchored her fringe down with clips while it dried and made it an orderly glossy brown cap, crackling with electricity. Her dark eyes skidded nervously from the mirror to the window. She'd had to explain to Giles where she lived.

'Yes, I know Paradise Parade.'

'The fish and chip shop.' She was watching his face, it showed neither surprise nor censure.

'Right, it's the fish and chip shop. I'll pick you up at twelve.'

It was now quarter past and she was standing at her bedroom window still waiting for him to come. She dared not go downstairs because the smell of stale chips would engulf her. She told herself she must expect him to be late, he was a rotten time keeper at work.

She was looking down on the glass verandah that fronted the shops. Rain had washed smoke and grime into long trails that clouded the glass. There were two broken panes above Wade's, through which she could see the yellow rubbish bin provided by their ice-cream supplier. She couldn't help but notice the chip papers blowing in the squally wind. He would notice the squalor more than she did. He was not used to seeing it every day. Suddenly his car was nosing to the kerb below. She went helter-skelter downstairs.

'Bye, Gran,' she shouted, as she shot past her in the living-room, and out through the yard and round the front of the Parade. It was easier than asking Gran to rebolt the shop door behind her.

Giles had got out and was staring at the shop. A large Closed notice showed in the door. Sweetpapers were thick in the gutter, it was beginning to drizzle. Two lads in torn pullovers had their noses pressed against Wade's window.

'There you are,' Giles said cheerfully, going to open the door for her. 'Sorry I'm a bit late.' She felt stiff with tension as she got in. She couldn't remember having ridden in a car before. Not ever. It ought to be a treat.

Giles pulled away with careful concentration, the windscreen wipers swished soothingly. Emily felt cold, she must make an effort.

'You found your way all right?'

'No problem.'

'Is it far to Churton?'

'Near West Kirby.' Once, in a summer long ago, Emily had gone to West Kirby on the bus with Alex. She couldn't remember how far it was.

'Don't worry. You'll be all right.' Giles turned to smile at her. It helped that he knew she was feeling on edge.

'My Aunt Harriet was just arriving as I left. She gives everybody a hard time, so you mustn't mind.'

'Oh dear!'

'She can be a bit sour. Father's sister, older than him, a spinster. Her fiancé was killed in the Boer War and she never got over it. She doesn't approve of any of us, I don't know why she continues to come.'

'Will your grandfather be there too?'

'Already is. He'll give you no trouble, probably go to sleep once he's eaten.' They had left the streets behind and were travelling along a lane with open fields each side. Emily sat up and began to take notice. She told herself it was a real treat to come out like this.

Nothing had prepared her for the house. Giles drove up a winding drive that broadened into a courtyard with tubs of flowers. The house was built of old pink bricks, with the centre set back between two wings. There were wide steps leading up to a massive porch. Emily thought it looked very grand. The sort of house you paid to be shown round.

In a sudden stab of nerves she felt her self-possession rip to shreds. She wouldn't know what spoons and forks to use, whether to shake hands or not. Her palms felt sticky. The thrill of excitement she'd felt when he'd invited her was gone, this was far worse than going to the office on her first day. Emily had the feeling of being on the edge of an abyss.

CHAPTER EIGHT

Alex was sitting at his father's workbench against the attic window, cutting tiny strips of yew veneer, making sure the size was exactly right and the grain went in a uniform direction. He stopped and stretched, sniffing the rich atmosphere of woodshavings, and marvelling at the infinite care his father was taking to glue the tiny marquetry pieces in place on the old table.

Ted had captured his interest in restoring old furniture years ago when he'd found an old sea chest in a junk shop. A roughly made piece with two drawers at the bottom, and a top that lifted so that trousers and coats could be laid flat. It had had the name John painted in faded letters on the black wood.

Alex had watched and learned as Ted had replaced the splintered top, made a new knob for one of the drawers, and another carrying handle that matched. He had shown Alex how to rub it down and apply black paint and then he'd finished it off with his own name in fancy letters. Knowing it was more than a hundred years old and had been taken to sea by a sailor named John, had captured his imagination. It had been a favourite piece in his bedroom since he was ten.

Since then he'd shared his father's hobby; often they spent a couple of hours on Sunday mornings up in their attic. The table was an elegant mahogany side table with slender Regency legs. The top had once had a dramatic marquetry design inlaid in yew, lime and apple woods. It had been damaged by water, years before they found it, so that the marquetry pieces had lifted. Some were distorted and curving away from the surface, and some were lost. It had been a labour of love that had taken several years of Sunday mornings. The problem had been to find the right wood and fit the bits together like a jigsaw puzzle.

He could hear the rasp of his father's breathing, and knew he couldn't even get up to the attic without resting between the flights of stairs now. He had had to take over all the sawing and much of the polishing, though Dad had served his time as a french polisher in his youth, and was rarely satisfied with his workmanship.

'Tea's ready,' his mother called upstairs.

Alex ran down. In the living-room, the fire was roaring up the chimney, the flames dancing a reflection on the polished wood of the sideboard. The chairs, everything, had been restored and made as perfect as possible by his father over the years. He knew that along the Parade it was thought the Frasers had the smartest and most comfortable home.

His mother was making apple pie in the kitchen. He got out three cups and saucers and poured tea. He felt they were a close family. For as long as he could remember, both his parents had guided and supported him. Now suddenly, he felt his position had changed. He and his mother were supporting Ted.

Back near the attic window, Alex drank his tea and used the little marquetry saw to cut more pieces. He would be sorry to see the table finished, working on it did not tax Dad's strength.

They had been working on a chest of drawers as well. His mother had helped him get it up here to their attic one day while Ted was out. They had repaired and polished the drawers, but were still working on the chipped mahogany veneer on the top.

Suddenly Alex noticed a car drawing to the kerb outside. He felt himself gritting his teeth as he recognised it as Giles Wythenshaw's, clenching his fists as he saw him get out and move under the glass verandah out of sight. He gasped; Giles Wythenshaw was calling at the chip shop next door but one!

'What's the matter?' his father asked, still concentrating on marquetry. He couldn't answer. Emily was running up the Parade wearing fancy shoes and a new plaid skirt that showed below her gaberdine. He couldn't believe it. He'd seen Emily yesterday evening and she hadn't mentioned this! Neither had her gran.

'Pass me that cloth,' Ted said. Alex got up from the window and put it in his father's hand. Back at the window he saw Giles holding open the passenger door, Emily sliding into the front seat as though she'd been doing it all her life. Alex was suffused with jealousy.

He'd eaten his supper there preferring to spend time with Emily rather than go round to the Bird again with Billy Wade. There had been the usual war reminiscences from Charlie and gossip from Gran. Emily had been distant, not saying much, making him realise how deep the gap between them had grown. Now he could see how far her affair with Giles Wythenshaw had gone. He was taking her out on a Sunday! Taking her to lunch somewhere.

Alex felt he'd been kicked in the gut. He had the sickening feeling that Emily really was lost to him, that Giles meant business.

'How's it look?' His father stood up.

Alex swallowed. 'Perfect.' The car was pulling away.

'Just these few pieces here to match. Don't even know what sort of wood this is. We'll have to be satisfied with matching the colour.' Ted was searching through their bits of wood. 'Do you want to cut a slice from this?'

Alex felt past doing any more. He couldn't even stand still. 'How about going for a drink?' This was another Sunday routine.

'Is it that time already?'

As he went downstairs the scent of roasting beef met him in the lobby. 'How long will it be, Mum? We're going to the Bird for a glass of beer.'

She came to the doorway tucking a stray tendril of auburn hair back in place. 'Half an hour, three quarters at most.' The living-room table was already set with a clean cloth.

Alex's mind was in turmoil, he couldn't think of anything but Emily's defection. He drank beer he didn't want, heard a discussion about football he wasn't interested in. Even ate the roast beef and Yorkshire pudding without tasting it. His parents usually dozed in front of the fire and read the Sunday paper in the afternoon. He couldn't sit still.

Giles Wythenshaw could have any girl he wanted. They were all swooning over him up at the factory. Why did he have to fasten on Emily? He loathed the man, was itching to crack his fist into Giles's handsome face. He even hated Emily for rejecting him.

'You're very restless, Alex.' His mother looked at him over her newspaper.

'Yes, I think I'll go for a walk.'

'In the rain?' He hadn't noticed the rain till now.

'It isn't much.' He went to get his mac.

'Sooner you than me.' Olympia returned to her paper. His dad was already snoring softly, spread-eagled in his chair.

The wind was raw off the river and gusted rain against him. The ships were dark smudges half-hidden in mist and rain. Alex turned up the collar of his mac and pushed his hands deep into its pockets as he strode along. The bad weather matched his mood.

He went past the boatyard and on towards the pier. He seemed to be the only person out and about. The rain grew heavier till it was drumming down, icy against his face. He stepped into the doorway of the ferry office to shelter for a moment, and was engulfed by its smell of disinfectant and cigarettes.

'Hello, Bert,' he said to the clerk selling tickets. Bert had worked here for years and was a good customer at the shop. 'Not much business today?'

There was one other person hovering in the corner with her back to him. Taking an interest in a faded poster. Pretending an interest, he thought. She looked familiar.

'Cathy?' he said. She turned guiltily, as though he'd found her doing something she shouldn't.

'Hello, Alex.' Her grey eyes wouldn't meet his.

'Hardly recognised you, Cathy, you look so smart.' She wore a tiny hat with veiling perched on her bushy curls, and carried a dripping umbrella. Along the Parade, it was thought that Cathy Tarrant was going up in the world. As a dental receptionist she was doing well for herself.

'What's the matter?' He couldn't help but notice the flush running up her cheeks. She was pretending an interest now in the ferry boat sliding into its berth at the end of the pier, though bad weather clouded the view.

'I've been stood up,' she whispered so the ticket vendor couldn't hear. 'Why else would I be hanging around here in this rain?'

Alex smiled ruefully. 'If it's any consolation, so have I.'

'I feel so . . . He seemed nice when he came to the surgery to have a tooth filled.'

He heard the clatter as the gangway rattled down on the ferry. Alex was starting to tell her about Emily. He had to tell somebody before it burned him up.

'Do you want to catch this boat?' Bert asked, sticking his head through the ticket window.

Alex paused, taking a breath. 'If you've nothing better

to do, Cathy, how about a sail to New Brighton and a cup of tea somewhere with me?'

'Yes,' she said, and smiled. With the tickets in his hand, he took her arm. They had to run the length of the pier in the driving rain. The gangway was raised again as soon as they'd crossed it.

They huddled on the lower deck in the lee of the wind, and watched the rain dimple the swirling brown water. There seemed to be only two other passengers as they crossed to Liverpool, and they were in the saloon.

'I thought you had a steady boyfriend. What happened to Joe Enders?' Alex asked.

'Haven't you heard? He's very ill with TB.' He felt a stab of guilt, he'd forgotten. Moisture was clinging in tiny droplets on Cathy's curls, she wouldn't look at him. 'My dad's forbidden me to go anywhere near him, he's terrified I'll catch it too.'

Alex felt himself sobering up, realising there were problems worse than his own.

'Yes, I had heard. How's he doing?'

'I think he's dying,' she whispered. 'My dad's even afraid I'll catch it from his letters. He doesn't like me having them.'

'Is that possible?'

'I suppose so, I don't know.' He could see her blinking back the tears, and felt for her hand. Forgetting Emily for the first time since he'd seen her get into Giles's car.

'About that cup of tea,' he said, as another thought struck him. 'I haven't enough money. Thought I was going for a walk by myself.'

Cathy gave him a watery smile. 'I'll pay, be glad to stand you a cup of tea.'

'Then I'll have to take you out again,' he said, feeling better. 'Perhaps the pictures or something.'

He had to put Emily out of his mind. Forget her. She didn't want him and that was all there was to it. He stole a glance at Cathy, knowing she had recognised they each needed the other. He'd known her since she was a child playing hookey from Sunday school. She was a decent girl, some would say prettier than Emily. He had to be satisfied with what he could get.

Emily could hardly breathe; Giles's home was far grander than she'd imagined. There were two big cars parked to one side of the massive porch; Giles drew up alongside them. She was out of the car before he could get round to open her door, it felt all wrong to have him waiting on her. She was paid to make his tea and run round after him, she didn't feel comfortable the other way round.

'It looks very old,' she said, shivering. She'd never feel at ease here as she did in Alex's home.

'About two hundred years.'

Emily was shocked. 'Have your family lived here all that time?'

'No, we aren't old landowners, far from it. Father bought it about twelve years ago. We used to live in Rock Park.'

'Did you?' Emily felt that went some way to close the gap between them. She knew Rock Park. 'Lovely big houses there too.'

'Not like this, and Rock Ferry isn't what it was.'

'I'd have thought you'd need to be a lord to live here. It's a mansion.'

He laughed. 'Father's business has thrived since the war.'

'Didn't it always?'

'It's doing better than it ever has before.' The huge front door opened on the latch. The height of the hall was dwarfing. A grand flight of oak stairs swept up to a gallery. Giles flung her coat over the immense newel post.

'This way,' he said. 'They'll be in the drawing-room.' He opened a door and ushered her inside. It seemed vast, with several tall windows. The living-room behind the shop would go into this room about eight times. Crossing the thick grey carpet was like walking in loose sand, it was pulling at her feet.

The fireplace was large enough to roast an ox. Several tree trunks were crackling in it. Emily looked at Jeremy Wythenshaw, owner of Wythenshaw's. This was the moment she'd been dreading, but he looked less formidable by his own fireside. He was actually getting to his feet to welcome her, hand outstretched.

'This is Emily,' Giles said as she went forward blindly, putting out her hand.

'Very pleased you could come,' he said. He seemed kinder than Charlie would be if she took somebody home.

'Let me introduce you to my sister Harriet.' Emily was almost overcome by what she saw as a resemblance to Queen Mary. Sitting bolt upright in an easy chair, she was wearing a hat on top of upswept hair.

'How do you do, Miss Wythenshaw.' Emily nearly choked as she saw Aunt Harriet lift a pair of glasses on a stick to scrutinise her kilt.

'And Arthur Calthorpe, Giles's grandfather.' Emily watched the old man struggling to stand. She wanted to tell him not to bother, but was afraid it might be wrong. He wobbled but finally managed to get upright.

'Hello, Emily,' he said. 'Come and sit next to me. Take pity on an old man.' As he collapsed backwards like a stone, she perched on the edge of the magnificent sofa, knowing he had taken pity on her.

'A sherry, Emily?' Jeremy Wythenshaw was asking. 'We have dry or medium.' Emily swallowed, there was a nervous constriction in her throat. She'd never tasted sherry of any sort, but she couldn't say that. She shook her head. 'Medium, then,' and he pushed a hand-cut crystal glass in her hand.

She sipped at it cautiously, it tasted medicinal, rather like the cough mixture Gran bought at the chemist's in Bedford Road. She hoped she'd manage to finish it. She had never felt less hungry in her life, but there was no smell of dinner yet. Perhaps it wouldn't be served for some time.

'I really don't see why not, Jeremy.' Aunt Harriet took an angry gulp at her sherry. 'A holiday would do me good.'

'Indeed it would, Harriet. You seem a bit liverish some days.'

'I would like to see the old house again. We had wonderful holidays there as children. Surely you can understand that? Didn't we enjoy walking in the Tuileries?'

Emily took surreptitious glances round the room, feeling intimidated by its size and luxury. The ceiling was high and finely moulded with two impressive chandeliers. She had never felt so utterly out of place.

'Big cities are very tiring places for people our age, Harriet. All that walking.'

'I could see a good deal from a seat on one of the *bateaux*. In comfort, and very pleasant too.'

'Not at this time of the year.'

'I was thinking of the spring. Paris in the spring. I haven't seen it since the war.'

'A cruise would suit you better. Paris is particularly noisy, and not safe for a lady alone.'

'I wasn't thinking of going alone. Alice Routledge has agreed to come with me. Don't you think he's being selfish, Arthur?'

'Harriet, I don't think I should be drawn into this,' he said mildly.

'The house belonged to Mother after all. Why shouldn't I use it?'

'Mother left it to me. She left you a place of your own.'

Harriet's lips pursed. 'You know I lost my house in the

war. The Germans blasted it to the ground.'

'I've made sure you've been fully compensated.'

'You had a house in France too, Aunt Harriet?' Giles said. 'I never knew that.'

'You're too young to remember.'

'My father is always talking about the war,' Emily put in, feeling she had to contribute something. 'Always reminiscing about what it was like.'

Arthur stirred at the other end of the sofa. 'Haven't heard you mention the war for years, Jeremy, though I know you served in France.'

'I don't like to think about it.' Jeremy shook his silver head. 'My grandfather was French, my mother half-French. Harriet and I spent a lot of time in France before the war. The country was torn apart.'

'Do you speak French, Mr Wythenshaw?' Emily was surprised.

'Yes, both Harriet and I were brought up to be bilingual.'

'And you too, Giles?'

'No.' His father answered for him. 'Elspeth, his mother was English, and I didn't want Giles . . .'

'Mother wouldn't want you to stop me using the Paris house.' Harriet returned to the attack. 'Not for a short visit. I'd be happy to go when you're not there. You hardly use it one week in six. I wouldn't interfere with anything.'

Emily was watching Giles through her lashes. He certainly looked as though he belonged here in his smart grey pullover and slacks. He caught her glance and smiled, coming to hover behind her seat. 'They go on a bit, don't they?' he whispered.

'You'd be more comfortable in a hotel,' his father retorted.

'I seem to remember the house being very comfortable. You go there regularly, it must be. You keep staff there.'

'No,' he said. 'I don't.'

'Of course you do. Really, Jeremy, you make me think you have something to hide. Do you keep a lady in residence? An inamorata?'

'Don't be ridiculous, Harriet! I'm thinking of selling Mother's house, if you must know.'

'Surely not?' She lifted her lorgnette to see him better.

'It needs too much doing to it. I don't want to be bothered doing the place up.'

'But what will you do? You go to Paris so often.'

'I shall stop going, retire. I'm getting on in life too, Harriet, though I'm not so far on as you.'

'You're not the sort to retire.'

'I recommend a cruise to you and Alice Routledge. Spring comes earlier in the Mediterranean.'

'A cruise is expensive.'

'You can afford it. I look after your affairs, I know your trust fund provides sufficient income for that.'

Aunt Harriet pursed her lips and lapsed into silence. With a jerk of alarm, Emily realised she had her lorgnette to her eyes again and was peering at her.

'What did you say her name was, Jeremy?'

'Emily,' she answered for herself. 'Emily Barr.'

A manservant in an immaculate dark suit came in to say lunch was ready. As they all trooped to the dining-room, Giles murmured: 'Don't worry, she doesn't bear you any ill will. She's both short sighted and a little deaf. Probably right about the woman. Father keeps the Paris house very much to himself.' Emily smiled, and thought it must be some sort of a family joke, she really couldn't believe that.

The dining-room, too, seemed vast and very formal, its dark wood panelling making it rather a sombre place. Through the big windows Emily saw the rain had stopped and a glimmer of sunlight showed through the clouds. She took her place at a table that could have seated a dozen in comfort. Jeremy sat at the head; there were two places set on each side.

Giles was shaking his starched damask napkin out of its creases and spreading it on his lap. Feeling awkward, Emily lifted the one on her side plate and did likewise. The servants were suddenly all round her. A severe-looking middle-aged woman in a plain black dress served soup from a tureen on the sideboard. Emily looked up and met her gaze, it seemed malicious and spiteful. She thought she must be mistaken and tried to smile, but the other's lips remained a thin straight line.

A younger maid wearing a cap and apron over her black dress slid a bowl of soup in front of her. Aunt Harriet was staring at her with haughty curiosity from the other side of the table.

'So you are Giles's young lady?' She had a particularly loud voice. Emily quailed, she didn't feel she could describe herself as that to his family. Things hadn't got that far.

'She is, Aunt Harriet,' Giles said easily. Emily warmed to him. He was certainly supporting her now, making her position very clear.

'And where did you meet him?' The lorgnette came closer. Emily felt she was falling short of Aunt Harriet's expectations.

'In the office, at work.' It made her more uncomfortable to hear her own voice. The accents of her hosts seemed more polished.

'Work? What work do you do?' Aunt Harriet's eyebrows had risen.

'Emily is my secretary,' Giles said calmly.

'Really? You typewrite?'

'And do shorthand.'

'Indeed, and Jeremy tells me you still live in Rock Ferry? Where exactly? We lived in Rock Park for years, so I know it well. Nathaniel Hawthorne was our neighbour. He lived at number twenty-six you know.'

'Yes, well I live more Tranmere way. Not far from the factory.'

'Oh my dear! And what does your father do?' Emily was afraid Aunt Harriet would like her even less if she told her. It was becoming an inquisition.

'He has his own business, Aunt Harriet,' Giles put in quickly.

'Mrs Eglin, tell Cook this soup is very good,' Jeremy told the severe housekeeper, who was bringing hot plates for the next course to the sideboard.

'Excellent,' Mr Calthorpe agreed. 'What sort is it?'

Emily was curling up inside. They all realised she was ill at ease, even the old man, and were trying to deflect the conversation from her. Her fingers clenched on the spoon. At home, the soup alone would be deemed sufficient for a meal.

'Asparagus, sir.'

'What sort of a business?' Harriet pursued relentlessly.

Emily felt she'd been backed into a corner. 'Fish and chips,' she whispered.

'What?' Aunt Harriet's palm brought one ear closer.

'Fish and chips.' Emily gasped and saw the housekeeper's dark eyes, full of disdain, studying her. For a moment, she showed the top of her teeth and upper gums in a fleeting snarl-like smile.

'Fish and chips? Good gracious,' Aunt Harriet exclaimed.

A large joint of beef was placed ceremoniously in front of Jeremy. The swish of carving knife on steel drowned everything else for a moment. He was almost covering a plate with thin slices of beef. Yorkshire pudding and a roast potato were added, and the plate placed with a flourish in front of Aunt Harriet.

Jeremy continued to carve. The manservant hovered. The housekeeper was bringing lidded dishes of vegetables to the sideboard.

Emily saw Jeremy's eyes on her, as the manservant flourished the plate between her knife and fork.

'The name Barr has been nagging at the back of my mind. You wouldn't happen to be the daughter of Alice Barr?'

'Yes,' Emily said. 'Fancy you remembering after all this time.'

'Impossible to forget. Gave me nightmares for years. Three people killed on our premises.'

'The kitchen fire,' Harriet said. 'What has that to do with your mother?'

'She worked there,' Emily said. Aunt Harriet might as well know she was not of their class. 'An assistant cook.' She saw the housekeeper's snarl-like smile come again, saw her look of contempt as she brought the vegetable dishes to her side.

'Very hard to lose your mother like that,' Arthur Calthorpe said sympathetically.

Emily, feeling all thumbs, tried to spoon sprouts on to her plate. To her consternation, one rolled off and settled – a dark green blot on the white cloth six inches from her plate. She couldn't look at the housekeeper, had no need to, the wall of scorn she felt projecting at her was paralysing.

'Terrible tragedy,' Jeremy said. 'How old were you?' She couldn't drag her eyes from the accusing sprout.

'Seven,' she choked, and watched with relief as Giles's fingers picked up the sprout and popped it in his mouth.

'I still feel guilty. It should never have happened.'

'Jeremy was very upset.' The old man was taking up his knife and fork. Emily forced herself to follow his lead.

'Hard to lose loved relatives at any time,' Harriet said. 'That's what so upset us about the war. Wiped out the French side of our family. I thanked God many times that He'd called Mother before it started. Our mother's family owned the Manoir de Frontenac at Lusec, near Arras, you know.'

'Tell us about it, Father,' Giles said. 'You never talk about the war.'

'Some things are best forgotten.'

'Come on, Father, what's the big secret?'

'No secret,' Jeremy said coldly. 'I found it very painful to lose my French relatives. Up until the war, we went every summer to stay at the Manoir de Frontenac, didn't we, Harriet? Every winter we went to Paris. They visited us too. I was very fond of them.'

'We both were,' Harriet said. 'I was specially close to Lisette, our cousin. In the war, she was driving a French general when the car was blown up. They were both killed.'

Emily thought Jeremy looked stricken. 'Never saw any of the de Frontenacs again. Never saw any of our cousins, and there were seven of them. The other girl, Mariette, was a nurse. Four of the lads went into the French Army, and the fifth into the Navy. They all died.'

'Once the war started, we heard nothing of them.' Harriet was eating her beef with obvious appetite. 'Lusec was in German hands. We worried about Aunt Celeste and whether they could survive at the Manoir.'

Jeremy laid down his knife and fork. 'You can imagine our relief when the Germans withdrew to the Hindenburg Line in 1917. They relinquished a huge salient between Arras and Soissons, freeing Lusec.'

'Fate is very strange,' Arthur said. 'That you should have been there.'

'I could hardly believe it myself. As they withdrew the Germans flattened whole villages, burning and vandalising everything, yet when I first saw the Manoir it looked much as it had before the war. Almost undamaged because they'd used it as a hospital. But the de Frontenacs had all gone.'

'You saw some of the servants, Jeremy.'

'Yes, and they remembered me. They told me they had heard that Pierre and Claude had been killed in the fighting in 1915. They took me to Uncle Henri's grave in the cemetery though there was nothing to mark the place by then. Of the rest there was no trace.'

'That is the story of your French relatives, Giles,' Harriet told him. 'Now you can understand why your father does not choose to dwell on the war.'

'But the Manoir was still standing, you said?'

'We were chasing the Germans, moving fast for the first time in the war. The Manoir didn't stay undamaged, the Germans fought a rearguard action. They began shelling our positions almost before we'd established ourselves. I think it was worse to see it disintegrate before my eyes, than to have come across it as a ruin.'

'Have I not told you I find all these currants indigestible, Jeremy?' Aunt Harriet asked when she saw the spotted Dick coming to the sideboard.

'Indeed you have. I asked for a milk pudding to be served today, didn't I, Higgins?' Emily thought Jeremy looked distressed as Higgins went off to the kitchen to investigate.

'I lost everything in the war,' Harriet said. 'Not only my relatives, but my house. Jeremy brought me a cut-glass knife rest as a keepsake. That's all I have now.'

Emily could see Jeremy was pulling himself together. 'How are you getting on in the design department?' he asked.

'I like it there.'

'I expect you've learned all about it by now. Are you ready to move on again, Giles?' Emily looked at Giles; he was showing no interest either way.

'Designing isn't something you'll do yourself,' his father went on. 'As I've explained before, what you need to understand is how design affects costs, and the other constraints on it. We can all look at a bracelet or a ring and know instinctively whether it pleases or it doesn't. And if it doesn't please us, it won't please our customers.'

Higgins was holding out a large, beautifully browned milk pudding; Harriet was spooning it generously on to her plate.

'The quality of our goods doesn't please me,' Giles said.

Emily heard Jeremy sigh. 'I've explained many times, Giles, we fill a niche at the bottom of the market. We undercut every other manufacturer.'

'But why? Aren't you ashamed of the stuff we turn out?'

'Our customers can't afford to pay more. Our market is the penny bazaars, Woolworths and the market traders. We export to Africa.'

'But our designs are very ordinary.'

'We don't aim to lead fashion, Giles, we follow it. A servant wants to buy jewellery similar to that she sees her mistress wearing.'

'Couldn't we do just a few lines that were better?'

'No, for two reasons. First, better quality jewellery is cast, not die stamped.'

Emily saw him look at her. 'The metal is melted and set in moulds,' he explained. 'We don't have the equipment, and the workforce doesn't have the skills. Secondly, our market is for cheap goods. We'd have to find new outlets for jewellery of better quality. Then we'd have to work in precious metals and real gems. Not only would that cost more, it would raise problems with security. To make money, Giles, you need to know your place.'

'Your father is a good businessman, Giles,' Arthur told him. 'Take heed of what he tells you.'

'I liked the brooch you designed,' Jeremy went on. 'Shows you're grasping fundamentals, but let the two Marys get on with it. Apart from the occasional suggestion, I do.' He put down his spoon and fork.

'When you are running the factory, the skill you will need is to pick out designs that sell, then hone them down so they're cheap to make.'

Giles's handsome eyebrows were lifting, he let out a gusty sigh. 'Where will you send me next?'

'Accounts, I think. A firm grip on finance is essential. I'll speak to Lockwood next week.'

'And I move too?' Emily asked.

'I think so.' A coffee pot on a tray was set in front of Aunt Harriet. She made a ceremony of pouring it into china cups. A maid delivered them round the table.

As the meal was finishing the sky had darkened; now sudden rain lashed against the windows. Aunt Harriet shivered, and Jeremy suggested they take their coffee and return to the comfort of the drawing-room fire. The maid carried in Arthur Calthorpe's, and within moments of his settling in the armchair, his eyes were closing. Gallantly, Giles assisted Aunt Harriet with her coffee.

'I've really enjoyed the last month,' Emily said to Jeremy. 'And learned a lot.'

Harriet's eyes were closed, her lorgnette dangling on her slack bosom. She blew a light ladylike snore. Sunday afternoon somnolence was settling on them all except Giles. He stood restlessly at the window looking out at the bleak garden. As soon as Emily put down her empty cup, he said: 'Shall we go, Emily?'

She stood up, wanting to ask where to. She thanked Jeremy, the only other person awake, in case Giles planned to take her home. He was holding her coat for her in the hall. So the visit she'd dreaded was over. She ran out after him into the rain. The windscreen wipers were working hard but the downpour was almost too much for them.

'What would you like to do now?' he asked.

She could think of nothing. She would have liked to see more of the house. What she had seen had whetted her appetite, but it wasn't the sort of thing she could ask, and it was too late now.

'We could take a walk in Rock Park. You could show me where you used to live.'

'Walk?' It was a damp and chilly afternoon.

'It's stopped raining. Save you paying the toll.' A toll was levied to keep unnecessary vehicles out of the park, and so keep it quiet.

Giles pulled up close to the gothic toll cottage. 'I don't mind paying,' he said, as water dripped from the trees. So he drove her to see the house where he used to live, pointed out where Nathanial Hawthorne had lived whilst he was serving as American Consul in Liverpool.

Emily thought the houses looked elegant and grand, and still prosperous and well cared for. But the tour took only a few moments, and then Giles was again wondering what they could do.

He parked his car with as good a view of the river as they could get from near Rock Ferry pier. The river was dimpling with rain, as another heavy shower started. The winter evening was drawing miserably in.

Emily worried whether she should invite Giles home for a cup of tea. There would be cake because Gran had had a piece of topside to roast and she always filled the oven when she had to put it on.

But the smell of chips would long since have overpowered the scents of the Sunday roast. Charlie would have taken off his slippers to sleep in the living-room chair. With the grandeur of Giles's home so fresh in her mind Emily decided it would be too stark a contrast. Besides, Charlie would not be welcoming.

'We could have tea at the Royal Rock,' Giles said. 'And a drink later.'

Emily couldn't face the thought of more food, and Gran would have a fit if she thought she was drinking. 'I think perhaps I'd better go home,' she said, and then worried anew, because she thought she sensed Giles was relieved.

He brought the car to a halt outside the chip shop. Three dogs were growling and snapping at each other outside Ethel's. She thanked him as fulsomely as she could and then ran round through the back entry.

It seemed an anticlimax to be back home. She was glad she hadn't invited Giles in. The unwashed dinner plates were still on the table. Gran was snoring with her hat pushed forward over her eyes. Charlie was just waking up and in a bad temper.

'Don't sit yourself down there,' he snapped. 'Can't you see things need doing? And put the kettle on, I could do with a cup of tea.'

The following morning, Emily was struggling in the nine o'clock crush in Wythenshaw's cloakroom, when she saw Sylveen making her way towards her. 'How did you get on yesterday?' she asked. 'What was it like?'

Emily put her head close to Sylveen's. 'A vast house. So grand you wouldn't believe. Wonderful things everywhere.'

'I know,' Sylveen whispered. 'Don't tell anyone, but I've seen it. Gilt clocks, antique vases, flowers.'

'Seen it? When?'

'Shush. Let's get out of here. We'll walk slowly. What else?'

'Filling food.'

'Tell me about his relatives.'

'His Aunt Harriet is a ferocious tiger, and I don't think she took to me. She almost had Giles's father by the throat. She wanted to visit his house in Paris and he wasn't willing. Do you know what she said? "I believe you must keep a woman there, Jeremy!"' Emily laughed. 'He's such a gentleman too. Not the sort to do anything like that.'

'Grow up, Emily. All men need a woman. Well, all normal men.'

'What?'

'Shush, keep your voice down. He took me there. Jeremy Wythenshaw.'

Something in Sylveen's manner alerted her. 'As his secretary? To work there?'

'No, you silly,' she giggled.

'Then why?'

'I'm his lady friend, Emily. He doesn't take me to meet his family, though Giles came in to talk to me the first time.'

'No! He doesn't seem that sort.'

'He is. Like I told you, all men are. You must have guessed.'

'No,' Emily said, horrified, as they came to the parting of their ways.

'Don't tell anybody. It mustn't get round.'

'Of course not,' Emily whispered and watched Sylveen turn away, her buttocks moving against her tight skirt.

'Thanks for the clothes,' Emily called. 'The outfit was a great success.'

She couldn't believe it, Sylveen and Jeremy Wythenshaw! Yesterday he had seemed fatherly, a family man, not that sort of person at all. She was astounded. She remembered what Gladys Wade had told a whole shop full of customers. It had shocked her at the time, but perhaps, after all, it was true.

CHAPTER NINE

Sylveen loved her present hectic life. In her own bed she dreamed of Giles, at her desk she fantasised about him, trying to read further meanings into everything he did and said. She expected them to share a golden future.

They were staying five nights at the Victoria in Gayton again. As they walked up to Heswall village, on Saturday afternoon, she turned to look across the River Dee, where pale spring sunshine sparkled on the water. All was rural peace here, so different to the urban Mersey.

She hardly dared think about marriage, but it was the natural next step, and she was hoping for it. Already her interest in homes and homemaking was sharpening. Almost without realising it, her step would slow as they passed estate agents' offices, and her eyes would eagerly scan the notices in their windows.

She pulled him to a halt in front of a window displaying properties for sale. 'That cottage sounds nice, three bedrooms, Dee views.'

'Sounds all right,' he managed, after she'd guided his attention to the right notice.

'Shall we go in and get more details?'

'No.'

'A house of our own would be lovely. Much cosier than going to a hotel all the time.' Sylveen gave her gutsy giggle. 'More private, and I'd love cooking dinners for us. We need one, don't we?'

'Need a house?' He looked suddenly harrowed.

'You could afford a cottage like that, couldn't you?'

'No.'

'What?' She'd thought everything possible. That for Giles Wythenshaw the sky was the limit.

'Why do you think I live with my father? No, I couldn't!' Sylveen felt she was choking on the unexpected disappointment. Giles spent money as if he could afford the best the world could offer.

'I asked Father to buy me a flat once. I thought he'd be glad to get me out from under his feet, but he refused. No, it's no good looking at houses unless you can persuade him to buy us one.'

'I don't know about that.' Sylveen couldn't think about her relationship with Jeremy. 'But you like this cottage?'

'I'd like anything if Father wasn't living in it too. Not to have him complaining all the time would be heaven.'

'You'd have me instead.'

'Seventh heaven, but don't bank on Father doing anything for us.'

'He pays you, doesn't he?'

'He allows me a thousand a year.'

'Giles! That's plenty to marry on. Three times what my dad gets.' She should have known he'd have strange ideas about the cost of living. He'd always had so much. Just to look at him set her pulse racing. He was in her soul.

'It doesn't go far,' Giles said, 'and he'll think I've lured you away from him. He's not going to like that. There might be nothing.'

'Nothing? But you work for it.'

'Father believes Wythenshaw's would do better without my help.'

'Nonsense!'

'He hates me, Sylveen. That's what I'm trying to tell

you. I don't think it would be wise to tell him about us.'

Sylveen closed her eyes. Everything she had hoped for was suddenly no more than a mirage. If Jeremy wasn't told, there could be no progress. 'You have money of your own, haven't you?'

'No.'

'Where does it come from, to pay for the champagne, the hotel bills?'

'I pay by cheque. My bank manager always gives me an overdraft.'

Sylveen was suddenly shivering.

'Father pays off my overdrafts. He doesn't want bad publicity.' She almost groaned, this wasn't how she'd imagined her future. This wasn't wealth. She felt sick with disappointment.

'So this is just an affair? You aren't thinking of . . . marriage.'

'Sylveen, I'd marry you tomorrow, you must know that! But I can't without Father's blessing. We'd have to have money. You must see that.'

Sylveen was blinking back the tears. 'I hope . . .' The future seemed suddenly less golden, less certain. She told herself there must be some way they could get married, and found it hurtful that he wasn't prepared to kick every obstacle out of the way. She was quite sure that if he truly loved her, he'd not have cared about his father, or having no money or anything else.

'Better say nothing, then. Hide it from your father.' She shivered again, wondering if Jeremy would want to go on seeing her if he ever found out. It didn't seem likely.

What a fool she was! Giles was another Denis Lake. She'd let herself love again, imagining him to be strong. Able to stand on his own feet and earn a living. How could she have been so stupidly blind?

Alex had made an effort to set out to work five minutes

earlier than usual. In the back entry, he propped his bike against the wall and went in to the Barrs' yard. Disappointment trickled through him when he found Emily's bike had already gone from the shed.

He had heard from Donkin that she was to start in the accounts department this morning, and before going to sleep he'd imagined how he would take her in on her first morning, and introduce her round. He was impatient with himself for letting her leave without him.

As he pushed open the double glass doors into the department, it was filling up with accounts clerks and typists. He couldn't miss seeing Emily.

In the largish hall with four rows of desks, each row six desks long, she was being settled in front of a typewriter on a desk only yards from his own. It hurt that her elfin eyes met his, but gave no sign she'd seen him. Miss Lamb, secretary and supervisor of the typists, looked up from the sheaf of papers she was giving to Emily.

'Mr Lockwood wants to see you first thing,' she told Alex.

'Now?'

Miss Lamb looked starkly efficient and bandbox clean. Her blouse was whiter than white and crisply ironed, her cardigan heavily pressed. 'Yes, and Norman Coates. Tell him as soon as he comes in, would you? He'll see you together.'

Alex sat down at his desk, unlocked it, and took out a file he had been working on. He watched Emily insert paper into her typewriter, her face screwing up with concentration as she studied the schedule she'd been given.

Suddenly he realised Norman Coates was already at his desk in the front row. He always wore a navy pin-striped suit that didn't fit too well, and from the back showed shiny patches round the elbows. He went over to tell him.

The typing-pool girls were not kind about Norman's

looks and said his mother must cut his hair. It stuck out toothbrush straight in solid spikes round his head, but Alex envied him his brain. Nobody needed to tell Norman Coates anything twice. Mostly he didn't need to be told at all, he worked things out by deduction.

Miss Lamb was back at her desk and asked them to wait, although he had seen Lockwood's iron-grey head and sickly complexion bent over his files through the glass panels. It seemed Giles Wythenshaw was expected too.

Alex saw Norman Coates cast his eyes towards heaven when he heard that. 'Looks like we could get lumbered,' he mouthed.

When Giles arrived, they were all shown in to see Mr Lockwood. He leapt up to shake Giles's hand, in a flowery welcome. Alex had never been in his office when there hadn't been an open packet of Rennies on his desk. Frequently he was seen sucking them, he never looked well.

'You know our two other management trainees,' he was saying.

Alex couldn't look at Giles Wythenshaw. Like almost every other employee, he'd known who he was from the moment he'd come through the front door a year or more ago. Alex had felt then an immediate bristling rivalry he couldn't explain. He'd never felt like this about anybody before. Usually he either liked a person or remained indifferent, and at that point he'd had no direct contact with Giles. Most of the workforce seemed to find him a likeable fellow; certainly the girls loved him.

'You're jealous,' Norman had laughed. 'Me too. But you'd better not show it, he's likely to be running the place before much longer.'

'He's called a management trainee too,' Alex said.

'But in a different class to us. He gets use of a private office and a secretary almost immediately, and he doesn't have to spend three nights a week at night school. He's going to go further and faster.'

'Older than us,' Alex pointed out. 'Been educated already.' Recently rumours had begun to circulate that Giles did not apply himself wholeheartedly to his duties, and Norman had commented that he wasn't progressing upwards as fast as he'd expected.

Now Alex had a reason to dislike him. It felt bad enough to be rejected by Emily; that Giles Wythenshaw was taking his place made it worse.

Alex's attention was drawn back to Mr Lockwood. 'In essence, one section of the department keeps check on the amount of products ready and available for sale, and, of course, collates sales figures. Fraser will explain it to you, and show you what goes on.'

He had heard it said about the office, that Lockwood was slowing down, that his grip on the department was not what it had been. 'The other three sections keep track of all expenses. Next week, you can attach yourself to Coates who will start explaining that side to you.'

'I'm sure I'll find it very interesting,' Giles said, lounging back in his seat, one leg crossed over the knee of the other in an attitude of exaggerated ease that Lockwood would never tolerate in himself or Norman.

'Right then, I'll introduce you to our Mr Donkin, then Fraser can show you round.'

'Donkin? I know him,' Giles said.

'Good, there's a desk in his office you can use while you're here. I'll just show you where it is. Quieter than down on the floor.'

Alex waited at the top of the steps leading down from the raised walkway. He couldn't help but notice Giles's lack of enthusiasm. He couldn't summon any himself for the task he'd been allotted.

He didn't find the next few days easy. He didn't like the way Giles's hostile eyes challenged everything he said, nor his condescending attitude. He had been told to explain how the storerooms functioned; how everything was accounted for, and he was doing it as well as he could, but it was a struggle not to lose his temper.

Four days later, in the storeroom, Alex pulled two cartons to the floor and showed Giles how to check their contents. Tossing one up on his shoulder, he went to the door and held it open. Giles was like a shadow, about to slide past.

'Bring the other carton, could you?' He wasn't finding it easy to keep the note of irritation out of his voice. He had already discovered Giles thought himself above humping cartons of goods about. He lifted the box as though it weighed half a ton yet a girl could have tossed it.

Swallowing his impatience Alex led the way to the main factory door. There was a lobby just inside, with the time clocks on one wall, and a counter with a bell where customers could ring for service when they came to buy goods.

He slid his carton on to the counter, got out the cash box and receipt book. Tucking the carbons between the pages of the book he pushed it along the counter to Giles.

'This is Mr McCarthy, a regular customer.' He directed Giles's attention to the man in a dirty raincoat on the other side of the counter. 'How many years have you been buying here?'

'Thirty or so, and my father before me.'

'Two cartons assorted, at two pounds ten shillings,' Alex dictated to Giles. When he saw he had no pencil, he gave him his own. 'This is Mr Giles Wythenshaw.'

'Quite an honour being served by the boss.'

'Boss's son,' Alex corrected rather sourly, and was rewarded by a dagger-like glance from Giles.

'Mr McCarthy has concessions in the fairground at New Brighton. What do you use our jewellery for?'

'Lucky-dip machines. You know, heap of goodies behind glass. Shove a threepenny bit in and for a minute you can control a crane and try to pick up a prize.'

'I wouldn't exactly describe it as "control", Mr McCarthy,' Alex chuckled. 'Have you ever tried hooking something out?'

'Can't make it too easy or there'd be no profit. Your brooches slip through the prongs at the last moment.' He laughed. 'Just the job. I use them on the penny-rolling stall too.'

Alex didn't miss Giles's supercilious glance at the customer's fingernails, which were badly bitten. He wished he'd hurry up and write out the bill.

'Yellow copy is the customer's receipt. Blue in the cash box with his money,' he said. Giles had stood by and let him make out the bills yesterday. There was no reason why he shouldn't do it. 'White stays in the book.'

'You certainly believe in buttering up the customers,' Giles complained, when the door closed behind him. 'Is it worth making all that fuss for a sale of five pounds?'

'He's regular, getting ready for the summer now. He'll be back every month, oftener if the season goes well.'

'All this trouble to sell small amounts,' Giles grumbled, wrinkling up his handsome nose in disgust.

'We've sold,' Alex totted up the cash in the box, 'thirty-five pounds' worth in three days. They're all in business in a small way, of course. They come because they get five per cent off for ex-factory sales. We save the cost of transporting the goods elsewhere, which gives us a better margin too.'

'But somebody has to serve the . . .'

'Nobody stands around waiting for customers. When the bell rings any one of the junior clerks in accounts answers it. Cash box and receipt book are locked in the cupboard here. Key is kept on that hook in Donkin's office.'

Alex watched him slouch off with the key. His irritation increased when fifteen minutes later he hadn't returned.

Alex never knew whether he'd gone to the gents or whether he'd gone home for the day. Last Monday they'd run a spot inventory in the storerooms, and after twenty minutes Giles had disappeared. Giles never bothered to explain his movements to him. An hour later, Alex had reason to go into Mr Donkin's office and found Giles alone there using the telephone.

'Yes, a double room. We usually have number fifteen overlooking the garden. Can we have it again? Yes Mr and Mrs Wythenshaw.'

Alex felt rooted to the spot. God! Mr and Mrs Wythenshaw as bold as you like, when everybody knew there was no Mrs Wythenshaw. Not yet. Anger was thickening in his throat. Emily? He didn't want to believe Emily would go to a hotel with him. Surely she had more sense than that?

Giles's eyes met his, flashing with hostility. 'I would prefer you to wait outside if I'm using the phone,' he said.

Alex's palms itched, he had a terrible urge to hit him on the chin, wipe the supercilious look off his handsome face. He left in a hurry, slamming the door behind him. Had to, or he'd have done it.

Which hotel and when? He wished he'd gone in sooner. He didn't know when the room was booked for. Only that it was.

He had to talk to Emily, but it was five-thirty and the typewriter on her desk was covered with its rexine cover. He rushed out to find her bike stall was empty. He pedalled hard, in a black rage, trying to catch her up. As he reached Paradise Parade he could see her cycling ahead. He managed it in the back entry as she was pushing open the gate to her yard. 'Emily!'

'Hello, Alex. Isn't it a lovely evening?' Her bike went through, the back gate scraped shut. They never did stop to talk at this time. It was rush hour along the Parade.

He had to swallow his frustration as he went into his own back yard. In the scullery, he washed his hands at the sink. Supper was cooking in the oven and filling the house with delicious scents.

He went through to the living-room. The fire had been made up, and three places set for supper at the table. In addition, there was a glass of milk and a sandwich.

He took them with him to a fireside chair, twitching up the top slice of bread to find boiled ham and mustard. Refuelling, his mother called it. He bit hungrily into the sandwich she'd made him, and a few minutes later tidied his glass to the scullery, and went to the shop. It was full.

'Half a dozen eggs, Alex, and a large loaf,' a voice called from the crush, before he'd taken three steps inside. Myra George, the assistant, was reweighing for a customer's benefit a half-pound pat of butter. When business was slack, she cut corners off the huge mound of butter that came in a box from New Zealand, weighed up half pounds, then with butter pats thumped them into neat oblongs before wrapping them up. She pushed her stringy brown hair under her white cap, and grinned a welcome.

Here in the shop Alex could forget Giles Wythenshaw. He lurched against his mother as they reached for the same box of matches. She lifted her heavy eye brows in a gesture of amused apology, and went on serving.

'Hello, son, glad you've made it,' his father puffed. He could only stand the pressures of rush-hour working for short periods now.

Alex knew he'd go back to the living-room fire and see to the supper so everything was ready to dish up when the shop closed. There wasn't room to have more than three people serving at once, and Dad was getting too slow. He found it rather pathetic, that his father had to find other ways to be useful to his family.

When the rush eased, Myra wiped down the bacon slicer and began tidying up. Her last job was to take a bucket and mop to the shop floor and front step, while his mother cashed up. His mother had the energy of a dynamo. By seven o'clock the shop was locked and they were sitting down to eat.

'Had a good day?' his father asked. When he put that question to Olympia, they all knew it referred to the day's takings. But Ted was looking at Alex.

'No, terrible.' He'd already told them he'd been given the job of taking Giles Wythenshaw round.

'What's happened?' His mother always wanted to hear every snippet of news about the Wythenshaws.

'He's a pain,' Alex said, biting into a roast potato. 'Treats me like dirt.'

'Not like his father?' she asked.

'No, Giles can't do anything properly.'

'Don't be silly.'

'It's true. He'll never run that factory.'

'Of course he will. You're showing him how, aren't you?'

'Everybody's showing him how,' Alex mopped up his gravy. 'But I don't think any of us is succeeding.'

'What'll they do then, when the old man retires?' Ted sniffed.

'Wisest thing would be to sell up, before Giles ruins a good business,' Alex said. 'Let him live like the gentleman he wants to be.'

'He'll have to have something to do, young man like that,' Olympia said. 'Can't sit around all day.'

'Giles could. Be happier if he doesn't have to work,' Alex said. 'I don't like him.'

'That's really what you mean,' his mother said pointedly.

'The Wythenshaws have it easy.' He knew his father didn't like Olympia taking such an interest in them. His mother's usual empathy was missing, she didn't seem to realise it was guaranteed to upset Dad. Alex knew it already had, he was becoming truculent. He felt caught in the middle when this happened. Emily had been right when she said his father hated the Wythenshaws.

'Why do you hate them, Dad?'

'I don't.' But his brooding face, his antagonism could only be explained by hate. 'I saved his life once.'

'Yes, Dad, in the war. He said thank you, didn't he?'

'Yes, bought me a beer, and Charlie Barr too, in a French café. But that's all.'

'What more could you expect?'

'He shows his gratitude for much smaller favours. Gives money away.'

'It was your duty. Perhaps it upsets him to be reminded of the war.'

'Why should it upset him to see me, when I saved his life? He's happy to have Higgins working for him. He sees him all the time, and he was his batman in the war. This afternoon I saw Higgins driving him home from work in his limousine. Went right past my shop and I was outside. You'd think he was the King of England now. It wouldn't have hurt him to give me a wave.'

'Does Higgins wave?'

'Yes, but not Jeremy Wythenshaw. Not him.'

When his mother went out to the scullery to wash up, Alex picked up a tea towel. 'What's up with Dad? He's always on about Jeremy Wythenshaw. I keep telling him, he's done a lot for me.'

'Bee in his bonnet.' Olympia turned the taps on full; water swirled noisily into the sink. 'The war changed him.'

'It certainly did.' Alex tried to picture him as he must have been once, a whole and healthy man. There was a frightening bitterness about him now. Had the war caused that too?

The next day Giles didn't show up at work all day; Alex felt quite pleased to have a day free of his company. The following morning he was at his heels again, and when a customer rang for attention in the lobby, Alex asked him: 'Do you want to attend to that?'

'Not particularly. I've grasped all I need to know about factory-gate sales.'

'Please yourself,' he said shortly. 'I'll go, you get the key for me.' Alex had the carton on the counter, and was making small talk to the market trader. He could do nothing till he could get at the cash box and receipt book.

He tried to swallow his irritation, and was on the point of going for the key himself, when he saw Giles coming down. Something about his manner alerted him.

Alex opened the cash box, fully expecting to find the cash gone. Some of it had. In its place was a cheque made out to J. Wythenshaw & Son for twenty-five pounds, signed by Giles. Despite his annoyance, Alex had to smile at his effrontery. Giles inhabited a different world to him and Norman.

He was tempted to say nothing, and let Giles feel the edge of Lockwood's wrath. The fellow was a fool and deserved all he got, but it would upset Lockwood too, he would feel it undermined his authority.

As the customer left he stabbed his finger at the cheque and said: 'I'd nip down to the bank if I were you, and cash this.'

'Why?' Giles's handsome face was frosty.

'Self-preservation. Could earn you a black mark.'

'Why?'

'Bad example to the rest of us. You'll save yourself trouble if you put the cash back before Donkin sees this.'

'Does he have to see it?'

'Yes, he checks all my figures.'

For a moment he thought Giles would see sense. Then he shrugged: 'Can't be bothered. Ought to stay with you. Might miss some vital gem of information.'

'I think you just have,' Alex said.

Waking from a deep sleep, Sylveen turned over and lay for a moment utterly relaxed in her narrow bed. A shaft of early sunlight came between the curtains, and sparkled diamond-bright in the mirror.

Flat on her back she stiffened, grew rigid and tense. Her mind frantically monitored her body. Did she feel all right? Were yesterday's horrific suspicions unfounded?

She could hear her father downstairs raking yesterday's ash from the living-room grate. Slowly she sat up and put her feet to the floor. Yes, she was all right.

She went to the cold bathroom, and while taking those dozen paces, knew with hideous certainty she was not. A queasy unease gripped her stomach. She stood holding on to the wash basin, pulling herself together. In the mirror above, her face looked green. She filled a tumbler with water, drank it back. Peristalsis moved in the right direction again, but the awful truth had to be faced. She'd felt queasy yesterday, but hoped it was the pork she'd had for dinner. She was overdue and still there was no sign of that.

Sylveen went back and lay down on her bed, feeling a slight prickle in her breasts. It had happened exactly like this last time. She was paralysed with dread.

'Sylveen, are you up?' her mother's voice called. 'It's quarter to eight.'

She had to rouse herself to answer, otherwise her mother would come up. The effort made, she reached for her handbag and turned to the calendar in her diary.

Oh God! It must have happened when Jeremy went to Paris. Giles's passion had hardly let her out of bed that weekend, and he was never so careful as Jeremy.

Oh God! She knew she had taken risks. She knew she should not have allowed Giles to grow lax. But lightning was said never to strike twice in the same place.

'Don't be such a fool,' she told herself as she started to dress. She had to get to work. Had to eat breakfast. Had to pretend nothing was wrong.

She'd known all the time this was possible, but a

possibility was easier to handle. Certainty brought its own pressures. Once, she'd believed it would accelerate her into the married state, and might not be such a bad thing. Now she shivered, remembering what Giles had said in front of the estate agent's window.

Oh God! Why did she give her love and trust to men who had no strength? She'd sworn never to make that mistake again, and she had.

'Are you coming, Sylveen? You'll be late.'

'I'm coming.' She clattered downstairs. Seeing her parents with awful clarity, sitting at the table as they had for thirty years. They would be furious she had let it happen again, after all their dire warnings.

She would not let Giles abandon her as Denis had. It was Giles she wanted, but if not Giles then Jeremy. They both had money enough to look after her.

She forced herself to behave as she did every other morning. Accept the cup of tea her mother poured. Go to the kitchen, her mother called it the kitchenette, fill a bowl with Force, flood it with milk.

'Are you all right?' her father asked, his eyes searching into hers. 'You look a bit peaky.'

'I'm all right.'

'You have too many late nights,' her mother said sharply. 'No wonder you can't get up in the mornings.'

She couldn't hurry. She only caught her bus because it came late. She wasn't ready to face all that again, being treated as a scarlet woman. The guilt and heartrend of holding a baby she could not keep, of wondering afterwards over the months and years how her baby was growing up.

She had called her daughter Frances, but adoptive parents always changed their names. She wondered who she was learning to call Mother.

But this time it would be different. Giles said he loved her. He wouldn't let her be sent to that awful home for unmarried mothers again, wouldn't let her baby be taken away.

She would wait a few days till she was absolutely certain. She had no strength for it now. Perhaps let Jeremy go to Paris again, it would get him out of the way. It was hard to cope with both of them at once.

It would be easier to tell Giles when they went back for their five nights at the Victoria, when she had him to herself. Quietly and in bed, when they were both relaxed after their supper and a bottle of wine.

She felt tears prickling behind her eyes. She'd felt on a knife edge like this last time. She was afraid, she wanted to feel his arms round her, she wanted reassurance from Giles. Most of all she wanted him to suggest marriage.

She was afraid, terribly afraid he'd give her nothing. She blinked furiously. She mustn't let herself be swamped by her own emotions.

Suffused with well-being, Giles felt his car respond to his touch, turn the corner heading down the steep hill. Through the windscreen, the wide view of fields and cottages sloping to the Dee estuary was curtailed by drizzle.

The disappointing weather didn't bother him when he had the satisfaction of knowing Father was gone for six nights, and he had scraped together enough money to pay cash for their room. He had to guard against Father finding out, that he moved into a double room at the Victoria, when he went to Paris.

When he had paid off his overdraft last time, Father had examined his statements. He didn't want him to guess it was Sylveen who prevented him enjoying his freedom at Churton.

'Do you want to drive for a bit?' he asked, as Sylveen stirred in the seat beside him.

'Not now.'

'If you want to learn, you have to keep at it,' he said, but in truth he was torn between wanting to please her and fear she'd hit another vehicle or wrap his car round a lamp post. It was not that he feared for the car exactly, more the questions that would be asked. Impossible then to hide that Sylveen had been in his car.

'This is like coming home,' he said as they went through the front door.

'Good afternoon, Mr Wythenshaw,' the receptionist said, and that took away some of his satisfaction. He'd never before cared whether his father knew what he did. Now with Sylveen it was different. He'd suggested going to a different hotel, but Sylveen liked the Victoria. Too late to sign them in as Mr and Mrs Smith here.

The bell pinged for the porter to carry up their cases. He took her arm as they followed him up. They had been given the same room. Sylveen admired its embossed wallpaper and dark silky curtains. He loved the open views over the back garden, and anything that pleased her.

Usually they fell on the bed laughing the moment the porter went. He followed Sylveen to the window, watched her toss off the little hat she wore over one eye. He unbuttoned her coat for her, his trickle of anticipation growing to a torrent.

The thought of Sylveen naked amongst the coverlets was what he'd lived for the last few days. The feel of her now exceeded anything he'd known before. She knew how to help a man reach his best. Satiated at last he held her luxurious body close against his own, and relaxed.

'Giles.' He was near dozing, his cheek against hers. 'Giles.' He wasn't ready to be disturbed, he pulled her closer, settling deeper. 'I'm going to have a baby,' her breathy voice came again.

It took him a moment to understand. 'A baby?' Black horror was coursing through his veins. He tossed himself back from her, wide awake now, his eyes searching her face, his heart pounding. 'You can't be.'

'I am.' His gaze went lower, her breasts were just as fulsome, her abdomen neatly rounded as ever.

'Have you been to a doctor?'

'Not yet.'

'Then how can you be sure?'

'I'm sure.'

'Sylveen, you can't be certain till you've seen a doctor.' She didn't answer, but moved across the bed to put her arms round him. Other hotel guests tramped past their door, their voices light-hearted. It made him realise the magnitude of their trouble.

'There must be somebody who can fix you up.' She was staring at him aghast. 'You know, have it taken away?'

'It's illegal, and girls die from it.'

He could see tears glistening in her eyes. It made him feel worse. 'How do you know I'm the father? Why blame me?'

He saw Sylveen recoil. 'I mean, it could be my father, couldn't it?'

She was trying to explain about dates. There was no talking to her. He felt sick. In her own mind, he could see she had no doubt.

'Jesus,' he said. 'What are you going to do about it?'

'I hoped you'd help.' Her face was grey against the white pillow, but her voice was steady.

He shrugged. 'I don't know how.' He watched her tongue come to moisten her lips. 'When will it be?'

'Christmas.' That seemed the final irony.

'Just what we need to bring joy into our lives.'

'Don't you want to marry me?' Suddenly she was sobbing.

'I do, Sylveen. You know I do. You know I love you, but . . .' She didn't help him, great sobs were shaking her, she'd gone out of control.

'Father will be mad at me. Mad at us. We daren't tell him. We have to keep this quiet.'

It took her two or three minutes to sob out one word. 'Why?'

He'd already told her why. 'You are his. He'll be mad at me.' Father could throw him out for this. He couldn't take on a wife and child until he was sure he wouldn't be thrown out of house and home.

That made her pull herself up the bed and blow her nose.

'Do be realistic, Giles. It isn't something I can keep quiet for long.'

'Well, of course, not for ever, I didn't mean that. Just for now.

'Jesus,' he said, reaching for his clothes. 'Jesus, what a mess.'

She sat up. 'Don't you feel you owe me anything?' He didn't like the accusing edge to her voice. He didn't like her tear-stained face; red eyed, she was no longer beautiful.

'It takes two. You can't heap all the blame on me. You've enjoyed yourself these last few months, haven't you? I've given you a good time.'

She collapsed against the pillows. She looked ill and utterly defeated. 'But what am I going to do now?'

'The same as I have to. Go grovelling to my father. He holds the purse strings. He'll fix you up, if you play your cards right. He's used to paying.'

'It's not his baby.'

'You don't have to point that out. He doesn't know you've been two-timing him.'

'What if he finds out?'

Giles felt his blood run cold. 'There's a lot he never finds out. Very wisely, we've kept quiet. About us, I mean.'

[illegible]

Book Two 1932–1933
CHAPTER TEN

Jeremy sat back in his reserved first-class seat, mesmerised by the scudding grey clouds and the flying landscape. The fields were soggy, but lush with early summer grass. Rain dripped from trees and hedgerows in full leaf. Roses bloomed in cottage gardens.

The sea crossing had been choppy, but he always enjoyed the boat. It woke him from his daze to pace on deck and breathe sea air. Trains he found wearying.

It was reassuring to know timetables exactly, and to know whether the taxi between Paddington and Victoria was travelling by the shortest route. He even knew which end of the Sud Express drew up at the most convenient part of the platform in the Gare du Nord.

But the journey was long, and he'd done it so often he was finding it tedious. He was glad to be back in England, and looking forward to seeing Sylveen again. She had promised to meet his train at Birkenhead Woodside. Higgins would be outside with the Rolls.

Perhaps it was Sylveen who made him dissatisfied with his trips to Paris. He certainly wanted to spend more time with her. There was only one other occupant in the carriage, an elderly man now hidden behind the pages of *The Times*.

Jeremy opened his attaché case on his knee and slid back the catch on the jewel case. He had chosen a pendant and bracelet for Sylveen. Enamelled gold set with sapphires, emeralds and rubies and hung with pearls in the French neo-Renaissance style. It dated from the mid-nineteenth century, and was perhaps by Marcel Tassigny.

It was a more expensive gift than he had intended, but its gloriously exuberant style would suit Sylveen. Elaborate and colourful, with rather too much ornamentation. If it were not hallmarked, he might almost describe it as ostentatious.

He shut the case carefully, imagining Sylveen's face when she saw it. Eyes shining, laughing aloud with pleasure. She would love it. He relaxed, closed his eyes.

With Elspeth dying of tuberculosis at thirty-seven, he'd expected that after a decent interval he'd marry again, but he'd never felt strongly enough about anyone till now.

He'd had a liaison with Olivia Reynolds that had lasted ten years, but Olivia had already had a husband. There had been others, but none had taken him with the storm Sylveen had. A man needed a woman to remain healthy and well balanced. He prided himself that despite his age he still appealed to women.

Sylveen had hinted she would like a more permanent relationship, but it would be a union of spring with winter. He wondered for the tenth time whether he should offer marriage. He wanted her with him always. He wanted to give to her, repay her for all she gave him. He wanted to feel they meant everything to each other. Sylveen's young firm flesh would keep him young.

When he had met Elspeth he had let nothing stand in the way of marriage. He'd wanted it, and gone all out for it, that was the way of youth. Age had made him wary, made him think twice about everything.

The years with Elspeth had been good, on the whole. Perhaps it was her illness that had made her difficult towards the end. He knew he was being kind to her memory, he could afford to be, after all this time. Elspeth had poked rather too much into his business.

Really Sylveen was impossibly young to be his wife. Only a year older than Giles. She looked older, more streetwise, and there was a ripeness about her that might later run to too much flesh. But however beautiful, her wide lips were too sensual. Everything about her had been designed by nature, or by Sylveen embellishing nature, to attract the opposite sex. She made it too obvious. Elspeth, if alive, would not consider her a lady.

But Elspeth was long gone and much of his life with her. Nothing could shield him from ageing. It would not take many more years to turn him into a dry husk like Arthur, he would need Sylveen more then. Marriage now seemed the right course.

As a companion she was delightful, bringing interest and pleasure to his life. He wanted to please her, to shower treasures of all kinds on her. Damn it, he wanted to marry her, she would add enjoyment to what was left of his life, but he would say nothing to her yet. He needed to think it over carefully. Sleep on it.

The train was slowing. His fellow traveller folded his newspaper, Jeremy did likewise. He felt stiff as he stood to remove his case from the luggage rack. It was time he organised something for his old age.

He saw Sylveen on the platform as the train jolted to a halt. She had not seen him, her eyes were searching the passengers as they thronged from the train. She seemed, even from a distance, to be less exuberant. His heart went out to her.

Her kisses were generous, and she laughed up into his eyes. She'd organised a porter to take his bags. He was pleased with her welcome, but Sylveen seemed different, not running over with her usual high spirits. Her eyes looked a little strained. Even her clothes were more subdued.

He no longer cared what Higgins thought. It was

difficult to have secrets from one's servants. He needed the comfort of having Sylveen at Churton. In the end it was more private, and fewer would know of his liaison. He'd looked forward all day to returning to his library. This was the world he wanted. He poured her a glass of white wine, and a generous helping of Laphroaig for himself.

He'd felt lonely in Paris and pictured Sylveen relaxed in his green velvet chair, as she was now. She was wearing a dress he'd not seen before, in some pale material, with a fashionable bolero.

She had brought his mail from the office, but he would not open it yet. Instead he heard that a repeat order for bar brooches with a fox's head had come from Penny Bazaar and had been put straight into production. That Miss Lewis was off with a cold. He asked about Giles and heard he'd been in every day.

Jeremy knew he helped himself too liberally to the whisky and also to the claret that went with the lamb Mrs Eglin put before them. He felt relaxed here in his own home with Sylveen telling him all was well with his world.

He should perhaps not have indulged in the brandy afterwards, nor poured such generous measures for Sylveen. He dismissed Mrs Eglin when she brought their coffee to the library. Only Higgins was to stand by to drive Sylveen home.

He'd taken the jewel case upstairs when he'd gone up to wash and change on arrival. He meant to indulge in a fantasy he'd had. Make love to Sylveen while she wore the jewels and nothing else.

In leisurely fashion they drank their coffee and had another brandy each with it. He heard Mrs Eglin locking up and retreating to the rooms allotted to her. He led Sylveen up to his room, settled her in his big armchair then kissed her as he put the jewel case in her lap.

He'd made no mention of a gift, he saw surprise in her

lovely eyes. She cried out with pleasure at the sight of it. He fastened the bracelet round her wrist.

'You're very generous, Jeremy.' He heard emotion in her breathy voice.

'I want to be. You're very generous to me.' She happened to be wearing a single strand of pearls so he hung the pendant on that. Imitation pearls unfortunately, but of a better quality than he produced. He pulled at her hand till she came to stand in front of his mirror. 'Look,' he bade her.

She seemed suddenly shy, only half lifting her eyes. 'It's beautiful, thank you.' Coloured shafts of light sparked off the pendant. 'Goes well on my old pearls.'

Jeremy thought it a sin to hang so expensive a piece on anything imitation. 'I'll get you a plain gold chain for it.'

He was taking her bolero off when he heard her sob, and tilting her face to his, was surprised to find it wet with tears.

'What's the matter, love?' He took her into his arms. 'What's the matter? I thought you'd like it.'

'I do. Of course I do.'

'Then?' He pulled her closely. 'Sylveen?'

'I'm going to spoil everything now,' she sobbed on to his shoulder. 'You're going to hate me.'

'I love you.' He hadn't meant to say it, and it brought her eyes to his, wide with gratitude and wonder.

'I hope you do. Jeremy, I hope you do,' she sniffed.

'I love you, Sylveen.' He kissed her.

'And I love you, but I must tell you.'

'Of course you must.' He found her a clean handkerchief and tried to mop up her tears. 'What is it? I want to know what's troubling you.'

He expected it to be shortage of money, that she'd overspent on her dress. Years of coping with Giles made him think on those lines. She wouldn't look at him, her face was burrowing into his jacket again.

‘I’m going to have a baby. I’m sorry.’ He clung to her, feeling the blood drain from his face. He was knocked sideways.

‘Not so easily remedied,’ he said at last, more to himself than to her. He could feel himself shaking. ‘Bit of a shock, love.’ Sylveen continued to weep. He led her towards his bed, and sat down beside her on the edge. ‘I thought I was being so careful.’

‘I’m sorry.’ Sylveen wept.

‘Don’t be. What’s done is done. You are sure?’

‘Certain. You see, this isn’t my first baby. I’ve never told anyone before, but I know how it feels. I know what will happen.’

Jeremy tightened his arm round her shoulders. It wasn’t the first time this had happened to him either. Strange he’d thought of marrying her in the train.

‘What did happen? Last time?’

It took her a long time to whisper: ‘Disgrace. A home for unmarried mothers, I had to give the baby up.’

‘This time will be different, Sylveen. I promise you.’ Her beautiful eyes wet with tears searched into his.

‘I’m quite tickled about becoming a father at my age.’ But he didn’t like knowing this child wasn’t her first.

‘Really?’

‘Of course I am. When will it be?’

Her smile was wavering and watery. ‘Christmas.’

‘You’ve started work on my present early.’

‘I wish I hadn’t. You don’t want it.’

‘Don’t say that, Sylveen, we have to take what fate sends us. I feel very guilty, because I see it isn’t what you want. I’ll see you’re all right, I promise. Do you want to stay here tonight?’

‘I’d better go home. I’m not going to be a load of laughs.’ She stood up. He was pressing the jewel case into her hand. He’d meant to tell her to look after it, because of its value. Now it seemed trite to put value on such trinkets.

It took her fifteen minutes in the bathroom to pull herself together to face Higgins. Jeremy rang down to tell him she was about to leave, then he paced his bedroom, trying to make up his mind. He'd come very close to saying, 'Marry me.' It seemed the least he could do. He hadn't meant to tell her he loved her, till he'd made up his mind about that, it had slipped out.

She came to say goodbye, her tears only just under control. He held her close for a moment, kissed her cheek. The words 'I want you to marry me' were on his tongue. If he'd wanted marriage before, this was an added reason to go ahead. Jeremy didn't know what held him in check, but something did. The canniness of age. He'd grown used to deliberating every move.

He took her downstairs, kissed her again. 'Trust me,' he said, turning up the big collar on her blue coat, shutting her face away from Higgins's eyes. 'We'll make this a happy time. I'll see you in the morning, at the office.'

He opened the front door, and saw Higgins leap out of the Rolls to open the door for her. A wave, as the car moved off.

Jeremy went slowly back to his room. Pondering how very close he'd come to proposing, and feeling dishonourable that he had not. Hardly able to understand why he had not. It was very wrong of him.

He ran himself a bath, relieved to be alone so he could think. Marriage for Sylveen was now an immediate need, not something he could mull over for the future. It made him feel pressurised. He was used to making up his mind about business matters, but could come to no conclusion about his bed.

In his dressing-gown he went downstairs for another whisky. Sat by the embers of the dying fire to drink it. He had not asked about Sylveen's earlier pregnancy. She had been too upset tonight to talk of it. He had never worried about the earlier affairs she might have had. What was gone belonged to a different life. He had known he was not the first.

She said she loved him and seemed to, but wealth was a powerful aphrodisiac, he mustn't forget that. How could he be sure he was loved for himself and not his money? Until he married her, the ball was in his court.

He was held back by the thought Sylveen might not be so eager to please once married. She could so easily become more demanding once her position was secure. Also it was difficult to hide everything from a wife.

Elspeth had poked too hard into his affairs. wanting to know exactly what he was worth, and how he came by it. She had been mighty curious about what he brought back from Paris, what he did there. Above all, the Paris house had intrigued her, she had wanted to have it modernised and redecorated, a smart place to invite friends to stay. Sylveen could be the same. That would prove dangerous.

It gave him a lift to take Sylveen into a restaurant and see the heads turn. He wasn't the only man who fancied taking Sylveen to bed, and there was no guarantee he'd be the last. Who could say whether she would remain faithful once that ring was on her finger?

And what of the child? He had to feel proud of fathering a child at his age, but it was not the first he'd fathered out of wedlock. Once, long ago, during his marriage to Elspeth . . . But he was letting his mind flutter off the track. He needed to make it up now. Should he or should he not marry Sylveen?

He went slowly upstairs to bed at last, wondering whether he had developed wisdom in his sixty years, or whether it was the chronic indecision common in the elderly.

Sylveen leaned against the washbowls in Wythenshaw's cloakroom and felt the girls eddy round her. She'd felt miserably sick as she'd climbed out of bed this morning.

Afraid she might really vomit. Afraid her parents might hear her in the tiny house. The thought of her mother knowing made her blood run cold.

'Hello.' Emily pushed in beside her, her pixie cheeks like rosy apples in the mirror.

Sylveen pulled herself together. 'Haven't seen you for a while. Are you going home for dinner now?'

'No.' Emily's brown eyes looked into hers, smiling. 'Giles takes me to the staff dining-room, most days.' Sylveen heard the gurgle of delight in her voice; it was like a knife turning in the wound.

She was gone before Sylveen could say anything else. She told herself she must not mind, though she found it aroused feelings of jealousy. She wanted Giles to take her to lunch, show his affection openly. It was hurtful to be kept out of sight as though he were ashamed of her.

The only good thing was that Emily was too engrossed in her own affairs to notice how dreadful she looked. Sylveen peered at her face in the mirror, her skin had lost its translucent glow, her sparkle had gone. She was sheet white.

She was bone weary too, but couldn't stay off work. Her mother would be all questions. Besides, Jeremy would have work for her, and she wanted desperately to know what he was planning.

She'd gone to bed not knowing whether she was disappointed or pleased. She hadn't really expected to be rushed to the altar, but she had hoped. Now she knew her news was not going to tip her into matrimony. She reckoned he'd have asked her last night if he'd meant to.

Just being at work made everything seem more normal. Miss Lewis's typewriter remained under its black cover while she was off sick. From her desk, the rattle of machinery was a subdued background hum. The office was quiet. She could go at her own pace. She set about opening the morning mail.

Jeremy came in as she was finishing, and hovered near her desk to take what she'd sorted for him.

'I haven't looked at what you brought last night.' He looked tired, as though he hadn't slept well. 'But when I have, I'm afraid there'll be work for you. Are you feeling up to it?'

She nodded. His smile was kindly. 'I'm all right. On an even keel again.'

'Good girl.'

Sylveen recoiled, that was the last thing she was. She felt a real bitch, foisting a child he hadn't fathered on him. She told herself she had no choice, it was this or facing her mother's cold insults, and they'd be worse the second time round.

'Come in for a moment first.' He indicated his inner office. She went gladly, it would stop her thinking about the home for fallen girls, and having the infant torn from her arms.

'Sit down, Sylveen.' He was hanging his overcoat on a bentwood stand.

'You will need a house, somewhere to live. It may take a few months to buy, so the sooner we start the better. I'm thinking of something fairly small you can manage yourself. Two or three bedrooms, but comfortable and in a pleasant area. Not West Kirby, not near Churton.'

Sylveen felt a burst of gratitude. Not marriage, but concrete practical help.

'Not Prenton either.' She managed a smile.

'Perhaps Heswall, then?' he suggested, and her heart jerked with relief.

'I want you to take a taxi this afternoon, go round the estate agents, see if there is anything on the market that pleases you.'

She nodded. 'There will be, I'm sure. Thank you.' She had to force herself to say: 'How much can I spend?'

He stroked his chin, and named a figure that made the

cottage she'd seen when she was with Giles a possibility.

'You pick out what you want, and then I'll come and see it. It will be better for you than coming always to Churton.' There was another pause, she almost got to her feet to go. 'I'll make you an allowance, when you can no longer work. I'll see you're all right, Sylveen.'

Then she found herself back at her own desk blinking back the tears of relief. What a fool she'd been. Her head had told her to choose Jeremy. He had offered easy orientation into a life of undreamed of luxury. Pleasant undemanding company, magical outings, exactly what she'd wanted.

At moments like this, she found it hard to understand why she'd fallen for Giles. Young and exciting perhaps, but another Denis Lake if ever there was one. She should have been satisfied with what Jeremy offered. She'd overplayed her hand.

Jeremy must never find out what she'd done. If he ever discovered that Giles had fathered her child, the new life she was setting up would collapse like a pack of cards. When he went off to Paris again, she hadn't wanted anything to do with Giles. It was enough now to work and wait for her future to take shape.

'I don't think so,' she said when Giles came to the office and tried to arrange their meeting.

'Why not?' Giles's blue eyes laughed down at her.

'You know why not. It's playing with fire.'

'It'll be a bit of fun.'

Whatever her misgivings about Giles when she was alone, she found it impossible to deny him anything when his tawny eyes were looking into hers. 'If I had any sense I'd send you packing.' But she laughed.

'I've no sense either, where you're concerned. You're beautiful, Sylveen.'

'You were as frightened of your father finding out as I was.'

'But he hasn't found out. Clever you. Let's go to the Vic again.'

'No, I'm scared. We've been there too often.' The last time had soured it for her. She didn't want to remember that.

'Somewhere else, then? Plenty of hotels in New Brighton.'

Sylveen sighed. 'I don't know.'

'He's gone for six whole nights again.'

'It isn't safe. Think of all the people who know us at the factory. Someone might see us.'

'Just for the weekend, then. We'll go on Saturday. Sit on the sand. Have dinner, spend one night. New Brighton is full of holidaymakers at this time of year. Father doesn't pay his workers enough to go to the Grand.' Sylveen thought of the alternative: staying at home with her mother, weeding the garden.

'Say you will. We always have a good time, Sylveen.'

'The risk . . .'

'Added excitement. It'll be safer when you get your own place.'

'I couldn't let you come there!'

'Only when Father's in Paris. Safe enough then.'

'Giles!'

'There's a garage, I can shut my car out of sight. Who's to know I'm inside?' Giles could make her believe anything. Giles was daring, seeming not to worry about possible consequences. 'The Grand at New Brighton then?'

The truth was that while she admired Jeremy, enjoyed his company and trusted him, it was Giles who provided the excitement, Giles she couldn't resist. Giles she loved.

She felt if she stayed close to Giles, all would turn out well for them in the end. Giles was reality; what she had with Jeremy was an insurance she wouldn't be left on her own. A means of paying the bills.

On Saturday afternoon they booked into the Grand, and later on took a walk round the Tower fairground. It was a wonderfully sunny afternoon, and they spent the last of it on the beach. Sylveen felt better, relaxed, full of sea air and sun.

The evenings were longer now. They had a drink in the bar and watched the sun set over the sea. Then went into the restaurant to eat roast lamb. Giles ordered a bottle of Médoc. Sylveen felt happier than she had for a long time.

'I'm so pleased with the cottage. I knew I'd love it the day I first saw it advertised.'

'Bit on the small side.' Giles frowned. 'I'd have gone for something larger myself.'

'I love the views across the Dee to Wales, and the thick solid walls.' She felt thrilled with its old-world charm. Thrilled with the redecorations Jeremy proposed to put in hand. Thrilled most of all that he was buying the cottage in her name, for her.

She was going to have a better home than her parents, and it would have no mortgage to keep up. Jeremy had not arranged her allowance yet, but she trusted him to be generous with that as he had with everything else.

He had driven her round furnishing stores and antique shops, guiding her choice. Buying for her what she most liked. She was wonderfully happy with what he was doing for her. All would be well, providing he never found out about Giles.

She ought to send Giles packing, but she could not. She needed him too. He was another reason she felt happy. She needed his love and his laughter. They had finished their lamb. The plates had been cleared and the menus brought to them again.

'What'll you have?' Giles asked.

'I'm full.'

'Come on, keep me company.'

'Perhaps fruit salad, then.'

'Apple pie for me. And coffee for two,' Giles said. As the waiter crossed the dining-room to fulfil their order, Giles's gaze followed him.

'Christ!' His sudden agitation alarmed Sylveen. 'Don't turn round,' he said sharply.

'Who is it?' Her heart was pounding.

'Aunt Harriet is over by the door, and she's smiling at me. What are we going to do?' he wailed. 'We should have gone to the Vic after all. We knew that was safe. What if she comes over to speak to us?'

Sylveen put her glass down with an unsteady hand. 'She's never met me.'

'She might see you at Churton. Once seen, you aren't likely to be forgotten.'

'We'd better go.' Sylveen picked up her handbag from the floor.

'We'll walk out together. Get your hat and coat, but make sure she doesn't see you go upstairs. From where she's sitting, I don't think she can.'

'Now?'

'I'll have a word with her as we pass. Don't you stop. I'll tell her we're in a hurry or something. Going to the Floral Hall. Late for the show. She'll see us leave, she's facing the front door. Are you ready?'

His fear was infectious. That was Giles all over. No immediate danger, and for him it didn't exist. Panic stations at the first sign though. Sylveen told herself that Aunt Harriet didn't know her. There was no reason why she ever should. Jeremy didn't want to introduce her to his family. She hadn't liked that, and had been envious because Emily was being treated differently.

'Come on, then.' Giles was pulling out her chair for her. Positioning himself between her and Aunt Harriet. 'Hurry up with your coat. I only want a moment with her.'

They came face to face with their waiter bearing a tray aloft with one apple pie and one fruit salad. She heard

Giles swear under his breath.

'Sorry, we have to go. Suddenly realised we're late.' He took out his wallet, fished for a note. 'This will cover it.'

'I can put it on your bill, sir. You're staying in the hotel?'

'Er . . . I prefer to settle now.' Sylveen had never seen him look so flustered. He pushed the money at the waiter and took her arm. 'Aunt Harriet has to see me pay, for God's sake.'

Sylveen could no longer think straight, she could feel adrenalin whizzing round her body as she heard him say: 'Hello, Aunt Harriet. What a surprise seeing you here.'

Sylveen allowed herself one glance before she took to her heels. Two old ladies sitting bolt upright. One in a pale toque looked like Queen Mary. She was examining Giles through a lorgnette, and he was waving his arms around and talking too fast.

Emily was not too pleased to find herself working in the accounts department, although she was told her presence was very welcome because there were two typists off sick with the cold that was going round.

She hated figures, copying them seemed to reduce her to two-finger typing. She had been summoned here several times when she'd been in the typing pool, and knew what to expect.

She didn't care for the desk she'd been given at the back of the hall, where female staff sat together on the left, male on the right. She faced the raised walkway and the offices belonging to Mr Lockwood and Mr Donkin. These were fitted with glass panels through which they could look down on the hall, and see who was working and who was not. She wished herself back in the quiet backwater of the canteen office.

Alex Fraser sat four desks to her right, and she was conscious of his presence the whole time. He was a distraction. This morning particularly so; he was laughing with Norman Coates as he got out his ledgers. She remembered the old times when she'd felt close to Alex, when he'd been always available, and always a comfort. She was glad to have plenty of work. It helped to be busy in such a public office.

It was some comfort to find Giles liked it no better. He had been allotted a desk in Mr Donkin's office, and after the fracas with the canteen accounts, he did not care to be so close.

Often, he came down to perch on the corner of her desk to commiserate, and turn over the documents waiting in her in-tray.

Every day he was in, Giles insisted on buying her lunch in the dining-room, waving away any suggestion that she should pay for herself. Once, on their way down, Emily had suggested letting Sylveen know so she could come with them again. He had said: 'Better not, two's company. Three's a crowd.' Emily had blushed and not mentioned Sylveen to him again.

The other typists seemed a close clique and did not include her in their conversations. She knew they whispered about Giles and wondered what it was in her that attracted him. Emily found that unsettling too.

Everything about the Wythenshaws was unsettling. Much harder to feel at home at Churton House than in Olympia's living-room. She'd grown up with Alex and Olympia, they spelled security.

Jeremy Wythenshaw had been kind, and more approachable than she would have believed. He'd tried to put her at ease, but she'd found the first lunch with him like walking on glass. With her sense of security shattered, she felt like a ship adrift.

Giles could be like a piece of elastic. Sometimes he was at her elbow foreseeing her difficulties, smoothing everything out, but at others he didn't seem to notice her floundering. Sometimes he seemed keen to have her company and at others, indifferent. Sometimes he treated her with warmth, only to ignore her the next day. With Alex, she'd known where she was.

It was Giles's powerful physical presence that mesmerised her. Once caught by the gaze of his tawny eyes he could make her emotions boil, lift her spirits, make her feel she could overcome any difficulties, and that everything was worthwhile. Giles could set her on fire and that too was unsettling.

Every morning at nine o'clock Emily opened the drawer of her desk and took out the work she had left over from the day before. Today she found five pages of closely written figures to type, four copies to make of each. She selected the page with the least figures on it, to start.

Emily stacked carbon paper between foolscap and rolled them all into her typewriter. Around her, phones began to ring, other typewriters clattered, people walked and talked as she worked. It was harder here to concentrate. The figures were growing along the page, when Emily looked up in surprise to see Mr Lockwood, grey faced and ill, standing by her desk.

'Miss Lamb will not be coming in today, she's sick. Succumbed to the cold that's been decimating this department for a month. I'd like you to stand in for her for a few days.'

'Yes, of course.' Emily stood up, looking uncertainly at the schedule she'd been typing. Half done and impossible to take out of the machine and put it back later, because the figures would be misaligned on the copies.

'I'll bring it with me, I can finish it in a spare moment.' She was about to pick up her typewriter, when she found Alex at her elbow.

'I'll carry it up for you. It's heavy.'

'Being gallant this morning,' she said.

'I'm going past the door anyway. Got to see Donkin.

You carry the cash box and ledger for me.'

She followed him up the four steps to Miss Lamb's office, having misgivings about the change, and thinking Alex was in a strangely quirky mood.

What was the matter with her? Wasn't this what she'd been hankering for? Letters to type instead of figures and an office of her own. It was the unknown she didn't like.

Seated in front of his desk with her notebook, she found his pace of dictation pedantic and told herself she was a fool to have been nervous. He was speaking slowly enough for her to take it down in longhand. All these changes were robbing her of the confidence she'd been building up. She'd typed about half his letters on Miss Lamb's typewriter when he came out to ask: 'Do you have an aspirin with you, Miss Barr?'

'No, I'm sorry . . .'

'Would you mind going out to get some? I've got a bit of a headache.'

'Be glad to.' It seemed like freedom to be going out in the middle of the morning, she was looking on it as a treat. Her gaze was drawn to Alex's dark red head, as she crossed the hall; for once he was craning his neck instead of working. She went to his desk.

'Does your mother stock aspirin?'

'Yes,' he said. As she decided to go down to Fraser's shop on her bike, she could see his attention was hooked on something else.

'What's happening?'

'The excitement is about to start,' he murmured.

It was Friday, the day Donkin was due to run his weekly check on the incoming cash. Giles had not heeded his warning, his cheque was still in the cash box. Alex foresaw trouble for Giles and was looking forward to the outcome.

Donkin had been on the phone when Alex had taken in the cash box and ledgers; he'd left them on his desk.

Giles, reading the *Guardian* in the corner, had given him a disdainful glance.

He'd watched and waited from his desk for half an hour. Everything seemed normal in the two management offices, and he was beginning to get bored with waiting. He had become engrossed in making up the other set of books that Lockwood himself checked on Friday mornings. He saw Emily take dictation from Lockwood, and then, after a bit of typing, go out for aspirin.

Suddenly Donkin was slamming out of his office with the cash box and hurrying to Lockwood's office. Alex pulled himself up in his seat. Although the glass panels were provided so the managers might survey the clerks, from the back row of desks Alex could see the managers if he straightened up. He knew Giles's cheque was causing consternation.

Donkin, red in the face, returned to his office, to send Giles sauntering along the walkway. Through the glass panel he could see Giles speaking across the office at Lockwood's scarlet face. Miss Lamb's empty desk was screened off in the entrance, Emily had not returned. Alex felt very tempted. He snatched up the figures he had ready for Lockwood's attention, and went up to hover at Emily's desk. He reckoned he was entitled to know the outcome, and this was the only way he would.

'Yes, all right.' Giles's voice sounded exasperated. 'I did it. My father won't mind.'

'I mind,' Lockwood said acidly. 'If I am put in charge of company money, I decide what happens to it.'

'It's only twenty-five pounds.'

Alex heard Lockwood convulse in fury. 'I don't care how little it's for, that's beside the point. I have to account for the money. I must ask you to get down to your bank, so the cash can be replaced immediately.'

'I can't. Nothing in my account. That's why I did it. I needed a few pounds in a hurry.'

There was a moment of dead silence. 'Are you saying this cheque will not be honoured? Then I shall have to tell your father.'

'Yes, well, he'll pay. He always does.'

'I don't approve of that, but any money your father gives you must come from his personal account, not from this. I don't know! Taking twenty-five pounds of company money, and replacing it with a dud cheque! You must realise that's dishonest! Words fail me.'

'They don't, Mr Lockwood. You use them very adequately.'

'Get out of my office, you cheeky pup!'

Alex felt a surge of satisfaction, it had expunged his need for revenge. He gave Giles a told-you-so smile as he rushed past.

On her return, Emily was about to push open the double glass doors of the accounts hall when Giles burst through them, almost cannoning into her.

'Giles,' she called, but he was already halfway down the corridor.

She went in to find the tea trolley was inside, dispensing morning tea. She got two cups, thinking Mr Lockwood would be glad of the tea to take with his aspirin.

Alex was watching her from the doorway of Miss Lamb's little office as she went up the steps.

'You've just missed the show of the month,' he chortled softly, his brown eyes laughing, his red head thrown back. 'And I'm sorry you have, Emily, it might have put you off the mighty Giles Wythenshaw.'

'What do you mean? You're being silly,' she said, putting her own tea on her desk and tapping on Mr Lockwood's door. She pushed it open and was halfway across the floor before she saw him slumped across his desk, with his head down on his arms.

'Mr Lockwood?'

Ridiculously, her first thought was that he was sleeping

at his desk. She felt the strength ebb from her knees as she realised he was not asleep. She threw the aspirins down, the tea splashed over into the saucer.

'Mr Lockwood?' She could feel panic burgeoning within her. She turned and flew out to the walkway. 'Alex!' she screamed. 'Alex!' He came bounding back up the steps.

'What's the matter?' She couldn't speak, just jab her finger towards Mr Lockwood, but the edge of her mind was beginning to function again. She lifted the phone on Miss Lamb's desk and asked the operator to send for an ambulance.

'Is he . . .?' She went to the door but she couldn't look at the form spread-eagled across the desk.

'No,' Alex said. 'No, get the nurse.'

'I've asked for an ambulance.'

'Get the nurse!' The fear in his voice lashed her. She could feel herself shaking as she lifted the phone again. She'd forgotten Wythenshaw's employed an occupational nurse who manned a first aid post in the factory.

'She's on her way.' The operator's voice had sounded calm against the storm that raged within herself. 'I rang through to her. Ambulance is on the way too.'

'Thank you,' Emily said weakly, as the blue uniform and white apron flashed past her desk.

Somehow she'd upset the cup of tea in her panic. It was soaking into the letters she'd typed. She began mopping at them with blotting paper.

She couldn't bring herself to look into the inner office, the sounds were frightening enough. Panting, desperate breathing, gasping. The waiting was awful, it was a relief to see the ambulance men carry in a stretcher. She turned cold as she watched them bring Mr Lockwood out, a limp form under a red blanket.

Alex came out to lean against the door, white faced and shaking, but intoxicated to fever pitch with excitement.

'It was his fault, Emily! Impossible to blame anything

else. He caused a blazing row. Enough to send anybody over the top.'

Emily roused herself: 'Whose fault?'

'Giles Wythenshaw's. I heard every word! All his own stupidity.'

'What's Giles got to do with Mr Lockwood?'

'I keep telling you. He took company money, they'd just had an almighty row. He drove him to this.'

'To what? What was the matter with him?'

'They think it's his heart. Giles caused it. Now perhaps you'll see what sort of a man he is.'

'Alex! Have you taken leave of your senses? Don't be so ridiculous.'

She could see him panting, his brown eyes stared down into hers. Then he seemed to pull himself together, and went out without another word. Emily sat on alone, cold and frightened.

CHAPTER ELEVEN

Giles sighed and closed the grey cardboard box file with a thump. He hated working in the accounts department, Father couldn't have chosen a worst place in the whole factory for him. He had never found figures easy, and it wasn't in his nature to be meticulous about details.

He lifted his head just enough to see the light flashing on Donkin's spectacles; he loathed having to sit in a corner of this glasshouse of an office, at a desk inferior in size and quality. Donkin was eyeing him with studied ease, fingers steepling against his chin. Waiting for him to make the slightest slip, confident he would.

He glared back at him and then deliberately opened the newspaper he'd brought in and pretended to read. Donkin had an inflated opinion of his own worth, and because of what had happened with the canteen accounts Giles felt at a disadvantage.

He had asked him to keep that matter to himself, and so he had, but he hadn't forgotten. Every little job Donkin asked him to do was prefaced with: 'Do you think you're capable . . .?' or 'Are you up to doing . . .?'

He couldn't complain that his duties weren't adequately explained to him. He was taken through the simplest jobs two or three times before he had to do them, but he felt Donkin's self-righteous manner prevented him concentrating on anything else. His palms itched to knock the glasses off his face. Donkin had power over him, and he always managed to find fault with what he did.

Worse still, from the day Lockwood had collapsed at his desk, Donkin's manner towards him had changed for the worse. He knew Donkin blamed him for it, though any fool could see Lockwood had been ill for a long time. He had done his best to smooth that over, rushing down to the bank and getting cash because otherwise Father would have heaped blame on his head too. That hadn't been without its difficulties because his allowance wasn't due to be paid in for another week.

Giles lifted his head a little further to look through the glass and see the top of Emily's brown head below him, her fingers flying on her typewriter.

He felt at ease with Emily, he knew she wouldn't stab him in the back, but he wouldn't want to be down there with her. Overlooked by his father's bosses, who only had to lift their eyes to see who worked and who did not. They'd list his failings for Father should he ask, without a thought for the trouble he'd land in.

Giles felt he was losing hope. In the office he was fighting boredom or swallowing indignities. Increasingly, the thought of returning after lunch for a further four hours was impossible to face. He felt Father's upper hand was growing stronger, that he was being beaten into a corner. Father was more testy with him at home.

Only with Sylveen did he still feel a man. In her company he could live a bit, have fun, but he was having nightmares about Father finding out what they'd done. Sooner or later Aunt Harriet would go telling tales to him. It was draining his sense of security. Father would never forgive him. At the very least he'd throw him out of house and home. Then what would he do?

He suddenly realised Donkin was fingering his sandy moustache, leering at him in his supercilious manner. 'A busy time, the end of the month. You're going to have enough to keep you at your desk today. Do you feel capable of making out a few cheques?'

'Of course.'

'You make them out, but you aren't required to sign them.' Giles felt himself bristle with dislike; Donkin spoke down to him, as though he were an idiot.

'Only senior members of staff are authorised to sign cheques on behalf of the company, and you are not one of them.'

'Yet,' he said. 'But every dog has his day.' Donkin had better watch out when his turn came.

Donkin stood over him, his finger stabbing towards a great heap of bills. 'Settlement day. These are passed for payment. See you get the figures right. When you've got the cheques made out, you'll need letters typed to accompany them. Do you feel up to all that?'

'Yes, of course.'

'Off you go somewhere else. I'm expecting a visitor. I need a bit of privacy.'

Giles almost snorted. Instead he said: 'I'll use Lockwood's office since he isn't in.'

'Anywhere you like.'

As he humped the files out, Giles told himself he was glad to get away. Lockwood's secretary looked down her nose as he went in, she was an old cow. 'Who said you could use the manager's office?'

'Donkin suggested it. Anyway, I'm doing his work, so I might as well use his space. Settlement day.'

'You can give the letters to me when you're ready.'

'I have my own secretary,' he told her frostily. 'She will do them.'

Writing the cheques proved tedious. He was glad to get them finished and send for Emily. She brought her pad and settled in the chair facing him.

'It's no big deal, Emily. Thirty letters or so to type, but they're all much the same. Just a sentence or so enclosing our cheque in settlement of your account. Boring stuff.'

'Anything is better than typing long columns of figures.'

He pushed a pile of files across the desk to her. 'Addresses, bills and cheques in here.'

'Hadn't we better check them? Bills against the cheques?'

'Course not. I spent all morning on them. Really concentrated.'

'I check every figure I type with somebody else. I don't always get them right.' Emily's brown eyes showed she only had his welfare at heart.

'All right.'

'Here's the cheques. I'll read out the names and amounts from the bills.' Her voice went on and on. He couldn't believe it when he saw he'd written the same name on two cheques. Got the figures wrong on another.

'Don't tear it up,' she said just in time. 'There's two-pence duty on each cheque, and they're numbered. Mr Donkin will know.'

'Christ!'

'Just cross out what's wrong and alter them. Better to find out before he does.'

'I'm not cut out for this,' Giles moaned. Everything about the place made him feel an incompetent fool.

Donkin's sandy eyebrows rose at the altered cheques. 'But I'm sure our suppliers will bear with us,' he said signing them in several places. He was slowly reading through the letters, checking everything carefully when the works hooter blew. Doors banged, and the office began to empty faster than water running out of a bath.

Giles watched him anxiously, but he failed to find further faults to complain about. He was creasing the letters in exactly the right place, edging them into envelopes and licking them down.

'You can put these in the post tray now, Wythenshaw,' he said. 'They'll go first thing in the morning. Glad you could spare us your time.' He took his white mackintosh from the bentwood stand. 'Quite an achievement for you to stay till closing time.' Giles bridled, he'd worked very hard.

'Raining, is it?'

'Pouring,' Giles answered. 'Lucky you.'

'I'm prepared.' Donkin lifted a neatly furled umbrella from the stand.

Giles was edging his Riley out into Paradise Street when he saw a lone figure in a white mac hurrying towards St Paul's Road, the umbrella held in front of his face. Most of the workers had gone. The rain was coming down in rods, his windscreen wipers could barely cope. There was an enormous puddle of muddy water in the gutter. Some spark of mischief made him head his Riley into it as fast and close as he dared. He saw the tidal wave build up and race towards the white mac, but felt a spasm of disappointment as it fell well short of its target.

Then he saw the umbrella lift, and the look of pure panic on Donkin's face. The silly man thought he was about to be run down! The next second he was jerking wildly on the steering wheel, just managing to correct his course in time. He hadn't realised he was on the pavement. In the rear mirror he saw Donkin's whole body screwing with terror.

Giles laughed to himself. What had started as half-veiled antipathy between him and Donkin had in four weeks deteriorated to open warfare. He was halfway home before he realised frightening Donkin might have been a mistake. It might have been better to go on swallowing his insults. He didn't want him to seek revenge.

The next morning Donkin was frostier than ever. He heaped work on his desk with even greater sarcasm. Giles thought the lunch break would never come. When he heard the background hum of machinery jerk to a sudden stop he cheered a little. He crashed his desk drawer shut, and stood up to find Donkin's pale eyes resting on him. 'You won't be in this afternoon, will you?'

He was taken aback. There had been several afternoons when he hadn't come back, but Donkin never assumed he would not. 'Aren't you going to Woodward's?'

'Oh yes.' Giles's spirits rose further. Anything was better than coming back here. Last week, Father had asked a business acquaintance, the proprietor of a button factory, if he and two other management trainees could be shown round his premises, to extend their understanding of business methods.

Father was keen on the other two, always praising their enthusiasm, and saying they were good management material, making it quite obvious that he rated their abilities higher than his own.

'How are we going to get there?' Alexander Fraser had demanded. 'On the bus?'

Giles had taken a dislike to Fraser's red hair and hostile brown eyes since he'd caused all that trouble over the cash. 'Good lord no! I'll run us to Wallasey in my car.' He needed to show them his position was a little different from theirs, even if they were all classed as management trainees.

If anything, he liked Norman Coates even less. The bright boy from the Dell council estate. If he was as bright as Father thought, he ought to be able to do something about his appearance. His suit was dreadful and his straight hair looked as though it had been cut with secateurs. Coates sat in front with him, obviously delighted with the car ride.

'My uncle bought a second-hand Ford Popular a couple of years ago. I helped him change the oil last weekend, and next week we're going to reline the brakes.'

'Can you drive?'

'No, he doesn't let me do that, only help with repairs and maintenance.'

'I take this to the garage if anything needs doing,' Giles told them. 'Can't be bothered with anything like that.'

He led the way into the button factory and asked for Mr Woodward. Introduced them all. He could show everybody he was management material too when he put himself out. He could make the other two trail behind him looking awkward.

Mr Woodward was a rough diamond too, Giles didn't take to him. When he handed them on to a man in a brown twill coat, he was even less pleased.

'Mr Jones, my floor manager, will show you round the factory, and be able to answer all your questions on production matters,' Woodward said heartily as he sent them off on their prolonged tour.

Giles tried to converse with him, but on the factory floor the constant background noise of machinery felt loud enough to burst his eardrums. He watched metal buttons being stamped out and covered with linen. Then another line making small shirt buttons by the thousand gross. He found the similarity to what went on in their own factory too great to be anything but boring.

The greatest difference he could see was that this was a humbler business, and whereas Wythenshaw's was kept clean and freshly painted, these premises were a squalid mess. The other two trailed behind, poking their noses into everything, making the long tour even longer. Giles wished he'd taken his boat out instead of coming with them. It was a fine afternoon, it might still be worth going, the evenings were lighter now.

At last they were taken back to the quieter confines of an office, where the other two started asking complicated questions. He went to the window and stood staring out into the dirty yard. The questions moved from production to other aspects of the business.

'Yes,' Jones explained. 'We sell in bulk direct to manufacturers of shirts and underwear. We make fancy buttons to order from dress manufacturers.'

'So you have a guaranteed market for your goods before you make them?' Alex asked. Giles hovered impatiently, wishing they'd cut it short.

'Only for a proportion of our products, Mr Wythenshaw.' Giles turned round outraged, about to protest.

'This is Mr Wythenshaw,' Alex said. 'I'm Fraser.'

Giles didn't like Fraser's look of half-concealed amusement, or Norman Coates's broad grin. The man went on oblivious: 'And with the depression, orders are falling. The rest are carded and sold through retail outlets for the home dressmaker.'

It was mid-afternoon when Jones took them back to Mr Woodward's office, saying he was the best person to tell them about their distribution system.

Giles thought his boredom might be banished when he saw Woodward's daughter, a tall healthy-looking blonde. He knew her vaguely from the sailing club, and would have inveigled her into conversation if she hadn't been rushing off somewhere else. She asked her father's secretary to make them tea and biscuits, and told them he had been called away to some problem but would be back in a few minutes.

'This is a total waste of time,' he fumed, losing patience and pacing to the window. 'What can we possibly learn from this?'

'They've got good ideas on stock control,' Alex told him. 'I think ours could be improved.'

'I don't expect I'll be involved in minor matters like that. I need to look at the business as a whole.'

'Stock control is quite important.' Alex's dark eyes glared up at him. Giles had always felt an edge of rivalry in the other's manner, and it annoyed him.

'This is a tuppence ha'penny outfit,' he said

disparagingly. 'I don't know why we bother.'

'There's a lot we can learn here,' Coates said and that annoyed him more. How could he judge?

'You've only to see this,' Giles maintained. 'It's messy. Place needs cleaning up and a coat of paint. The man says himself, the depression is cutting their profit.'

'The depression is cutting everybody's profit,' Fraser said. 'The object is to learn how to keep going until times improve.'

'That's what I mean,' Giles said. 'It's easy to see he doesn't make as much as we do. The whole place looks run down.'

'Wythenshaw's doesn't make all that much,' Alex said.

Giles said impatiently: 'Of course it does, it's thriving. Look at Wythenshaw House, the running costs alone are enormous and it pays for that. Then there's . . .'

'I don't know how your father does it,' Alex told him, his eyes bristling aggressively.

'What do you mean?' Giles spat out.

'I've been collating the figures for product sales,' Alex told him. 'They aren't as high as I expected.'

'Not when you take into account the expenses,' Norman added. 'I work on that side, as you know.'

'You mean you've worked this out between you?' he demanded.

'We can't work it out.' Alex smiled. A totally aggravating self-satisfied smile. 'We see only part of the picture. We don't know what wages and salaries come to for instance, and we don't know whether the premises are rented . . .'

'They're owned outright, of course.'

'It's a private company. We work on the accounts but when the final figures are put together, they aren't shown to the likes of us.'

'But you'd like to know, wouldn't you?' Giles sneered.

'Put it down to curiosity. Just an idea to play about with.'

'Father's ploughing the profit back into the business,' he told them. He'd heard it was a sensible thing to do.

'No, he's certainly not doing that. He's not expanding.'

Giles felt a rush of fury; who was Fraser to contradict him?

'He's not renewing machinery or starting up new lines. We've come to the conclusion he's over-staffed. He's paying us now, and we're here looking round another factory instead of working for our pay.'

'Your pay is petty cash to Father.'

'Perhaps,' Alex said.

Two pairs of eyes challenged his. There was no mistaking the crusading light in them, they both believed what they were saying. They weren't trying to put him down.

'The jewellery factory isn't making enough to allow him to do all he does. Your father's too generous. He has too big a staff, which he pays over the odds. He puts too much subsidy into staff emoluments. Pensions are too generous, training schemes are too generous. And in addition he's set up Wythenshaw House as a home for elderly pensioners who can no longer look after themselves. It can't be done on what the factory earns.'

'And all in the worst depression the country has ever known,' Coates added.

'Don't be silly, it is being done,' he pointed out. 'Everything is working well, the workforce is happy.'

'The workforce doesn't realise just how lucky it is, but if the business can't afford it, it will eventually close and everybody will lose their jobs.'

'Nonsense,' Giles said, but he felt a sense of shock.

'Have you ever seen any trading figures?' Alex asked, pushing his red head close to his. Giles took a step back. He had not.

'A balance sheet or profit and loss figures?' Norman was pressing, his comic hair sticking out all over the place making him look like a guy.

'No.'

'Surely you must have noticed and wondered?' Giles's lips straightened, he had not.

'Why don't you ask your father? He'll show the figures to you. Then unlike us you wouldn't have to surmise.'

'I will,' he said, then realised he'd shown that he'd given credence to their ridiculous idea. 'Just to prove you're wrong.'

'We reckon your father is earning his income elsewhere. Doesn't he have a posh shop in Liverpool?'

'Yes.' Giles pondered for a moment. Could they be right? It was a thought. Grandfather was very proud of his shop and his family had lived on its income for years. It could be that Father was keeping him away from the real money-earner. Perhaps he should ask him if he might work there? Couldn't be worse than accounts, and it would get him away from Donkin.

Jeremy liked to move about his factory, and go where he was not expected, but he didn't make a habit of it. To be permanently on the prowl would defeat his object. He liked to keep his eyes and ears open and see for himself what was going on.

The accounts office buzzed with activity, he had paused at the door for a moment behind the rows of desks, and everyone was working, apart from two clerks on the front row who were whispering together. Their heads jerked back over their ledgers as soon as they saw him.

He had no trouble picking out the chocolate-brown head bent over the typewriter.

'Hello, Emily,' he said, as she stopped typing abruptly. This was the first time he had stopped to speak to her since she had had lunch at Churton. 'Are you settling in the new job?'

'Yes, thank you, Mr Wythenshaw.' She looked flustered. 'Yes, I'm getting used to it.'

'Good. Is Giles in the office?' He watched the scarlet tide run up her cheeks.

'Not at the moment.' With sinking heart, Emily watched him go up the steps and along to Donkin's office. He would find out Giles had not come to work this morning, that he habitually came in late and left early, and was spending a lot less time than he should at his desk.

She watched Jeremy rap on Donkin's door. Through the glass panels, she saw Donkin, in neat grey suit and gold-rimmed spectacles, leap to his feet to greet him.

'Good morning. Would you like a seat, sir?'

'I have good news of Lockwood,' Jeremy said. 'He's out of hospital.'

'Good, I'll have a collection made for him round the office.'

'I arranged straight away for the firm to send fruit to the hospital and flowers to his wife. He's sent in a note from his doctor. Seems he did have a mild heart attack.' Jeremy was surveying the accounts hall from his vantage point, noting that Emily's fingers were flying again on the keyboard. 'I've been thinking,' he said. 'Lockwood has less than a year to go to retirement. Probably wiser to retire him now on health grounds.' He sat back and waited.

Donkin asked: 'Who will take his place, sir?'

'You are the most experienced man.' Hard to believe, looking at him like this. He looked young for his thirty-five years, despite his bookish glasses and sandy hair. 'I would like you to take charge of accounts.'

'Yes, thank you, sir. Immediately?'

'Yes. Your remuneration will be increased by two

hundred and fifty pounds per annum from the beginning of this month.'

'That's very generous. Thank you.'

'Now, who are we to promote to internal audit?'

'Coates has worked with me for nearly a year, he's very competent. I know he could do it.'

'Coates it is, then.'

Donkin said: 'He'll need an energetic person to help him, there's a lot to see to. Someone keen and reliable.'

'I was wondering, do you think my son Giles would be a suitable person? I'm afraid he'd not like working under young Coates, though.' He looked at Donkin whose mouth opened and then closed without saying anything.

Jeremy went on: 'I'd like Giles to have a job with definite responsibilities. A year or so in internal audit would teach him all he needs to know about the firm's finances.'

He saw the flush run up Donkin's cheeks. 'Do you mind if I speak frankly, sir?'

Jeremy had an empty feeling in his stomach. He said quietly: 'I want you to.'

'Well, it isn't easy to teach Giles anything. He doesn't want to learn, and he certainly doesn't want to work.' Jeremy sank back into the chair.

'I find him rude. No ordinary employee would get away with what he does. In fact he deliberately baits me.'

'Go on.' Jeremy felt a sinking of despair. What was he going to do with Giles?

'Very rarely does he put in a full day. The day before yesterday, he came in mid-morning and stayed till closing time, but that's unusual. He even did a little work. Made out the end-of-the-month cheques.'

'He can do it if he wants to?'

'Yes, with the help of Emily Barr. But today, he hasn't come in at all.'

'And Emily Barr? How do you find her?'

'A competent shorthand typist. Hard working, conscientious. A nice girl, but she covers for him.'

'What do you mean, covers?'

'Does his work for him. He's allotted a job. It comes in, and then later it transpires the girl has done it for him.'

Jeremy's heart sank further as he heard what had happened about the canteen accounts. He had believed Giles was settling down, but it seemed he was wrong.

'In fact, sir, I would be happier if you could find a slot for him somewhere else. He's a bad influence on the young clerks. They see him getting away with murder.'

Jeremy felt angry, he was doing his best for Giles, but he was making no effort. He despised his son's idle ways. He didn't want to make anything of himself or his inheritance, he wanted to be out enjoying himself. Jeremy could no longer pretend he'd ever run the factory. He wished he'd get off his back, join the Army, go somewhere else.

It took him a moment to bring his thoughts back to the matter in hand. 'Who else? Can you suggest anyone working in the department now?'

'There's Alexander Fraser. A year or two in internal audit would give him a good background for administration later on. Otherwise, we could advertise for an accountant.'

Jeremy went back to the glass panel overlooking the hall. Alexander Fraser's dark red head was bent over a file. He liked his air of eagerness, his willingness to work hard. He ought to be given every chance to further his career and make a decent living. The lad was worth ten of Giles. He was toying with the idea of making him his personal assistant.

'Alexander Fraser? I'm thinking of something else for him.' He had deferred the decision because he knew it would upset Giles, and it would make Fraser look like the heir apparent. On the other hand, he had to have somebody capable of running the business.

'Yes, let Fraser do it, but only for a few months. We'll reconsider later.' There was the other problem, that he wanted no past scandal to surface now. He wanted nothing to prevent him getting his knighthood.

As the bus turned into Heswall Bus Station, Sylveen stood up, eager to be away about her business. This morning Jeremy had called her into his office and given her a key to the cottage. She wouldn't be able to move in for a few more weeks because he had arranged for work to be done.

'Might as well get the place fixed up properly while we're at it,' he'd said. 'Needs quite a lot doing, a new bathroom for a start. The vegetable garden needs turfing over, and the whole place needs painting and decorating.'

Sylveen had hugged the news to herself all morning, and since it was Saturday, she'd decided to come and see it again. She needed to think about colour schemes.

It was a warm sunny afternoon, people were walking about in summery clothes for the first time this year, although July was almost here. Sylveen felt reassured, all would be well.

As she walked down from the upper village, she could see the tide was in. Being in Heswall was almost like being on holiday. The more she saw of it, the better she liked it. Her way took her through the lower village, past the sandstone church then down a lane towards the shore.

'Won't you find it too quiet?' Jeremy had asked. 'I would have thought on the bus route, near the shops in the upper village.'

But she had set her heart on the cottage. She'd liked it when she'd first seen it advertised for sale. From the outside it was very pretty. White-washed under a blue slate roof with a tiny garden in front, entered by a little wicket gate. Behind was a larger garden and a recent owner had added a garage, which was reached from an adjacent lane.

'A discreet arrangement.' Jeremy had smiled. 'Your neighbours will never notice if I put my car in there, and come in the back way.'

'Does it matter if they do?'

'No,' he'd said, but she had the feeling that he would prefer them not to know. She pushed open the wicket gate and went up the path. She didn't need to use her key, the front door was open and the sound of hammering came from inside.

Jeremy had said the front of the cottage had not been changed much since it had been built about 1750. Sylveen stepped through the front door into what had been the living-room, but she would use it as a dining-room because another larger sitting-room had been built on behind.

'Sympathetically done.' Jeremy had approved. There were low ceilings and open beams everywhere. A lovely old fireplace.

Sylveen followed the sound of hammering. A new Aga was being fitted in the kitchen to provide heating and hot water. The workman told her he had more plumbing to do upstairs for the new bathroom. She felt the first thrill of ownership. Funny, if Giles had agreed to marry her, it would have belonged to them both. This way, it was all hers.

She was making her own plans. She would not tell her parents anything until she was able to move. Marriage was the only outcome they would be happy with.

'You'll be a kept woman.' She could hear her mother's voice condemning her now. Or would she say scarlet woman?

'Why doesn't he marry you? Is he ashamed of you or something?'

Sylveen would have preferred marriage. She'd made herself say so to Jeremy, but he'd laughed and said living in sin was more exciting. She couldn't press him, he was being very generous.

It really would have been one in the eye for Miss Simpson and Miss Lewis if she could have announced she was marrying Jeremy. As it was, she had to keep her mouth shut about everything.

'But I'll be kept at a higher standard than Dad keeps you,' she would say to her mother, and it would be true.

Jeremy had opened an account for her in a Heswall bank. She would have more money than her mother had to run her house. There would be no need to scrimp and save.

'You must stop working soon,' Jeremy told her. 'Mustn't do too much and run yourself down.' But she was feeling better than she had during the first months. She would wait till the cottage was complete and she could leave home too.

Already he was talking of hiring a nurse by the month to move in and look after her when the baby was due. Marriage would have been better, but having this baby would be luxurious compared with last time.

Giles admitted it had given him a jolt to have Aunt Harriet catch him with Sylveen at the Grand. It had ruined the whole weekend, leaving him jumpy and irritable. His nerves hadn't settled down since.

Sooner or later Harriet would tell Father, because she had nothing else to talk about. Only the fact that Father was keeping Sylveen hidden too, had saved him. He felt it had been a near thing.

'Why don't you ask your girlfriend to Sunday lunch again?' his father asked one morning.

'Is Aunt Harriet coming?'

'Yes.' Giles didn't want to be present if Aunt Harriet mentioned the Grand, and it wouldn't do to have Emily there.

'I won't, then. You know what Harriet's like, I think she put the fear of God into Emily. If it's a nice day I might take her out in my boat. Shall I bring her for supper afterwards?'

'Up to you.'

'I will, then.' It would be a good thing for Father to see them together. After all, if he was inviting Emily out, it would hardly look as if he was interested in Sylveen.

Giles felt relaxed as he drove Emily to Churton. The afternoon had gone well. Emily had never been out in a small boat, but she'd taken an interest and tried to help. They'd had a good laugh.

'Can I tidy myself up?' Emily asked as they crossed the hall. 'I feel so windblown.' He showed her to a bathroom.

'Can you find your way down to the library?' He pointed it out. 'Father usually has a drink there before supper.'

He went in. The *Sunday Times* rattled down. 'Haven't seen much of you this week,' his father said. 'I want to talk to you.'

That alone caused Giles's bile to rise. 'Not now. I've brought Emily.' His father stared at him belligerently as he helped himself to a drink.

'How's Aunt Harriet?'

'Surprised you're interested. She asked if you had a new girlfriend. Saw you eating out in New Brighton with someone different.'

Giles turned away to hide his face. 'It was Emily. Not a new girlfriend.'

'She said a blonde.'

'You know Aunt Harriet, blind as a bat. Not a blonde, it was Emily.' He was glad to get this over without Emily being present to deny it. It made him jumpy to know she was so close.

'About Emily.' Jeremy folded his newspaper. 'I had a word with Donkin about you both on Friday, and I've been trying to catch you ever since.'

Giles felt his heart lurch, but he told himself it could be

worse. The problem of Sylveen had receded. He must try and ride this. He'd done it before.

'Have you deliberately kept out of my way?'

'Of course not, Father. I've brought Emily to have supper with us.'

'It's now Sunday evening, and you haven't appeared at any meal since Thursday. You never come home in the evenings now.'

The door opened and Emily came in. Giles knew he was off the hook for the moment. Father would never discuss personal matters in front of a guest. He meant to keep Emily with them as long as possible.

Jeremy cleared his throat, he would have to swallow his impatience with Giles for a little longer.

'Get Emily a drink,' he bade him. She came to sit opposite, crossed her hands in her lap. An odd waif in a creased cotton dress, but she had her wits about her. He should have realised, her attraction for Giles was that she protected him.

Jeremy knew he was always reaching out to touch Sylveen, his eyes never left her when she was close. Giles was giving no sign he wanted to reach out to Emily. He doubted Giles knew what it was to love another, Giles loved himself. He was using Emily as a shield.

Emily was telling him about Giles's boat, her little elfin smile enthusiastic about their afternoon. Her brown eyes following Giles about the room. Their fingers touched as he gave her the glass, but it was because she wanted them to. He hoped it would be enough for Emily.

He almost rushed them to the dining-room for the cold roast beef and salad to which they helped themselves from the sideboard. He watched Emily eating the apple pie that followed, looking out of the long windows at the last of the evening sun disappearing from the gardens.

Higgins was on duty alone this Sunday night. He brought them coffee and poured it out.

'Will that be all?' he asked. Usually Jeremy dismissed all staff on Sunday night.

'No,' Jeremy said. 'I'd be glad if you'd drive our guest home.' He saw Giles straighten up in alarm.

'I'll take Emily home,' he said. 'I was going to show her round the garden first.'

'Some other time,' Jeremy said smoothly. 'I'm sure you'll forgive me, my dear, but I'd like to have a few words with Giles. Tonight seems the only opportunity.'

Emily was on her feet as soon as she'd finished her coffee. Giles took her to the door. Jeremy followed, just to make sure Giles didn't think of something more urgent he had to do. They both watched the back of the Rolls disappear down the drive.

'Right, come in the library and let's have this talk.' Giles hovered, unwilling to sit down. 'Sit,' Jeremy snapped, pointing to the chair opposite. Giles collapsed into it.

'I am disappointed. I hoped you were taking an interest in work. Now I hear that little girl does most of the jobs assigned to you.'

'Not any more,' Giles said. 'Donkin keeps us apart.'

'Very wise too. If you're ever going to learn anything.' How many times had he said all this before? 'What are you going to do with your life? Waste it idling around?'

'I can't work in that factory.'

'What can you do, then? What would you like to do?'

'I don't know.'

'That's your trouble. What about a one-way ticket to Australia?' He wanted Giles off his back. 'Would you like to work your way round the world? Enjoy travel and adventure?'

'How would I get back?'

'That would be up to you. Work your way round.'

'Be reasonable, Father.'

'Well, what?'

'Could I try the shop in Liverpool?'

Jeremy was surprised, he almost snapped a refusal. There was too much he needed to hide there, but Giles did not have an enquiring mind. He'd be none the wiser if he worked there for ever. On past showing, he'd only last a month or so.

'It's very specialised. There's a lot to learn about the stock.'

'I'd be interested, Father.'

'It's taken me years to learn what to buy.'

'The difference between fakes and the genuine article, you mean?'

'Yes, but genuine antiques come in all qualities. Superb, good, average and indifferent, that's often harder. There's more to learn, and a smaller empire to manage at the end. You'd be better in the factory.'

'I hate all the industrialisation, all the noise and the shoddy stuff.'

'All right,' Jeremy said, deciding to capitulate. 'But only so long as you remember the customer is always right, and he won't necessarily treat a shop assistant as his social equal.'

'Yes, Father.'

'And you stay behind the counter all the time the shop is open. No sneaking off.'

He saw Giles's face drop at that, but he said quite cheerfully: 'Yes, Father.'

'We'll give it a trial. I'll take you with me on Tuesday. Introduce you to the staff. You'll have to travel by train from West Kirby. That means you'll have to get up earlier.'

'Can Emily come with me?'

'No, she can't. She's not a shop assistant.'

'She could still be my secretary.'

'Don't be a fool, Giles. You'll be working as a sales assistant. There's nothing else you could do. Give up pretending you need a secretary.'

'She helps me. I like her company.'

'Then you'd better marry her.' Even as he said it, Jeremy realised how he would benefit. It would get Giles off his back. 'You need a nursemaid, that way you'd get one.'

CHAPTER TWELVE

Giles hummed to himself as he drove the Riley to Heswall. He enjoyed driving, and it was a novelty since he travelled to Liverpool by train. A road tunnel was planned, and it couldn't come soon enough for him. In the meantime he used his car only to get from home to the station and back.

He found he quite enjoyed the shop. Mr King and Miss Roberts were polite, Father came only twice a week. The aura of luxury suited him better than the factory. Of course the hours were long and it was hard on his feet, but on the whole he found it more congenial.

The beautiful silver and antique ornaments almost sold themselves, and everything was priced. Unusual items carried a note of when and where they had been made, and what they were for. Giles felt he had a flair for selling, but as for understanding why one ornament cost a fortune while something similar was relatively inexpensive, he never would.

His father was expected back from Paris tomorrow. Giles always felt happier when he was away, but there was still tonight. His sixth and last night with Sylveen for a month.

The cottage was a huge success. Sylveen loved it. His father had persuaded her to give up work, and she was thoroughly enjoying her new life. She cooked for him;

usually dinner was almost ready when he got there. He liked the privacy, and they both felt much safer than in a hotel.

There was the added advantage that he didn't have to find money for hotel and restaurant bills, so there was less risk of Father finding out that way. Giles felt well pleased with the way things were turning out.

As he was approaching Heswall, he decided he'd buy flowers for Sylveen, she'd given him a marvellous time this week. He pulled in opposite a flower shop and bought an enormous bunch of gladioli and carnations. They filled his car with a sharp fresh scent, and because he was thinking how pleased she would be with them, he missed the lane leading to the back of her cottage.

Never mind, he was telling himself, when his reflexes made him stamp on the brakes. His tyres screamed in skidding grit and the bouquet jerked from the front seat to the floor.

No, don't stop, was his panicked reaction.

His father's Rolls was parked at the wicket gate, with Higgins waiting draped over the wheel. He hammered the accelerator and shot past the Rolls and the front of the cottage.

He dared not look in the rear mirror. He was scorching down the narrow lane, barely able to hold the car on the bends. Had Higgins recognised him? His heart thumped, his forehead was damp with sweat, the strength was ebbing from his knees.

He slowed, not knowing whether it was possible to get back to the main road without having to pass Higgins again. Higgins could recognise his car at a hundred yards, but perhaps his eyes had been closed, sometimes he did doze off. He'd been a fool to brake so violently, he'd made more noise than sounding his horn. Higgins would have had to be sound asleep not to have his attention jolted to the Riley. He wondered how long he'd been waiting.

Father had come home a day early. God, that had been a close thing! He began to think he could reach the main road by a different route. He didn't care where he was heading, so long as he put distance between him and the Rolls. He found himself on Parkgate promenade, the tide was out. He pulled in to look at the mud. His hands were damp with sweat.

Sylveen would be cooking a meal for two. Often the dining-table was set before he arrived. Father would have to pass the table on his way in. He had left his shaving tackle in her bathroom, and a case with clothes in her bedroom. Had Father telephoned before he'd gone there? If he hadn't they could already be up the chute.

Giles could see his fingers shaking as he rested his hand on the steering wheel. Thank God he hadn't driven his car straight into her garage and gone bounding in with his flowers. That was what he usually did, what he had meant to do. He would not have seen the Rolls from the back lane.

If Sylveen had managed to cover his traces so far, she must be going through purgatory now, expecting him to do exactly that. What miracle had stopped him? And why had they felt safe?

Giles sat shaking and worrying for half an hour. He felt sick, he was afraid he was about to be revealed as the father of Sylveen's unborn child. He could see a public telephone kiosk, but dared not ring her in case his father was still there. It would be an added hazard if she was managing to cover his traces.

He would look in the garage at home first. If Father's cars were both there, he would risk it. He had to find out what was happening.

Sylveen said the cottage was hers. The deeds had her name on them and were lodged in her bank, but if Father learned how he had been tricked into providing it, they each risked losing the allowance he was paying them.

Giles tried to work out how he could safeguard their position. They should have been much more careful.

The sharp fresh scent of flowers filled his car. He picked them up, only one gladioli stem was broken. He pulled it out, and shook the dust from the rest, they still looked good. He would give them to Emily.

He hadn't seen her for the five weeks he had been working at the shop. He would ask her to lunch next Sunday. Let Father see them together again. To have a different girlfriend was the best insurance he could think of. He could trust Emily, and his father had taken to her.

'You'd better marry her,' he'd said. If they got engaged, Father would not believe he was interested in Sylveen.

Giles put the Riley into gear and headed towards Paradise Parade. The lights were on in the chip shop though it wasn't really dark. The door was open, the most wonderful scent of crisping chips reminding him he had had no dinner. His stomach rumbled as he went inside.

An old crone turned round from the fryer to serve him. Her old-fashioned straw hat decorated with cherries held his gaze, it looked out of place. He guessed she was Emily's grandmother as he asked for fish, chips and peas. He was looking round for Emily, taking in the sheets of newspaper carefully torn in half for wrapping, the tables in the alcove.

'Do you want them on a plate?' The old woman was staring at him with rheumy eyes.

'What?'

'Are you going to eat them in?' The cherries slid across the brim as she nodded towards the tables. Understanding came.

'Yes.' He sat himself down. Emily said she always served in the shop but she wasn't here. A plump man with a thatch of grey hair was serving the only other customer. Giles watched him, deciding he must be her father. He ought to tell them who he was.

The plate slid in front of him. Luscious crunchy batter round flaking fish. Saliva filled his mouth. The old woman hovered. 'Do you want tea?'

'Do you have tea here?'

'Course, penny a cup. And bread and butter.'

'I'll have a cup of tea please. Are you Emily's grandmother?'

'I am.' She was staring at him as though he'd come from another planet. The fish was melting on his tongue.

The man had moved closer, to listen, but more customers were coming in. She wiped her hands down her floral pinafore and went behind the counter to help serve them. When the shop emptied again, she brought his tea over and he asked: 'Is Emily in?'

'Do you know her?' A strand of white hair hung down below her hat.

'Yes. Tell her Giles is asking for her.' He was beginning to feel better with food inside him.

A moment later, Emily was standing in the doorway, her brown eyes saucer-wide in her puckish face. She looked almost as untidy as the rest of her family with her hair scraped up under a turban, but the sight of her brought relief flooding through him.

'Hello, Giles.' She smiled.

As the evening rush slackened, Charlie had sent Emily to rekindle the living-room fire. She was bringing in another bucket of coal and thinking of all the changes that had taken place recently at work.

She couldn't get over Sylveen leaving like that, nor the reason she'd whispered and told her to keep to herself! Sylveen had telephoned her at work today and invited her to tea this Sunday. Emily was looking forward to seeing her cottage.

About the time Sylveen left, Giles had told her he was being transferred to the Liverpool shop. The typing-pool girls were asking continually how he was getting on, but she'd heard nothing from him. She found that very hurtful, but now she didn't expect to, not after all this time.

He had built up her expectations. Seeming to like her company, taking her home to meet his family and telling them all she was his girlfriend. He'd paid for her lunches at work too, sat on her desk and talked. She couldn't get him out of her mind. His tawny eyes laughed up at her from the columns of figures she typed. She was so sure Giles had felt the same.

'Turned your head,' Gran said indignantly when she told her. She'd had to because she kept asking about him.

The week after he went, she expected him to contact her at work, or write or something. She found herself looking for his car as she went through Wythenshaw's gates. Expecting to see him in the corridors. She couldn't believe she'd hear no more of him, but as time went on, it seemed more likely.

She told herself angrily, she should have telephoned him at Churton while his father was away. She'd done it many times when they worked in the canteen. Now after five weeks it was too late. It was clear he wanted no more to do with her. Emily had decided she must accept things as they were.

She was putting more coal on the fire when Gran's head came round the living-room door. 'He's here,' she hissed. 'A posh feller's asking for you. It's him I'm sure.' Emily leapt to her feet, the adrenalin zinging round her body, this wasn't how she'd imagined he'd contact her. 'Here, let me do that, you go and talk to him.' Emily shot into the shop forgetting what a scarecrow she looked. It took Giles's tawny eyes rising to her turban to remind her.

He was the only customer sitting at the tables. 'I came to see if you'd come out for an hour. Haven't seen you for a long time, Emily.' His smile was captivating; after a moment he added: 'Have you had supper?'

'Not yet.'

'I shouldn't have done this,' his fork waved at his plate, he was only part way through his meal. 'I could have taken you somewhere for a meal.'

'Where else could we go at this hour?' Gran was attending to the pan of mince cooking on the stove in the back, but there wasn't time for that now. She put some chips on a plate for herself and slid into the chair opposite him, aware that her father was eyeing them and hovering closer, trying to hear what they said. There were fewer customers now, but each one stared at them while they waited for their chips to be wrapped.

Emily ate quickly. 'I'll have to change. Can't go out like this.'

'I'll wait,' he said, but she darted behind the counter for the huge aluminium tea pot to refill his cup.

'Bring it with you,' she told him, wanting to get him out of the shop. 'Come and say hello to Gran.'

As he followed her into the living-room, she was aware how dark and cramped and shabby it must appear to him. 'Won't be a minute,' she said.

As she shot upstairs, she heard him say to Gran: 'I've missed Emily. Haven't seen her since I started my new job in Liverpool. Couldn't stay away any longer.'

She had to make herself presentable. She reached for Sylveen's kilt and white blouse. Combed out her hair, put on lipstick. Draped her black cardigan round her shoulders; she would manage without a coat, it was warmer now.

'Don't be late, Emily.' Gran's voice, with its geriatric waver, followed them through the shop. It was just closing.

'You heard what your gran said,' Charlie grunted as he locked up behind them. Emily felt uncomfortable because she hadn't introduced him.

'I'll bring her back in good time,' Giles answered. 'Good night.'

Emily watched as Giles opened the car door for her. 'What lovely flowers.' They filled the front seat, the whole car was redolent with their scent.

'They're for you.'

'I've never had flowers like this, thank you.' She gathered them up in her arms. 'Perhaps I should take them in, put them in water first?'

'No, they won't hurt for an hour or so, get in.' She held them on her knee, burying her face in their sharp fragrance. He got in beside her.

'I've been so tied up with my new job, Emily. Can't believe it's five whole weeks. I should have been in touch.'

'It doesn't matter.' She smiled at him. 'Not now.'

'You should have phoned. It was always your job to remind me. I need reminding. I need you too.'

Emily clutched the flowers more tightly. 'I missed you,' she whispered.

He stopped the car near Bond's boat yard. 'Let's walk, it's a lovely night.'

Emily got out still clutching her bouquet. He opened the rear door. 'Push it on the seat,' he told her.

'Come on.' He tucked her arm through his. 'What have you been doing all this time?'

'I'm still in accounts.'

'I meant in your spare time?'

'Nothing.' Emily pulled her cardigan closer. Mostly she'd mooned about thinking of him, but she couldn't tell him that. They strolled along the almost deserted Rock Ferry Esplanade. The night seemed too perfect to be real.

It was full tide. Dark waves were splashing into lacy foam on the rocks below. The moon was full and high in a sky from which daylight hadn't quite gone. It cast a faint glow on the surging tide. Stars were just coming out, not yet bright enough to shine against the pale sky.

Emily felt a ball of excitement building inside her, the night air felt balmy against her cheek. She sensed Giles had brought her here for some purpose, and was almost certain he meant to kiss her. She looked up at him, tall beside her, his shoulders broad against the sky, his chin held high.

'Emily, I want you to marry me,' he said.

She stopped, feeling fluttery inside, yet puzzled. It was all too sudden. From being neglected for five weeks, to being proposed to within the hour. She stared at him in disbelief. He hadn't even touched her, let alone kiss . . . But his arms were going round her now. His lips were warm on hers.

'Bit sudden . . .' she was starting.

'I know, and you must forgive my being clumsy. I've never done this before. Emily, say we can be engaged at the very least.' He was clinging to her. 'I love you.'

She pulled him tighter, telling herself not to be silly. Wasn't this what she wanted? Hadn't she thought it couldn't happen except in her wildest dreams? She relaxed, as Giles began raining kisses on her face. When next she looked up, the sky was black velvet with thousands of glittering stars.

'The whole sky's lit up for us,' she laughed. 'In celebration.' The full moon sent a band of golden light across the waves. It shimmered and sparkled almost to the Liverpool bank.

'Like a path into the future,' Emily breathed. 'Beckoning us on. A golden future.'

'Or the primrose path to Hell,' Giles said. 'Let's go to the Royal Rock and have a glass of champagne.'

She agreed, but was nervous about what Gran would say. Surely it couldn't be wrong to have champagne when they'd just got engaged? It was what everybody did in films.

When he was taking her back to Paradise Parade an hour or so later, Giles said: 'Come for lunch on Sunday. We must tell the family.'

'Sunday? I've been invited out to tea on Sunday.'

'You can go on afterwards. I'll drive you.'

'Won't have much appetite for it after lunch at your house.'

'We've got to make it official, Emily. Where's your tea party?'

'Do you remember Sylveen?' Emily thought she felt him stiffen.

'Yes.' His manner was suddenly abrupt.

'She's asked me over to see her new house in Heswall.' Emily was stiffening too, remembering what Sylveen had told her. Giles would be half-brother to her baby. She wondered if he knew.

'I'll drive you there,' was all he said, so she decided he did not. She wondered if he would mind, and was glad she hadn't let it drop by accident. His father must explain these matters to him.

When Emily crept through the yard hugging her bouquet of flowers, the ground floor was in darkness though Gran's light was still on in her bedroom.

In the back kitchen she looked for vases large enough to take the long-stemmed gladioli. They had nothing suitable, so she filled the washing-up bowl with cold water and used that, leaning the flowers against the taps.

She found two small vases, and cut down some of the carnations and the stephanotis. She needed to take some of the flowers up to her room, as proof she wasn't dreaming. She would take a few up to Gran too. The flowers and her face told Gran everything. Except how it had happened so suddenly.

'He said he suddenly realised how much he'd missed me,' she said dreamily. 'Do you think I should, Gran? Marry him?'

'You'd be a fool not to,' Gran said robustly. 'You don't want to spend the rest of your life in a fish and chip shop, do you? Why do you ask?'

'I don't know.' Emily knew she had reservations, but it wasn't easy to put them into words. She loved Giles, and he had said he loved her, but she didn't feel his love. It wasn't clearly there for her to hold on to.

She wished she'd had more experience. All she had to base her instincts on, was her one and only affair with Alex Fraser. Then, she'd been very sure of what Alex felt. But that had not lasted. She'd been wrong about Alex. Perhaps Giles felt more than she realised.

'Think of it,' Gran said. 'Marrying him you could afford anything. Anyway, I think he's a lovely lad.'

'You do?'

'Handsome too. I think you're very lucky to have this chance.'

'Yes, I am,' Emily said, making up her mind not to let it trouble her. Hugging her little vase of carnations she ran up to her room and got ready for bed.

Giles did not feel any safer as he drove home. All evening he'd felt poised over a huge chasm. He knew what he'd arranged with Emily would not save him if Father had discovered his pyjamas in Sylveen's bed.

He parked his car at the foot of Churton's steps. Only the lights which were kept on all night still burned. There was only one safe way he could find out whether Father was asleep in his bed, or whether he was still with Sylveen.

Keeping to the shadows and the grass verges Giles went round the back, into another courtyard of outbuildings. Several years ago, the old stables had been opened up inside to take cars. It took him only a moment to find the Alvis was alone.

So Father must still be with Sylveen. He tried to make up his mind whether that was a good sign or a bad. Since he had taken Higgins with him, it must mean he did not intend to stay all night.

Giles knew he had longer to wait. He went up to his

room, which was at the back of the house, well away from his father's quarters. He left the doors open so he could hear. Took a long hot bath, and got ready for bed. It was one o'clock when he heard his father coming upstairs. He held his breath, listening for his step, half expecting to see him coming along the corridor.

It didn't happen, Father went to his own room and closed the door softly. That had to be a good sign, though Father could be a cold fish. He could fulminate for days before he erupted in temper. Giles wished he knew what had happened.

Now he knew Sylveen was alone, but the telephone at Churton was in the hall and the only extension in Father's bedroom.

He dared not use it. Giles understood the extension made quite definite sounds when the hall phone was picked up. He couldn't risk Father lifting it and hearing him speak to Sylveen.

He pulled on his clothes again and crept down to his car. The nearest public phone box was only a mile down the road, but once the car was moving, it seemed silly not to go to see Sylveen.

Nothing moved on the road. Almost every house was in darkness. It was a beautiful night, with plenty of light from the moon and stars. He pulled up at the wicket gate, the cottage was in darkness.

Surely she would not be able to sleep after what had happened? He tapped softly on the door. An owl hooted somewhere close. He tapped louder.

'Who is it?' Fear sharpened Sylveen's voice.

'Giles. Just me, love.' She was drawing the heavy bolts, and then the old door creaked open. She fell into his arms, sobbing with relief.

'Giles, it was awful. I've never been so frightened in my life.' He pulled her close. She was wearing nothing but a thin nightgown and a wrap with swansdown. It was cold now, bed was the only possible place for them. He half pushed half carried her into the bedroom, wriggling out of his own clothes. Pulling the coverlets over them both. Hugging her close.

'Did you get any warning?'

'Yes, he phoned. Said he'd brought a little gift for me, and he was going to drop it in. I'd put a roast in the oven and set the table for us. The whole place was reeking of roast lamb.

'I had to ask him if he'd had dinner, and thank goodness he said no. I invited him to eat with me. It was the only way it wouldn't look suspicious.' Sylveen was still shaking.

'I couldn't think straight. I went round in circles snatching up everything that belonged to you. I found a pair of your shoes in the kitchen, seconds before he arrived. I was panic-stricken. I'm sure he thought me very strange.'

'So everything's all right?'

'No, Giles, I can't live like this. I rang the shop, but you'd all gone. I even rang Churton, after allowing time for him to start. I panicked when you weren't there. When your housekeeper asked if I wanted to leave a message, I put the phone down.

'The worst part was expecting you to walk in through the back every minute. I can't cope with this sort of thing,' Sylveen sobbed.

'You have coped with it, Sylveen. I think we're in the clear.'

'No, tell him about us, Giles. It's like living on a razor's edge. This cottage is in my name. He can't take it back. With a house and a car, we can manage.'

'We can't tell him, for God's sake. He'll cut me off without a penny. He's hardly likely to feel any happier about you, when you've just got a house out of him. What'll we live on?'

'I don't like doing it to Jeremy,' she said. 'He's such an upright person. I like him.'

'Too late to worry about that,' he said, cuddling her close. Giles felt relief, he was able to think of other things. He kissed her.

Sylveen dragged her lips away. 'I almost choked on the lamb. Couldn't swallow it. I locked the back door, so you couldn't breeze in shouting "Hello, darling", as you usually do. I was afraid you wouldn't know he was with me.'

'Locking it would have warned me, love.'

'But from the sitting-room, he would have seen you come up the garden path. I couldn't draw the curtains until it began to get dark.'

'It's all right, Sylveen. Relax, we've got away with it. Somebody up there was looking after me when I missed the back lane turn off.'

'I was afraid you'd hammer on the back door,' she shuddered. 'Or worse, come to the window.'

'We'll be more careful next time.'

'I don't want a next time. I couldn't go through anything like that again.'

'You won't have to, love.' He kissed her again, but her response was slow in coming. It had shaken Sylveen to the roots. He really had to work at her but, once soothed, nothing could hold back their passion.

Giles was driving to the station the next morning when he realised he hadn't told her he'd proposed to Emily. He hadn't wanted to tell her last night when she was already upset. Sylveen wasn't going to like it, she was keen to marry him herself.

Sitting beside Giles in the Riley, Emily was not dreading having lunch at Churton this time. Now that she had been before, she knew what to expect. She knew his father would be welcoming, his grandfather very polite. This she told herself was going to be her life from now on.

She had been saving up for a new dress, and decided she had to have it for this occasion. As soon as she saw it swinging on its hanger in Ethel's hand, she knew it was just what she wanted. It came with one of the very fashionable shoulder capes.

She was smoothing the folds of sunshine-yellow cotton across her knees, telling herself she was lucky it was in her size, because she couldn't wait for Ethel to order anything different.

'I've told Father about us.' Giles's tawny eyes smiled down at her momentarily before switching back to the road. 'He's pleased.'

She had told herself she was getting used to Churton, but really she wasn't. The size and grandeur of the house and the sweep of the gardens took her breath away when she saw them again.

Jeremy rested a hand on each of her shoulders and kissed her cheek. 'I hear we are to congratulate Giles?'

'Yes,' she told him shyly. She couldn't remember actually saying yes to Giles. He had proposed, and she had been too surprised to say anything. He had taken it for granted. Now she had thought it over, it was what she wanted. Already her new life was opening up. Aunt Harriet sat bolt upright on the window seat. Emily put out her hand, and on impulse bent to kiss the papery cheek. She smelled of eau de cologne.

'I thought Giles had changed his mind about you,' she said.

'I told you I had not,' Giles said quickly.

Giles's grandfather kissed her and wished her well. 'No ring yet?'

'No,' Giles answered for her. 'We haven't had time.'

'What sort of a ring do you fancy, Emily?' Jeremy asked.

'I don't know.'

'Well, you'd better think about it, and come to the shop on Tuesday. You and Giles can choose it,' he told her. A bottle of champagne was opened to drink their health.

Emily felt lapped about in luxury, and a little bemused, how very different life was for these people. Their spotless fingernails fascinated her, but then they didn't have to handle potatoes, light fires and wash floors.

It was only when it was time to move on to Sylveen's that Emily felt awkward. 'Just say you're going out to tea,' Giles had advised, 'better not mention who with.'

But Emily thought Jeremy might be surprised if later he found she had been to see Sylveen. She had worked out what she meant to say.

'A friend invited me to tea a week ago,' she told them all. 'She's just moved into a cottage in Heswall, and I'm looking forward to seeing it.' She turned to Jeremy. 'She worked in the office at Wythenshaw's with me. Helped your secretary for a few weeks. Her name's Sylveen Smith, you might remember her?'

Emily knew immediately that what Sylveen had told her was true, but his words betrayed nothing.

'Yes, I remember her. Pretty girl.'

And as she left a few moments later, he said: 'Don't go into the office on Tuesday, Emily. Come straight to the shop in Liverpool. You'll be able to find your way?'

'Yes, thank you, Giles has explained where it is.'

'Did you see his head jerk up when you mentioned Sylveen's name?' Giles chortled as he drove down the drive. 'Guilt all over his face?'

'I didn't quite believe Sylveen till that moment.'

'How else would she get a cottage?' Giles laughed. 'Look, I don't want to get too involved with my father's girlfriend, I'll just drop you at her gate.'

'You know where her cottage is, then?'

Giles seemed very intent with some switch on the dashboard. 'Yes, I know Heswall quite well,' he said eventually. 'We're just coming to it here. You go through this wicket gate.'

'It's lovely,' Emily breathed. 'Sylveen must be thrilled.'

Giles leaned over to peck her cheek. 'I expect she'll show you where to catch the bus home.'

Sylveen felt her nerves were raw. Finding herself pregnant again had been a shock. Negotiating this cottage, moving in, leaving work, they had been big steps for her to take. Some, she'd felt, were daring steps and had taken all her courage.

She was very glad she'd taken them. This time she had a home of her own. The baby would be hers to keep, but she couldn't hide from herself that she had hoped for more.

Her parents had disowned her. She had asked them to come and see her cottage and they had refused.

'Not again?' her mother had screamed when she told her. 'Not again. Don't you ever learn sense?'

Jeremy was quietly supportive, she knew he would not let her down. She could relax with him as long as Giles wasn't likely to burst in on them, but she had wanted more than he was willing to give. She'd hoped for marriage or, at the very least, she wanted to share his life, meet his relatives. The cottage was wonderful, but she didn't want to be hidden away, as though he were ashamed of her.

But Jeremy knew only half her problems. It was Giles she loved, and it was her relationship with him that exerted the pressures. If it came down to what she really wanted, Sylveen knew it was marriage to Giles. Anything with Jeremy was second best. She had not recovered yet from the nightmare that Jeremy was about to learn the worst.

And everything was happening too quickly. Sylveen wanted to hold the pace of change until she grew more used to it. Jeremy had spent last night with her and she'd been more relaxed. They had both enjoyed themselves. He had noticed nothing, suspected nothing.

She had asked Emily Barr to tea. She wanted to show

off her pretty cottage. What was wrong with that? She didn't have to pretend with Emily, neither did she want to hide the fact that she was visiting her.

'I've asked a friend to come and see my cottage,' she'd said to Jeremy. 'I hope you don't mind.'

'Why should I? I want you to lead a normal life.'

'The trouble is, you know her too. It's Emily Barr.'

'Giles's little waif? Does she know about us?'

'I've told her . . . Everything. I felt I . . .'

'Had to talk to somebody?'

'Yes.'

'She's still working in the office.' Sylveen saw his frown. 'I hope she isn't going to start gossiping about us there.'

'Emily knows how to keep her mouth shut. It won't go any further.'

'As long as you're sure.'

'Yes, I know her well. Worked with her. When I started as Mr Bunting's secretary, he wanted me to set up a new card index of sales outlets. Emily was sent from the typing pool to help. I sorted out the information and she . . .'

'Typed the snippets on to the cards.'

'Yes, we moved a table and typewriter into my office for her. It took us three weeks, and we never stopped talking. I didn't know anybody. Didn't even know my way round. Emily took me by the hand and eased me in. Smoothed things for me. We get on well.'

'I wouldn't want to turn up while she's here,' he said. 'But you can't cut yourself off from everybody you know.'

'I knew you'd understand. I like Emily.'

'Funny little thing. I wouldn't have thought she was Giles's type.'

'No,' Sylveen agreed.

She had enjoyed her morning making a sponge cake. Jeremy had bought her a new electric cooker as well as the Aga and she had all the latest gadgets for her kitchen. She loved trying things out. Time didn't hang heavy while she was alone.

As the time for Emily's visit drew closer, she made cucumber sandwiches without crusts, and set the food on her tea trolley. Through the kitchen window, she saw Emily getting out of the car and coming up her garden path.

Sylveen rushed out to meet her and gave her an excited hug. 'Was that . . .?'

'Yes, Giles. I've been to Churton to lunch again.'

Sylveen smothered her envy. She would love to be asked to lunch at Churton to meet Jeremy's sister and father-in-law. Really she could not see why Emily could go and she could not. Emily looked such a little elf, surely she looked more out of place at Churton than she would? Her father was a teacher, a professional man, and her mother had special tea knives and doilies, even if they only came out for visitors.

'Come and see the garden first,' she made herself say. 'It's too sunny a day to sit inside.'

'It's lovely, Sylveen. So private in the back, with lovely leafy trees round it.'

'Good to have shade on a hot day too.' Sylveen led her towards some rustic seats against an ivy-covered wall, stopping to adjust the lawn sprinkler on the way.

'I'm going to put daffodils in this rough grass. Lots of them, and climbing roses on the fence there, I haven't got it as I want it yet.'

'Have you done all this?' Emily asked, amazed.

'It was full of old sprout plants until Jeremy had it turfed by a landscape gardener.'

'Should you be doing gardening, Sylveen? I mean with the baby . . .'

'You sound like Jeremy. "Get somebody in to cut the grass and do the heavy work for you, Sylveen. Especially just now. Can't have you overdoing things." ' She laughed, despising herself for showing off in front of Emily. Showing off about how Jeremy took care of her. Trying to prove she'd made a good bargain. 'I just want a pretty place to sit out on fine afternoons.'

'I'm dying to see inside,' Emily grinned back at her.

'Come on, then.' Sylveen was on her feet again in a moment. That really brought out the worst in her, made her take Emily through every nook and cranny in the cottage, to show off all she'd gained. Emily went into raptures about the kitchen and the bathroom.

Emily was such a little innocent. The sort who would think her mother's semi was smart, easily impressed by the velvet curtains.

'You're a real woman of the world, Sylveen,' she told her, 'I'd never dare do what you've done.'

That made Sylveen feel better. 'What's your news?'

'I thought you'd never ask,' Emily said. Her brown eyes met hers shyly. 'I'm engaged.'

Sylveen felt the bottom drop out of her world. 'To Giles?' As if it could be anyone else! She felt sick. Why had he done this to her? She wanted to scream: 'He's mine!'

'Are you all right, Sylveen?'

She pulled a face. 'Something gave me a turn inside. Yes, I'm all right. So when did this happen? Have you fixed the date?' She wanted to scream: 'No, not Giles. You can't marry him.'

Emily was chattering on. Sylveen could no longer take in what she was saying. She had to sit down; she led the way back to her sitting-room, and collapsed into an armchair. She felt she was being torn in half.

'Do you think I should?' Emily's brown pixie eyes were on her face. She was waiting for an answer.

'Marry Giles, you mean?' Sylveen's mouth opened in surprise. She couldn't believe Emily would have doubts. Knowing all Giles's faults she would jump at the chance for herself.

'I love him of course, but he's all over me sometimes then he seems to forget I exist. I'm not sure what he feels about me, and it's all so sudden. I feel a bit fluttery when I think about it.'

'Oh, Emily.' Sylveen covered her face with her hands. From being torn in two, now she was being splintered. How could she tell Emily that Giles didn't love her?

Giles was in love with her. She knew his weaknesses. Something had driven him to propose to Emily. She thought it must be that Jeremy was suspicious about her. Giles had done it in self-defence, but she was stricken.

'I don't know, Emily. How can I advise you about who you marry? You must make up your own mind.'

'I can see all the material benefits, and I want them of course, but I don't know . . .'

Sylveen felt faint. What was she letting her friend get into? She could no longer think properly.

'Marriage can be a bit of a lottery, Emily,' she mumbled at last. 'Who knows whether you and Giles will be happy?' Emily's face made her add: 'If it comes to the worst, at least you can be miserable in comfort.'

Sylveen had a terrible afternoon. She was devastated by what Giles intended to do. What she had kept hidden from Emily was worse. She was no better than Giles.

CHAPTER THIRTEEN

Emily pedalled home from work on Monday through a blustery shower, feeling put out. She had decided to go over to Jeremy's shop tomorrow, wearing the same yellow dress she'd worn for lunch on Sunday, but the weather had broken. It would be chilly for the dress on its own, and she had only her old gaberdine to wear over it.

'My perennial problem,' she groaned to Gran, as she finished serving a customer. 'I never have anything to wear.'

'Ethel's got some new coats in. There's a nice one in her window. You'd better see if it suits you,' Gran said, and during the first slack moment she went upstairs to her room. When she came down, she beckoned Emily into the lobby and pressed three pounds into her hand. 'Ethel won't mind waiting if you're still a bit short.'

So when they'd washed up after supper, Emily changed into Sylveen's kilt, combed out her hair and went next door to study the red coat displayed in the window. It looked very smart, so she reached to the skylight above the shop door, and rang Ethel's house bell. Quick firm steps sounded on the shop lino, and the door pinged open.

'Emily, come in.' Ethel was middle aged and had a puff of faded brown hair round a good-natured face.

'I was wondering if that coat would fit me. You don't mind my coming after hours?'

'Course not. Do you want it in red? I've got other colours. Olympia's here, come and have a cup of tea with us first.'

Emily followed her into the room behind the shop. It was identical in shape and size to all the other shops along the Parade, but Ethel's shop smelled excitingly of new cloth. Her room was immaculate, full of little china ornaments and satin cushions. Charlie said it was the room of a fussy spinster.

Olympia's generous frame overlapped the seat of a little tub chair.

'Hello, Emily. Your gran is bragging about your news. Hope you'll be very happy.'

'We're all pleased for you, Emily,' Ethel added. 'Excited for you.'

'You'll be giving Ethel good business now,' Olympia smiled. 'You'll want to smarten up.'

Emily's heart sank. She wasn't sure how she was going to manage. It would take her years to get a decent trousseau together, never mind the wedding dress.

'You aren't the only one giving me business,' Ethel laughed. 'Cathy Tarrant's spending on a new wardrobe. Romance is blooming along the Parade at the moment, and that's always good for trade.'

Emily suddenly found she was struggling for breath. 'You mean . . .?'

She was staring at Olympia with her mouth open. She'd seen Cathy Tarrant walking down Paradise Street with Alex one day, and Gran had said she'd seen them in the Bird. She hadn't attached much importance to it, because they'd known each other all their lives.

'We were just talking about Cathy, how much happier she looks.'

'Alex?' she croaked at Olympia.

'Yes.' Olympia's brown eyes glittered at her strangely. 'Funny, for years I thought you and Alex were going to make a go of it.'

Emily swallowed hard. 'I thought so too.'

'I'm so pleased for Cathy,' Ethel went on. 'She's a lovely girl. Such a shame, her fiancé dying like that. It's the best thing that could happen to her, finding another boyfriend. Her mother's delighted, says Cathy went through hell. Well, we're all pleased for her, they'll make a lovely couple, won't they?'

'Are they getting engaged?' Emily hardly recognised her own voice. She ought to want happiness for Alex, but . . .

Olympia laughed. 'He doesn't tell me everything. I hope so. I'd like to see them settled.' She smoothed a straying wisp of red hair back into its severe bun. 'Our Alex has been like a bear with a sore head till now.'

'Not because of me,' Emily retorted.

'I think he was disappointed when you turned to Giles Wythenshaw.'

'He was going out with other girls before then,' she said.

'I don't know . . .'

'Yes, Billy Wade's friends. He was taking Alex to the Bird to meet girls.'

'He was, Olympia.' Ethel nodded her puff of faded hair in agreement. 'I remember seeing him outside here with Billy and a couple of tarts, and thinking Emily might be upset.' She got to her feet.

'One in the eye for him, Emily. You've done very well for yourself. Come and look at the coats.'

Emily followed blindly. Why couldn't she stop thinking about Alex Fraser? The obsession she felt for him dogged her still.

Olympia laughed. 'I told him he could do better than those floosies. Ted and I are very glad he has.'

'Nobody could say Cathy Tarrant isn't good enough for him,' Ethel agreed.

Emily felt stretched with tension. She'd known for years Alex was drifting away from her, and she hadn't been able to stop it. Why should she mind if he was fond of Cathy Tarrant? She only knew she did.

She told herself firmly, she had to accept it was over. A childhood romance she'd grown out of. To keep thinking of Alex was an indulgence that was rebounding on her, feeding on itself, increasing her hunger for him. Ridiculous when she was about to marry Giles.

Ethel switched on the shop lights. 'These are the latest three-quarter length, very smart.' Emily found Ethel was sliding her arms into the sleeves, and pulling the coat round her. 'What colour do you want?'

'I want it to go with this kilt, and my black skirt, and I also have a grey one.'

'Not black, Emily, you're too young. Try this cream one, there's cream in your kilt.'

'I thought it was white.'

'Creamy white, then. It goes very well.'

'It's very pale. Won't it get dirty quickly?'

'You won't have to worry about cleaning bills when you're a Wythenshaw,' Olympia said dryly.

'It'll look good over a black skirt. It's summery, you'd be able to wear it over the yellow dress you bought the other day, any summer dress. You'll find it useful.' Ethel was smoothing it over her shoulders, buttoning it up. 'A very new line.'

'I like it.' Emily twirled in front of a mirror. 'But I need a hat to go with it.' Ethel didn't sell hats.

'I've got one you can borrow,' Olympia volunteered. 'Not matronly at all. Ted says it's much too frothy for me. Do you want to come and see it?'

'Do you mind?'

'Course not. It's cream, same colour as the coat. Rain's forecast for tomorrow, so I'll lend you my umbrella too, to keep it dry.'

'You're very kind, Olympia.'

'You're one of us. You've got the chance to go up in the

world we all hoped for. I don't suppose you'll find it easy.'

'No.' Emily was glad to find Olympia so understanding.

'Come on, then.'

They went out through the entry, and into the yard behind Fraser's. To Emily, their living-room seemed the most comfortable in the Parade. She was envious of Olympia's polished furniture, sparkling brass and carpet. It always seemed cosy. When a fire was needed, it was lit early in the morning; it blazed up brightly now.

Alex looked up from the table, where he was writing in a notebook. 'Hello, Emily.'

'I'll get the hat,' Olympia said, heading for the stairs.

Emily joined him at the table. She couldn't look at him. She'd said little to Alex for weeks, but every day she worked at her desk in accounts, she was conscious of his brooding presence at the other end of the hall. She was searching for the right words, to end it once and for all.

'Congratulations, Alex. I hear you've taken up with Cathy Tarrant.' His eyes were dark pools of hurt.

'And you've made up your mind to marry Giles Wythenshaw.'

'Yes,' she said, immediately on the defensive.

'The Wythenshaws aren't what they seem.' There was pent-up feeling in his voice. 'Everybody thinks they're wonderful, but they don't always treat people as they should.'

'You're doing all right from them, Alex,' she pointed out. 'Picked for management training and rapid promotion.'

'That's not what I'm talking about, Emily,' he said.

'What do you mean?'

'You'd better watch out, I could tell you a few things about . . .'

'Alex!' Olympia returned. 'What are you needling Emily for?' For a long moment, Alex's angry brown eyes burned into hers. Then he slammed his notebook shut and rushed upstairs.

'Think he's still got that sore head.' Olympia was frowning as she took the little cream hat from its paper bag and twirled it on her fingers. 'What do you think?'

'Just the thing,' Emily approved, and submitted while Olympia fastened it on the side of her head, and adjusted the tulle.

'Suits you better than me,' Olympia was telling her, but Emily was worried. Alex seemed suddenly dead set against the Wythenshaws. He believed he'd turned up some secret, some awful sin they had committed. She was afraid he'd heard about Sylveen.

The next morning Emily walked slowly up from the Liverpool ferry feeling apprehensive. In the first shop window, she glimpsed her reflection and could hardly believe her eyes; her new coat and Olympia's hat provided a transformation. She looked quite elegant.

She was hesitating again outside Calthorpe's, pretending to study the display of rings in the window, but she was feeling shy about walking into a shop that sold nothing she could afford. It took her a few moments to gather her courage. As soon as she opened the door, she saw Jeremy's silver hair sparkling under the shop lights. 'There you are, my dear,' he said. 'Come on in.' Emily felt herself relax.

'We'll go up to the office, I think. More private. Alice, perhaps we could have some coffee?'

She saw Giles was serving a customer. An array of silver candlesticks was spread across the counter between them. His father signalled him to come up when he was free, and led Emily towards the stairs. Her office shoes sank into the carpet. The shop lights glittered back off precious metals and cut glass. The atmosphere was discreet and expensive.

'Have you decided what sort of a ring you'd like?'

She smiled. 'Wouldn't it be better if Giles chose? I shall be pleased with any of the rings you have here.' Emily did not wish to seem grasping, after seeing what the prices were in the window.

He signalled her to pass into the office ahead of him. 'It won't hurt Giles's pocket, whatever you choose. The business can stand this as an engagement present.'

'That's very generous, Mr Wythenshaw.'

'Come on, Emily, I want you to like it. Diamonds or sapphires? A solitaire or three matched stones?'

She took off the cotton gloves that Olympia had offered to complete her outfit.

'You have small hands. Probably three stones would suit you best. I'll get a few for you to try on.'

Emily sat down, her hands looked very brown and rather roughened. A ball of apprehension was building up again in her throat. She felt out of place here.

The door opened, a young girl slid a tray of coffee on the desk. 'Good morning,' Emily said, but the girl cast an envious look in her direction and fled.

She was glad to hear Giles's quicker step on the stairs. He honed in on the coffee tray and poured out three cups. 'I think Father's going to be generous,' he whispered.

Then as his father came in with the black velvet tray glittering with diamonds, he moved a cup of coffee in front of her and said: 'Here you are, darling,' and pecked at her cheek.

Emily was embarrassed, she sensed that Giles had kissed her only because his father was here to see him do it.

She caught Jeremy's smile, and then gasped when she saw the rings. He slid one on her finger. Three large stones flashed iridescent pinpoints of colour as she moved her hand. 'It's . . . it's absolutely beautiful.'

Jeremy had removed all the price tags. 'I'll leave you and Giles to choose,' he said. 'Giles can come down for more if you can't make up your mind.'

'Not that sapphire.' Giles broke the silence. 'The diamonds are worth more. In fact, there's a couple of very expensive solitaires he hasn't brought up. I gave the rings a good look over this morning. Shall I go and get them?'

'No, Giles, how can you be so mercenary? These are all beautiful.'

'You might as well have the most expensive while you're at it. You mightn't get another chance like this.' They could hear footsteps on the stairs again. Jeremy brought in another tray.

'Try a solitaire, Emily, it's the popular choice this year.' She slid it on her thin finger. It seemed enormous, sticking out like an opulent plum.

'Wonderful,' Giles said. 'I like that.'

Emily shook her head. 'I prefer this.' She put on the three diamonds that Jeremy had first picked out. 'Though I'm tempted by the sapphire.'

'You can wear diamonds with anything, Emily. Sapphires need blue to be seen to their best advantage. Have the diamonds,' said Jeremy.

'Are you sure?' Giles was frowning.

'Yes.' Emily wished she was as sure about everything else. She loved Giles but he did silly things, like suggesting she go for the most expensive ring. She wondered if he could be testing her.

'Now it's official,' Giles said. 'It will be announced in tonight's *Echo*.'

'Perhaps you'd like to take Emily out to lunch? Grandfather and I will be going to the Exchange, but I expect you'd prefer to be on your own?'

'I've booked a table at the Adelphi,' Giles said, 'and a photographer is coming to take our picture.'

'You can set the day now, Emily.' Jeremy was jovial, but it made Emily quake. Things were happening too quickly. The ring felt an enormous lump under Olympia's glove. She felt full of doubts, there seemed to be nothing but space between her and Giles. Surely she should feel close to him?

'It will take me a long time to save for my trousseau,' she said, wanting to slow things.

'I'll take care of all that,' Jeremy said, 'I insist. You won't want to work after you're married. Your job will be to look after Giles, and the sooner you start the better.'

'It'll take time to arrange.' Emily felt the ground was being cut from under her feet. 'A big wedding, such a lot to think about, where to live and . . .'

'I think the best thing would be to fix up a suite of rooms for you both at Churton. That shouldn't take too long.'

''I think, Father, Emily would prefer to have a little place of her own,' Giles suggested, his tawny eyes commanding her to agree with him.

Emily swallowed hard, her spirits spiralling downwards. She had expected to have a little house like Sylveen's. She couldn't see why Jeremy would want them to be together. Surely it would be more sensible for Sylveen to share his life at Churton, and for her and Giles to have their own place?

'Nonsense, it's such a big house we can be quite private when we want to be,' Jeremy said quickly. 'Yet there's company when we feel like it. Why don't you bring your family to lunch next Sunday, Emily, and we can get started on the arrangements?'

'My family?'

'You have a grandmother, haven't you? She'll want to be involved, and your father. I think we should meet.' Emily closed her eyes, agonising about what Charlie was going to say to that.

The next morning at work, Emily found the new life had started in earnest.

'Saw your picture in the paper last night, Emily. Aren't you lucky? You make a lovely couple.' Everybody had some comment to make.

Emily was aware again of Alex's eyes smouldering at her across the hall. What he'd said had been at the back of her mind all yesterday, adding to her sense of unease. Without giving herself any more time to think, she leapt to her feet and strode over to his desk.

'What was that you were trying to tell me on Monday?'

'We can't talk about it here,' he said.

'In other words, you're just going to drop hints? You're trying to get me worried, and there's nothing concrete you can tell me? It's a haze you're blowing up because . . .'

He gripped her wrist with vicelike fingers, and towed her down the passage to a stationery cupboard that had the reputation of being a lovers' tryst. Emily was reminded of what she'd done to Giles in a storeroom; it made her more angry.

'What is so important you want me to know about it?'

'I think you already do know about it.'

'Then there's no problem, is there?'

'There is, the way I see it.' He was choosing his words carefully, the intensity of his feeling showing in his scarlet cheeks. 'He's been taking you to a hotel for a long time, hasn't he? You're sleeping with him?'

Emily felt a wave of indignation surge through her. 'Whatever makes you think that?'

'I heard him on the phone, booking the room. The one you always have.'

'You overhear a personal phone call, and you jump to conclusions?' She was angry.

'No, I know what I heard. For Mr and Mrs Wythenshaw, he said.'

'I am not Mrs Wythenshaw yet.'

'That is what bothered me.'

'Don't let it, Alex. It has nothing to do with you. And you've got it all wrong.'

'So which hotel do you go to?' His brown eyes scorched down at her.

'Don't be so stupid. I keep telling you, he doesn't ask me to . . . I suppose you think because I let you, I'd let anyone. Well, we don't.'

She saw the fight go out of him, but couldn't stop. 'Giles is more honourable than you, and in future, mind your own business. What I do has nothing to do with you now. Let me be.' As she pushed past him to run back to her desk, she saw Alex close his eyes and lean his head against a shelf.

Emily sat over her typewriter for a long time, trying to still her shaking fingers. Alex was just trying to make trouble. She had to forget him. Vowed she'd forget him, put him out of her mind once and for all.

Saturday night came, the chip shop was closing. Ted arrived alone. Alex had not come with him since the night she'd asked him to take her out. Since Gran's illness, Ted had been bringing a bottle of stout for her as well as the beer.

Feeling on edge, Emily carried in plates of fish and chips to the table. Charlie's suit was on a hanger suspended from the picture rail, airing in the heat of the living-room. Emily had tried to tell him the flashy chalk stripe on dark wool was too formal, that the Wythenshaw men would wear sports jackets or just pullovers, and even old Mr Calthorpe would wear only a blazer.

'Be different with us going.' Charlie wouldn't hear of wearing his best pullover.

On the other side of the room, Gran's best black crepe had developed a greenish tinge over the years, and now swung in the draught from the door. Gran had untacked the cream lace jabot to wash it. It was now spread like a shawl round the clock on the mantle. The smell of moth balls was fighting the scent of chips and had the upper hand at the moment.

'Will my hat do?' Gran wanted to know. 'Mrs McFie will lend me her best if you think this won't.' From the back, Emily eyed the hat pin that skewered it in position. Over the years it had torn noticeable holes in the straw.

'Perhaps you'd better,' she said.

'I don't like Mrs McFie's, mind.' Gran grumbled. 'Doesn't suit me, but if you think . . .'

'My God, Emily, that's a knuckle duster not a ring,' Ted said.

'Isn't it?' Charlie agreed. 'Bet you could buy a house with what that cost. But she won't tell us.'

'I don't know what it cost,' Emily insisted. It weighed her hand down like an anchor. She was conscious of it always.

'Who would have thought a cheeky little madam like you would have done so well for herself?' Charlie marvelled.

'She'll look after you, Charlie, in your old age.'

'You'll have to try your suit on,' Gran said. 'Tonight before you go to bed.'

'It'll be all right. It's not that old.'

'You had it for your wedding, Charlie. We all know how long ago that was.'

'You've put on a bit of weight since then,' Ted agreed. 'Fancy Captain Wythenshaw welcoming the daughter of Corporal Barr into his family. I'd never have believed it.'

'Our Emily works in his office. Makes all the difference.'

'Where's the reception to be, Emily?'

'She's not saying,' Charlie said. 'But the likes of them get married from home. I don't suppose they'll want it here.' He laughed with his mouth wide open, showing a half-chewed chip. 'Eh, Emily?'

Emily groaned. She hadn't given any thought to all these preliminaries. She certainly hadn't expected them to be so embarrassing. She would like to keep things as they were till she was more used to the idea.

'Why do you have to invite them all here?' Harriet asked with distaste. 'Hardly necessary, surely?'

Jeremy always took the opposing view to Harriet's. 'I think it is. A wedding takes some organisation.'

'For the bride and her family. Why don't you let them get on with it?'

Jeremy sighed. 'Not easy for a girl like that.' He didn't think Emily was keen on an early wedding. 'It would take her a long time.'

'Does it matter?' Harriet shrugged her shoulders.

Jeremy had decided it mattered to him. Giles had been a cross he'd had to bear for years. He was tired of worrying about him, of trying different ways to help him grow up. Marriage might do it. Emily had her wits about her, she'd cope with Giles better than he could. He saw it as a means of handing over responsibility to Emily.

'They aren't our sort, you know, Jeremy,' Harriet was saying distantly, watching through the window as they got out of the car in the courtyard.

'Watch your manners, Harriet,' he said. 'Don't be rude to them.'

'I'm never rude. I won't say a word to upset them. Good gracious, is that her father? The vendor of fish and chips! He looks like an American gangster in that striped suit.'

Giles brought them in, and though Harriet said little, her lorgnette was held to her eyes in a lengthy stare. Charlie riveted her attention, she examined the way his beer gut bulged over his trousers and the buttons wouldn't meet on his jacket. Gran seemed to pass muster though she said her borrowed hat had too high a crown and made her look like a gnome. Emily, in a new yellow dress, she seemed to ignore, perhaps because she'd seen her before.

Jeremy had decided on champagne instead of sherry. Drink the couple's health and happiness. Never did any harm to make a fuss of the bride. She was ill at ease today, he could see, her brown eyes hardly knew where to look. Jeremy decided to get things moving.

'We ought to settle the main details today, while we are all together,' he said. 'Now, when's it to be, Emily?' He saw the blood run up her cheeks. Sensed she felt she was being rushed.

'A Thursday,' her father suggested. 'Early closing day,

best time for us, and Emily's friends along the Parade.'

Jeremy was opening his diary. 'Giles?'

'As soon as possible, I suppose.'

'August the fifteenth, then? What do you think, Emily?'

'That's very soon, not much time to . . .'

'You don't have to come in to work every day,' Jeremy was trying to treat the girl gently. 'Take off as much time as you like. You'll need to have fittings for your trousseau. We'll have the reception here, of course. I'll get caterers in.'

Through the windows the sun shone on the well-kept acres. Jeremy got up to refill the glasses. Harriet was right about the father, he didn't feel they'd have much in common. He noticed Charlie Barr was looking up at him eagerly, his pasty face damp with perspiration. 'You don't remember me, Captain Wythenshaw?' Jeremy's hand jerked; the champagne he'd been pouring made a pool on the table.

'Corporal Charles Barr. Cheshire Regiment.'

'Yes, of course,' Jeremy said, but he couldn't equate this middle-aged man with any he'd known in the trenches. He'd tried to sweep that period of his life out of his memory.

'Corporal Barr, and you're Emily's father?' He couldn't quite believe it. Why had the name not alerted him? He remembered now far too much. 'Of course, yes, Alice Barr was your wife.' That was another thing he'd blotted out of his mind for years. 'I'm so dreadfully sorry about . . .'

'Alice, yes. Dreadful way to lose your wife.' He saw Charlie stifle a shudder.

'I wish I could have done more . . .'

'You helped with my keep.' Emily's brown eyes were smiling up at him. 'We have to thank you for that.'

'Keep?' He was searching his mind, not understanding.

'Yes, you paid us ten shillings a week. Till I was old enough to come to work.'

'No,' Jeremy frowned. 'No, I didn't do that.'

Emily's eagerness was brimming over. 'Yes, didn't he, Dad? I saw the money orders coming every month.' Jeremy straightened up, trying to think. Rang the bell for a maid to mop up the champagne he'd spilt.

'That would have come from my insurance. Same source as your lump sum.'

He saw Emily's elfin face transformed by surprise. 'I don't think there was a lump sum,' she was whispering, when her father put in quickly: 'Do you remember Private Fraser? Ted Fraser? We talk about you and the old days quite often.'

'You served with Jeremy in the war?' Harriet's voice was heavy with interest, her lorgnette was examining Charlie's face. Jeremy felt uncomfortable.

'Yes, but, of course, the war was different for the likes of officers.'

'The war was different for me because of our family connections,' Jeremy said, wishing the grandmother would take her eyes from his face.

'Yes, of course, your mother was French,' Emily said.

'Half French,' he corrected. Mrs Eglin came bustling in, and he directed her gaze to the spilt champagne. She was tutting officiously at the mess, rushing to get towels and polish, inferring Charlie Barr's clumsiness had caused the accident, but he was oblivious. Then he noticed Emily's stricken face, and knew she'd noticed. He waved Mrs Eglin away before she could apply polish.

'Do you remember the Manoir de Frontenac? Were you billeted there with Jeremy?' Harriet barked.

'That big house? Course I remember it,' Charlie's eyes were amazed. 'At a place called . . .?'

'At Lusec. The Germans had been using it as a hospital, and withdrew suddenly to some line or other,' she said.

'The house was almost undamaged when we moved in,' Charlie nodded.

'Didn't stay that way for long.' Jeremy closed his eyes, trying to visualise it as it had been, steep roofs of dark shiny slates, thick grey stone walls. 'They gave us a hard time.'

'Blimey, was that yours?'

'No,' he said. 'It belonged to relatives of our mother's. She had a small house in the grounds which she bequeathed to Harriet.'

'We used to spend our holidays there before the war,' Harriet put in. 'Had some very happy times.'

'Blimey,' Charlie said again. 'Fancy that, you knowing the place before.'

'Owning it,' she corrected tartly. 'My mother was Louise de Frontenac before she married. The Germans shelled my house. Jeremy says only one wall was standing after three days.'

'Shelled us too,' Jeremy reminded them. 'I billeted myself and a few friends in it. I thought I'd protect Harriet's belongings, but the Germans razed it to the ground. There was nothing I could do.'

Charlie beamed round at them. 'That was the place where there were all those stories of buried treasure.'

Jeremy quaked as he met his gaze. 'Just stories,' he said, not wanting to revive all the old rumours. They were what everybody remembered of the Manoir de Frontenac.

'No, we found a huge cache of booze hidden there. Fine wines they said, and brandy.'

Jeremy shuddered. The first they'd known of that was when half the battalion was drunk, with more men passing out in drunken stupors by the hour. They'd had to find the cache and remove the wine to the officers' mess in order to maintain a sober fighting force. It had been drunk there with more moderation, and probably greater appreciation.

'Not just rumours, I saw it with my own eyes. Solid silver cutlery blown out of a wall,' Charlie told them, his eyes wide.

Jeremy couldn't get his breath. 'Really?'

'When we was shelled. Shared it out we did and said nothing. Officers never knew about that. There were rumours of other stuff, jewellery and antiques that the Germans had looted. That sort of thing.'

'I don't know.' Jeremy couldn't stand any more, he had to change the subject.

'Of course Jeremy had a house of his own in Paris,' Harriet said. 'Still has, he was lucky.'

'A wonderful asset in the war.' He helped himself to another drink. 'Made me popular with my fellow officers. It was an oasis of civilisation in the midst of chaos. We'd go to the house when we were supposed to be on rest, live it up, have a night on the town.'

'Trust you,' Arthur chuckled. 'You always manage to enjoy yourself.'

'In the middle of the war?' He could see Emily's eyes couldn't equate that with the stories she'd heard from Charlie. But it was true enough.

'Rest was like leave, Emily,' he tried to explain. 'But we were kept close, in case we were needed as back-up.'

'What I remember,' Charlie said, 'is three days in the trenches followed by three days in billets just behind the firing line. That went on solid, month after month.'

'Then suddenly we'd get a month's rest, sometimes six weeks, and we'd fall back twenty or thirty miles to more permanent billets for that.' Jeremy smiled. 'Surely you haven't forgotten your rests?' It didn't seem the moment to remind Charlie that as quartermaster Jeremy hadn't seen much of the trenches, that most of his war had been spent in billets. 'Once we rested only ten miles from Paris, I enjoyed that.'

'Of course I haven't forgotten. It was a relief to get away from them trenches,' Charlie sniffed. 'But rest was all drill and manoeuvres and gunnery practice.'

'Didn't you drink beer in the estaminets? Swim in the canals and enjoy the concerts?'

'I drank beer whenever I could.'

'I bet you did,' Gran laughed. 'And you wouldn't miss a concert.'

'Didn't get a chance to live it up like the officers though.'

'In the early years of the war, our front line was only forty miles from Paris. It hardly moved, we'd fight for months over a few hundred yards. Of course we lived it up, took all sorts of risks to do it. Why not? We were risking death in the trenches, it made sense to enjoy ourselves when we could.' Jeremy lay back in his chair, sipping his champagne as it all come flooding back to his mind. Sometimes they'd gone to Paris when his friends had been in billets for three nights.

'Strange times, Emily. The French peasants tended their fields and animals just the same, even where trenches were being dug only a mile or so away. Life went on for the country folk, war or no war, they had to earn their living. Cafés and bars were open, beer and wine available only a few miles from the front.

'The transport officer was a friend of mine. He allocated transport to me for ferrying supplies from depots up to the trenches, mostly horse-drawn though, and that was too slow. But he also controlled trucks and cars and motor bikes with side cars for official use. Occasionally we used them for our own pleasure and went to Paris, wonderful to get out and away from the front.'

'What's wrong with that?' Giles was watching his father closely.

'Most of the time we lived in tents,' Jeremy said, feeling he was on safer ground now. 'But we acquired bits of carpet to go on top of our ground sheets, under our camp beds. As quartermaster I was popular because I always had a supply of empty cardboard cartons. We arranged them like nesting boxes round the tent sides, they kept our belongings off the ground and to hand. Excellent for books and shoes, bottles of cognac and glasses. Many of us had gramophones and records. We did our best to make ourselves comfortable.

'Colleagues asked me to store their things if they were sent to hospital, or on a course. I was quite happy to oblige. The only problem was transporting the stuff. Petrol and diesel got tighter as the war went on, harder to come by for clandestine trips, and Arras was much further away from Paris. I hardly ever used the house then.'

Charlie said: 'We never got tents to ourselves, pushed us in like sardines. Mostly we lay down where we could, fully dressed. Didn't see many beds, I can tell you.'

'We always tried to find the men decent billets when they came out of the lines,' Jeremy protested. 'Some French families would take men in, give them board and lodging.'

'Not very often,' Charlie said.

'Always a barn or something with a roof so you wouldn't get wet.'

'Wouldn't think we were both fighting the same war,' Charlie grumbled. 'All Ted and me got was body lice, empty bellies and seeing our friends killed. I got frostbite in my toes and Ted got a dose of gas.'

Jeremy felt he was choking. 'I had a taste of those things too. All my French relatives were killed, and many of my fellow officers. Sometimes I wonder why I was chosen to survive.'

He'd thought all this was years behind him, forgotten by everybody. Now this man was making his family take more interest in the war and the Manoir de Frontenac than they were in the wedding arrangements.

Jeremy looked down at his notebook. 'August the fifteenth it is, then,' he said. The champagne was making the grandmother's transparent cheeks burn, and her hat no longer seemed straight on her head. Anxiety was twisting at his gut.

'Can we have the Paris house for our honeymoon,

Father?' Giles's eyes were sparkling. He was quick enough when it came to picking up anything like that. 'You'd like to honeymoon in Paris, wouldn't you, Emily?'

'No,' Jeremy barked, then, realising just how vehement he'd been, he added: 'Too hot and dusty in August.'

'He won't let you go, Giles, if he won't let me,' Harriet laughed. The last thing Jeremy wanted them to discuss was the Paris house.

'Torquay would be pleasanter,' he said hurriedly. 'Near the sea, height of the season, plenty going on.'

'Torquay would be wonderful, I've never been further than New Brighton.' He warmed to Emily. 'We'd enjoy Torquay, wouldn't we, Giles?'

Jeremy found lunch an uncomfortable meal. Harriet was right, he never should have invited them here. If he'd known her father was Charlie Barr, he never would have. Suddenly he was no longer sure he should have made so much of this match.

After lunch, he took them up to view the wing in which they would have their suite. 'Shouldn't take too long to organise,' Jeremy said. 'Just get Emily to make up her mind what she wants. A new bathroom and kitchen. And arrange for a door in the passage to cut it all off from the rest of the house.'

'Just like your own flat,' Gran said, looking round with obvious enthusiasm. 'Better really.'

He was even having second thoughts about this. She'd probably want her family to come and visit.

Jeremy's first inclination had been to buy them a house well away and let them get on with it. It was only when he'd thought it over that he'd decided it might be kinder to Emily to have them where he could keep an eye on things. Make sure Giles didn't get into too much trouble. He'd thought it better to see how Emily settled down before all Giles's problems were revealed. He was so totally disorganised about money.

While afternoon tea was being served on the terrace, Jeremy took Emily to the library. 'I want to make some arrangements for your trousseau.'

'What do you mean?' Her little pixie face was screwing up in embarrassment.

'I could open an account for you in one of the Bold Street shops, so you can go in and choose what you want.'

'Oh no, Mr Wythenshaw, I couldn't do that.'

'Why not?'

'I just wouldn't be comfortable in those expensive shops, and I can't let you pay for everything.'

That surprised him, Emily was the first person he'd come across who wasn't trying to sting him for the maximum he'd part with. She was far too good for Giles.

'You must have a wedding dress, Emily. I want you to look pretty.' He smiled down at her.

'I usually get my clothes from Ethel's in the Parade. Through her business. She'd expect it, you know.'

'I'll give you a cheque, if that would be easier.'

'I could manage by myself, Mr Wythenshaw. Gran has offered me a bit. It's just that I'd have to save up first. It would take time.'

'Better not take your gran's savings, take this.'

She was looking at the cheque he'd put in her hand. 'Why, this is far too much.' He saw a scarlet tide run up her cheeks. 'I couldn't spend all this on clothes.'

'Of course you can. You want to look smart, don't you? You owe it to Giles now.'

'Yes,' she said. 'Of course. Would you mind if I spent some of it on a new dress for Gran? For the wedding.'

He laughed, and patted her arm. 'Buy what you like, Emily. You know, I'm quite looking forward to having you here, taking care of Giles.'

'I want to do that of course.' She hesitated, but she knew this was an opportunity which would not occur often.

'Mr Wythenshaw, there's something I'd like to know. Could you tell me more about the insurance that was paid for my keep?'

'Employer's liability? Well, I could lose everything, the whole factory could go up in flames, and if my employees were injured or lost their lives, I would in addition have to meet claims for compensation. That's the law. So I insure.'

Emily swallowed hard. 'Was there a lump sum too?' She'd heard nothing of a lump sum till now, but she'd seen Charlie's face when it was mentioned. Suspicion had thumped through her. She knew only too well what he was like with money.

'There's usually both.'

'How much of a lump sum?'

'I can't remember. I insure for larger sums now.'

'Mr Wythenshaw, could you . . .? Is there any way I can find out what exactly was paid for my mother?' That brought his blue eyes searching into hers, but she saw sympathy in them. It took him a while to answer.

'Mr Lockwood used to see to my insurances, but you could ask Donkin. It's a long time ago, but I expect he'll find the records stored somewhere.'

'Thank you,' she said. 'I'd like to do that.'

'I'm glad you felt you could work for us too,' he said.

Emily tried to smile. 'You must know Wythenshaw's is the best firm to work for in Birkenhead.'

She was angry that Charlie had never mentioned receiving any lump sum. She and Gran had worked long hours for him, believing it was necessary for survival. Now she suspected it was not. Stop it, she told herself. Wait till you know exactly, but she couldn't forget it; her resentment was fermenting on what she had already learned.

CHAPTER FOURTEEN

Emily felt very curious about the insurance money Charlie had received, but was shy about asking Mr Donkin because it was a personal matter and he always seemed busy. It was two weeks before she brought herself to do it.

'Nineteen twenty-one, you said? Yes, I remember the kitchen fire, but I'll have to clear it with Mr Wythenshaw.' His fingers were steepling under his chin as he spoke, his manner was authoritarian.

'He told me to ask you.'

'The documents will be in the basement somewhere. Won't be easy to find after all this time. Right, I'll let you know if we can find them and Mr Wythenshaw agrees.'

Emily had to be patient for another three days before he sent for her. When she went into his office, he opened a file tied up with pink ribbon and started spreading papers across his desk.

'Now then, what is it you want to know?' Emily felt keyed up with expectation as she told him.

'Here we are.' He extracted a letter. 'Compensation paid on the death of Alice Barr, kitchen assistant.' She watched him reading silently while her heart raced. At last he began reading it to her: 'One thousand pounds to Mr Charles Thomas Barr, husband, in compensation for his loss.' Emily felt her cheeks flame. So Charlie had had money!

'A further one thousand pounds to be held in trust for her daughter Emily Jane Halston, known as Barr.'

Emily gasped in astonishment; that she hadn't even suspected. A wave of cold fury washed over her, leaving her shaking.

'And in addition a weekly payment of ten shillings to be paid until the eighteenth birthday of Emily Jane Halston, known as Barr, or until her twenty-first birthday, if she remains in full-time education.'

Emily could hardly speak. He pushed the letter across the desk to her. It was there in black and white. The words danced before her eyes.

'That's all we have about it,' Donkin said, sitting back in his chair.

Emily stared at him. It was all she needed. She pulled herself together sufficiently to thank him and drag herself back to her desk. She felt a terrible urge to storm home and face Charlie with it right away. But as it was the middle of the afternoon, she had to gulp down her rage and settle to typing two more schedules. She couldn't believe it of Charlie.

Always he was pleading poverty. Always he was pleading for help to get his business on its feet. Yet all these years he'd had that insurance money, and said nothing about it to her and Gran.

She had let Charlie suck her dry. She had been handing over half her wages every week for her keep, when the insurance was still paying him ten shillings towards that. In addition, she was working two or three hours every day in the shop, more on Saturdays when she had a half day. She couldn't afford decent clothes on the money she had left. It made her angry now that she'd done it willingly, but she knew why.

Charlie had said it was necessary if the family was to survive, and she'd believed him. She'd wanted to help him.

She'd always tried to please Charlie. Since she was a child, she'd done every job he gave her. Done it as well as she could without fuss. Never once had she refused. She knew it was his approval she'd sought, his affection as a father. She should have realised before now she'd never get it. Charlie only valued her for the pounds, shillings and pence she could save him. Charlie had never liked her.

Hadn't Alex told her years ago that along the Parade it was usual practice for parents to waive any contribution from working children towards their keep, if they regularly helped in the shop during rush hours?

She wished she'd found out before now. With only a few weeks to her wedding, she'd soon be leaving home anyhow.

When the hooter blew at five-thirty, and she reached the shop, it was full of customers. Gran was serving as she always did.

Emily changed out of her office clothes, and went to sit in front of the living-room fire. She poked up in a fit of rebellion what Charlie had banked down, turned on their old wireless. A few moments later he came to the door with a face like thunder.

'What you doing here? Get yourself in the shop. Can't you see we're run off our feet?' She jumped out of the chair, but stood her ground.

'No, never again. I found out today that you got two thousand pounds insurance, Dad, and half of it belongs to me. That you're still getting ten shillings a week to pay for my keep, and yet you have the nerve to take another two pounds out of my pay.'

He was staring at her. He was no taller than she was, but his shoulders were powerful. His thick swatch of iron-grey hair fell over his angry eyes.

'If I got a bit of insurance, it was to help pay for your keep. I've kept you, haven't I? Come along, hurry up.'

'No, Dad. You've got a good business there, you can afford to pay for help to run it.'

Charlie shut the living-room door quietly and came closer, hovering over her. 'Go on,' he said.

'Well, I'm not handing over any more of my pay, and I'm not going to work two hours every night after work.' Emily stopped to take a breath. 'I bet you're stacking it away.'

'What this shop makes is little enough and it's none of your business.'

'I'm going to tell Gran. She knows you're mean, but robbing your own daughter, that's dreadful.'

'I got saddled with you, and you're not my daughter.' His greasy face was stiff with rejection.

The hurt stabbed home; she'd tried to be what he wanted, and never succeeded. 'Thank goodness for that,' she shouted now. She didn't see Charlie raise his hand, but she felt the sharp clip on her ear, it sent her reeling.

'Now you listen to me, Emily. I've kept a roof over your head these last ten years. Nobody else wanted to. It hasn't been easy keeping your belly filled and your back covered, but I did it for you.' He stepped forward till his beer gut bounced against her.

'The insurance I got all went to keep you, and if you don't want to be put out on the pavement tonight, you'd better come and pull your weight now.' He was breathing heavily, he seemed threatening. 'And don't you go worrying Gran, accusing me of taking your money. You've had your share of what's going. She'll tell you that.' Charlie's face was livid.

'Get yourself in there, and let's have no more of this nonsense.' Emily felt his hand whack against her rump, the force of it pushing her forward and out into the shop.

'A twopenny fish and a pennyworth of chips,' someone called, and she reached for the paper and started serving like a automaton.

Charlie, his lips in a straight line, didn't speak to her again all evening. He was short with his customers and downright rude to Gran, telling her she wasn't quick enough.

The rush of customers thinned and almost stopped. Gran was selecting two pieces of fish to boil in milk for herself and Emily.

'Got to do it, Charlie, fried fish gives me indigestion at night.' She departed to the kitchen to put the kettle on. Emily began wiping down the tables, lifting the chairs on top so she could sweep beneath. Her fury was coming to a slow boil.

As Charlie locked the door behind the last customer, she turned on him. 'I suppose you think you've won? Well, you haven't.'

'Give over, Emily. I've told you what's what.'

'No, you listen to me, Charlie. Once I leave you'll have to pay somebody else to work in this shop. You are going to find yourself an assistant straight away, because I'm not standing for it any longer. Knocking me about the ears, forcing me in here. Moaning at Gran because she can't scuttle round fast enough to please you. What gives you the right?'

'You're getting too big for your boots. Acting like you're a Wythenshaw already,' he grumbled. 'I've told you, I can't afford to throw money about.' His face was working with fury; Emily made herself stand her ground.

'Eight weeks,' she spat, 'and I'll be gone. What difference will eight weeks make to you? Do it now.'

'No. I'd have eight weeks' wages to find.'

'What would it cost? You could get a school leaver for fifteen shillings. A pound would get you a strong lad.'

'No,' he said, and went behind the counter to cash up. 'I've told you, I can't afford it.'

Emily was shouting.' 'You've got my insurance money, stolen it. With that and what you've saved from this shop,

I bet you could buy up the whole Parade.'

'Bloody cheek!' he said. 'I haven't stolen your money. I should have sent you to the orphanage where you belonged. Thought I was doing you a favour giving you a good home.'

Gran came to the doorway, pulling her shoulder shawl tight. 'What's the matter?'

'Getting big Wythenshaw ideas,' Charlie said. 'Already thinks money grows on trees.'

'Thank goodness I am going. I wish it were sooner. Ethel would let me lodge with her for two pounds a week, I'll bet, and give me discount in her shop. I'll tell everybody you've stolen my money. I'm not staying any longer to pay over my wages and be put upon, so make up your mind.'

'Shut up, I can't count while you're blethering on.' She could feel his sharper antagonism, and knew he didn't like being accused of theft.

'He clipped me round the ear, Gran.' She couldn't calm down, her blood was boiling. She tried to tell Gran about the insurance money but was hardly coherent.

'Doesn't he work you from morning till night?'

Gran's eyes wouldn't meet hers. 'Our Charlie's all right, Emily. Just a bit tight with his pennies.'

That pulled her up short. She'd expected Gran to be on her side. She'd thought she was fighting Gran's battle too.

'He works you too hard. Olympia says so.'

'At my age it's different. Want to be thought useful now. Nice to be wanted. Our Charlie's all right really.'

Emily felt she stood alone, she could understand Gran's divided loyalties, and she wasn't supporting her over this. Suddenly she was fighting for self-control, she wasn't going to give Charlie the satisfaction of seeing her cry, though she knew she wasn't far from it.

'I know I am right,' she said desperately. 'Get help in the shop, Charlie, or I'll look for lodgings for my last eight weeks. I'm not putting up with this any longer.'

She turned and ran upstairs, threw herself across her bed and let the tears pour out in a release of nervous tension.

Emily felt she lay there a long time shaken by her sobbing. She was drying her eyes when she heard Gran's footsteps, slow and heavy, coming up the attic stairs.

'Brought you a cup of tea, Emily,' she said. A cup of tea was Gran's remedy for everything. Emily sat up and blew her nose.

'Goodness, girl, you'll catch your death of cold.' Gran rushed to the window and slammed it shut. 'Put something on.'

'I'm all right.' Upset Emily might have been, but she'd tossed off the clothes she wore in the shop before coming into her room. It was an ingrained habit now. She was wearing only her petticoat.

'Ugh.' Gran pulled her shawl closer and tossed a cardigan to her. 'Put that on, it's freezing in here.' Emily felt the springs of her bed go down as Gran sat on the edge. 'You've no chance with Charlie.'

'Didn't you see his face that Sunday? I knew he had something to hide. I saw it written down in black and white, Gran! Did you know he had two thousand pounds for my mother?'

The cherries on Gran's hat slithered as she shook her head. 'I knew he got something, but he never said how much. You've no chance of getting it back, Emily. Charlie hates to part with money.'

Emily sniffed and reached for the tea. 'Don't I know that? But what's he want it for? He never buys anything.'

Gran shook her head again. 'Said he wanted a café once. Said he was saving for it.'

'A café? Was he?'

'Yes, used to go through the adverts in the *Echo* regularly. We went to see two or three. There was a good one in New Ferry, good position, good turnover. Just right, he said he was very tempted, but when it came to the point, he couldn't part with his money.'

'What's the good of money if you never spend it?' Emily demanded.

'I wasn't sorry about the café, I wanted to stay here. I knew then we'd never move, no matter how much he went on about a café.'

'But what good is money to him?'

'I expect he thinks of all the things he could buy if he really wanted them. Just accept you've no chance of parting Charlie from any of it. He's too tight-fisted. Anyway, you'll be a Wythenshaw soon, practically are already. Didn't Mr Wythenshaw give you a fat cheque? What you're going to have will make Charlie's look like chicken feed.'

'Yes,' Emily said. 'But he's going to get help in the shop now. And I'm not giving him any more of my pay. He's got to be fair. And he does work you too hard.'

Within three days Charlie had installed a girl to help in the shop. Emily knew Charlie hated the thought of paying wages for work she'd always done for nothing, but he didn't want a new story circulating along the Parade about taking her insurance money.

'Have you got a new girl serving in your shop?' everybody was asking her. 'We bought chips the other night and you weren't there.'

'Yes, her name's Pammy Green.'

'She's mean with the chips.'

'Has to be to please Dad.'

'Your replacement?'

'Yes, he has to have somebody else when I go.'

Emily felt things were better, she was glad she'd stood up to Charlie. Both she and Gran were spending less time serving in the shop. Gran seemed happier, she gave a hand if they got pushed, but mostly she pottered around in the living-room. The last weeks were rushing past, already her life was changing.

At work, everybody accepted her now as the Wythenshaw bride. More people than ever told her how lucky she was. If she expressed any doubts, she was told all brides had them and her future couldn't be rosier.

One early-closing day, Ethel took her to Liverpool. They went into the specialist bridal-wear shops as well as the big stores. Ethel went through their stock minutely, picking out gowns for Emily to try on.

Then, when Emily had decided what she liked, Ethel took notes of everything she would need to complete her outfits. In one afternoon they chose her bridal gown and going-away outfit. Then Ethel ordered everything through her own business the following day.

Emily felt very happy about her clothes; she had learned to trust Ethel's judgement, but she was uneasy about everything else. Everybody was making such a fuss, everything was happening very quickly, and she seemed to see very little of Giles.

Her wedding day was on her before she felt ready, and it dawned sunny and hot. The shops along the Parade opened for business as usual, but there was an air of expectancy everywhere. At the last minute Ted came round to borrow cufflinks, looking like a cadaver in his black suit. Olympia came looking for him, larger than ever in deep red.

Emily was in the living-room, already dressed in her finery, in the stage beyond nervousness when everything seemed faintly unreal. She was blinking hard as Olympia bent to kiss her cheek and wish her well. She and Ted were coming to the wedding, but not Alex.

When she'd opened the envelope to find his formal refusal, it had felt like a slap in the face. It doesn't matter, she kept telling herself. There wasn't room in her life for

Alex now. Better a clean-cut break. She had to stop thinking about him.

The cars were outside and Charlie was calling to her. 'Come on, Emily, stop mooning about. Let's get it over with.'

Sylveen walked slowly from the bus stop with dread in every step. The bells were peeling out joyously from the massive church tower, making her cringe. They sounded a death knell to everything she wanted. She stood for a moment looking at the handsome ivy-covered walls of West Kirby parish church, gathering courage to go in. Already a few cars were parked outside, and sightseers were collecting. In ten minutes Giles's wedding service would begin; the air of excited anticipation made her shudder.

An usher met her at the door, presented her with a prayer book and the order of service. She found herself sitting alone in a pew at the back on the bride's side. The church was full of flowers. A bee was trying to collect honey from the arrangement nearest to her. Her fellow guests were exotically dressed. 'Jesu Joy of Man's Desiring' soared magnificently from the organ. She could still hear the bells.

Sylveen covered her face with her hands, sinking to her knees in an attitude of prayer, trying to blink back the tears stinging her eyes. She felt she was being torn in two.

'Why?' she had demanded of Giles when Emily had first told her. She had been astounded, unable to believe her ears and boiling with frustration and anger when he'd come to spend the night at her cottage again. 'Why marry Emily?'

'My father wants it,' he'd said. She couldn't believe that either.

'But why?'

'That time Aunt Harriet saw us. I told him it was Emily, when it was you.'

'But that doesn't . . .'

'There were other reasons. I wanted to keep her as my secretary.'

'What's that got to do with it? How can you marry Emily when you love me? It doesn't make sense. Not when I'm having your child.'

'Father thinks the child is his. He wants me to marry Emily.'

'But do you want it?'

'You know I don't.' He sounded petulant.

'Then don't do it.'

'You don't understand, Sylveen.' She had washed up noisily after their meal, clattering the pots together and thinking what a fool she was to love a man like Giles. He lowered his newspaper when she went back to the sitting-room.

'When you get yourself in a hole, it's sometimes difficult to get out,' he said seriously.

'If your father told you to put your head under a bus you would.' She'd been angry. Angry with him because he wouldn't stand on his own feet and angrier with herself for putting herself in this position.

'Shall we run away together? Do you want that?'

She couldn't help clucking with impatience and frustration. 'Giles! Where would we run to, and what would be the point of it? Tell your father you're going to marry me. That I'm going to have your child.' Had she no pride left? Beseeching him like this? 'I have this cottage, and you have a car. You can get a job if your father throws you out. For God's sake, if you're a man, do it. We'll manage.'

'Is that what you want?'

'You know it is.'

She despised herself more for being persuaded into bed with him later that night. Despised herself for loving a man who justified rejecting her by saying: 'Lots of people labour from dawn to dusk for a pittance. I'm close to money, I don't get all I want but I get some. Wouldn't I be a fool to cut myself off from it and join those who have to work?'

Neither of them had given a thought then of what it would do to Emily.

The church was filling up. A couple edged into her pew with apologetic smiles. The music was soaring; she loved Bach, it should have soothed her soul. Abruptly it stopped at the end of a bar, the last vibrations died away in a rustling as the congregation rose. An expectant pause, then Wagner's Wedding March from *Lohengrin* came flaring through the church.

She turned to see a pale-faced Emily behind a veil, clutching desperately at Charlie Barr's arm, nervous eyes down at the floor. She wore ivory slipper-satin, elegantly fashioned into a dress with a train. Four page boys in blue satin and two little girls in gold followed her up the aisle.

'I want you to be my bridesmaid,' Emily had said in a heart-jolting moment.

'No,' she'd said vehemently. 'No.' She'd wanted nothing to do with Giles's wedding, not even wanted to come. Emily had been pressing but she'd had the excuse of her pregnancy.

'We'll call you matron of honour, then. I can introduce you as Mrs Smith, nobody need know.' She'd asked Amy Tarrant from the greengrocer's in her place, Cathy Tarrant's younger sister. She was one of the two adult bridesmaids.

When Emily had pushed the printed invitation into her hand she'd said, 'This is your chance to meet all Jeremy's relatives. I shall tell them you're my friend.'

She'd cried when Emily had gone home. Any girl could be excused one pregnancy to a man who turned his back, but to do it twice a girl really had to be a fool. She ought to hate Giles as she hated Denis Lake, but he had only to turn his hot tawny eyes on her to twist her round his finger. How could she be such a crass fool?

Sylveen stood to sing 'Love Divine All Loves Excelling', and wondered if she knew what love was. She'd known coming here would be like turning a knife in the wound, but Emily would notice if she did not. She must not betray the secret.

She had no guts either or she'd have told Emily at that moment in the cloakroom when she'd said: 'Giles has asked me to lunch at Churton.' She'd been jealous then, but that was nothing to what she felt now. She ought to hate Emily too, but instead she carried this weight of guilt for what she'd failed to do. Emily had been so grateful when she'd given her that kilt. She couldn't look at her now in her wedding finery.

Instead she stared down at the pew, tracing the whorls in the oak with her finger. Impossible to shut her ears to the words of the service: ' . . . if either of you know any impediment why ye may not be lawfully joined together in Matrimony, ye do now confess it.'

Was her unborn child an impediment? She didn't know, but she knew now what Giles had meant. Impossible to open her mouth at this late stage.

The worst part was knowing she'd brought it all on herself. She had made the basic mistake of approaching Jeremy when all the time she would have preferred Giles. Every girl in the office believed she could do it and she'd not had the guts to try.

She hadn't believed for a moment she stood a chance. She had imagined his life full of girls from wealthy families. Had thought Jeremy would not approve of a secretary from his own office as a bride for Giles. Yet if he could accept Emily, he would have accepted her. She knew now with hindsight she could have been in Emily's shoes today. That was the awful part. Knowing she had played it wrong from the beginning.

Emily was coming back down the aisle on Giles's arm to Widor's Toccata in F, veil thrown back, looking flushed but relieved. Giles, looking magnificent in his grey tails and top hat, had eyes for nobody but Emily. He held on to her arm and seemed to be enjoying all the excitement and fuss of the occasion. Sylveen trailed out behind them with the rest of the congregation.

The Press was waiting and a crowd had gathered to see the big wedding. Women with shopping bags, children with lollipops all gaping at a happy couple starting married life with every possible advantage. Sylveen felt physically sick and would have slipped off home but for an usher guiding guests towards the cars.

It was the first time she had seen Churton House in the light of day; it looked very beautiful in the bright sunlight. Emily stood on the steps with Giles and Jeremy to greet guests, it all seemed very formal. Inside she was offered sherry and found herself walking out into the courtyard again through french windows. The wedding breakfast looked magnificent, but she couldn't eat.

Sylveen didn't know how she got through the afternoon. She was introduced to the aunt who looked like the dowager Queen Mary. She spoke to Emily's gran who was wearing a new black straw hat with violets on the brim.

It was hurtful to see Jeremy enjoying himself, moving from one group of guests to another. He even apologised for not being able to spend more time in her company. Sylveen felt an outcast and wanted to get away, but the drive was in full view of the courtyard and she'd have to walk down it. She felt trapped.

Emily seemed to have more self-possession, she was a Wythenshaw now and this was her setting. She must have noticed her standing alone and taken pity on her for Sylveen saw her coming over.

'Come and help me change into my going-away outfit,' she said, and took her by the wrist. Sylveen followed her up the stairs and was surprised to find she was the only one invited up.

'I want to show you our suite. Not quite finished yet, but it will be by the time we come back.' Emily was rushing her from room to room, flushed with her triumph. 'Giles and I wanted our rooms to be different from the rest of Churton.'

Sylveen felt she was touching bottom at that. 'It's all going to be lovely,' she said, giving Emily a sudden hug.

'We want them to be simpler, less cluttered, bang up-to-date in the latest nineteen thirties' style. We want a lot of pale-cream paint and chintzy chairs.'

'I thought I had all the answers,' Sylveen said sadly. 'But here I am fat and ugly and on my own.'

'You couldn't look ugly if you tried,' Emily smiled. 'Perhaps pregnant, but not ugly.'

'Does it show?'

'Only because I remember what a good figure you have normally.'

Sylveen knew her face looked puffy. 'I don't have the radiance women in my condition are supposed to have.'

'What's one day off form? Cheer up.'

'Emily, you're Mrs Wythenshaw now. Sometimes I get depressed. Like my mother said, I've done it again, and I'm no nearer getting married.'

'You've got what you said you wanted,' Emily reminded her. 'Jeremy's looking after you. You don't have to go to work every day.'

'Sometimes I wonder if I know what I want. To think I used to tell you how to manage things. Look more like me, I said, if you want my chances. I was a fool, Emily. Why didn't you tell me?'

'No, you're not. Look at the lovely cottage you have. I wish we had something like that.'

'I'd settle for what you have, any day.' Sylveen laughed nervously, wishing she hadn't said that. It was too near the truth. 'You've really landed on your feet, Emily.' She kissed her goodbye. 'Be happy.'

It was equally painful to see guests waving them off in another round of congratulations. To see the car move slowly away down the drive dragging three old boots somebody had tied to the bumper. To see Giles alone with Emily.

Emily sat in the front of Giles's Riley, watching it eat up mile after mile of road while the evening sun slipped lower in a blaze of golden light. The hum of the engine was making her sleepy.

The wedding, what she'd thought of as her first hurdle, was over. Half the population of Birkenhead had been present, most of whom she hadn't met before. Those she knew, had been dressed in their best and not always easy to recognise. She was relieved all the fuss and pomp was behind her and she hadn't disgraced herself.

She'd hardly had a chance to exchange two words with Giles all afternoon. She was glad to be alone with him at last, and half expected him to pull in to one of the laybys they were passing so that he could kiss her. She'd been the focus of everybody else's attention, yet strangely she'd felt ignored by him.

She stole a glance at him now, and though his handsome face was set with concentration, he noticed and smiled at her. 'Only another five miles.'

'You've driven a long way, Giles, you must be tired.'

'Wanted to reach the Castle Hotel for the first night. Want things to be right for you.'

Emily nodded. She'd never spent a night away from her narrow bed in the chip-shop attic. Any hotel was an adventure.

'Booked the bridal suite for us. A fourposter. You'll like it.'

'Sounds wonderful.' She was a little worried about the second hurdle. He was attaching great importance to the bed. She hoped she wouldn't disgrace herself there. She didn't want him to be disappointed. They had spent very little time alone. She felt she hardly knew him.

The hotel was a castellated mansion of breathtaking beauty. Its bridal suite was sumptuous. Emily had never seen a fourposter except on the cinema screen. She stood at the bedroom window looking down over the darkening lawns, expecting to feel his arms go round her now.

'Only ten minutes to get down to the dining-room,' Giles fussed. 'I don't know why they have to finish serving dinner at ten.'

'Are you hungry?' Emily asked dreamily. The wedding at two o'clock, for the convenience of the Parade shopkeepers, had meant the wedding breakfast was served in the middle of the afternoon.

'We must have dinner,' he said. 'Hurry up and change.'

'Won't this do?' She felt she was wearing her finery already. Her blue linen suit was her going-away outfit and had been chosen with great care.

Giles was petulant. 'I imagined for our first dinner together you'd wear a long romantic evening dress, and now there isn't time.'

Emily washed her hands and followed him down to the dining-room, where he seemed more interested in the bottle of red wine than the food. She noticed other people turning to look at Giles, particularly women. He didn't seem relaxed, didn't even seem to be enjoying all the luxury. It put her nerves on edge.

Giles was yawning before the meal came to an end. When it did, Emily wanted to delay the moment of going to bed. 'A stroll along the terrace?' she suggested.

Giles hesitated, frowning. 'It's dark. Let's go to bed.'

Emily unpacked her new nightdress. He surely wouldn't be disappointed with its low neckline and frills. She had bought it in Grange Road, not wanting Ethel's attention directed on it. She went to the bathroom to make herself ready, hardly able to look at Giles undressing.

She took a bath. Used the perfumed bath salts and powder she found provided there. The thick carpet of the bridal suite felt luxurious against her bare toes as she came back to the bedroom. Giles was already in bed. Only the bedside lights were lit and because of the festoons of silky curtaining on the bed, the light was dim inside. It took her a few moments to realise he was already asleep.

Emily got in beside him feeling it was a very strange thing to do. She couldn't tear her eyes away from Giles, with his bare torso, broad strong shoulders, and pale hair beautifully sculpted to his well-shaped head. He slept elegantly with his lips parted in a slight smile.

She had expected Giles to be an ardent lover, the typing pool had cast him in that role. Yet here he was, not showing any great eagerness. Emily felt strung high by the events of the day; she couldn't settle to sleep, though she wanted to now. Her mind was crawling with new impressions, experiences and sights. What she had expected to happen had not, she was beginning to worry that she did not measure up to his expectations.

She lay awake for hours, listening to Giles's steady breathing and watching the draperies of the bed waft slightly in the breeze from the window, musing on the mysteries of marriage. He was a glamorous stranger. She couldn't keep her eyes away from him, but it seemed that she didn't excite him.

She was still dazed with sleep when she felt him turning her over, and his arms tightening round her. She was jolted back to wakefulness to hear his muttered apologies: 'Over tired. Long hard day.' Emily was relieved to find that the only problem, and that he found her attractive after all.

As a lover she thought perhaps he did not have the great prowess she'd anticipated, but Emily expected to live happily ever after. They were man and wife, that was irrevocable.

Their journey continued to Torquay, and Emily thought the view across Torbay very beautiful. She'd never imagined England could be like this. Their hotel was luxurious, even Giles couldn't fault it. The weather was hot and sunny, but Giles seemed easily bored. She tried very hard to think of things to do that would interest him.

They went to expensive restaurants and swam in both pool and sea. He hired a boat several times, a motor boat for fishing trips, and a sailing boat to explore the bay. He liked the shops and they spent a lot of time in them. Emily found if she stopped to look at a dress or coat, she was likely to find him buying it for her. He spent a great deal of money and was very generous with his gifts.

At the end of the fortnight, she felt no closer to him. He said the honeymoon had been a great success, but Emily wasn't sure. Giles was restless and didn't seem to enjoy her company. Several times he'd suggested they go to the bar where there were other people to talk to. She felt apprehensive about the future.

that [illegible] but [illegible]

[illegible]

[illegible]

They [illegible] and spent [illegible]
[illegible]
for fishing [illegible] and a [illegible]
[illegible]
[illegible]
[illegible] that had [illegible] making [illegible]
[illegible]

[illegible]
[illegible]
[illegible] Violet was rescued and [illegible]
[illegible]
[illegible]
[illegible]

CHAPTER FIFTEEN

On the drive home, Emily made herself think about the third hurdle. She would not have chosen to live at Churton House. She had certainly wanted to go up in the world, but the change was too sudden and too great. Churton made her feel Cinderella-like.

Jeremy had a kind and pleasant manner but she was in awe of him. He was a rich and powerful man who could make or break the fortunes of others. The distance separating her from Jeremy was even greater than between her and Giles. The thought of living in his house made her apprehensive, she would have preferred a cottage some distance away, like Sylveen had. She felt she couldn't cope with the grandeur of Churton any more than she could with its master.

She made herself think of the suite she was to share with Giles as a flat, somewhere she could shut herself away. The servants were another anxiety.

'I could look after our flat quite easily,' she told Giles. 'What else will I have to do if I'm not to come to work?'

'Don't be silly,' he'd frowned. 'It would embarrass Father. You're my wife, you can't possibly clean the house. You've a position to keep up now.' She sighed, wondering how she was to learn to manage servants.

'Mrs Eglin will explain it all to you,' he said irritably. That made her freeze.

Mrs Eglin had been there the first day she had gone to Sunday lunch, when Aunt Harriet had asked her what her father did for a living. Emily had seen the look in her eyes when she'd said he owned a chip shop. Ever since, she felt Mrs Eglin had treated her as a usurper, as though she felt she was not good enough for Giles.

Her whole attitude said, Giles Wythenshaw's bride should be a lady, you would be better suited as a kitchen maid. Not in words, of course, but Emily was sure Mrs Eglin felt she was demeaning herself if she had to do some service for her. There was a bristling in her manner as she proffered vegetables at the table. A reluctance to show her the way to a cloakroom. Emily knew she could not expect help from her.

It was late afternoon when they reached Churton after the long drive back from Torquay.

'Welcome home.' Mrs Eglin came bustling out on the steps to greet them, baring the top of her teeth and upper gums in a smile that was all for Giles. For Emily there was a frosty nod before she summoned a housemaid.

'Betty, take the bags up.' The girl shot a curious glance in her direction before rushing out to the car.

'Your father asked me to tell you he's arranged a special dinner tonight. Seven o'clock, with drinks in the library first,' the housekeeper said to Giles.

'Is he home yet?'

'No, sir. Will that be all, madam?' Emily could see their cases left in the middle of the bedroom floor.

'Yes,' she was saying uncertainly.

'No,' Giles overruled, striding from one room to another. 'Get these bags unpacked and cleared away. I'm pleased with the sitting-room, Emily. It's turned out well.'

So was she, though she had tried to make the decor plainer and simpler. Jeremy had asked her opinion on every detail, but if it differed from Giles's, then Giles had his way. He had gone round the rest of the house picking out pieces of furniture he liked, and had them brought here. They had chosen new upholstered chairs and settees. There was an entirely new bathroom and kitchen.

'I don't see any drink up here.' Giles opened a cabinet with cut glassware set out in rows. 'I need a drink now, Mrs Eglin. Whisky, and bring a selection of bottles up. Sherry, brandy, everything. Do you want a drink, Emily?'

'I'd love some tea.' She looked up into the housekeeper's frosty face. 'Please.'

'I'll serve it in the drawing-room downstairs as usual, shall I, madam?' Emily felt numbed by the hostility in her eyes. 'Earl Grey, orange pekoe or do you prefer China tea?'

'Just tea,' Emily said weakly. 'I don't want anything to eat.' She watched the woman close the door softly behind her before she said: 'Do I have to go downstairs to the drawing-room for a cup of tea?'

'Only if you want to. You are a little silly.' He strode straight to the bell push and kept his finger on it for a long minute. When the housekeeper returned he said: 'Madam has changed her mind, she'll have her tea up here.'

'Yes, madam,' and Emily thought she saw the flicker of triumph in her eyes.

'You've got to tell her what you want, Emily,' Giles said when they were alone. 'Otherwise it will be what's easiest for her. Save their legs not having to carry tea upstairs.'

'I could make my own tea here,' Emily said miserably, looking round her little kitchen, and thinking it would be much easier.

'If that's what you want tell her to stock the shelves. Bring up tea, coffee, milk everything.' Giles, she knew, couldn't see her problem.

She felt tired after the journey and would have liked a quiet evening, but it was not to be. Jeremy had wanted a celebration dinner. 'I'll have a bath and change. Do you think my red evening dress tonight?'

'No, there'll only be the three of us. Something simple. What about that blue dress with pleats I chose in Torquay?' It made Emily realise how much she had to learn.

Later, wearing it and feeling better, she went down to the library with Giles. Jeremy rose to kiss her cheek, she felt they were both trying to be welcoming.

It was very different to sit down and enjoy a drink before dinner. She told herself it was much better than coping with rush hour in the shop. She started telling him how beautiful Torquay had been.

When Mrs Eglin announced that dinner was ready, she trailed into the dining-room behind the men and found them waiting for her to sit down. Three places had been set at one end of the table. Lighted candles in silver candelabra blocked off the expanse of polished mahogany stretching up the room. Emily toyed with Parma ham, surprised anyone should think of eating it raw.

'I want you to think of Churton as your home,' Jeremy told her. Emily looked round the panelled dining-room with its portraits of earlier Wythenshaws. It wasn't going to be easy. 'Use the sitting-rooms down here when you want to. I don't want you to be shy and shut yourself away in your own wing.'

Emily murmured her thanks, telling herself he meant it kindly. Once the main course had been served, the staff withdrew while they ate it and Jeremy went on:

'I'd like you to take an interest in running the household. The staff need livening up a bit. Having just a couple of bachelors to take care of has made it too easy for them.' Emily froze, feeling appalled.

'They've all given years of faithful service. Loyal and trustworthy, all of them, but they need a woman to keep them on their toes.'

She felt scared, unable to swallow. Jeremy was expecting more of her than she could give.

'How do you like the pheasant?' She shaved the smallest possible piece from the breast on her plate and put it in her mouth. Was pheasant thought to be a delicacy?

'Very nice, I've not had it before.' She preferred chicken, and though Jeremy spoke of the wine as something special, it was like bitter aloes on her tongue.

'Now there's a woman in the house, I expect things to improve. When you find your feet, we'll give a few dinner parties.'

Emily's fork paused halfway to her mouth as she was gripped with new misgivings. 'Like the Sunday lunches you invited me to?'

'No, Sunday lunch is a family occasion with plain solid roasts, simply served. I want to entertain properly, live with a bit more style. Without a hostess, it's difficult to manage a dinner party. I want to introduce you to my friends.'

Emily, gulping at her glass of water, compared this table with the oilcloth in the living-room behind the shop. Everything at Churton looked so stylish, it was going to take time to feel at ease with it. She knew nothing about style, she certainly couldn't improve on this. She felt desperate.

'The kitchen needs new life breathing into it. Too many plain roasts, though Cook is good at them. Can you cook, Emily?'

'Yes, fish and chips,' she said. He laughed, thinking she was making a joke of it, but Emily felt her spirits plummet, it was just about the only thing she could cook.

'I'm sure Mrs Eglin and Cook can do it. It's just a question of getting them organised, explaining to them what you want.'

Emily was trembling, she felt incapable of organising Mrs Eglin to do anything. She had never had to tell anybody what to do. Up till now, her lot in life had been to jump when others ordered it. She was panic-stricken about the new role she was expected to step into. She tried to explain this to him.

'I don't want you to worry about it, Emily,' Jeremy said when they were preparing to go up to bed. 'Give yourself time to find your feet. Take over the reins gradually, there's no hurry.'

She was in a state of agitation when she reached her bedroom. 'I can't,' she said to Giles who was calmly getting undressed. 'Mrs Eglin doesn't like me, she's trying to make me feel uncomfortable.'

'Nonsense, Emily. You're imagining things.'

'I know it. Take up the reins! I wouldn't know where to begin.'

'Course you do,' he said, getting into bed. 'Anyway, Father says take your time.'

Emily quaked, afraid a hundred years wouldn't be long enough. She couldn't sleep. It was another night spent listening to Giles's steady breathing. She was even dreading Giles and Jeremy going off to work in the morning, leaving her alone with Mrs Eglin and the servants.

Betty the housemaid brought morning tea. Emily felt sleep-sodden; she'd fallen into a heavy sleep at dawn. Only half-awake she pulled herself up on her pillows to drink the tea the girl was pouring out for her. Betty, a girl near her own age, looked at her shyly: 'Shall I draw the curtains, madam?'

'Yes,' Giles said. 'I suppose I shall have to go to work. You don't have to get up, Emily. I'd stay where you are.'

When he'd dressed and gone, she lay back, dozing for an hour and worrying about how she'd ever cope with a dinner party. That brought all her anxieties flooding back. She got up and dressed, feeling she could lie there no longer with it on her mind. She rang the bell for service, having decided she'd have breakfast here in her own rooms.

The housemaid Betty came in shyly. 'Mrs Eglin asked me to say breakfast is waiting for you in the dining-room downstairs, and please can I tidy your bedroom while you're away?'

Emily took the line of least resistance and went downstairs. The deserted dining-room looked formidably formal. A white damask cloth covered a third of the table this morning. One place was set. There were chafing dishes under silver covers on the sideboard; she crept over and lifted one. Bacon was frazzled to a crisp by being kept waiting. She rang the bell as she had seen Jeremy do last night.

'Good morning, madam.' Mrs Eglin appeared in person at the door.

'I'd like some fresh tea and some grapefruit please.'

'We haven't any grapefruit, madam. It's something we don't order in this house.' The top of her teeth were bared momentarily in a snarling smile.

'Why not?'

'The gentlemen don't care for it.'

Emily stared at the plasterwork on the ceiling. 'I do,' she said. Not that she'd had it very often, but she'd enjoyed it on her honeymoon. 'Perhaps you'd order some for me?'

'We received our weekly order yesterday, madam, and won't be ordering again till next week.'

'Next week, then,' Emily capitulated. 'In the meantime, I'll have toast with the tea.'

'Yes, madam,' and there was no mistaking the half-veiled insolence in her manner.

Afterwards, Emily went slowly from room to room absorbing the gracious atmosphere of high ceilings of ornamental plasterwork, of tall windows overlooking park-like gardens, of antique furniture and comfortable sofas. She was more than uneasy, feeling restless and unable to settle to anything. She felt she'd been bested by Mrs Eglin which would make it harder than ever to do what Jeremy expected.

The day stretched ahead, empty till Giles returned, and she was used to bustling offices, busy shops and a lot of hard work.

Suddenly she remembered Sylveen and how interested she was in cooking and home-making. At that moment Sylveen seemed a lifeline. Emily rushed to the telephone.

'Come round and see me.' It brought relief to hear her familiar breathy voice. 'I want to hear all about it. Did you have a wild time?'

'I don't know about wild.' Emily was guarded. She was having reservations about everything in her new life. It wasn't going to be as easy as the typing pool had predicted.

'Come straight round and spend the day with me. Salad all right for lunch?'

'Yes, fine thanks.'

'You've made my day. I'm looking forward to this.'

Emily felt cheered and was racing upstairs to get ready, when she saw Mrs Eglin crossing the hall.

'I shall be out for lunch,' she said. Then as an after-thought added, 'Where do I catch the bus to Heswall?'

'Turn left at the bottom of the drive, the stop's a hundred yards further on.'

'Do you have a timetable?'

'There's one in the kitchen. I'll send Betty up with it.'

'Thank you,' Emily said, wondering if she was paranoid about the housekeeper. For the first time, she was being helpful.

When she saw Sylveen, she felt quite alarmed. She had never seen her look so pale and her sparkle had gone.

'Aren't you well?'

'I'm all right, I suppose. You can't expect me to look wonderful when I'm seven months pregnant.' Emily studied her, she looked tired. Her blonde hair had less life.

'It's more than that, isn't it?'

'I'm just a bit down. Here I am again like this. It's not a lot of fun on your own.'

'You're not on your own. Hasn't Jeremy been to see you?'

'Yes.'

'It won't be like last time. Only a few more weeks and it'll be over. You'll feel better.'

'I feel better now, having you here.' Sylveen's smile was tremulous. 'I wish I was a married woman like you.'

Sylveen's cottage was homely and comfortable. 'I wish I had a cottage like yours,' Emily smiled. Over coffee, she poured out her own problems.

'Churton is a wonderful place,' Sylveen breathed. 'You'll love it once you're used to it. All those servants . . .'

'Jeremy says they've got slack having only two bachelors in the house.'

'Have they?'

'How would I know? Everything is immaculate. The meals are lovely. You know, you've been.'

'Perhaps he just wants a bit of change. What do you think of the housekeeper?'

'She terrifies me. So superior.'

'You're imagining things.'

'No.'

'She's all right with me, a bit starchy perhaps.'

'Not with me. She can't get me any grapefruit until next week.'

'Buy some as you go through Heswall,' Sylveen advised. 'Show her you mean to have your own way. You'll have to let her know you're the lady of the house.'

'How?' Emily wailed. 'There's nothing I can complain about.'

'Show her you've got the upper hand.'

'But I haven't!'

'Look at her as though you're used to a fleet of servants.'

'She knows I'm not, heard me say my father had a fish

and chip shop. She's looked down her nose at me ever since.'

'Oh dear! She can't be that wonderful or Jeremy wouldn't think she needs livening up. And if he can't sort her out, he must know how hard it would be for you.'

'Women's work, that's why he can't do it. He sees you providing stylish meals here without help and thinks all women can do it. And he's on about having dinner parties for twelve. I've never even been to a dinner party, Sylveen. You've got to help me.'

'I'd love to.' Sylveen was coming alive before her eyes. Emily realised then it was what Sylveen needed. To involve her in the household management problems at Churton would be very good for them both. 'Lots of light courses, each with a different wine. Dress up the table.'

'You'll be my salvation, Sylveen. Ask Jeremy if you can come and help.'

'You must ask him, Emily.' Her depression seemed banished. 'He's asked you to act as his hostess. You'll have to tell him you need me. I could make lemon sorbet and push that in as an extra course to clean the palate. Seems more impressive than it is.'

Emily smiled. 'You'd be better as lady of the manor. He's got us in the wrong places.'

'I can show you. We'll have a bit of fun doing it together.' Emily went home with borrowed books on cookery and household management. In Heswall, she bought four grapefruit. It was later than she'd expected by the time she got back to Churton, but she had a quick bath and changed into a fresh dress.

She found Jeremy in the library drinking whisky. He rose to his feet as she went in, offered her a drink and then poured it for her. 'Where's Giles?' he asked. 'Isn't he home yet?'

'No, what time does he usually come home?'

'With a new wife here, I'd have thought before now. Have you had a quiet day here on your own?'

'I've been to Heswall to see Sylveen.' She took a deep breath and the words came tumbling out. 'Can I ask her here? Would you mind? I think I'm going to need help, you see. I've never lived in a big house, and I know nothing about dinner parties. Never even been to one. Sylveen's interested in things like that, and it would do her good to come here and show me. She wants to, I think she's bored by herself at home. It's difficult for her to get out much now.'

Jeremy sat swirling the whisky round his glass for so long Emily thought she'd upset him. 'I didn't realise you two were such friends.' His piercing blue eyes met hers at last. 'You're right about Sylveen, she's spending too much time alone. Yes, ask her here, get her to show you what's needed.'

Emily felt a weight had been lifted from her shoulders. With Sylveen's help, she thought she might cope.

'I'm glad she lives so close. It's easy to get there, though I did just miss the bus on the way back. I was afraid Giles would be home before me.'

'You went on the bus? I left a message with Mrs Eglin to tell you to use the Alvis if you wanted to go out.'

Emily felt suddenly cold. That proved it.

'Just send one of the maids to find Stanley. He's a gardener, but he can drive you about locally.'

She'd not imagined Mrs Elgin's hostility. She'd even sent Betty up with a bus timetable! It was firming up her mind. She must not allow the housekeeper to treat her like this. It took an effort to make her voice sound normal.

'That's very kind. She must have forgotten. Can I send him to collect Sylveen tomorrow?'

'Yes, use him as you wish. Here's Giles now. I was beginning to think we'd have to start dinner without him.'

Giles's face felt cold against her own as he pecked her cheek.

'Have I got time for a bath first, Father?'

'No,' Jeremy barked, 'you've kept us waiting long enough. Where have you been till now?'

'Stopped at the club to see somebody.'

'Get yourself a drink if you want it and we'll go straight in,' Jeremy said, and Emily realised for the first time just how tense the relationship was between Giles and his father.

Next morning when Betty brought her morning tea she gave her the bag of grapefruit and asked her to prepare one and bring it back upstairs in about an hour. Giles had barely left for breakfast in the dining-room when it came back on a beautifully set tray, with tea and toast. She telephoned Sylveen. 'You can come,' she said. 'I've asked him.'

'Wonderful!'

'What time? I'm sending his car for you. Said I could do that too.'

'Say an hour, give me time to tidy up here a bit first. Have you been down to sort Mrs Eglin out?'

'Not yet.' She told her about the message from Jeremy she hadn't passed on. 'She thinks I'm not good enough to ride about in a fine car. I knew she was being difficult.'

'Emily, you're a Wythenshaw now! Don't take any more from her. Do it now, when you arrange the car for me.'

Emily gathered her courage and went down to the kitchen. She'd never invaded Mrs Eglin's territory before. She found her, the cook and two maids at breakfast.

She pulled up a chair and sat down, introduced herself to the cook whom she hadn't yet met and ignored the frost in Mrs Eglin's manner.

'Do carry on with your breakfast,' she said, since the

woman had laid her knife and fork down. 'Pity to let it get cold.'

She was on the attack immediately. 'At what time, madam, will you vacate your rooms in the morning? So Betty can get in to tidy up,' the housekeeper added, sipping her tea in ladylike fashion.

Emily showed as much surprise as she could, knowing it was now or never. 'I prefer to come and go when I'm ready, not at any set time. Betty can come immediately she's finished her breakfast, whether I'm there or not.' She saw the housekeeper straighten with surprise and knew she'd hit the right note. It gave her the courage to add: 'Mr Wythenshaw has asked me to take an interest in the housekeeping.'

She could see her bristling at that. 'I'm sure I've always given Mr Wythenshaw satisfaction.'

'I'm sure you have, Mrs Eglin. It's just that he thinks Wythenshaw wives should control the household. What have you planned for dinner tonight?'

'Mr Wythenshaw will not be in for dinner,' the housekeeper was quick to pounce.

'Oh.'

'So it will be for Mr Giles and yourself. Did you have anything special in mind?'

Emily felt she'd cut the ground from under her feet. Jeremy had not told her he'd be out. 'No, what do you have in?'

'Do you care for fish? Perhaps hake?' Cook suggested.

'I'm expecting a friend for lunch. We'll have the hake then.'

'Does madam want chips with it?' Emily's eyes jerked to look at Mrs Eglin's face, there was no mistaking the insolence in her manner.

'No thank you,' she said frostily, turning back to Cook. 'Parsley sauce and mashed potatoes please.' She was fighting a terrible urge to run back to her own apartments.

'And for dinner, madam?' Cook pressed.

'Giles likes steak, so we'll have that.' It took the supreme effort to look Mrs Eglin in the eye and add: 'He likes chips, so perhaps those too.' She knew now she could leave with her dignity intact. 'If you'd like to come up with me now, Betty, I'll explain what I want done in my rooms.'

It was only when the thin-faced Betty stood at the door of her sitting-room clutching dusters and hoover, that Emily remembered about sending the car for Sylveen. Betty was dispatched to find Stanley before starting anything else.

Seeing Sylveen get out of the Alvis at the front steps altered everything. Her figure had thickened, she now looked noticeably pregnant, but this morning she could still run up the steps. Emily met her in the hall and was swept into an exuberant hug. 'You're better today,' she told her.

'Decided to snap out of it,' Sylveen said. She'd washed her hair that morning, and was wearing an elegant lavender dress. 'Life's too short. Now, I want a complete tour of the house, inside and out, before we think of anything else.' She giggled. 'Didn't dare say that to Jeremy.'

'Haven't seen it all myself yet,' Emily laughed. 'Where do you want to start?'

'The main rooms, but skip the library, I've seen all I need in there.' Sylveen bustled round, full of energy, exclaiming with joy at the size of the rooms and the grandeur of the furniture.

When Emily took her up to her own suite, Sylveen sank into a chair and said: 'You've got it made, Emily, mistress of all this. With a housekeeper, a cook and two maids.' She counted them off on her fingers. 'Then there's Higgins, and two gardeners. All to look after two men.'

'It's a big house,' Emily said.

'I bet they don't push themselves.'

'There's our lunch to prepare today.'

'There's a cook with nothing else to do. She'll be cooking a meal for the staff anyway. It's a wonderful house. You ought to be thrilled, Emily.'

'I'd be more thrilled if I knew how to run it.'

'Let's go to the kitchens. Get out all the best glasses and silver. See what table linen there is instead of those starched white cloths. See if there's a different dinner service. Everything is bound to be dusty if it isn't used much. Be sure to tell Mrs Eglin it needs washing, if you get the chance.'

'I've had one brush with her this morning, I'm not sure I'm ready for another.'

'Get yourself ready, Emily.' Sylveen gripped her arm. 'You've got to know the routine and what's here before you can do anything. Poke round, ask how they manage. Right?'

'She isn't going to like this. I don't think she likes me going into the kitchen.'

'You want her to hate it. That's the only way you'll stop her giving you the runaround. The only way you'll get more style on the table. Come on.' Sylveen headed down the passage.

Mrs Eglin and Cook were having coffee at the table. There was an open biscuit barrel between them. One maid was at the sink peeling potatoes. Emily took a firm grasp on her nerves.

'We've come to see round the kitchens, Mrs Eglin, I hope it's a convenient moment?'

She stood up. 'If you had let me know, madam, I could have had everything ready for you.'

'Better we see it as it is,' Emily said as firmly as she could. 'Do you cook on the Aga?'

'Usually, but we do have a gas cooker too.'

'And a refrigerator?' Sylveen asked. 'Would it be possible to make ice cream?'

Cook's face fell. 'Yes, I suppose so.'

'Mr Wythenshaw wants to give a dinner party,' Emily explained as they toured the old-fashioned chill room and preparation rooms.

In the butler's pantry Sylveen peeped in a cupboard and found it filled with glassware. Emily opened another and found a china dinner service in a biscuit colour with a relief pattern of flowers and a gold border.

'There must be half a dozen dinner services here,' Mrs Eglin said. 'Fancy stuff, we don't use them.'

Sylveen lifted a tureen down to the table. 'Lovely, just look at this. Must be hundreds of pieces to this service. Is there enough for twelve, Mrs Eglin? Wonderful for a dinner party. That half-moon dish is for salad, but what about this? A finger bowl, do you think?'

Emily shook her head. 'I don't know. To me matching plates are a dinner service.'

'This is how you put style on the table, Emily,' Sylveen whispered. 'Bet he hasn't seen any of this for years. Look at these wine glasses. Is this Waterford crystal?'

Emily felt the jab Sylveen made at her ribs. 'It could all do with a wash, Mrs Eglin,' she said, unable to look at Sylveen. 'Can you show us where the table linen is kept?'

The housekeeper took them to the passage outside her sitting-room where there were drawers full of white damask tablecloths. 'Each about an acre in size,' Sylveen commented.

'Beautifully laundered and starched,' Emily added quickly, and saw Sylveen raise her delicately arched brows at her. 'Are there any place mats? Or a lace tablecloth?'

More drawers were pulled open. 'Marvellous,' Sylveen cried, picking out dark-brown linen place mats. 'Are there a dozen of these?' Mrs Eglin began to count them.

'A bit plain, aren't they?' Emily asked.

'Jeremy loves subdued things. Let's try a few on the table. I hope they match the colour of the wood.' Emily followed Sylveen's bustling figure to the dining-room and agreed the mats were hardly visible, once on the table.

'The silver and cut glass will sparkle twice as bright on a dark background,' Sylveen enthused, leading the way back to the butler's pantry. 'Just a few cream-coloured flowers in low bowls. We'll need brown or cream table napkins, Mrs Eglin, are there any here?'

'There are a dozen mats,' she said coldly.

'We'd better have them washed and starched again to freshen them,' Emily ordered. 'Crumpled, been lying in a drawer for years.'

Back in her own wing, Emily made coffee while Sylveen opened up the cookery books. 'This is the exciting part, mustn't be too rich, nor difficult to cook. We don't want any disasters.'

'Shouldn't we have consulted Cook?'

'Not yet, you can tell her when we've given it some thought,' Sylveen murmured. 'Must have a salad to use those half-moon plates. Endive and citrus? And start with a prawn and cucumber mousse, I think. How many brace of grouse to feed twelve?'

'Cook will know about that,' Emily said faintly.

'So will *Mrs Beeton's Household Management*. The book I gave you last night.'

They spent hours drawing up a menu, Sylveen deciding what she would ask Cook to do and what she would do herself.

'A shopping excursion the day before, so we know we've got all we need and a rehearsal so the table is set exactly as I want it.'

'I'll ask Jeremy who he wants to invite and when,' Emily said. 'You will be here too?'

'Try and stop me,' Sylveen said. 'I'm loving all this, but I'll have to go home. Jeremy's coming for dinner tonight, and I have things to do.'

'I have things to do too,' Emily sighed.

'Don't forget, you must sort her out now, once and for all.'

'I've done it already, surely? She thought we were interfering this morning.'

'No, Emily, that just got her back up. Make her worse because she'll try to get her own back. You've got to lay the law down or she'll probably win in the end. Promise you'll do it now or it'll drag on.'

As soon as Sylveen had gone home Emily rang for service. As she expected, it was Betty who answered.

'Please tell Mrs Eglin I want a word with her up here,' she said, and then in a flurry of nerves paced the floor waiting for her to come. It took her twenty minutes. As they dragged over, Emily realised that Sylveen was right; the skirmishes she'd had with her this morning had solved nothing.

Sylveen had spelled out to her what she must say. Taken her through the interview step by step. 'Don't ask her to sit, and don't you stand.'

The knock on the door was aggressive and Mrs Eglin stood before her, black eyes blazing with antagonism because she'd been asked to come upstairs.

'Mrs Eglin,' Emily began, her teeth almost chattering with fright. 'I asked you to come up here because we have something to discuss in private.' She calmed down a little when she saw the colour draining from the older woman's face.

'Yesterday Mr Wythenshaw left a message with you that I might use his car. He was very surprised to hear I'd gone to Heswall on the bus.'

'I forgot,' she said. 'I'm sorry.' There was no hint of remorse in her manner.

'I'm surprised it didn't jog your memory when I asked for a bus timetable.' The woman was silent, and would no longer meet her eyes. 'Didn't it?'

'No, madam.'

'Why have you taken a dislike to me?'

'I haven't,' she protested. 'Of course I haven't.'

'Then is it because you've had no mistress to answer to for the last fifteen years? You've run this house exactly as you wished. The staff have had it to themselves all day during the week?' Still she didn't answer. Emily tightened her grip on the arms of her chair.

'I would have preferred that my husband and I had a small house of our own, Mrs Eglin, one I could have run without staff. My father-in-law wanted this arrangement. He also wants me to take an active part in running this house, and I'm going to do it.' Emily took a deep breath. Horrors, it was developing into a monologue.

'People don't like change, but we have to accept it. You are going to have to accept me whether you like it or not.' She paused for breath. 'Are you afraid of losing your job?'

'I'm sure I've always given satisfaction . . .'

'Of course you have. Mr Wythenshaw says you are trustworthy and loyal, but it doesn't give me satisfaction when you forget messages. Neither do I enjoy your snide references to fish and chips.' Emily could see the housekeeper was beginning to look uncomfortable.

'You're a lot older than I am, you know more about running this house, about Mr Wythenshaw's likes and dislikes, but I intend to learn and I expect you to help me. In future, don't try to score off me. And don't ever try and thwart me.' Emily stood up, she'd run through the list Sylveen had made for her. She felt she'd got a load off her chest. 'I'm sure we'll get on now we know where we stand. I may look like a slip of a girl to you, but don't forget I'm Mrs Wythenshaw.'

Emily collapsed back in the chair when she'd gone. It took her a long time to recover her equilibrium.

[illegible] have you got against [illegible]?

[illegible]

[illegible]

[illegible]

[illegible] Emily [illegible]

[illegible]

[illegible]

CHAPTER SIXTEEN

'About these dinner parties.' Sylveen's blue eyes were sparkling. 'Let's do one soon.'

Emily stiffened; her instincts were to put them off, but she knew Sylveen needed something to occupy her during the last months of her pregnancy. Also, she was afraid that once Sylveen's baby was born, she would put only half her mind to dinner parties at Churton, and if she delayed too long Jeremy might put on pressure.

'All right,' she agreed, though the thought made her shiver with nervous excitement. 'As soon as we can. You'll be coming to partner Jeremy?'

'No, don't infer anything like that. Let it be known I'm your friend, the spare lady to make up the numbers.'

That evening, Emily asked Jeremy for his list of guests and he said he was pleased they were going ahead so quickly. Sylveen had already shown her how to type up the invitations on Churton notepaper. Mr Jeremy Wythenshaw and Mrs Giles Wythenshaw request the pleasure of the company . . . Emily was shocked to find he'd given her ten names.

'In case somebody declines,' Jeremy explained, but nobody did and that meant fourteen to sit down.

'What's another two if you're catering for twelve?' Sylveen asked calmly. In return, Emily gave Jeremy the menu and asked him to choose and organise the wines.

'What am I going to talk about?' she'd asked Sylveen.

'Anything. Tell them about Torquay. Talk about cooking or anything else that interests you.'

It was Emily's biggest worry. After all, these people were the cream of Merseyside society.

'Just to be on the safe side,' Sylveen pushed two newspapers into her hand on the morning of the party, 'let's enjoy a quiet hour perusing these.'

Emily had been stiff with tension as she'd come downstairs just before the guests were due to arrive.

It was a comfort to hear Sylveen's gutsy laugh from the hall below as she had a word with Jeremy. She had spent hours in the kitchen throughout the afternoon, and was only now on her way upstairs to bath and change.

'Is everything all right?' Emily asked nervously.

'Everything's coming on well,' Sylveen smiled. 'Come on, relax and enjoy it.'

Emily took a deep breath: 'What would I do without you?' Sylveen had been wonderful, finding books and magazine articles on entertaining and etiquette for her to read. She felt very grateful, though this first dinner seemed like a test at school where she had to put all she'd read into practice.

Giles came down behind her looking wonderful in a dinner jacket. He took her arm and led her into the drawing-room, where he made a great fuss about mixing a cocktail for her. When the guests started to arrive, he was at her side, introducing her as his bride. Emily's nervousness was mixed with love and pride. Giles was a husband to be proud of.

'Have to circulate,' he murmured suddenly, and went to join a group of wives and daughters on the other side of the room. She couldn't help but notice the women were eyeing him in the way the office girls had and sending surreptitious glances in her direction, as though wondering what he'd seen in her.

She felt deserted and very much alone, though a man she couldn't name came to talk to her. He was holding forth earnestly on how the River Dee had silted up over the centuries, land-locking Parkgate, once a port from which ships sailed to Ireland. It seemed irrelevant, and she couldn't concentrate.

She couldn't drag her eyes away from Giles. His hot tawny eyes were burning down into those of the girl by his side. His expression the same as when he'd come to perch on her office desk. She hadn't expected him to do that any more. Not now he was her husband. She shivered, it felt like a kick in the teeth, like rejection. She wanted him here at her side.

Her head rang with names of the guests. She knew those well enough after sending out invitations and receiving the acceptances and Jeremy had told her a little about his friends. But they had all arrived on time, one couple after the other, and she wasn't sure she was fitting the names to the right faces.

Was it Philomena Bird that Giles was paying so much attention to? She tried to recall what Jeremy had told her about the family. Walter Bird, her father, had provided the printing and packaging used at Wythenshaw's for two decades. He'd died suddenly a few years back and his wife, Elvira, had run the company very successfully since.

Yes, Elvira had joined her daughter and was talking to Giles too. A plump lady wearing a shiny dress that emphasised her surplus flesh. Fortyish, growing heavy round the jowls but not unattractive, her dark eyes were fastened on Giles too. Emily emptied her glass with one gulp and told herself she was foolish to feel jealous. Giles was a handsome man. She must expect the ladies to make much of him.

There was no reason why he should be bowled over by Philomena. The name Bird suited her too well. Her nose was large and beakish. Her dark eyes were beady, like those of a sparrow hawk, but they were laughing up at Giles, showing her interest.

Sylveen was nodding that it was time to take the ladies up to powder their noses before the meal. Emily took a deep steadying breath, she must not forget her duties as hostess. She did what was expected of her and led the ladies upstairs.

Sylveen had decided on the bedroom and bathroom to be used as a cloakroom and had the bed made up with pretty covers to take away the unused look. 'So nice for Jeremy to have a hostess,' Elvira Bird said to her, as she put up clouds of face powder in front of the dressing-table mirror, but there was nothing friendly about her manner.

Emily, feeling very keyed up, got everybody to the table without too much trouble. The hum of conversation must mean it was going well. She had never seen the dining-table fully used before.

Sylveen had been right about the brown linen place mats making the glass and silver sparkle more brightly. The biscuit-coloured dinner service with its raised pattern of flowers and the low bowls of cream roses gave it an air of restrained elegance.

She had always thought the dining-room sombre and dark, but tonight with the women in jewel-coloured evening dresses it came to life.

Not that she felt comfortable sitting at the bottom of the table in the chair that marked her out as hostess. Looking up its length, she could see the lamplight shining on Jeremy's silver hair at the other end. He was talking with great animation to the woman on his right and seemed to be enjoying himself.

On her left, Emily had the managing director of a

margarine factory, on her right a senior official of a bank, but both seemed happy to have her listen to them.

Sylveen had giggled as they'd drawn up the seating plan. It was she who had put Giles next to Elvira Bird. Philomena was pecking at a bread roll well down the table, teamed up with the son of a transport company director.

The food came, course after relentless course; she couldn't see why anybody should want to eat so much, but it was beautifully presented, tasted good and there were no problems with the service. From napkin-wrapped bottles, Higgins was filling then refilling the battery of wine glasses set at each place.

Emily took a grip on herself. She must not mind about Giles. He had always been like this, he was a ladies' man. She had known that from the beginning. She should not expect marriage to change him, but she felt disappointment that it had not.

It helped now to see Sylveen halfway down the table, chatting to somebody in shipping. She looked relaxed and beautiful in a royal-blue gown in the empire style. There was nothing in her manner to show she had changed all the lampshades in the room to plain cream, picked and arranged the flowers and folded the napkins into water lilies. She was staying very much in the background, letting it seem Emily had made all the arrangements.

The meal was coming to an end, but Jeremy was recounting some anecdote, holding the attention of most of his guests. Tension was tightening in her chest again. She was relying on Sylveen to give her a nod confirming the time was right to lead the ladies off for coffee in the drawing-room. Jeremy's voice died away. In the general laughter that followed, Sylveen's head nodded almost imperceptibly towards the door. Emily tossed her napkin on the table and stood up.

'Ladies,' she said in the way the etiquette books recommended. 'Shall we leave the men to their port?'

Sylveen was on her feet in seconds, the rest followed. As they trailed out behind her, Emily knew the whole thing had been a success, she need not have worried.

When everybody went home, Jeremy praised their efforts, saying he was very impressed. They had another dinner the following week and then a third. Emily found it got easier with practice and asked about a fourth.

'I've returned all the hospitality I owe for the moment,' he said. 'We'll leave it for a while. About once a month should be enough from now on.'

'Thank goodness for that,' Giles said. 'I'm tired of all your old cronies. Full of their own self-importance . . .'

'I specially invited the young too,' Jeremy flared back at him. 'I went out of my way to include sons and daughters so that Emily and you would meet people of your own age.'

Over the following months, Jeremy's hospitality was returned. Emily and Giles were usually invited with him. Emily got over her initial nervousness and began to enjoy these occasions.

They paid a return visit to the Bird household; Emily hadn't enjoyed that. Philomena seemed more than interested in Giles. Hadn't the whole of the office expected him to marry the daughter of one of his father's rich friends?

Emily knew she could manage a dinner party on her own now if she had to. She felt closer to Sylveen, who had helped her solve the problem of handling the housekeeper too. Sylveen was spending more and more time with her at Churton. She brought her own cookery books with her and pointed out recipes Jeremy had particularly enjoyed at her cottage, so Emily could hand them on to Cook to enlarge her repertoire of family menus.

They had both taken a dislike to the huge dining-room.

It was over-formal for family use and the table off-putting when set for one or two. She and Sylveen toured the other ground-floor rooms; there were a good many that were hardly used.

Emily liked what Betty referred to as the pink parlour. It was much lighter, with silvery-pink wallpaper and a beige and pink Indian carpet. It was no further from the kitchen, had french windows on to a terrace and faced south-east to catch the morning sun.

She called the gardeners in to take out some of the sofas and move in an oval mahogany table and chairs, designed to seat six. Jeremy approved and told Emily the woman's touch was improving the comfort at Churton. Emily wasn't sure whether the woman's touch belonged to her or Sylveen.

As the birth of Sylveen's baby drew closer, preparations for it took precedence over everything else. Emily felt she was living and sleeping babies and even Giles seemed swept up in the fever. Everybody was making a tremendous fuss of Sylveen, and Emily had to tell herself she was a fool to feel envious. Wasn't Sylveen envious of her own married state?

They were going shopping for the final items in the layette on the morning Emily first thought it possible she could be pregnant too. It seemed the answer to her niggling envy. She was thrilled at the thought of having a baby of her own.

'Everything will be wonderful for you.' Sylveen gave her a kiss of congratulation. 'An heir for the Wythenshaw fortune.'

When she told Giles, he swept her into a boisterous bear hug and danced with her round their sitting-room, his face lit up with joy.

'You're pleased?' She could see he was, but she wanted to hear him say it.

'Delighted,' he laughed. 'Wonderful news.'

Emily felt joy bubble through her. A baby could change everything for her and Giles.

She had expected married life to provide more loving and more romance. Hadn't she and Giles been swept up in a heady love affair of flowers and champagne? She was conscious of thinking about Giles all day, wanting him home with her. Of being impatient when he was late, hurt if he stayed out all evening. How many times had she run to him as he came through the door, but found no answering passion in him, no fever of emotion. She found it hurtful to find he didn't want her as she wanted him.

She couldn't accuse him of never making love, but while she had waited for the moment, tingled at his touch and could never have enough of him, he seemed like a man already satiated. For him it held no thrill, no excitement; he took her for granted, brushing her fingers away if she reached out to touch him. Jeremy seemed to make more fuss of her than Giles.

She might be a success in domestic matters, but Emily felt she was failing as a wife. She could not rouse her husband to the peaks of passion he roused in her. And worse, he didn't seem to want her company. She saw more of Sylveen than she did of Giles.

A baby would be something they could share, it would bring them closer, weld them together. With a baby, she would be more part of the family. She hoped it would be the answer to their difficulties.

'I'm delighted,' Jeremy said, taking both her hands in his as he kissed her cheek. His beaming smile left her in no doubt he meant it. He called for champagne to be put on ice immediately and then rationed her to two glasses.

'You must cosset her now, Giles,' he told him.

'Of course I shall,' Giles had agreed, but it hadn't changed his ways.

Emily turned to Sylveen for information about child-birth in the way she had for help with clothes and dinner parties. Sylveen was a mine of information on every aspect, from the assembly of the layette to the birth itself. Emily began to feel more settled in the married state.

Not that it was always easy. Jeremy was often out in the evenings. Emily knew he went to Sylveen's cottage to be alone with her, but often Giles was out in the evenings too without explanation. It seemed to be that if Jeremy was in having an early night, then Giles stayed out.

'You must have felt the sparks flying between us, Emily. Father and I are not compatible. Better if we don't see too much of each other, we only row and that upsets me.' Emily knew nobody could miss the tension twisting between them when they were both tired after a day's work.

'If you are having a meal out, couldn't I come with you sometimes?' she asked.

'Emily, you are so good with Father. He likes your company. You keep him happy at home when he has his early nights. Think of that as your job now.'

About once a week, Emily would ask Stanley to drive her to Paradise Parade. Gran would change into her best frock and come with her for an afternoon outing. They would drive to New Brighton, have a stroll along the promenade followed by afternoon tea. Sometimes they would go to Parkgate or to the shops in Chester.

Emily found pleasure in watching Gran's face. For her, such trips were beyond her wildest dreams. 'We can go as often as you want,' she told her.

'Could we ask Ethel and Olympia to come too, once in a while?' Gran asked.

'Of course. What about next early-closing day?'

'Go and ask them,' Gran said when they returned to the Parade. So Emily went into Fraser's to arrange it.

'Beats the old life does it, Emily?' Olympia asked. Emily remembered her Jekyll and Hyde existence between the office and the shop. Now she had a car at her disposal and lots of pretty clothes she could wear all the time, and best of all there was the coming baby. The difference was unbelievable.

'Into a cocked hat,' she laughed, turning to see Alex, who had just come home from Wythenshaw's, standing in the lobby doorway.

'Glad you're enjoying life, Emily,' he said, but his tone was cold. In the instant before he ran upstairs she saw his face stiff with anguish. It made her feel suddenly saddened that her happiness should bring hurt to Alex. She wanted to follow him up to his room as she had done when they were children. She dared not now and she doubted her presence would be welcomed.

'How's Cathy Tarrant?' she asked Olympia.

'Fine, she's coming to help Alex paint the living-room for me at the weekend.'

The midwife moved into Sylveen's cottage, so that there would always be someone with her. They were all waiting. It happened that Emily was with her the afternoon she went into labour. All keyed up, she telephoned Wythenshaw's office to let Jeremy know, and he came to the cottage when the factory closed.

Emily scarcely had time to make him a cup of tea before the midwife came downstairs to tell them Sylveen had been safely delivered of a seven-pound baby girl and that she'd had an easy time.

They had to wait another three quarters of an hour for mother and baby to be bathed and changed. Then the midwife called them up to see her. Emily was surprised to see Sylveen so radiant, in a pretty new nightdress. Surprised too, to see Jeremy blinking back emotional tears as he held the infant for the first time.

'I'm going to call her Nadine,' Sylveen said contentedly.

'Isn't she pretty?' Emily agreed, studying the perfect pink face and the covering of golden down on her head.

'She's all Wythenshaw.' Jeremy was delighted. Emily felt she was intruding on a precious moment and decided to go home, making the excuse that Giles would wonder where everybody was if they were all missing.

Jeremy stayed for several hours and his dinner had to be kept hot for him. Even Giles seemed interested and wanted to hear every detail. Emily looked forward to the time when she would hold her own baby in her arms and hoped hers would be as perfect.

Giles drove slowly home to Churton when the shop closed. He hadn't been able to slow down all day or think of anything else. The ball of excitement in his stomach felt like wind. He couldn't rid himself of it, couldn't rest. He was alternately brimming with elation and cold with fear.

It was Sylveen's twenty-sixth birthday and Emily had arranged a quiet dinner for four as a celebration. He had bought a modest box of chocolates as a public offering.

Last night he'd taken her an eternity ring from Calthorpe's. Baguette diamonds interspersed with the same gems emerald cut. It cost more than he could afford, but he deemed it money well spent if it went on Sylveen. He'd been shocked when she opened the door to him. She looked wretchedly pale and drawn.

'Is the baby all right?'

'Yes, she's asleep upstairs.' Her eyes looked red and puffy, as though she'd been crying. 'Giles, I'm frightened. I'm pregnant again!'

He'd felt a jerk of elation before he realised just how upset she was.

'Nadine's only twelve weeks old. I can't go through it all again.'

'You can't be sure, not yet.'

'Sure enough, I was sick this morning,' she wailed. 'I know the signs. How am I going to tell Jeremy?'

Giles felt his mouth suddenly dry. 'Have you been with him? You know . . .?'

'Of course I have. You know I have.'

'Well then, it's his.'

'It could be yours again. I don't know.'

'He believes Nadine is his, why not the next?'

'I feel so awful,' she wept. 'I wish it hadn't happened. I can't face it.' But they both knew she'd have to. He wondered if she'd announce it tonight.

They were all gathered in the sitting-room of his suite when he got there. Emily was pouring champagne for them.

He thought Sylveen looked better as he pecked her cheek and wished her a happy birthday. She'd been to the hairdresser, and was wearing a red dress he hadn't seen before but there were heavy shadows under her eyes.

He felt a jab of sheer bliss as he watched Father holding baby Nadine awkwardly, playing with her, trying to establish some rapport. Giles couldn't drag his gaze away from the besotted look on his father's face. It showed clearly he believed himself to have fathered the infant. He wanted to crow.

He accepted the drink Emily put in his hand and shot off to his bedroom before somebody noticed how cock-a-hoop he looked. Nobody knew about the second pregnancy but him and he didn't doubt the child was his. He loved Sylveen. It made him feel like God. All powerful, the giver of life. The stud. He started to run a bath.

Emily's figure was still skinny and gave no sign of approaching motherhood, no doubt it wouldn't for months yet. He'd been very surprised when she'd announced she was expecting. It hardly seemed possible that such low-key lovemaking could prove fruitful so quickly. He would have three children born to him in one year. The thought gave him satisfaction. Proof he was better at some things than Father.

He dressed in casual sweater and slacks; he was looking good too, he decided as he combed his pale loose waves. Father was an old man, women should find him more attractive. Of course Sylveen's second child was his too. She could still set him on fire. He took his empty glass back to the sitting-room for a refill.

Sylveen was staying overnight in their spare bedroom. She said it was easier to bring the baby with her than to find a babysitter and leave her at home. She got up to settle the child in her cot.

'That's a pretty dress,' Emily told her.

'I'm still a bit on the plump side,' Sylveen complained as she stopped to see its effect in one of Emily's mirrors. Giles thought she looked more curvaceous, more alluring than ever Emily would. He couldn't help comparing her soft luxurious breasts with Emily's little knobs.

Emily was all right, but he was not finding the ball and chain a great blessing. He found he was no longer free to spend all his spare time with Sylveen when Father went to Paris.

'It would be too obvious to Emily,' Sylveen had protested. 'It's bad enough that you come here on the evenings Jeremy does not.'

'She thinks it's Father I'm avoiding. I tell her I'm playing golf, that I have a drink afterwards with friends there, or even a meal. No problem there.'

'As long as she doesn't decide to take up golf herself. The alibi wouldn't stand up then,' Sylveen said dryly.

'I've hardly been near the place all this year. Got better games to play now,' he'd said lewdly. 'Anyway, there's a Ladies' Club at Bidston, I'd persuade her to go there.'

★ ★ ★

Emily was bustling from dining-room to kitchen, where the maids were clattering plates. It was the first time they had had anybody to a meal in their suite and she was making much of celebrating Sylveen's birthday. Her pixie face was flushed with pride as she ushered them to the table.

'It looks wonderful, Emily,' Sylveen enthused, and her beautiful face had all its old sparkle for a moment.

Giles didn't know why women attached such importance to table setting, Emily was flushing with pleasure at her praise. He'd not seen the pretty china before, nor the lace place mats, and their informal dining-room suited the arrangement.

'Lovely, Emily,' he agreed, glad she was learning fast. He felt hungry and hoped she'd arranged a decent meal.

'How are the tennis lessons?' Jeremy asked Emily over the smoked salmon. She had been persuaded to try tennis by Olivia Semple, the daughter of one of his friends whom she had entertained at dinner. Everybody thought Emily needed to expand her social life – Giles certainly agreed with that. It would give him a freer rein if she had somewhere to go and something to do that didn't involve him.

'I'm learning, but I'm not all that good,' she said.

'You mustn't overdo things,' Jeremy cautioned. 'Not with the coming baby.'

'Jeremy,' she laughed, 'everybody agrees gentle exercise is beneficial.'

'Is it gentle enough?' he asked.

'Course it is. A lesson lasts only three quarters of an hour. Olivia takes me home for tea afterwards.'

Nobody could fail to see Emily's look of triumph as the cake was set before Sylveen. Giles felt she'd taken to married life with more enthusiasm than he had.

'We'll have our coffee in the sitting-room,' Emily said, leading them back. Sylveen sat one side of the fireplace, filling the great armchair like a brilliant butterfly, Jeremy sat the other. She and Giles shared the sofa pulled up between the chairs, Giles in the corner nearer to Sylveen.

Emily sighed, but not with discontent. She had not expected to find so much pleasure in domestic matters. She was pleased with the success of her little celebration for Sylveen. Pleased too, there had been no eruption of ill-feeling between Jeremy and Giles during it. She could always feel the underlying tension that smouldered between them and knew it only took a spark to set them off, but tonight, thank goodness, it seemed well damped down. They were on their best behaviour.

The worry about Giles niggled. After his first rapturous excitement about her pregnancy, he behaved very much as he always had. The coming child had not strengthened their marriage. Giles almost seemed to have forgotten it. Emily had a recurring dream about putting out her arms to him, but finding he was always out of reach. She kept telling herself it would be different once the baby was born.

She tried to relax now her dinner had been well received. She could see Jeremy watching Sylveen, all his attention on her words, adoration in his eyes. It took her a long time to notice that Sylveen was directing much of her conversation towards Giles. In one unguarded instant she saw Sylveen smile up at him through her lashes. Emily almost felt something pass between them. She held her breath, feeling jealousy bite into her gut.

It left her shaking, but Jeremy had noticed nothing. She told herself she was being a fool, it was all in her mind. Sylveen could not help being the centre of attention, her beauty drew the eye. And Giles's tawny eyes sought and held every woman's gaze.

Emily felt older and wiser than she had been at her wedding. She was glimpsing the truth. Giles was a mirage, a wonderful-looking man who always escaped her, entering another side of his life where she could not follow. She had always known there were things he didn't want her to share. It left her frustrated and dissatisfied.

She had allowed Gran and the adoration of the typing pool to persuade her, but she had known from the beginning what Giles was really like. From the moment she'd scratched his face in the storeroom and he'd turned on her. She'd known but ignored her knowledge. She couldn't understand why she hadn't thought it through more fully at the time. She had nobody to blame but herself.

In the second bedroom, the baby began to whimper for her ten o'clock feed. Sylveen stood up and stretched, came over and kissed her cheek.

'Thanks, Emily, it was a lovely birthday dinner.' Emily watched her kiss Jeremy's cheek too.

'Good night, I'll get into bed to feed Nadine. These four-hourly feeds are killing me.'

'Nadine has gone over her time,' Emily said, watching to see how she would take her leave of Giles. She touched him on the shoulder as she passed and murmured, 'Good night.' Emily told herself her imagination had been working overtime.

Jeremy was hovering on the hearth. 'Giles, did King give you an envelope to bring home?' Emily remembered he'd not been to the shop today as he usually did on Tuesdays. He'd gone to a meeting instead.

'Yes, I'd forgotten. I'm sorry.' He fetched it from their bedroom. Jeremy tore open the envelope and started to study the page. 'What is it, Father?'

'Just the sales figures for the last day or two.'

'Could I see them?' Giles asked.

Jeremy's eyes jerked up from the page, sparking with sudden antagonism. 'Why?'

'Well, I'll never learn where the money comes from if you don't let me see the accounts.'

'Why would you need to know where the money comes from?' He was glowering.

'I thought you wanted me to know. So I can run the business.'

'Giles, I wanted you to run the factory but you've opted out. Are you aiming to manage the shop?'

'Yes, eventually.'

Jeremy's sigh gusted round the room. 'It's much more specialised. Would take you longer to learn and you need a greater interest in antiques.'

'But it's where you make your money, isn't it?'

'Who told you that?' Jeremy demanded, his face like thunder.

'Nobody told me,' Giles retorted. 'It's obvious you don't make enough from the factory for all this.'

Emily felt shocked by the sudden deterioration in the atmosphere. 'I think I'll go to bed,' she said, but neither took any notice.

'Have you been talking to King?'

'No.'

Emily saw Jeremy's face turn crimson as she stood up. 'Good night,' she said hastily.

'Nothing like that would be obvious to you,' Jeremy barked before she'd reached the door. 'You've been talking to somebody. You've heard something. Tell me, I want to know.'

'No, Father,' there was agony in Giles's voice.

'Is it King?'

Emily closed her bedroom door and went through to the bathroom. Turned on the taps to shut out the voices that followed her. She had thought Giles exaggerated when he spoke of rousing his father's wrath without meaning to, but he'd certainly stirred up a viper's nest with a fairly innocent question this time.

She was glad Sylveen had gone to bed before the storm blew up. She told herself that life with the Wythenshaws was not without its problems, but it had its compensations too. She must make the best of it.

When Sylveen whispered that she thought she was pregnant again, Emily felt no envy. Sylveen herself didn't seem too pleased, but it seemed to prove it was Jeremy she loved. She had imagined there was something between her and Giles. Anyway, everybody loved Sylveen.

Emily felt the last months of her pregnancy were dragging. She felt heavy and ungainly. Jeremy continued to cosset her with kindness, but Giles seemed to spend more time away from her than ever.

Pregnancy certainly wasn't binding Giles to her. He wasn't in any way quarrelsome, they didn't bicker at all. If anything, he was over-polite, as one is with strangers.

In bed, he told her he didn't want to make demands on her while she was carrying the baby. If she pushed him into any love-making, he was distinctly half-hearted about it. When she tried to talk to him about the coming child, he no longer seemed interested. It was only when they discussed naming a boy, he seemed to care one way or the other.

'Not Piers, Emily!'

'Alistair then?'

'No.'

'All right, what about Theodore? Teddy when he's small?'

She saw Giles wrinkle his nose in disgust. 'I like the name Peter,' he said. 'It's short and plain. Pete sounds good whatever age he is.'

'Peter?' She let the syllables roll off her tongue. She wasn't sure. It wouldn't be her first choice, but it pleased her that Giles felt strongly about one aspect of parenthood.

There were certain things she couldn't bear to think about: that she was no longer attractive to him, no longer important either. Instead she told herself continually, everything would be different once the baby was born. They'd be a family then, it would alter everything.

Sylveen comforted her with the same thought.

'It will all seem worth while once you're holding the babe in your arms.' Emily smiled and thought of Giles cuddling the child.

Preparations were being made for the birth. A midwife was hired to oversee them. Sister Jones had dark curls creeping out under her starched cap and her apron crackled as she walked. Emily thought she looked young but super-efficient and was happy to entrust herself to her.

Under her guidance, the spare bedroom in her suite was stripped bare and a single bed brought to stand in the middle of the room.

Emily was living for the day her baby would be born. The date on which her doctor had told her to expect it came and went. Never had she felt such impatience for anything, but when at last she realised the moment was upon her, she was overcome with nerves.

'You'll be fine,' Sylveen whispered. She sat with her all that afternoon while the midwife went back and forth to the kitchen on rubber soles, boiling kettles and setting up trays.

'Waiting is the worst part, and that's over,' Sylveen comforted. 'Soon all this will be too. You'll forget the bad parts. I know, I've been through it twice and I'm well on the way with the third. Easy as shelling peas.'

'Phone Giles,' Emily gasped as she came out of a bad contraction.

'I have, and Jeremy. I thought I'd send Stanley with a note for your gran as soon as there's news. Unless you want her here now?'

'Just Giles,' she managed, as another contraction gripped her. 'Charlie might not like it if she's fetched away at rush hour.'

'He'll be here any minute,' she said.

Jeremy returned from the factory and came up to see her.

'We're making good progress,' the midwife told him.

'Can I get you anything, Emily?' he asked as he patted her hand. Emily took a long shuddering breath and shook her head.

'Isn't Giles home yet?'

'Not yet, but he won't be long now. Soon be over, Emily. Then we'll wet the baby's head with a bottle of Moët et Chandon.' Emily tried to smile but, racked with pain and anxiety, felt the last thing she needed was champagne.

Then Sister Jones was bundling both of them out of the room. 'The second stage,' she told them. 'Won't be long now.'

Emily, totally engrossed in the urge to push, wanted it over. It was an exhausting, pain-torn twenty minutes. She felt hot and sweaty; her mouth was dry and impregnated with the taste of rubber; her head was whirling from the gas and air. She was filled with relief to find it was all safely over.

'A boy.' The midwife sounded a long way away. 'A lovely little boy.'

Her baby, swathed in a bath towel, was put in her arms. Emily hugged the bundle feeling a rush of love. His eyes were bright blue and wide open, staring up into hers; his tiny lips made sucking noises.

'Seven pounds six ounces,' the midwife said with satisfaction. 'A good weight.'

Then Emily felt her fixing the tiny lips to her breast and encouraging them to suckle. Her head swam as she tried to focus, marvelling at her own baby.

Never had a cup of tea been so welcome. It seemed to sober her up. Later when Sister Jones had bed-bathed and changed her into a new nightdress, Sylveen and Jeremy came back, to marvel with her. Soft snufflings and grunts came from the bassinet beside her bed.

'His name's Peter,' she told them. 'Giles wanted it, if it was a boy.' His face was not the scarlet face of the newborn, but each of his features was distinct and beautiful. Gold down covered his well-shaped head. Every limb rounded to perfection.

'Just like Giles when he was a baby,' Jeremy said, peering over his tightly wound blanket. 'I shall put down a pipe of port for him. Be just right in twenty years.'

'Thank you,' Emily smiled, she couldn't begin to imagine what this scrap of humanity would be like that far into the future.

'And this is for you, Emily.' He pushed a small leather case into her hand. 'You deserve it. You've given me my first grandson.'

Emily slid back the catch and opened it. A necklace of rubies linked together with gold chains sparkled up from a bed of black velvet.

'Thank you,' she choked. 'It's beautiful. You're very kind, Jeremy.'

'Let me help you put it on.' Sylveen's cool fingers were brushing the back of her neck as she fastened the clasp. 'There, it looks lovely.' It filled the wide lace-edged neckline of her nightdress. Sylveen held her hand-mirror so Emily could see the rubies glowing against her skin.

Emily was half aware of Higgins bringing in the champagne bucket and a tray of glasses as Sylveen placed a gift-wrapped box in front of her.

'Now you must open my gift.'

'It's like Christmas,' Emily said, pulling at the ribbons. A baby's silver-backed brush and comb was revealed. 'It's lovely, Sylveen, thank you. I feel overwhelmed.'

When Jeremy put the glass of cool champagne in her hand, miraculously she did enjoy it. She enjoyed the fuss as they all raised their glasses and drank to the baby. Even the midwife looked a little flushed after that.

Then Higgins was tapping on the door and ushering Gran forward, looking unnaturally smart in the outfit she'd chosen for Emily's wedding.

'Too many visitors too soon.' The midwife was shaking her starched cap, so when Jeremy had poured a glass of champagne for Gran, he took Sylveen downstairs.

'Emily, whoever would have thought you'd have it this good?' Gran's eyes surveyed the infant in his cot. 'Born with a silver spoon in his mouth,' she said with satisfaction.

She had brought more gifts. Ethel had sent a pair of blue rompers and Gran had knitted a matinée coat to match. Emily felt fussed over and made much of.

But dinner time came and went and Giles still did not come home.

'You did ring him?' Emily asked.

'Yes,' Sylveen confirmed. 'I spoke to him myself, not just left a message.'

'Could he have had an accident?' she worried. They both stared back at her sympathetically.

'Probably just Giles,' Jeremy said gruffly. 'Don't you worry about him. He'll be all right.'

Emily swallowed. She'd hoped Giles was looking forward to the birth of his baby as much as she was. She'd put all her faith into this moment bringing them together. Giles hadn't even come home. It didn't augur well for the future.

The midwife helped her feed the baby. Settled them both for the night. Still Giles didn't come. Emily felt a stabbing hurt. She slept till midnight, when the baby wakened her in his bassinet beside her bed. The midwife heard him too, and came in to see how she was.

'Is my husband home yet?'

'No,' she whispered, and Emily saw the pity in her eyes. She had to blink hard. Tell herself the thrill of holding the baby in her arms made up for her disappointment in Giles. He had given her this miracle.

Giles came to her bedside as she was giving Peter his early-morning feed.

'Where've you been?' she asked, trying hard not to sound aggressive.

'Out celebrating. You've done wonderfully well, Emily. I'm delighted.' He looked exhausted, his words sounded flat. Sister Jones's eyes met hers as she got up to leave, giving them a moment alone.

Emily could smell alcohol on his breath. He was wearing the clothes he'd gone to work in yesterday. She wanted to cry. He hadn't wanted to be with her. He'd stayed away while she was giving birth to his child. She knew now having the baby would not bind them together as she'd hoped.

The morning brought flowers from Jeremy and Sylveen, flowers from Giles and flowers arrived from Olympia and Ted. Her bare room was turned into a hothouse with huge bunches of exotic, out-of-season blooms, long-stemmed roses, gladioli, chrysanthemums, lilies and sweet-smelling freesias.

That afternoon Gran came again, bringing more gifts from her neighbours along Paradise Parade. A box of fruit from the Tarrants, a shawl from old Mrs McFie, violets growing in a modest terracotta pot.

As Emily balanced the pot on her counterpane to read the card, the violets seemed simple and homely. She preferred them to the hothouse blooms ranged round her room. She recognised the writing immediately.

'From Alex,' it read. 'To mother and child. With love

and best wishes for the future.'

She buried her face in them, breathing in their fresh sharp scent, needing to hide the tears prickling at her eyes. She ached for Alex at that moment, wanting his constancy and support. Quite certain he would not have left her if the child she'd given birth to had been his. But it was no use craving for Alex if he didn't want her either.

'How is Alex?' she managed, keeping her gaze on his flowers.

'Fine,' Gran said. 'As usual.'

'Not engaged yet?' It seemed a long time since she'd seen him and unless she'd asked, Gran wouldn't have mentioned him.

'No, and less talk of it now, though he's still going out with Cathy.'

When Gran went home she wept into her pillow. Sister Jones comforted her, telling her it was a touch of baby blues, and all women had them after having a baby. Emily knew it was more than that.

She kept the violets near her bed, finding them a comfort because Alex had cared enough to send them. Wondering how much he did care about her. Hoping, yet knowing there was no hope, because she had married Giles.

Emily knew it was fanciful, but she felt if Alex's violets thrived, so might his love for her. She watered them carefully. Over the following weeks the violets grew and multiplied. She asked Jeremy's gardener for advice on how to keep them growing and applied it, tending the plant regularly.

Peter thrived too and grew more beautiful every day. He learned to smile up at her whenever she was near his cot.

Jeremy wanted to hire a nanny for him but Emily couldn't bear the thought of anyone else attending to her baby's needs. Betty could sit with him if she wanted to go out alone, otherwise she would look after him herself.

Emily was sure she was going to enjoy motherhood, but was afraid that marrying Giles had been a terrible mistake.

Book Three 1934–1938

CHAPTER SEVENTEEN

Sylveen sighed and tiptoed out of her children's bedroom. She was in luck today, it seemed they would take their nap together instead of one at a time. Now Nadine was twenty months and Natalie nine months, she couldn't pretend it wasn't hard work looking after them, but she found them rewarding. It wasn't the children she found difficult.

It was going to be another hot August afternoon, and the pleasantest place to spend it would be in the garden. Emily was bringing Peter to tea, and she wanted to fill the paddling pool because all the children enjoyed it. Jeremy was concerned that she empty it as soon as she went indoors to do other things.

'A child can drown in three inches,' he kept telling her. 'And you let Nadine play in the garden by herself.'

So almost every day she had the chore of refilling the pool, but even that was not a problem. It was Giles who was bothering her.

Sylveen turned on the hose tap and watered her asters en route to the paddling pool. Giles was giving her the jitters. As soon as Jeremy turned his back, he was in the house. She was afraid because he was careless and totally irresponsible.

It was Giles who set the pace. When Jeremy had an early night, she had Giles. Giles was demanding; if he didn't get his own way he would sulk. She wanted to simplify her life, rid it of stress. She had come to the conclusion she would be happier with just Jeremy and the children.

It had taken her a long time, but she was beginning to realise that Giles was the permanent dependent. He would always need someone to lean on, to protect him, to tell him what to do. He'd never manage on his own. He expected too much of other people. What they gave him was never enough. He had this bitter enmity for his father who had bent over backwards to help him. Still would, if he knew what would help.

Giles seemed to swing between fear of doing things in case he failed, and over-confidence. There were times when he felt capable of anything and gave the impression that what he was being asked to do was beneath him. Sylveen sighed. Believing Giles was the love of her life had been a bad mistake.

'Lovely afternoon, isn't it?' Jean, her neighbour, called from the next-door garden, a middle-aged woman in a large straw sun hat. 'Does your father have a Rolls? I've noticed it at your gate quite often.'

Sylveen choked out, 'Yes,' because anything else would need an explanation. It made her twist with guilt again. She couldn't stand the lies and the subterfuge any longer. She wanted a normal decent life.

'My father saw it the other day. Very envious. He has a bull-nose Morris.'

Sylveen laughed politely with her neighbour, but she felt more like crying. She wanted to be able to look Jeremy in the eye. Treat him honestly. The Alvis was pulling up at the wicket gate.

'I have a visitor,' she said to make her escape. She thought Emily's company would cheer her up, but Emily gave her such a hug at the front door, she was suffused with guilt again. It was on her conscience still that she should have warned Emily before she married Giles. Any true friend would have done so.

'You're jealous,' Giles had said, but what woman wouldn't be? How could Giles tell her he loved her and yet marry her friend? Sylveen saw that as a despicable thing to do to them both.

Stanley carried Emily's bag of nappies and toys through to the garden and the large rug Sylveen had spread in the shade of the old oak. Then he went off to buy gardening supplies for Churton.

Sylveen examined Emily's face, she didn't seem unhappy. Her dark skin had tanned well; there was a healthy shine to her hair, which was shaped more attractively. Emily never confided any problem about Giles, and though Sylveen would have liked to know how she felt about him, she couldn't bring herself to ask.

Her eyes kept going to Emily's left hand, with the big diamond engagement ring and the matching plain gold band beneath it. How could Giles be so blind about how she felt if he truly loved her? Her disenchantment with him had started with his engagement to Emily.

'Can I hear Natalie crying?' Emily asked, and Sylveen ran upstairs to bring her children down. All three splashed busily in the paddling pool and played with the toys while she and Emily idled the afternoon away in the sun.

When Sylveen was bringing the tea out, her neighbour came to the fence again.

'Such beautiful children, lovely to see them playing together.' Natalie was tipping water over Peter's back. 'The little boy is a relation, is he?'

'Yes,' Sylveen said shortly. The Wythenshaw likeness was strong. They all had golden hair, but Nadine's was curlier than either Natalie's or Peter's. They were all lovely and chubby without being fat. Usually they were good tempered and happy. Nadine and Natalie would be taken as Peter's sisters if they hadn't been so close in age.

Emily laughed. 'Like three peas in a pod, aren't they? Yes, they're related.'

Sylveen shuddered. Emily had no idea how close the relationship was. She gulped at her tea. Months ago, she'd decided to tell Giles he was no longer welcome.

She'd tried to half a dozen times but he'd swept her objections aside. She would have to spell it out more clearly. She could no longer face what he'd done to Emily. And it wasn't just what Giles had done. She couldn't go on cheating Emily herself. Damn it, Giles had married Emily. Why couldn't he stay with her like a normal husband? She would have to force him to stay at home.

Later on at home that evening, Emily was hugging her crying child to her shoulder. Now that Peter was a year old he was heavy to hold like this to pace between his cot and the window, but it had always been the most effective way to soothe him.

Usually he went off to sleep without any fuss, so she wondered if he was over-tired, or whether he was teething again. Or had he had too much sun this afternoon? Anxiously, she looked at Peter's fair baby curls and tear-stained face. Nadine had only just recovered from chicken pox and she hoped Peter was not about to succumb to it.

Emily laid a hand on his forehead, but he didn't seem to have a temperature. He was just cross and out of sorts. Emily pulled the curtains tighter to shut out a ray of light, slid him into his cot again and hoped he'd go off.

'Bunny,' Peter turned his round blue eyes to her face and started to whimper again. Usually Peter went to sleep cuddling his favourite toy, a fluffy white rabbit. She pressed a small teddy into his arms, but he tossed it away.

Emily sighed. The toy rabbit had gone with them to Sylveen's cottage and she'd not brought it back. She blamed herself for being careless. She knew Peter could be difficult to settle without it. She rang the bell for Betty, the maid.

'Sit with Peter for a while, will you? I can't get him off.'

It was at moments like this that she wished she'd not decided against a nanny for him when Jeremy had suggested it. But Betty was always available to babysit when she wanted to go out without him, as she did tonight.

Jeremy had donated funds to build a convalescent home for children recovering from serious illnesses, whose parents were poor. It was to be opened tomorrow by the Mayor. Tonight there was a dinner in his honour and he had asked Emily to partner him. Since she had started to entertain for him, she was usually asked to accompany him when hospitality was returned.

Betty pulled a chair near to the cot and started telling Peter the story of the Three Bears. Emily went to the phone in her sitting-room.

'Sylveen, have we left Peter's toy rabbit with you? I can't get him to sleep.'

'Yes. Found it in the kitchen two minutes after you'd gone. I've put it out of Nadine's reach on the sideboard.'

'I'll get Stanley to drive down straight away. Give it to him, will you? Can't get Peter off without it.'

'Of course.'

Emily went down to the kitchen. She had given Cook the evening off because Giles had said he would be out for dinner too. Only Mrs Eglin was there.

'Could you tell Stanley I want him to go on an errand right away?' She had had no reason to complain of the housekeeper's attitude over the past year or so. In fact, she felt she was popular with all the servants now.

'I'm afraid he isn't here, madam. I sent him to the hospital with the new gardener. He speared his foot with a garden fork. I'm sorry, I didn't think you'd need the car again.'

Emily went back to her own wing. From the door, she could hear Peter whimpering. On the spur of the moment, she dialled Wythenshaw's, the line went straight through to Jeremy's office. In the last year or so she'd felt closer to him.

'You're coming home to change, aren't you, Jeremy? Will that be soon?'

'You've just caught me. I was about to leave.'

'Would you mind awfully collecting Peter's fluffy rabbit from Sylveen's? We left it there this afternoon and he won't go to sleep without it.'

'Yes, I can hear him complaining now.'

'I've just told Sylveen that Stanley will collect it, but he's had to take the new gardener to the hospital. Stabbed his foot with a fork.'

'Oh dear, is he bad?'

'I believe so.'

'Right, I'll get Peter's rabbit for him. I'm on my way now, see you in half an hour or so.'

Jeremy locked his desk and went out to the yard where Higgins waited with his new Rolls. He'd worked late, the factory had closed. All was quiet. He relaxed against the upholstery and thought of the changes the last few years had brought for him. Suddenly he was surrounded by infants. Little Peter and Sylveen's two children were giving him enormous pleasure.

To have Nadine, a daughter of twenty months and just able to talk, was a wonderful blessing at his time of life. Little Natalie had come as a shock, but now she was nine months old, he was able to enjoy her too.

He went round to see them almost every evening unless he was away. Sylveen seemed to look forward to his visits. He played with the children and had a drink with her at the very least. Usually she cooked him a meal. The children kept her tied to the house and she needed his company.

Sylveen fitted in well at Churton. She was there with Emily on many days. Often stayed on to dinner, but there was toing and froing with babysitters. He was beginning to think it was all an unnecessary complication. Life would have been more restful if he had married Sylveen and let her be a real wife.

He was contented with the other decisions he'd made. Emily coped very well as his hostess. He was growing fond of her too. The girls got on well together, there would be no problem there.

Even Giles was less trouble since he'd married. He was doing nothing with his career, of course. Working as a shop assistant would get him nowhere and he'd never be able to handle that business. The lad was a fool, but he wasn't causing problems any more, and little Peter was a delight.

Jeremy sighed, he was slowly accepting that he'd have to set up a trust fund for Giles and his family. When the Liverpool shop had fulfilled its purpose, he'd sell it and use the proceeds for that. Though he wouldn't want to sell while Arthur was still alive, it would upset him too much. Higgins swung the large car into the lane and pulled up at Sylveen's wicket gate.

'I'll not be long,' he told him as he got out. The garden was lush with late-summer flowers; Sylveen had better asters than he had at Churton. He rang her bell.

He had to ring again, but she'd be putting the children to bed at this hour, and as it was Stanley she was expecting, she would not worry if she kept him waiting a few moments.

At last the door half opened and Sylveen's blonde head came round. She was hugging her damp baby to her shoulder, wrapped in a bath towel.

'Jeremy!' She seemed stunned.

He stepped inside the dining-room, though she was slow to step back so he could.

'Is something the matter?'

'I thought Stanley was coming.' Her frightened blue eyes went to the white rabbit on the sideboard. He could feel her tension coming at him in waves.

'Uncle Jeremy.' Nadine, also wet from the bath and wrapped in a towel, came downstairs carefully one step at a time. He swept her up on his shoulder. He had wanted the children to call him Father, but was afraid it might be an embarrassment. He'd discussed it with Sylveen and decided it was safer not. There were some things he regretted about this arrangement.

'Hello, love, your Uncle Jeremy's come to put you to bed. I've time for one drink, Sylveen.' He turned round and noticed the dining table was set for a candlelit supper for two. He felt suddenly cold.

'I'm sorry, didn't I tell you I was dining out tonight?' Warning bells were ringing in his mind. Sylveen's face was paper-white.

'Yes,' she mumbled, turning from him and leading the way into the sitting-room. 'I'll get you some whisky. Come and sit down.'

Jeremy felt a searing pain in his gut. His feet were like lead. He struggled as far as the doorway. Nadine was playing with his hat, her baby face crowned with damp curls was laughing down at him.

Sylveen had put Natalie in a corner of an armchair and was at the drinks cupboard with her back towards him. She was very nervous, he heard the neck of the bottle clatter against the tumbler. He knew with cold certainty she was expecting another man.

'Who are you cooking for tonight?' His voice sounded strangled. Suddenly the child in his arms was struggling to get free. He lowered her carefully to the floor and she scampered to the stairs.

'For Giles.' Nadine's baby voice came back at him as clear as a bell.

Jeremy couldn't breathe. There was an iron band round his chest. Now he understood Sylveen's panic at finding him on the doorstep.

She had frozen, her head bent over the whisky bottle. He wanted to cry out that he loved her, had trusted her.

Giles! Giles of all people! The dragging silence was

broken by Nadine's gurgling laugh from upstairs and suddenly he understood why Sylveen was so frightened. Giles was here now.

He almost ran up the steep winding stairs. Went striding along the narrow landing to find the bedroom door already open.

In the middle of the bed where he'd so often shown love to Sylveen, Giles's body was stretched out, bare apart from a towel wrapped round his waist. A cruelly youthful body compared with his own. Nadine had clambered up and was sitting astride Giles's torso. His bare arms hugged the child to him, playing with her.

In the stunned silence, father and son stared at each other, as though neither could believe his eyes.

Jeremy felt himself go hot and then cold as he fought a terrible urge to throw himself at Giles. He wanted to kill him. Tear him apart. He could have done it with his bare hands at that moment. He wanted to rave at him, let all his ill feelings erupt. Perhaps it was the presence of the child that prevented him. Instead he collapsed silently against the brass bed rail, shaking in agony.

What could a man say when his world had collapsed? Nothing could put back the clock and make it as it had been five minutes earlier. As he had supposed it to be, five minutes earlier. Sylveen had followed him upstairs; he could hear her sobbing in the doorway.

Fury was raging through him. It was his age that made him delay. Made him fight for calm control. Nadine giggled and rolled away as he took a deep breath and said to Giles: 'I never want to see you again.' His voice was flat, beyond anger. 'Churton is no longer your home.' Another spasm shook him. 'And what about Emily? What's she going to say about this?'

'Emily?' Giles lifted his head, supporting it on one arm. 'Emily knows, she doesn't care. She isn't bothered about any of us, as long as she's got money to throw around.'

Jeremy's knuckles showed white as he grasped the bed rail.

'Make arrangements for your family to move elsewhere. I'll not support any of you in future.' Still holding the bed rail he turned to Sylveen.

'I believed you loved me. You could have done nothing more hurtful. Don't expect me to support you after this, either.'

Slowly, Jeremy pushed himself as near upright as he could get, went slowly downstairs and out to his car. He felt dazed as the Rolls made its stately progress towards Churton. It was too awful to believe.

He knew other men found Sylveen attractive, but he couldn't stomach that it was Giles she'd chosen. His own son! He felt like Methuselah. They had taken advantage of him, probably laughed at him behind his back, thought him a foolish, self-satisfied old man.

He'd congratulated himself on his way with women, on his libido, when all the time it was his money Sylveen had wanted. His money Emily had wanted, and certainly Giles had wanted nothing else. His vitality was gone now, collapsed like the myth it was. He felt an empty shell of himself.

Suddenly he realised Higgins had opened the car door and was waiting for him to get out. It was an effort to climb the steps to the front door. He was putting his hat on the hall stand when he heard Emily's quick footsteps.

'I'm all ready. Do you like my dress?' She twirled in front of him in a slim crimson evening gown. 'Daringly backless, isn't it?' It had a big pompom on one shoulder.

Jeremy closed his eyes in another wave of agony. He wanted to lash out at Emily because he'd grown fond of her. She'd seemed to like him, but he'd never stopped to ask himself whether it was an act she put on. It was another stab at his pride to find she knew all about Giles and Sylveen. They'd all kept it from him. The last to know.

He bit back on the bitter words rising to his tongue. At his age, verbal battles racked him, made him feel even worse.

'Did you get it?' Emily's figure had filled out in the last year or so. Her hair had been thinned to a pretty brown bob. She was changed into an attractive young woman.

'Get what?'

'Peter's white rabbit.'

'No.'

'You did go for it? To Sylveen's?'

Her brown elfin eyes were wide with alarm. Despite his anger, it touched him. He didn't know what to say. He couldn't bring himself to talk about what had happened. Not yet, it was all too painful.

'Are you all right, Jeremy?'

'Yes.' He was roughly impatient with her. 'All right.'

'We are going to this dinner?'

He pulled himself up to his full height as another wave of distress engulfed him. He'd forgotten about the dinner! For a moment he thought of going. Of bathing and putting on his dinner jacket, but he knew he couldn't eat. Hadn't the strength to listen to all that chit-chat tonight.

'No.'

'But it's arranged specially in your honour.'

'I can't go. Not up to it tonight.'

'I'll make our apologies, say you aren't well.' He stared into her face, almost convinced she was showing concern, but Giles had said they were all in this together. They were a different generation, unbelievably immoral.

'It doesn't matter.' He was making for the stairs.

'Jeremy, it does matter. We are expected to dinner within the next hour. Charles Bradbury is hosting it, isn't he?'

He couldn't think. He had to lean against the stair rail for a moment.

'Yes, Charles Bradbury, or his wife.'

'I'll ring for Dr Powell too.'

'No, I don't want a doctor.' He knew his tone was thunderously rough. The girl was trying to help. 'I'll go to bed. I'm all right.'

'I've sent all the staff off except Betty, because Giles was planning to eat out too. I'll make us something.'

'I don't want to eat. Leave me alone.'

'Well, I want to eat, and I think you should too. You want to keep your strength up, don't you? Then you must try.'

He would never have believed Emily could be so persistent. 'What's happened, Jeremy?'

He didn't answer. Couldn't trust himself not to break down. His whole world had crashed. Who could blame him if he wept?

'Something has. You were quite different when I phoned you an hour ago.'

He had to give some explanation or she'd call the doctor. He closed his eyes, trying to clear his mind.

'Giles and I have come to the parting of our ways. He's battened on me long enough. I've told him I'll not put up with him any longer, neither here nor at the shop.'

Her pixie eyes looked into his, filled with horror. 'What's he done?'

'You'd better ask him.'

'What about me and Peter?'

She was Giles's wife and he wanted to destroy him and everything belonging to him. He had wondered at the state of their marriage, because Giles so often absented himself from home. Now he knew, he felt sick.

'You'll go with him, Emily, you're his wife.' He wanted nothing to remind him. Nothing of his past, no infants and especially no young girls to remind him how he failed to capture his lost youth. He turned and stumbled up to his room.

Sylveen sagged on to the bed, wanting to scream with

frustration. She'd let Giles talk her round once too often. Why hadn't she pushed him out when she'd first made up her mind to break with him? Stupidly she'd let him drag it out, now it had blown wide open.

'One in the eye for him at last,' Giles crowed from the pillow beside her. 'Did you see the way he was hanging on to the bed rail? Could hardly stand.'

'He trusted me. He was generous and kind. Oh God!' Sylveen felt terrible.

'He doesn't realise even now, these kids are mine. I can kick him down again with that,' Giles chortled.

'Don't you have a conscience?'

'He's been on my back for years. He was overdue for this.'

'I asked you not to come. I pleaded with you to be careful,' Sylveen wept. 'I knew we were pushing our luck. Too often . . .'

'I was careful. I put my car in your garage. He didn't see that. You shouldn't have asked him in.'

'When I open the front door, he just comes in like you do. It's not a question of asking.'

'Then you shouldn't have answered the bell.'

'Emily said she was sending Stanley.'

'Then it's Emily's fault.'

'It isn't, and it's no reason to be spiteful. Why did you tell him Emily knew all about us and was only interested in his money? You know that isn't true.'

'To let him think everybody knew but him. To turn the knife in his chest.'

'He's very fond of Emily, and she of him.' Sylveen sighed. 'What are you going to do now?'

'Can't do anything tonight, Father's taking Emily out. Let's eat, enjoy our evening as planned.'

'I'm not enjoying it,' she wailed. 'Grow up, Giles.'

'Now Father knows and he's done his worst, there's nothing to stop me moving in.'

Sylveen froze. 'No.'

'You suggested it once. You've got a house, he can't take that back, and I've got a car. We could manage, you said.'

'That was before you married Emily. Yes, Giles, I still feel bitter about that. You never give a thought to anybody else's feelings. And what about Emily and Peter? You gave him reason to throw them out too. Are they to fend for themselves?'

'There's a spare bedroom here.'

She sat up with a jerk. 'Bloody hell, Giles, what are you suggesting? All three of us here together?'

'One big happy family. Why not?'

'How do you think Emily will feel? She's your wife!'

'You've both borne me children. I feel I have two wives.'

'Absolutely not! You're crazy if you think I'd agree to that!'

'I thought you liked Emily.'

'I do. She's my friend.'

'Just me, then? Emily could go back to her chip shop.'

Sylveen closed her eyes in mounting anger. 'I should have had the sense to show you the door a long time ago. Get out. Go on now. This minute.'

She was furious with herself too. Why hadn't she been firmer instead of letting him talk her round? None of this would have happened if she'd put her foot down, refused to allow him to come when she first felt she wanted things to finish. What a shilly-shallying fool she was.

Several days later Sylveen was dispiritedly sipping her breakfast tea while she spooned porridge into Natalie's mouth. Meals were not solitary with a high chair on either side of her, but not social either. She'd taken to eating them in the kitchen. It was easier to clean up the mess afterwards.

Since that terrible evening, she'd had no energy. Her

daily routine was shot to bits. Dust was thickening on polished surfaces, the carpet needed hoovering. Toys stayed where the children dropped them. She couldn't get on with anything, those awful scenes played over and over in her mind. She was stuck in limbo.

She had had to summon all her determination to get Giles out, but she'd done it. He'd pleaded with her to let him stay just one more night. He kept saying he loved her.

She had put Nadine to bed while he dressed. She'd found Natalie asleep in the corner of the armchair, with nothing but a damp towel round her; she hadn't moved from the moment Jeremy had come in. Sylveen carried her up to her cot, dressed her in nappy and nightdress and hardly disturbed her.

'I'm hungry,' Giles said, coming down and seeing the table all ready for a meal. He wandered into the kitchen, and inspected the two fillet steaks arranged in the grill pan. Nibbled a piece of lettuce from the salad bowl she had ready.

'I'm not, and I'm not cooking for you, Giles, not any more.' She had to stand firm, end it now, or she'd never get rid of him. Giles would find somebody to support him, she knew him well enough to know that. It wasn't going to be her.

Sylveen was gripped by rage; she shot upstairs to pack his belongings. Dragged them down and found carrier bags for what couldn't be crushed in his case.

'Go,' she spat at him. 'Go.' Eventually he had.

She had collapsed on the sofa feeling it had taken the last ounce of her strength.

From having a sociable life, she'd spoken to no one but her children these last two days. From being a busy home-maker and cook, she'd done nothing but feed her children.

Everything had changed. She worried about Jeremy. She wondered if she could get a job, but did nothing about it. She tried to telephone Emily to find out what was happening but Mrs Eglin told her she had moved out and was unable to give her an address. The only way she could measure the passing of time was in the increasing dust and dishevelment of her house.

Nadine had finished her breakfast and was shouting to be released from the chair. Sylveen picked up a damp face cloth and removed most of the porridge from her face and hands. She untied her bib, her dress was stained, but she'd have to wear it because she'd done no washing. Nadine's blonde curls were a tangled mess, she hadn't brushed them for days.

Sylveen was letting her out into the back garden when the postman pushed two letters through the front door. One was the gas bill, she still had enough money to pay that, she put it on the sideboard. The other was from Jeremy. Her fingers felt weak as she ripped it open.

'Perhaps I was hasty, Sylveen,' she read. 'I'm very fond of Nadine and Natalie and would like to continue seeing them as they grow up. Would you agree to bring them to Churton on the first Saturday in each month, just for a couple of hours, until they are old enough to come alone? Or the second Saturday, if I should be in Paris?

'If you would, I will continue to support my daughters until they are of an age to support themselves. Your present allowance will continue. I have no wish to see you or them in financial difficulties and if further sums are needed for education later, I will provide them.

'Let me know if you are agreeable. Sincerely, Jeremy.'

She put it down slowly, then snatched it up to read again. Her first feelings were of relief. It meant salvation. She had no need to worry about where the next penny was coming from. She and the girls could continue to live here in comfort. Her second, that she would be taking his money on false pretences. Guilt was churning her stomach again.

She ought to tell Jeremy they were not his children. Tell him the truth and hope that he'd still find it possible to be generous. But she knew she would not. She couldn't find the courage. The truth would bring Jeremy additional pain. He could cast them off if they were Giles's children.

But if she did not tell him, Giles might well do so at a later date. He'd threatened as much. Once again, she felt herself being torn in two.

CHAPTER EIGHTEEN

Giles tried to close the largest of his matching set of leather cases, it was hopelessly overfilled. Every wardrobe door stood open, every drawer pulled out. Clothing and personal possessions were heaped on the satin bedcover.

Emily pushed her fringe off her forehead. 'What did you do to upset your father?'

'Doesn't matter,' he muttered, tipping the entire contents of his socks drawer into a case.

'Of course it matters.' She climbed over a half-packed box, her brown eyes angry. 'Suddenly we're leaving home. Surely I have a right to know why?'

'You said you preferred to live somewhere else. That you found it hard to settle here.' He could see distress on her face as she looked round the chaos in their usually elegant bedroom.

'That was ages ago. I have settled, I don't want to move.'

'Father's throwing us out. We have to.'

'I know that, but why?' She was cramming another case too full to close properly.

'It's a private matter between him and me.' He could see her brown eyes challenging that. 'Business,' he added, to throw her off the scent.

'That means money.' Emily seemed to pounce on him. 'Did you take what doesn't belong to you?'

'No, and the less you know about it the better. Ring for somebody to carry all this down to the car.'

'Is it to do with Sylveen?'

'Why should it be?'

Emily was going to be hard to satisfy this time, but it was better she didn't know. She'd be kinder to him if she remained in ignorance. He couldn't risk her turning against him as Sylveen had.

'She seemed sort of guarded when I phoned her. And we aren't going to stay with her.'

'Father wouldn't be pleased if we did. How could he visit, if we were there? Anyway, I've rented us a house. You'll like it.'

'But how are we going to pay the rent?'

'I'll get a job. It could be a blessing in disguise. We won't have to put up with Father any more.'

'I shall miss him.' Emily sounded sad. 'So will Peter. I still think it would have been wiser to ask Sylveen if we could stay with her for a week or so. Give you time to find a job first. I'm sure she wouldn't have minded.'

'That won't be necessary. You're bringing all your jewellery? We can raise money on that if we have to.'

'The best of it belonged to your mother. I can't take that.'

'Of course you can. Father gave it to you, didn't he?'

'He said, as the present Mrs Wythenshaw, I ought to wear it.'

'There you are, then.' He was trying not to be impatient with her. Emily was over-honest. A gift was a gift after all.

'He wouldn't want it sold, Giles. They're family heirlooms. Some pieces have been in your family for generations.'

'Those are kept in a safe deposit at the bank. What Father gave you was Mother's everyday stuff. See you bring it with you. Now, have we got everything?'

'It won't all go in the car, not at once. Peter's pram and

cot. You'll have to make another journey.'

'Surely you don't want to take this old plant?' Emily had put Alex's violet on the boxes they were taking. 'It's finished, not a flower on it.' It had flowered twice a year since Alex had given it to her.

'It'll come again,' she said. 'I've had it for ages. Don't want to part with it now.'

'All right, then, carry on packing. I'll get Stanley and the Alvis. We can load that up and have it follow us. We don't want to come back again.'

'Funny us going like this,' Emily said from the passenger seat, as he drove down the drive with the Alvis behind him. 'Not saying goodbye to your father. Leaving everything.'

'We'll be better off, Emily, on our own. Wait till you see the house. It's in Caldy, lovely views of the river.'

'Why didn't you tell me what you were doing? I could have helped you choose.'

'Had to fix it in a hurry, you know how impatient Father can be.' He was driving along a pleasant suburban road, tree lined, with impressive houses half hidden in large gardens. 'Here we are.' He turned into a drive.

Emily saw the name 'Beechcroft' on the double gates as they passed.

'Do you like it?'

'It's a lovely house.' He found the tremulous pleasure in her voice touching. Her face brightened into an elfin grin.

'I knew you would.' It took away some of the rawness he felt about the move. He got out quickly to lift Peter from her knee, hoisting him on to his shoulder.

'It's quite big.' Her eyes were travelling over the modern façade of white stucco with six tall windows on the ground floor.

'Roomy,' he said, 'but nothing like Churton.' The hall had a grandfather clock and Persian rugs on a parquet floor. Wide stairs swept up to the first floor. 'There are five bedrooms and three bathrooms.' Giles pointed upwards.

'Three bathrooms?' Emily's eyes met his in alarm. 'And five bedrooms, we'll never use half the space.'

'Come and look at the sitting-room.' Emily stood in the doorway, her eyes like saucers.

'Aubusson carpet,' he told her. 'Silk curtains and upholstery, a baby grand piano. Do you like it?'

'Yes,' her voice was a whisper. She went to look through one of the two windows. 'We could still be out in the country. I can't see another house with all these big trees, and the back lawn stretches to infinity.'

'There's a gardener that comes with the place, and a cook-general.'

'Giles! How much is this costing?' He told her and she collapsed into an armchair, her smile gone.

'Don't you want to see the rest of the house? There's a panelled dining-room and a study and a splendid nursery for Peter.'

'Is Jeremy paying for this?'

'No, I'll get a job, Emily. I'll earn some money.'

'To pay for this? You must be crazy! We can't stay here.'

'Of course we're staying. I've signed a lease.'

'For how long?' Her voice sounded hoarse, the colour had gone from her cheeks.

'Six months.'

He watched Emily close her eyes in resignation, heard her gasp: 'How much do you think you're likely to earn?' It was guaranteed to raise his anxiety level another notch. He'd been on a knife edge since Father had caught him on Sylveen's bed.

Emily felt as though she were waking in the middle of a nightmare. In the vast kitchen Mrs Drouet introduced herself as their cook-general. Plump and genial and wrapped in a white apron, she took Emily on a tour of the kitchen cupboards and then presented her with a list of what she called necessities.

'Is it all right if I phone the order through to a local grocer? We've always dealt with Murdock's, they're very reliable.'

Appalled, Emily was studying the list as she was introduced to her husband Jim, the gardener, also plump and genial. Mrs Drouet explained they occupied a flat over the garage and that their combined wage was two pounds a week plus their keep.

Emily was horrified, she couldn't think. She backed out of the kitchen, purposely being as noncommittal as she could.

'How much cash have you got?' she croaked at Giles, as soon as they were alone in the sitting-room again. He took out his wallet, it was stuffed with money.

'There's more in the bank,' he said crossly. 'You make such a fuss, Emily, we aren't on the bread line.'

'Not yet,' she said weakly. 'I want you to drive me to Paradise Parade, Olympia Fraser will give me discount on an order as large as this. You'll have to pay cash, but at least we won't be running up a bill.'

'It'll be a bind,' he complained.

'What else were you thinking of doing? Come on, I'll tell Mrs Drouet we'll have lunch out. We can have fish and chips with Gran.'

Giles agreed with ill grace. All along Paradise Parade Emily felt they were treated like royalty. They had arrived before the lunch-time rush. Everybody shook Giles's hand. The greengrocer and the butcher carried their parcels out to the car for them.

Olympia's large face was wreathed in smiles as she hugged Peter and sat him on the counter. Emily collapsed on the bentwood chair, feeling she'd come home. 'I don't stock all these brands,' Olympia told her. 'Too expensive for round here.'

'I'm used to your brands,' she said. 'Rather have them anyway.'

Olympia was totting up the bill. 'I don't suppose you're interested in discount now?' She looked up and smiled, Emily found it disconcerting.

To tell her she was, would need explaining. It was all too painful to talk about, and anyway she couldn't in front of Giles, he'd be furious.

But she found Olympia was teasing, the discount was subtracted. Giles paid, tossing the notes on the mahogany counter as though he had plenty more. Olympia would have carried the boxes out to the car for him if Emily hadn't lifted one herself and suggested Giles take the heaviest.

Gran was pleased to see them. Her old eyes kept looking Giles over, as though she couldn't believe he was real. 'You must come and see where we're living now,' he told her, turning on all his charm.

'When will you be able to fetch her, Giles?' Emily forced herself to act normally. 'What about lunch on Saturday? Charlie won't mind now he has Pammy to help, will he?'

'My, you've got it made, Emily,' Gran told her happily. 'You are lucky.' Emily shuddered, she couldn't confide in Gran. It would upset her too much to know the truth.

After breakfast the next morning, Giles drove off without saying where he was going. Emily decided she must finish the unpacking. She was arranging her stockings and handkerchiefs in the ample drawer space provided, when she came across the leather case that held her engagement ring. She flicked open the lid with the Calthorpe label printed on the lining; the matched diamonds sparkled back at her.

She shivered; Giles had suggested selling her jewellery to provide funds. Emily was in no doubt the need would come. On the spur of the moment, she took the ring out of its box. She would hide it, so that she could decide when it was to be sold and what the money raised should be used for. She was afraid Giles would fritter it away too soon.

She took up the cream coat she'd bought from Ethel before going to Calthorpe's to choose the ring. She wore it often, it suited her well. With her nail scissors she slit open the seam in the lining of the right sleeve, till she could reach the shoulder pad. Then she slit that open, and inserted her ring inside. A few stitches, and it was held firmly in place. When she'd restitched the lining, there was no sign it had ever been touched. She crunched the shoulder pad between her fingers, impossible to feel it either. Giles would not sell it without her knowing.

She felt she had to talk to somebody, bottling it up was making her feel worse. Sylveen was her friend, she'd always shown her the way round her problems. Perhaps she could think of some way out of this. Emily picked up the phone and invited her to come and see her new house.

'I'll come this afternoon on the bus.' Sylveen's voice, breathy with enthusiasm, was reassuring. The nearest bus stop was some distance away and Sylveen arrived with rosy cheeks, pushing her children in a push chair designed for twins. They smiled up at her, the September sunshine full on their faces, fair skinned and blonde like Sylveen, but Nadine's hair was a mop of curls, and Natalie's straight, like gold silk.

'What a wonderful place! Aren't you thrilled, Emily?' Sylveen's blue eyes were excited as they took in the wide hall and magnificent staircase. She ran up. Emily picked up Natalie and followed more slowly; Nadine scrambled up on all fours.

'Five bedrooms! You'll certainly live in style here. Jeremy relented, then? He's really a big softy, terribly generous.'

Sylveen had reached the nursery door when Emily got the words out: 'Jeremy hasn't relented.'

Sylveen's mouth had opened ready to praise the bright and airy nursery. Emily saw her swallow, her blue eyes came to meet hers, they were dazed with shock.

'And Giles hasn't got the money? To pay for all this?' She was relieved that Sylveen understood without a long explanation.

Emily closed the door and perched on a chair designed for an infant.

'I'm terrified,' she whispered. 'Giles has signed a lease on this house. We're going to run up enormous debts.' With a whoop of delight Nadine advanced on a doll's house. Peter left the truck he was playing with to stagger towards her.

Sylveen sank down on a nursing chair. 'Just the sort of thing he would do,' she breathed. 'Rush out and choose the most expensive on the market. Never give a thought to the cost. It's too easy for him, he's well known round here. Just give the Wythenshaw name and every trader knows he'll be paid.'

'I don't know what to do for the best,' Emily worried. 'We've got two servants to pay wages for and Mrs Drouet is providing for us on a princely scale.'

'Couldn't you surrender the lease and find something cheaper?'

Emily straightened in her tiny chair. 'Is that possible?'

'Maybe.'

'I knew you'd be better at this than I am.'

'Have you got a copy of the lease?'

'Yes, it's in the study, I'll go and get it.'

'Must be costing a fortune.' Sylveen was leaning over the banisters as she came back upstairs.

Emily led the way back into the nursery. Natalie had curled up on the floor and seemed ready to sleep. Nadine's head was inside the doll's house and Peter was making a traffic jam with toy cars round it.

'Let's have a look.' Sylveen opened out the lease and

began to read. ''Fraid not. You're legally liable for six months' rent whether you live here or not.'

'What am I going to do?' Emily asked, anguished.

'You'd have to find another tenant for the place.'

'How am I going to do that?' Emily wailed. 'I don't know anybody who wants a big house with a baby grand. Mrs Drouet says the last tenant was a consul from some country in South America.'

'Better make up your mind to enjoy it while you can,' Sylveen said, stretching out her elegant legs.

'Enjoy it? I feel trapped. We're going to get into awful debt and there's nothing I can do,' Emily fretted.

'Giles has plenty of expensive toys he can sell. His boat for a start and the car.'

Emily groaned. 'Giles keeps saying we'll sell his mother's jewellery. He told me to be sure to bring it with me, but I didn't. At the last minute when he went out to the car, I collected it all up and put it in Jeremy's drinks cabinet in the library. He didn't really give it to me, just suggested I might like to wear it for the dinner parties. I know he wouldn't want it sold.'

Sylveen's blue eyes were heavy with sympathy. 'You could leave him, Emily. Let him run up his own debts.'

'I don't know. You know what he's like, hopeless on his own. Anyway, where would I go?'

'You and Peter could stay with me.'

'He's my husband . . . I feel I've got to stay, help if I can. He's no one else.'

'You're too damn loyal.'

'Jeremy might not like me staying at your place. I mean, he wants to see you on your own. How is he taking all this?'

Sylveen hesitated. 'He hasn't been near these last few days. I expect he's upset about it too. He understands about Giles, how helpless he is without money and servants to run round after him.'

'Giles has been brought up to expect everything laid on. He's like a spoilt brat who can't cope with the daily grind. Sometimes I feel like his nanny.'

'His mother was an invalid. Was ill for years. I think Jeremy cushioned them both from reality. The offer's open if you change your mind, Emily. You can come any time. Just you, mind, not him.'

'That's very kind.'

'You don't want to go back to your dad?'

Emily shuddered. 'No.'

As the days passed, Emily grew more desperate. She did her best to hide it, because she had to pretend hope if only to keep Giles's confidence up. He ordered several newspapers to be delivered daily and studied every job advertised, marking those he fancied. She offered to type out his applications for him, but was shocked to find how high he was aiming.

'I've had management training at Wythenshaw's, be sure to put that in all the letters,' he told her when she protested that managing a flour mill might be beyond him. 'I've met the owner. So have you, Emily, he came to one of those dinner parties you gave. It's not always what you know but who you know that counts. Father won't refuse me a decent reference.'

They were settling into a daily routine at Beechcroft. The house seemed to call for a grand lifestyle. Living among the trappings of wealth, Emily found it hard to believe she was poor. She understood why Giles found it impossible to economise. It was left to her to exercise thrift when she bought provisions, turn out electric lights others left on and find the wages for the gardener and cook every week.

Emily was surprised when Giles was called for interview at the flour mill. He was cock-a-hoop, certain he'd be offered the job. She tried to recall the owner, but could remember nothing but his deep laugh and large cigars.

Giles bought himself a new business suit, though Emily told him he had three that were more than adequate. She wished him well as he set out, half believing he'd get it. Even beginning to worry about how he'd cope when he had.

He was gone for over six hours and when he did return she knew he'd been drinking. 'You didn't get it then?' She knew by his face he had not.

'You wouldn't believe it, Emily,' he hiccuped. 'I went, on the understanding I was being interviewed for the job of manager at seven hundred a year. Not enough experience, they said. Do you know what they did? They offered me a junior management post at half the salary.'

Emily felt weak with relief. 'But you've got a job. At least you've got a job.'

'I told them what to do with it,' he said indignantly. 'Three seventy a year? We couldn't survive on that!'

Emily felt suddenly sick. 'You didn't turn it down? The rent is due again and we can't pay. We need money for food.'

'I can do better,' he said stubbornly. 'Three seventy a year? I'm not working for that. Father paid me a thousand.'

She covered her face in her hands. 'Nobody else will,' she told him. 'That's a top salary. It's only paid to people with qualifications, those prepared to work hard and take responsibility. Do you know how much I earned? Three pounds a week, and that's generous for a shorthand typist.' Giles looked pale and subdued.

'Three hundred and seventy pounds! It was a wonderful opportunity, and you turned it down.' She wanted to cry. She'd known Giles had extravagant tastes. She hadn't realised how poor his grasp of money was. He carried on as he always had, buying whisky and wine by the case. New clothes on impulse, whether he needed them or not, and talked of getting a new car.

'No,' Emily shouted. 'No. We may have to sell the one you've got.'

'Nonsense, Emily.' But he sounded uneasy. 'Look, there's more jobs here. Apply for all these. Curator of a museum, that sounds interesting. Accountant for the Borough.'

Emily was astounded, surely he couldn't believe he'd be taken seriously? 'Don't be ridiculous! What about experience and qualifications?' But once, everyone had assumed he was capable of running Wythenshaw's; things looked different with hindsight.

'Yes, well, something will come up, you'll see.'

Emily took a deep breath, ashamed of her outburst, it wasn't helping. 'You might get a job in a shop. You've had two years' experience of that.'

'We couldn't live on the wages.'

'We'll have to,' she insisted.

'Father will pay off my overdraft,' he told her. 'He always has.'

Emily shivered. 'You've had a fall from favour since then.'

'He will,' Giles said confidently. 'Bad for his image to have a son running up debts.'

But at the end of the month Giles received a letter from his bank manager, informing him that his overdraft facilities had been withdrawn because his father had refused to underwrite future debts. He also informed him he'd returned two cheques because there were no funds in his account to meet them.

Giles was angry. 'No consideration. I shall change my bank.'

'No bank is going to give you money, Giles. Give up using one,' Emily urged. 'If you only spent cash from your pocket we wouldn't be running up bills.'

'I haven't got any cash,' Giles said irritably. 'You'll have to sell some of Mother's jewellery.'

Emily closed her eyes, the moment had come to tell him she'd left it at Churton.

'You fool!' Giles screamed out in fury. 'What did you do that for? Didn't I tell you to bring it all?'

Emily tried to explain that what she'd left wasn't really hers. 'Anyway, you have several pairs of cufflinks, a signet ring and a Rolex Oyster. You can sell those.'

Giles calmed down. 'I wouldn't want to part with my watch,' he said indignantly. 'But the rest, well, I'm not very interested in cufflinks.'

'Good, sell them, then. You've got a Leica camera and some binoculars too.'

Giles frowned. 'Can you do it? I've never sold anything, I wouldn't know where to begin.'

Emily pushed the fringe off her forehead. She didn't know where to begin either, she'd have to find out.

'You know, Emily,' he went on. 'I've left things behind too, in my old bedroom. I hardly ever went there after we got married. I had a good fishing rod and lots of tackle, and a clarinet.'

'Can you play it? Well enough to play in a band?'

'No, I only had a couple of lessons. Gave it up, didn't like it.'

Emily sighed.

'I've got some silver tankards and a George III christening mug. And a stamp collection. We could raise money on those.'

'I didn't know you collected stamps.'

'I don't. Grandfather did when he was young. He gave me his collection when I was about fifteen. I added a few but never really got interested. Might be worth a bob or two though.' Emily could see his mind ticking over. 'Come on, we'll get them while Father's out. He'll be at the factory now.'

'Ask him first,' Emily urged. 'He could have given orders not to let us in. There's always someone there,

Higgins or Mrs Eglin. No point in asking for trouble.'

'You phone him, Emily. He won't refuse you.'

'He wouldn't refuse you either. Not something like that.'

'You could ask him for Mother's jewellery while you're at it.'

'I'll not do that and you'll have to collect your own things. I don't know what's yours.'

'All right,' Giles agreed. 'Whatever you say.'

The stamp collection he brought to show her was extensive. Emily found the address of a specialist stamp dealer in Liverpool and agreed when Giles asked her to go with him to sell it. He pushed her forward to open negotiations, but hovered close behind to make sure the cheque was made out in his name.

It raised more money than she'd dared hope, but Giles hung on to it, doling out small amounts weekly to her. She had to nag him to pay their larger bills. The proceeds kept him in comfort for several months, but gradually he began talking of tightening his belt and making more effort to get a job.

The day came, just as she had known it would, when Giles was unable to give her money to meet their weekly expenses. Emily decided to take the bus and Peter's pushchair into West Kirby and see the jewellery shops. She wanted to sell if she could, the gold slave bracelet and cameo brooch Jeremy had given her as Christmas gifts. She also had the ruby necklace he'd given her when Peter was born, and some pearls from Giles.

In the window of one jeweller's shop she saw a notice: 'Experienced staff required. Apply within.' She felt cheered, this was a job Giles could do if she could persuade him to apply. Times were getting harder and she knew he regretted turning down the job at the flour mill.

Selling small items of personal jewellery, she found more embarrassing than selling a stamp collection. The stamp dealer's attitude had been that they were realising value on an investment. This was raising cash on trinkets to buy necessities. Only those on the brink of destitution did it.

She screwed up her courage while she waited for the shop to empty of customers. When it did, she went in and put her slave bangle on the counter. She had to wait while the assistant took it to an office at the back for assessment. But the sum he whispered was more than she'd expected and the transaction was quick. She knew she wouldn't feel so bad about it when the time came to sell her rubies. The money she raised paid for their food, necessities for Peter and a week's wages for the Drouets.

Giles's confidence was draining away with his cash. He agreed to apply for the job selling jewellery and went down to the shop the next morning. Calthorpe's had an excellent reputation and he'd been given a reference to cover the period he'd worked there.

Emily was watching anxiously for his return from the nursery window. His face was grim as he got out of his car and came in; she went slowly out to the banisters as he came upstairs.

'You didn't get it, then?' She was expecting the worst.

'Yes.' He swept her back into the nursery and closed the door carefully. They were both paranoid about hiding their money problems from the Drouets.

'That's good.' She was smiling. 'I'm pleased.'

'It's pointless, Emily,' he raved then, his tawny eyes full of pain. 'Four pounds ten shillings a week. We can't live on that.'

'It's something . . .'

'We need more for food and rent, and gas and electricity. It's hopelessly inadequate.'

'It all helps,' she said as calmly as she could. For a start, it helped her to know he was at work instead of out spending money they couldn't afford. She knew it would help Giles too, to get out of the house and have his mind occupied with other things. To know he was earning something should have a settling effect.

'Why do you stay up here all the time?' he demanded irritably.

Emily looked round the plain room. There were robust carts and blocks of solid wood, a rocking horse that had been used by generations of children. Broken dolls and well-worn teddy bears. Odds and ends, parts of toys she didn't recognise.

'Peter loves the toys and there's nothing he can damage, it makes sense.' She liked the old Victorian story books from which she read him tales with a moral.

'There's no comfort here,' Giles said petulantly. She vacated the wooden armchair with faded chintz cushions, so that he might use it. He thought the nursing chair too low. The floor was covered with linoleum, the furniture unpretentiously solid from the turn of the century.

Emily found it assuaged the opulence of the rest of the house. She felt almost afraid of what money could buy.

In a few short years she'd grown soft on it too and did not know how she'd cope without it. She didn't feel rich in the nursery with the bars on the windows and an electric fire in the hearth behind the solid old fireguard.

'When do you start?' she asked. Peter was pulling himself to his feet on Giles's leg.

'Tomorrow morning.' He brushed the child off roughly. With a whimper he crawled into Emily's arms. She pulled him on to her knee, and buried her face in him; he smelled sweetly of talcum powder and soap. She was glad she'd never had a nanny. It would be harder for her now if she had, and Peter had to learn to stand on his own feet.

'Is it worth it?' His handsome face was black with frustration. 'I mean, what's the point? I'm not going to earn enough.'

'You must, Giles.' She felt desperate. 'Try it, please.'

'We'll never make ends meet.' She noticed his Rolex Oyster had gone, he was wearing a cheap watch.

'You might have to sell your boat too.'

He resisted that as she knew he would. 'I'll miss sailing it. I'll miss the sailing club.'

'It's an expense you can't possibly afford now,' she told him firmly. 'And how often do you take your boat out?'

It was several more months before he got round to it. Summer had gone. Shortage of money in his pocket eventually drove him to advertise it. The boat sold quickly.

Emily was sitting near the fire mending a tear in Peter's trousers when Giles came and banged the cheque down amongst her needles and cotton reels. 'Now are you satisfied?'

'Giles, there was no other way.'

'I don't think you realise what a wrench it is to me. It was a twenty-first birthday present. I love sailing. Summer won't be the same without it.'

'It's not my fault, Giles,' Emily was stung to answer.

'No, it's my father's.' Giles collapsed in the armchair opposite. 'How can he do this to me? But I'll get even with him. One day I will, I promise you, I'll get my own back.'

Emily laid down her sewing. 'It isn't worth getting upset, Giles. Try to accept . . .'

'I'll never accept what he's done to me. I can't . . .' He leapt to his feet and strode to the window. 'Let's go out tonight, Emily. Mrs Drouet will sit with Peter. Let's have dinner at the Royal Rock, we can afford it now. Be like old times.'

Emily protested. 'We need every penny, we can't fritter it away.' She couldn't face paying seven and six each for dinner. He'd want drinks before and wine on top. It would be like eating money.

'Well, I can't stay in night after night. I'll go by myself if you won't come,' he threatened.

Emily didn't want that either. He'd be buying drinks for other people in the bar and possibly end up spending even more.

'Why don't we go and see Gran?' she suggested. 'We haven't been for ages. It's Saturday, so Ted will be there for supper. We could join them, take Peter with us.'

'I don't know, Emily, that isn't . . .'

'Come on, it's somewhere to go that won't cost the earth. Take a bottle of wine, Gran enjoys that.' Giles was reluctant, but she persuaded him.

They arrived at Gran's an hour before the shop closed. She didn't serve in it much now Pammy was working full time, and was delighted to see them. She made tea, played with Peter and asked countless questions about Beechcroft.

Emily knew the questions were winding Giles up. She had not confided in Gran, because she knew if she shared the insecurity she felt about not being able to make ends meet, Gran would be thrown into a panic.

Ted arrived with beer. Giles put out a friendly hand but he ignored it.

'I knew your dad. A real toff he was.' Bitterness twisted Ted's cadaverous features.

'Really?' Giles seemed not to notice the breach in manners. 'Didn't you meet at the wedding?' He poured wine for them all. Ted put his on one side and poured himself a glass of beer.

'Knew him long before then, I did.'

Emily slipped into the shop. Pammy Green, the stringy-haired, fourteen-year-old school leaver Charlie had hired to take her place, was serving the only customer, but there was a great heap of chips cooked ready and she knew Charlie wouldn't close before they were sold. She paid for three helpings of fish, chips and peas, though Peter would not eat much. Charlie would not feed them for nothing.

She went back to the living-room and began setting out

knives and forks on the table. Before long, Charlie was bringing in the heaped plates.

'Bully beef is what we got in the war, you know,' Ted said, turning over the fish on his plate. 'Tinned bully beef, tinned butter and tinned jam too.'

'Wasn't bad,' Charlie said, 'corned beef, really.'

'Bet your father did better.' Ted nodded towards Giles. 'Officers always did.'

'Other regiments left empty tins all round the trenches,' Charlie said. 'Officers made us clean up after them.'

'Threw the rubbish out on no man's land, that's all we did,' Ted chuckled. 'Strewn everywhere it was. Pioneers cleaned up, sprinkled chloride of lime in white showers on the mud. Trenches stank of it.'

'Place still swarmed with rats,' Charlie said. 'It was no picnic for the likes of us.'

'What are rats?' Peter's baby treble asked, his eyes going from one to the other.

Emily pulled a face. 'Like cats. Like pussy cats.'

She speared another chip. Nothing had changed here; Ted and Charlie were off on another trip through their war memories. Looking round the familiar living-room, it seemed even shabbier than she remembered. Everything smelled of stale frying, but that no longer worried her. She wouldn't be staying long enough for it to permeate her clothes.

'Course, it would be different for your father.' Giles's presence was making Ted more aggressive. Emily could see him bristling. 'Toss him in a midden and he'd come up smelling of roses.'

'What do you mean by that?' Giles sounded resentful.

'Knew how to feather his own nest he did. Got the best of everything for himself. Best food, best billets, everything.'

'I've heard him say his first responsibility was to see the men provided for,' Emily put in, she couldn't imagine

Jeremy taking part in the life they described. It seemed a different war altogether.

'He might well say,' Ted sniffed. 'But we know better, don't we, Charlie? Saw him do it many a time.'

'Do what?' Giles demanded.

'All sorts of things he shouldn't.' Ted chuckled macabrely. 'Officers had ways and means.'

'Emily,' Gran said. 'Nip round to Olympia's and see if she's got a tin of fruit or some cake left. We ought to have a pudding since we've had a glass of wine. Make an occasion of it.'

'Hasn't Olympia gone to the pictures?'

'No,' Ted said. 'She's starting with a cold, didn't feel too good. Thought she'd stay by the fire tonight.'

'Right, I'll see what she's got.' Emily pushed her chair back from the table.

'Fruit salad, that's my favourite.' Gran was reaching to the mantelpiece for the housekeeping purse.

'I'll get it,' Emily said. Gran believed she had more money than she knew what to do with, she'd expect her to pay.

She could see the Frasers' living-room light showing between the curtains as she went up the back yard. She knocked on the back door, opened it and called: 'Olympia, are you there?'

She crossed the dark kitchen to the living-room door and put her head round it. Alex was alone, beside a bright fire. Hurriedly he stood up, his book sliding to the floor. She hadn't seen him for a long time; his shoulders had broadened, he seemed taller than she remembered.

'Emily! What a surprise.'

'I thought Olympia . . .' She could feel a hot flush running up her cheeks. 'Ted said she'd be home, not very well.' She had forgotten how attractive Alex's brown eyes and red hair were, and was cross with herself for being so put out.

'Mother's succumbed, gone to bed. She's been fighting a cold all day.'

'I see . . . I'm sorry . . .' She felt flustered. It took an effort to pull herself together. 'Gran wanted a tin of fruit or some cake. We're all having supper round there.'

'Right, come and see what we've got.' He led the way rapidly across the dimly lit hall, stopping to flick the shop light on. Emily only just stopped herself cannoning into him. 'Sorry,' Alex said, placing his hand on her arm to steady her.

His touch was like fire. Sparks went spiralling through her. The luscious scents of Fraser's shop made the years fall away. How could she have forgotten what she'd once felt for Alex?

'Tinned peaches, pears or pineapple?'

She forced her eyes along the shelf. 'I'll have a large tin of fruit cocktail please.' Emily felt in her purse for money. 'What about cake?'

'Only these four eccles cakes left.'

'I'll take them. Giles likes eccles cakes.'

She paid, scooped up her purchases and followed Alex back through the dark hall. He was seeing her out the way she'd come, opening the kitchen door and standing back against it.

'Thank you.' It left little space, she had to turn sidewards to pass.

'Emily?' He put his hands on her shoulders, trapping her against him. She was tingling with excitement. 'Why did you have to marry him?' There was no mistaking the agony in his voice.

Emily hugged her purchases, unable to move. His nearness was intoxicating. Slowly his mouth came down on hers. It was a sad and gentle kiss, underlining his loss.

'I couldn't have given you so much, but we would have been happy.' His face was heavy with emotion, his brown eyes searched into hers. 'Wouldn't we?'

Emily felt in a turmoil, tears were prickling her eyes. She longed to feel him close again, another moment and she knew she'd put her head down on his shoulder and have a good cry, tell him everything. Already his arms were trying to pull her closer.

Suddenly alarm bells were ringing in her head. She was Mrs Giles Wythenshaw and could not seek comfort from Alex now. She pushed herself out of his arms, wanting to escape before he saw her tears.

In the dark of the back entry she paused to wipe her eyes and blow her nose. Those few minutes in Alex's company had altered everything for her. She'd felt his love for her. Seen it with her own eyes. How could she have been so blind that she'd turned her back on Alex? She heard a creak and realised too late the door to Fraser's yard was opening again.

'Emily? Are you still here?' He was a denser shadow in the dark.

Her heart was suddenly pounding, she wanted to escape. She couldn't possibly explain to him why she lingered in the dark by herself. She knew it was too late when she felt his arms pull her close against his own strong body. She heard the squelching thud before she realised she'd dropped the tin of fruit salad.

'Emily, love.' His lips came down urgently on hers and she was carried along on a bow wave of desire. It left her weak and shaking and almost unable to breathe. She put her head down on his shoulder and heard his heart racing.

She felt his yearning, recognised the craving that had gone unsatisfied over the years. Knew for the first time with certainty that Alex loved her as she loved him.

She had thought she loved Giles, but the champagne bubble had burst leaving nothing. She doubted whether Giles had ever loved anyone but himself.

Alex's arms tightened round her. 'You love me more

than you do him,' he whispered. 'Tell me you do, I want to hear you say it.'

But she couldn't. Couldn't stop his kisses either, couldn't stop herself reaching out for him. She knew what she was doing was very wrong. She couldn't blot out her marriage to Giles.

'I have to go. They'll wonder where I am.'

'When can I see you?' There was urgency in his voice. 'Emily, meet me at . . .'

'No!' He released her reluctantly. She was groping on the ground for the tin of fruit.

'Tell them you were talking to me.' There was a sadness in his manner again. 'They know we were always friends.'

In Gran's scullery, she spent time opening the tin and finding plates. Anything to give herself a few moments before she faced Giles again. She told herself firmly she must not show the turmoil she felt. Alex had no place in her life now. She was still fighting for self-control when she went back to the living-room table. She spent the rest of the evening in a daze, thinking about Alex.

'Did you hear what Ted said about Father?'

Giles could hardly wait to close the car door before the words came bubbling out. He was buzzing with interest, she hadn't seen him so alive for months.

'Ted goes on about the war,' she said wearily. 'Like a bad record, the same thing over and over. Forget it.'

'I think Father took them to the Paris house.'

'I didn't hear him say that! Anyway, it's all ancient history.'

'Father's hiding something. I know it. It could be a way to get back at him.'

'You're as bad as Ted.' Emily lost patience with him. 'Your father was very generous to you, Giles. He only had your good at heart, believe me. If you put as much energy into standing on your own feet as you do in trying to knock him off his, living with you would be easier.'

Back at Beechcroft, Giles clumped angrily upstairs straight away. Emily paused at the hall table to lift the terracotta pot of violets to her face. The dark green leaves were lush and rampant with life. The purple flowers nestled between, in full bloom. It had not been just a fancy. The violets had thrived and so had Alex's love for her. She was holding the proof in her hands.

But she knew living with Giles would not be easy now. Seeing Alex again had set fire to her emotions. Everything she'd ever felt for him was bursting into life. She couldn't get him out of her mind.

CHAPTER NINETEEN

Giles had been working at the jeweller's for a couple of weeks, when he asked Emily one morning if she would see that his suit went to the cleaners.

'Have you emptied your pockets?'

'Do it for me, I'm going to be late.' Giles was shaving in the bathroom. Emily did as she was bid and found amongst the collection of pens and used handkerchiefs three visiting cards in his breast pocket. She turned them over.

'Who is Carteret Mathews?' she called.

'I don't know.' He came to the dressing table to stare down at them. 'Yes, I remember. He came into the shop last week.'

Giles had told Emily at length how inferior the stock was to that at Calthorpe's and what a large proportion of it was secondhand.

'There is even,' he said, 'a printed notice in the window offering the best prices for secondhand jewellery and old gold.' Emily nodded, that was how she'd disposed of her slave bangle. When she'd wanted to realise money on her rubies, she'd thought it politic to find another buyer, since Giles was employed there.

'It brings in the public with items to sell, and we have to take everything to the proprietor to fix the buying price, because he doesn't trust anyone else to judge it right. He's got one of those windows between the shop and his office, that looks like black glass on the shop wall, but he can see what's going on from his desk.'

Emily stared down at the visiting cards as she began to fold the suit.

Giles had plenty to say about him: 'Carteret Mathews brought in a little clock, and when I took it to the boss, he turned his nose up at it. "Isn't it any good?" I asked, because it looks better than the general run of stuff we sell.'

' "Too good for the likes of him," he sniffed. "Tell him there's no market for it here."

' "But I sold something similar last week, not as nice as this," I said.

' "It's Carteret Mathews, he's a bit dodgy. Could be stolen. Rather not touch anything from him." '

Emily was pushing the cards towards the waste-paper basket.

'No, don't throw them out. He buys almost anything. Could be a handy person to know.' Giles transferred the cards to the pocket of his clean suit.

Emily felt they could survive for a few months on the job and the proceeds of the boat. Then Giles got bored and complained the staff at the shop treated him without respect. He'd completed three months when he told the owner his stock was tawdry and walked out.

He got another job quite soon selling bacon and cheese at the Co-op, but he didn't bother going in on the third day. All the time their debts were mounting, and their assets shrinking.

Emily was frightened, she hardly dared think of their finances. Talking to Giles about money was a waste of time, he continued to spend what she thought of as an exorbitant amount on clothes, whisky and wine. He could think of no way to balance their budget, other than selling off their valuables, and they had precious few of them left.

He began to cut down a little when she talked of selling his car.

She was seeing less of Sylveen, it was more difficult now she didn't have a car and chauffeur at her command. Even bus fares seemed an expense they couldn't afford.

Emily found herself thinking of Alex more and more, of the security she could have had with him. She gritted her teeth, told herself there was no way out of the mess she'd got herself into. No good hankering for what she couldn't have. She had chosen Giles and there was nothing she could do but wait for the lease to end.

During the last week, she took her engagement ring out of her shoulder pad and sold it. It paid what they owed at Beechcroft. When all their debts were settled, Emily still had thirteen pounds in her purse.

'Now we have to find something cheaper.' She turned to the adverts in the local paper, while Giles watched her helplessly. 'We're going to have move to a cheaper district. I think I'd like to go back to Rock Ferry.'

She picked out two dwellings that sounded reasonable and Giles drove with her to look at them. Emily thought she knew what to expect, but to eyes used to the opulence of Beechcroft they looked dire.

'We can't live here.' Giles turned up his nose in disgust at the first. They looked at five more that afternoon and none pleased Giles.

'We've got to get a roof over our heads.' Emily felt desperate. 'It's no good looking at houses we can't afford. The same thing will happen again, and your car is all we have left.'

With blue-slate roofs gleaming in the rain, New Street looked depressing. None of the gardens were cultivated. The grass and weeds grew three feet high in summer and died back in winter to a rough tangle. The houses were substantial, with enormous windows. Number thirty-six was like its neighbours, a sombre dark Victorian semi of gothic design, long since fallen into disrepair. Built of smoke-blackened brick, it was four storeys high and occupied by four different families, though no attempt had been made to adapt the building for multiple family use.

Here, the garden was hard-packed earth because children played on it all the time. Today it was turning to mud in the downpour. Emily had been given two keys by the agent. She turned the first in the front door and pushed. It had swollen with the spring rains and stuck. Dark green paint was peeling off to show dark blue beneath.

Inside the house was colder than outside. Emily saw Peter wrinkle his nose. It smelled of damp and mice. Emily hoped it was only mice. Giles said rats.

He led the way up wide stairs with a graceful handrail that felt sticky with the sweat of countless hands. There were damp patches on the wallpaper growing black mould. The narrow strip of threadbare carpet was dun coloured with dust.

On the first-floor landing was an ancient gas cooker and three doors. One already stood open, it was the bathroom shared by all tenants. Emily went in and shuddered.

The bath was large like everything else and stood on curving iron legs. Rust had eaten through the enamel, trails of it ran from each tap to the plug hole. There was a cracked washbowl with brass taps, one labelled hot, the other cold. Emily turned them on: cold came from both.

The lavatory was smelly; a rusting chain hung from the leaking cistern. A bucket was wedged underneath to catch the drips. There was blue lettering just above the accumulation of lime that read: Patent Water Closet. The floor was covered with worn lino.

Emily's second key opened the other two doors. A living-room overlooked the front garden, with a sink behind a curtain. The huge windows rattled in the wind, but an overgrown monkey puzzle tree in the garden cut out most of the light. The bedroom was at the back.

The rooms were large. When the house was built in 1856, Rock Ferry had had its share of prosperous merchants. Then Liverpool had been growing fat on the industrial revolution and new iron ferry boats were being built with engines that were reliable. Rock Ferry could be reached quickly and in comfort, and became for more than half a century a high-class residential holiday resort. It was the coming of the motor car that opened up newer and smarter residential districts further afield.

'I think we'll have to take it,' Emily said.

'Nonsense, I can't live here,' Giles retorted. 'There must be something better that doesn't cost the earth.'

'You find it, then,' she said shortly, but though he told her he'd tried, he couldn't.

Once they moved in, Emily found inconveniences she hadn't thought of. At first glance, she had liked the large rooms and high ceilings, but they were hard to heat and draughts rattled through the ill-fitting window frames. Originally, all the rooms had been designed as bedrooms, and the one they now used as a living-room had a small iron bedroom grate that would hold only a few coals. Emily found the damp hard to dry out, warmth impossible to achieve.

She felt like crying when she looked round her new home. She had thought their own possessions amongst the rented furniture would improve the decor, but not so. Giles was always out, Peter fractious, and she knew their changed circumstances would upset Gran. She'd be hurt, though, if Emily kept it from her now she was living this close. She had to tell her before somebody else did, and that bothered her too.

There was the added irritation that she had to carry all the coal upstairs and all the ashes down. Giles had been suspicious and angry on their first day. He suspected the other tenants would help themselves to the coal she had bought and had to leave downstairs in the communal coal shed. He insisted on locking their two separate doors behind them as they moved from room to room, convinced if they did not, their other possessions would disappear.

Emily found having the communal bathroom so close a major disadvantage. All day and half the night fellow tenants came and went, thoughtless of the noise they made. At first, Giles made a point of getting out of bed to complain to them all, saying they were waking him and Peter. Again and again it happened, always the same, heavy footsteps crossing their landing. The slamming bathroom door, the lock shooting home, and a few moments later, a rush of water like the opening of a bore hole. The old pipes rattled and the cistern slowly refilled and settled into silence.

If Emily needed to use it herself, she could guarantee the door would remain locked for half an hour, while a bath was taken or hair washed. After which a fog of steam hung about their landing.

She was determined to lay out her thirteen pounds as thriftily as possible, but her calculations were ruined on the second day when Giles needed nine pounds to pay for upkeep to his car. He talked her into parting with another pound for petrol, and she had to lay out money for coal and food.

Together they scanned the job vacancies in every newspaper they could get. Emily wrote letter after letter on his behalf, by hand now, because their typewriter had been sold. Giles said he would go out and deliver them by hand, and promised to follow up every lead he could get.

'I'll take any job I can get,' he said. 'I'll have to now.'

On her third day in New Street, Emily felt she could not put off a visit to Gran any longer. She dressed herself in Sylveen's plaid skirt and topped it with the coat she'd bought from Ethel; she still felt smart in the outfit.

Turning out Peter to look decent was more difficult because he was growing out of the clothes he'd had at Churton. She did her best. Then she carried his pushchair down to the front door, and ran back to pick him out of his play pen, which was the only safe place she could leave him when she had to go down to the garden to hang out washing or get coal.

She hugged him to her, trying to find comfort in his baby kisses, but she was losing hope. She pushed him round to Paradise Parade and as she went up the yard, saw Gran through the scullery window, brushing her hair in front of Charlie's shaving mirror. The back door swung open before she reached it. Gran's hair stood out round her shoulders in thin white wisps.

'Emily! I was just thinking about you. Such a long time, come on in. Hello, Peter, isn't he growing? Oh, he's lovely.' Emily hugged Gran's bony shoulders. She seemed more fragile than ever.

'You've brought your pushchair? Didn't Giles bring you in the car?'

Emily swallowed the misery rising in her throat. At least the opportunity to tell Gran had arisen naturally. She started on her tale of woe, how Jeremy had disowned Giles, and Giles's lack of money sense.

'Sense of any sort,' Gran lamented. 'I'm a fool too. Bragging how well you'd done to Ethel only yesterday. Drawing comfort from the thought you had everything, that Peter would never go short.'

As she began telling her what a disaster renting Beechcroft had been, Emily could no longer hold back her tears.

'Poor love.' She felt Gran's thin arms come round her, pulling her head down on her bony shoulder. It took her back decades. She sobbed openly as she listed the sums Giles had committed himself to pay. It had been a nightmare she'd never brought herself to talk about till now.

'You should have,' Gran sniffed, and Emily realised there were tears in her eyes too, one rolled down her wrinkled cheek. 'Anyone with sense would have told you to sell everything you had, straight away. Stamps, boat, ring, car, everything. You could have bought a little house with money like that.' Gran was rocking her, but crying too. 'Put a roof over your heads, once and for all.'

Emily knew Giles would not have considered it for an instant. He'd been unable to appreciate how changed his position was. Hadn't even told her his intentions, until it was too late.

'You could have made it decent.' Gran's head shook with disbelief. Absentmindedly, she picked up her brush again. With the ease of long practice, she was twisting her hair and drawing it up into a knot high on the top of her head. She had worn her hair like this since she was eighteen. Now it was thin and wispy and the knot had shrunk to button size. She reached for her black straw hat, and speared it to her hair with a long hat pin.

'Too late.' Emily couldn't help sobbing. 'Too late now.' Yet the telling of her troubles made her feel better. Gran understood what hard times were, she'd lived through plenty herself. 'Giles doesn't want anyone to know along the Parade. He's afraid of losing face.'

'Bound to find out you're living in New Street, love. Where else would you get your bread? No point in walking up to Bedford Road every day.' Gran dried her own eyes, though they looked still looked rheumy. She made tea, her panacea for everything.

She started unravelling an old cardigan Emily had outgrown years ago, promising to reknit it as a pullover for Peter. When she was leaving, Gran said: 'If you want to leave that feller, you know you'll always be welcome here, don't you?'

'Gran, how can I leave him?' But Gran's understanding was making tears start to her eyes again. She left in a hurry while her self-control still held and was halfway up the entry before she realised Gran had pressed three pound notes in her hand. That brought the tears raining down again. She wouldn't tell Giles she had them, it would be her reserve.

Within a week, Emily realised Giles was going to find it very difficult to get another job. There were two and a half million unemployed. She saw them on the streets of Rock Ferry every time she went out.

When she went down the Parade to shop, Olympia would tot up her order, then add a couple of eggs to make lunch for her and Peter. When she went to buy potatoes in Tarrants', they always pressed a piece of fruit into Peter's hand. Emily felt their sympathy, was comforted by it, but it brought tears to her eyes. Even harder to cope with was their growing hostility towards Giles, which they didn't bother to hide.

When Sunday came, she got out of bed feeling full of nervous energy that drove her to work all morning. She washed clothes in the bath, but the hot water ran out before she'd finished. She considered putting more money in the geyser, but her burst of energy had run out too.

As she carried the bucketful of wet clothes downstairs, she could hear somebody coming up. Looking over the balustrade she saw the top of Alex's glossy red head bounding towards her. Her steps slowed, her heart churned and seconds later he was on the landing looking up at her.

'Mother told me.' His dark eyes were smouldering with emotion. 'Why didn't you?'

She ran past him. 'How could I?'

She heard his footsteps following her down again, and out into the back garden. The communal washing line already had a row of grey napkins flying in the wind.

She squeezed water out of Peter's pullover with cold and crepey hands and started to peg it out. Alex's strong brown hands took it from her to wring it harder.

'Don't you have a mangle?' She shook her head. He carried on helping her, wringing the last vestiges of water from Giles's shirts and socks.

'Is he in? Giles?'

'No.' She hadn't seen Alex since he'd held her close in the entry that Saturday night, but in her mind she'd relived every word and every kiss countless times.

At first, she'd thought it a comfort that Alex still cared about her. It had gladdened her heart, warmed and uplifted her, but now she could think of nothing else. The love she'd once felt for Alex was growing into passion and underlining her indifference to Giles. He was all show and no substance. It was no longer his love-making she craved, but Alex's.

'Come up and have a cup of tea.' She was torn between wanting to keep him with her and the knowledge that she'd be tormented by everything he said and did. She knew the more she saw of him, the more she wanted him. She had to go back anyway, because she'd left Peter alone in his play pen. She led the way, glad she'd lit the fire and tidied up this morning; Alex had come when the room was looking its best.

'Where's he gone?'

'Down to Donovan's for a drink.' Just to see Alex again made her feel on top of the world. She was tingling all over.

'He's drinking too much?'

'He doesn't think so, Alex.' Even one drink was too much if it took money they could have spent on food.

She wanted to laugh at the surprise on Alex's face when she grabbed the kettle from the gas stove on the landing and dashed to the bathroom to fill it. He didn't seem to notice she had a Sunday dinner roasting in the oven, though the two lambs' hearts were filling the landing with a delicious scent.

When she took him into their living-room she saw his eyes going round the shabby furniture, saw the censure on his face. 'I can't believe Giles Wythenshaw lives here.'

'He does.' Peter was asleep, curled up in a ball on the play-pen rug, his head on a teddy bear. Alex stood over him.

'Your baby looks well.' Emily flushed with maternal pride; he was a beautiful child with long gold lashes curling on his cheeks. She had bathed him this morning and dressed him in clean clothes, not noticing till now his trousers reached only to mid-calf, and his toe was pushing through his slipper.

'Do you remember these? The violets you sent me?' She lifted the terracotta pot to show him, sniffing their scent.

'When your baby was born? Is that the same plant? It seems much bigger, more luxuriant now.'

'It's thrived over the years,' she smiled.

'More than can be said about you.'

On her way to make the tea, she accidentally brushed against Alex. Her heart was pounding and she could feel her arm burning where it had touched him.

'What about Jeremy Wythenshaw? Does he know you've come down to this?' She knew from his eyes, Alex had felt the same trembling shock.

'He doesn't want to know.'

'He would help you, Emily.'

'He put us out. Cut us off.' She brought the teapot back, sat down at the table.

'What did Giles do to deserve it?' His gaze was probing hers. Hadn't she asked herself that countless times? She felt deep down that Giles must have made a pass at Sylveen, but he'd denied it. Either that or Giles had taken, or rather stolen something from Jeremy. He denied that too and put their present misfortune down to a whim on the part of his father. She couldn't believe that.

Alex put his hand on her arm and let it lie there; his touch scorched with the intensity of his feelings. She couldn't take her eyes from it, a square practical hand, showing signs of physical work. It brought the sting of tears to her eyes, and the next moment he was pulling her close.

She was conscious of his jacket, rough Harris tweed scratching her cheek as she let her troubles pour out, and his hand, gentle now against her hair.

'Where did we go wrong?' His lips brushed her forehead with a kiss of comfort. Emily knew, now that it was too late, that she would have found happiness with Alex. Why hadn't she come to her senses before it was too late? He kissed her lips, pulled her closer, and the passion she'd sensed just below the surface rose up to engulf her. She felt on fire, alive.

Suddenly she was pushing him away.

'I'm Giles's wife.' That put her out of Alex's reach for ever. 'You shouldn't come here, Alex. It's wrong.'

'I know, but I never have been able to keep my hands off you.'

She felt heady with excitement as his lips came down on hers again. What could be wrong about this when they both ached for it? Some sound broke the spell, made them turn round. Peter was sitting up, watching them through the play-pen bars with wide blue eyes.

Giles pulled himself to the side of the bed. It sagged in the middle, so during the night he and Emily slid together in an uncomfortable tangle. They hadn't had a decent night's rest during the week they'd spent here. Emily stirred under the shabby eiderdown.

He looked round the bedroom, appalled. Peeling wallpaper, a chest of drawers that listed to one side, net curtains grey with age.

'I can't live here,' he complained. 'It's disgusting.'

'Shush, don't wake Peter. At least there's plenty of room for his cot.'

But he knew Emily didn't like it either, she was putting on a brave face. She was pushing herself up on her pillows; her face had lost its colour, she no longer looked well. Peter had had a cough since they'd come.

'Surely you can find something better?'

'Not for fifteen shillings a week. At least we aren't running headlong into debt.'

'But getting there just the same. I can't stand it.'

'We didn't have to sign a lease like at Beechcroft. If we see something better we only have to give a week's notice.'

Giles felt desperate for money again. He almost spoke of it, but managed to bite the words back in time. He knew what Emily would say, and didn't want to hear it again.

'The only thing of value we've got left is your car. You'll have to sell it.' He couldn't contemplate parting with his car, though it wasn't running well and he didn't know how to cure it.

'I think I'll see if I can get a job.' Emily's voice was resigned. 'We've got to have income.'

'Who will look after the baby?'

'Couldn't you?'

'Every day, and all day?'

'Sylveen wouldn't mind if you took him there. She said it was as easy to look after three as two.'

'But that means more petrol. More expense.'

'Gran would have him like a shot, but she's so old. I couldn't ask her to do it every day. We've no food left, we've got to get money from somewhere.'

'There's my dole,' he said.

'It doesn't help me much.' Her tone was sharper than she intended. Giles kept most of his dole as pocket money.

'Olympia?'

'I can't ask Olympia again. We already owe her two pounds.'

Giles sighed heavily. 'I'll see what I can do.'

'You'll sell the car?'

'I've got an idea.' It had occurred to him that he had a source of income he'd never attempted to tap. He would go over to Liverpool and see his grandfather. He said nothing of his intentions to Emily. Better keep quiet about it, in case he couldn't screw anything out of him. Father might have asked him not to help them.

He had a bath, it was something he was doing less often. Although Emily said she'd scrubbed it with bleach, the lavatory stank, making it a penance to stay in the bathroom. He had to ask Emily to light the geyser because it was beyond him, it took a threepenny bit he could ill afford, and then it provided only a couple of inches of warm water.

He shaved in luke-warm water with toilet soap. The blunt razor blade left his chin feeling rough. At least Emily had bought more toilet soap, for two days they'd only had Sunlight. His hair needed trimming; he added a little water to the dregs of bay rum remaining in the bottle, damped his hair down well, it would have to do.

Today was Monday, it would be as good as any day to go. Grandfather went to the shop on Tuesdays and to Churton on Sundays. He had no idea what he did during the rest of the week, but assumed he sat at home doing nothing. He spoke of Father as though he provided the only social events in his life.

Giles wondered whether he should telephone first, but it was no longer convenient when he had to go round to the post office to do it. Also, it would give Grandfather the chance to think about the purpose of his visit. He would say he was passing and had just dropped in.

Emily wouldn't part with the half a crown he needed for petrol and tunnel fees. She said it was all she had left and argued against it. In the end he had to take it from her purse when she wasn't looking. It made him feel better to find she still had another shilling. Once in his car, everything seemed normal again. The new tunnel had just been opened by George V and Queen Mary. It was quite a novelty driving between Birkenhead and Liverpool for the first time.

In the fluorescent light, the tiling was bright white. He'd expected it to be full of fumes deep under the Mersey, but the air seemed no different. He was impressed by the orderly traffic flow, the ease of getting to Liverpool now.

It was not so easy to find his way to Rodney Street because he hadn't been to Grandfather's house since he was a boy, but he got there in the end.

A manservant answered the door, in striped trousers, dark waistcoat and jacket. Giles was left to wait in the hall deciding that, like his present accommodation, it was in need of redecoration. Unlike his place though, it was clean and warm, with good-quality rugs and pictures and lovely Georgian furniture of the same period as the house.

'Mr Calthorpe will see you now.' The manservant returned to show him in.

'Giles, this is a surprise.' His grandfather was struggling to his feet. His shoulders were bowed, he could no longer straighten up. There was nothing left of him, he was wearing a suit that seemed several sizes too big.

The room was lighter than the hall with a huge fire roaring up the chimney. He was offered an armchair pulled close to the hearth. Within minutes Giles could feel the sweat breaking out on his brow.

'Why haven't you been before? Don't seem to have seen much of you, don't see much of anybody. Only your father bothers now.' Giles felt at a loss, and wished he'd rehearsed the needed words.

'You see Aunt Harriet when you go to Churton, don't you?'

'Harriet, yes,' the old man snorted. 'Very wrapped up in herself. Not much pleasure in her company, says she can't hear very well. Think she's becoming a hypochondriac. I'm tired of hearing about her indigestion and her bowels.'

Giles tried to think of something to say. It wasn't easy to ask for money when Grandfather was complaining about Aunt Harriet.

'Going on another cruise I believe. She was seasick you know, last time.' The old man sighed gustily. 'If only Elspeth had lived . . .'

The manservant brought morning coffee and biscuits. Giles felt hotter than ever as Grandfather started on a discourse on his domestic arrangements. He could no longer get upstairs. He'd had to have his bed brought down to the dining-room and the table and chairs moved elsewhere. He used only the two rooms now.

The manservant knocked again and came in. 'Higgins has arrived with the car, sir.'

Giles went cold and hot again, leapt to his feet and went over to the window. Why hadn't he got on with it? Sure enough his father's Rolls was outside. He hadn't wanted him to know he was here!

'Have him wait. I don't suppose you'll be staying long?' His grandfather turned back to him. Giles swallowed, he had to get on with it.

'Are you going to Churton today?'

'No. Your father thinks I should get out and about more. Since the tunnel opened, he's been sending Higgins every few days to take me out for a run. Thinks it will do me good.'

'Where do you go?' Giles kicked himself for procrastinating further. Higgins would have seen and recognised his car of course. His father would find out about this. No point in asking Grandfather to keep quiet.

'I don't care where I go,' he said with a sudden burst of irritability. 'Jeremy will no doubt have instructed him to take me to Southport or some such.'

'He takes you shopping?'

'Certainly not, my shopping days are over, far too tiring. Anyway, I've got all I need. I'll sit on the prom if it's warm enough, or perhaps listen to the band in the park.' Giles wondered if he should offer to accompany him. No, he'd only put off asking and more of this would drive him mad.

'It sounds very interesting,' Giles said, and his grandfather's sunken eyes swung to his face.

'I'd prefer to stay at home in comfort but your father hounds me. Thinks he knows better than I do what I want.'

'He treats everybody like that,' Giles said dryly.

'He does it for the best, I suppose. With both Ellis and Higgins I can get almost anywhere.'

'Yes, I suppose so.' Giles knew he couldn't put it off any longer.

'You haven't told me any of your news.' The ancient rheumy eyes were on him again. 'How do you like your job at Westman's?'

'You know about that?' Giles felt knocked off course again.

'They checked on the reference you gave them. Your father was pleased to know you had a job.'

Giles launched forth at last. 'They didn't pay enough to cover our living costs. A wife and child cost money to support.' He took a deep breath. 'I'm in a bit of a fix financially, Grandfather.'

'Your father was afraid you might be. Worried.'

Not worried enough, Giles thought grimly. It was his fault he was in this position.

'Is that what you've come to tell me?'

Giles swallowed hard; he wasn't surprised the old devil had no visitors. He wasn't making it easy.

'I was wondering if I might ask for your help, Grandfather?' He felt pleased with that, he'd phrased it well.

'Help? I need the help. Old age is hell, Giles, as you may find out one day.'

'Yes, I'm sure, Grandfather, but the sort of help I need . . .'

'You're asking me for money?' The rheumy eyes met his again, searching sourly. 'Of course you are. What other help could I possibly give?'

'I'd be grateful. Emily and I would be very grateful.'

'Not that I have a lot, but at my age the need has gone. A cheque?'

Giles was riveted with hope. 'Thank you. That would be wonderful.' He was going to come out of this all right after all.

'Help me to the desk.'

The old man was nothing but skin and bone. He swayed across the room, sitting down slowly, doing everything in slow motion, taking twice as long as anyone else. Giles was almost screaming with impatience as he watched him find his glasses, his pen, his cheque book, sit with pen poised between purple fingers. At last, very slowly, he began to write.

Giles saw the figures of one hundred pounds being formed on the cheque and felt his body run with sweat and joy. It was more than he'd dared to hope for. More than he'd got for his boat and that had lasted them months.

With the cheque in his hands he was lyrical with thanks. The old man's sunken eyes looked up at him.

'Don't come asking for more, because in this life I need it myself.' His skin was greyish brown, his hair sparse clumps of white on a dry scalp. 'But you might as well know I've remembered you in my will.'

Giles couldn't stop his face breaking into a wide smile. Better and better.

'I've left my furniture and personal effects to your father. He'll appreciate my things.' Giles saw the antique glass and silver for the first time, the french clock, the pictures and the Regency furniture.

'But your father is not in need of money, so apart from a few bequests to my staff, I've willed what remains to you.' Giles felt his heart leap with satisfaction. 'Together with this house.'

He could hardly get his thanks out, could not believe his luck. Then he was letting his eyes travel round the room, it was old-fashioned but marvellously comfortable compared with where he lived.

'I don't suppose you'll want to live here, but you could sell it and raise capital to buy something more to your taste.'

'Most thoughtful of you, Grandfather, I want you to know I'm very grateful,' Giles kept repeating as he took his leave.

'Who else would I leave it to? You're Elspeth's boy. My nearest blood relation.'

Giles asked to use the bathroom, so that he could see more of his inheritance. He really couldn't remember much about the house.

He sat in his car outside for as long as he dared, letting his eyes wander up and down the Georgian terraces of Rodney Street. He moved on before he was ready, not wanting Grandfather to find him still here, when Higgins brought him out to the parked Rolls.

He felt exultant, wanting to laugh aloud. He had a hundred pounds in his hand, but that was nothing to what he'd get when the old man died. Surely not more than another year or so to wait. Could come in weeks, if he was lucky; the old man looked as though he wouldn't last much longer. But he'd looked half-dead ever since Giles could remember, and that manservant of his, Ellis, was coddling him too much. Poor old Grandfather had outstayed his time in this world. He was well over ninety after all.

CHAPTER TWENTY

Giles felt euphoric. As he drove back through the tunnel, he kept pushing his fingers into his top pocket to crinkle the cheque.

He emerged in Birkenhead in golden sunshine, and headed straight to his bank to present it. After the trouble the manager had given him, complaining he was overdrawn and returning his cheques, he didn't intend to leave money in his account. He'd asked Grandfather to make it a bearer cheque. He felt even better with the thick bundle of notes in his wallet.

The last thing he felt like doing now was going home to those miserable rooms and the new tougher Emily, who would talk him into giving up some of his windfall. Though it was early, he went instead to the Royal Rock and had a beer in the bar followed by a decent lunch. It felt almost like old times.

He came out into the early afternoon sun to see small boats with sails billowing, tacking upriver. The breeze was laden with salt and the scent of seaweed. He yearned to be out on the water.

There was no reason why he couldn't go to the sailing club. He no longer had a boat and he hadn't paid his dues, but he knew a lot of people there, perhaps somebody would let him crew for them.

He was heading towards his car with this in mind when

he heard somebody say: 'Hello, Giles.'

'Oh, hello.'

She looked a sports-loving girl, with long brown hair drawn back in a no-nonsense plait. Her face was tanned, free of make-up and familiar, but he couldn't place her.

'Audrey Woodward,' she said. 'I've not seen you at the club for ages.'

'Of course, Audrey. Lovely to see you again. I've been away in Australia. Just thinking about the club as a matter of fact. Wondering if someone would let me crew if I went down.'

'I would,' she smiled. 'I was just on my way.'

'Really? What boat do you have now?'

'The same. An International Fourteen.'

'A smashing sailing dinghy. Thanks. Do you want a lift?'

'Have you got your kit? You can't come like that.'

'Er . . . I'll have to run up Bedford Road and get some sailing shoes.'

'I'll go ahead and get the sails up,' she said. 'Don't be long.'

Giles felt he was living again after months in the dark. He also bought a towel, a windcheater and a pair of cotton slacks that didn't fit very well. Out on the river with the water slapping against the boat and enough wind in the sails to make it skim over the choppy waves, it felt pure heaven.

It was a long time since he'd been sailing and he'd missed it. He'd been a fool to let his boat go without a struggle. Audrey's handling of hers was a pleasure to watch. She swung the boom across with a precision that made him feel he'd let his sailing skills rust.

He would have liked to go further upriver, but Audrey said no because the autumn afternoon was drawing in early.

She was faster at stowing the sails than he'd ever been.

He tried to help but found it hard to remember exactly what needed doing. The wind seemed suddenly cold, but with his face made taut by the sun and wind, he felt exhilarated by his outing. He leaned forward and kissed her full on her lips.

'You're very lovely, you know that?' He didn't want to go home to Emily. 'Come to the Royal Rock. I want to buy you a drink.'

'I'm expected home, Giles, thank you. Dad worries if I stay out.' Giles felt his pleasure fade. This day had been an oasis of delight in a slough of despond. He didn't want it to end yet.

'Why don't you come home with me?'

'Could I?' he asked. 'Now we've met up again, I don't want to lose you.'

He let his gaze burn down into her wide brown eyes. He felt his pulses quicken. In the past, he'd never gone for the healthy outdoor type, but Audrey's lustre of perfect health was attractive.

'You can have a drink with Dad, you know him anyway. And I'll ask Mummy if you can stay to supper. She'll let you as long as it isn't chops. If there's enough for another, I mean. She likes me to bring my friends home.'

He changed quickly into his suit at the club. It gave him a chance to rinse his face and smooth down his hair. The house she directed him to in Beryl Road was a modern villa. He thought it modest compared with Churton or Beechcroft, but comfort seemed to cushion him as soon as he was inside the door. Everything was new and slap up-to-the-minute in style. Audrey led him across the hall to the sitting-room door.

'Dad, this is Giles Wythenshaw, I think you know him. Could you give him a drink?'

Giles remembered going to his button factory. He'd thought her father a rough diamond that day. He still did; he wore a shapeless cardigan and carpet slippers.

'Ah, Jeremy's lad. How is your father?'

Giles had no idea and didn't care. 'Very well, sir, thank you.'

'Haven't seen much of him recently.' Giles smiled with relief. He'd never been more than an acquaintance anyway. 'Would you like whisky or beer?'

'Whisky please,' he said before he noticed her father was drinking beer. He kept his drinks on a glass-shelved trolley, with metal bars shaped like wheels holding them together.

Giles sank into a deeply sprung armchair in pale plush. The carpet was thick, the light fittings art deco. He was impressed in spite of himself; the room was a stylish epitome of the best the thirties could provide.

Audrey's mother came in and he leapt to his feet, going to meet her with hand outstretched. She was austerely thin and tall, there was nothing rough about her, she seemed stylishly dressed.

'So pleased to meet you, Mr Wythenshaw,' she said.

'Call me Giles.'

He managed to capture her dark eyes with his and hold her gaze for a few seconds before it slid away. 'I'm delighted to be here.'

'You'll stay for supper? Pot luck, I'm afraid.'

'I'd love to, thank you. Most kind.'

The aroma that followed her in brought saliva to his mouth. Giles felt cosseted. The whisky measure was more than generous, it was topped up with soda and ice. Life here was a vast improvement on New Street.

Audrey had disappeared upstairs, now she returned in an emerald-green dress, with her long brown hair loose about her shoulders. Giles jerked to his feet in surprise. She had worked a transformation from the sporty to the romantic type. He felt his interest quicken and could hardly drag his eyes away; she really was pretty. Her father poured sherry for the ladies, topped up his whisky for him. His question took him by surprise.

'How's your wife?'

Giles hesitated a moment too long. He'd been working out a storyline in which he was a bachelor, rather smitten with Audrey. Once he'd been eligible, his hand sought. He wanted to be encouraged to stay here.

'I'm afraid she died,' he said sadly, changing his line of approach. 'Very painful . . .'

'Oh dear, I am sorry.' Mrs Woodward was all sympathy. 'She seemed so young . . .'

For a moment Giles was afraid they might know Emily too.

'We came to your wedding,' she added. 'Such a pleasant girl. May we know what happened?'

'An accident . . . A riding accident out in Australia.' He forced a choke into his voice and looked suitably solemn. Audrey's eyes were soft with sympathy. They wouldn't leave his now. This was more like it.

'Such a tragedy,' her mother said.

'I'm hardly over it yet. Quite lonely.'

'You still have your father . . .'

'He goes to Paris so much. Very lonely.' Audrey was giving him encouraging smiles.

'I hear you aren't working for him any more.' Mr Woodward's eyes when he met them seemed needle sharp.

'Not here in Birkenhead,' he conceded, 'but I am.'

Three pairs of eyes watched him, he knew he'd captivated their interest.

'In Australia?' Audrey asked.

'Yes.'

'I didn't know your father had interests there,' her father put in.

'He hasn't yet. He sent me out to assess the possibility of starting a factory. He wants to expand.'

'Expand in Australia?' Mr Woodward laughed outright,

his mouth wide open showing gaps in his dentistry. 'Does he have a market in Australia now?'

'No,' Giles said before he could stop himself.

'Putting thousands of miles between two factories won't make the business easy to run.'

'The intention is that I will run the Australian end,' Giles said with all the confidence he could muster.

Woodward's dark eyes surveyed him in the long drawn-out pause.

'I can't see the point of starting up in Australia in the middle of a worldwide depression like this. Not when Japan and the Far East are undercutting us all. Sooner or later they'll swamp the market for artificial jewellery. Your father knows that. No flies on him. He'll not be wasting his time and money on building a factory out there.'

Giles shivered, feeling repulsed and a little afraid of his know-it-all air.

Supper, when it came, was an excellent meal of soup followed by beef olives. Giles enjoyed the spotted dick and custard served for pudding. A maid waited on table and there seemed to be staff in the kitchen.

He wondered whether he might wangle an invitation to stay the night; with staff it wouldn't put her mother out too much. He took the opportunity to whisper to Audrey as they left the table.

Their guest room was comfortable. Giles changed into the large pair of silk pyjamas Audrey furnished him with. Padded across the carpet on the landing to use the new toothbrush her mother found for him. He got between the linen sheets and lay down with a well-satisfied stomach but an uneasy mind.

He'd noted which bedroom belonged to Audrey, but was nervous about crossing the landing to it. The parents' room was closer, the cook seemed to sleep dangerously near, and her father had not yet come up.

He decided not to try. There had been a knowing look in her father's eyes when he'd spun that yarn about Australia.

Still, Audrey was on his side; he'd suggested he drive her to Llandudno tomorrow and her mother seemed pleased at the interest he was taking in her. He was looking forward to getting Audrey alone in his car.

It was high time he ditched Emily. He certainly couldn't stay in those dreadful rooms she'd found. A pity he had to grovel to the old parents, particularly her old man, but tomorrow would be another grand day out.

Giles woke to find bright fingers of light showing round the curtains. He drowsed on, only half-aware of a strange household wakening round him.

He heard quick footsteps approaching his room. Welcomed them, expecting a tray of morning tea to be slid on the table by his bed.

The door crashed back on its hinges, making him jerk up on one elbow with shock.

'Get up and get out.' Mr Woodward, his face puce with rage, was fully dressed for work and advancing belligerently on his bed.

Giles scrambled out in a pall of horror, shivering as he held up the too-large pyjama trousers; his heart seemed to bounce out of control.

'I've just spoken to your father. What a pack of lies you told us last night. You must think we're all stupid.'

Giles felt caught up in a tornado. His heart thudded, his legs felt too weak to support him. 'I . . . I can explain,' he began.

'Don't bother. Get yourself out of my house and back to your wife. Don't dare show your face here again, or come running after my daughter.'

Emily was worried stiff. She couldn't understand where Giles had got to. He'd gone out yesterday morning saying he'd be back in time for lunch, and now twenty-four hours later there was still no sign of him.

Now that money was tighter he mostly came home for meals. At first she thought he might have met some old crony and gone on what he called 'a bender'. This seemed more likely when he missed supper too.

But when she'd woken up this morning to find she still had the bed to herself, she began to fear he'd had some sort of accident. She was beginning to wonder whether she should go to the police.

Lunch time again, she'd set out the knives and forks on the table an hour since, after scrubbing the oilcloth so hard the blue pattern had disappeared in one place. The mince and mashed potatoes had already waited twenty minutes. She had been bursting since yesterday to tell Giles their troubles could be over.

Usually happy by nature, Peter began to whimper; he was hungry. She dished up a portion of mince in his enamel bowl and left it to cool while she wiped his hands on a face flannel and sat him in his high-chair. Eagerly Peter began spooning the slack mixture to his mouth. He was managing to feed himself now, though he made a mess. She was dreading having to leave him all day, that would be the hardest part. But where had Giles got to?

The smell of dinner decided her, she would wait no longer. She dished up her own, turned the gas out under the pans. She'd finished eating when she heard Giles's footstep on the stairs. He came in and slammed a bottle of whisky and two of wine on the table.

'Guess what? Our luck's turned.' His manner seemed a strange mixture of nervous bravado. She put it down to guilt because he'd stayed out all night.

'Where have you been?' The sight of the bottles made her feel sick.

'Didn't you hear what I said? Our luck's turned.'

'You've got a job?'

'Better than that. Grandfather's given me a hundred pounds.'

She shivered. 'Does he expect you to pay him back?' She couldn't get used to the way Giles could spend on luxuries as soon as he had a few pounds in his pocket, not when they owed money.

'Of course not. Also, he's going to leave me his house and money in his will. Our difficulties are over.'

Emily felt she was being teased. 'He could live to be a hundred. Lots of people do.'

'He could go next week. Anyway, we've got his hundred pounds.'

'So where did you go last night? I was worried. Decided to give you till four o'clock and then go to the police.'

'Don't ever go to the police, Emily! No need to worry about me. Met an old sailing friend. Had a night out. Enjoyed myself.'

'Spent some of your money, you mean?'

Giles laughed and, lifting Peter out of his high chair, he danced round the room holding him high. When he caught his heel in a torn rug and stumbled, he hastily dumped the child on her knee.

'How long will it last us, do you think?'

Emily shook her head. If she controlled it, she could spin it out six or even nine months. In Giles's pocket, it was impossible to judge.

'I've got good news too, I've got a job.' Emily felt he'd taken the wind out of her sails. Perhaps she'd been too hasty.

Giles sat down looking thoughtful. 'How much are they going to pay you?'

'Two pounds fifteen shillings. In a baby linen shop in Bedford Road.'

'As a shop assistant? You can do better as a typist.'

'Not many typists needed round here. I'm starting on

Monday. Nine till five-thirty.' She looked up to find Giles beaming at her.

'I've worked out that if we only pay fifteen shillings for rent, we can just about manage on my wages. With your hundred pounds too, we'll be in clover.'

'We could move somewhere decent, Prenton or Bebington.'

'But then I couldn't walk to work,' Emily protested. 'And you couldn't push Peter round to Gran's if you wanted to go out.'

'We can't stay here.'

Feeling at the end of her tether, Emily rounded on him. 'I can and will. I can't afford anything better. Not while you buy drink for yourself.'

'For you too.' He was picking at the foil on a wine bottle neck. 'Where's the corkscrew? We'll have a glass to celebrate.'

'Wine would choke me. If you move to Prenton, you go by yourself.' It was the first time she'd found the courage to say it outright, but not the first time she'd thought it. She'd gone to Olympia's for bread and discovered he'd taken the half crown she'd refused him from her purse. It had frightened her, made her go looking for a job.

'Emily, don't be like that.'

'We didn't pay the rent last week. I'm afraid we'll get behind.'

She busied herself with Peter. Wiping dinner from his face and hands, taking him to the bedroom and putting him in his cot for his rest. Giles followed.

'We owe money to Olympia and half a dozen others. And you want to celebrate.'

'Emily, we've got a hundred pounds.'

'You have now, but a fool and his money . . . You must know the saying. We need food, Giles, not whisky.'

She threw herself face down on her bed in desperation.

She heard him shut the door softly, felt the bed sag under his weight.

'Emily . . .'

'Go away.' The bottles had slammed home the message. She could work and scrimp to keep them all on her wages, Giles would always fritter away anything that came his way. Not that a lot would come his way if he couldn't get work.

With two and a half million unemployed, she'd known she'd find it easier than Giles, but she couldn't earn as much, women didn't. And someone had to look after Peter. Suddenly it all seemed hopeless.

She heard the rustle and lifted her head. Through the dazzle of tears she saw him counting pound notes on to the pillow beside her.

'Fifty,' he said. 'For you.'

She stared at it, hardly able to believe her eyes. Giles had always resisted handing money over to her, he wanted to keep control himself. He wouldn't admit she could handle it better. She found herself always begging him for meagre amounts to pay for essentials.

'If you want to stay here, I'm staying too.'

Emily sniffed into her handkerchief. Peter gave a little snore.

'I'll look after him while you go to work. We'll make out all right between that and my little windfall, and if things get bad, well, I've still got the car.' His arms went round her in a tight hug. 'I couldn't leave you, Emily.'

Emily sat on the edge of her bed and dried her eyes. Perhaps they would make out. Perhaps.

By the next morning Emily felt a blessed respite. When Giles went out in the car, she put Peter in his pushchair and went out. She paid the rent they owed and a month in advance. She felt she was buying trust from the agent should they fall into arrears again, as well as having the satisfaction of knowing the rent was paid.

She owed money all along Paradise Parade. It felt wonderful to buy all she needed and clear her slate at Tarrant's the greengrocer and McFie's the butcher. She owed most to Olympia because she'd loaned her money as well as groceries. She'd been worrying herself stiff about how she would pay her back.

She started her job. After working in a fish and chip shop, a baby linen shop was easy. On Thursday afternoon, her first half day, she called in on Gran and found her still in bed. She looked pathetically small and frail under the bedclothes, her wrinkled skin shiny with sweat.

'What's the matter, Gran?' Emily felt alarmed.

'Just a bit down. I honestly thought you were on easy street.'

'Don't you worry about me.'

'I persuaded you. Jump at him I said, and was pleased when you did. You'd not had an easy start, losing your mother like that.'

'Gran, I'll get over this.'

'I thought Giles was a lovely person. I couldn't see anything wrong with him.'

'Neither could I then. I'll ask the doctor to come.' Emily knew Gran must be feeling ill because her teeth were still in the tumbler on the bedside table. Without them her cheeks sagged inwards, making her look older than ever.

'No, there's nothing he can do, Emily. He'll just say stay in bed and keep warm.'

'How's your throat?' Gran had bad throats every winter.

'It's a bit sore.'

'I'll get some lemons and make lemonade for you. And you need a fresh nightie. You've sweated into that one. Have a wash first, come on, you'll feel better if you do.'

Emily went in several times that day to look after Gran.

At tea time Charlie and Pammy were desperately busy in the shop and he asked her to help serve through the rush hour, though she had to leave Peter up in Gran's room. Charlie rewarded her with fish and chips to take home for Giles.

On Friday morning, Emily got up an hour earlier to see to Gran before she went to work. When she rushed round to see her in her lunch hour, she made Charlie send for the doctor.

He diagnosed tonsillitis, and the following day Peter went down with it too. By Sunday, Gran was worse. Emily knew she could not do her job in the baby linen shop and leave them both. On Monday morning she sent Giles up with a note to explain why she couldn't come in. Giles said the proprietor was angry and said she needn't return at all, she'd get someone else.

She was torn then between attending to two patients. Some days Giles was persuaded to stay home with Peter while she went down to Gran. Others, she wrapped him up warmly and ran down with him in the pushchair. Peter was hard work when he was ill, fractious and whining, so Giles soon lost patience with him. His cough kept them awake at night. Emily took him to the doctor but the linctus he prescribed didn't seem to help.

There was Gran's washing to do as well as her own. Meals to make for Gran as well as at home, and Giles still wanted her to write applications for jobs, though he was no nearer getting one. After a week of that Emily was worn out, but Gran was on the mend.

Another day and Emily's own throat felt raw. She wasn't feeling well, and stayed in bed an extra hour. She had to get up to see to Peter, because at last Giles had an interview. She had washed out Peter's nappies and a few other essentials and was sitting by the tiny fire trying to summon the strength to go down and put them on the line in the garden. She heard the tap on the living-room door, but couldn't rouse herself to answer. Probably be the children from upstairs wanting change for the bathroom geyser.

Sylveen enjoyed her children's bedtime. She had bathed them, tucked them into bed and read them a story. Nadine was already breathing deeply, Natalie's eyes were closing. As she came down the steep cottage stairs she told herself it was all over for another day. At one time, she had loved the evenings, now they were empty.

No, not exactly empty. She could have coped with emptiness. She spent them alone, it gave her time to think. The trouble was they were filled to overflowing with remorse for the wrong she had done Jeremy, and utter dread he would find out he was not the father of her children.

She drifted round the neat kitchen, but there was little to tidy apart from the children's supper things. She made herself a cup of tea and went into her sitting-room. Over the months of empty evenings she'd worked through the cottage room by room, putting the last touches to the decor. Anything to keep her mind occupied and her conscience from pricking. Now it was exactly as she wanted it. Yet she still felt dissatisfied.

She had a beautiful home, a generous income and two wonderful children, but everything was falling flat. She was gregarious by nature. She craved more of the evenings she used to spend with Jeremy, was guilt-stricken when she thought of him eating alone at Churton. Common sense told her Jeremy had plenty to fill his day. He had a social life that hadn't included her. Perhaps she was missing him more than he missed her?

She felt guilty about Emily. She longed for another gossipy afternoon with her and was desperate for news. Sylveen knew Emily's position was far worse than her own.

She had lost her friends and was lonely. How many

times had she told herself it was her own fault? She knew it was. She had told Giles to go and he had. She had seen little of Jeremy. On the first Saturday of each month she called a taxi and took the children to Churton. They were stiff and uncomfortable occasions. Heart rending too, to see Jeremy try to play with the children he thought of as his own.

When he had been coming to the cottage almost every evening, playing with them had come naturally, and when any of them tired of it, that was the end. On a set visit everything was formalised. It was no longer play, Jeremy seemed to see it as duty. He was not enjoying the Saturday visits any more than she was.

Once she had felt close to him, but no longer. Now she was conscious of an unbridgable chasm yawning between them. His back was straight, his manner remote. She had tried: 'Next month come to the cottage instead,' she'd urged. 'You'll find it easier. The children are more relaxed at home with their toys.' His blue eyes swung to hers, frosty and hostile. 'No strings attached,' she'd added.

She intended to offer him dinner, but better not to mention it yet. She missed her little candlelit dinners. It was difficult to go out in the evenings with all the paraphernalia of babysitters to arrange, and she had no friends left.

She was making an effort. Jean next door invited her in for coffee, and she had her back to tea. She had a similar acquaintance with Margaret down the road, but they couldn't replace what she'd lost.

After five monthly visits to Churton, Jeremy had agreed to come, but he was on edge at the cottage. He went upstairs to see the children being put to bed, but couldn't get down fast enough once they were. Last month, he had stayed for a meal too, but the occasion was only marginally less frosty.

Sylveen wanted to talk about Giles, tell Jeremy how sorry she was. Tell him they were finished, that Giles meant nothing to her now. She tried several times, but Jeremy choked off any approach. It brought home to her how much she had hurt him.

Sylveen kicked herself for wallowing in worry about Emily, instead of finding out what was happening and offering help. She went to her phone and dialled the Beechcroft number. It shocked her to find another family now had the tenancy, and had no idea of Emily's whereabouts. They suggested she ring the agent. Sylveen knew she'd delayed too long, Emily could be anywhere now. She felt she'd let her down yet again.

She made herself more tea and decided she could find out from the chip shop, but she'd have to call there because they had no phone. She made up her mind she'd do it tomorrow morning. She was ashamed of the way she'd treated Emily after five years of friendship.

What she'd done to Jeremy was unforgivable. Perhaps it was as well he didn't know the worst. The trouble was she knew, and was conscious of it all the time she was with him. She'd poisoned her closest relationships. She could hardly believe it of herself, because she'd valued them. It was a terrible thing to do.

Her children always woke early. Sylveen got them up and dressed them carefully. After breakfast, she combed her blonde hair, set her new blue hat at a jaunty angle and took the children out to the bus stop. She was taking them on more outings like this. Usually to the shops in town, or to Arrowe Park; it helped fill her day.

Paradise Parade looked shabby. The chip shop was closed with the blinds down. A notice in the door said it would open at eleven-thirty, but it was only ten-thirty. Why hadn't she thought of this? There didn't seem to be a bell or a knocker. She banged on the door till her hand hurt, but there was no response.

The other shops were open. She could see Fraser's Grocers of Distinction next door but one, and knew Emily had been friendly with Alex Fraser. She parked the pushchair outside and went in to buy biscuits and ask if they knew Emily's present whereabouts. Olympia said she remembered her, they'd spoken at Emily's wedding reception. Sylveen got the address she sought, and directions on how to walk there.

She trudged up New Street, thinking what a come-down this must seem after Beechcroft. Thankful she didn't have to live here. The front gate of number thirty-six was tied up with a wet scarf. Four toddlers scrambled after a ball on the bald earth.

The window on the stairs hadn't been cleaned in years; it let in enough light to see dust, thick enough to leave footprints on the stairs. On the landing, she knocked then opened a door to a bedroom. The bed was unmade, but she recognised Peter's cot, it was the only decent piece of furniture in the room. She closed it quietly, not wanting Emily to know she'd seen the unsavoury mess. She moved to the next door on the landing.

It was a living-room; at first glance she couldn't believe it was Emily huddled in the chair by the miserable fire. Her thick brown hair needed shaping, there was a streak of food down her jumper. Peter was more easily recognisable, though he needed a bath.

'Can I come in?' Smiling, she already was, and so were Nadine and Natalie. 'Is it all right to leave their pushchair downstairs?' The children were beautifully turned out, matching blue coats, new white socks and black ankle-strap shoes.

'Goodness, Emily! You look all in.' Emily shivered. She felt an unwashed mess. Their breakfast dishes were still on the table, and Peter had emptied his toy box all over the floor. 'You're not well?'

'Tonsillitis. Caught it off Gran.' Her voice was like

sandpaper. 'Can I get you something? Tea?' Sylveen sat down opposite and restrained Nadine by pulling her on her knee.

'I'm taking you home with me.' She saw Emily open her mouth to protest. 'Just for a few days till you're better. You and Peter. I want to, Emily, seen nothing of you for ages. You need a rest and somebody to look after you. Where's Giles?'

'Gone for a job interview.'

'Do you know when he'll be back?' She watched Emily shake her head hopelessly. 'Could be celebrating if he's got it and drowning his sorrows if he hasn't?' she suggested.

Emily continued to shake her head as she croaked: 'He hasn't any money.' Sylveen straightened up sharply, stabbed with pity. It meant Emily had no money either. None for food or to keep the baby decent.

'None at all? Can't he get dole? He must have paid in to it while he was working.'

'Yes, we're getting it now, but it's means tested and we get only twenty-one shillings. Giles hates having to queue for it every week.'

'Won't hurt him, Emily, but is it enough?'

She shook her head. 'I can't make it stretch to cover rent and food. It's something.'

'I'm surprised Giles doesn't want to keep it as pocket money.'

Emily's half-hearted smile was lopsided. 'I make him hand most of it over now. But nobody is allowed it longer than six months, and time is running out for Giles. After that we'll be on Assistance.'

'Can't imagine it, Giles without money. His sort always gets it from somewhere.'

'Not any more.'

Sylveen couldn't look at Emily, she looked poverty-stricken. She had been better off working at Wythenshaw's. Why had she let her marry Giles?

'Let's put your things together. If Giles isn't back, I'll walk up to Rock Ferry station and get a taxi.'

'The washing . . .' Emily pointed at a huge bowl of wet nappies.

'We'll take them with us. I can dry them at home.'

Sylveen found a suitcase and packed into it all Emily brought out of her drawers, making up her mind to replace the worst. There were lots of things Nadine had grown out of that were better than these, even if they were girlish. She was about to set off in search of a taxi when Giles came home.

'No job, then?' She knew by his long face before he opened his mouth.

'Not this time. Wasn't much of a job anyway.'

'I'm taking Emily and Peter home with me. She's ill. She needs rest and decent food.'

'What about me? Where am I to go?'

'Giles, I don't mind as long as you don't come to my house.' She saw Emily blanch at her words. Well, she might as well know there was no love lost between them now.

'Don't go, Emily, I don't want you to.' Giles's tawny eyes were appealing to her.

'Just for a week, till she's better,' Sylveen insisted. 'You don't want to catch tonsillitis, do you?'

'I can't stay here by myself, it's a terrible place.'

'It's just the same for Emily. Worse, she does all the carting up and down those stairs.'

'No it isn't. Emily's used to living in this sort of place. I'm not.' Sylveen saw from Emily's face that the insult had struck home. 'She chose it,' he said, looking pathetic.

Sylveen felt a rush of anger. How could she ever have imagined herself in love with such a helpless fool?

'Come on, Giles, make yourself useful. Carry this case down to your car. You can drive us.'

'I haven't any petrol.'

Sylveen let out an explosion of annoyance. 'I'll buy a couple of gallons for you,' she spat.

Emily lay back in Sylveen's guest room, watching the filmy curtains moving in the breeze. The first warm spell of the year had come, bringing hazy sunshine. Though the trees were bare, she could see the daffodils in flower in the garden. New Street seemed like a bad dream.

Here there was order and cleanliness, thick carpet and pretty furniture. Sylveen had brought her here, run a bath for her, telephoned for a doctor, made hot drinks to soothe her throat, and light meals.

Sylveen had led her to the door of the children's room, to see the new twin beds she had chosen for her girls, though Natalie was still using her cot. Peter had slept there, and for the first two days he'd almost been taken off her hands. She felt rested, her throat was better, outside the birds were singing in the trees.

Emily could hear Sylveen playing with the children below in the garden, she could hear affection in her voice as she spoke to Peter, and was filled with gratitude. Sylveen was a wonderful friend. She'd never be able to repay such kindness. She decided she'd get up.

The pin-neat bathroom, the uneven white walls, contrasted with the thick crimson carpet. Emily tried to stem the tide of envy washing through her. It was churlish to envy Sylveen her home.

'Once I envied you.' Sylveen's voice was brittle. 'A married woman. I thought you'd done better than I had.'

'But not now,' Emily said in a flat voice. 'Being Mrs Giles Wythenshaw has disadvantages.'

'Not now,' Sylveen agreed.

Emily met her gaze and smiled: 'You've changed.' Sylveen's clothes were no longer chosen to attract men's attention. Her style was softer, more sophisticated, she was more beautiful than ever.

'We all grow older. Other things become more important.'

'Your children?'

'The most important thing in my life now.' Sylveen's smile was honest and gentle. 'I enjoy them, I've a lot to be grateful for.'

'Your lovely cottage, and the peace.'

'Not peace.' Sylveen straightened up, her blue eyes anxious.

'I feel peace all round me here.'

'You can stay longer if you like. Permanently.'

Emily felt another rush of gratitude as the silence lengthened. 'What would Giles do?'

'Let him do what he likes. He's causing the problems.'

'I can't,' Emily groaned after a long silence.

Sylveen's blue eyes darted daringly to hers. 'You love him?'

'Oh God, I don't know. I don't know what I feel any more. Numb most of the time, or panic-stricken. Terrified the day will come when I've no money for food.' She could see Sylveen's face going white with horror. 'I'm sorry, I'm . . . You knew anyway.'

'Leave him, Emily.' The vehemence in Sylveen's face frightened her. 'Leave him. You can stay here, I want you to.'

The phone was ringing in the dining-room; she thought Sylveen wasn't going to answer it, but eventually she got to her feet. Emily closed her eyes and leaned back in the garden chair, the gentle spring sun warming her face. She wanted to stay, desperately. If she did, she wondered if they would continue to get on so well.

If Sylveen would look after Peter, she could go back to work. She needn't sponge on her too much, needn't get under her feet. Emily caught a glimpse of a secure and happy life for them all. Except Giles.

'It would put the skids under Giles if I left,' she said as

Sylveen returned. 'In an odd sort of way he leans on me.'

'What do you mean, odd? He needs a crutch. You're carrying him,' Sylveen retorted. 'He'll let you do it for the rest of your life. I really mean it, Emily. I'd like to have you and Peter here. It's lonely, just me and the girls.' Her voice changed. 'That was Jeremy on the phone. He's coming tonight, for dinner.'

'I'll stay in my room,' Emily said awkwardly.

'No, I've told him you're here. Nothing else, just that you're here. He wants to see you.' She went striding off down the garden to break up a disagreement between her children. Peter was digging in a flower bed.

'Tell him, Emily,' she said, when she came back. 'Tell him how awful things are for you. He'll help, I'm sure.' Emily was surprised how well she understood Giles. How well she saw the position he was putting her in. Sylveen was changed in other ways. She seemed to have new depths, was quieter, more introspective. Her blue eyes were full of sympathy.

'He threw us out.'

'Giles, not you and Peter. He's a generous man.' But Sylveen was more on edge, more nerve-wracked than she used to be.

'I can't go begging.'

'It isn't begging, that's your pride talking. It's good advice, Emily. Please do it, he'll help you.'

Emily thought about it all afternoon, while the orders were telephoned to the butcher and the greengrocer. All through the cooking and the preparation, she even thought she might.

But when Jeremy arrived, she could see he was changed too. Not in appearance, though perhaps he was a little more portly. His silver hair was still thick, vitality crackled out of him, but his manner had cooled. He kissed Sylveen's little girls, but hardly looked at Peter.

He encouraged Nadine to climb on his knee and pull on

the gold chain that looped across his waistcoat until his half-hunter burst out of his pocket. Then he made it chime the hour while a delighted Nadine held it to her ear. Natalie pulled at his trouser leg for her turn, but when Peter tried to join in, he picked him off his knee and held him out to Emily.

She almost snatched him, hugging him extravagantly, hardly able to believe his dislike of Giles extended to his child. She caught sight of Sylveen's face; that had floored her too. Jeremy was very changed.

Sylveen produced a meal that was as beautifully cooked and served as in the past. She was a thoughtful hostess but Emily felt uncomfortable sitting between them. The conversation seemed stilted, the whole occasion flat. She couldn't bring herself to talk of her difficulties to this remote and austere stranger. He showed no sign of affection for her or Peter. Nobody mentioned Giles all evening.

'How long are you staying here, Emily?' he asked, as though he resented her presence. His attitude reminding her he'd bought the house for Sylveen, that he was paying for its upkeep. Over the years, neither had made a secret of the reason.

Sylveen had always welcomed her during the day while Jeremy was working, and she'd always left in the late afternoon, so that Sylveen could give her attention to Jeremy if he should come.

'Not much longer,' she said stiffly, feeling a gooseberry. A moment or two later she said good night and went up to her room, in order to clear the way for him.

She put out her light so he would not be embarrassed, but though the children were asleep, Jeremy made no effort to bring Sylveen upstairs.

She was surprised to hear him leaving shortly afterwards. Then the clink of china as Sylveen cleared the table. Emily put on her dressing-gown and went downstairs to help.

'He was embarrassed at finding me here, Sylveen. I spoilt the evening for him.'

Sylveen was at the sink dowsing plates vigorously in hot sudsy water. 'He was just a bit off tonight,' she said, but Emily felt the constraint in her manner too, and knew there was more to it than that.

The next day Giles telephoned, pleading with her to return to New Street. She told him to come and fetch her, and started packing her things.

CHAPTER TWENTY-ONE

Shortly after coming home from Sylveen's, Emily found herself another job.

'A builder's yard,' she told Giles. 'I'm receptionist, typist and I sell paint and putty and stuff to the public. Nine to five with a half day on Thursday.'

Giles was staring at her. 'You'll work on Saturdays?'

'Yes, all day, three pounds a week. Start on Monday.'

Emily even told herself she enjoyed her new job. She was kept busy there all day, mostly on her feet. With her mother's old bike she could get home in her lunch hour and make sure Peter had something to eat.

The main problem was that by evening she was exhausted and she still had a lot to do at home. Giles reckoned Peter kept him busy all day, but he left the bathing of him till Emily returned, together with the washing and cooking and cleaning. She had been used to working till seven o'clock in the chip shop after a day's work at Wythenshaw's, now she was lucky if she could sit down at nine.

Sundays were busy too, though she usually went round to see Gran, or took Peter on the bus to visit Sylveen.

At first, Emily felt she and Giles would manage. She had to nag him about dumping Peter on Gran too much. Though Gran said she didn't mind, Emily felt it was wearing her out. Peter needed watching every minute, he was into everything now. Life for her was all work and very little comfort, but she was making ends meet.

She was combing her hair before setting out to work one morning. Peter was still asleep in his cot. Giles never got up with her, he said there was no point. In the mirror, she saw him pulling himself up on the pillows.

'Emily,' he said, 'could you possibly lend me ten shillings?'

She froze, holding her comb high. It seemed the death knell to all her hopes. 'You haven't spent . . .?'

'I'm just a little short at the moment.'

'But the fifty pounds you had?' She saw herself in the mirror, white faced, aghast.

'It doesn't last for ever.'

'It's only a month, Giles!'

'I haven't got a regular wage like you.'

'You aren't spending it on rent and coal and food like me.' She felt bitter, and sounded it.

'Just ten shillings,' he wheedled from his pillows. 'I need petrol, and surely you don't begrudge me a few pence in my pocket?'

'I do.' She knew she sounded a harridan. 'How much do you think I spend on myself?' His tawny eyes drew hers, there was a hurt look on his face.

'If I could get some petrol, I could go and see Grandfather again. I'm sure he would help me out.'

'If you're so sure why don't you get it on tick?'

Giles sat up. 'I would if I could. Old Jones delivered an ultimatum yesterday. No more credit till I settle my bill.'

Emily sank down on the bed in horror. 'How much?'

'Fifteen – a little more.' In the mirror she saw her mouth hanging open. What a complacent fool she'd been.

'Sell your car, Giles, if you need money,' she said harshly. Peter turned over, his eyes flickered open. She wanted to seek comfort from her baby, lift him up and hug him, but she was already late for work. She blew him a kiss.

'Please,' Giles urged.

She had to get away; she pulled on her hat, snatched her bag and rushed headlong downstairs.

Giles felt very bitter; his life was making him depressed. He was walled up in these awful rooms with a crying child, day after day. He hadn't a penny left and couldn't even go down to Donovan's for a drink. Emily had money, but she wouldn't part with it. Not even for bus fares to take the child to the park.

'Take him along the shore,' she'd said. 'Peter loves the sand, and it's on the doorstep. You could take a bag and pick up driftwood to help with the fire.' She had even accused him of sulking because he had no money. He hardly dared mention the word.

'You'll have to sell your car,' she said, every time he did. She wouldn't part with money for petrol, and without that it was useless. Worse than useless, as she kept pointing out, to have it parked permanently outside, buffeted by the weather and the local children.

Unbelievably, from their living-room window, they'd seen children climbing on it; he'd hammered on the glass and eventually they'd run off. It was now five years old and needed a decoke, a new silencer and four new tyres. The insurance was due.

Emily had grown hard, tough as old boots really, and eventually she'd broken him down. He hadn't got as much for it as he'd hoped. The car had left its epitaph on the street: in wet weather, iridescent circles showed where petrol had leaked. The only good thing was it put him in funds again, and this time Emily certainly wasn't getting half. He felt his wallet in his inside pocket, it was wonderfully thick.

Giles shook the raindrops from his hat and shivered as he climbed the dark stairs. He'd gone out and got drunk when he'd first got his money, but he knew he had to be more careful with it now. Today he'd had a couple of hours in the public library on the newspapers and magazines, then he'd tramped round Birkenhead in the rain till the pubs opened. He'd had more beer than he'd meant to, but hunger was gnawing at his stomach now. He listened as he unlocked his door; the building was alive with little sounds but none of them came from his rooms.

The living-room was in darkness, last night's ashes were cold in the grate. He shuddered with frustration; it wouldn't be so bad if Emily were here to greet him with a fire blazing up the chimney and a hot meal simmering on the stove. He didn't have to wonder where she was; if she wasn't at work, she'd be down at her grandmother's. She'd be mad with him too because he'd left the baby there all day.

For a moment he thought of lighting a fire. Cooking something, but he was tired as well as cold. He'd bought himself half a bottle of whisky, it swung heavy in his coat pocket as he turned. He found a tumbler and poured himself a drink. It was warm and comforting in his throat.

His stomach rumbled as he wrenched open their food cupboard. Lifting the lid on the cheese dish, he found little left but rind, but there were a few eggs, half a loaf and some plum jam. He felt a rush of anger, intense enough to leave him shaking. His father had done this to him, compelled him to live like a pauper. With growing resentment, he recalled the comfort of the dining-room at Churton, the roast ham and pork pies left under net covers on the sideboard for late snacks, the bell he'd rung for service, the four- and five-course meals.

It was Saturday night, he ought to be out enjoying himself like everybody else. He felt his fury boiling up, sending burning flushes up his cheeks, making him stride about the ugly room. He had to find some way of getting even with his father. He had pushed him, his only son, into this dreadful existence and at the same time was giving thousands away to charity, to people he didn't even know. Giles clenched his hands, there must be some way he could hurt him.

Ted and Charlie knew just how bad Father was. Ted kept blethering about the terrible things he'd done in the war, but he never spelled them out. He ought to make him.

Father was desperate to keep everyone away from his Paris house. His whole manner changed, he looked guilty when Aunt Harriet talked about it. Giles was certain there was something there Father wanted kept hidden. If he could find out what it was, he'd have him where he wanted him.

He looked at the clock. The chip shop wouldn't have closed yet. The thought of chips brought saliva flooding to his mouth. Emily might shame Charlie into feeding him for free.

He picked up his whisky; he might need it to loosen their tongues. The shops along Paradise Parade were just closing as he reached them. The newsagent next door to Charlie's was taking in his placards. The enamel sign on the door drew his eyes. Park Drive ten for fourpence, reminding him he was out of cigarettes. He shot inside to get some, still able to smell Charlie's chips above the newsprint. Wade's shop was locked behind him as he left. There were two customers in Charlie's shop; Giles lit up and waited till they left.

'If you've come looking for Emily, she isn't here,' Charlie said, wiping the perspiration from his forehead.

'Where's she gone?'

'To the pictures with Olympia and Ethel.'

'What about the baby?'

'Oh, he's here, same as always.' Giles felt another wave of resentment; tonight of all nights Emily wasn't here and Charlie wasn't exactly welcoming.

'I'd better get my supper here, then. Give me a fish and a pennyworth of chips.'

'Taking them home, are you? Or staying to eat with us?,

'With you, since you're asking,' he said. Perhaps after all it would be better without Emily putting her oar in. 'I'll go through if I may?' His step sounded loud on the lino in the lobby.

Ted, gaunt as a skeleton, was sitting at the table with his beer poured out. Gran, her battered straw hat askew, was trying to toast her knees at the meagre fire, but she had a glass of stout.

'How's the baby?' He had to say something, he might have been invisible for all the notice they were taking of him.

'Asleep on my bed.' The cherries on Gran's hat slid the other way as she moved. 'Thought it would do Emily good to have a break, and she wanted to see Shirley Temple.'

Giles offered his Park Drive to Ted, hoping he'd reciprocate with a glass of beer. There were four pint bottles lined up on the sideboard, only one had been broached.

'Not just now, thanks.' He waved them away, sitting tight, glowering at him. 'Get on my chest a bit.' But Gran was shuffling across to the sideboard.

'I suppose you've come to eat with us?' She flung another knife and fork on the oilcloth, got out another glass and three quarters filled it with beer for him.

'Thanks, Gran, you're the tops. I'll take you across to the Bird when we've eaten. Buy us all a drink.'

'Who's going to look after the baby, then? We can't take him with us.'

'I'd forgotten he was here.' Giles gulped at the beer.

'You're always forgetting about him,' Ted grunted, making things worse. He was glad to hear Charlie kick at the door, and when he opened it found him balancing four plates at once. Giles felt his stomach contract, his gastric juices spurt at the sight of the glistening golden chips. He hadn't eaten since noon, and only a sandwich then. They tasted fabulous.

Only the scratch of cutlery against plates, the occasional slurping of beer broke the silence, but antagonism blazed from Ted's eyes every time he met his gaze. Charlie seemed to be counting the cost of every chip he swallowed, and Giles and Gran had been given smallish helpings. He still felt hungry and, insult on insult, Ted put his knife and fork down with his plate only half-cleared.

'Ted, if you don't want that fish, do you mind if I have it?' He switched their plates and forked it up hungrily. The indignity of having to eat other people's leftovers to keep body and soul together! If Emily had been here, she'd have seen he got a decent helping in the first place. Charlie was miserably mean; after all, he had paid.

'Had a good day, Charlie?' Gran wheezed, rubbing her stomach.

'So so.' Charlie got up and started to refill their glasses.

'Come over to the Bird and have a drink on me,' Giles invited; he'd get them talking tonight. The bottle hovered to his glass, a little beer splashed in.

'Better if you nip across the road and get another bottle or two,' Charlie said. 'It'll be full being Saturday night and the smoke gets to Ted's chest. Not good for him.'

'Right then.' Giles drained his glass and stood up. 'Another Guinness, Gran?'

'Ta, I wouldn't mind.'

'Have you got a bag?'

Charlie got to his feet. 'Must be going to treat us to a skinful, if you need a bag.'

'It's Saturday, why not?' They were both going to take some loosening up anyway.

Charlie was right about the Bird. Giles could hear the singing as soon as he let himself out of the back door and, once inside the pub, he had to push his way to the taproom bar. The air was blue with smoke. He got six more pints and on the way back he slipped his half bottle of whisky into the bag with them. Giles hoped what he would hear would be worth the investment in booze.

He took their empty glasses to the sideboard. Slid a generous measure of whisky into Ted's before filling them with beer. They were all pulling their chairs round the fire. It seemed a bit warmer with his feet resting on the rag mat Gran had made. It was time he got on with what he'd come to do.

'You knew my father,' he prompted.

'Too right, we did.' Ted glowered at him, excessively aggressive for so weak a man, but he was launching into his usual reminiscences.

Giles sipped moderately at his beer and listened. He'd heard it all before, several times, the fatigues, the work parties, the shelling, the gas attacks. Ted and Charlie were the biggest bores out. He got up to refill their glasses. Gave Ted another slug of whisky in his. He hoped it wasn't all going to be wasted.

'I killed a soldier with my bare hands, you know,' Ted said. 'Saved your father's life.'

'When he took you to his house in Paris? It happened there?' They were getting round to it at last.

'No, of course not,' Ted said irritably. 'We don't know anything about his house.'

'It was in the trenches you killed that German, wasn't it, Ted?' Charlie was leering at him. That seemed a stopper, he'd really believed they knew something. Now he wasn't sure.

'Tell me about him,' he tried. 'I want to hear what he did in the war.'

'You're just like my father,' Ted spat. 'Full of confidence, talking with a plum in your mouth. Buying booze to butter us up. Your dad was a right bastard.'

'Still is,' Giles grinned. 'He's causing me and Emily no end of trouble. What did he do to you?'

'Give over, Ted,' Gran said. 'You've said enough.'

'Charlie knows what he's like. He'll tell you.'

'All officers were like that,' Charlie said. 'Ordering you about, think you can go on digging like a machine. All they have to do is to keep you at it. Wythenshaw was like the rest.'

'Never did you any harm, Charlie,' Gran said. 'And he was all right when Emily got married.'

'Got up my nose. He was a real stickler for authority. Had a big opinion of himself.'

'Hadn't they all?'

'But he was generous with his cigs. Always passing them round.'

'Yes, free issue "Glory Boys". He was in charge of them,' Ted said. 'Who's to say he only took two packets for himself?'

Giles got up and poured more drink. This time he gave Charlie a slug of whisky too; he was turning Ted off.

When Gran started to cackle with geriatric laughter he realised she'd seen him do it; the cherries fairly danced on her hat. 'Have a little touch, Gran?'

She was holding out her glass to him. He gave her a good dose to keep her quiet. So far it had all been a terrible waste. He was almost ready to give up, but Ted's jaw was jutting forward belligerently, his usually grey cheeks were crimson.

'What did he do to you, Ted?' he asked.

'Unforgivable,' he hiccuped.

'What was?' Giles thought he'd overplayed his hand, that he'd got him too drunk.

'Amazing you both fancied little Emily. Both wanting to marry her!'

He could see Ted tingling with hate and frustration. 'What can a man like you see in a working girl like her?'

Ted nosed closer to Giles. 'Emily wasn't even a raving beauty, but she looked better in her posh clothes. More like all the other toffs.' Some of the polish had rubbed off on her, but she was no great catch for the likes of Giles Wythenshaw.

'What did Father do?'

'Olympia made me promise. On oath. Never to say a word.' Said she'd kill him if he ever opened his mouth, particularly to anyone along the Parade. They'd be on that bit of news like ferrets. 'Your father . . .'

But nobody must know. Jeremy Wythenshaw had poisoned everything for him. Left him bitter, a broken man in body and mind, and he couldn't tell a soul. Everybody thought the war had warped him, but it was Jeremy Wythenshaw, and he'd never dared say it.

Ted felt overcome with hate and frustration. Everything had been lavished on this one: money, education, clothes. He'd been brought up a gentleman. He'd done little enough for the other.

'Captain Wythenshaw wasn't too bad, Ted. Doing his job like,' Charlie put in.

'Wasn't his job to get at Ol— Olympia.' Ted's face was puce. 'Oh, you don't know the half of what I've suffered at your dad's hands.'

'Not his hands,' Charlie guffawed.

'Well, what did he do?' Giles didn't understand. He was getting something at last, but he wasn't sure what.

'Our Alex, that's what.' Tears rolled down Ted's furrowed cheeks, they were grey again. 'He's his father. Can't forgive that.'

Giles stared at him dumbfounded. It took him a moment to say: 'You mean Alex Fraser . . .?'

'He's your half-brother, lad. How do you like that?' Charlie's greasy face was cruelly close to his, he was laughing.

'I don't!' Giles was indignant. 'It's not true.' They were making it up to rile him.

'It is.' The old woman cackled like a hyena, tossing back

in her chair, lifting her sticks of legs up from her rag mat.

'Nonsense.' They had known all along he wanted to hear about what Father got up to in Paris. They'd deliberately strung him along to get his beer. Now they were going all out to upset him.

'I don't believe you!' It couldn't be true. 'Anyway, that would have been long before the war. Long before you knew him.'

'We didn't have to,' Charlie cackled. 'It was Olympia who knew him. She worked in the office up at Wythenshaw's.'

Giles felt as though he would choke, he was burning with fury. That his father could stoop to this. Alexander Fraser of all people!

Emily felt better, she had enjoyed sitting in the Palace Picture House with Ethel on one side and Olympia on the other, she had escaped the daily grind. Her head still swam in a dream world where Shirley Temple danced and sang and Adolphe Menjou reminded her of Jeremy.

Even Ethel's living-room seemed infinitely preferable to her own. Curtains fresh and frilly and a real carpet square. She and Olympia were still talking about Little Miss Marker. 'It's a Damon Runyon story, you know.'

Ethel made scalding tea in matching china cups. She provided each guest with a tea plate for the meadow creams and chocolate digestives she offered. Spinsterish and fussy, Gran said, but Emily thought it civilised.

'I'll have to go,' she said; already she was feeling twinges of guilt at leaving Peter with Gran yet again. 'Gran will want to go to bed.'

'Won't Giles have collected Peter by now?' Ethel asked.

'I don't know.' In Ethel's world, things that needed doing were done. 'What time is it?'

'Late enough.' Olympia stood up too. 'Gone eleven. We'll both go, Ethel. Thanks for the tea.'

'Come with us again next week, Emily.'

'Yes.' Olympia took her arm. 'It's Errol Flynn.'

Ethel opened her curtains to light their way down her neat and tidy yard. With the gate closed, the back entry was black. Emily saw a tall figure looming against the gate to Charlie's shop; she was pulling Olympia closer when he spoke. 'Mum?'

'It's you, Alex. What is it?'

'Dad's not home, I was just going to see where he was. Usually he's back before this time.' Even in the dark Emily felt Alex's gaze riveted on her. She had tensed at the first sound of his voice.

She led the way up the yard because they still thought of it as her home. From the scullery she could hear voices and wild laughter. She couldn't believe it of Gran, but there she was lifting her legs up from the floor in a frenzy of mirth.

Charlie seemed to be holding Ted up and Giles was scarlet with rage. Olympia was blinking in the sudden light, trying, like her, to make sense of what was going on.

'Say it isn't true,' Giles raved at her. 'Tell them it isn't.'

'What?' Olympia's large face had paled. 'Ted?'

'He says,' Giles pointed an accusing finger at Ted, 'that my father is also Alex's father. Is that right?' Olympia's face was crumpling. She opened her mouth and closed it again.

'You whore,' Giles ground out, flying at her. 'You whore!'

Emily watched Alex step out from behind his mother, aware he was as shocked as she was. She heard the crack as his fist landed on Giles's chin; it was all over in a flash.

Gran was suddenly silent and on her feet. They were all staring down at Giles who had crumpled in a heap on the rag mat.

'Alex!' Emily let out a long shuddering breath.

Alex could feel his heart thumping like a sledge hammer. His fist ached where it had crashed against Giles's chin; the blood was coursing through his fingers, no, coursing through his whole body.

'Come on, Dad.' He put an arm round Ted's bent shoulders. 'Let's go home.' His mother was off without another word, leading the way.

His head buzzed, he couldn't believe it! Had never even thought that Ted might not be his father. Yet his mother's crumpling face told him it was true.

In a way it was believable, he had never seen anything of Ted in himself. But Jeremy Wythenshaw! And Mum, the self-possessed, capable matriarch of the family! Now he knew why Ted had been dead set against him working at Wythenshaw's.

As a child he remembered Ted always in his armchair by the fire, always coughing. Breathing with a whistling wheeze he could hear from his bedroom. Always kindly towards him, interested in what he was doing, wanting to be involved in his games and his school work. Grumbling if he left too much to Mum, or didn't help enough in the shop. Ted had treated him as he would a son, even if he was not.

Alex was manoeuvering him towards his armchair in the living-room when Ted's eyes met his; pale, apologetic, full of suffering.

'I suppose you think I'm an old fool?'

Alex was filled with a sudden searing pity and said stiffly: 'I think of you as my father – with great affection.' He could see his mother's usually tranquil eyes filling with tears.

'He should never have told Giles.' She was indignant. 'Charlie had no business . . .'

'I told him,' Ted straightened up for an instant, more like a cadaver than ever.

'Why? Why did you tell them, Ted?'

'I don't know. He was needling me.'

'Let's get him to bed,' Olympia said. 'You want to go, don't you, love?'

Alex couldn't look at her as they supported him upstairs between them, breathless and wheezing. Mum had always been protective of Ted, perhaps he'd learned from her to be that way too.

Jeremy had a restless night, sleeping only fitfully, but he was wide awake again at dawn, out of bed and bathed before Higgins brought his morning tea.

'An early breakfast this morning,' he ordered. 'Kippers.'

But he didn't feel like kippers, didn't feel like eating anything. 'No, I'll have egg and bacon.'

It was a fine blustery morning; he went out through the french windows to the terrace and down to the garden. The grass was damp but immaculately trimmed. There was a splendid display of roses. In his vast grounds, nature was controlled and ordered, but his mind was chaotic. He had no energy even for strolling.

In the past he'd never failed to find peace in his garden; this morning it wouldn't come. He shivered and went to his library where it was warmer. Settled in his armchair, but he was on his feet again in moments to look at his treasured collection of antique glass. He lifted a Bohemian goblet so that a shaft of sunlight fell on it. Always its perfection had brought him a surge of appreciation and pleasure. This morning it seemed merely a dusty curio. Higgins was getting slack again. All servants needed a woman to keep them on their toes. Perhaps that was his problem too?

No, he would not think of Sylveen again; she had infiltrated his mind these last weeks, taking away his energy for work. He had to keep her at bay.

He'd been overcome with fury when he'd found Giles in her bedroom, choked with it, blinded with it. He'd showered everything he had on Sylveen, yet she'd preferred Giles. His own son!

That had been the dagger blade, his own son. After several happy years and two children, she found she preferred Giles's company. His pride had taken a beating, his ego had been slashed. He'd been floundering in a pit ever since. Sylveen had seemed happy, yet she'd done that.

He'd congratulated himself on not marrying her, of course. Told himself how much worse things would have been if he had. He'd been right not to trust her, but he was torn too by the thought that if they had been married, this might not have happened. He had trusted her and loved her too, and without her he was lonely. But it had happened, it had cut him to the quick, making him want to lash out at her in return. He was quite sure, knowing Giles as he did, that she'd rue the day.

Sometimes he wondered about Emily, and whether Giles had told the truth when he'd said she only wanted his money. He missed her and Peter too. That was the top and bottom of it, he was lonely.

Jeremy caught sight of himself in the gilt-framed mirror. He was looking older. He put his shoulders back, made himself stand straighter. He didn't want to become bowed like Arthur. One drawback of seeing him regularly was that he showed too clearly the frailties of old age he could expect. At sixty-six it was coming closer.

He ought to go to Paris again, and the sooner the better. He had been enjoying his trips there less and less, till now he felt a great reluctance to go at all. Yet he had to finish what he'd set out to do. The travelling exhausted him now. He hated the long hours on the train, and the last few sea crossings had been rough. He ought to think of flying, in his younger days he would have.

A tap on the door, and Higgins's head came round to tell him his breakfast was ready. He went gladly, though he was not hungry. The one place set at the table underlined his loneliness.

Higgins, hovering to make conversation about the weather and the dahlias, made it worse, yet he meant it kindly. He was glad to be left alone with *The Times*. Or he was until he opened it and saw the banner headlines all screaming of war.

The talk of coming war was unsettling; more than that, frightening. The papers were prophesying a fast-moving war, an air war, very different from the last. It would be a disaster if it came before he'd completed what he'd set out to do. He might conceivably get stranded in Paris, he'd certainly be cut off from visiting.

Another war would cut him off from his markets in Africa, but to manufacture artificial jewellery would be too frivolous a waste of manpower and resources anyway. The Great War had almost finished off Calthorpe's, another would be disastrous for him on every level.

Breakfast over, he was ready to be driven to work, along the road where every bend was familiar. Though long experience made it easy to control his little empire, he no longer found much pleasure in doing so. The point had gone if it wasn't for his heirs.

Yet he must work, he was wasting time and energy on worry. He must keep his mind on the factory. Its centenary was coming up in August. An achievement, to keep a business thriving for a hundred years. He must work out some way to celebrate.

Impossible to put his mind to celebrations of any sort when he felt so low. It occurred to him then it was a job he could delegate. He'd get Alexander Fraser to arrange something. Good experience for him, and it would leave his own mind clear for other things.

His Rolls swept through the gates of Wythenshaw & Son and drew up outside the main entrance. He could hear the rattle and thump of machinery from the factory, but it was early for the office staff, not many were about.

'Good morning, ladies.'

He opened the door to his secretaries' office. Both Miss Lewis and Mavis Finegan, who had replaced Sylveen, were at their desks. He found Miss Finegan no temptation with her mousey hair pushed straight back anyhow behind her ears.

'Book me another trip to Paris,' he told her. 'To leave on Monday, and I want to see Alexander Fraser. Get him to come up as soon as he comes in.'

He reached his own office but Miss Lewis had come to the door to remind him: 'You have a meeting of the Wythenshaw Trust. Nine-thirty at the Town Hall.'

Jeremy froze, what was he thinking of? He'd meant to go straight there, it would take most of the morning. He hadn't much time, but he might as well do something since he was here.

'I'll see Fraser first.' Better talk to him about the centenary while it was on his mind. He should have done something about it before now.

He was looking through some literature on a new and cheaper process for making metals untarnishable, when he heard the tap on his door. 'You wanted to see me, sir?'

'Come in, Fraser, have a seat.' Jeremy waved towards the chair, watched him sit down. He could never stop himself searching the boy's face.

He had always this effect on him, but there was no likeness, and he had his mother's dark red colouring. He seemed ill at ease, sitting on the very edge of the chair, strangely different this morning.

Jeremy started to tell him how Wythenshaw's had started in business in August 1837. He even felt a touch of pride.

'I thought we could set up a line to make centenary favours, as we do at Christmas. You know, handouts to our suppliers and of course the workers. I had in mind a teapot stand. Something they can take home and keep. Lattice work with our name and the dates. Talk to the two Marys, get them working on a design.'

'Yes, sir.' He'd made up his mind years ago how he would handle Alexander Fraser. He wouldn't let himself get close. Only make things more difficult. Jeremy took another look at the boy, and hesitated. There was a wildness in his eyes, he was shuffling on his chair, unable to sit still.

'Then a trip to the seaside for the workers and their families. I thought perhaps Rhyl. It falls on a Saturday so I could give everybody the morning off. You find out how many would like to go and arrange the charabancs and perhaps a meal too. And I'd like to put on something for the children. Always pleases the men to see their children included. Could you get balloons printed with an appropriate message? And we'll have a party. Do you think it's a good idea to have it in the canteen?'

'No.' Alex's voice was agonised. 'No.'

Jeremy jerked to a stop, feeling the first stirrings of unease. He cleared his throat. 'Why not? Do you have ideas of your own? I'd like to show my appreciation to the workforce.'

'With respect, I'm sure they appreciate their jobs. And above everything else, they want to keep them.' Fraser's cheeks were scarlet.

Jeremy was shocked, the boy wouldn't look at him. 'What's that mean?'

'The sales figures are fifteen per cent down on this time last year,' his voice sounded strangled.

'Who told you that?' Jeremy felt as though he had a tight band round his chest. There was a painful truth in what the boy was saying.

'Nobody, sir, I see some of the figures. You pay me to collate them. I know it's only half the picture, but I feel the business can't afford it.'

Jeremy had believed he was keeping all that hidden. Nobody else had noticed in all these years. He had to keep accounts for tax purposes, but he kept them as private as possible. Wythenshaw's had always paid its way, even through the worst of the depression. Though the boy was right, its income was still falling, he could not afford to be lavish on its profits now, if it were not for . . . He was having trouble getting his breath.

Jeremy knew he should tell the boy roundly that he was wrong. Insist Wythenshaw's could afford what he wanted, with ease. Instead he sank back in his chair, feeling he'd received a body blow.

'Well, yes,' he said, 'but that need not stop . . .'

'With respect.' Alex was beyond caring, he had dropped his guard, dropped the inhibitions he usually felt in Jeremy Wythenshaw's presence. They'd been swept away on a tide of indignation and wrath. Saturday night had turned his world on its head. 'What you are suggesting are frills, Mr Wythenshaw. The centenary may be important to you, but you're far too generous to your workers, and times are hard. There are more important things to spend time and money on.'

'Such as what?' He knew he barked, hadn't he spent hours thinking about the future?

'There's talk of another war . . .'

'Yes,' he prompted impatiently.

'Jewellery such as we make . . .'

'Do you think I haven't considered all that?'

'We should be thinking of our role in another war . . .'

'And how do you see that, Mr Fraser?' His tone was frigidly sarcastic. He usually treated his juniors more gently than this. The boy stared back at him, cheeks scarlet.

'I think we should diversify. Make badges, insignia, uniform buttons and buckles. It's a big market now. Police, firemen, railway staff, bus drivers, boy scouts, all use such things. If war came, there would be huge expansion in military uniforms. We already have most of the machinery to do it, and the skills of your workers are more in keeping with that than making better-class jewellery.'

Jeremy leaned back in his chair and closed his eyes. Why had he never thought of it? It seemed the obvious course to take.

'I think time would be better spent seeking markets for this sort of product, rather than making centenary favours.'

Jeremy looked at the boy with new eyes, no employee had ever tried to change his mind for him before. Nor offered his own opinion on how Wythenshaw's should be managed.

'Anyway, you're far too generous to your workers. They'd prefer to know their jobs are safe.'

'Yes,' Jeremy sighed. He was too old for all this. He sat staring at the boy who stared silently back.

It seemed five minutes before he spoke again: 'Do I have your permission to go ahead? Look for markets?'

'Yes, go ahead.' His mouth felt dry. 'It's an excellent idea. What made you think of uniforms?'

'We talked about how Wythenshaw's could best move on. Norman Coates and I.'

'Norman Coates?' Jeremy felt shaken, he'd never thought of discussing policy with his staff. Trainee staff at that.

'You told us to query everything and think things through,' Alex said earnestly.

Jeremy sighed, he had done that.

'There's another thing,' the boy was gathering confidence as his faded, 'I want to discuss something personal.'

'Well, what?'

'I saw Giles on Saturday night.'

'Giles?' He could feel himself cringing, waiting for the blow to fall.

'He'd been in Barr's chip shop. It seems he heard something he didn't like.'

The boy paused, his brown eyes searching his again, seeking something. Jeremy saw him take a deep breath. 'They told him you had fathered me, that I am his half-brother.'

It was the last thing he'd expected. Jeremy felt as though ice-cold water was showering on his head, he was pinned in his chair. From his past, one sin, long hidden, had caught up with him.

'Yes.' What else could he say?

'He called my mother a whore and I went for him. Knocked him out.' He could see the perspiration standing out on the boy's cheeks.

'Good.'

'What? He's all right, just a few bruises.'

Jeremy cleared his throat, the silence seemed endless. He had to say something.

'It's not a story I want bandied about the factory, but I'm glad you know. You can look upon me as your father.'

The boy's dark eyes stared into his, aghast.

'I already have a father.' There was frost in his voice that lashed him. 'Ted Fraser has been that to me all my life.'

Jeremy had been getting to his feet, intending to come round to shake his hand. Now he slid back in his chair, overcome by the cutting rejection. Why had he never asked himself what effect it would have on the child? He had lavished all his care on Giles, hardly giving this boy a thought. He shivered with shock and fear.

'I don't think I can cope with two fathers.'

Alex was beyond caring. He'd thought of Jeremy as remote and powerful. A man who could shape or break his career. Like everybody else, he'd treated him with great respect, with kid gloves even.

He felt one of the knots in his stomach loosen. All night

he'd had nightmares, half-expecting him to deny it. After all, he'd never been treated any differently to Norman Coates.

He looked at Jeremy with fresh eyes. A distinguished old gentleman holding his silvery head at an angle that showed his privileged background. A man who even seemed old for his mother. Impossible to believe he was fourteen years older than Ted. What made him suddenly more approachable, was the shock in his eyes as they riveted themselves on his face. The sudden tremor in his fingers.

He'd had to tell him he knew. He certainly could not go on working for him without.

'I should have done more for you.' Jeremy's voice was hardly above a whisper.

'Mother told me you were generous.'

'She did?'

'You bought her the business.'

'It was what she wanted. Saw herself expanding till she had a turnover to rival mine. Your mother had ambition, guts too.'

'Still has.'

'She took on Ted Fraser. Two dependants, before the business was on its feet.'

'It's on its feet now, sir.'

'We did agree, your mother and I, it would not be a generally known fact. For Ted's sake and her reputation. I wanted to do more for you. Send you away to school, but she wouldn't hear of it. At fourteen, she said, when he's old enough to work, you can mould his future then.'

'I thought I'd been singled out because I was bright, like Norman Coates.' Alex was suddenly choking as another thought occurred to him. 'Or is he . . .?'

'Certainly not! Norman Coates is just a bright lad. I set up the scheme years ago so I would not seem to be singling out only one. Other boys have benefited, but so has the company. Past trainees have stayed loyal. So though I did wrong by Olympia, some good has come of it.'

The silence dragged between them, then he added, 'You're a fine lad. I ought to be proud of you. Proud of Olympia, bringing you up. She's coped wonderfully.'

The silence lengthened again. 'When you were born, I was married, I could not have much contact, later there was Ted.'

Alex understood that. 'He wants the world to think I'm his son.'

How often had he heard Ted rile against the Wythenshaws? Don't trust them, he'd said, and it seemed he had grounds on which to base his opinion after all. 'Ted was always bitter about you. I never understood why till now.'

'Yes, well, life has not been kind to him. The war.'

'Everybody thinks he blames the war because it ruined his health,' Alex said slowly. Only now was he beginning to understand. 'He's built it up as a protection, an obsession almost, because he can't say it's you he blames.' Only now after years of listening to Ted holding forth about his sufferings in the war, did he realise the hurt had come from Jeremy.

Alex had lost his fear of hurting Jeremy. He deserved to be hurt. 'Ted even said he regretted saving your life.'

He saw that bite home. The silver head lifted, the blue eyes sparked with new anger.

'When did he save my life?'

'In the war, said you were never grateful, though you did buy him a drink.'

Alex watched Jeremy's chin go up. 'I may have bought him a drink, though I don't remember. However, if he had saved my life I would certainly remember that.'

Alex felt agonised. 'With his bare hands,' he whispered. 'A German soldier who was about to kill you?'

The silver head was shaking a strong denial. 'No, nothing like that happened.'

Alex unfurled his palms in front of him just as Ted so often did. He saw gaunt, lined hands that were not his own.

'He didn't save your life?'

'No, not that I know of.'

Alex felt numb. He was only beginning to understand what Ted had gone through.

'Did Ted know my mother, before . . .?'

'Yes,' Jeremy said soberly. 'She was his girlfriend. That was the hurt I did him. It was wrong of me; put it down to hot-blooded youth.'

CHAPTER TWENTY-TWO

Giles pulled the bedclothes round his ears trying to shut out the sounds of another day; thinking about his problems and the injustice of his present life. He'd always looked down on Alex Fraser, it was a shock he couldn't adjust to.

He turned over angrily in bed, moving to his own side. He'd told Emily she disturbed him when she got up to go to work. Now her exaggerated mouse-like movements in the semi-dark were a greater burden to bear. He was always thankful when he heard her go off downstairs. Especially if she went without disturbing Peter.

This morning he was out of luck. He pretended not to hear his baby voice. Why couldn't the child leave him in peace for once?

Peter still slept in his cot because they couldn't get him a bed, but he could climb over the top of the rails now and Emily said it was safer to leave them down, in case he fell.

He heard Peter's bare feet squeak on the lino, the bedroom door open as he went to the bathroom. Giles lifted his head from the pillow, the damn child had left it open. On so public a landing, he felt on show. He felt his patience snap, it violated his privacy, he'd have to get up and close it. But the sound of rushing water was thundering in his ears and nearer at hand the squeak on the lino as Peter came back and closed it. Thank God.

He was glad he no longer had the fag of worrying about the baby's bladder, Emily had tried to tell him it cut out all the inconvenience of looking after him, but she didn't have to do much of it.

'Daddy?' Urgent baby fingers were tugging at his bedclothes, letting in cold draughts. There would be no more peace today. He felt the child snuggle up to him, put ice-cold feet in his groin.

'We'd better get up,' he gasped. The thought of another day shut up in these awful rooms with the baby appalled him. He'd been thinking half the night about where he could turn for more money, and it came to him as his feet touched the floor; he had resources he'd not tapped yet. Aunt Harriet for instance. He could go and see her. Surely she wouldn't see him starve?

As he warmed up the porridge Emily left for him and the baby, he tried to decide whether he should take the child with him.

It might bring out Harriet's better nature to see Peter in an impoverished state. For best effect he should, but Peter was a bind, always up to something he shouldn't be. Giles sighed, he didn't feel cut out to look after babies. Couldn't even get peace to read the paper without Peter pulling at it for attention.

He'd probably race up and down her drawing-room driving them both mad, and might even break one of her ornaments. Easier to leave him with Gran.

He ate, while the huge living-room window rattled in the wind and water gurgled in the gutters. He could see the blackened brickwork of identical houses opposite gleaming in the rain. New Street depressed him, but he could not visit Aunt Harriet unless he found his address book. It was years since he'd been to her house, and although he had an image of it in his mind, he had no clear idea where it was.

The porridge stuck in his craw. The baby was making a

mess with his, he'd have to leave it for Emily to clear up when she came home. Giles hungered for something tasty like egg and bacon. He got up to wrench open the food cupboard door. For once it was possible, but he hesitated, deciding after all he couldn't be bothered. He poured himself another cup of tea instead.

He had more important things to do. He rummaged through every drawer in the bedroom, creating chaos, before he put his hand on the address book. He had to dress Peter. A pity Emily couldn't teach him to tie his own shoelaces and button his coat.

They were ready, but it was raining so heavily he decided to make himself a cup of Camp coffee and wait for it to slacken off. Then another five minutes wasted while he searched for his mackintosh.

He took Peter round to Paradise Parade in his push-chair, going through the back entry, though the shop would be open by now. Charlie was best avoided, he always had some rude comment to make every time he took Peter there.

He was lucky enough to catch Gran in the back kitchen. She lifted Peter up on the drain board to sponge his face at the sink. At least she never refused to have him.

He had to walk to Rock Ferry station then, because trains ran to a system he understood, while the bus routes defeated him. He was about to pass the Royal Rock when another heavy shower started, and since he didn't want to appear on Harriet's doorstep looking like a drowned rat, he decided to pop in for a beer. He'd bought a newspaper at Wade's and he was able to read it in peace and comfort.

He decided then he'd better have another beer, because he didn't want to arrive at Harriet's while she was eating her lunch. It was bothering him now that he'd never got on well with Harriet. Still, he had to go, his money was running out.

He thought of having lunch here, but after the beer he

wasn't hungry. Eventually he walked up to the station and caught the train to West Kirby, then took a taxi from the station to Aunt Harriet's address.

He recognised her house as he paid it off. A biggish Edwardian villa of shiny red brick. An elderly parlourmaid answered the door. It was a long time since he'd seen a maid, but even longer he thought since this maid had shown in visitors. She made no effort to relieve him of his mac and kept him standing about in the hall. Giles felt its middle-class atmosphere of furniture polish and recently baked scones close round him and felt immediately at ease.

He remembered her sitting-room, comfortably warm, with a piano open as though she'd just been playing. He knew his timing was good when he saw her tea tray had just been taken in. The hot scones were there with homemade strawberry jam.

He smiled, submitting to Aunt Harriet's examination through the blasted lorgnette she affected. She was looking very regal, sitting ramrod straight in an upright chair, wearing clothes that had been fashionable two decades ago. She was showing no pleasure at his visit.

'Giles,' she said. 'What brings you here?' He ignored her question, it was disconcerting. He had planned to lead up to his purpose after an interval spent demonstrating affection and concern for her.

'How are you, Aunt Harriet?'

'Not too well.' That wasn't the right opening either, Giles realised, as she enlarged on digestive symptoms he'd rather not have heard. He tried to keep the sympathetic smile on his face. It slipped a little as she turned to her scone with relish. Her eye caught his.

'Have you had your tea? No?' She rang her bell and when the maid answered, asked for scones for him. He felt his mouth water at the prospect.

'What's the matter with you, Giles? You're looking pale, not yourself.'

'Lost my tan,' he said lightly, but anybody could see it was more than that. He had cultivated the image of an athlete on top of his form, expensively dressed. It had been shattered. The barber he'd found in a back street hadn't cut his hair properly. It hung lank instead of curving in perfect waves round his head. It needed trimming again, when he could spare the money.

'Lost more than that, I hear.'

'What?'

'Jeremy tells me he had to ask you to leave.'

'Yes, I'm afraid . . .'

'Why? He's not giving his reasons. Just unpardonable behaviour.'

'A difference of opinion,' Giles managed, as the maid came back and placed another tray on the table beside him. Thin fine china, his own small teapot and hot-water jug and two fragrant scones.

He was savouring the first bite when Aunt Harriet said tartly: 'It's no good coming to me for money. I suppose that is why you've come?'

Giles felt butter and strawberry jam ooze from his lips. No point in denying it, but he'd meant to handle it more gracefully.

'I'm finding it very difficult, Aunt Harriet.'

'I'm sure you are.' The light glittered against her lorgnette as she examined him again. 'But I've only the income from the trust fund Jeremy set up for me.'

'It's just that Peter has not been well. There's been bills for doctors and medicines, and he advises a nourishing diet to build him up. His chest, you know.'

He could see Aunt Harriet's lips pursing. With her severely upswept grey hair, her resemblance to Queen Mary seemed stronger than ever. He hoped her charity had royal beneficence. She was reaching for her handbag, which she kept always to hand.

'How is Emily?'

'Upset of course, about the baby. Said she'd rather be ill herself than see Peter suffer. He has a dreadful cough.'

He heard the rustle of notes and felt a lift of exultation, he'd managed it again. Then he saw the five pound notes she was pushing in his hand. Disappointment sliced through him, cutting him down. The mean old bitch!

'Thank you.' He knew she was waiting to hear him say it. 'Thank you.'

'Sorry I can't offer you more . . .'

The tight-fingered bitch! He wondered what her income was. Father wouldn't be mean with her. Even old Arthur had been more generous.

'How's Grandfather?'

'He was very well last Sunday.'

So his luck was out there too, there'd be nothing more from him just yet. Waiting, always waiting, and grubbing about like this for a fiver.

He tried to pour a third cup of tea from the pot. It was too small, she was mean even with tea. He drank back the mouthful in the cup. Stood up.

'Jeremy will be sorry to hear Peter isn't well.'

'Yes,' he said, but he'd be glad to hear Giles was short of money. His father wanted him to suffer. He should be able to live like Harriet with a maid to take care of his needs. He wouldn't worry too much about Emily then, she could please herself.

He kissed Harriet's soft cheek, she smelled of eau de cologne. The old skinflint! She had everything she could possibly want, a comfortable home with pretty ornaments everywhere. His eye came to rest on two miniatures in silver frames, one of the Duke of Wellington, the other of his lady. They'd be worth a bit.

He left the sitting-room, and Aunt Harriet followed him down the hall to the front door; she was slow on her feet. He paused there, holding it open, asking after his father's health, enlarging on how sorry he was they'd had their differences.

'Goodbye,' he said, and then, pretending he'd only just thought of it: 'Oh dear, I'm going without my mackintosh.'

He strode quickly back to her sitting-room to get it. As he'd half expected, she waited at the open door to see him out. It took only a second to hook the miniatures off the wall. He held them in his hand with his mac folded over, keeping them out of sight.

He could feel his blood coursing round his body, excited by his own daring. He kissed her again. Thanked her again. Walked slowly to the garden gate.

As soon as Aunt Harriet closed the door, he broke into a run. Serve her right for being so mean. It wouldn't have hurt her to give him more. He was clear of her road and heading back towards the station.

Giles was feeling heady with success until he met two schoolboys with satchels on their shoulders. They eyed him curiously, turned to look at him as he ran past. He forced himself to slow down. There were not many people about in these residential roads, but he mustn't attract attention. He was growing breathless, he couldn't stop himself pounding along the pavement, he needed to put distance between himself and Harriet.

A car overtook him. It was slowing. A few yards ahead it swung round, ran up the pavement and stopped in front of a gate. He hardly noticed the passenger get out to open it, so intent was he on his own thoughts. He passed behind the car hardly slowing his step.

'Giles?' The driver was winding down her window. 'It is Giles Wythenshaw?'

He turned, taking in the smart two-seater Morris Cowley. His heart was already racing, it went into overdrive, fluttering with guilt and panic. He was searching into the woman's face in alarm, thinking he'd been caught.

It was her house he recognised first. He'd been here for dinner with Emily and his father more than once. Suburban Edwardian red brick, with a bay-windowed tower at one end, topped with a turret. The Bird family. Elvira Bird and her daughter.

'Good afternoon.' He raised his trilby, was relieved to feel cool air drying the sweat on his forehead. 'How odd to meet you like this.'

'What brings you to these parts?'

'I've been visiting an elderly aunt who lives not far away.'

The daughter had opened the gates of the garage as well, she came round to his side of the car. Her body, swathed in a short brown cape, jutted forward from long thin legs. She had a rather beakish nose and beady dark eyes and a way of putting her head on one side like a Christmas-card robin. He trawled through his memory for her name. It came to his tongue in the nick of time.

'Philomena,' he said. 'How lovely to see you . . .' His eyes swung to include her mother. 'See you both again like this.'

He was wiser now; he knew he had to aim for the one holding the purse strings. The business with Audrey Woodward had taught him that.

The mother smiled. 'Are you in a hurry? Would you be able to come in for a cup of tea, so we can catch up with your news?'

Giles's fingers tightened on Harriet's miniatures. He pulled his mackintosh closer. He was almost overcome by the tumult of emotion, but he recognised this could be his big chance. He needed to calm himself. Hadn't he already decided that another woman, one with money in her own right, was his way out of the mess?

'A cup of tea would be very welcome,' he smiled.

'Splendid.' Elvira put the Cowley in gear and it moved up the short drive and into the garage. Their house reminded him of Aunt Harriet's. It was of the same era, but a little larger, homely and comfortable rather than grand.

'Would it be possible to use your cloakroom?' he asked. Philomena pointed out the door at the back of the hall.

He bolted it behind him and took a deep breath. He had to hide the miniatures somewhere. He couldn't let them be seen. He wished now he'd left them on Aunt Harriet's wall.

There was a row of pegs along one wall; he hung up his mac. Apart from that there was a lavatory, a washbowl and a towel rail. And a windowsill with hats and gloves piled on it. He pushed the pictures under a purple velour, and then had second thoughts. They were out of sight, but what if one of the Birds should move that hat? To put those they were wearing on the sill too?

He looked again at his mac. The pockets were deep but the diagonal vents into them only wide enough to admit a hand. He forced one miniature through and down, stretching the material and breaking a stitch but it slid out of sight. Hastily he pushed its partner into the other pocket. Sighing with relief he folded the pockets inwards, out of sight. It was unlikely the Birds would touch his coat; he immediately felt more secure.

Hastily then he used the facilities, splashing cold water on his face to calm himself. He could still feel his hands trembling as he reached for the towel.

In the hall he saw a housemaid scurrying with extra china into the dining-room. Philomena, looking more girlish without her cape, beckoned him in. Tea was taken at the dining table in this house. He eyed it with pleasure. Crustless sandwiches of bloater paste, seed cake, fruit cake and jam tarts. Something like a tea.

He sat down facing Elvira. Taking in her pale hair permanently set in exactly uniform waves. She had the same rather large nose as her daughter and her smokey grey eyes were smouldering sensuously at him. When he'd seen her at Churton years ago, he'd felt she was a kindred spirit. She was perfect for his purpose.

She'd put on weight since then, and though more matronly, had the air of one clinging fiercely to youth. Her stylish pink afternoon dress would have suited Philomena better. He watched her tucking into her tea with relish and wondered how old she was.

For his own part, his appetite had been damped down by Harriet's scones. He felt too nervous to eat much. This chance had come too suddenly, not giving him time to think, and too much depended on the way he handled it. He had to seem interested. He let his tawny eyes burn into Elvira's and couldn't help but notice he was bringing a flutter to her eyelids and a flush to her cheeks.

They would get round to asking about Emily sooner or later. He needed to get his story running along a believable track. He would tell them they had not got on, that Emily had deserted him for another man. He smiled, letting his gaze hook into Elvira's again. It had to be Elvira, not her daughter, though he found Philomena more to his taste.

Philomena was being chivvied to get changed. It seemed she'd arranged to go to the Liverpool Playhouse with an old school friend and her family, and they'd be having supper out afterwards.

Giles was relieved, it would make it easier to get on better terms with Elvira if Philomena was not watching every move he made.

'Do please stay and keep me company. Do say you'll stay for supper,' Elvira pressed. Giles was flattered; it was going to be easier than he hoped to get his feet under this table.

When the meal was over she was fussing him. Settling him in a comfortable armchair in her sitting-room, with the radio and the *Echo* for company. She poured a glass of scotch for him and left the decanter at his elbow. Made up the fire till the flames danced and roared. Giles felt born again. He was never going back to Emily and those miserable rooms if he could help it.

'You are a dear,' he told Elvira, and stood up to kiss her cheek. She giggled girlishly.

Elvira felt more alive than she had for years. Philomena was showing unusual reluctance to get ready and they'd already sat over the tea table too long. She almost had to push her upstairs.

She had been going to eat a poached egg for supper. Now she swept into the kitchen to see if something better could be arranged. Steak and kidney was simmering on the stove for tomorrow's dinner when both she and Philomena would be home. She ordered it served under a pie crust tonight, with a soup to start and a pudding to follow. Queen of pudding had been Walter's favourite, she asked Cook to prepare that.

Mrs Tatling gave her a sour look. Because Philomena had arranged to go out, she told her this morning she might take the evening off. That Mabel could manage the poached egg for her.

Because Giles was staying, she had just rescinded that privilege. Resentment at the change of programme was coming across in bitter waves.

Elvira sniffed; she'd hired Mrs Tatling a month earlier and she was not giving satisfaction. She lived locally with her husband and what she'd really wanted was a nine to five job. Since she and Philomena worked those hours, Elvira required a cook to prepare tea and dinner. To look after them when they came home from work.

Mabel the housemaid had fitted satisfactorily into her household for the last fourteen years. She'd tried her at cooking, but what she dished up was plainer than plain and eventually she'd sought relief.

Mrs Tatling's cooking was better, but she brought an atmosphere of antagonism to the kitchen. She and Mabel were continually bickering. She would have to go, but tonight, with an unexpected guest, was not the moment to tell her.

Elvira went up to her room to change. She had a quick bath and half dressed again. She had a tendency to puffiness round her eyes and had read in a magazine it could be improved by relaxing flat on her bed for ten minutes with a round of cucumber on each eyelid. She had brought up the cucumber to try it now, but it seemed a waste of valuable time.

Everybody knew Giles and Jeremy had parted, and rumours as to the reason had circulated wildly at the time. Both she and Philomena had been agog at the news. Now she didn't care. It was assumed Giles had been thrown out of the business for some misdemeanour. He'd told her tonight it was a family quarrel, a feud with his father.

They had both thought Giles exceedingly attractive at the time of his marriage, and his bride rather unworthy of such a catch. In the four years since, Giles's shoulders had broadened and he'd filled out generally. He no longer seemed in the first flush of manhood. Perhaps his perfection was marred by his need of a haircut, but he had the face and body of an Adonis.

Elvira slid off her bed to sit at her dressing table. She let her smokey eyes search into the mirror for signs of aging. Because she had put on weight, her face showed few lines, but horrors! She could see two or three grey hairs in her pale brown waves. She plucked them out at the roots, with her eyebrow tweezers, and sat back to survey the result.

Not too bad, but her charms had failed to attract another husband in the five years since Walter had died. How many times had she told herself there was no reason to feel desperate. The business kept her in comfort. The income had grown under her control. But she missed the company of a man.

Forty-two, but she'd pass for mid-thirties, she thought. Giles must be thirty now, he need not feel there was too big a difference in their ages.

She put on her smartest frock. A comfortable one to wear, dressy blue silk cut on the bias. Giles's eyes showed appreciation when she returned to the sitting-room.

'Such a long time since you last came here to a meal,' she said.

'Two years at the most.'

'Too long.'

'How old is Philomena now?'

Elvira took a deep breath, she found this a sensitive area. With a daughter as old as Philomena, it eased the pressure to knock a year or two off.

'Seventeen,' she said. 'Sometimes I think she looks older.'

Giles's eyes locked into hers again. 'You look more like sisters.' Elvira had her attractions, her breasts were voluptuous, crying out to be fondled.

She wound up her gramophone and put on a record of Bing Crosby crooning 'In the Blue of the Night'. Giles advanced on her with his arms wide. 'Let's dance.'

'Lovely idea.' Elvira carried the machine out to the hall where there was a parquet floor. Giles rolled up the rugs and stood them in the corner against the stairs, then he took her in his arms. She felt soft and cuddly like an outsize bolster, her heady perfume wafted up strongly as she moved. She felt as light as thistledown on her feet. He pulled her closer, let his lips linger against her forehead. This was more like it.

When the wine and the dinner had been consumed, there was no suggestion he should leave.

Within days, Giles felt he'd cracked it, felt on top of the world. Life had changed for the better. He was never going back to New Street and Emily. Elvira took him round her carton-making works with its printing shop. It was a man's world but she controlled it. Philomena worked in the office.

Giles was flattered when she asked his advice, but he thought it wise to tell her she knew more about packaging than he did.

His duties, Elvira told him, were to help run the house, but it ran like clockwork needing little attention from him.

Mrs Tatling had been dispatched and Mabel had taken over the cooking again. He bossed the gardener as well as Mabel, hired a daily cleaning woman and worked her hard.

He helped where he could. Ran little errands for Elvira, offered to teach Philomena to drive. Chauffeured them both about.

He felt happier than he had for a long time. Elvira was generous, buying him clothes and giving him money to put in his pocket. He rejoined the Golf Club, and started playing again with Walter's old clubs.

All Elvira needed in return was cosseting and he was good at that. He liked being the only male in an otherwise female household.

The days ran into weeks. Elvira talked about him getting a divorce. Suggested he should see a solicitor at her expense. Giles did so, he felt he was making a success of his new life. He meant to write to Emily. He didn't think she'd object to the divorce.

Emily was coming out of a deep sleep. She knew, because enough light was coming through the thin curtains to see across the bedroom, that it was time she got up for work. Peter was a still mound in his cot, but the sound of steady breathing from the pillow beside her was missing.

She sat up with a jerk. Giles was not in his place beside

her. This was the second time he'd not come home to sleep.

Impatiently, Emily tossed off the bedclothes and started to dress. She was furious with him. He knew she relied on him being here to look after Peter while she went to work.

Before she went, she would have to dress Peter and take him down to Gran. She shot back from the bathroom telling herself Gran wouldn't mind looking after him all day for once, but Giles's absence made it more difficult to cope.

Gran was hardly out of her own bed. 'Not come home? Where is he, then?'

'I don't know.' He'd promised last time it wouldn't happen again. His absence rankled all day, an added irritation. She collected Peter at closing time and went home to her cold dark rooms.

She was fuming at Giles, thinking he hadn't been near all day. When she went into the bedroom an hour or so later to put Peter to bed, she saw the note.

'Emily — Please don't do anything silly like informing the police. I'm perfectly all right. Just came to collect some of my things. Love, Giles.'

She almost exploded. He was all right, but what was she to do? He didn't say whether he'd be away for a few days or whether it was for good. And where was he anyway? Not too far away, if he could come home for his clothes.

Emily checked his drawers, he'd taken all the shirts she'd ironed for him last night. Several suits and pairs of shoes. Quite a lot. She thought he must be planning to stay away some time.

Only half listening to Peter's baby chatter, she decided she'd give him a day or two before giving up her job. She didn't want to think about what she could do after that if he didn't return. As the days passed, her first panic-stricken anger receded; she was not sorry Giles had gone.

The following week, she told them in the builder's yard

she could no longer work full time. They gave her her cards, and she started to look for part-time work. She felt very lucky when she was offered a morning job.

'In a carrot-canning factory, just starting up,' she told Gran. 'I'll be the only typist, and doing general office work too.' Office work was less tiring, it left her with energy to do other things.

'Of course I'll look after Peter,' Gran told her. 'He was here a lot when Giles was supposed to have him.'

She understood only too well Emily's need for money. Every lunch time, Emily went back to Paradise Parade and in return did some of Gran's heavy household tasks. She washed sheets and changed beds, washed Charlie's clothes, swilled out the yard, swept the living-room and stairs.

She began to settle into her new routine, at times even enjoyed it. Her rooms were uncomfortable, but at least she had a roof over her head. Money was tight, but she wasted nothing. Without Giles's profligate spending habits, she could just manage. The weeks ran into months; Emily no longer expected him to come back. Didn't want him to.

Giles opened his eyes slowly, aware of Elvira's bare feet padding round the bed to draw back the curtains. The morning light was bright, showing up her flaccid flesh quivering against her filmy nightdress.

'Good morning, darling,' he said pulling himself up on his pillows.

In the evenings, after a whisky, Elvira was all any man would ask for. In bed she could be demanding, but he loved all her cushioning flesh. It was only when the morning sun caught her full in the face, as it did now, that he was reminded how much older she was than him. This morning there were bags under her eyes and her face seemed slack. It was easy to see the tiny wrinkles. He found them off-putting.

'Time to get up,' she said. 'I heard Philomena go down a few minutes ago.'

The routine on Sunday mornings was different. It was Mabel's morning to lie in. She stayed in bed until it was time to put the joint in the oven for lunch. She set the breakfast trays on Saturday nights and left them on the kitchen table. Philomena had been making tea and toast and carrying the trays upstairs since she was ten. It was her contribution to the running of the household.

'I don't like Philomena seeing you in my bed. Go down and fetch our trays, Giles.'

Giles sighed and swung his legs out on to the thick rug. 'She knows I'm here, though.'

'Not a good example to set a daughter. She's at an impressionable age.'

'I'll go.' Giles felt down the sheets for his pyjama trousers, then pulled on the dressing-gown Elvira had chosen for him.

The scent of toast drew him towards the kitchen. Philomena was standing at the stove with a cup of tea in one hand and the Sunday paper in the other, her attention divided between that and the grill.

'There's tea in the pot,' she said.

The cord on her dressing-gown was so loose it didn't hold the two sides together. He could see white lace and deep cleavage between two firmly jutting young breasts.

'Mother wouldn't like to see you eyeing me like that,' she went on without looking up.

Giles moved nearer, pulling the cord to free it, and taking the tea cup from her hand and putting it on the table. He loosened his own dressing-gown and pulled her to him. It wasn't the first time he'd kissed the little bird. She'd come home from work with a bad headache one day. She said he'd cured her of that.

He'd had a wonderful afternoon in her room. Forbidden fruit was always sweeter. But he meant to be careful, he knew well enough Elvira was the one for him.

'I don't know what you see in my mother,' Philomena had sniffed that day. 'She's old enough to be your mother too.'

'No,' he said. 'I'm years older than you, and she was married very young.'

'Yes, a child bride, I've heard that before. How old did she tell you I was?'

'Seventeen.'

He watched Philomena double up in a fit of giggles. 'How old are you, then?'

'Twenty-two. She finds it embarrassing to admit she has a daughter as old as me.'

'Have another headache, Philo,' he urged. 'How about tomorrow?'

He was pulling her closer so he could feel her firm young flesh against his chest. She laughed up at him. The sun was full on her face too, but she could take strong light. Her skin was wonderfully taut and young, her dark eyes bright and perky. He straddled his legs round her, rubbing her firm body against his own. He found it wonderfully titillating to live with two women.

The acrid smell of burning toast made Philomena tug away. It was on fire under the grill. Laughing aloud she flung it into the sink and ran water on it. Giles pursued her, trapping her in his arms, pushing her dressing-gown off her shoulders.

'Mother wouldn't like this either,' she said, putting her arms round his neck.

'Too damn right she doesn't,' Elvira blazed from the doorway.

Giles felt Philomena tear herself from his arms; the strength ebbed from his knees in the silence that followed. He could have kicked himself.

'Isn't anybody safe from your attentions?' Elvira screamed, looking an embittered harridan. 'And you, you young hussy, get up to your room.'

He watched Philomena knot her dressing-gown cord and go without another word.

'Get out,' Elvira spat at him. He scrambled for the stairs feeling frantic, could have kicked himself for losing a comfortable home this way. He could think of nowhere to go but back to Emily, and the dreadful rooms in New Street.

CHAPTER TWENTY-THREE

Emily was finding life easier without Giles. With her part-time job and Peter to take care of, she was salvaging something from the mess. She'd developed her own routine.

On Sundays, when she'd finished her chores, she devoted herself to her child, taking him on outings if the weather was fine. She hadn't seen Sylveen for a long time and today she planned to take the bus to Heswall in the hope they'd catch her at home.

She was dishing up their dinner of stew and dumplings on the living-room table, cutting Peter's helping into small pieces so he could feed himself, when she heard footsteps crossing the landing.

The door banged back and Giles burst in on them. She leapt out of her chair, her heart pounding with shock; she felt his arms go round her and his kiss on her mouth. After one stunned second, Emily was fighting to free herself.

'What have you come back for?'

'This is my home, I'm your husband, Emily.'

She saw his tawny eyes taking in the damp patches on the wall, the shabby furnishings.

'I thought you'd found yourself something better.'

She could see he had. He looked well, his hair was beautifully trimmed into loose waves curving round his head. He wore a new tweed sports jacket and fawn trousers.

'Where've you been?' She was filled with revulsion at the thought of having him back.

'Working,' he said. 'But unfortunately I've got the sack.'

'Why didn't you let me know where you were?'

'I kept meaning to. Kept meaning to send you money.'

'It's been four months,' Emily said outraged. 'Four whole months!'

He swept Peter up in his arms and waltzed round the room. 'Lovely to see you both again.'

'I can't afford to keep you, Giles. I've only got a part-time job. It just keeps me and Peter.'

'Don't worry, I've got money.' He pulled out his wallet, showing her the wedge of pound notes in it. He withdrew six, and tossed them on the table. 'I can pay my way. Let me stay, Emily, it needn't cost you anything.'

'How long will that last you? Five minutes?' She shrank from him, recalling how quickly money could go through his fingers.

'Then I'll look after Peter, and you can get a better job.'

'No, Giles! You'll disappear again and I won't be able to keep the job. I'd rather you'd stayed away.'

'No you wouldn't.' His tone conveyed that he thought she was teasing. 'I love you, Emily, we're a family, we belong together. You aren't going to turn me away?'

She wanted to. She had no appetite for her dinner and none to offer him.

'Don't worry about me, Emily, a cheese sandwich will do. I'll take you out for a decent meal tonight.'

Emily closed her eyes and lay back in her chair. It was starting all over again.

'I don't want this, Giles. I've settled down by myself. I prefer to be on my own.' She could feel reluctance building like a wall between them.

'Nonsense, love. I'll give you a good time, you'll see.' He went to the food cupboard, got out the loaf and some cheese. Emily let her resistance collapse, she didn't know how to fight him.

It seemed she would have to grit her teeth and keep them going on her wages. She didn't dare think of what would happen when Giles's money ran out. She could manage the food bills and shillings for the electric meter. The carrot-canning factory where she worked was expanding. She had more typing and basic accounting than she could cope with. Bill Hadley, her boss, was working twelve hours a day.

'Soon I'll need you working full time, or I'll have to get another girl,' he worried.

He was six foot, square jawed and middle aged. Emily was tempted because she needed the money, but she was afraid Giles would disappear again. Office work wasn't easy to come by on her own doorstep and she liked this job. It would be too much for Gran to look after Peter all day and every day.

Two weeks later Bill Hadley asked: 'Would you mind working this Saturday afternoon to keep the books up to date?'

Emily agreed, glad of the chance to earn extra money. Giles could look after Peter. It was longterm commitment she was afraid of. She didn't want to let Bill Hadley down and be forced to abandon this job as she had the others.

They shared an office, but he was talking of new premises too. Her desk was in front of his and as she worked she could hear him give an occasional cough or a little sigh. She had had her week's wage yesterday, but at closing time, he came and put her overtime money on her desk.

'You work very hard, Emily, thank you,' he said wearily. 'If you didn't, I'd have had to get another girl before now. You deserve a rise, how about another five shillings a week?'

Emily felt a real lift and laughed with pleasure. She decided to buy fish and chips at Charlie's, because she'd left Giles to get the weekend shopping. He was always tempted by little luxuries and if the money gave out before he'd bought all the items on her list, he was quite likely to have bought nothing for supper.

She felt happier as she pedalled towards Paradise Parade. Though it was nearly six o'clock on a Saturday evening, all the shops were open and doing good business. The lights were full on, streaming out a welcome into the cold night. There were several customers waiting at the counter when she opened Charlie's door. He looked harassed, his face was running with perspiration.

'Thank God you've got here,' he said belligerently. 'Where've you been till now?'

Emily's heart sank. 'What's the matter? Is Peter all right?'

'No thanks to you. Come on in.' He edged behind Pammy, leaving her to serve on her own, and made for the living-room door. Emily pushed through the customers to join him.

'What's the matter?' She found Ted in the living-room with a sleeping Peter in his arms.

'Your gran's ill again and I can't be looking after your offspring as well as the shop. We need eyes in the back of the head with him.'

'Is it her throat? Gran?'

'Went down in a dead faint she did and nearly flattened the baby.'

'Is he hurt?' Alarmed, Emily went closer. Peter had a graze on his forehead, it had been washed clean.

'Screamed for a bloody hour, he did, on and on. Hardly hurt at all.' Emily felt guilt-ridden and was about to lift Peter into her arms.

'Just managed to get him off,' Ted complained. 'Be careful, we don't want to start him off again.'

'It's Ma,' Charlie said. 'Happened before like this, sudden like. Thought she wasn't coming round.'

Emily felt fear spear thorough her: 'Dad, you'll have to get the doctor, if she's bad.'

'She's had the doctor. She is bad. Don't keep telling me what I must do.' Charlie's oily face twisted with anger. He wagged his finger at her. 'You cause the trouble. Dumping the baby on her, expecting her to look after it all the time. I can't cope with your problems as well as my own. Had to get Ted here early to help.'

Emily felt as though she'd been slapped. 'Giles looks after Peter, doesn't he?'

'Not so you'd notice. Leaves him here every morning while he goes to Donovan's. Collects him at dinner time so you can feed him, then back for the afternoon. Usually picks him up before now though.'

'Couldn't find your fancy man,' Ted added spitefully. 'We sent Myra George up to your rooms. No one there.'

'He had to get some shopping,' Emily said faintly, feeling cold inside.

'He's done that. Was round with Olympia early this morning. I told her she shouldn't give him more credit.'

'He didn't need credit, I gave him money.' Emily clapped her hand over her mouth, but it was too late now, she'd told them.

'Said you hadn't got any money, and you know what Olympia's like.'

Emily felt sick, it was a nightmare she'd dreaded. 'How much does he owe?'

'Eleven pounds fifteen shillings and fourpence,' Ted said, his pale eyes staring her out.

Emily gasped. It would take four weeks of her wages to cover that. She wasn't sure whether Ted's cadaverous face showed pleasure that Giles had lapsed or dismay that the debt was to Olympia.

'He's a bloody leech sucking you dry, Emily,' he sniffed. 'Why do you let him?'

'He's spending ten times what you earn, you fool,' Charlie hissed. 'Take your head out of the sand.'

'The Wythenshaws are all the same.' Ted's face twisted with hate. 'I did warn you.'

'You ought to be round here giving a hand with your gran, not pandering to that fancy man. What did he ever do for you?' Charlie pushed his angry face close to hers.

That stabbed home. 'Gran,' Emily choked, 'I'll go up and see her.'

'She won't be well enough to look after your kid on Monday,' Charlie called after her. 'So don't bring him here.'

Emily stumbled upstairs. Gran hardly seemed to know her. That was the hardest blow of all.

Half an hour later, Emily was throwing her weight against the pushchair, wheeling her sleeping child back to New Street. She could feel her anger coming to a slow-rolling boil. Giles made no effort to help himself, he battened on other people. Gran, Olympia, herself, anybody who would give him something.

Now all Paradise Parade knew how Giles Wythenshaw rated as a husband and provider. Once they had envied her luck, now they pitied her. She had supported him for too long. They'd had four years of disastrous marriage. To believe he could change was hoping for a miracle.

She carried Peter upstairs, heavy and slack in her arms; she would put him straight in his cot. The bedroom door was not locked, she could hear Giles's heavy breathing as she fumbled for the light switch. He was lying on their bed, fully dressed, shoes still on. In the sudden light his mouth snapped shut and he turned over. She could smell the alcohol on his breath from here.

It fuelled her anger. While she had been working he'd been out getting a skinful. Spending money they needed. She had little patience left for Peter, but he hardly stirred as she undressed him, put him in the unmade cot. Giles never bothered to make it when he got Peter up.

Giles was hunched in a ball now, still heavily asleep. Some instinct took her to the listing chest of drawers, made her fingers drag at a drawer, push away her underwear. She had opened a Post Office savings account and banked the fifty pounds Giles had given her from Arthur's handout. She felt for the outline of the book beneath the wallpaper a previous tenant had used to line the drawer. It was in its place. She felt a trickle of relief, then another thought stabbed at her: a bank book meant nothing.

She slid it out, opened it and gave a gasp of horror. The list of withdrawals blurred before her eyes, sometimes four pounds, sometimes three. He must have forged her signature. Her account was only two shillings in credit.

All the months he'd been away she'd been stretching her wages, priding herself on drawing as little as possible from her reserve. He had drained her account in the last two weeks.

Tears of rage sprang to her eyes, it had been her nest egg. Knowing she had twenty-two pounds in reserve kept her juggling with pence in order to keep it. It was her security. Now it was gone. She was sobbing as she rushed to the living-room table and crawled underneath.

Since the day Giles had taken money from her purse, she had not felt safe keeping it there. She kept a reserve in an Oxo tin taped to the underside of the table. Although the mahogany veneers were cracked and broken on top, underneath solid Victorian workmanship had provided struts and strengtheners and a mechanism for winding in extra leaves. The tin could not be seen, neither would unsuspecting fingers touch it if the table was moved. She didn't think Giles would think of it as a hiding place. Her fingers closed on the Oxo tin, prising it open so roughly she tore a nail. A deep breath of relief, Giles hadn't found it. The two pound notes and two half crowns were still inside, but provided scant security now it was all she had.

She shivered, the fire had not been lit today. She was too weary to do it now. She took her toothbrush and went to the bathroom; she would go to bed.

She lay down beside Giles, feeling bone weary, but she was in an emotional turmoil, and sleep wouldn't come. She knew she would have to make the break now, or accept that this was how she'd live for the rest of her life.

She had Gran to consider too, she was poorly. She could not go to work on Monday and leave Gran to Charlie's care. Her thoughts raced, she could decide nothing.

Men took the initiative in all things, especially Wythenshaw men, but this was something she had to decide for herself. Men could be bastards but their wives stayed. Women accepted marriage for better or for worse, that was what she'd promised at the altar.

Emily knew she must have slept after all, because when Giles flung himself off the bed and switched on the light, she felt sleep-sodden.

'What's the matter?'

'Nothing,' he said. She heard him slam the bathroom door, then water sluice down like a mill race, the pipes rattle. Peter began to whimper and Emily had to get up to settle him. Giles was gulping water, he brought a full tumbler back to his bedside table, and started to undress.

'What have you been celebrating?' Emily asked, kissing Peter and rolling back on her bed.

'Nothing, just went for a drink. Nothing to celebrate, have we?'

'Oh, I don't know. We're touching bottom.'

'What's that mean?'

'The worst has happened. You've taken my reserve.

Bled it out of my account. We've nothing to fall back on.'

'My money,' he muttered, getting into bed, but leaving the light on. 'Grandfather gave it to me, if you remember?'

'Yes.'

'I gave it to you for safe keeping.'

'I thought I was doing that. Thought I was buying all our groceries too.' He didn't answer.

'Did you have to run up a bill with Olympia? What could you possibly spend eleven pounds fifteen shillings and fourpence on?'

'Eggs and bacon for breakfast, a few biscuits for the baby. Not a lot.'

'You said the biscuits were a present from you.' Emily was choking with indignation.

'So they were.'

'But you hadn't paid for them,' she shouted. While she worked for necessities, Giles had spent ten times her wage on luxuries.

She felt calmer, more collected than she had. Past anger now. Something else occurred to her. 'Any other . . . debts?'

'A little at the off licence and the pub. Only a fiver or so each.' Giles's eyes met hers, they had a hangdog look. 'Well, perhaps a little more.'

'They let you drink on tick?' Emily was astounded. 'Well, you've drunk us dry, the party's over. Are you going to put the light out?'

Giles was snuggling down under the blankets. It meant Emily would have to cross the cold lino to the switch at the door, or burn electricity they couldn't afford.

She got up again. It didn't matter. Giles had helped wonderfully to concentrate her mind. Tomorrow she would leave him. Move her own and Peter's things back to Paradise Parade.

Peter woke her early, she got him up and dressed. Giles

hardly stirred. She found the larder well stocked. Emily cooked them both a good breakfast of eggs and bacon, and then started packing. She felt better, her mind was made up.

She had less to take away than they'd brought, because she'd already sold Peter's high-chair and play pen as he'd outgrown them, but this time she had no car to transport her things. She went in and out of the bedroom, packing their clothes. Giles's head came up from his pillow: 'What are you doing?'

'I'm leaving you.'

He groaned and closed his eyes again. 'You'll be back.'

'Never, I've had enough.' She collapsed Peter's cot, she would have to take that, though he'd outgrown it too. There was no other bed he could use. The mound of boxes and bags looked enormous.

She looked out the rent book and slipped it in her pocket. The tenancy was in their joint names, but she had always paid the rent. Tomorrow, she would see the agent, she didn't want to find she was liable for rent months hence because Giles hadn't paid it. It was one of the things she'd thought about in bed last night.

As she packed some of Peter's bedding in his pushchair and fastened him on top, she remembered the trolley on which Ken Tarrant from the greengrocer's wheeled sacks of potatoes from their yard to Charlie's. She would ask if she could borrow that. She took a suitcase, half balanced it on the pushchair and set off. Charlie was up and drinking tea, but hadn't got round to taking a cup to Gran.

'I've come to look after her,' Emily announced. 'I won't go to work tomorrow. I'll put a note through the office door this afternoon.'

'How long you staying?' Charlie asked.

'Till she's better.' Emily sat Gran up and gave her sips of tea. Washed her and made her bed. Made bread and milk and fed her with that. She seemed a little better.

Her old attic bedroom smelled damp and dusty under the all-pervading smell of chips. She threw open the window. Then she went to see if the Tarrants were up. They were eating their breakfast. Ken Tarrant had the same tight curly hair that Cathy had; he promised to bring the trolley up to her rooms in half an hour. Even said awkwardly that he'd help.

She rushed to fetch the pushchair. Peter was playing in the back yard and Charlie promised to keep an eye on him through the window while he read his paper.

There was no sign of Giles, but she didn't go into the bedroom again. Ken Tarrant ran up and down stairs loading the mound of goods she'd built up on the landing. He set off ahead of her with a huge load on his trolley. She was juggling with so many boxes on the pushchair she could hardly see where she was going. It was a fine breezy morning, and church bells were peeling out from St Peter's. Emily thought it must be a good omen.

As the weeks began to pass, she knew it was nothing of the kind.

Gran didn't improve. She was torn between looking after her and the demands Peter made on her time. Charlie expected her to take care of household tasks and help in the shop at rush hours.

She felt guilty about the money owed to Olympia, and too tired to do anything but drag up and down stairs.

Giles pulled himself up on his crumpled pillows and looked round the room. Shafts of bright light were coming through the sagging curtains; he'd been wide awake for hours, but he'd kept his head down hoping sleep would return. It hadn't, but he'd come to bed early last night, to get warm. He could feel the beginnings of a headache because he'd been too long in bed.

God, he missed Elvira and her comfortable well-ordered home. If only the bird-like Philomena had kept her distance, he'd be there now. Silly little bitch that she was, she'd not been worth what he'd lost.

He even missed Emily, though there was more room in the bed, and the sagging springs mattered less when only he rolled to the middle. At least she kept the rooms warm and tidy and provided food.

She'd said she was going for good, but he hadn't believed her. But she'd been gone two days and he was beginning to fear Emily would not relent. He'd walked down to the chip shop last night to see about her coming back and Charlie had been quite rude.

'What do you want?' he'd demanded as soon as Giles had got inside the door.

'Is Emily in? Can I go through?'

'What do you think this is, a hotel? I don't want any more of Emily's dependants here.'

'I wasn't thinking of living here,' he'd retorted.

'Not good enough for you? Just as well.'

'I want a word with Emily. I want to know when she's coming home.'

'She's staying here. Her grandmother's ill. Somebody's got to look after her. I can't, with the shop.' He'd turned away to serve another customer newly come in. The shop was bright and warm and the chips smelled good.

'I'll have a pennyworth of chips and a fish,' he told the little slut Charlie employed, who'd been leaning against the counter listening to every word.

He sat himself down at a table to eat them because he knew his presence annoyed Charlie. When the girl brought his plate over, he said: 'Tell Emily I'm here and want a word with her.'

'The boss won't like it.'

'Tell him I'm not going till I see her.'

He'd asked for tea when he'd finished his meal, and the girl had given him the stewed remains of an old brew. He'd sat on, determined to see Emily. She came at last, standing at his table looking weary.

'I'm not coming back, Giles, didn't I make it plain?'

'Emily, I need you.'

'I can't now anyway. Gran's very poorly.'

'Soon then? When she's better?'

'No, Giles. Not ever,' and she'd marched off.

Nothing for it then, but to ignore Charlie's self-satisfied smirk and come back to this awful place. The mess everywhere was overwhelming. How did Emily expect him to cope on his own? It drained his money, having to pay for every mouthful of food, and it was almost gone, he couldn't survive more than a few more days.

Giles pulled at the thin blankets, wanting more warmth round his shoulders. The sudden cold at his feet told him the bedding had come loose. Damn it, he thought in sudden fury, the bed needed making up properly. Somebody ought to put clean sheets on it.

He felt lost. Nobody cared any more. He'd been turned out by his father and abandoned by his wife. Everybody had turned against him, even though he'd tried so hard. He felt a trickle of fear; he didn't like being alone, didn't like this place Emily had dumped him in. He was cold and hungry here and he needed more money.

Even Sylveen had told him to get out of her house, and he'd loved Sylveen. She preferred his father, that was the really awful thing. He couldn't stand that.

This was all his father's fault. He'd been all right till he'd turned on him. He'd get his own back if it was the last thing he ever did. He was hitting rock bottom; he shuddered, wondering where his income would come from in future. He still had a little money but it wouldn't last much longer.

He thought of the dole. He'd been claiming that, but hadn't bothered while he'd been at Elvira's. It was demeaning, a weekly insult for a few shillings. He was only entitled for six months anyway, and the time had probably run out by now. There was only the Poor Law left to try now and he didn't know how to go about it anyway. Even the poor themselves abhorred that, he had to think of something else.

It came to him then like a shaft of light. Making him leap out of bed on to the cold floor and start hunting for his mackintosh. It was hanging on its peg behind the living-room door and Aunt Harriet's miniatures were still in its pockets.

He knew exactly what he would do; he would take the train into Birkenhead and take them to Carteret Mathews.

It was a long time since he'd last seen the visiting cards and he'd forgotten the whereabouts of the shop. He started hunting through the pockets of the suits he'd thrown over the bedroom chair. He drew a blank in those. He tugged at the wardrobe door and started to hunt through the pockets of those hanging there.

Emily had folded the clothes he hadn't taken to Elvira's into a cardboard carton and put it on top of the wardrobe. He was exultant when he found he didn't have to get it down. The three cards were still together in the top pocket of his grey pin-stripe.

He started to dress. Yesterday he'd bought himself a shirt and a pair of socks. It seemed easier than trying to wash the clothes he already had. His unwashed shirts were piling up in the corner, heaped as high as the chest of drawers. The alarm clock told him it had gone midday.

Crossing the landing on his way to the bathroom, he filled his kettle and lit the gas, hoping the shilling would not run out till he'd cooked his breakfast.

The living-room felt dank and cold because he hadn't had a fire since Emily had gone. With the grate full of ash and the scuttle empty, it didn't seem worth trying to light it, though there was coal in the coal hole downstairs if the other tenants hadn't pinched it.

He attacked the pile of unwashed dishes in the sink to find a cup and plate to rinse for breakfast. There was no milk because he hadn't paid the milkman, but he had half a bottle of Camp coffee and was getting used to drinking it black. Not bad, if he didn't let himself think of the freshly ground coffee at Churton.

Now, what was there to eat? He opened the food cupboard; it was empty except for more unwashed plates and half a stale loaf. He remembered then the frying pan with a thick layer of bacon fat set hard. It was where he'd left it yesterday, out on the gas stove on the landing. He cut himself two thick slices of bread and went out to fry them. He'd got them crisping nicely, sending up a mouth-watering aroma, when the cheeky girl from upstairs came skidding past to the lavatory.

'Yummy, bacon butties, I'll have one,' she sang out. Giles didn't bother to reply, he dished up his breakfast and took it back to his living-room.

It was drizzling as he left the house twenty minutes later. He wore his mac belted tightly, feeling the miniatures still in the pockets bumping against his knees as he walked.

The shop itself was hard to find and he had to ask directions three times. It was not what he'd expected, very much a back-street shop with a wired-up window. From what he could see of the stock displayed there, it hardly seemed worth protecting. The bell clanged as he opened the door. It was dingy and very small.

'Yes?' Carteret Mathews seemed larger in the cramped space behind the counter.

'Would you be interested in buying these?' Giles unwrapped the miniatures from the newspaper and laid them on the counter.

'What you asking for them?' Mathews got out a magnifying glass.

Giles had polished up their silver frames last night and

assessed their value. He decided they must be worth a hundred pounds, but he'd been well schooled in the West Kirby shop on the difference between a buying price and a selling price. Especially in a shop like this. 'Fifty pounds.'

Mathews laughed. His scanty hair was parted an inch or so above his right ear and the thin dun-coloured locks spread to best effect across his fawn scalp. From the front it gave him a huge dome of a forehead.

'Solid silver frames,' Giles said. 'They must be worth something. London made.' If he'd had a list of hallmarks, he would have been able to date them. He had a feeling they could be contemporary with the Duke.

Mathews was taking them out of their frames, grunting with what seemed satisfaction. He turned round; from the back, another large area of bare scalp could be seen. 'Where did you get them?'

'They belonged to my aunt.'

'Twenty-five pounds.'

Giles was shocked. 'Each?' he tried.

'They're a pair. Twenty-five pounds the pair. Take it or leave it.'

Giles hesitated. He could take them to Calthorpe's, on a day when his father was not there. If Father recognised them later, so much the better. But it meant a trip over to Liverpool, more trouble.

'I'll take it,' he said; twenty-five pounds would see him through for a while.

Mathews counted the pound notes on to the counter. As Giles was putting them in his wallet, he said: 'If you've anything else to sell, you know where to bring it.'

Giles was glad to get away from the dingy shop. He walked as fast as he could till he saw a pub, went in and ordered a pint of bitter. He'd managed, he'd got more money.

He sat over his beer for a long time, savouring it, making decisions. He was not going to stay in that hellhole in New Street. He'd seen lodgings advertised for working men, breakfast and evening meal included. He would look for somewhere clean, nearer the station. He was going to think more carefully about his future, about getting even with his father, about enjoying life more. He was going to be stronger about getting his own way.

CHAPTER TWENTY-FOUR

Emily came upstairs and paused at Gran's door, listening for Peter in the attic bedroom above. Ten minutes ago she'd put him in his cot for the night. He'd gone off quickly, thank goodness; all she could hear was Gran's laboured breathing. Then from below, she heard the shop bell sound again, and the spitting roar of boiling fat as Charlie threw a new batch of chips in the fryer.

She tiptoed in leaving the door ajar; Gran had scarcely moved since she'd left her. She had her small black shawl tucked tight round her shoulders, showing only an inch of pink nightdress.

Emily pulled a chair close to Gran's double brass bedstead and sat down. Once long ago this bed had seemed a haven of comfort. When her mother died she used to come and snuggle into Gran's arms.

Her scant white hair straggled across the pillow. Emily reached for her hand, its joints misshapen with arthritis, the fingernails purple. The sunken eyes flickered open momentarily, her blue lips tightened in the ghost of a smile.

'Emily,' she said. Her lips moved again, the cheeks sucking in, but no sound came. Moments later she seemed asleep. Her black straw hat with the cherries was hooked over the brass knob on the bed head. Above was a framed text that had hung here for as long as Emily could remember: Prepare To Meet Thy God.

Poor Gran, she refused to put her teeth in now, saying she was more comfortable without. They smiled at her from a tumbler, porcelain perfect, the gums brick red. She was afraid Gran would never put them in again.

Agonised, Emily's eyes examined the well-loved face. Thin and pinched now, with soft slack cheeks, her nose bluish at the tip. She did look ill. Charlie had said it was her fault Gran had come to this.

'You should never have let your fancy feller bring your kid here. On the go all day long she was. Never had a moment's peace with him.'

'You could have told me sooner.'

'You should have known he wouldn't do it. Lazy devil.'

When the doctor called again, Emily asked him if Gran would get better. He'd looked suitably solemn and said: 'She is eighty-nine. It's a good age, we can't hope for too much.'

Gran's eyes were open again, but clouded yellow.

'A drink?' she suggested. Gran tried to pull herself up the bed, but had no strength. Emily sat her up, plumped her pillows, settled her more comfortably. Held the glass of milk to the thin blue lips while she sipped.

'More friends on the other side now,' she mumbled. Emily stiffened, bending closer to hear. 'All gone from this world now. My time soon.'

'Gran! No!' Emily shivered with dread.

'I'm tired. Can't go on.'

'You'll get better. I want you to.'

'Only like falling asleep, Emily. Don't want to be a burden.'

'Gran, you aren't a burden,' she told her hotly.

'You've been very good. Meant a lot to me.'

'You've been the world to me.'

'Don't be sad. Lying here, feeling weak, no pleasure in it.' Emily thought she'd drifted off again, but after a moment she opened her eyes again. 'Glad my time's up. Can't go on for ever.'

'What'll I do without you?'

'I'll be watching over you,' Gran said, with another ghost of a smile. 'From up there. You be glad for me. Best thing now.' Emily was blinking hard, doing her best to stop tears running down her cheeks.

'Emily, love, don't grieve. Not sorry to go.' A door slammed downstairs. Gran's door creaked wider as the blast funnelled upwards.

'I'm not bloody having this.' Charlie's voice was raised in anger. 'Who do you think you are?'

'I'm not bloody staying,' Pammy screamed in response. 'I want me cards. You work me like a horse, yet begrudge a few chips. You're as mean as muck.'

Emily tiptoed to close the door. When she came back Gran's eyes were closed. She slumped back on the chair in despair. Without Pammy, Charlie would be after her to help in the shop much more. She'd have to make it clear it was only for a day or two until he could get someone else.

Gran's breathing rasped. Emily held her hand, needing her here. What would she do without her? Always she'd been behind her providing love and support. Emily knew she was being selfish, Gran had given all she could.

It happened. Emily sat with her all night; by first light she had gone. Gran never spoke again, she just slipped away. Emily was bereft, her only comfort that Gran had had a long life and was ready to go. She thought often of her last words.

Charlie managed to arrange her funeral for Thursday afternoon, early-closing day, and all Paradise Parade turned out to pay their last respects.

Emily had hardly spoken to Amy Tarrant since she'd been her bridesmaid, but she came in offering to look after Peter for the afternoon. She said she'd take him for a walk along the prom and then give him tea in their place. Emily accepted gratefully.

Mrs McFie, the butcher's wife, boiled hams and roasted pork in the cellar below her shop to sell cold by the slice. She brought generous amounts round to Emily for the funeral tea. Ken Tarrant brought salad vegetables and Olympia added tins of peaches and cream and came round during the slack part of the morning to help her wash the salad and set things out in the living-room. Ethel came from next door while they were at it.

'Your gran believed in a good send-off. Mustn't disappoint her,' she said putting two bottles of sherry on the sideboard and folding Emily into her arms in a hug of silent comfort.

Alex was standing with Cathy Tarrant at the grave, looking like a stranger in a new dark overcoat, but his eyes were awash with sympathy. As they walked back to Paradise Parade he put an arm across her shoulders, pulling her close with the liberty of one who had known her all her life. The gesture sent the years spinning away for Emily, bringing the loss of Alex's love as sharply in focus as the loss of Gran.

'You made her last six weeks more comfortable,' he said. 'I admire you for coming back.'

Emily was fighting tears again. 'I owed her that much, and . . .' No, she couldn't say it. Looking after Gran had given her an excuse to get away from Giles.

But all Paradise Parade knew that, so Alex must too. Why else would they all rally round like this? She felt surrounded by a wall of warmth and friendship. She felt one of them. The one pinprick was that the Fraser family seemed on closer terms with the Tarrant family than she remembered.

Olympia was the last to leave the living-room; her large pale face had a Madonna-like aura of peace.

'Don't dare fret for her, Emily. She wouldn't want it,' she said.

Charlie had gone out. Left alone, Emily sat on by the

fire. It was for herself she fretted as she took stock of what was left to her.

She was back with Charlie and worse off than she'd been at seventeen. Her eyes went round the living-room; nothing had changed since she was a child, except that it had grown shabbier with time.

Her eye came to rest on the terracotta pot high on the shelf holding the wireless, where Peter's fingers couldn't reach it. She leapt to her feet and snatched it down. Her precious plant was a dusty cluster of withered leaves. She touched one, it crumbled to dust between her fingers. The pot was bone dry, the old compost returning to dust too.

Emily couldn't stop the tears coming then. How could she have forgotten to water her violets? She'd nurtured the plant for three and a half years, ever since Peter was born.

Alex's violets. She remembered the fancy she'd once found comforting. While the plant thrived, his love for her would thrive too.

In her misery she'd let everything go. Gran had gone, and left a terrible void. She'd lost Alex, and all the plans she'd made with him had come to naught.

She'd not seen Giles since she'd moved out of New Street, nobody had along Paradise Parade. She'd lost touch with Sylveen and Jeremy. Lost her job. There was nothing left to hope for.

By the next day Emily had little time to dwell on anything. Following the fracas with Pammy, Charlie had given her the sack.

'It was good riddance,' he told Emily. 'She was a rotten worker, had to watch her every minute. Always up to something she shouldn't be. Good job you're here to give a hand.'

'You can get somebody else,' she said, but over the next days was forced to spend more time in the shop. It was no place for an active three-year-old while she was trying to serve. Charlie complained he was underfoot.

She decided the safest thing was to close her attic window, dress him warmly, lock him in, and leave him to play with his toys on the floor. Once she would have been able to fasten him in his cot, but now he could climb out; it was safer to leave the cot side down.

Whenever there was a lull in the shop, she ran upstairs to look in on him. She felt guilty leaving him so much alone.

'You'll have to get another girl,' she told Charlie.

When he wanted her down in the cellar peeling potatoes, she let Peter play about her feet. It was a dangerous place for him, but better than the shop, with its boiling fat. Impossible to leave him on his own all the time.

'Can't afford another girl when I'm keeping you and yours.' Charlie nodded towards Peter who was pulling the wooden truck Sylveen had given him along the lino.

'You mean you're not going to try?' Emily had hardly been aware of the days passing. She seemed to be in a haze of exhaustion and despair. She could feel herself sinking into misery and hopelessness.

'I've got you here, haven't I? What would you do if I did? Sit ànd play with the baby all day?'

'But you don't pay me wages.'

'You don't pay me rent. Or help with the food bills. I can't support two more if you aren't going to lend a hand when I need it.'

Emily sat back and closed her eyes. She didn't want to stay here. She tried to think of the alternatives.

She couldn't foist herself on Sylveen however generously she offered. Hadn't she seen what happened when Jeremy came? If she lived there permanently, she'd spoil what Sylveen had. She'd be there between them always.

Jeremy had set the cottage up for Sylveen and her babies. He had a right to be there, to have things as he wanted them. Emily knew that had been part of the bargain from the beginning.

Nor could she face going back to juggling pennies to make ends meet. She just hadn't the energy. Here at least the bills were not her responsibility and Charlie made sure there were no debts.

They were finishing breakfast one morning when he said: 'Well, girl, what are you going to do? Get out or work?'

She tried again to think, any decision was difficult to make now. Could she find them a couple of rooms, a motherly person to look after Peter and another job to pay for it all?

No, it was too much. She felt too tired to do anything. Once, she'd thought of her existence here as being like that of Jekyll and Hyde. Now she knew going to work at Wythenshaw's had been her salvation. Having Peter made a job doubly difficult. Yet Charlie owed her something. He'd never given back her insurance money. She shook herself awake.

'I haven't got that sort of money,' he snorted when she demanded her thousand pounds.

'What happened to it?'

'Went into the business. New fryer, that sort of thing. You're getting the benefit of the business now, aren't you?'

Emily doubted the truth of what he was saying. Charlie knew better than anyone how to hang on to his pennies.

'Giles still owes Olympia twelve pounds. I've got to have that, and a weekly wage. I can't work for nothing, Peter needs things.'

'A pound a week and your keep. And the baby's keep.'

'Two pounds,' Emily bargained. 'And Olympia's money.'

'Thirty shillings, and the money for Olympia. See you pay it, though, I don't want Ted on my back.'

'Of course I'll pay it.'

'Right, then it's settled.'

Emily sank back exhausted, wishing she'd held out for more. Feeling low didn't describe how she felt. She was numb. It wasn't grief that made her so, but the realisation she was trapped. She saw it as being trapped at the bottom of a mineshaft in darkness, with no possibility of escape.

'Want more tea.' Her son pushed his enamel mug against her plate. 'Please, Mummy.'

Emily was reminded she still had something to be thankful for. She had Peter. But Peter's fluting treble often made demands on her she couldn't meet. Charlie's demands on her energy and her time were more strident. He wouldn't let her evade them. She felt she was failing in her duties as a mother as she'd failed in everything else.

She felt tired when she got out of her bed in the morning, tired all day and somehow blunted. She said as little as possible to customers as she served them. She was working hard physically for long hours and feeling less than half-alive.

She felt she was being overwhelmed, her mind paralysed with misery and loss. She was beginning to think it helped not to feel emotion of any sort. She had no energy left to worry about Giles. No energy even to think of Alex. He was out of her reach. She had lost everything, even hope. Nothing mattered any more.

Alex came with Ted again on Saturday nights to eat fish and chips at the living-room table. Emily didn't know how to treat him. Their old childhood ease was gone. Too much had happened.

But she knew he was trying to help her. She saw him as offering a hand to her from the top of her mineshaft, but always his hand was just out of her reach. Half of her wanted to be left alone.

'Snap out of it, Emily,' he said. 'You're turning in on yourself.'

When Ted and Charlie began reminiscing about the

Great War, Alex talked about what had happened in Wythenshaw's office during the week. She didn't want him to lift her back to normality. It was less hurtful to feel blunted.

She couldn't believe now she'd been such a romantic fool as to marry Giles Wythenshaw. Not when she'd known from the start exactly how Giles would react when things didn't go his way.

'Come to the pictures with me,' Alex suggested one night. 'You need to get out.'

'What about Peter?' Emily shook her head.

'Put him to bed first. Charlie and Ted are here.'

She knew Ted would find it difficult to get up to the attic, and Peter would have to cry a long time before Charlie would bother.

'There's still Giles. It would set tongues wagging.' It was an excuse really, she didn't want to be bothered.

'Emily, we have to do something.' She heard desperation in his voice.

The following Saturday, as they were eating supper, Alex said: 'Emily, how about coming across to the Bird for a drink with me afterwards?' She continued to eat, half embarrassed at being asked in front of Charlie. He held strong views on the duties of a wife.

'You'll listen for Peter, won't you, Dad? Send Charlie up if he cries?' Alex asked, his dark eyes never leaving her face.

'She only drinks champagne,' Charlie said vindictively. Emily was the only one who had not had beer. 'And her gran wouldn't like it. Not Emily going to the Bird.'

That made her push the curtains of apathy aside. She'd let Charlie exert the same influence over her he had as a child. He was deliberately treating her as if she was fourteen now, he wanted her completely at his beck and call.

'Thank you, Alex, I'd like to. Just for an hour, Ted, if you'd listen out.'

Alex came to help her wash up in the scullery before going. Already she was regretting it. 'I'm Giles Wythenshaw's wife. Everybody will talk,' she said. 'Seeing us together.'

'Don't let's worry about Giles.' There was an awkwardness in his manner. 'He's gone now, Emily. Come to our place if you'd rather. Mum's gone to the pictures. I want to talk to you, on our own.'

He made up the fire when they got there, put the kettle on to make a cup of tea. Emily sat down on the sofa. He came, hovering with his back to the blaze.

'If I made an appointment for you, would you see a solicitor?'

She shied away, startled. 'What for?'

'About a divorce.' His dark eyes were scorching into hers.

'A divorce?' The word was alien, it stuck on her tongue. She didn't know anybody who was divorced, apart from film stars. And she'd never had any dealings with a solicitor. It would be too difficult, too much to think about. She couldn't. 'It's a big step. Giles wouldn't want it. Neither would Jeremy.'

'I would,' Alex said. 'You'd be free.'

She shivered, trying to think. 'What would it cost?'

'I don't know,' he admitted. He came and sat beside her, put his arm round her shoulders.

'A great deal, I expect,' she sighed, edging away from him. She couldn't face it. Not yet, she hadn't the energy.

'I could find out. Giles should help support his son, you know, that's the law.'

'What does the law know about it? Giles can't support himself.'

'Emily, why are you locking me out? Why can't I reach you? What have I done?'

Emily sighed. Misery had deadened her. Even Alex's gentleness no longer warmed her. The plant had shown her the truth. It hadn't been mere fancy.

'It's dead,' she said, looking up at him.

'What is?' His eyes were dark with shock. 'Your love?'

'Your plant, the violet. All withered and dead.'

'It doesn't matter, it's very old anyway.'

'It does.' She tried to explain. The plant was dead and the love they'd felt for each other was dead too.

'I'll get you another.'

Emily shook her head. 'Another wouldn't do. It was your love token, a very special plant, and I let it die.'

'You can still make me burst into flames.' He smiled at her. 'If you'll let me, I'll show you the plant doesn't matter.'

She was beginning to feel the tenderness he was projecting. She could see it in his eyes, in the way he watched every movement she made.

'Emily, you've got to let me help you.' He took both her hands between his, she felt his strength and warmth begin to flow into her.

'You seem locked away in sadness. As though you've lost hope. It's like trying to waken a sleeping beauty.'

Emily smiled at that. 'I feel anything but beautiful.' She knew her hair needed cutting and washing, she'd grown careless of her appearance. 'I'm a mess.'

'Not to me,' he said. 'To me you're always beautiful.'

He was letting butterfly kisses flutter down on her face and running gentle fingers up her back. It touched a chord, made her lift her face to his and put her lips against his cheek.

'That's more like it, Emily, love. The first response you've made for weeks.' She stared up into his dark eyes, surprised. 'The first response you've made to anything.'

She felt the touch of his lips on hers then, growing more positive. Was aware of the masculine scent of shaving soap. He was running his fingers through her hair. The tenderness she'd felt him holding back spilled over.

'I frightened you once with my hunger, my wild savage passion. I wasn't gentle enough.'

She felt the first pulsing of desire and knew she was alive.

His touch grew firmer, more demanding. Soon she felt the blood begin to course in her veins again, he was bringing her back to life.

'You've always been mine, Emily. Nobody else will do.' He was taking off her knitted jumper. The touch of his fingers on her bare skin was electrifying.

Emily felt not only alive but a wildness, a lifting of joy she'd never felt with Giles. His caresses were sending hot tremors running through her. She knew now she'd been tied with invisible strings to Alex all her life. He hadn't been able to let go of her any more than she had of him.

He made love to her on the sofa, just as he had when she was fifteen. It brought her exquisite pleasure, took her to heights she hadn't achieved since. Alex had finesse. Alex cared. His love for her showed.

If it was wrong when she was fifteen, it was a greater sin now, but she didn't stop him. It warmed and comforted her, but underlined how hopeless her life had become.

'It's too late for us,' she told him.

'I'm not giving up now, Emily.'

The next day he brought her another terracotta pot with violets in it.

A week later, towards the end of the lunch time rush, Emily was making up an order for four builders working in a house round the corner. As she slid the newspaper parcels on to the counter she met Sylveen's smiling eyes as she came into the shop, with a little girl swinging on each hand.

Emily smoothed her hair, she no longer bothered to cover it while she was in the shop. What was the point, she was going nowhere else? She wished she'd put on a clean overall this morning, she knew she looked a drudge.

'I've been to your flat. It was empty.' Sylveen looked like a fashion plate, in a Prince of Wales check suit. Neatly groomed golden hair showed round a smart grey hat. 'It's such a long time since I heard anything from you. I don't want to lose touch, Emily.'

Her children in blue alpaca coats reminded Emily of the two little princesses she'd just seen in a photograph in one of the newspapers she'd used to wrap chips.

'How they've grown.' She went round the counter and swept Nadine up in her arms. She saw the child wrinkle her pretty nose.

'You do smell funny, Auntie Emily,' she laughed. Emily recoiled in horror. Guilt made her kiss the upturned face. She found no revulsion in her baby smile, but her words cut deep. It seemed she'd chained herself to Charlie and this grinding existence for the rest of her life.

Sylveen was pulling out chairs at one of the tables. Lifting Natalie on to one.

'We'll all have fish, chips and peas,' she said. 'And cups of tea.'

'She thinks she's come slumming,' Charlie said out of the corner of his mouth as Emily produced plates.

'I'll have my dinner with them,' Emily told him. 'You can manage now the rush is over.' Sylveen was like a visitor from another world. Suddenly Emily was desperate to hear news of it.

'Where's Peter?' Emily's hands covered her face, she couldn't believe she'd forgotten him. She ran up to the attic, brought him down, sat him on her knee. Sylveen was pushing two tables together, even for four the space was cramped. Emily slid Peter on to the chair opposite, got another plate and slid some of the food from her plate on to his.

Now he was facing her, she was ashamed to see his hands were filthy with dust. She leapt to her feet, whisking him to the scullery to sponge his hands and face. When she came back to the table she could see streaks of dirt on his pale cheeks, and his jersey was stiff with morning porridge. He looked pale and plain in comparison with the pretty girls. Nobody would believe he was related to them now. Emily wanted to cry, she was failing Peter too.

'This won't do.' She found Sylveen's shocked gaze studying her. 'I'm taking you home with me. As soon as you've finished eating, we'll go upstairs and pack your things. I want you to stay for good.'

Emily dropped her head in her hands. She couldn't go, knowing she'd ruin things for Sylveen. Sylveen hadn't thought things through.

'Oh no you don't.' Charlie had come to the end of the counter. 'I need Emily here. I can't manage the shop without her.'

'Can't you get somebody else?' Sylveen asked.

'I don't want anybody else. Emily said she wanted the job. I'm paying her, so she's got to stay and do it.'

'Is that right, Emily? He's paying you? You want the job?'

'Yes.' She couldn't meet Sylveen's probing eyes. Why couldn't Sylveen see she'd lose Jeremy's love if she was there, always between them? How could she be so blind?

'Yes, that was the bargain.' She rested her head against the wall behind her, as she saw for the first time exactly what she'd done. As a child Charlie had dominated her, worked her, drained her. She'd fought to free herself once, and now she had put herself back in the same position again.

'Come for a rest, then. Just a week, you're tired out.'

'We're all tired out.' Charlie's face glistened with sweat and grease. 'I can't just close up shop, we've got a business to run. You're not taking her away to soft soap her.'

'She doesn't look well, Mr Barr. Peter doesn't look well.'

'Emily's staying. I paid off her debts, I give her a wage. I've put a roof over her and her kid for months. Fed them both, the least I can expect in return is a hand in the shop.' He smoothed down his iron-grey thatch.

'A holiday.' Sylveen stood up. 'Just a break, can't you see she's nearly out on her feet?'

'Get out of here,' Charlie said, his voice rising. 'Before I put you out. The likes of us can't afford to go swanning off on holidays when we feel like it. Go on, be off with you before I call the police.'

Emily saw Sylveen's blue eyes fill with horror. 'Come any time you can, Emily. You know you'll be welcome.'

She gathered a daughter with each hand and went towards the door Charlie was holding open. His beer gut bulged against an apron splashed with fat.

'She's not going anywhere, and don't you come down here again like Lady Muck on a slumming trip. You'll not be welcome.'

Sylveen paused at the door, her lips in a straight line.

'Emily, you've got to tell Jeremy. He'd be horrified to see you and Peter like this.'

Charlie slammed the door in her face. Above the jangling of the bell, Sylveen heard him rave: 'Take no bloody notice of her. None of her bloody business. You know which way your bread's buttered, don't you?'

Emily felt her treadmill never stopped. She had only enough energy to keep putting one foot in front of the other. Another three Saturdays had passed since Alex had taken her home. He'd wanted her to do it again, but she had refused.

She had always known that there were times when Peter could bring her back from the numbed state. She had learned that Alex could do it too, but it could lead to nothing but trouble, and anyway she hadn't the energy. She lived for Sunday, the wonderful day when the shop didn't open and she had time to play with Peter.

Not that she had the whole day free; this Sunday morning, she had had clothes to wash, and the house to clean, otherwise there was no comfort for any of them. For dinner, she made stew and dumplings followed by rice pudding.

Charlie ate more than his share. 'Nursery food,' he complained, before falling asleep in his armchair.

Emily didn't feel like walking, but Peter needed fresh air. She tried to take him out every afternoon for twenty minutes or so, but Sunday was the only time they could get away from the shop for several hours. She sponged his face and buttoned him into his coat before going out through the yard to get his pushchair from the shed.

Once outside, Emily began to feel better, especially as Peter decided to push his pram rather than sit in it. This way, he would be tired out by the time she got him home. He'd go out like a light once she put him to bed and she'd have an hour for herself to wash her hair. She kept a finger on the handle of the pushchair to guide it, enjoying the way the brisk breeze tossed and tore at her hair.

'Emily, wait for me.' She turned, surprised to see Alex running after her. 'Can I come with you?'

'We're only going for a walk along the prom,' she said wearily. He fell in step beside her.

The Mersey tide was almost full. The breeze was whipping the waves into white horses as they raced in to crash against the red sandstone wall of the promenade. It was a popular place to walk on sunny weekends; today the grey clouds were scudding up river, the sun weak and fitful. One man and his dog followed a quarter of a mile behind. The waves sucked and thundered as they broke beneath them, sending spray twenty feet into the air.

'A wonderfully boisterous day.' Alex gave her a lop-sided grin as she guided Peter away from the spray and the wet edge of the promenade. 'Blow the cobwebs away.'

'Got plenty of those,' she admitted, quickening her pace, watching the seagulls wheel overhead, taking great lungfuls of air that smelled of ozone and seaweed.

'I know. That's what I wanted to talk to you about.' He was tense and frowning, his dark eyes stared straight ahead. He stepped out briskly, too briskly for Peter.

'Not just a spur of the moment urge to come walking, then?'

'No, I was watching for you from my bedroom window. I knew you'd take Peter out.' He put his hand on the pram handle, hustling it along.

'What then?' she had to ask.

'I'm saving up for your divorce. Costs more than I thought.'

Emily kept walking, her eye on the horizon. She couldn't begin to think about a divorce.

'You can't go on like this. You ought to get away from Charlie. He's a hard taskmaster, and you're letting him turn you into a drudge. It's no life for you, or the child.'

Emily felt herself curling up inside. As if she didn't know that.

'It's easier said than done,' she said sharply. 'You don't understand how difficult it is to earn a living and look after a child at the same time.'

'I think I do,' he said quietly.

She turned on him angrily. 'Of course I don't like having Peter there. It's not from choice. I know it isn't ideal.' It was none of his business, she didn't want him to interfere.

'I have a suggestion . . .'

'I haven't the energy now. It takes me all my time to keep going. Perhaps when Peter goes to school.'

A huge wave roared in to crash over the promenade, spraying into the gardens behind. The houses in Rock Park backed on to the promenade. They would have been soaked if Alex hadn't rushed them forward.

'Don't you want to hear me out, Emily?' he asked evenly.

She felt mutinous. Her answer would have been no, but she couldn't bring herself to be rude to Alex. She knew he was trying to be kind, but what could he do?

'If I were to rent a place, would you come and live with me?' The soft squeak from the pram wheel stopped abruptly as Emily brought up short.

'Live with you?' His eyes met hers, she saw love and concern there.

'I've seen a little house in Tyburn Street,' he went on quickly. 'Two up, two down. It wouldn't take much to fix up. I could afford the rent and we'd still have enough to live.'

Emily felt an emotional surge. It was a life line! Her first instinct was to grab at the chance. It would be blissful to live with Alex.

'You can't go on like this, you're driving yourself into the ground. You aren't looking after yourself or Peter properly.'

Emily felt the heat rushing through her body. She felt overcome that he cared enough about her. Then she was fighting the urge to throw her arms round his neck and put her head on his shoulder. Hadn't she always loved Alex?

Suddenly she was shivering. She knew it was impossible.

'How do you think it would look to Jeremy and his friends? Mrs Giles Wythenshaw throws over one son to live with the other?'

'We won't tell him.'

'Somebody will! Tyburn Street's close to the factory. His employees live all round there. We couldn't hide it.'

'Then we won't try.'

'I'd be frightened for you, Alex. He'll throw you out too. Give you the sack. Anyway, what would you get out of it?'

'You.'

Emily felt the tears start to her eyes. She walked on, so he couldn't see. He'd be thinking she was always in tears. 'I'm Giles's wife.'

'I'm not likely to forget it.'

'Neither will anybody else. Think of the scandal.'

'Think of yourself and Peter.'

'I'd like to.' She was blinking furiously. 'Don't think I'm not grateful, Alex. It's just that I'm frightened for you.'

They'd covered another hundred yards before Alex said quietly, 'You know, there's never been anyone else as far as I'm concerned.'

Emily swallowed hard. All those years ago, she'd been torn apart with jealousy, quite convinced there was.

'What about Cathy Tarrant?' There was suspicion in her voice now.

'No, she never thought of me as more than a friend. We had a mutual need once, but Cathy's happier, got a new boyfriend now.'

'Yes, Reg Bartlett.'

'I needed her when you took up with Giles. Say you'll do it, Emily. What have you got to lose?'

She marched on, quickening her pace.

'Nothing. I have nothing to lose, but you have. You work for Jeremy. He's hoping for a knighthood, the last thing he'll want is a family scandal. He'll throw you out.'

'No, I'm his son, he admits it to me.'

'That makes it twice the story. Twice the scandal. He threw me and Giles out. Why should he treat you differently?'

'I don't think he'd do anything to harm us.'

'I know how his mind works, Alex. He's already thrown me out once.'

'We'd make out, if he did.' Alex's mouth straightened to a stubborn line.

'You'd put your career on the line for me?' There was

wonder in her voice. 'It used to be important to you.'

'It still is.' His voice thickened with emotion. 'But you are more so. I've missed you, Emily. I hated to see you turn to Giles. Hate to see you in trouble now.'

They had come to the end of the Esplanade and into the gap, a small sheltered beach of golden sand running down to the river.

'We haven't been here for years.' Alex's smile was wan. 'Remember the old days?'

Emily gazed out across the Mersey. Once there had been regular ferries to Dingle and the Pier Head, from New Ferry as well as Rock Ferry. She could just remember New Ferry Pier, damaged in the twenties when a steamer ran into the end of it. It had been a decaying landmark for years, gradually being broken up by the tides. Ferry travel had been in decline and eventually the whole had been demolished. Only the ticket office remained now.

Most of the sand was wet but the tide had turned. Alex picked up the pushchair and found a place up against the wall where they were out of the breeze and the spray. Peter began digging with the red tin bucket and wooden spade Emily had brought along.

'You've had time to think, Emily. Shall we do it?'

'No.' Her voice was agonised. 'We can't.'

Alex kept his face turned away from her. 'You still love him, then?'

'No. I never loved him the way I loved you. And Giles soon found out he'd made a mistake. It was a terrible mistake, a fiasco.'

'What happened to us, Emily?' Alex sighed. 'I thought I had our future all organised. It hurt like hell to see you marry him. I could have told you he'd be no good to you. No good to anybody.'

Emily didn't answer for a long time. He had told her that, but she hadn't listened. It was too cold a day to sit still. She no longer knew what she thought about anything. 'I must have been blind.'

'I love you,' he said.

'If only you'd said that when Giles was . . .'

'You knew, Emily,' he insisted, his face agonised.

'I should have known,' she said sadly.

'Let's look at the house in Tyburn Street on the way home.'

'It's too late, Alex.'

'Not for that.'

'It's too late because it could all rebound on your head. Jeremy won't have your interests at heart if we ruin his plans.' Peter came and snuggled against her, his hands red with cold.

'We'd better go home,' she said. 'The sun's gone.'

It was Alex who decided Peter must walk to warm himself up before getting into his pushchair. It was Alex who decided they would walk home through the Dell instead of along the prom. It would be more sheltered away from the river, and Emily would see Tyburn Street.

'Don't decide against it right off. I want you to think it through carefully. It could work, you know. The neighbours needn't know we aren't married. They needn't know Peter isn't mine. We'll look at the place and you think about it. You'd be better off with me.

'After that I'm taking you home. Mum and Dad have gone round to Aunt Edna's for tea, so there'll be nobody there. We'll have something to eat and talk it over. All right?'

There was nothing Emily wanted more than to put off the decision. She felt too exhausted to think straight.

After Churton House and Beechwood, Tyburn Street was no great temptation. It was a terrace of red-brick bay-windowed houses; there was a To Rent sign hanging outside number sixteen. She looked through the front window into a small sitting-room. She imagined a fire burning in the Victorian tiled grate. Peter in his pyjamas ready for bed. Sharing it with Alex seemed a very daring thing to do. She wanted it. She wanted it very badly.

She wouldn't let herself think of Charlie as they went back to the Parade. He'd expect her home to get his tea. As always, Olympia's place was much more comfortable.

Alex poked the fire and made it up. Spread a white cloth on top of the green chenille. She helped him set out dishes, telling herself this was what Sundays would be like if she went to live with him.

Peter ate a ham sandwich and some cake and nodded off in an armchair in front of the fire. She knew Alex would make love to her again on the sofa.

'I can't let you risk it,' she whispered when, full of love, Alex tried to persuade her again. 'You'll not get the chance of another job like that at Wythenshaw's. Ordinary jobs are hard enough to come by.' Hadn't she seen Giles try?

'It would end your problems,' he said, kissing her nose. 'We'd be happy.'

'End the problems I have now. Possibly give us a whole new set,' she said, shivering. 'No, Alex. I'd love to, I love you for suggesting it, but no.'

She couldn't let Alex risk losing what he had. He didn't understand how empty everything seemed when things went badly wrong. He didn't realise how hard it was to get another job.

CHAPTER TWENTY-FIVE

Jeremy stretched his legs under the desk. The figures were dancing before his eyes, he couldn't think properly and welcomed an excuse to break off. He was finding it harder to get down and do a good day's work. He might as well have stayed at home today for all he'd achieved. The knock he was expecting came. He looked up as Alex Fraser came into his office.

'Afternoon, sir.' Over the last year he'd been pushing more and more responsibility on to the boy. He was turning out surprisingly well, with the capacity for hard work of the young and hungry. In a way, Jeremy felt compensated for his disappointment about Giles and was grateful to have someone to share his workload. Alexander was in and out of his office fairly frequently now, but he kept the relationship strictly formal and confined to business.

Today Fraser had asked to see him on a personal matter and he was wondering what it might be. Perhaps he was going to ask for a rise in salary; Jeremy decided if he was, he'd agree, he was worth more. He was soberly dressed in a grey suit with a suspicion of shine to the seat and the elbows, white shirt and neat tie.

'Have a seat.' The boy held himself well, his dark red hair was neatly trimmed. He'd inherited his mother's build, taller and broader than the Wythenshaws. Impossible not to be reminded of Olympia every time he set eyes on him. But he did not have Giles's magnetic good looks that made all eyes turn when he came into a room.

'What did you want to discuss?' Today his dark eyes were anxious, that was unusual. Jeremy often saw some of Olympia's tranquillity.

'Emily.' Alex was perching uneasily on the edge of his chair. He had the air of one who has something to get off his chest and is not at all sure of the reception it would get. He was making Jeremy feel uneasy.

'You probably think it's none of my business,' he went on. 'Emily thinks it's none of my business, but I can't bear to see her struggling like this.' Jeremy straightened in his chair, wondering why he'd never stopped to think about Emily.

'Giles can be difficult to live with.' He knew Giles had been getting money, he'd heard from both Arthur and Harriet that he'd been round to sponge on them, telling them the baby needed medicine and food.

'It's not that. Emily went back to the chip shop to look after her grandmother when she was ill, but her gran died and now she's stuck with Charlie.' He was gathering confidence.

'Her father's got some sort of hold over her. Except of course, he isn't . . .'

'I understand the relationship,' Jeremy said.

'Well, he makes her work in the shop to earn her keep. He's a bit tight fisted, gives nothing away. While the shop is open and Emily's serving, Peter has to be shut away in the bedroom at the top of the building. It isn't safe to have him playing about under all that boiling fat, but it isn't good for him to be so much on his own either. And Emily's working herself to a standstill. It's too much for her, she works in the shop, keeps house and tries to look after her child.'

Jeremy could feel himself trembling. In the outer office,

he heard Miss Lewis start pounding her typewriter. He had to ask: 'Couldn't Giles give a hand in the shop from time to time? Or take the child out for a walk?'

'Emily left him – when she went home.'

Jeremy felt suddenly cold. 'Left him for good, you mean?'

'Yes.'

'Where is he?'

He saw Fraser shrug. 'Emily's heard nothing, but as far as she knows, he's still living in the same place. Nobody's seen him recently.'

'Since how long?'

'About six months, I suppose.' Jeremy swallowed hard. Giles must already have been on his own when he'd called to see Harriet.

'Emily needs help. I've tried, but she won't accept anything from me.'

'Money, you mean?'

'No.' The lad was flushing. No mistaking the scarlet tide sweeping up his face. 'If you must know, I offered to rent a place for her. She wouldn't take it.'

Jeremy couldn't stop staring at him. He made himself lean back and think. Was Alexander telling him he'd asked Emily to live with him? He couldn't ask him to clarify that. 'Thank you for telling me,' he managed.

'Emily said Sylveen had asked her to live with her, but she hasn't gone. I think she's past making any effort for herself. She won't listen to anyone.' The silence hung between them, heavy with expectation. 'Please help her,' he urged.

'I'll see to it.' He was brusque with the boy and he wanted him gone. He couldn't let anyone see him like this. He felt vulnerable, an old man, too wrapped up in his own problems to think of anyone else. Sorry for himself, that's what he'd been.

With the office to himself Jeremy began to pace up and

down. He was shaking, it had come as a shock to find people in the office talking about Giles. Telling him the whereabouts of Peter and Emily, things he didn't know. He should have made it his business to know.

He'd been quite taken with Emily, he remembered her elfin smile and eager ways, and Peter was his grandchild. He'd missed them when they'd gone. He knew what Giles was like better than anybody, yet he'd left Emily to cope with the child as well as Giles. She'd had no means of support.

He'd said he would see to it, so he might as well go now. Jeremy looked at his watch, four o'clock, he was restless now, good for nothing else here today. This had shaken him, he had to see Emily. Do something for her, but what? Offer her money? He should have done that before now.

He ordered Miss Lewis to bring in any letters she had ready for signing before he went. Couldn't even read them through with any concentration. Once in the car, he ordered Higgins to take him to Paradise Parade. As he pulled up at the kerb, Jeremy could see the chip shop door was closed; a large sign behind the glass said it would reopen at five.

He sat in his car, undecided about what to do next. Olympia's shop had a bit of style to it, but the chip shop was the shabbiest in the row. As he watched, a child walked slowly past his car, holding on to his mother's hand; it was only when they went to the chip shop door and the woman took out a key, that he realised who they were.

'Hello, Emily,' he called, getting out of his car. Peter had grown much taller but he was thinner. His girlish coat was too small for him. It had been washed instead of dry cleaned and was dirty again, shabby, unwholesome even. He couldn't believe he'd let this happen to them. They looked unkempt.

'Jeremy? Hello.' He'd never seen such a change in anyone as he now saw in Emily. There was a numbness about her white face, she looked a decade older than when he'd last seen her. No longer girlish, she looked down at heel, exhausted, even downright ill. He felt himself recoil with horror that he'd done this to her.

'I want you to come back to Churton with me,' he told her. She stood staring up at him, as though she didn't understand. Alexander had not been exaggerating. 'Is there anything you want to bring?'

'I can't, not now. The shop . . .'

'I want to take you away from the shop.'

'It opens at five. Charlie needs help.'

'Emily, you need help. You can't go on like this. Look at Peter.' The child stared back at him with wide blue eyes, as though understanding why he was here. Emily seemed in a daze.

'Here, let me have him.' He took the boy clumsily from her. He wasn't used to children any more and he was wary of spoiling his new vicuna coat. 'You, go and put your things together and I'll have a word with your father.'

He was inside, the smell of stale chips closed round him like a fog. The floor in the dark lobby behind the shop was slippery with grease.

'Off you go.' He pushed Emily up the dingy stairs. The child went too, he couldn't part him from his mother. 'Get his favourite toys and something to wear tonight.' He watched her stumbling blindly up, aghast. He had never realised she'd lived like this! A chip shop she'd said, but he couldn't remember ever being in a chip shop before, certainly never behind it like this.

The door to the living-room was ajar, he pushed it further. Charlie Barr was stretched out in an old armchair before a dying fire. His red-checked shirt was unbuttoned to mid chest, showing an expanse of pale oily flesh. With his beer gut hanging over his belt, his mouth sagging open and eyes closed, he seemed like a fat slug.

'Mr Barr,' Jeremy said loudly. 'Mr Barr.' His grease-splattered carpet slippers were moving, his mouth closed and eyes opened to stare at him blankly. Then suddenly he straightened in his chair.

'Mr Barr,' Jeremy announced. 'I've come to take Emily and Peter back to Churton.'

It took a moment for the message to sink in, then Charlie was blustering: 'You can't do that. Emily's got to stay here to help in the shop.'

'Emily's just about out on her feet. She needs a rest.'

Charlie stood up, his face turning turkey red. 'Aye, this isn't the army now. You can't come bursting in here taking my staff away at a moment's notice. Anyway, she's my daughter, she's staying here.'

'She's my daughter-in-law. Peter is my grandchild. They're coming with me.'

'You're not doing that. I've got to open the shop in an hour. I've got to have Emily here, I'm paying her to help.'

Jeremy felt for his wallet and threw some pound notes on the table that hadn't been cleared after the last meal. 'Get yourself another helper, she's coming with me,' he said.

Charlie went immediately to pocket the money; it didn't stop him complaining: 'How can I find somebody else? I've only got an hour. It's not right, you coming here like this.'

Jeremy saw Emily in the lobby with a small case in her hand, the boy clinging to her skirts.

'Don't go, Emily,' Charlie said. 'You know I need you.'

'Get in my car,' Jeremy instructed.

'If you go, you needn't come back. Next time he throws you out, I won't take you in.' Jeremy winced at that as he turned to follow her.

'Give me my key,' Charlie shouted. 'Don't you dare take that.' Emily was feeling in her pocket. Silently she placed his key on the shop counter.

'You needn't think you're ever coming back here. I won't have you,' Charlie was raving behind them. 'You keep turning up like a bad penny, but I won't have you back again.'

Jeremy shut the shop door on him. His knees felt weak as he crossed the pavement. He felt he was being seen off, especially as Charlie snatched the door open again and stood snarling on the step watching till Higgins pulled away.

'I'm sorry.' Emily's face was deathly pale. Her brown eyes stared mutely at him from the far corner of the back seat; she was hugging the child on her knee. He felt what he'd said to Charlie was a wall between them, too awful to talk about, but he had to if they were to get back on their old terms.

'That was dreadful,' he managed at last. 'Didn't handle it very well . . . I had to insist . . . that you come with me.' He sighed, feeling drained, he could no longer take the hurly burly that life threw at him.

'Thank you,' Emily whispered. There were dark rings under her eyes. He was glad of the glass panel between them and Higgins, impossible not to be aware the car was filled with the smell of stale cooking.

'You haven't heard from Giles?' He had to ask, though he didn't know why he should feel guilty about Giles, he'd done his best with him.

'Is this your car?' A small hand was tugging at his sleeve.

'Yes.' Tears had washed paler channels down Peter's cheeks, there was a grimy smudge where his small fist had wiped them away. Even so he could see the family likeness, his pale hair waved round his head as Giles's did.

'Who are you?'

'This is your grandfather, Peter.' Emily roused herself and took a handkerchief from her own pocket to rub at the grime on his cheek. 'I'm afraid he's forgotten you.' She meant it as an apology, but she saw Jeremy's mouth tighten and knew he was blaming himself for their separation.

'Grandpa's at home,' Peter said. 'In the shop.' Emily was drawn into an explanation.

'Who is that driving?' The piping treble came again.

'His name is Higgins,' Jeremy said.

'Why do you let him? Don't you like driving?'

'Not all the time.'

'I would. Can I learn?'

'When you're old enough.'

'I'm four.'

'Old enough for school,' Jeremy said. 'Has he started yet?'

'September, he's down for Ionic Street.' That had been another worry. The school she'd attended in Mersey Road had closed. Ionic Street was a long way for him to come home at dinner time, when she'd be busy in the shop.

'We'll find a kindergarten,' Jeremy said. She was taking in the changes in him. It was two and a half years since he'd banished them from Churton, and he'd faded from middle to old age in that time. Then vitality had crackled out of him, now he was looking frail. He'd still been able to get his own way with Charlie though, and he still looked distinguished.

Emily pulled herself together, made herself sit upright to watch the kaleidoscope of refreshingly different sights. She felt she'd been shut away for a long time.

She thought she could remember Churton House, but its fresh sparkle surprised her. The newness of the paint, the manicured grounds, everything about Churton was neat, clean and ordered and had an impact far stronger than she remembered.

Jeremy led the way up to her old suite; she followed with Peter carrying her own case. It seemed too small and shabby a thing to hand over to Higgins.

'You can have a room elsewhere, if you wish.' Jeremy was diffident, probably thinking it would remind her too painfully of Giles. Emily felt she'd been hardened against fads of that sort.

'No, it's like coming home.'

'Nothing's prepared, I'm afraid.' The bed was not made up, there were dust covers over the upholstery. 'Mrs Eglin can see to it while we have tea. It might be warm enough in the garden this afternoon.'

Emily felt she'd shaken off her shackles as she sat on the terrace eating cucumber sandwiches and victoria sponge from the trolley. Peter was clinging to her skirt, looking round him with saucer eyes, not eating. She'd hoped for some miracle to get them away from Charlie, but she'd not expected it.

With her second cup of tea, another thought came to her. She must have been fazed not to find it strange. She turned to Jeremy: 'What made you come to Paradise Parade?'

'Alexander Fraser told me you needed help.'

'Alex?' She felt her heart jerk. 'So it was Alex?'

'He gave me the prod I needed,' Jeremy told her miserably. 'Not the man I was, Emily, can't think for myself any more.'

'That makes two of us.'

'A rest, that's what you need, fresh air and good food. A few weeks here will put you on your feet.'

'And you? What will put you on your feet again?'

'Having you and Peter back. I've been an old fool, Emily.' She looked at him, concerned, afraid it might take more than that.

When she went back to her suite, her bed had been made up with freshly ironed linen sheets scented with lavender. A cot bed had been brought in for Peter and was placed near hers.

She wandered from room to room; it had all been dusted and hoovered since she'd arrived. There were vases of flowers and bowls of fruit. Her suite was as she'd remembered it. Its perfection blotted out the horrors of New Street and the dark living-room behind the shop. Emily took a deep breath, she felt better already.

She bathed Peter and put on his pyjamas. Strange she'd never noticed the trouser legs came only to mid-calf. Perhaps tomorrow she would get him some new ones. She ran a bath for herself in the pretty bathroom, scenting the water with handfuls of crystals. She washed her hair, soaked for half an hour, feeling she was washing the old life away.

She felt squeaky clean herself but she hadn't clothes equal to eating with Jeremy. 'A quiet supper,' he'd said. 'Just the two of us.' But though she'd brought her three favourite dresses, here in the suite they all showed signs of the wear they had had over the last years.

She took out a dinner dress. Really rather too grand for a quiet supper, her evening dresses had survived in better shape because she hadn't had occasion to wear them. Until, that is, she'd discovered the girls in New Street were only too glad to give her a few shillings for them. Her full-length dance and party dresses went like hot cakes, the girls and their mothers exclaiming over the quality of the material, but she had never found a buyer for her dinner dress.

It was of such a dark red as to be almost black, plain with a high neckline and long sleeves. She put it on now and her years in exile were no more than a bad dream. She turned from the mirror in a flurry of fine pleating. Her dress felt wonderful, all clinging flattery.

Peter was fast asleep but she asked for Betty to sit with him in case he should wake up and find her gone. He might be frightened in a strange place.

Jeremy was in the library with a glass of whisky beside him. He got to his feet. 'A glass of wine, Emily?' She was hesitating. 'Sherry, then?'

'No, I'd like to try wine again.'

She saw his lips straighten, and knew what she'd said had stabbed home. She rushed on: 'It was the cost I resented. Giles couldn't stop spending and we needed the money for food.' Too late, she realised she'd elaborated on the wrong theme. Her wine was slopping over the glass his hand was shaking so much.

'Don't worry about me, Emily,' he said awkwardly, slumping down in his chair. 'I'm upset at what I did to you, when you always tried to please me. I was fond of you, yet I didn't stop to think. Forgive me if you can.'

She got up to kiss his forehead. 'You thought of me as belonging with Giles. You thought I'd take his side in everything.'

'Yes.'

'You only did what I expected. What anybody would expect under the circumstances. Nothing to forgive, Jeremy, but I'm glad I'm back.'

'We've all made a lot of mistakes,' he said. 'Tomorrow I'll see my solicitor, I'm going to set up a trust fund for you and Peter. I want to give you the security of knowing you'll never be without money again.'

'You're very kind.'

'I've been thoughtless about you till now. I mean to remedy that. The income will be sufficient to make you independent. It will all come to you till Peter is twenty-five, then it will be split between you.'

'That's more than fair, I don't know what to say.'

'There's nothing to say, Emily. Except I'm glad to have you back. It's been lonely, very lonely.'

They sat in silence for some minutes. Then she asked: 'Do you see anything of Sylveen?'

'About once a month. She brings the children to see me.'

'Do you mind if I ask her here?'

He was such a long time replying that she thought he would refuse.

'No,' he said at last. 'I can't shut you up here by yourself, can I?'

'I'm so used to working, Jeremy, I think I'll need to do something. Perhaps the office . . .'

'Not yet. I want you to take it easy, have a good rest. Spend more time with Peter. You both need new clothes, that should give you something to think about. I bought a Rover last year, sold the old Alvis. Stanley is still with me. He'll drive you to the shops.'

He got up to help himself to more whisky. 'Drink up, let me refill your glass. You haven't told me anything yet. I know you've had a bad time; if you could bear to talk about it, I'd like to know.'

Already Emily could feel the wine loosening her tongue. She began telling him about New Street.

Sylveen was fond of her garden. This spring, she had set herself the task of reorganising the small patch in front of her cottage. It was divided in two by a path and steps of York stone going from the gate to the front door. Each side had a tiny square of grass surrounded by flower beds. She wanted to make it less formal, more a cottage garden. It looked too suburban.

She had dug out the grass on one side and meant to make a rockery near the steps, planting more flowers, to give colour in the summer months. She encouraged Natalie to dig with her beach bucket and spade, it all helped to loosen the soil. She was busy putting in primulas that Jean, her next-door neighbour, had given her.

Sylveen enjoyed the physical work of gardening, it kept her busy in the fresh air when it was too cold to sit about. The years were passing, Nadine had started at the village school. She quite enjoyed taking her there and collecting her again, it gave point to the day.

Other mothers chatted to her as they waited together. Nadine had been invited to three birthday parties, Sylveen felt they had a growing circle of friends. She wore a wedding ring now, telling her new friends she was a widow if they should ask about a husband. It seemed the simplest explanation. She was happier.

Sylveen looked at her watch, she just had time to plant up a patch of the geraniums. She was pressing the soil round the roots and imagining how her garden would look when they were in flower, when she heard the gate latch click. Giles Wythenshaw was coming up her path.

'Mummy!' Natalie was tugging at her skirt. 'Who is this?'

'Hello, Sylveen,' he said, and his hot tawny eyes were searching into hers.

'What do you want?' Slowly, she stood up, shaking with a sudden attack of nerves.

'Just come to see how you are. For old times' sake.'

'Who is this, Mummy?' Natalie asked more urgently.

'Hasn't Nadine grown?'

Sylveen straightened up, shocked. He didn't even know his own daughters! 'This is Natalie. I'm afraid I can't stop and chat, I have to collect Nadine from school now.' She picked Natalie up bodily and rushed to her front door. When she tried to close it, it bounced off his foot.

'Let me in, Sylveen.'

'You are in,' she retorted, rushing upstairs to the bathroom. Fear was stabbing through her. The water was splashing noisily into the wash bowl as she pushed her child's hands into it.

'I don't like him, Mummy.' She stopped the words with the face flannel and then the towel, she couldn't bear to hear them. The water was brown with soil as she washed herself. When she went down, he was sitting at the dining-room table.

'I came to ask you out for a meal.' He turned to look at her. She found him changed, the gloss had gone. Once she'd thought him handsome.

'No thank you.' Her manner was brusque. She'd been lonely, had her doubts about many things, but she'd never doubted she'd done the right thing when she'd told Giles to get out.

'I'll walk down to the school with you.'

'I'd rather you didn't.'

'Who is this?' Natalie demanded. 'I don't like him.'

'Just somebody I used to know.'

'Send him away, Mummy.'

'You see, you're just causing trouble. Please go when I ask you.' She'd thought she was back on an even keel, but now she realised how fine the line was. Giles was making her feel on edge.

'Soon,' he said. She couldn't look at him. She hustled Natalie out of the door, and he came too. She locked it and set off at a spanking pace.

'I'm not letting you into the house again,' she said, looking straight ahead, almost dragging Natalie off her feet.

'If you don't, I'll explain the set-up to my father.' His voice was low, full of menace.

'What?' That brought her to a stop. She could feel terror pulsing out of her.

'He's still enjoying fatherhood, isn't he? You're still enjoying his generous allowance?'

She set off again, almost at a run. She should stand her ground. The words came to her lips: Tell Jeremy what you like. She should shout them, dare him to do his worst. If she didn't, he'd be able to make her do anything. Even come back and live with her, and she mustn't let him see how frightened she was. She could feel herself quaking.

The children were already streaming through the school gate. She was only just in time, but it meant she didn't have to speak to the other mothers, or introduce him.

Several said hello. She did her best to appear normal as she grabbed Nadine's hand and set off home again. He was still behind her as she went up the path to her front door. 'Please, Giles,' she implored.

'I'm not going to make any trouble.' He pushed his way inside. 'I'm not going to hurt you. Not unless . . .'

'What do you want, then?' She went to the kitchen to get the children their tea. It was what she always did at this time of day.

'A bit of company. Come out for a meal at the Vic for old times' sake.'

'I can't, I'd need a babysitter.'

'Can't you get one?'

'No, I haven't needed a babysitter for years. I can't just leave them with anybody.' Sylveen felt a growing desperation.

'Then you could ask me to have supper here. It's what we used to do in the old days. We had some good times, Sylvie, didn't we?'

'They've gone.' She shivered, feeling she was in the cleft of a stick. She wanted him gone, but he was threatening to tell Jeremy.

The only sensible thing was to tell Jeremy herself before he did. She quailed at the thought, she'd worked herself up to do it on more than one Saturday when she'd taken the children to see him. She'd never been able to get the words out. She didn't want him to know. She had hoped to repair the rift between them.

She was also afraid that if he did find out, he'd cut her off without money as he had Giles and Emily. It lay heavily on her conscience but she'd been putting off doing anything until both children were in school. If the worst came to the worst then, she could try and get a job. 'How's Emily?'

'She's left me. Walked out and left me in that dump in New Street.'

'Good for her,' Sylveen snapped. 'So there's nobody to look after you?'

'Just a meal, Sylvie. What's the harm?' She thought he looked abject.

'All right, if you promise to go afterwards.' What else could she say?

'Yes, all right.'

'It'll have to be omelette and salad.'

'That's fine. I'll help you bath the children first.'

Sylveen felt her insides clamp into a tight ball of foreboding. The children were her protection, she dreaded putting them to bed, and having nothing between her and Giles. The way his eyes kept seeking hers frightened her.

She had whisky in the house for Jeremy, and two or three bottles of wine. Purposely, she offered him nothing, afraid alcohol would make him harder to cope with, but Giles had been a frequent visitor. He knew where she kept everything. When she came down from tucking up the girls, a bottle of red wine had been opened to breathe on the kitchen table, and he had a stiff whisky near his hand.

She got out the salad vegetables and took them to the sink to wash. He came behind her, his arms pulling her close against him, fondling her breasts.

'Get off.' She jerked away. 'You promised, Giles! A meal only.'

'A meal but other things first. You always used to. You were the best, Sylveen, we really had something wonderful, you and me. I thought you loved me.'

'I did. Dear God, I must have been blind!'

'You've got another boyfriend?'

'No, I haven't. I've given all that up.'

'You shouldn't have, you're more beautiful than ever.' He was coming towards her again, his arms wide to hold her.

Sylveen backed away. 'What if I refuse?'

He was smiling. 'You know the answer, there's something I can tell my father.'

She shook her head, agonised. 'If you loved me you wouldn't be blackmailing me.'

'Blackmail? I wouldn't do that! You were my father's mistress, but you loved me more than you did him. God, you had passion. Come on, Sylvie, you know you want to. Let's go up to your bed.'

Sylveen stared at him, feeling the heat rush through her body. 'Yes, I loved you, fool that I was.' She erupted in sudden fury: 'Don't come an inch nearer. We're not starting that again. It took me a long time to see what you're really like. Perfectly beautiful on the outside, but inside?' She came closer to him, screwing up her face in distaste. 'You're psychologically flawed. Temperamentally twisted, nuts, whatever you want to call it.'

'Don't be silly.' He was laughing but his face had paled with shock.

Sylveen straightened up. She should have had the guts to stand up to him sooner. Didn't she know his aura of self-confidence was fake? That at the first sign of trouble he was frightened and tried to push all responsibility for it on to someone else? He couldn't stand up to opposition, problems were never of his making.

'I don't think you love me. You're in love with yourself, always have been. Never see anybody's needs but your own.' She knew it was getting home, he was recognising the truth in what she said.

'You had every possible advantage, do you know that, Giles? You didn't have to achieve anything, it was handed to you on a plate. I bet from birth, everybody loved and fussed you.' He was staring back at her in silence.

'Yes, you're a very handsome fellow. Your mother told you that?' He had a wonderful body, broad shoulders and slim hips; his face had lost its golden tan and showed signs of strain; his chin was still arrogantly high; but he'd lost his pleasing waves and his healthy sparkle. He was getting older.

'I bet she spoiled you. I bet love and possessions were heaped on you, everything you wanted, and a lot more you hadn't even thought of. Once you had the world by its tail.

'Now you have no friends. You're at odds with your father and with me. Emily has left you. You have no idea how to nurture a relationship, you've never had to.'

She took another deep shuddering breath and went on: 'You're like Peter Pan, you've never grown up and you don't want to.'

Sylveen was conscious of silence, broken only by the ticking of her clock; he looked dazed.

'Now get out of my house and never come back. Go to your father and tell him exactly what you want to. You've no proof, it's your word against mine.' She was gasping for breath. 'Grow up, Giles, that's all everybody wants. Stand on your own feet for a change.'

He went without another word, slamming the front door behind him, so that the glass rattled. Sylveen slid into a chair, propping her head in her hands over the kitchen table.

Oh God, she'd done it now. She'd survived an emotional upheaval, but her insides were still churning. She mopped at her tears with a kitchen towel, knowing what she'd done guaranteed Jeremy would hear how she'd let him down and taken him for all the money she could. She felt ashamed at letting Emily down too, and she didn't want to hurt either of them.

Twice she'd fallen in love with a wastrel. Her mother had been right when she said she was making a mess of her life. She was frightened to think of what would happen next.

CHAPTER TWENTY-SIX

Giles felt despondent as he walked up to Bedford Road to get a newspaper and some cigarettes. It was further than going down to the Parade, but he no longer felt comfortable in the shops there. Everybody knew he was a Wythenshaw, everybody knew he was Emily's husband and that she'd walked out on him. They stared at him. Their expressions told him he'd come down in the world, and they thought it his own fault.

He no longer felt comfortable in the rooms in New Street either, the place was a complete tip and he couldn't afford to have it cleaned. He went out more so it was handy to call in the newsagent's in Bedford Road as he walked up for the train.

It was a damp humid morning without sun; its greyness matched his mood. Emily had rejected him; that was painful enough but he was coming to terms with it. When he thought of Sylveen turning against him too, he was filled with despair. Every word she'd said had cut him to the quick.

When he'd gone to see her yesterday, he'd been so sure she'd help him. Damn it, he needed her, and now things had cooled down with Emily, there was no reason why he couldn't move in with her. It was even an advantage that Father knew, no need to hide the fact. No need to get out of the way because he was coming. Sylveen had ended up with a pleasant home and a comfortable income and he'd thought that now at last they could enjoy it. They were already a family, what could be better?

He'd half expected her to jump at the chance. At the very least he thought he could persuade her. Until he'd seen that steely glint in her eyes. She didn't want him!

Sylveen could still set him on fire. As soon as he'd seen her with a smudge of soil on her nose, he'd known it could be just the same again. They'd had a little tiff but that was ages ago, he'd never believed it need part them for ever. With Sylveen he'd felt wrapped in love, lifted to new planes of excitement. She'd been fun, everything he'd ever done had been to give her pleasure.

If she'd just let him make love once, he'd have changed her mind, even now he was certain of that, but she wouldn't let him. She'd grown hard, but he still couldn't believe she'd turned against him. Not Sylveen!

He'd tossed half the night in his uncomfortable bed, with the sheets knotting round him, and every time he'd closed his eyes, Sylveen had been there smiling at him, taunting him with her fragile beauty. He ached when he thought of her. She'd put in the knife while he was down. He'd cried in bed last night.

He hated her, hated them all for what they were doing to him, but he'd get his own back. He would be killing two birds with one stone when he told his father. He couldn't understand why he hadn't done it already, it was the obvious way to get back at him. Easier than worrying about what had happened in Paris all those years ago.

He'd go to Churton this evening. Let Father have it, and take Sylveen down a peg too. See how they liked it when he kicked back.

He paused outside the newsagent's and read the notices in the window. 'Wyncliffe Street, Rock Ferry. Clean lodgings for working man, breakfast and evening meal included.' He asked the woman serving him where

Wyncliffe Street was and she pointed further up the road. 'Just after the station.'

'Couldn't be better,' he told her. She took the card out of the window and told him the number at which he should apply. He didn't feel like making the effort really, but it was what he'd wanted. He decided he might as well call round there now, since he was so near.

The houses were terraced and much smaller than those in New Street, but dated from the same period. Mrs Hood was in scraggy middle age, with grey hair drawn tightly away from a stern face. 'I keep a clean house,' she told him, before he was over the doorstep. 'You could eat your meals off my floors.' Giles felt her sharp black eyes raking him.

'It's a single room,' she said as she puffed up the stairs ahead of him. 'I have two other lodgers, they share the back bedroom.' It was a slit of a room over the hall, with just enough space for the single iron bedstead, a tallboy with a mirror and a chair. He felt a stab of disappointment, he'd expected more space, more comfort.

'There's a wardrobe on the landing.' She opened the door to show him. 'You can hang your best clothes in here.'

He didn't care much for Mrs Hood, her manner was that of a strict schoolmistress, but the room smelled of fresh distemper and the lino shone. The window was open, he looked out on a tiny patch of garden, all neat and orderly, a privet hedge, a bit of lawn and some flowers.

'Thank you,' he said, turning down the bed. Clean sheets, clean blankets and a reasonable eiderdown. Mrs Hood sniffed with disapproval as she led him off to see the bathroom, cold and old fashioned, but clean and tidy.

He followed her down to the kitchen where she turned down the gas under a big pan bubbling on the stove. The scent of stew was drifting appetisingly all over the house. It wasn't grand – decent working class, her advertisement had said, and it was that, a vast improvement on what he had. A little more expensive but he'd be getting two meals a day. He threw off some of his depression.

'Always a cooked breakfast. Always porridge, and eggs, bacon or sausage, something like that.'

'I'll take it,' he told her.

'What's your work?'

'Well, I haven't got a job at the moment.'

Her interest faded visibly. 'Working man, is what I want. Out all day. Can't do with anyone under my feet when I'm working.'

'I'm out most of the time,' he said quickly. 'Looking for work. Shop work.'

She looked doubtful. 'What about paying if you haven't a job?'

'I can pay.' He took out his wallet. 'Two weeks in advance. Then you'll not have to worry.' It wouldn't leave him much of Carteret Mathews's money, but he had to get out of those awful rooms.

'Always a week in advance, mind,' she said. 'That's my rule.'

'Right, I'll bring my things round this afternoon.'

'Tea's at half-five.'

'Tea?'

'Evening meal.'

'Oh!'

'Shop work starts at nine, I suppose?' He nodded.

'My other lodgers work on the railway. Start at eight, breakfast's at half-seven. It would be more convenient if you came down the same time.'

'Half-seven?' He was having second thoughts.

'If you're not on time for meals I can't keep them hot. That's the understanding.'

Meal times were not what Giles would have chosen. 'I'll have my breakfast in bed,' he said, it seemed the logical answer.

She looked astounded. 'I can't be running up and down stairs for you. If you want breakfast you'll have to come down for it. That's my rule.'

'Yes, of course,' he said hastily, swallowing his pride. The woman had no idea how to provide a service. She was looking at the money he'd given her almost as though she intended giving it back. He mustn't lose his temper, though he could feel himself bristling. It was worth moving just for a clean room. He had to get away from New Street.

He had brought round what he wanted of his possessions and was trying to stow them in his room, when the stew was served. It seemed the square front room was used by the lodgers. The back room was for family.

The two middle-aged railway employees were a bit rough, and because he'd had no lunch, he found the helping of stew rather meagre, the rice pudding that followed watery. He didn't like the oilcloth on the table or the thick white plates, but at least he didn't have to think about washing up.

Afterwards he took the train to West Kirby, determined to see his father; he was in exactly the right mood to let fly at him. He needed to put Father in his place. Make up for all the insults he had had to swallow because of him.

He had to take a taxi from the station because Churton was too far to walk and he knew nothing about bus timetables. As he came up the drive the house looked bigger than he remembered; the grey clouds had gone, it was bathed in evening sunshine. An atmosphere of wealth emanated from the pink brick house and the immaculate grounds. He'd never noticed it when he'd lived here. Now he could weep at the difference between Churton and his present quarters.

The taxi came to a halt in the paved courtyard, formed by two wings jutting forward from the main block. He paid it off and climbed the front steps, going straight in and up the hall to his father's library. He'd expected to find him sitting in the green velvet armchair with a glass of Laphroaig beside him. The chair was empty, and the fire hadn't been lit.

Giles could feel his frustration boiling up, nothing was going his way. He heard a step on the stairs behind him and went back to the hall thinking at first his mind was playing tricks on him.

Emily was on her way down, gripping the banister looking as though she'd seen a ghost. But it was not Emily the drudge, this was an Emily he hadn't seen for two years. Her hair looked as though she'd come straight from the hairdresser's, an elegant pale silk dress swirled above high-heeled shoes.

'What are you doing here?' She recovered first.

'It's my home.' She was giving him the guilty feeling of being caught doing something he shouldn't.

'It hasn't been for some time.' Her brown pixie eyes were flashing with apprehension.

'What about you? You're here.'

'Your father invited me to return. Me and Peter.'

He was filled with a virulent indignation. 'He let you come back? I don't believe it!'

'It's true,' she shrugged.

'Why didn't you say? I'd have come back with you.'

She looked at him long enough to make him feel uneasy. 'I don't think Jeremy wishes you to return.'

'Of course he does. If you're back, he'll expect me too.'

'No, Giles. I've told him we're separated.'

'What did you do that for? If you're here, there's no reason why I shouldn't be. Churton is much better than where I am now.'

It wasn't easy to accept that nobody wanted him any more. Another wave of hate washed over him, he was on the outside looking in. They meant him to stay where he was. 'Where is Father?'

'In Paris. What did you come for? Jeremy said he hadn't seen you for two years.'

'I came to tell him something about Sylveen. I'm sure he'll be interested.'

'What?'

'Never you mind. Have you seen her?'

'She came for lunch today.' Giles exploded with livid wrath. It seemed the last straw. He couldn't believe it, they were all back together. Emily, who could live on the smell of an oily rag, was living like a lady. He'd been pushed out in the cold. Left by himself.

'It's not fair. Wait till I see Father.' Resentment was thickening his voice. 'What time did you say he'd be in?'

'Not tonight.' She was looking at him as though he was out of his mind. 'He's in Paris, won't be back till Thursday.' When he turned back to the library, she added, 'Where are you going?'

He sensed a change in Emily, a new animosity. He didn't believe his father was in Paris. She was like Miss Lewis at the office, trying to protect him from unwanted visitors. He could be out at a dinner and be expected home late.

She stood in the library doorway watching him. He'd soon find out. He moved the hinged picture of the golden helmet and sword from the wall to see Father's key box. He kept his keys hanging in a glass case, all clearly marked – factory, shop, Paris house – rows of them.

Giles collapsed in disappointment. He had gone to Paris after all; Father had duplicate sets of keys for the Paris house and one was missing. This was always how he checked if his father really was away.

Sore and smarting he turned on Emily. 'How long have you been here?'

'Only a week. Please go, Giles, I'll tell Jeremy you want to see him when he comes back on Thursday.'

A wonderful idea had come to him. 'Perhaps I'll go to

Paris and see him there. That would be rather fun, wouldn't it?' He could find out once and for all what Father was hiding in the house. Yes, an excellent idea.

Father was paranoid about keeping the family away from that house. If Giles were suddenly to appear, it would give him a nasty shock. Oh yes, it was a wonderful idea.

Giles reached up slowly, but the case was locked. He picked up a silver candlestick and broke the glass with one blow. Then, slowly, he unhooked the duplicate set of keys and slid them into his pocket.

'Giles!' He saw Emily's pink tongue moisten her lips, he was having the same effect on her that he'd had on Sylveen. They were frightened of him.

'Where is my passport?' Emily was shaking her head numbly. He hadn't been abroad for years, he wondered if it was still valid. It would be in his old room, the one he'd used in his bachelor days. He headed for the stairs. 'Get some food for me, I'm hungry.'

'I want you to leave, Giles.'

'Ask Mrs Eglin for some ham or a slice of pork pie, something like that, and a bottle of burgundy.'

'You'll go when you've had that? I'll ask Higgins to drive you home.'

His old bed wasn't made up, the curtains were drawn to stop the sun fading the furniture. There were old books and bags, tennis and squash racquets, a fishing rod.

Aunt Harriet had taken him to Baden-Baden when he left school. That had been a bore. After he'd read about the man who broke the bank at Monte Carlo, he studied roulette and had gone to Deauville determined to do the same. It had been a disaster. He tried to think how long ago that had been.

He pulled open a drawer; it was full of neatly ironed shirts. His, of course, or they had been years ago. More than he owned now and in better condition than most. Just the thing to take with him. He put his hand on his passport almost immediately, it had eight more months to run. He could go.

Now he knew he was on course to deliver a body blow to his father, his wrath had tempered to vindictive hate. He found a bag and started to pack a few clothes, almost everything he'd need was here to hand. He swaggered downstairs to find Father's housekeeper toing and froing to the dining room.

'Everything's ready, Mr Giles.' Her smile was like a snarl, showing the top of her teeth and a large expanse of gum.

He poured himself a glass of wine. 'Emily, do join me.'

'No, no thank you.' He cut himself a good portion of pork pie and sat at the table. This was more like it.

'You don't realise how lucky you are to get back here. I've had a dreadful time on my own, but I'll be all right now.'

'Is there anything else? Coffee?' Emily was flapping nervously about.

'Timetables, trains and boats, find me Father's Baedeker for Paris.'

'I don't know.' But she went off to his library and returned with several booklets and pamphlets. There were several boat trains each day between Victoria and Gare du Nord. It shouldn't be difficult.

'I'll need some money too, quite a lot. But you'll give me that won't you, Emily, if I promise to leave you alone afterwards?'

He was getting organised now; if Emily didn't produce enough money, he'd have to visit Carteret Mathews again; there was a silver tea and coffee service on the sideboard, a silver egg cruet and a butter dish. He could take them, but it would lose him a day.

She came back and flung a bundle of notes up the polished table to him. He counted them carefully, deciding it would be enough. He'd get Higgins to drive him back to Rock Ferry, then he'd get up for his seven-thirty breakfast, walk round to the station and be at Woodside in time to catch a morning train down to Paddington.

Emily was as frightened of him as Sylveen had been. What he wanted most of all was to reduce Father to the same state. He reckoned it was possible now.

Giles enjoyed the journey, it was an experience he wouldn't have missed. He felt he was treated royally, the food and service being excellent. Getting out in the bustle of Gare du Nord and having to contend with French taxis was not so pleasant, but he'd written down the address of his father's house; all he knew was that it was not far from the Bastille.

It was getting dark by this time and he felt tired and less like a confrontation with Father than he had last night at Churton.

Paris seemed alien, the scent of Gauloise cigarettes filled the air, but the worst part was being unable to communicate his needs. He'd learned French at school, but had retained little. Other passengers scurried past but he had no idea which way to turn. He found it hard to believe his father could feel at home here. Yet by his own account he did.

Giles paid off the taxi at the end of the street. All the buildings rose high against the night sky and had windows in the roofs. He wanted his arrival to be a surprise and he needed the cool night air to clear his head. The district seemed incredibly old, not what he'd expected, though he remembered now Father saying the house dated from 1750. Light blazed out of windows, people hurried past him, talking fast in their incomprehensible language.

He found the house. Like those all round, it was built of dun-coloured stone, six storeys high, with tall narrow windows all heavily shuttered; steps led from the pavement to a huge front door. He strolled past it in case his father happened to be looking out into the street.

Everything at Churton sparkled with care and new paint; this house was the shabbiest in the rue Cordemais, nothing had been done to it for decades. Even in the dusk he could see it was in crumbling condition. Not a flicker of light showed anywhere. It came to him with a jolt – there was nobody in the house.

Caution kept him on the opposite side of the street. Perhaps Father had gone out for his dinner? He felt jumpy and couldn't decide what to do next. He got out the keys, picked out the one which must open the front door, but he could not bring himself to cross the street, put it in the lock and go in.

He walked on, into a square where there was a café-bar throwing out light. He went inside, ordered himself a brandy and some coffee. Later, because he saw a workman eating *croque monsieur*, he decided to have one too.

He felt better and decided to go back to the house. If it was as deserted as it appeared, there seemed no reason why he should not sleep there. Father had maintained to Aunt Harriet that he stayed in a hotel when he came and kept no servants at the house. Nobody had believed him, but it seemed to be the truth. Then when Father came, he'd be on hand to meet him as he opened the front door.

The house was still in darkness when he got back, nothing had changed. There were fewer people about now, and the streetlights were on. He waited until there was no one in sight, took a deep breath and marched up to the front door. The key turned easily, the door creaked open. He closed it quietly. Inside, the air smelt stale and musty. His heart was thumping like a steam engine. He'd bowled into Churton without a qualm yesterday; he seemed to have less right here.

Giles struck a match, it was the only means of light he had. The stairs wound upwards, wide and shallow with a wrought-iron balustrade. He went up, crossed the landing to a bedroom at the front. The door opened outwards; inside it was pitch black.

He struck another match. There was a bed with draperies, he was choking in the stale musty air. He tried to open a window, it had not been touched for decades and wouldn't budge. There were two in the room, he went to the other. Knowing he couldn't sleep without air, he pitted his strength against it. It gave at last with a resounding creak and he found a shutter beyond. Good, the open window would not be seen from the street. He opened it as wide as he could, gulping fresh air. He was tired enough to sleep anywhere, which was just as well.

He lay down on the bed and covered himself with his mac, but he could feel damp and cold driving up from the mattress, it was worse than New Street. Mice were scuttling in the skirting boards. He had to roll some of his mac under him before he could get to sleep.

When he woke it was broad daylight, dust motes danced in shafts of sunlight coming through the shutters. The bed was disgusting; the warmth of his body had drawn out the odours of damp and age.

He got up, smoothed down his suit and went to see what was in the other rooms. There was so much dust he felt he must be leaving footprints. There were many damp patches on the walls, cobwebs everywhere, dead flies and spiders. Woodlice and more spiders that were still alive.

This house had belonged to his mother's family. He couldn't understand why Father had let it all decay. Nothing seemed newer than the turn of the century. Certainly it all dated from before the Great War.

He crept round the silent house. There were gas brackets on the walls, but the mantles had long since shattered. He tried a gas tap and found it had been turned off. No electricity had ever been installed and no water came from the old-fashioned taps. Giles stood aghast, wondering why his father kept a house in an unusable state, doing nothing to maintain it. It didn't make sense.

He closed the windows, pushed his bag out of sight under the bed and shook out the wrinkles he'd made in the cover. Then he buttoned himself into his mac and returned to the café he'd been to last night. He managed to get *petit déjeuner* and to rinse his face and hands in their washroom.

He would go back and search the place, he decided. Find out as soon as he could what significance it had. Today was Wednesday; Father was here somewhere in this city, doing something. He'd surely come to the house at some time. He'd lie in wait for him. If he didn't come today, he wouldn't come. Not if he was to be home on Thursday. Then, Giles decided, he'd go to a hotel and stay as long as his money held out.

He found the steps going down to the cellar and knew Father came here more frequently than upstairs. There were clear footprints on the floor, as though he'd come when it had been raining. The cellar door was locked; in addition it was secured with a huge padlock.

He tried the keys on his bunch one by one. He knew he had a complete set and eventually he got in. There were other doors, all locked. He found wooden crates, some open, some empty. He found half-empty boxes containing a few candlesticks, clocks, ornaments and silverware. There was a small safe bolted to the floor. He even had the key to that; there were a few oddments of jewellery on the shelf inside, mostly it contained documents.

He straightened up, stiff with disappointment. This was the sort of stuff he'd sold at Calthorpe's when he'd worked there. The shop had specialised in continental *objets d'art*. Giles had always known Father came here to buy stock for the shop. There was no secret, the house was just a store. Nothing more or less.

He laughed to himself now, that he'd imagined Father keeping a woman here! Definitely wrong about that.

He felt let down, rather flat. The only good thing was he could stuff his bag full of goods for Carteret Mathews before he went home. Father would find out sooner or later his store was not as safe as he imagined it to be.

Giles went upstairs to the bedroom again and stood looking down at the street. The house depressed him, he could swear nobody had stood in this room for twenty years.

He couldn't be bothered waiting to surprise Father. He found a large bag, filled it with what seemed the lightest most valuable pieces he could find. He took a leather case containing pearls, but he didn't know whether they were real or not. He took silverware, a small clock and an ornament or two.

No point in hanging about, he could see Father at Churton when he wanted to. Carefully, he locked the place up behind him and walked down to the café in the square, carrying both bags. There he asked them to call a taxi. While he waited he had a glass of red wine and enquired about hotels. He decided he deserved a decent lunch, then he'd see something of Paris.

He spent four very enjoyable days before his money was running out. It didn't worry him, he had return tickets all the way back to Birkenhead. It was only when he reached Calais and joined the other passengers heading towards Customs and Immigration control, that he gave any thought to customs clearance. He could feel waves of panic washing over him; what should he say if they opened his bag? Fortunately customs clearance seemed a mere formality on leaving France.

He sat up on deck, with a stiff breeze blowing during the crossing, and tried to think. He'd heard Father talk of applying for licences to import stock for his shop, or was it to export the stuff from France? Giles had no idea what was required. He knew Father did it legally, that he had documents to cover goods he brought in, and he had not.

In the men's lavatory, he opened his bag and removed the case containing the pearl necklace, slipping it into his jacket pocket. Then he tucked some of his dirty laundry over what remained in the bag.

He thought it safer to carry his own bags, and since many seemed to be waiting for porters to carry theirs, he arrived in the customs shed to find several customs officials waiting to deal with him. He'd meant to go through when the crush was at its height, but he'd misjudged that. He swallowed hard and slid his two bags on to the stand in front of the youngest officer he could see.

'Anything to declare?'

'Yes,' he said, bringing out the leather case from his pocket and opening it for inspection. 'Just this one thing.'

He thought he knew from his years at Calthorpe's what pearls would sell for. He'd already converted that to francs. He opened his wallet and searched his pockets endlessly for a sales receipt he couldn't produce. He kept on talking, telling the man his fiancée was a blonde and how soon they meant to marry.

He was cross-examined as to where he'd bought them, but he knew the names of the firms Father dealt with. He said it was a present for his fiancée. The pearls were taken away to an office. It was all taking a long time, luggage kept being wheeled in, the shed was growing busier. He could feel sweat breaking out on his forehead.

The man returned, and told him duty must be paid on the pearls. Giles argued about the amount, grumbling and fussing, though he had enough to pay. Eventually he did. His bags were not opened.

As he walked to the train he told himself he was a very clever fellow. He'd had a drinking acquaintance years ago who'd told him he'd come through customs on such a ruse. Richards, was that his name? No, Pritchard. Anyway, it had worked for him too.

He couldn't wait to see what Carteret Mathews would give him for this lot. Perhaps he'd get more cash if he leaked it to him a little at a time?

Jeremy knew he'd been going downhill for some time, but suddenly he felt he was falling apart. When he went to the store to pack what he meant to bring back, he couldn't find what he was looking for.

It took him an age to realise some of his stock had gone. He thought at first he was making a mistake, that he was looking in the wrong crate. He got out his records and began checking through everything he had left, but there wasn't much now and he knew it all intimately. It was only then the awful truth sank in, some things had gone. He'd seen them here six weeks ago, when he last came to Paris, and now they were gone.

He was struggling for breath as he examined the locks on the cellar door, went rushing up to the front door to examine that. The locks were as he'd left them. He went round all the windows, there was no sign of forced entry. He went through every other room in the house. Somebody had been in, doors were open that normally he kept closed. There were signs the intruder had rested on one of the beds.

He hardly knew what to think, he only knew he was frightened. Over the last twenty years, this had been his worst nightmare. He couldn't think what to do, he felt totally distraught.

He had sleeping-car accommodation booked on tonight's London train, only a few hours to make up his mind what he should do. He felt sick with worry.

He had to get away from the place, couldn't think with the problem staring him in the face. He locked everything up and left. Out in the sunshine, with life going on around him, he felt more normal.

He walked slowly towards the river, towards Notre

Dame. It was a place he'd always meant to visit again, but never seemed to have time. Time was standing still today. Inside it was cool, the smell of age overlaid with the scent of incense. He sat down feeling insignificant in so vast a place. He let his eyes absorb the beauty of the ceiling soaring above, feeling numb.

For decades Jeremy had encouraged his mind to skeeter away from anything unpleasant; it had been his way of cutting down on worry, protecting his peace of mind. Now it took a huge effort to think through what he should do; he was sweating even in the chill of the ancient building.

Someone had been in his house, and he didn't know who, that was the awful part. It was the unknown he couldn't take. He'd thought he had it all worked out, that his system was foolproof, now he knew it was not.

The obvious thing was to buy three new padlocks for the cellar doors. Those locks he could easily change. He would like to change the front-door lock too, but that meant finding somebody to do it immediately.

His mind made up, he left the cathedral, walking back the way he'd come, looking for a *quincaillerie*. It took him too long to realise he was walking himself to a standstill and that he was in the wrong quarter for such a shop. He found a taxi and asked to be taken to one, kept it waiting outside while he made his transactions. Madame behind the counter told him her husband could change his front-door lock. Jeremy sat in the back of the cab with his eyes closed while the locksmith packed his bag and made ready to come with them.

There was one other obvious precaution; he must take as much of his stock with him as he could. It would be safer in Liverpool after this. Over the last few days he had bought more, from Lefarge & Drogue, as well as a few items from Clochette. All bona fide stock that could stand any amount of investigation. He had to have the cover they provided.

Having got the locksmith to the front door, he seemed reluctant to start work. Jeremy was ridden with anxiety to pack what he could and get the new padlocks on the cellar doors. He had little patience with the torrent of French, though he prided himself on speaking it well. Eventually he was forced to listen, and understood that the man had brought too small a lock for the massive old door, and was suggesting he leave the old lock in, setting the new one above it. Jeremy didn't care as long as the new lock went on.

He felt fraught. The banging from the door was pounding through his head. He surveyed the pieces he had to pack and thought it almost impossible, there wasn't much time. He began cramming as much as he could into the one crate he had prepared. Every visit over the last twenty years he had taken one crateful back with him.

The only way to take what remained was to nail it up in the original boxes, though he had no papers for it. He would have to get it through customs without. He felt very much on edge.

Even so, he'd have to come back once more to put the house on the market. He wanted to be rid of it, he could no longer cope with the pressures. It was too much at his time of life.

Time was running out, the lock was in place and the man paid off. He found the job physically exhausting, the boxes would have to be nailed down and he could no longer lift them. He had to have help.

Jeremy walked up to the square for a taxi to take him to Lefarge & Drogue. He had got to know Emile Lefarge fairly well; after all he'd been coming to Paris for years and bought from him regularly. Lefarge & Drogue always crated up what he bought and delivered them to the Gare du Nord for him. The salerooms were closing for the night. His crate had been loaded into a van and was about to set off.

Jeremy asked for the services of a couple of porters, but they had all gone home for the night. Emile Lefarge offered the services of his sixteen-year-old son Claude, who said he was capable of nailing down crates and loading them into the van with the help of the driver. Jeremy directed them to the house, wondering if he'd done the right thing.

He felt very shaky; this was the first time in twenty years he'd brought anybody here, but he had to have help. The three crates were nailed down and carried out to the van. Jeremy felt exhausted as he was driven through the Paris boulevards, squashed between Claude and the driver on the front seat. But if he got this safely to the shop, there was the great consolation of knowing he'd cleared that house.

One last trip, to put the house on the market. That was all he'd need. To be rid of it and the need to keep coming was his greatest ambition now.

He saw his crates loaded in the guard's van, tipped the boys handsomely and said goodbye. One of the reasons he travelled home by sleeper was that the sleeper carriages were shunted on to the boat and his crates would come straight through to Victoria with him.

There was barely enough time to get through Customs and Immigration. It didn't bother him; he'd done it too often before and knew it was only a formality here, to allow passengers to remain undisturbed through the journey.

He'd always congratulated himself on being able to sleep anywhere, but now he kept waking as the train sped through the night. He was worried that the documents he carried did not tie up with the goods he was importing, that he was hopelessly under-insured. He had always been so careful about such things.

It was a relief to see dawn breaking over the Kent countryside. He got himself up in time for breakfast, as he usually did. He was known on this route, having travelled it regularly for the last twenty years. He put the theft and its consequences out of his mind, determined to behave as he always did. Customs officials boarded the train before he was allowed to leave. He proffered his documents, they were duly stamped and the crates cleared without them being opened. Sometimes they were opened, but not always.

He always brought heavy crates with him. Always organised a brake to meet him at Victoria. He was driven with his crates to Paddington to take the Great Western Railway north to Birkenhead.

Never had he been so glad to see Higgins waiting for him at Woodside. He felt totally drained and exhausted by what had happened. It was Higgins's job now to see the crates into the van and on their way direct to the shop. He was too old for worries like this, he felt ill.

'Mr Giles called round to see you,' Higgins told him almost as soon as he pulled away from the station.

Jeremy leaned back in the luxurious leather and took a deep breath to steady himself. Giles! He had been wondering if Giles was behind his loss. If his duplicate keys were missing from the library, then it would be.

An anxious Emily met him in the hall, but he went past her to the library. Swung the picture of the Golden Helmet back to see the broken glass in his key case. So it was Giles. Should he be relieved or otherwise? He didn't know.

Emily was pouring him a glass of Glenlivet; she came to sit with him with her glass of wine, but he could think of nothing but Giles going to Paris and stealing his stock. He had no contacts there, he must bring what he'd taken back here.

'What made Giles come back after all this time?' Emily asked. 'I wish you'd been here. He wanted to see you.'

Jeremy closed his eyes. Harriet had accused him of

stealing her miniatures, but he'd only half believed her story. He had told her quite strongly it might just as well have been some other caller. But if Giles had taken them, and had now taken his stock, it meant he had some means of disposing of it. He needed to think the whole thing through and he couldn't with Emily here beside him.

'He called on Sylveen too,' Emily said, her brown elfin eyes wide. 'She said she was frightened, that she couldn't get him to leave.'

'He didn't hurt her?'

'No.'

'Or the children?'

'No.'

'What did he want from her?'

Emily was shaking her head. 'I think he wanted a home. He wanted her to put him up.'

'Did he take anything?' Jeremy roused himself. 'Anything of value he could sell?' He told her of the theft from Aunt Harriet, the theft of his stock.

'She didn't mention anything like that.

'Jeremy,' Emily said after a pause; he could see she was trying to find the courage to say something to him. 'I think Sylveen misses you. She has been finding life a bit flat. She's glad I'm back here and we can see each other again.'

'So am I,' he said, rousing himself.

'Can I ask her and the children to lunch on Saturday?'

'It's not her day to come.'

'She wants to forget the monthly visit, Jeremy. She says you're both so stiff and formal. Can't she just come here as my friend? I'd like to see you both relax, as you used to. Enjoy each other's company. Can I invite her?'

'It's my birthday on Saturday.'

'Is it? Then all the more reason. We'll make it a real birthday celebration. Shall I ask Aunt Harriet and Grandfather too?'

'No. Absolutely not.' He sounded an irritable old man,

but he didn't want Harriet drawing conclusions.

'I just thought you might not feel like visitors for lunch again on Sunday, better if . . .'

He understood what Emily was trying to do, she wanted Sylveen introduced into the family circle. She wanted things to be as they once had, but nothing would turn the clock back.

'No, Emily, I'll not have that.'

'Just Sylveen, then?'

He sighed. 'Ask her if you must.'

'I want you to want it too.'

'All right,' he said, but really he could think of nothing but Giles handling his stock in Paris. It was clouding everything for him. 'I think I'll have a hot bath and go to bed, Emily. It's been rather a trying journey.'

'What about dinner?'

'I'll have something light on a tray. What I need is rest.' His new problem was pushing Sylveen to the back of his mind for the moment.

CHAPTER TWENTY-SEVEN

Emily didn't yet feel settled at Churton. The first night back she had slept like a log. Peter had wakened her in the morning and she'd seen to him without dressing herself. It had been bliss to ring for breakfast to be laid out in their own dining-room. Wonderful to be asked what she would like to eat.

Then she had asked Betty to take Peter out for a walk, and gone back to bed to sleep till lunch time. It had taken that routine for three days before she'd felt she'd had her sleep out.

She was enjoying having time to play with Peter. Already he seemed livelier with the greater stimulation. It was marvellous to see the colour coming back in his cheeks with better food and more fresh air. Wonderful to have the money to go out and buy them the clothes they needed. She had discarded almost everything she'd brought with her, wanting no reminders of a very difficult period in her life.

But she wasn't yet at ease here either. It had shaken her to see Giles walking in, made her realise her problems were not all behind her. She was still his wife.

It hadn't occurred to her until Jeremy came back from Paris that he might have problems of his own. That night, it had been obvious Jeremy was a worried man. Jeremy said Giles had stolen from Aunt Harriet and stolen some of his stock in Paris. Emily was shocked.

'Is this what happened before?' she asked, but Jeremy stared at her blankly. 'Is this why we had to leave Churton?' He didn't say either yes or no and his mind had seemed miles away.

She had felt his tension, he'd seemed in a state of dazed frenzy and she couldn't reach him. She wanted to help Jeremy, repay him for his kindness. Having Giles steal from him was bad enough, but Emily had the feeling there was more to it than that. But he wouldn't say any more, so there was nothing she could do to help.

The best she could do was to provide a calm and pleasant home life. His birthday was next Saturday; she decided on a family lunch party to mark the occasion.

When she'd been in New Street, she'd thought of Sylveen's life as one of ease and contentment, but Sylveen too was a nervous wreck. She wanted to help them both. Get them to relax, and, if possible, get them back on more friendly terms.

She had decided it would seem more of a party if they sat down to eat with the children. She had arranged to keep the food simple, poached salmon with new potatoes followed by queen of puddings. Sylveen had insisted on making a birthday cake with candles. The children would love it and Jeremy would enjoy their delight.

It had given her something to do this morning. With Peter following her everywhere, she was getting the conservatory ready for Jeremy's party. There was more space and nothing for the children to damage if they spilled their food or became boisterous. She decorated the white tablecloth with coloured ribbons.

They would play a few games afterwards. Keeping it a big secret from Peter, she wrapped up a sugar mouse in many layers of paper, as a prize for Pass the Parcel. She brought Giles's old gramophone down, wound it up and put a record ready. She drew a donkey on a large card with Peter's new crayons, and his loose tail was ready for them to stick on. She mustn't overdo this, Jeremy was likely to have a short tolerance for nursery games and the object was to entertain him.

Emily had arranged a more sophisticated menu for tonight's dinner, and hoped to persuade Sylveen to stay. She'd had the spare bedroom made up in her suite for her and the girls. Everything was ready; she had sent the car off to fetch Sylveen half an hour ago, she would be here any minute.

Jeremy had insisted on going over to Liverpool to the shop for a few hours though she hadn't wanted him to, but she could see his Rolls coming up the drive. He was back in time as he'd promised.

Peter, bursting with excitement, went rushing to the door. 'Happy Birthday, Grandpa. Happy Birthday.' He was hardly allowed time to remove his coat. 'I've got a present for you.'

Emily thought Jeremy looked white with worry, but he allowed himself to be made much of. She poured him a drink. With Peter on his knee, he unwrapped the box of homemade sweets she had helped Peter make. She kissed his cheek as she offered her own gift, a goblet of antique glass made in Poland. She was no expert on glass and didn't know how Jeremy would rate it, but he seemed pleased.

It was only then, they began to worry about Sylveen. She should have been here long since. Emily went to the phone and dialled her number, but there was no reply.

'She'll be on her way,' Jeremy said, and accepted another glass of wine. But she didn't come. Eventually he sent Higgins with the Rolls to see if the Rover had broken down.

Sylveen knew she was working herself up into a state. Since she'd thrown Giles out and told him to do his worst, she'd hardly slept, expecting every moment that the bombshell would fall.

She hardly dared go to the door when she heard the postman drop something through her letterbox. She was afraid Jeremy might send a formal letter telling her he would no longer pay her allowance, now he knew the children were not his responsibility.

She was even nervous about lifting the phone when it rang. Afraid Jeremy would announce a visit. It rang several times before she forced herself to lift the handset.

'Sylveen?' She recognised Emily's voice and felt relief seeping through her. 'I'm back at Churton. Just Peter and me.'

She was jolted with surprise. 'I'm so glad for you, Emily.' It was a load off her conscience. Living in her suite at Churton, without Giles, Emily was better off now than she'd ever been.

Emily's voice tingled with excitement. 'Jeremy brought us back.'

'How is he?'

'Not all that well. This quarrel with Giles has upset him.'

'But he's all right?' She knew she was sounding too anxious.

'Yes, he said he'd seen you two weeks ago. That he'd been to your cottage and you'd given him dinner.' Sylveen took a deep breath. It seemed Giles had not told him yet. His attitude had not changed.

'Come over and see us,' Emily went on. 'I've missed you, we've a lot to catch up on. Jeremy's told me to use his car. Can I send it for you?'

'Why don't you come here?' she invited quickly. 'I'll lay on lunch, just like old times.' She felt safer in her own cottage, here she wouldn't be mesmerised by the thought of Jeremy walking in on them. Giles could tell him any time.

'Thank you, Jeremy says I must get out and about again.'

She and Emily had always got on very well. As she opened the front door to her, she knew nothing had changed, Emily might have been here eating lunch with her every week. She'd really missed her over the last years and would have been delighted with her invitations to Churton if she were not so frightened of Giles dropping his bombshell.

Again Emily invited her to Churton, and Sylveen couldn't put her off the second time. She felt on a knife edge as the car took her up the drive. It was a relief to find Jeremy had gone to the shop, and she left before he came home.

When Emily told her he'd gone to Paris again, she thought of it as a six-day respite. They went on a shopping spree; Emily said it was quite like old times, except she wanted to see her and Jeremy back on friendly terms. Then yesterday Emily had phoned again.

'Come to lunch on Saturday, it's Jeremy's birthday.' Sylveen had felt the blood drain from her face and was glad Emily couldn't see her. She would not be able to avoid him any longer. 'I've cleared it with him, he wants you to come.'

It all served to make her more nervous. Sooner or later Giles would say his piece, she had no doubt of that. She'd seen revenge on his face as she'd forced him out of her house. Just to think about it brought her out in a cold sweat.

Since Giles didn't appear to have done it yet, she must look upon it as her last chance to tell Jeremy herself. Some birthday present she had for him.

'Bring the children, he loves to see them,' Emily went on. 'I'm planning a celebratory family lunch to mark the occasion.'

Sylveen replaced the phone slowly; she was going to

mark the occasion in her own way. It was not the day she would have chosen, but better by far if he heard it from her.

The days were slipping away quickly and she was growing more jittery by the hour. She decided a small gift from each child would be appropriate. From herself, probably it would be better if she offered nothing. She would make him a birthday cake, ice it and get some candles. The children would love to sing Happy Birthday for him. She could feel dread building up like a wall inside her.

Saturday came before she felt ready to cope. The girls were awake early. She heard their excited voices from the next room and realised they were turning out their toy box looking for a toy to give Jeremy.

She got up, found some thin card and set them crayoning personal birthday cards for him. Sylveen had taken some photographs of the children in the garden, which had turned out well, and she'd had the best enlarged.

After breakfast, she suggested they go up to the shops in Heswall so Nadine could choose a frame for it. She edged Natalie towards a book about birds, telling her Jeremy was interested in them, which he was.

Back home, she helped her daughters wrap their gifts; it seemed a charade, her own thoughts were miles away, trying to decide exactly what she would say to him. She knew she was getting more and more keyed up.

Emily had arranged for Stanley to come over for them at twelve. Sylveen couldn't keep her eyes away from her watch; as the time came closer the ball of dread in her chest expanded.

She got herself ready, washed her children, oversaw their attempts to put on the identical dresses she had bought for them. She'd chosen deep-blue velvet falling from a high yoke, with white lace collars.

She brushed their hair. Natalie's had grown almost to

her waist, a long straight mane of sparkling gold. Usually she plaited it; today it was held back with a velvet Alice band. Nadine's hair was just as golden, but it had a natural wave in it, as Giles's had. Sylveen thought it suited her better short.

Stanley was on the doorstep; she gave the gifts into his keeping. The Rover waited at her gate; she led the way down the path with the same enthusiasm she'd have faced a firing squad.

She wished the day over, as yesterday she wished it would never come. She was going to face Jeremy. Admit she'd fallen in love with Giles, admit he'd fathered both girls, ask for forgiveness. Nothing else was possible if she was to get rid of this time bomb hanging over her. It was the only hope she had of staying on friendly terms with Jeremy.

She sat on the back seat with a child on each side, unable to watch the few miles to Churton being eaten up so rapidly. It was a pretty country road winding through lush farmland, with the River Dee on the left and ahead the estuary and the Irish Sea.

Nadine was glued to one window, but Sylveen couldn't look at anything. She was cradling Natalie against her, drawing what comfort she could from the warmth of her body. Telling herself she'd still have the children whatever Jeremy did.

The violence with which Stanley was braking took her completely by surprise. The brakes were screaming, both her children were screaming, and in the split second before the clash of tearing metal, it seemed second nature to clutch Natalie tighter. Terror paralysed her as the crash threw everything forward, jolting her forehead painfully against the seat in front. She was hanging on to Natalie who was screaming with shock, while the car was flung off the road and turned round to face the way they'd come.

Sylveen didn't know how long it took her to recover, to

realise she wasn't really hurt. To understand that Natalie, despite the noise she was making, had only minor grazes. She was conscious at last of looking for Nadine, and felt the scream tear from her throat when she found she was no longer in the car. One rear door had been torn off its hinges and the crumpled bloody heap of blue velvet and lace out on the grass verge was Nadine. She scrambled out, crying, and tried to lift her.

'No.' A girl she'd never seen before prevented her clutching Nadine to her. Nadine was bleeding and ashen, with blood matting her golden hair. 'No, don't move her. Better not.'

'Is she . . .?' Sylveen gasped, unable to get the awful word off her tongue.

'She's breathing,' the girl said.

Sylveen hugged and cried over Natalie but it was Nadine she was desperate to touch. She dared not look at Stanley, still slumped behind the wheel, grey and sweating, his eyes closed and his head resting back against the seat. A lorry was slewed across the road, another car with the whole wing crumpled beyond. People were walking about.

'The ambulance is coming,' the same girl told her. Sylveen sank down on the grass feeling ice-cold inside, unable to do anything. The waiting seemed interminable.

Then the nightmare of the ride in the ambulance. She was terrified Nadine, whose face was now paper-white, was bleeding to death. Her leg was torn and twisted, the ambulance man was applying a tourniquet to her thigh. Natalie wouldn't stop howling, Sylveen felt distraught.

Moments later the ambulance drew up in front of a building and Nadine, a tiny mound under the red blanket, was wheeled away. Sylveen was left to wait again, her head throbbing, the hospital smell catching her throat. After what seemed hours, a nurse took the howling Natalie from her and another nurse led her into a treatment room to lie on a slippery couch.

'I'm all right,' she told the doctor who came to examine her. He found a large graze on her forearm she hadn't known about, and she waited again in the white-tiled room full of stainless-steel instruments and dressing drums till the nurse cleaned the graze on her forehead and dressed the one on her arm. 'What is happening to Nadine?'

'The doctor is examining her now.' The nurse took her back to the waiting-room and brought her a cup of tea. Sylveen listened to the alien sounds. The soft squelch of rubber soles on wooden floors. The soft voices, the rattle of screens being wheeled. The view through glass doors of two rows of beds each with a white counterpane and a locker. Each occupied by a suffering face.

A stout sister with starched head-dress came with authorisations for her to sign, cards to fill in, wanting to know names and addresses, dates of birth. Sylveen muddled them up, no longer able to think. 'Is she going to be all right?'

'She's lost a lot of blood. Doctor is coming to talk to you about a transfusion. Here he is now.'

'Mrs Smith?'

'Yes,' Sylveen said. 'Nadine, how is she?'

'In a state of shock, I'm afraid. We've set up a dextrose and saline drip, but she'll need blood. I take it you'd be prepared to give blood for her?'

'Of course.'

'We'll have to cross-match. See if you'll suit as a donor.'

'I'm her mother, so I will, won't I?'

'Not necessarily. She may have her father's blood group. We'll have to see.' Sylveen felt her stomach muscles contract painfully. Any mention of Nadine's father was another nightmare.

'Could you telephone her father, ask him to come? Just in case. Your other little girl Natalie is not hurt. A graze on her head, another on her knee. Nothing to worry about. It would be better if her father, or someone she knows, could take her away.'

'Where are we?' Sylveen followed the navy skirts to an office. Took the seat indicated by the desk. Saw the phone being pushed towards her.

'The Cottage Hospital at Hoylake.'

She should have rung Emily before now. She'd be worried. The sound of Emily's voice, concerned and grave, made her dissolve in tears.

'I'll come straight over,' Emily said. Sylveen went back to wait by the hospital screens. She'd had her finger pricked and watched her blood drip into the test tube.

'Has Nadine broken her leg?' she interrupted as the doctor was explaining about cross-matching.

'Yes, she has a compound fracture of her leg, possibly her arm is broken too. We are trying to stabilise her condition first, before we can treat her fractures.'

'But they are bad fractures?'

'She'll need to be X-rayed before we know the full extent of her injuries.' Sylveen felt dreadful. A policeman came and tried to take a statement. She had no idea what had caused the accident.

Then suddenly Emily was there hugging her close, and Jeremy's image was distorted by her tears. It seemed strange to be held against his alpaca coat again. As she saw the doctor's white coat, the stethoscope swinging from his pocket, Sylveen blew her nose and wiped her eyes.

'I'm afraid Nadine is blood group AB negative, the rarest group. And you are Group O positive, Mrs Smith, so you aren't a match.'

Sylveen shivered, she felt like ice again. 'So my blood won't do?'

'Well, as Group O, you are the universal donor. A few years ago, we would have used your blood. Nowadays, we don't like the fact that you are Rhesus positive and Nadine is Rhesus negative. It can lead to problems if Nadine needed another transfusion in the future. We prefer a perfect cross-match. Her father . . .'

'I am her father,' Jeremy said without flinching. Sylveen stared out of the window. He'd never admitted it before to anyone. He said it openly and proudly. 'I would be happy to give blood for Nadine.'

'Thank you, Mr Smith.' Sylveen was swallowing her agony as Jeremy filled in a form, giving his name as Wythenshaw. Another test tube was produced and a needle to prick his finger.

Jeremy was asking about methods. 'Transfusions are much safer now we know about the Rhesus factor. Yes, sodium citrate in the test tube to prevent coagulation.'

Sylveen shut her ears to it, she had to tell him now about Giles. 'Jeremy.' There was a sob in her breathy voice. 'There's something . . .'

'It'll be all right, Sylveen. After a pint or two of blood she'll be all right, you'll see.' Jeremy moved closer to her on the hard seat, felt for her hand.

This might bring them together, she thought. Jeremy was no longer holding himself aloof. He felt bound to her, sharing her distress about Nadine. She tried to work out the chances of Jeremy's blood providing the perfect match. He was Giles's father, after all. Logic seemed to tell her Giles could have got his blood group from his mother, but she couldn't think properly. She began to pray their blood would cross-match. The waiting seemed endless, another cup of tea was brought for her. 'Where is Emily?'

'She took Natalie back to Churton. She'll be better there.'

As she saw the doctor coming down the corridor to speak to them, Sylveen felt a quiver of dread. Sister, her stiff apron rustling with importance, followed one pace in the rear. Jeremy stood up, Sylveen did the same.

'We've grouped both your blood samples, and both of you are Group O Rhesus positive.' Sylveen shivered, he was looking beyond them, through the window.

'Is that unusual?' Jeremy asked.

'No, forty-three per cent of the population are Group O positive. What is unusual is that your daughter's group is AB negative. Neither of you cross-match with her.'

Sylveen felt cold sweat breaking out on her forehead. 'There's also agglutination with the serum. We can't use either of you as donors.' Sylveen felt the waiting-room eddy round her.

'I understood you to say,' Jeremy was frowning with concentration, his face chalk-white, 'one or other of the parents can expect to provide a match?' His voice sounded a long way away.

'Yes,' the doctor said. The long silence was broken only by a starchy rustle from Sister.

'Then I can't be Nadine's father?'

The doctor opened his palms. 'Genetic inheritance makes it impossible.' Jeremy's agonised eyes met hers; the bottom had fallen out of her world; Sylveen knew she was falling.

Emily felt thoroughly shaken up. Seconds ago, she had been concerned with refilling Jeremy's glass and hoping the salmon would not be overcooked because they were waiting for Sylveen. Then she had answered the telephone to find the local police asking for Jeremy. He had seemed immediately distraught, as he jumped up from his chair.

'Yes,' he said. 'I am the owner of the car.' Emily watched the colour drain from his face, and her stomach turned over; she knew there had been an accident.

'Hoylake Cottage Hospital? Are they badly hurt?'

From Jeremy's face, she knew the answer must have been yes. She turned away appalled and saw the Rolls coming back up the drive. A few minutes later Higgins was coming through the green baize door from the kitchen.

Jeremy put the phone down slowly, his anxiety was infectious. Peter was swinging on her skirt, his face crumpling with tears. Higgins was telling them about the wreckage at the side of the road when the phone rang again.

'Emily, something terrible has happened.' Sylveen's shuddering breath transmitted a pall of pent-up feeling. 'Could you come and get Natalie?'

'Of course I'll come. Is she all right?'

'Yes, it's Nadine.' The tears were in her voice now.

'How is she?'

'I don't know,' Sylveen sobbed openly. 'She's badly hurt.'

Emily shivered, gripped by fear. 'We're coming now, Sylveen, right away. We've just heard about the accident.'

Jeremy was already putting on his coat. She swung Peter up into her arms, though he was a heavy weight now, and made for the kitchen.

'Betty will look after you, love,' she crooned. 'Auntie Sylvie needs me, and you need your lunch.'

'You said we'd have a party,' he complained.

'We'll have to have it later.'

Jeremy was already sitting in the back of the car as she grabbed a coat and ran down the front steps with it.

'It's Nadine,' Jeremy said unnecessarily.

'What about Stanley? Is he hurt?'

'Shocked, a few bumps and grazes, nothing much. It wasn't his fault. An oncoming lorry was out of control. It went straight into the Rover.'

It was a short drive to the hospital. Moments later Emily was through the front door, crossing highly polished floors with a smell of disinfectant assaulting her nose. Sylveen was sitting on one of the hard chairs arranged round the walls of the waiting-room, hugging Natalie on her knee. She seemed to have pulled herself together since the phone call.

Emily went to take the child from her, but Natalie buried her smooth blonde head in the crook of Sylveen's arm. Emily sat next to her trying to entice the child away, as Sylveen's shaking voice told of Nadine's compound fractures and her need for blood.

She had Natalie on her own knee when the doctor came in and began talking about blood-matching. To her it hardly made sense, but she sat up straighter when Jeremy said, 'I am her father.' She watched the cotton print curtains fluttering in the draught from an open window, feeling she was intruding on a personal confession.

'I'll take Natalie home,' she said.

The child had sobbed herself to sleep against her shoulder by the time they reached Churton. Higgins carried her upstairs as she led the way to her own bedroom. She hoped Natalie would feel better after a sleep.

In her own small sitting-room, Betty was reading a story to Peter. She had him engrossed, and said she would listen out for Natalie. Emily felt superfluous and very restless. She couldn't settle to anything. She had sent Higgins back to the hospital in case Jeremy should need him. She called a taxi and returned too.

The atmosphere in the waiting-room was totally changed. The doctor was still there but seemed at a loss. Sylveen, grey faced, was recovering from a faint, attended by Sister. Jeremy was distancing himself, sternly aloof at the window.

Emily's heart missed a beat as she imagined the worst. 'Nadine?' she asked, fearful she was dead.

'Her condition is stabilising. We're sending her to the Children's Hospital in Birkenhead,' the doctor said.

'What about the transfusion?' Jeremy asked, tight lipped.

'Today, it's possible to use frozen blood up to two weeks old,' the doctor replied. 'They'll get a match for her there and call in an orthopaedic surgeon to set her leg.'

Emily listened, feeling at a loss. Something terrible had happened to thrust Jeremy and Sylveen apart, something she didn't understand. 'Are you going with her to the Children's Hospital, Sylveen?'

'I think it would be better if you took Mrs Smith home,' Sister said. 'Her child is under sedation.'

Jeremy turned abruptly. 'We'll all go. Nothing we can do here.'

It shocked Emily to see Sister helping Sylveen to her feet. She took her other arm. Jeremy stalked out ahead to the car.

'I'm sorry, Jeremy. I'm sorry.' Sylveen was sitting between them sobbing quietly. 'I'm glad it's out in the open.'

Emily had never seen Jeremy so stiffly severe. He was checking that the glass separating them from Higgins was wound tightly up.

'I'm glad you know. I've been trying to tell you. Trying to make myself do it, but the words wouldn't come.' Sylveen's tear-stained face turned towards him, beseeching. 'I've ached with the worry about what I did.' Jeremy's chalk-white face gave no sign he heard; he was watching the passing countryside.

'I'm glad it's out. I couldn't go on hiding it.' Emily took Sylveen's hand between her own in a gesture of sympathy, but Sylveen's attention was all on Jeremy. 'I know I did a terrible thing.'

Jeremy stirred, his face suddenly flushed. 'Who was it? I loved your children, believed they were mine. I even loved you. Now I find . . . Who fathered them?'

Emily sat holding her breath. It seemed a long time

before Sylveen whispered: 'Giles.'

Emily felt her mouth dropping open, the blood draining from her face. 'Giles?'

Sylveen's voice, low and shaky, went on: 'Giles was looking for revenge . . .'

'On you?' Jeremy asked.

'As well as on you. He threatened to tell you, when I wouldn't do what he wanted. In the end, I dared him to go ahead, I couldn't stand it.' She was sobbing openly. 'But he didn't, did he?'

'No,' Jeremy said.

'I'm sorry.'

'Giles! Why is it always Giles? If it had been anyone else . . . I can't stomach it. His children foisted on me.'

Emily felt she'd been kicked. The car had drawn up at Churton's steps. She had to get out, stumble up them behind Sylveen. How could Giles be Nadine's father? She felt sick.

It made a nonsense of her marriage. She'd believed Giles had loved her, but he could not have done. He must have made Sylveen pregnant at the time he was proposing to her.

Emily felt tears sting her eyes. What a credulous fool she'd been. She'd been duped from the beginning. Their marriage had been a farce, it had never stood a chance.

'Why did he want to marry me?' she demanded. Sylveen and Jeremy were staring at her, aghast. 'I suppose you think I don't have feelings? That I don't matter?'

Jeremy took her arm and pulled her towards the library. 'I know how hurtful it is,' he said. 'Aren't I feeling the same thing?' He sat her down, got her a glass of brandy she didn't want.

'I didn't know,' she said. 'Why didn't you tell me? I must have been blind.'

'Years ago, when I caught Giles in Sylveen's bed,' he said, 'he told me you knew all about it. I thought I was the last to find out.' She felt his arm go round her shoulders, pulling her against him in a gesture of comfort. 'I was wrong?'

'Yes,' she mumbled. 'I'm sorry, I know you're upset too.' She could see that his eyes were wet.

It was all too obvious now: Giles had used her to cover his affair with Sylveen. Her big romance had been a farce. Sylveen was sniffing into her handkerchief on the other end of the sofa. She turned on her. 'How could you do it? How could you let him do that to me?'

Emily felt submerged in a tide of loathing for Sylveen. She saw with dreadful clarity that Giles had deceived her from the beginning. He'd had his own reasons and they had nothing to do with loving her. It was obvious Sylveen had known all along, and that added stabbing hurt.

She'd have trusted Sylveen with her life, their friendship went back years. Yet Sylveen could have warned her at the beginning and had not. Could have told her how things stood between her and Giles. She'd told her everything else.

'I'm sorry,' Sylveen sobbed. 'You must both hate me. Jeremy, can I use your car? I want to go home.' He reached over and touched the bell.

'Yes, you'd better go. Emily and I will be better on our own.'

Emily sighed, trying to pull herself together. 'We'd better see if Natalie is awake. I put her down on my bed.'

'Let Sylveen see to her,' Jeremy said, his hand detaining her. 'She can ask Higgins to take her home.'

She glimpsed Sylveen's face as she went out; she looked totally bereft. Jeremy had turned his back on her. He was poking viciously at a fire that did not need it. The door closed softly behind her.

Emily felt exhausted, tension had crackled like forked lightning between them. She sat on the sofa, nursing her brandy glass, shutting her eyes to Jeremy's ash-white face.

He looked ill. She felt like a piece of flotsam washed up on the shore after a storm.

'I can't believe it.' Jeremy was suddenly raging with fury again. 'I still can't believe Nadine is Giles's daughter!' He had loved her and Natalie, had never for one moment questioned that they might not be his children. Old fool that he was, proud of producing them at his age. Now that he knew they were his grandchildren, he felt a decade older.

He felt betrayed. What Sylveen had done was ten times worse than he'd first supposed. Bad enough to think that a two-year love affair with Sylveen had cooled to let Giles move in, but they had been lovers all along, keeping him in ignorance! He couldn't swallow that. Searing jealousy was knifing him apart. Giles was evil, and Sylveen had loved his money not him. He poured himself an over-generous measure of whisky, went to refill Emily's glass.

'We've eaten nothing since breakfast,' she protested. 'It's going to my head.'

Guilt was fuelling his rage because he'd given no thought to Emily sitting there beside him. If he'd stopped to think, on that dreadful night when he'd found Giles in Sylveen's bed, he'd have known what he'd said about Emily was a pack of lies. He knew Emily had never grasped for his money, yet he'd accepted Giles's story without even asking her.

He hadn't been thinking straight then. And this afternoon he'd raved at Sylveen, making her admit Giles had been her lover for years, with no thought of what it could mean to Emily, finding out she had been betrayed too.

'Are you hungry?' he asked her.

She was shaking her neat brown head. It was gone three o'clock. He rang the bell. 'We'll have tea.'

For his own reasons, he'd manoeuvred her into a hopeless marriage. He'd believed she'd relieve him of the responsibility of coping with Giles, settle him down. But he had believed Giles loved her.

Emily's face had crumpled, she had taken it hard. It didn't surprise him, he knew how hurtful it was to be rejected. And how much worse to know he'd never been loved, that he'd been taken in by a pretence of loving. What could he do to help Emily now? What could anybody do? She was taking it more calmly than he was, though she'd had no prior warning.

It was one thing after another. The settled life he'd built up over two decades was collapsing like a pack of cards. He was another step nearer the brink. He ordered tea in the family dining-room.

Emily went off to find Peter and bring him down; they all ate a nursery tea of boiled eggs and lit the candles on Jeremy's birthday cake. Afterwards she took Peter out with his ball into the grounds and tried to calm her racing thoughts.

Sylveen had not found happiness with Giles either. She was filled with remorse for what she'd done to Jeremy, probably regretted what she'd done to her.

Only Peter seemed normal, their problems did not touch him. He laughed, kicking the ball towards her. She kicked it back, feeling better out in the fresh air. They'd all been living in a web of lies.

They had all made mistakes but she had made the biggest. She had rejected Alex who loved her, to marry Giles who did not.

She thought of Giles, a cheat, a liar, a man without principles. What a gullible fool she was to be taken in by him. When she had known exactly what he was like. A man who pushed his work on to her and then blamed her when she did it wrong.

Hadn't Alex tried to tell her? She'd shrugged that off too, taken in by Giles's good looks, his glamour and his wealth.

She hadn't even realised it was his father's wealth he

was spending. She couldn't blame Sylveen. It was her own fault she was tied to Giles and would have to face a divorce.

She would talk to Alex about it again.

CHAPTER TWENTY-EIGHT

Sitting in the back of his Rolls, being driven up James Street to the shop, Jeremy remembered the old days when he'd come by train and had to walk up here, stepping out like a youngster, swinging his walking stick, priding himself on his robust health.

But the years were totting up. In two years he'd be seventy, he was beginning to feel his age. He'd given up the silver-headed cane when he found he had a tendency to lean on it. He needed to keep up and going.

Too many things were going wrong, he felt he was being swamped with catastrophe. His rule had always been, never think of the awful things in life except to consider the action needed to deal with them, but he could no longer do it.

Jeremy shivered as he thought of Giles. Something had made him go to Paris and steal things he had thought safely hidden. He wished he knew what it was, and what he meant to do next. Giles could finish him. Yet it was his own fault, he had done wrong, and all the more frightening for that.

He'd done all he could, emptied the Paris house immediately and taken the stuff to the shop. He'd put it on sale as soon as possible. Get rid of it. Why hadn't he stayed another day and put the house on the market?

It was a great convenience now to drive to the shop

door, it conserved his energy for working when he got there. The Birkenhead to Liverpool tunnel made the journey much more comfortable. The car crawled in the evening rush hour. Like him the city had lost some of its vitality and he no longer enjoyed going to the shop as he had.

It still looked good: 'J.A. Calthorpe, Established 1729' in gold lettering above the handsome double doors. Customers were going up the marble steps as the car pulled slowly out of the Lord Street traffic to stop round the corner.

Jeremy crossed the pavement to the window. Miss Roberts's elegant thin fingers were dismantling a handsome display of diamond rings, pearl necklaces and cameo brooches to lock them in the safe for the night. It was a good business and would continue to thrive even when it no longer had the thrust of his continental *objets d'art*. Like many things in his life, the business had turned sour on him. He wanted to be rid of it, sell it, but with Arthur still alive, he couldn't.

Inside, the air of opulence closed round him as always; Mr King, his manager, came to greet him, hand outstretched, as he did each time he came. Jeremy was reminded King was due to retire in a few months' time, and he must decide now whether to promote Alma Roberts to the position or advertise for a replacement. Perhaps next time he came, he would have a word with her. He would be safer with her in the job. New staff could be too keen, ask too many questions.

He made for the shallow stairs, luxuriously carpeted, leading up to the floor where the most expensive pieces were displayed. He could never walk through this department without pausing to take pleasure in what he had on offer. French nineteenth-century silver chocolate pots, coffee pots, teapots and ewers ornamented with repossé decoration, gleamed under the shop lights, looking stunning. Miss Roberts looked up from the till where she was cashing up.

'Good evening, sir, the three silver vinaigrettes have sold to a collector. He was asking if you could get more.'

Jeremy remembered them: silver boxes each only an inch long, made to hold tiny sponges soaked in scented vinegars, the vapours of which escaped through ornamental pierced grills. Ladies of Regency times used them to ward off fainting spells. He turned to the shelf on which they had been set out; he still had an impressive display of seventeenth-century pomanders, spice boxes and scent bottles. Small articles sold steadily.

He almost asked Alma Roberts to come up to the office now to talk about promotion. He grunted, impatient with himself, because he had more important things to do. He'd come in the evening when the shop was about to close, so he could be alone. It was a job for which he'd need peace and privacy.

He went behind the far counter and through a door marked: Staff Only. The carpet ended abruptly. Here was stark linoleum and dim lighting. A staff cloakroom opened off the landing, but Jeremy headed up another flight of stairs to the office and storerooms on the top floor. He found himself hanging on to the rope that served as a handrail, deciding he must renew the lino treads grown slippery with age. The narrow steep stairs were difficult enough without that hazard.

He stood at the window to get his breath back. Evening mist shrouded the river and the wet city roofs would have seemed pleasanter without the security bars on the window. Taking off his hat, he ran his fingers through his silvery hair; it felt thinner. He was hanging his coat on the bentwood stand when King came up.

'I hope everything's all right, Mr Wythenshaw?' Jeremy could see his visit, unusual at this time of the day, was raising the other's anxiety.

'Yes, I'll just glance at the books. Lock up, King, and send the staff home.'

'I'd be glad to stay, sir, if you need my help.'

It was the last thing he needed. 'No, no thank you. I'll be quite happy on my own.'

'Shall I ask Miss Roberts to make you a cup of tea before she goes?'

Jeremy hesitated, half tempted, but he'd be better pressing on with the job. 'The crates I brought from Paris, have they been opened?'

'Not yet, you said to keep them . . .'

'Send up Mr Cook with his jemmy or whatever it is he uses.'

Between seven and eight, he'd go out and get a meal, then come back and try and finish. Higgins had driven him here, but he'd dismissed him. The car was round the corner, he could go home when he was ready.

In the meantime he sat at King's desk and looked through the books. He always did when he came. He wanted everything to seem as normal as possible.

Outside, the traffic thinned, the streetlights came on, sending up a yellow glow to the office window. Inside all was quiet.

He had to sort out what he brought. Label each piece so the staff had some idea of what they were selling. He needed to give its use or purpose, the date and place of manufacture, and decide what he could charge. For insurance purposes he had to list any specially valuable items. The shop had to have records, showing the cost at which he had acquired each item, and from where. The clerical work needed was prodigious.

It was work he was used to doing. He still welcomed Arthur's help with pieces he was not absolutely sure about, but he always examined them very closely first. He had never before had such a large quantity to cope with at one time and, looming large as a problem, he'd kept some of these things aside in the Paris cellar for years as being too easily identified, or too valuable.

There was a large collection of miniatures, all of one family, made in the mid-eighteenth century and arranged in a yew portrait cabinet. Many were painted on ivory, most had eighteen-carat gold frames. He had been trying to decide whether to risk offering the collection complete or whether to break it up. It seemed a sacrilege to break it up, but now Giles had stolen four of the miniatures, it was no longer complete.

Jeremy sighed, pushing away a French desk ensemble of polished malachite. He was wasting time admiring the goods.

He worked on until he was very tired as well as hungry. It was getting on for nine when he locked up and went out. He walked up North John Street towards the Exchange Hotel, intending to have a meal there. It hardly seemed far enough to make it worth the bother of getting in his car, but the pavements were wet, and there was drizzle in the air. He was passing a place that served sandwiches, when he decided to go no further.

He spent twenty minutes munching on beef and horse-radish and thinking about a French cut-glass epergne, ormolu mounted with three separate vases and two bowls. Was it a table decoration of the eighteenth century? Or could it be a Victorian copy? He would like Arthur's opinion on that.

Walking back slowly, he decided he would not stay late. He could not afford to make mistakes and he was weary. He would have to come again, perhaps on Sunday because he had more energy during the day.

He was pushing the shop key towards the lock, when a shadow moved, and the weight of a body crushed against him. Suddenly he couldn't breathe, panic was rising in his throat. The key scraped in the lock, the door pushed open; he thought he was about to be burgled. 'It's only me, Father.' There was scorn in Giles's voice. It turned his fear to fury.

'What do you think you're doing?' he blustered. 'Coming here like this.' They were inside, he was blinking in the light. 'What do you want?'

Giles's tawny eyes burned into his. Defying him to look anywhere else. 'A little chat.'

'Why here?' He had to choke that out; he was suddenly certain Giles knew his secret and was about to blow everything wide open. He sensed Giles was thirsting to hurt him in any way he could, and the way must be obvious to him now.

The handsome eyes were looking beyond him round the shop wares, but the very valuable were shut away in the safe for the night. He hadn't seen Giles for over two years; he seemed less concerned with his appearance, his clothes looked tatty. He had always sought confrontation, but there was a new wildness in his manner.

Jeremy felt another spiral of fear fork through him as he remembered why he was in the shop at this hour. 'You went to my house in Paris,' he accused. 'You took some of my things.' The tawny eyes turned on him. He could feel hate projecting at him and knew he returned it all and more.

This was the man who had occupied Sylveen's bed, who had fathered the children he thought of as his. The man who had stolen and lied and married a girl he didn't give a damn about. He might be his son, but he was an enemy too, who might yet do more harm if he wasn't careful.

'Yes, Father,' he agreed. 'We might as well go up to your office and sit down for our little chat.'

'You can say all you have to here,' he told him. But Giles laughed and ran up the stairs with the ease of youth. He had to follow and was panting with rage and exertion by the time he'd pulled himself up the last flight. He pushed past Giles in the doorway to flop into the chair behind the desk. Giles was rattling the shop keys, tossing them from one hand to the other.

'You've no business to go there or take anything. I know what you've got.' He'd taken some nineteenth-century powder boxes, vanity jars and photograph frames, nothing to worry too much about, but the four missing miniatures could be identified, the name of the artist and the sitter were on the back. The pearl necklace had belonged to Aunt Lisette, he could remember her wearing it. He'd have given that to Harriet if it weren't for the fact that she asked so many questions. 'I want them back.'

'Too late, Father.' Giles's smile infuriated him further.

'I've got to have them back. Do you understand? Got to. They're no good to you, you can't sell them. Where are they now?'

'Don't be silly, Father. They don't have to go through your shop. I know somebody who's glad to handle them.'

'Who?'

'Carteret Mathews.'

Jeremy felt sweat breaking out on his forehead. 'God! You shouldn't have let him near them!' As soon as the words were out, he knew he'd betrayed his fear. He could feel himself literally shaking. Carteret Mathews was a known fence, and he didn't want the police looking closely at those pieces.

He had always been so careful. In twenty years his care had paid off. No suspicion, a wonderful reputation, no trouble. He was letting Giles see he was frightened, rather than angry. He'd know he had him in the cleft of a stick.

Giles was surveying him curiously. 'You've always belittled everything I've done. He paid me for them.'

'A fraction of what they're worth, I'll guarantee. Everybody knows they're buying stolen property when they buy from him.'

He could see Giles eyeing the safe. It contained his most valuable pieces, the sapphire and diamond torsade necklace, and the canary-yellow diamond ring. Fear sliced through him; Giles meant to take more, why else would he come here? At least he'd locked everything out of sight before he'd gone out.

'There's something I want you to know about Sylveen.'

Jeremy could feel his heart pounding, he knew what was coming. Hadn't Sylveen said he'd threatened her with this? 'I don't want to hear it,' he said, trying to still the shaking in his hands.

'Do you remember introducing me to Sylveen in the library at Churton? She said it was the first time you had taken her there. I was quite impressed that an old man like you could pull a girl like that. But you couldn't keep her.'

Jeremy stood up. 'Get out of here.'

'Oh, but I haven't finished. I want you to know that every time you went to Paris, I had six nights in her bed. I made her love me. We had a wild time, Father.'

'Get out, I say.' Jeremy advanced on him, barely able to see for rage.

'Those two children you think of as yours.' Giles's eyes taunted him, showering hate on him. Jeremy felt his control snap as he lunged at him, thrusting his palm into his handsome face as hard as he could. Giles fell back a few steps to the doorway, laughing.

'You should know you can't win with your fists. You're too old for that.' He laughed again. 'You're going to hear me out. I fathered those children you're happily supporting. How does that make you feel?'

Jeremy took another step towards him. He knew he was being goaded. He already knew the worst, but it made no difference; it was cutting him to the quick as it had when he'd heard it from Sylveen.

'You do believe me, don't you?' Giles pushed his face close to his; his eyes smouldered, demanding eye contact. For Jeremy, knowing it was the truth made it worse. 'I need some money, Father. Say a hundred pounds.'

Jeremy turned livid as he spat: 'You'll not get another penny out of me.'

'If you don't I could drop in to Wythenshaw House. They still believe in you. Think God has issued you with halo and wings, giving money to the poor the way you do. It would surprise everyone to hear you kept a mistress. I could drop in at the factory too, they'll remember Sylveen there. Make a tasty snippet of gossip.'

Jeremy lashed out at him again, swinging his hand wildly. He knew Giles was laughing at him, knew he no longer had the strength to hurt him. Blind fury kept him lashing out, but Giles moved lightly on his feet, away out of his reach.

The top of the stairs was only two or three steps away. Suddenly Giles's laugh turned sour and became a scream. Paralysed with horror, Jeremy watched him fall, hands clutching for the rope handrail but missing it. He crashed like a sack of coals on to the landing below and lay in a silent twisted heap.

Feeling sick, Jeremy groped his way back to the office chair and slid into it. He didn't know how long he sat there staring at the cleared desk, trying to get his breath back. Then he was listening, but the moaning had stopped. He couldn't say he felt calmer as he crept downstairs to take a closer look. Giles hadn't moved, blood had oozed from the back of his head into a pool on the brown lino. He didn't seem to be breathing.

His mind raged, he felt desperate. He didn't know what to do, couldn't think. It took him another five minutes to pull himself back to the office. He felt overwhelmed, his mind a riot of conflicting feelings: fear, anger, hate and guilt. Mostly guilt. He reached for the phone and asked for an ambulance. Slowly then, he went down to the front door to await its arrival.

★ ★ ★

Emily got up from her armchair, yawning. A play on the wireless had kept her out of bed. For an hour it had cheered her, taking her mind off what Giles had done to them all. Hadn't she half guessed years ago that Jeremy had caught Giles with Sylveen? Hadn't she sensed their intimacy the night Sylveen had filled her armchair like an exotic butterfly?

Giles had denied it. She wanted to laugh now because she'd believed him. All the time, what he'd done was worse than either she or Jeremy had suspected.

The fire had died back to nothing. Yawning again she got up, switched off the music coming from the speaker and went on her way to bed.

Giles had used her as he'd used Jeremy. It seemed he'd used Sylveen too. What fools they all had been, to be taken in by his guile.

Out in the passage the curtains had not been drawn and she could see down into the courtyard. She stopped to admire the ethereal beauty it had at night. One lamp burned over the massive door, lighting up the front steps, enhancing the old pink bricks. She marvelled again at the events that had brought her here to call this mansion home.

She was about to move on to her bedroom when a movement caught her eyes. She thought at first it was Jeremy coming home, but it was a taxi she could see pulling up in front of the steps. It seemed a long time before there was any further movement.

She always left her bedroom door open; she could hear Peter's deep and regular breathing from the soft darkness within.

The taxi driver was getting out and opening the rear door. Helping Jeremy out. He was bent over, cowed, almost dazed. The driver took his arm and began to help him up the steps. She couldn't believe the change in him.

Unusually, he'd come home to lunch. She and Peter

had gone down to eat with him in the dining-room downstairs. He'd seemed weary and tense as he'd spoken again of Sylveen and Giles.

He'd said he was going to work in his bedroom for an hour or so and then intended to go to the shop as there was something important he wanted to do there. But this didn't seem the same man. This was an utterly beaten, deflated version of Jeremy.

She ran full tilt down to the hall and had the door open before he reached it.

'What's the matter?' Close to, his face shocked her, he was a broken man. 'Jeremy! What's happened?'

'An accident.' He came closer, gathering her into his arms, leaning on her heavily.

'Another road accident?'

'No, it's Giles, he came to the shop. Fell on the stairs.'

Emily clung to his alpaca jacket feeling numb. She ought to feel sorry for Giles, but poor Jeremy, it couldn't have come at a worse time for him. He seemed to be taking one knock after another. She felt she was holding him upright.

'Where's your car?'

Behind them the taxi driver cleared his throat. Jeremy felt for his wallet, then pushed it into her hands.

'Pay him, will you? Didn't feel I could drive tonight. And I went to the hospital with Giles.'

Emily looked up the stairs. The staff had all gone to bed.

'Help me get him up to his room first, would you?' she asked the taxi driver. With one supporting him on either side, they were getting him up.

'So how is Giles?' she asked. 'Is he badly hurt?'

Jeremy was swaying. 'That's what I'm trying to tell you, Emily. He fell down the shop stairs. The fall killed him.'

Her mouth was suddenly dry, she was rooted to the spot, staring into Jeremy's shocked face. She felt knocked for six, her hands trembling against his sleeve, but she didn't feel any regret.

'Giles is dead?' She couldn't take it in. No wonder Jeremy was in a state of collapse.

She got him up to his room, saw the taxi driver out. Telephoned for Jeremy's doctor and got Higgins out of his bed to help Jeremy undress. Only then did she let herself think of Giles being dead. Guilt came, a heavy black pall. She wasn't sorry at all. She was free.

Until last night Emily had never been in Jeremy's bedroom. Now she knocked rather diffidently and went in. The magnificent bed had a gothic mahogany trellis at the head and a lower one at the foot; its size dwarfed him. His face, almost as white as the pillows, lifted towards her.

'There you are, Emily. I want you to do something for me.' She crossed the huge carpet, pulled out the chair he was indicating and sat near him.

'Are you all right, Jeremy?' What a stupid question to ask when Giles had just been killed. She wasn't used to the idea herself yet. She had never known Jeremy stay in bed during the day, never known him be ill before.

'Phone Miss Lewis and tell her I want to see Alexander Fraser. Get him here.'

'Alexander Fraser?' His name cut again at her frayed nerves.

'Yes, I can't think of the factory. Somebody must.' Emily stood up, looking round for the phone. She knew he had one here. 'On the desk.'

She was surprised to see it was not just a bedroom; there were easy chairs and a sofa. She went to the desk, and stood looking through the window into the front courtyard as she dialled the factory. It was the second time she'd done it this morning. From downstairs she'd rung Miss Lewis and told her that Jeremy wouldn't be in today and why. It seemed strange to ask openly for Alex.

'He could be anywhere,' Miss Lewis's voice said. 'I'll ask him to phone you when I make contact.'

'Thank you,' Emily said.

'How is poor Mr Wythenshaw? Tell him we send heartfelt sympathy. To you both. Such a shock to us all.'

Emily went back to his bedside to wait for Alex to ring. She started to tell Jeremy as calmly as she could what she'd done yesterday afternoon. All the time, she felt consumed with longing to hear Alex's voice.

'It was visiting-day at the Children's Hospital. I asked Stanley to take me to see Nadine.' Jeremy was staring across the room, showing no sign he'd heard. 'Don't you want to know how she is?'

His blue eyes turned to her then. 'How is she?'

'My heart was in my mouth as I went up the ward. She has a plaster spica to the waist, but she was propped up and seemed quite lively. Sylveen came in while I was there.'

He said nothing but his face turned to hers again.

'She looked drawn and seems to have lost weight,' Emily sighed. 'I can't hate Sylveen.' She had cared more for her than any other friend she'd ever had.

'I got up from Nadine's bed and hugged her as though nothing had come between us.' It had brought tears to Sylveen's eyes.

'You're too loving and forgiving, Emily,' he grumbled.

Her voice was suddenly tart. 'If you truly love a person . . . feel friendship or affection, whatever you want to call it, you can't make it conditional on that person's good behaviour.'

She saw him swallow as he turned away, and knew she'd struck home.

'Is that what you think I do?' he choked.

'You're doing it to Sylveen.' He'd done it to Giles too. She went on quickly: 'I offered Sylveen a lift home instead of letting her take the bus. She didn't want to accept, but I insisted. She asked me in for a cup of tea, and I said hello to Natalie and the babysitter.'

'Sylveen's all right, then?'

'No, Jeremy! She's in a terrible state. Her eyes keep filling with tears, she's at the end of her tether.'

'What do you mean?'

'You know, emotionally adrift.' Her smile wavered weakly. 'Like you.'

'I don't see what she's got to worry about. Nadine's on the mend.'

'She's afraid you're going to cut her off without a penny. She thinks the only reason you haven't done it already is because of Nadine's accident. She thinks you'll get round to it soon.'

'I wouldn't do such a thing!' he protested.

'She saw you do it to me and Peter. She's worried about how she'll support her children. She's looking for a job.'

'I learned something from what I did to you. Tell her, Emily, I won't stop her allowance.'

'Can't you tell her yourself?'

'No, I'll do what I did for you, set up a trust fund for her and the girls, then she'll have the security of knowing it's always there.' She could see his face screwing up with anxiety. 'You've repaired the rift, Emily, forgiven her?'

She shook her head. 'It's not that easy.' Sylveen had been defensive and wary. 'But what good will it do to have a feud?'

That brought his anger brimming over again. 'What she did to you was unforgivable. What she did to both of us.'

'You're hard on her and hard on yourself,' Emily flared back at him. 'We're blaming each other, but we've all made mistakes. I've had a lot of pleasure from Sylveen's company and so have you. If we aren't careful we'll make another mistake and never speak to her again. She's sorry, she knows she's hurt both of us.'

Emily saw Jeremy's lips tighten. 'It will take me some time to get over this.'

'But we will.'

It was easier for her, Emily told herself. She benefited from Giles's death. It released her from the promise she should never have made.

When at last the phone rang, she got up in a rush of excitement, then tried to hide it. 'Shall I tell Alex that Higgins will fetch him?'

'Yes.'

His voice, achingly familiar, made her heart lurch. She knew talking to Alex was bringing a sparkle to her face. She was careful to keep her back to Jeremy.

'He'll come straight away,' she told him as she rang for Higgins. Joy was bubbling through her at the thought of seeing him again.

Once Higgins was dispatched to the factory she could hardly conceal her impatience. She could hear the added lilt in her voice as she read out pieces from the morning's *Guardian* to Jeremy, and wondered if it was as obvious to him.

It seemed a long time before Higgins brought him to the bedroom door. Alex was holding his auburn head proudly, but he looked strangely out of his depth.

Emily got up. 'Don't go without having a chat,' she said. 'I'll be in my rooms.' She looked at the clock on Jeremy's bedside table, it was almost twelve. 'Will you stay and have lunch with me?'

'Thank you,' he said as he slid on to the chair she'd vacated. 'I'd like that.'

As she left, she heard Jeremy say to him: 'You take charge of the factory, I can't. Not any longer.'

Buoyed up with anticipation, she rushed towards her suite to get things ready, then suddenly changed direction and headed for the kitchen instead. Preparations for lunch were well under way. It was too late to change anything.

With Peter in mind she'd ordered mince stew and rice pudding.

'We have a guest for lunch, Mrs Eglin,' she said breathlessly, before rushing back upstairs. In her dining-room, the table was set for two; she set a third place. Then she got out some smarter place mats and reset it all.

Emily could feel excitement rising in her throat as she went to her bedroom. She changed into a dress she'd bought last week, of brown and cream striped linen. She put on more lipstick and some perfume.

She could hear Peter's childish laugh down below on the grass. Stanley was taking him away from the house and flower beds. He'd made him a set of goal posts which were set up in the park where there was plenty of space to kick his ball. Emily watched them from the window, thankful Peter now had so much space to play and that Stanley seemed to be enjoying the game too.

She sat down to wait for Alex, but was up on her feet in seconds, fiddling aimlessly with the table settings. Then back to her bedroom to recomb her hair and apply more perfume. Her cheeks had never looked rosier, she felt intoxicated before he even came.

She had left the front door to the wing open, and now she heard footsteps coming up the corridor. She rushed to meet Alex.

'Thank you,' she said to Mrs Eglin who had shown him the way. 'Will you send Betty out to fetch Peter and wash his hands? And we'll have our lunch as soon as you are ready.'

There was a simmering expectancy in Alex's dark eyes, but a wariness too. As soon as the door closed, she kissed his cheek. He was clinging to her, but his eyes were going beyond her, taking in her surroundings.

'It's all very grand, Emily. And so are you. I had no idea you lived like this.'

She laughed. 'A recent improvement.'

'You look like a duchess, very elegant and polished. The way you spoke to that woman, you could have had servants waiting on you all your life.'

'You know different. When you came to see me at New Street, you didn't tell me I looked a drudge.'

He laughed. 'I could hardly do that.'

'I'm still the same person underneath. I haven't changed.'

He fished a ring box from his pocket, pressed it into her palm.

'I want us to be married. As soon as all this dies down and we decently can.'

She threw her arms round him. 'Wonderful! I was hoping . . .' She was tingling all over. His lips found hers.

He was murmuring: 'I went through purgatory when I lost you.'

'I had plenty of time to regret it too. Plenty of time to realise what I really wanted. Made me grow up in a hurry.'

'Don't know how I dare ask, I can't compete against all this.' He looked beyond her again, through the window, taking in the grandeur of the grounds.

'You don't have to, Alex. Money isn't everything.'

He pulled her closer. 'You can say that after all you've been through?'

'It taught me a lot. Money was desperately important when I didn't have any. With a little in my pocket I'd rate loving and being loved more important. Then there's security and happiness.'

'I think I can offer those. I've always loved you, Emily. Always will.' His lips crushed down on hers, but even as she felt sparks bursting through her, she could hear Peter running down the corridor outside. She pulled away as Betty brought him in.

Alex looked awkward, but was making much of her child. He'll make a good father, she thought as Mrs Eglin came bustling past with a laden tray for the dining-room.

When Betty took Peter off to the bathroom, she drew Alex into her sitting-room.

'With servants you never get your home to yourself,' she whispered.

'We could remedy that,' he smiled. Emily opened the ring box he'd given her; it had come from Pyke's, not Calthorpe's. A dark blue sapphire sparkled in a plain setting; there was a diamond on each side.

'It may not seem much of an engagement ring after what you've been used to, but I promise you, you'll never need to sell it.'

She smiled. 'I love it, Alex, thank you. This is more my style. Not too ostentatious.'

'I can consider myself engaged, then?' Alex picked the ring off its velvet pad and was about to slide it on her finger. She was still wearing Giles's wedding ring.

'Of course we're engaged,' she said quickly. 'But would you mind if we keep it quiet for a little while? I'll wear it on a chain round my neck. Just till things settle down, I don't want to embarrass Jeremy.'

'I wanted to stake my claim,' he said. 'I know I'm too quick off the mark. I was going to suggest we keep it to ourselves too. There's still the inquest and the funeral. The only good thing to come out of the mess is that you're free of Giles.'

'We're all free of Giles.' She was thinking of Sylveen and Jeremy as she took her wedding ring off.

'But Jeremy is taking it very hard.'

'No he isn't,' Emily said slowly. 'I think in some terrible way he's relieved about Giles's death. Something else is bothering him, something worse.'

'What could be worse than that?' There was a shiver in Alex's voice.

'I don't know, but I'm worried stiff. He's frightened. I think he's done something terrible, and he isn't out of the woods yet.'

CHAPTER TWENTY-NINE

Jeremy felt too weak to move, too tired for anything. He had thought a day or so in bed would rest him, but no. Even now after almost two weeks, he couldn't get dressed, never mind think of going to work. He was spent.

He sighed, plumping up his pillows, but nothing made him comfortable.

It was Giles! He had to get Giles out of his mind. It was too awful to think about. He'd trained his mind to skid over black spots, because it played havoc with his sense of security to mull over painful matters. But the spectre of Giles would not leave him in peace.

The inquest had been pure hell, the coroner's verdict: accidental death. Giles's injuries were said to be consistent with the fall as he'd described it. He'd offered no explanation of why Giles might have fallen, except that the lino was worn and slippery and the stairs steep and narrow. Youth was well known to take less care than age with such things.

But he had not told the whole truth, and that was very wrong of him. He had led the coroner to believe his relationship with Giles was a normal one. That they had been working together on the stock while the shop was closed. He felt so guilty. No murderer could feel worse.

The coroner had seemed to pity him, losing a son in an accident as simple as falling downstairs. No doubt he thought it ironic it should happen to his son and not to him.

Perhaps it was the coward's way, to opt out, but he felt he could stand no more. Emily was running the house, Alex was running the factory and King was running the shop. The one thing he had to do himself was to get over to Paris and put the house on the market, and that he couldn't face.

It was Emily who insisted on sending for his doctor. He'd prescribed sedatives which made him feel worse, when what he'd really needed was something to get him on his feet and going again. Emily had been very kind, she was sitting with him, reading from Buchan's *Thirty-Nine Steps*, when the phone rang.

He heard her say, 'Police,' in a surprised voice, and felt himself suddenly go ramrod stiff beneath the sheets. Blood was thundering through his veins. With the inquest over and Giles buried, he'd not expected further contact with the police. He knew immediately something must be dreadfully wrong.

Emily put the handset down and came to the foot of his bed. 'There's been a theft from the shop, Jeremy. Mr King called in the police. They have his statement, but they'd like to come and see you.'

He could feel sweat breaking out on his forehead, he felt aghast, wanting to scream out a refusal.

'Shall I tell them you don't feel up to it?' Her brown velvety eyes were searching his, concerned. But that wouldn't do either. He had to know . . .

'Ask them why,' he said and closed his eyes. Listening to her voice, he picked up the words theft, last night. Black horror was rolling over him, somebody was after his French antiques again. He'd thought them safe at the shop. Worse, it couldn't be Giles, and that made it doubly disturbing. He couldn't take it, not on top of everything else.

Emily was trying to explain something to him, but shock had thrown veils across his mind and he was barely taking in what she was saying. Identify items taken from the shop! He was sweating again.

'What's the matter, Jeremy?' She was holding his hands between her own. 'Oh God, what's the matter? Shall I get the doctor again?'

'No! No, that old fool's no good to me.' He was clenching his teeth, desperate to know if it was the yew cabinet with the family of miniatures that had been taken. His luck had held all these years, why did it have to desert him now? This could be the end for him.

'What is it, Jeremy? Something's frightening you.' Emily shivered, her voice was a whisper. 'Tell me.'

His breath came out in a sob.

'You've got to tell someone. Perhaps I can help.'

'No one can help me. I've done a dreadful thing. For the last twenty years, I've kept it hidden.'

'It can't be that bad.' He saw Emily's little pixie smile trying to humour him.

'I'm a murderer and a thief.'

'Nonsense! Could you have saved Giles, stopped him falling?'

He shook his head slowly. 'If I hadn't been there . . .'

'You had every right to be there, and he had not. You're worrying yourself . . .'

'I took that which was not mine. I am a thief.'

'You're giving away thousands. Everybody says how generous you are.'

'That was the whole point, Emily. What I wanted it for. It doesn't make me less of a thief.' She was beginning to believe him now, he could see a new wariness in her eyes. She was right, he had to tell someone. He took a deep breath, and forced the words out: 'During the war, I fought in France. The Great War, I don't suppose you remember much about that?'

'I've heard plenty,' she said slowly. 'Charlie and Ted were always on about the mud in the trenches, the shellings and the gas.'

'Oh yes, Charlie.'

The pixie smile came again. 'But what did you do that makes you so frightened after all these years? What happened?'

Suddenly his past seemed to be coming up and hitting him in the face. 'A terrible thing. My mother was half-French. She had relatives who owned the Manoir de Frontenac at Lusec.'

'You told us,' Emily said gently. 'She left you the house in Paris and Aunt Harriet a house on the Frontenac estate.'

'I was billeted there in 1917.' He paused again, seeing it in his mind as it had been then.

'Yes,' Emily prompted, shifting in her chair. 'Both Charlie and Ted said the place was rife with rumours about buried treasure. Didn't Charlie say a bundle of silver cutlery was blown out of a wall? And somebody else came across a cache of fine wine?'

'They were digging latrines,' Jeremy chuckled half-heartedly, 'when they found the wine.'

'But what did you do that was so terrible?'

'I kept everything else.'

'But what did you find?'

'I didn't find anything.' He could see Emily blinking impatiently as she tried to make sense of that. 'Or when I did, it was already stored in the cellar of my house in Paris.'

'Somebody else put it there for you, you mean?'

'Yes. I used to take my friends there from time to time for a night out on the town. I stored their personal belongings if they went away. Gramophones, records, books that sort of thing.'

'Yes, you said.'

'It happened like this, Emily. The enemy fell back to a stronger position on the Hindenburg line. We overran the Manoir as we chased after them, but it was then in the front line and being destroyed all round us by enemy shells. We were due for rest. Long overdue, but we had to wait till things settled down. We heard it was definitely coming a month or so later, and we'd be withdrawn some thirty miles from the fighting for a month or six weeks. One of our platoon officers, a friend of mine called Tom Thirkell, was being sent on a gunnery course. He expected leave in Blighty too, and was hoping to get away from the front for a couple of months.

'I knew other officers who were going on the course, and they all wanted to store their things till they were posted back. Nothing of any value, they took that with them. Just stuff that made life more bearable in the lines.

'I was quite happy to do it, the only problem was transporting it there. We were all keen on another night out, we hadn't been able to go for some time. Lusec was further away, that made it more difficult. Another friend, Bill Makin, was in charge of transport but diesel was tighter and he couldn't see how he could get enough for a clandestine trip to Paris.'

Emily was nodding, happy that he was getting on with it.

'It had been a quiet evening. Makin and I took a stroll up to see Thirkell who was on watch. We wanted to discuss what we could do about the Paris trip. I thought I knew every inch of the ground because I'd played there as a child, but the landmarks were all changed, it was an odd sensation.

'The Manoir was bordered by a wood to the west that was providing cover for the enemy to snipe at us. We glimpsed them from time to time through the trees. A week earlier, an officer sent his sergeant to reconnoitre, and when he didn't return, went to see what had happened to him. Neither were seen again, that upset us all.

'Our commanding officer put the wood off-limits, we were forbidden even to try and retrieve the bodies for burial, the danger from hidden snipers was too great. But gradually the trees were being thinned out by shells that were falling wide and we hoped, sooner or later, to keep the Germans out.

'We were told Thirkell was raking the wood with his field glasses from the nearest sniping post, but as there was only room for two men in it, I waited in a nearby trench, while Makin went to talk to him. They thought I was old then, Emily. I was one of the oldest there.

'Suddenly Makin was back saying they'd seen enemy activity. He thought trucks were being driven into the wood without lights. We were still keen to avenge our officer and his sergeant, and determined to get Fritz this time.

'Hurriedly Thirkell fell in a party of his best marksmen, knowing it would be impossible to hide vehicles in a small patch of woodland. For once everything seemed to go our way. It was a black night, but we knew they were there. They had posted guards but we got rid of them quietly and went on into the wood. We saw eight men loading the trucks with boxes from a disused mine shaft.

'The fight, when it came, was bloody. I only saw half of it. I got a bullet in my thigh and spent the next few hours writhing in pain. Thirkell had me carried back. He was crowing with success; he'd taken two prisoners and decimated the rest. He'd captured two civilian trucks loaded with boxes, and a German staff car. He was talking about keeping a truck with a full tank for the Paris trip. That, he said, was definitely on, but not for me.

'I was taken to a field hospital, and from there sent back to Blighty. It was nine months before I returned to France, over a year before I went to my house in Paris again. That's when I found the cellar was full of crates.

'I was devastated when I heard Tom Thirkell had been killed; I'd thought he had a charmed life too. I'd been posted back to a different company, so I hadn't seen him, and he'd been dead a month before I saw his name on the list. I went to Paris to see if anything of his remained in my cellar. Often things were put there and never removed. I had his home address and wanted to send his books and anything else worth having to his wife.

'I found a few cardboard boxes of clothing and books, a wash stand, some candlesticks, that sort of thing. And rolls of mud-stained carpet that had been there since 1915, the belongings of my dead comrades, but I was also opening crate after crate of antiques and jewellery. I couldn't believe my eyes.'

'A fortune?' Emily's face was incredulous.

'Not one fortune. More than that. I kept levering boxes open and finding more. I sat there running my fingers over old silver and wonderful jewellery, and thinking about Thirkell and Makin. They must have brought both the trucks there.

'I had a letter from Tom Thirkell while I was in England, with some cryptic message about the crates in my cellar but I hadn't understood it and couldn't remember what I'd done with the letter.

'I'd heard no mention of any find back in the lines, but as I said, I was with a different battalion and nowhere near the Manoir. I thought Thirkell and Makin would have kept it to themselves. It was possible nobody knew I had it, but I wasn't sure. There was no way I could find out.'

'What happened to Makin?'

'He was posted to Palestine and died in the fighting there.'

'What about Charlie? And Ted Fraser? Could they have known about it?'

'I don't think so, possibly there was gossip at the time. Makin returned my key to me while I was in hospital and said he'd been to collect his own and other people's belongings. If he'd used military vehicles for that, he'd have used army drivers. He may have taken others to help with the loading, but they'd have been from the Transport Corps, and he'd have led them to believe it was a military manoeuvre. I never saw any of them again, so I don't really know what happened.'

'Surely,' Emily said, 'if the antiques came from the Manoir de Frontenac, you had a right to them? Your friends must have thought so too, otherwise they wouldn't have taken them to your house.'

'I should not have kept them, Emily. I sat there awestruck, telling myself the crates had been there a year already, so there was no hurry to report them. Difficult to explain too, how I had come by them. I should have gone straight to my commanding officer, but I didn't.'

'Jeremy, if the de Frontenac family were obliterated, would you not have inherited their wealth?'

'It wasn't all de Frontenac wealth. They were rich but not that rich. At the shop I have a gallery of miniatures all of the same family – not the de Frontenacs. It was less than honest of me.'

'But you recognised some of the pieces?'

'Yes, some came from the Manoir.'

Emily's chocolate-brown head was bent over her fists for a long time. 'After the war, somebody must have inherited the Manoir?'

'There was only Harriet and me left with any claim. The house had been pulverised, I didn't want to go there. I sold the land eventually; the money went towards setting up a trust fund for Harriet.'

Emily sighed: 'I thought you'd done something terrible. You've just got a prickly conscience. Not everyone is as honest as you. You gave most of the wealth away again.'

'I spent the rest of the war hugging my secret, wondering how I could realise its value. I saw myself as a modern

Robin Hood. Even the wisest of us can make dreadful fools of ourselves.'

'What you did was not so very wrong,' Emily said. 'Some of the valuables were de Frontenac property and would have been yours legally. The Germans must have looted the rest, they hadn't come by them honestly. You gave to the poor. Used it to benefit a lot of people.'

'I could have been sentenced to death.'

'Death? Never!'

'I've studied the 1914 Manual of Military Law. It confirms that a soldier on active service found guilty of "breaking into any house or other place in search of plunder", may be sentenced to death.'

'You didn't break into anything,' Emily was denying, she looked frightened.

'No, but I kept plundered goods. However, I think no British soldier was executed for looting during the Great War. I've checked, dear God, I've checked everything, but we would have been disgraced. Reduced to the ranks, possibly a prison sentence.'

'What about the officers who were killed?'

'Disgraced, the other reason I had to keep my mouth shut. It must have given some comfort to their wives and mothers to have them die as heroes.' He closed his eyes, sank back on his pillows. It had not made his life easier. Why had he not realised how many years it would take, and the pressures and stresses it would bring?

'And after all these years of building myself up as a saint, I'm frightened the world will find out now that I'm not.'

Emily was frowning. 'Why?'

'The police coming here, wanting me to identify . . .'

'Jeremy, you didn't listen. I said somebody threw a brick through your shop window and grabbed a handful of Rolex watches and some engagement rings. Nothing to do with . . .'

'Was that it?' He let out a pent-up breath. He was done, tears were clouding his eyes. 'See what happens when something weighs on your conscience for years? I'm finished, Emily.'

'No you're not! You've told me all this, and do you want to know what I really think?' Emily was feeling for his hand. 'I think you'd better get up out of that bed and start living again.'

'What's the use?'

'You always have Arthur to lunch on Sundays. You don't want to let him down again, do you? He telephoned to ask whether you were well enough this week, and I said you were. I've asked Aunt Harriet too.'

Jeremy sighed. 'I'm surprised you haven't asked Alexander Fraser as well.'

'I have,' she smiled. 'Now he's running your business for you, I thought you'd want to hear news of it.'

'Anybody else?' He knew he sounded suspicious.

'If you're asking if I've invited Sylveen, the answer is yes I did.' He opened his mouth to object. 'But you're quite safe, she isn't coming.'

'Didn't want to, I suppose?' he flared.

'It's not that. Visiting-time at the hospital is two to four on Sunday afternoons. She didn't want to be late. Nadine expects her on the dot, and it's only twice a week. I said I'd fix something for another time. So get up now if you want Higgins to help you. I want to send him over for Arthur.'

'Send him now,' Jeremy said irritably. 'Do you think I'm not capable of dressing myself?'

'That's more like it, Jeremy,' she said tartly.

He had half smiled at that. 'I'm glad you're here with me, Emily I did myself some good when I brought you back. I've got you and Peter instead of being alone.'

But he couldn't believe how exhausted bathing and shaving made him feel. It took him a long time to dress.

He sat to rest in the chair in front of his desk and wasted more time. It was only when he saw the Rolls drive into the courtyard with Arthur, that he put on his shoes and went down.

It ought to feel like any other Sunday, with the family collecting in the drawing-room. Harriet sitting ramrod straight, wearing a pale blue toque and strings of pearls.

'A fine how-do-you-do this is, Jeremy,' she said. 'You ill on top of everything else.'

'I'm not ill,' he retorted.

'I told Aunt Harriet you were not yourself,' Emily said, trying to smooth things over. 'Nobody expects you to be, after such a terrible accident to Giles.'

'Poor lad.' Arthur was settling himself with exaggerated care into the corner of a sofa. 'Thirty, no age at all.' It made Jeremy feel half afraid of old age. He didn't want to be like Arthur, with sunken eyes and wrinkled, transparent skin. 'Good of you, Jeremy,' he gasped.

'What is?'

'Having me to lunch every Sunday.'

'Nonsense. I need a bit of company.'

'Look forward to my visits. Good of you to keep in contact now Elspeth's been gone so long.' Jeremy felt the pall of guilt come down like a portcullis. He had used Arthur's expertise. Couldn't have got away with it without his help.

'You've been a good son-in-law to me. Kept me going the last few years.'

'Oh, come on.' His voice was thick with embarrassment. He hauled himself to his feet to hide it. Threw another log on the fire in the huge fireplace. Arthur liked a fire even in summer. 'You taught me. Gave me the benefit of your experience for nothing.'

He ought to feel better now he was up and dressed. It felt strange after two weeks, and he'd almost forgotten how comfortable his drawing-room was with three tall windows looking out over the park and two more into the courtyard.

He saw Alexander Fraser drive up in the baby Austin he'd authorised him to buy. Watched him get out carrying a briefcase as though he was coming to work. He felt a pang that he'd done so little for him till now.

Beside him, he heard Emily gasp. 'I thought he was coming on his motor bike. Have you given him this?'

'Goes with his new job,' he said, but she was bolting off like a rabbit to meet him.

Her cheeks were scarlet when she brought him in to be introduced. Jeremy pulled himself together and was careful to explain to Harriet that Alex was running the business now.

'How's it getting on?' he had to ask.

'Everything's fine, sir.' Alex didn't seem at ease yet at Churton. 'Quite a lot is happening, I've got some of the new markets we discussed. Perhaps we could have half an hour afterwards and I'll tell you all about it.'

Jeremy nodded and pulled himself to his feet again to pour more sherry. The boy made him feel guilty, he was doing so much for him.

'How's your father?' Emily was asking him. Then she spoiled it by adding, 'Ted?' He had to strain his ears to hear the reply; it was almost an aside to Emily.

'He seems much better.' He heard a note of optimism in Alex's voice. 'Less angry, more accepting, since everything came out in the open. I think it's been good for him.'

'Your father's not well?' Harriet's voice carried like a fog horn.

'No,' Alex said. 'It's his chest, he was gassed in the war.'

'I just want you to know I'm grateful,' Arthur was saying slowly, as though nothing had interrupted their conversation. 'Grateful you sorted out my business. Good to know it's in safe hands. Can't believe you're old enough to retire too.'

Poor devil, just as well Arthur didn't know he'd set out to use him, but as he said, he had nobody else. Arthur would be a lonely old man if he hadn't needed him. Rationalising it thus made him feel better. Money no longer bought what Arthur needed.

'I should have been more welcoming when Elspeth first brought you home. Was I too scathing about your bangles and baubles factory?'

'Yes.' It depressed him more to find Arthur dwelling so much on the past. Elspeth had died in 1920.

'Costume jewellery, you called it,' the old man chuckled ghoulishly. 'I thought that a bit pompous.'

'You thought it junk.'

'Yes.'

'So it was. Still is.'

'Good money-earner though. You're a good businessman,' Arthur nodded. 'You've had the last laugh.'

'But more status in fine art.' He was glad Emily and Alex were here, he needed them to keep him young.

'And now you have both, they complement each other.'

Jeremy sighed. He wouldn't have put it like that. He wanted them both taken off his hands.

'Didn't realise how much I'd grow to like you that first night.'

Despite himself, Jeremy was transported back to the night Elspeth had taken him home to dinner to meet her parents. He'd been on his best behaviour, only too conscious that fine art gave the Calthorpes status. It allowed them to talk of good taste, even formulate other people's taste. He could do that now, but he'd passed the stage when it brought him pleasure. Like Arthur, he was finished.

Higgins came to announce lunch was ready and to help Arthur into the dining-room. Alexander came to Jeremy's chair and hovered as though he felt he needed similar help. It made him feel worse.

They were only five, so they used the small dining-room Emily had organised for family use. Well, Emily and Sylveen between them, but he couldn't think of Sylveen. It was a light and pleasant room; Emily never ceased to surprise him, she was proving a great comfort.

He wasn't used yet to the idea of her marrying Alexander. When she'd told him last week, he'd thought it a complication he could do without, but they were being sensible about it. They would wait until the fuss about Giles had died down.

'Alex may be your son,' Emily had said, 'but you both need to know each other better.' Now he couldn't take his eyes from the dark red head bending towards Emily. He couldn't blame the boy for rejecting him as a father. What else could he expect after ignoring him for twenty-odd years?

'We're both adults now,' Alex had said, half-apologetically.

'Too late to develop any filial relationship, you mean,' he'd barked at him.

'Perhaps, but not too late to be friends. It's taken me time to accept that we are related.'

'I'd like us to be friends,' he'd answered gruffly. It seemed more than he had a right to expect. Alex was a good lad. Emily would be better off with him than she had been with Giles. It was only right the boy should live at Churton. He wanted to see them both happy.

Back in the drawing-room, with the fire drawing up to make it rather too hot, both Harriet and Arthur were dozing off.

'Let's leave them to it,' Jeremy said, determined to make more effort. 'Come to the library and tell me what's happening at the factory.' Emily came too, but said little. She and Alex couldn't keep their eyes off each other.

They weren't going to keep their engagement a secret for long. Even Arthur was bound to notice. It surprised him Harriet hadn't already.

Jeremy began to feel better. Alex's plans to diversify would give Wythenshaw's a new lease of life, and, even if war came, it would survive, maybe even flourish.

'I shall be very pleased to see you married to Emily,' he said. 'I want you to know you'll be welcome here. You'll be as good for Churton as you are for the factory.'

'That's kind of you, sir.' Suddenly Jeremy couldn't help but see the boy was trying to cover his embarrassment. It made him feel cold. 'But I don't want to come and live in Emily's suite.'

He felt slapped down, deflated. 'Well, there's plenty of space here, we can do up another wing.'

Alex's cheeks were burning now. 'You're very kind, and very generous, but Emily and I want a small place of our own. I don't feel I should step into Giles's shoes.'

Jeremy was fighting for breath again. He felt defeated. It hadn't occurred to him that they wouldn't want to stay with him. He was shivering. It was all over for him. He didn't want to be alone.

Emily had taken his hand. 'Jeremy,' she was saying, 'don't you think Arthur would like to move into the suite, when I leave? It would be better if he was closer. I think he'd like it. He's looking older and he's a bit doddery on his feet today.'

'Well, he is coming up for his century,' he managed. Soon he'd be like Arthur, but there'd be no one to take any interest in him.

Jeremy felt stiff and old and very low again.

Emily happened to be crossing the hall when the postman pushed the letters through the door. She picked them up and stared in wonder at one oversized envelope of superlative quality, then went running upstairs to Jeremy's room with it.

He had promised last night to get dressed after breakfast, but as yet he'd made no move. She found him lying back against his pillows staring into space, his breakfast tray pushed to the foot of the bed, the boiled egg half eaten, only one slice of toast touched.

'There's a letter for you from Buckingham Palace,' she said. He took it but made no move to open it. 'Jeremy, I'm dying with curiosity. Is it what you hoped for?'

He opened it, then slowly drew out the thick note paper, read it carefully, taking his time.

'From his principal private secretary. Asking me if I'll accept a knighthood in the Birthday Honours List.'

Emily laughed aloud. 'And of course you will.' She felt lifted with pleasure, glad it had come in time to help him out of this slough of despond.

'It's come too late.' He was folding it back into the envelope.

'No,' she protested. 'You've had your sights set on this for years. Pounce on it.'

He sighed. 'Does it really matter?'

'Of course it matters.' Excitement touched her but had left Jeremy cold. She flopped on his bed, causing the egg to roll down the tray.

'Everybody thinks of you as a philanthropist, you've set up Wythenshaw House and the Wythenshaw Trust. You've put in a lifetime as a public benefactor. It's now bearing fruit. It's what you wanted.'

'Once I wanted it,' he sighed, 'I've changed my mind. Over a lifetime that's bound to happen.'

'You're depressed because you've had a bad time recently.' Emily took his hands in hers. 'But this is fundamental, you haven't changed your mind about this. Remember when you came to Charlie's shop and brought Peter and me back here? I was quite unable to help myself. You got me going when I'd lost heart. I want to do that for you.'

'I'm old, Emily. Best left to settle into retirement.'

'Compared to Arthur, you're young, and you know it. You've got a lot to live for. I'm going to type a reply to this and accept for you. Sir Jeremy! I want you to get dressed and come downstairs. Shall I ring for Higgins?'

'There's so much hanging over me, Emily.'

'Such as what?'

'I've got unfinished business in Paris.'

'Only the house to put on the market. You've done the hard part.'

'But I'll have to go again.'

'You needn't go alone. There's nothing to hide any more.'

She'd got his attention at last. 'Will you come with me?' Emily hardly knew what to say, she had to think about it for a moment.

'Yes, if it's what you want, but it would be better if you took Sylveen.' She saw his lips settle into a hard straight line.

'We told her to go, Emily, that we didn't want to see her again.'

'I've changed my mind,' she said. 'I'd like you to change yours.'

'Can't forgive what she did.' He was shaking his silvery head.

'You've done things you wished you had not. Isn't that why you're so upset now?' He stared at her, not answering. 'Aren't the rest of us allowed to feel the same? We've all done things we regret, Jeremy. Sylveen has and I have, but we can't spend the rest of our lives locked in remorse.'

He didn't answer.

'I'm going to do for you what you did for me. Whether you like it or not, I'm going to see you accept this knighthood.'

'What I did for you was a sap to my conscience. I caused your problems in the first place.'

'Reasons don't matter.' She watched him flop back against his pillows.

'What use is a knighthood now? I shall be alone here, a lonely old man.'

'No you won't,' she flared at him angrily. 'Come on, get up. You've stayed in this bed long enough. I'm going to ring Sylveen and make a booking somewhere for lunch. Jeremy, you've got something to celebrate.'

'But I can't say anything about it, not till it's announced.'

'You don't have to say anything. We can tell her about me and Alex. Anyway, you've told me, a little whisper to Sylveen wouldn't hurt.'

'No, it's against all the rules. You're bullying me, Emily,' he complained.

She rang the bell. 'Just putting a bit of pressure on. To get you going in the right direction. Higgins is coming. Come on, get up, you'll feel better if you do.'

He was grumbling at Higgins about the nicotine on his fingers as he shaved him. Grumbling to himself as he bathed and dressed, but he knew Emily was a crutch to him. Who would have thought the little pixie would order him about as she did?

Emily was down in the drawing-room, all excited, telling him she'd booked a table at the Victoria Hotel in Gayton. He sat sipping a glass of wine waiting for the car to return with Sylveen.

'Wouldn't it have been easier to pick her up on the way?' he grumbled.

'No, she wants to bring Natalie here to play with Peter,' she said. 'Betty will look after them both.' She was keeping on at him.

'Look, Sylveen hurt you, I know, and it's human nature to kick back when we're hurt, but Sylveen is sorry, she knows it was wrong, she loves and needs you. Jeremy, you need her.'

Emily was making him nervous, elaborating on home truths when Sylveen could walk in at any moment.

'I want you to invite her to go to Paris with you.' Her brown eyes were fierce. 'You need her.'

His Rolls was pulling up outside. He felt fluttery, his knees were shaking as he stood up to greet Sylveen. He told himself he was an old fool.

Emily was right, he'd stayed in bed too long. He heard Natalie's piping voice as she spoke to her mother. Then they were standing before him.

'Hello, Jeremy.' He'd forgotten how attractive Sylveen's breathy voice was. 'Thank you. I was praying you'd find it possible to forgive me. It takes a very generous person to forgive what I did.' It seemed churlish then to say he had not, and anyway, he could feel his animosity melting.

He straightened up to look at Sylveen; her piercingly blue eyes met his, he felt their sensual pull as he always had. She came closer and kissed his cheek. He tried to stem his tide of longing in Natalie's long blonde hair and baby kisses, but already she was pulling away to kiss Emily.

Sylveen was wearing the elaborately enamelled pendant and bracelet he'd chosen for her at Lefarge. The sapphires, emeralds and rubies sparked and flashed at him, reminding him how once he'd wanted to marry her. Nadine's conception had rushed him into making a decision before he was ready, and an old man's thinking had made him err on the side of safety. Nadine's accident had forced him into another decision. Perhaps they had both been wrong.

Her silver-grey dress showed off her jewellery to perfection. She was more plainly dressed, more elegant now. There was no cleavage showing, but her figure looked wonderful all the same. He could feel her warmth, as he had the day she'd pinned the poppy in his lapel, though she was not as exuberant as she used to be and her fragile features had lost their childlike innocence.

Emily was organising everything. Betty and Peter came down to carry Natalie off with them. Sylveen sat down to drink a glass of wine, her elegant legs neatly crossed at the ankle. Then Emily was leading them out to the Rolls.

It was no good telling himself he was not interested in Sylveen. Of course he was, she was a luscious girl. He felt the old stirring of pleasure as he walked across the restaurant behind them both. Heads turned, Sylveen still had that sort of attraction. It made him feel better just to see it again. Perhaps there was life left in the old dog yet.

After two weeks shut away in his bedroom it was a novelty to be in a restaurant, surrounded by other people. He hadn't much to say as he tackled the trout, he was too busy thinking. Perhaps he didn't deserve the luck he had, but it was with him still. Against the odds he'd survived, and with panache. A man with nine lives. Enjoyment was what he'd always sought from life. He was enjoying this.

Once, long ago, he'd toyed with the idea of taking Sylveen to Paris, of unfolding the beautiful city before her. Wanting to enjoy the thrill it gave her. He wondered if she were still hungry for life.

But Sylveen seemed subdued, she'd never been this quiet. They none of them had anything to thank Giles for; his shadow lay between them still. He had to scotch it once and for all.

'How do you feel about a few days in Paris?' he asked her. He saw Emily's pleased smile waver for a moment.

'I'd love it.' Sylveen's cheeks ran with colour. 'When?'

'I'll look after Natalie,' Emily hastened to volunteer.

'But Nadine will be coming out of hospital in two weeks' time.'

'I'll have you back by then,' Jeremy promised. 'Nadine will need you.'

'I'll visit her in hospital,' Emily said. 'While you're away.'

'I've never been abroad before,' Sylveen breathed; her eyes sparkled; she still had her youthful enthusiasm.

'Perhaps we should fly Imperial Airways.'

Sylveen could hardly speak, the smile wouldn't leave her lips. 'Could we? I've never flown before.'

'Neither have I,' Jeremy said. 'Always had so many crates to bring back.'

Sylveen had always been hungry for new experiences; he needed them too. The King George V Hotel of course, he couldn't do without his comfort. 'I'll get Miss Lewis to book our tickets,' he said as the old excitement swirled through him.

He'd been a fool to let Sylveen slip through his fingers. Emily was right, he must not let it happen a second time. He caught her pixie smile, and her hand rested on his for a moment. He knew she was pleased.

Emily was delighted Jeremy was arranging to take Sylveen to Paris, because she wanted to think of Alex. Their news was leaking out. They'd set the day and she had things she wanted to see to.

But she wasn't sure Jeremy was on an even keel again until they came back from Paris. They both had all their old bounce, and Sylveen positively sparkled as she whispered: 'Can't wait to see my mother. Her face will be a picture when I tell her I'm going to be Lady Wythenshaw.'